3/27/19
12:15 pm

Katie,

Keep churn.
those bear.

# The End Zone

## An Ahmad Jones Novel

# Kevin Fitch

SPIRIT OF
BROTHERHOOD
PUBLICATIONS

# The End Zone
## *An Ahmad Jones Novel*

*Kevin Fitch*

Library of Congress Control Number: 2017905756

ISBN: 978-0-693-94439-4

*Printed in the United States of America*

Cover art by Jarrett Holderby
Layout and Editing by Denis Ouellette
Proofing by Nancy Kolze

*Visit* **TheEndZoneNovel.com**

## DEDICATION

**To Nancy and Robert**
*My Mom and Dad*

**To Jarrett Holderby**
(1958–2018)

*My dear friend, Jarrett was a fine-art illustrator and Renaissance man, who contributed the cover art for this book. His refined perceptions and sensitive delineations of line and color are the stuff of divine experience. He was the apotheosis of a world-class artist.*

**"Planets don't make things happen, people do."**

—Noel Jan Tyl, world-renowned
astrologist and author

DSS SPECIAL AGENT FRANK SCUDDER discovered a parking space from the side street and sped to the intersection. The black SUV that had been tailing him was still within surveillance range. In New York's South Bronx, Scudder made a sharp left from Cauldwell Avenue onto 149th Street and quickly merged into the dense current of late-night traffic. The man behind the wheel of the SUV, a hitman, approached the intersection to make the same turn but the light changed. Scudder tactically appraised the location of the space while squeezing the full-size car into the right lane. The space was at the front of the line and there was a no-parking sign ahead of it—ideal in case he required a quick egress. Behind the parking spot was a long line of vehicles and a lamp post that kept them and the sidewalk well lit. Scudder would have a clear sightline at his four-to-five o'clock angles.

The hitman watched his target's car slowing down. Scudder pulled into his ideal space. At the intersection the hitman switched gears then backed away from it and into an empty portion of roadside on Cauldwell Avenue. His cigarette was half gone now. He held the filter tip inside the bend of his forefinger and took several puffs, until a bulky cloud filled the interior. The hitman cracked the window. When the smoke had cleared and he could assess his mark through the moving partition of vehicles, he saw something that put a hideous grin on his weather-beaten face, something he hadn't seen before. It was the rhythm of traffic. Now, the hitman had a clever advantage— his moving target had become a sitting duck.

Scudder cut the engine with a brusque flick of his wrist, took one hand off the steering wheel, and switched off the headlights. He suspended all movement for a thoughtful few seconds. His thumb and forefinger remained on the key. This time, he considered driving back to the small restaurant and waiting inside with his protectee, Ms. Marakie Dewabuna, even if his presence there made her uncomfortable.

Scudder's operational routine was rigid. He was to accompany Ms. Dewabuna to the small restaurant and sit away from her at the bar or at a different table. When she was ready to depart, he was to leave first with her following behind. After driving Ms. Dewabuna to her apartment, he was to escort her to the front door, take her key and open it, pre-search the rooms and wait for the first shift guys, who would cover Ms. Dewabuna's protection until morning. Agent Frank Scudder, an employee of the Diplomatic Security Service, had one assignment: to keep Ms. Dewabuna out of the jaws of harm.

She had developed an aversion—not to him—but to the stipulations that had directed her life for more than a year of close personal protection. Security for her was less stringent back in her country. Still clutching the key, Scudder recalled what Ms. Dewabuna asked him four days ago in Downtown Brooklyn, while she huddled in the backseat, against the door.

"Frank. You're doing your job protecting me and all, and I am fine with it—"

"But?" Scudder said.

"But?"

"Yes. There's going to be a *but* in there somewhere."

"Okay, well, can I ever go somewhere by myself, besides the bathroom and my sleeping quarters, without all this direct protection? I am a grownup."

Scudder said, "Even grownups need personal protection, especially when they *do* need it." He had turned back around, waiting for the light to turn. It was a long light. He adjusted the angle of the rearview mirror and saw her staring out the window, sulking. Scudder thought hard and devised a scheme to change her mind. The light was still red. He turned again to face her, just as an EMS emergency vehicle bolted past them with its siren blaring.

"Okay, Marakie, I will lend you some space."

Marakie took her palms from her ears. "Lend? Did you say lend, Frank?" She nudged her arm from the inside door panel and sat up. Her sullen look vanished. Another EMS truck followed quickly after the first. Marakie covered her ears again. Scudder waited for the noise to subside.

"That's right—lend, but you've asked me to alter my intelligence package, which will in turn change threat levels, lesson mitigation of security risk, and could potentially get me fired, or you and me killed."

Marakie flips her long hair away from her expressive eyes. She looks up and follows the surface of the car's roof lining. She points and adds, "Not while you have that shotgun up there. And what threat levels? Only my dad, you, Ms. Lorena, and the others at Fort Lee know who I am. But anyway, thanks, Frank, for bending the rules on behalf of my privacy."

The light turned green and Scudder continued north on Jay Street past Myrtle Avenue. A familiar logo of an upheld white torch with purple fire, loomed high up on the building ahead. The signage was attached to the building's south face, above a façade of many feet of glass panels. He parked and got out of the car but Marakie had already let herself out and had shut the door. "You're lending me space, right?" Scudder's little gambit backfired. She waved and said, "See you at ten." He buttoned his jacket and watched her stroll toward the door at the far end of the glass façade of NYU's Tandon School of Engineering, which she attended.

Now, four days later, with his thumb and forefinger still on the key, Scudder laughed at himself for his poor attempt at reverse psychology. He decided that tonight he would continue the *loan*, just one last time, but tomorrow he would take it back and be in Marakie's shadow again. His moment of levity ended quickly. He was wrestling with other concerns. He checked the blind spot over his left shoulder and ran his eyes over to the small restaurant where she was, then took his digits off the key and pushed up against the seat back.

Scudder was on edge about something from the far side of his general awareness. In addition to watching the restaurant, there was this strange and remote sensation of imminent danger. It was similar to what he had faced in guerrilla-infested cities as he snaked through the tight corners of stifling narrow alleys at night with less than a second to tell friend from foe. What he was edgy about barely registered except for its faint alert in his gut, which was swallowed up by his incessant thoughts and his own reactions to them— too much mental noise! Because of that suspicion, though, he sat crouched in his vehicle like a deadly feline with raised hairs on its back—alert, poised, taking in its surroundings.

Scudder turned his head to the left and right and a little behind each shoulder, smoothly, like a periscope. There was no apparent risk to this present intelligence picture. He looked toward the ceiling at the rugged vehicle gun rack with his Remington 12-gauge shotgun mounted on it. He grimaced as a faint light allowed him to inspect his work on the stock's walnut finish. He lowered his head and noticed the flow of traffic while reaching his hand sideways, underneath his jacket, to touch the handle of his Glock. He marked the time then decided to call in his whereabouts. He said something, then muted the phone on the dashboard mount, snatched up his radio from the console unit, and notified the New York Field Office.

The luxury sedan shielded Scudder and his protectee from most types of assaults by assailants using conventional weapons. It also bought him time to orchestrate, in the midst of crisis, an effective strategy of defense for himself and his protectee—and call for backup, so long as the windows and doors stayed shut. The sedan was roomy. It was 17.375 feet in length and weighed just under 4,000 pounds. It had ballistic glass and a reinforced shell. 2002 had been the final year for this fully equipped, multi-functional, government-issue model. It would be discontinued for the next fifteen years. Unfortunately, Scudder's life was about to be discontinued, too.

It was 11:25 in the evening. In six minutes something would happen to Scudder, which would, in a freakish way, positively affect millions of people. By some outlandish affair, Scudder would become an unknown hero—not for his distinguished record of defeating belligerents after he and his team's boots landed on foreign soil, all of which was utterly classified. No, he would achieve the stature of a hero simply by dying in his car.

Scudder was the head of security support for Ms. Dewabuna, a resident diplomat—the protectee. From the car window, he was separated from her by nearly fifty yards, about half the length of an American football field. She was eating late-night food at Lorena's Place, situated at the corner of a cut-through street.

Scudder was sharp, sharper than most. He had a law degree from Harvard and had done many tours with a Navy SEALs unit—an overachiever. He was nicknamed, "Granite Scudder." He was fierce, like an Italian Mastiff guard dog, trained to kill with its powerful muscular frame and jaws. Scudder was stronger than most men for his height, which was slightly above six feet. His wife often commented about how his wavy brown hair, youthful looks and baby-blue eyes sometimes blurred the fact of his solid frame and austere manner.

He was toughly experienced concerning mundane tactics in the world of combat—even tougher than necessary—an overcompensation. But with all his sharpness and strength, Frank Scudder had an innocence, which some might call a weakness. It could turn his granite temperament into mush. That innocence was a placeholder in his heart, reserved for a special woman. It gave a philosophical balance to his relatively short and intensely disciplined life, by way of its dynamic and conspicuous counterpoint. It was for his stunning wife, Gloria.

As an agent for a federal arm of the U.S. State Department, Scudder's attire and tactical accoutrements were of the finest quality and always neatly arranged. He considered every aspect of his assignment to be reflective of every other aspect. He was an elegant soldier in his charcoal-grey Armani and Stefano Ricci white shirt and yellow tie. He loosened the tie, unbuttoned the shirt and pulled down on the vest, which was riding up on him. He waited in the blue Lincoln Continental to escort Ms. Dewabuna home. He shoved the radio back into the console unit and pressed unmute on his cell as his feeling of uneasiness mounted.

It was a Friday night in April. The Full Moon was refreshingly clear and bright. A cool breeze meandered along 149th Street from west to east. Scudder's breath and whatever heat was still left of his coffee had reacted to the cool air outside. Muffled tire sounds, screeching brakes, loud music and muscle-car engines at high idle could barely be heard from the inside of Scudder's armored windows. With all of them rolled up, the space inside was almost acoustically dead. It had to be, so he could hear Gloria, besieged by illness, talking to him on his cell. They'd been conversing since 11:15.

The glare of headlights raced up and down the main drag. Then the noisy thoroughfare got quiet and barren. The cycle of noise and quiet occurred in 30-to-45-second gaps. Scudder had been measuring that interval for several days. It was something to do while waiting for his client—noting the relative interplay of vehicles at rest and vehicles in motion. That interval could be a useful algorithm for something, but to whom and for what? Scudder was proud of his wit, able to find meaning in a simple, pedestrian occurrence that was otherwise taken for granted. Tonight, that very interval would be used against him. Inside the government vehicle, a newspaper was opened to the sports section, quarter-folded on the passenger seat. Scudder was a sports fanatic. The paper was docile and lifeless and needed to be acted upon, to be unfolded and read as many times as possible. To delay its own final chapter in the trash, the half broadsheets needed the psychic life-current of attention, which right now Scudder could not afford to give. His head had to be on a swivel or suffer a potentially high cost to security.

Scudder relaxed a bit, listened to his wife and checked his watch—a Casio with a small camera crammed into it. It came out in 2002. His wife surprised him with it for his 29th birthday. That was thirteen days ago. Three minutes had passed since he parked. In his professionally trained voice that suggested a highly specialized level of intelligence and education, he said, "Baby, I'll see you not long after midnight. We'll talk about it then." He paused a beat and said with emphasis, "You know I love you."

Straining to speak, after this long overdue declaration, Gloria says, "Yes... I know... I never doubted, my darling, that you love me."

Scudder periscopes his eyes over the street and walkways, checks his mirrors and the side and back windows. He turns to Lorena's Place at his ten o'clock, to the corner of the next block, where Trinity Avenue and Pontiac Place meet, for any sign of Ms. Dewabuna, his young protectee.

He rechecks his wing mirror and sees the black SUV at his seven o'clock, still parked near the edge of Cauldwell Avenue, one block behind. He had noticed it during his last security sweep around the block. As he turns back around and looks up at the blued finish of the magazine under the 14-inch barrel of his Remington, he says to Gloria, "I'm coming home with a surprise, baby." Then he whispers, "You're going to be okay."

A thin haze gathers on Scudder's driver's side window. Traffic resumes its predictable pattern. Scudder looks at the single-bottle box of champagne in the footwell below the glove box—an Extra Age Brut Rosé. He adds, "And I've got the anniversary bubbly right here. It spent five years in the cellar." He reaches behind his headset cable to scratch an itch below his hairline. "And, honey, I worked out all our problems. You'll see." Scudder is getting his hopes up. Now, he is both worried and happy for his wife. But he *worked out* his wife's problem. While talking, he's about to open the glove box.

"Gloria, honey, I know we've got about a half hour before midnight, but happy 6-months anniversary, baby. You know I love you. Gotta go." He hears nothing, no response. He checks the display. The line is still open. He says, "Bye." She says, "Goodbye, honey."

He puts the cell on the passenger seat, reinserts his tactical behind-the-ear speaker, leans diagonally with his harness still engaged and reaches inside the glove box. He takes out a goldenrod envelope and lifts the flap and thumbs through six packs of hundred-dollar bills. They're separated into sets wrapped with mustard-colored currency straps, the standard color for one-hundred-dollar bills. Each strap reads $10,000.

On First Avenue in Manhattan's Upper East Side, Gloria takes the plugs out of her ears and tosses the cell phone near the foot of the bed. She uncrosses her ankles and turns her body to the edge of the bedside. Gets to her feet. She switches the lamp on and grabs the remote off the table and presses the button for the CD player, then tosses that on the bed. She feels her belly, then walks out of the bedroom through the dark hallway into the dining room. She reaches for the armrests and gingerly lowers herself into the dining chair. Darkness surrounds her. She feels for a match, the long green ones with the silver tips. She pulls one out of the ceramic strike container and lights two candles. She gazes a few feet in front of her. Elton John's "Your Song" plays in the background from the bedroom. Frank and Gloria slow-danced to that at their wedding. The candles brighten the room. The aroma of crusted, spiced and plank-grilled salmon pours out of the oven. Their champagne glasses are ready. Gloria feels she still has a bombshell figure. She's wearing White Linen, Frank's favorite scent, under a vibrant, red form-fitting dress with a plunging neckline.

Her long hair, the color of midnight, accentuates the deep red of her dress. Her eyes are gentle, luminous and saturated with deep feeling. She continues to look at their wedding picture, at the center of the table. Her smile brings out the symmetry of her rose-colored lips. She's cheerful and lighthearted for the first time in several weeks because her husband told her that he loved her. Those words are still affecting her by degrees. She evokes the spell of Frank's severe but caring gaze when their eyes met for the first time, in the low light. How he showed up in the doorway where power lines were swinging and making hissing sounds. And how he grabbed her shaking hand, tightly, and yanked her over the wide chasm in the floor, and how she fainted afterwards; not knowing how that man got her to street level, and hearing, as though in a dream, the terrifying noises of the buildings collapsing upon their foundations, and the blast of blinding smoke and dirt, agony and destruction, while he carried her out of certain death, to life. And now, death is nearby again.

She remembers his valor, service to country and devotion to her. She reaches for the picture, kisses and hugs it. Takes it with her as she saunters into the kitchen, livelier than she can remember ever feeling. Places it on the counter, so it faces her. She pulls open a cutlery drawer and takes out a six-inch slicer knife; it must be freshly sharpened and perfectly balanced, she thinks.

# 1

## The Fifty-Fourth Hit

ON THE MAIN DRAG THE TRAFFIC WAS FULL. Moist air had been hitting the cold glass for a while. Condensation had gathered on the driver's side window. It blocked Agent Scudder's sightline to Lorena's Place where the young woman was still dining. *She should be out soon.* He loosened his tie some more and twisted his body, creating warping sounds against the leather. Then he turned his head in a half circle, sped his eyes over every square inch of whatever his eyes could see at his four-to-five-o'clock angles through the back windshield, including the entrance to a New York City Housing Authority apartment, a full parking lot, an old woman slowly pushing a grocery basket and an empty bus-stop shelter and bench. He did the same for his left flank. His Kevlar rode up near his neck again. He wiggled while pulling it down.

There are intermittent splashes of heavy trucks, vans and cars. Through the spaces between the moving vehicles, Scudder spots that same black SUV. It's just sitting there like his Remington, neatly stowed in its compartment above his head. That same subtle something below his outer awareness keeps directing his attention to the SUV. He's distracted by his thoughts of Gloria—and by *what if?* Scudder is thinking of his wife's illness and the money he was given for an operation that may or may not be successful. What if she doesn't survive the operation? Preoccupied, his mind tells him that the black SUV is just part of the furniture of the city. He needs to see the small restaurant and take in some fresh air.

All clear. Agent Scudder, again with a brusque flick of his wrist, makes the car chime sound as he lets his window down. Condensation will never be an issue again. His sightline to the small restaurant is restored. But Frank Scudder's move is ultimately the wrong move at the wrong time.

One block behind Scudder's fully armored Lincoln, parked at the edge of Cauldwell Avenue, a big man with big hands and that weather-beaten face, the hitman, flicks his cigarette out the window, slides on a pair of gloves and quickly starts the engine of his black Cadillac Escalade. It's 11:31. Releasing the brake, he waits for a vintage red Dodge Dart to pass the intersection from right to left. He pulls out onto 149th Street. He stalks three car lengths behind the vintage car. He's coming to the empty bus shelter and bench. Vehicles behind him clutch together in a tight grouping behind a new red light. Lucky break. He's in that interval between resting vehicles and moving vehicles. The signal timing cycle, for this section of the South Bronx, is about 30 seconds. The hitman takes his time. He powers down the right-back passenger window, stretches his arm out backwards, and then slows to five mph.

Scudder switches on the interior light and grabs *The Post* off the seat. Scudder has always been a sports fanatic. He's compelled to finish the story about Mets pinch hitter Mark Johnson's home-run win over the Cards. Marakie Dewabuna is still inside the small restaurant. He checks the solid maple door to Lorena's Place in case she comes out early. It's time to close the window, Scudder surmises, but he unfolds the paper to the sports section—just what the paper needed, attention.

Newspapers can be unintentionally ruthless.

The front tires of the Escalade roll on the smooth asphalt opposite the rear tires of the Continental. Scudder looks out toward the restaurant again, his finger on the power-window button. The Escalade blocks his view due to its elevated position. Its rear tires are at his eight o'clock. He catches the outline of a big head with a nose whose tip extends an inch further from its chin line. It shows up against the glare of oncoming headlights. The rear tires are now opposite Scudder's door. He puts the envelope back inside the glove box but doesn't close it instantly. He picks up the paragraph where he left off. The big man targets the newspaper and lowers his arm like a precision instrument. He senses where the Kevlar vest is riding up from the waist. Every vest does it to a greater or lesser degree. The pistol is almost invisible in the hitman's hand, like a baseball inside a catcher's mitt. He pulls the trigger fast on the Walther P22A, twice. Blue-white flashes confirm the hollow points' jaunt at 1,600 feet per second. Scudder hears the flight of two projectiles in the air.

The hitman retracts his arm. The barrel is hot. Thin curlicues of smoke billow out of the muzzle. He engages the safety and places the pistol with its hot extended suppressor under his legs. The smell of incinerated powder mixes with the residue of cigarette smoke. He revels in the combined smell.

The weapon gave no sonic boom or ballistic crack, but a sound like a golf club striking dirt under the impetus of a terrific swing. The old woman with the grocery basket about to pass the Lincoln saw the blue-white flash. It looked like a passenger was lighting a cigarette. A new traffic cycle began, as the light turned green and the drivers behind the man with the battered face stepped on the gas like thoroughbreds dashing out of the gate. Another lucky break—getting mixed up in traffic. He took the next left turn. Scudder dropped his eyes to the single hole in his paper, and then dropped them some more to the hole in his gut.

Scudder's vest had moved up an inch. He put two and two together— the black SUV and the physical and psychological pain welling up from his belly. His uneasiness, no longer out of range of his awareness and no longer a faint intimation, took a definite shape. The newspaper rustled its own death knell. How could he have been so stupid? He, a member of a Navy SEALs unit, with a law degree and a sharp mind, who'd faced and defeated foreign ene-mies. The newspaper, the unwitting foil of a murder and the stealer of Frank Scudder's attention, would soon be photographed along with its victim. Its image as evidence ensured that it would have a kind of immortality.

"No! Not yet... Can't be!" Scudder reaches out to the dash mount to call Gloria, but maybe he can still make it if he grabs the radio. It's closer. He can call it in but something in his back is severed. He can neither call Gloria nor the field office. He speaks into the space in front of him, "Gloria. I'm sorry. I'm not coming home, darling. I love you." He plays in his mind again how he was given that $60,000 for Gloria's experimental procedure. Now she won't get it and will most likely die, because that money will be confiscated. His superiors will determine that he was involved in some graft, malfeasance, something dishonorable—an agony of thought. He got the money by break-ing the rules, which all DSS agents were cautioned not to break. He can ex-press his primal emotion, his dread, only through a profanity—the only word fit to describe his bizarre circumstance.

Scudder watches the traffic and a few pedestrians moving about on streets and sidewalks, oblivious to his approaching denouement. What iso-lation. *Fuck! I'm... I'm not gonna die. I'm gonna live. The pain, getting worse. I'm not gonna... fucking die... Fuck,* Scudder says. The reduction of the street noises meets and commingles with an emerging silence. He shifts his focus. He can't move his back or his limbs but he can still think. Frank Scudder was always aware of the possibility of being killed in the line of duty. Now, years of trained discipline take over. Before he breathes his last breath on the streets of New York, Scudder visually follows the Escalade.

Like a weak hand that struggles to turn a tight lid, the agent musters the strength to wrench his eyes left, just in time to see the shooter's rear-side window roll up as it accelerates and rounds the corner with a soft skid onto Trinity Avenue. Ms. Dewabuna is in danger. Scudder knows it. It's 11:32. He's unable to protect his client. He will fail to help two women in less than two minutes. Both will die from his stupidity. He tracks the vehicle even as traffic crosses his sightline. Vision is still good. He follows the bright red lights of the Escalade even as the sparkle in his eyes dims. He wrenches his eye fur-ther left and the last thing he sees is the black awning with the splash of neon ruby-colored letters above it: Lorena's Place, which the Escalade drives past at the end of the cut-through.

Scudder's eyelids want to close now, for good. He is the shooter's fifty-fourth victim. Physical pain partially recedes. The seat, the paper, and his lap are covered in blood. He slips into another space. Acceptance. He surrenders any more attempts to command his body. His head and upper back bend forward and down. With his final thoughts, he begs Gloria and the woman he duly swore to protect to forgive him for not wiping the condensation off the armored window.

Gloria Scudder pulls the salmon fillet out of the oven and rests it on top of the stove. She slices several portions with a chef's precision. The test results were confirmed. She was pregnant. She had known for more than a week but she hadn't told Frank. She would break it to him tonight, after they made love, not before. She could reconcile a new life and her own death if Frank was there. He said he loved her, after several weeks. It was almost a foreign language.

She picked up a napkin, dried her tears and tucked it inside her neckline. She reflected about how utterly terrific her short life with Frank was. Gloria, too, was accepting. She was given a little less than a year if she followed the protocols to the letter. What surprise, she wondered, would Frank come home with? She felt excited. How would she love him after they dined? She blushed, then smiled and shoved the fish back in the oven, after shutting it off, and waited for her husband, the love of her life, to appear in the doorway, like he did in the North Tower, then yank her into his arms.

The man with the weather-beaten face, the hitman, places a call to the driver of a beige van parked half a mile away. The driver, in his late twenties, puts an orange box of fried chicken on top of the dashboard.

"Yeah?"

The hitman's voice is aggressive, with a slow, commanding cadence. "This is your supervisor speaking and that's one. Be at Concord Avenue in exactly ten minutes and wait there. She'll be leaving Lorena's wearing a black trench coat. Where are you?"

"Popeye's, on Prospect."

"That's nice, getting your nourishment, eh?"

"Yeah, eating some chicken. Got the munchies."

The hitman looks at his cell in disgust, "That's two. You fuck this up, you get nothing. Oh, and let me put more meaning into my statement. You and your three friends get to be dead. Do you understand?"

Silence. The driver has lost his appetite.

"What's going on out there? I don't like hearing myself talk."

*"Y... Yeah."*

"That's three. The answer is *yes*. You say *yeah* to me again and you'll be giving me one of your own fingers for every ten grand I give you. But you get to choose the fingers. After all, I have to be fair."

Silence. The driver feels like he's going to be sick. He opens the door but he fights the reflex and then says, *"Yes. Sir."*

"That's more like it. The money, and, of course, our hearty thanks, will be waiting when you complete the job. Now *get* ready to *go* to work."

Shaking and trying not to stammer, he mutters again, "Yes, sir."

Satisfied that the driver got his meaning, the hitman ends the call. He slows and slips into the space on the other end of Cauldwell. He has a clear view to Lorena's Place.

# 2

## 007

THE TIME WAS 11:38 PM. At the end of the cut-through street, some fifty yards from the blue Lincoln, and nested in a booth against the back wall of Lorena's Place, Ms. Marakie Dewabuna drank the last drop of a hot and spicy beverage. She picked up the little paperback again and read eight more paragraphs, laid out in the form of a letter. There was one page left in the final chapter. She stopped reading and reinserted the leather strip between the last two pages. She placed the paperback on top of an outsized, pricey textbook and snuggled her back up to the cushiony fabric, considering the emotional impact of the final scene of the novel.

A jazz quartet begins playing. A drummer's brush swirls over the snare drum while his other brush pats out a complementary rhythm on the high-hat cymbals. The standup bassist plucks a solemn, but hopeful, melody, backed up by soft, deft keystrokes from the pianist. Black walls and a ruby-red ceiling give the single room of the bistro a comfy feeling. Marakie's mood is dreamy. Her heartstrings are astir.

Lorena's Place, at the juncture of Trinity and Pontiac Place, was outfitted with speakers in every corner. A feeling of live music poured through. If your eyes were closed, the clarity made the music feel as if the players were there in the bistro. Marakie opened her eyes as the singer streamed her sultry soul-currents through each word.

Carmen McRae's definitive voice moved through Marakie's body: *The night is like a lovely tune—beware, my foolish heart!* The words deepened in her the sentiment of the novel's eight sad paragraphs.

Marakie, naïve and perfectly stunning, was surprised at the cold, matter-of-fact way that the double agent confessed her deceit in the spy novel. If Vesper truly loved James, Marakie thought, then how could she put the one she loved in danger, as well as his fellow spies? Yes, the song was *just like* those eight paragraphs—was it love or fascination? To her, the song was about boundless, unconditional love versus a sophistry of love—a flash-in-the-pan and crude love that impersonates, in its paltry manner, the real thing. The events in the book in relation to the witchery of the musical selection dropped deep into the center of Marakie's chest and awakened in her a huge warehouse of feeling.

*How white, the ever-constant moon. Take care... my foolish heart.* But Marakie had never been in love.


Precisely at 11:48 pm, the driver of the beige van parked on the corner of Concord and 149th, two blocks away from the blue Lincoln.

The dome light inside the Lincoln was still on. Out of Scudder's two-way radio the question was asked several times: "Do you copy, Agent Scudder?" A few minutes earlier the old woman with the grocery basket staggered back past the apartment complex. She came upon the agent's car and saw that the interior light was on. She was curious. The driver wasn't moving. His head was pitched forward and down. His seat harness kept him from bending forward onto the wheel. She looked around, then teeter-tottered over to the passenger window and placed a hand on each side of her head to block out light from the lamp post. She brought her palms closer in front of her face to make it easier to look through the tinted glass. She could make out the paper, a dark liquid and the phone. She peered more to the right and saw the envelope but couldn't exactly conclude that she was looking at the ends of paper money.

But her heart began racing, though, not because of fear, or that the man was obviously dead, but because she felt something long unfamiliar—excitement. If it were money, then it was right in front of her. The window was shut, but the driver's side wasn't. She stood up from the big car, almost tripping backwards, and then grabbed the handle of the basket as she checked the sidewalk for people. She watched the street traffic and waited for the light to change. She, too, knew how to gauge the traffic interval of rest and motion.


Marakie would be the last customer to leave. It was 11:51. Inside Lorena's Place she had enjoyed lamb and garlic, Ethiopian bread and nut-butter. She dined at the far corner at the back of the establishment near the kitchen's double-doors for a reason—she had an unobstructed view of the front entrance, and should the occasion arise, had an expedient exit through the narrow kitchen and out into the back alley. Her driver, DSS Special Agent Frank Scudder, had instructed her to find the strategic spot in all public places where she could flee from danger if the need presented itself, but he hadn't instructed her on how to read the signs of danger at a distance before it was in her face. A lesson he had recently failed.

She sat on the single black-leather bench and pored on through the final page of her novel. Carmen McRae's ethereal, behind-the-beat phrasing took up the background of her awareness.

The double doors swung back and forth in ever-shortening arcs. Lorena, the owner of the bistro, asked, "How was the food, honey?" Lorena had been born in Iberia Parish, Louisiana. She had been an Army drill sergeant and was now working through her second marriage. Her take-control persona, flamboyance and sense of the dramatic had marshaled an atmosphere of excitement inside the bistro. She ambled to the corner booth and collected Marakie's dishes and tableware.

Marakie looked up, "The food? Miss Lorena, it was delicious!"

"Oh, child... just Lorena." She finished loading the empty plates and mug on her arm. "So, what you readin' this time?"

"It's *Casino Royale*, a James Bond spy novel by Ian Fleming. See?" Marakie took the book off the table and with soft, artistic-looking hands modeled the cover: four cards of different suits and a dagger arranged against an orange background. After her tour of duty, where clear English was demanded, Lorena resurrected her native Cajun accent and other speaking habits peculiar to her. She tended to leave out useful parts of speech on purpose, for brevity. "Good book?" Lorena, a full-figured, thirty-five-year-old former NCO, at five-eleven, was wearing a mind-bending bright-yellow tank dress with a low neck. She was highly attractive and assertive in an abrupt, Bette Davis manner. She exuded sensuality, had bronze skin, full lips, hazel eyes, and a boxy hairstyle à la Grace Jones. She flaunted her chestnut hair with pale-gold hoop earrings. Lorena told herself that her getup was good for business. She smiled, nudged the kickplate with her foot, and strode back into the kitchen, lip-syncing McRae's lovely words.

Marakie answers her question, while raising her pitch a little, "Yes, it was a good book, but sad in the end. James' heart is broken." She positions the novel on top of her textbook and fastens the elastic strap around them.

She's curious about something, so she asks Lorena, still in the kitchen, "Why do you... expose so much of yourself? You're beautiful, but excuse me for saying, aren't you giving your patrons the wrong signal?"

The song ends. There's a moment of silence, then Lorena swings the doors open and wipes her hands with the dishtowel. She sashays toward her questioner and stands opposite her and nods, "Woman to woman? Okay, then maybe you'll understand. I know what works. They can look all they want. I'm in love with one man. One... man! But I *knows* what works and I makes sure I use what has worked these past four years to maintain my bottom line."

Lorena peers into Marakie's eyes—a striking hazel into soft and lustrous baby browns.

"Honey, my food's what brings 'em here. If it weren't for my dishes," Lorena shakes her head, "nobody would care a lick about what I put on. I enjoy wearing bright colors and going free boob most of the time. Something to do with my Aries rising, or somethin' or other, my astrologer told me years ago. Anyway, my first husband was dissin' my free spirit." Lorena's eyes meandered around the room, and then came back to Marakie. "He wanted a divorce. He didn't understand me. Guess he was insecure."

"Maybe worried about your safety."

"Maybe but, honey, I can take care of myself. He knew that before we got married. What's going on underneath my appearance is just the reason why no patron of Lorena's has ever made a pass at me or acted improper. I keep order in here, just like I did with my recruits. Attitude is my master key. As I said, I am in love with only one man—that's my husband. He and I agree that my food, good looks, and the intimate feel of this place are responsible for our success. Marakie, I'm like a healthy mom to my patrons. I feed 'em and make 'em feel cozy. I'm old school." Lorena turned as if to push through the swinging doors, into the kitchen, then she stopped herself and faced Marakie.

"And I believe that any husband of mine should be able to do something more with his hands besides fondling my breasts and grabbing my ass."

Blushing, Marakie says, "Miss Lorena!"

"It's just Lorena, honey." She turns left and points toward the front door. "Do ya see that hostess' podium?"

Marakie turns right, "Yes, it's beautiful."

"Well, my husband, Errol, built it with his own hands. An' he did it, don't ya know, in three days. Out of Honduran mahogany, Miss Marakie. I hope you, too, can find someone who knows how to work with his hands. Get my meaning?"

"Yes, ma'am."

"I'm old school, but not *that* old school, just Lorena. Never liked being called ma'am." Lorena stares at Marakie. "You ain't dressed like a nun, now, are you?" Marakie looked at her clothing. Lorena took the seat opposite her young patron. "How you carry yourself makes all the difference. No matter what you're wearing. Has anyone disrespected you since you've been in the states?"

"Never."

"Why?"

"I don't know. Maybe because of my escort. He's tall and strong and he's got a pistol under his jacket."

"Well, maybe so, but I reckon it's more than that."

"Well, I'm not seeing anyone yet. My focus is on my studies. I have a high GPA to maintain but I guess, in my mind—"

"You waitin'," Lorena said as she got up and walked slowly toward the double doors, "for the right man to come along." Marakie dropped her eyes. She couldn't hide.

"I think that's why... Attitude is the reason that men are behaving that way toward you. You can't conceal what you think or how you feel. You're waiting for the right man to come along and everybody can tell. They may interpret it differently—like maybe you're stuck up or you're already datin' someone, or you're just too serious. The point is they feel you searchin' for something. Something, *ah...* authentic. You telegraph it. The riff-raff just get out your way. I believe in the power of thought, Marakie. All people can tell when you're for real or full of crap. It's built into every human. Everyone has a built-in crap detector."

Marakie laughed. Lorena started for the kitchen door.

"You heard me. It's the truth." Lorena looked up at the digital clock on the wall above Marakie's head. "Now, let me get back to my chores."

From inside the kitchen, there is gushing water from the faucet and dishes and tableware crashing into each other. Lorena calls through the doors, "We were talking about James Bond's heart, Marakie. What keeps the heart going is the constant, unending act of being pushed. I know it's true, girl. I did lots of pushing."

Marakie was fascinated by that statement. Lorena was an effective communicator. Marakie felt those words push through her, just as Lorena had described. They were poignant, standing forth on the screen of her mind as if written on a ribbon of blazing light. Like those words, she felt as if *her* heart were not exactly being pushed but directed, like a lock searching for its only key, leading her she knew not where.

Lorena's bronze face is all smiles as she returns to the dining area with refilled salt-and-pepper shakers for all thirteen tables. She glides between and around each table set, inserting the shakers into their little racks, and then circles back to Marakie's table. She takes up a steaming wet cloth from the side of a small divided bucket and runs it over the surface after Marakie lifts her books. She pushes her foot again against the silver kickplate.

Lorena adds, "That part about the heart being pushed is from *Beneath the Lion's Gaze,* by Maaza Mengiste, an Ethiopian-American. So, James Bond's heart may have been broken but he *will* push on and find love again. Always does."

Marakie shrugged, "But it never lasts. Anyway, Bond girls always end up dead."

"That's because it's fiction, dearie. You will find love, too. There's someone out there looking and he's worth his salt. He's looking for you. One day, maybe soon, you'll meet." A commercial dishwasher is turned on. Lorena walks slowly out the kitchen, between the double doors, and checks the digital clock again. She smiles at Marakie.

Marakie said, "I'd be devoted to him and love him with all my heart. If I met someone like that. I wouldn't betray—"

Lorena bit off her words, "Of course, you wouldn't." She placed her fist on her hips like she was about to give orders to a line of recruits, "Well then, it's closing time."

That gesture and the finality of Lorena's words was Marakie's cue. It was like a therapist telling a patient that their session was over. She stood up serenely, at five-eight, with her books in her arms. She was slim and shapely, with a subdued sensuality and grace in her demeanor.

Since arriving in the South Bronx, Marakie often came to Lorena's Place to unwind after classes. But Lorena's presence did just the opposite. It got Marakie all wound up. Tonight, her garb blended perfectly with the two main colors of the place. Her red blouse accented her black trench coat, skirt and pumps. Her long charcoal hair fell softly around her shoulders. Her brown face and cheekbones could have been copied from some ancient template for depicting sublime beauty.

Marakie put $33.00 under the saltshaker, wrapped her arms around her books and meandered between two sets of tables and chairs down the center of the bistro, past the hostess podium to the front entrance. "Goodnight, Lorena." And with that she pulled open the solid maple door.

"Thank you and Godspeed, my dear," Lorena answered.

"You're welcome and the same to you!" Marakie stepped out into the cool night. She looked in both directions of Trinity Avenue but didn't spot Agent Scudder's Lincoln at first. He never parked in the same place. She thought of calling him but reconsidered. Her apartment was only two blocks away, to the west on Cauldwell. Maybe Frank was giving her more privacy, she thought. She heard a knock and turned around to see Lorena's bright yellow dress and her hand waving goodbye through the side window. She waved back, then heard the door lock, and saw Lorena's hand turn the sign around, with the clock face showing the bistro's reopening, tomorrow at noon. Next to the clock was posted Zagat's stellar review.

Marakie walks south toward the corner between a caravan of trucks and SUVs and an apartment, then past a grocery store, and then a sheet-metal products garage near the corner of 149th Street. She has a perfect gait, which she learned at a finishing school in her home country, Afarland. Her cultured demeanor appears out of sync with this tempered, rough environment, but she is happy to be on her own, without a diplomatic escort.

The moon is soft and luminous. It steals her attention. She lowers her eyes to street level and waits for the light. She can see her apartment and is about to cross the intersection of 149th and Trinity.

Standing at the corner, for reassurance, she looks around for Frank, expecting to see him in the blue, luxury sedan rolling to a stop any second, then hopping out the door into a brisk walk toward the back and around to her, dressed to the nines, all the while smiling and surveying the perimeter and speaking kind yet firm professional words, "Miss Dewabuna, allow me," as he unostentatiously shields her and opens the back door for her to get in. She is used to this ritual, which is well choreographed and deftly executed. She feels safe. He is skilled, experienced and a devoted husband to his sick wife. Marakie admires that quality in him. She hopes the extra money her powerful father has given him will help.

Looking for her federal escort while standing on the busy street, Marakie now realizes her psychological dependency on the federal protection. Would this be her life? If she was giving her power to someone else, she naturally relied less on her own power, her own resources. She imagined a bird in its cage, hopping about and flying for nanoseconds inside its wire mesh, safe within its confines, playing out its life of domestication. Could she move about the world without that wire grid, without so much supervision? This silent question made her feel differently and she *desired* to feel differently.

The driver sees the trench coat, yanks the chicken wing out of his mouth and drops it into the orange box, then puts his greasy fingers, all ten of them, onto the wheel and gear, shifts into drive and flows with traffic. The van's high beams are on as it slides into a screeching stop in front of Marakie. Startled, she staggers back a few steps. Again, she looks for Agent Scudder. Her eye is led to the Housing Authority apartments. There she spots the car and sees her protector's head bent over.

She shouts, "Frank!" and tries to run to him but the driver presses on the gas and blocks her, almost hitting her with the van. She steps sideways, then back. In the past, Lorena would talk about the basic combat training skills that she taught recruits. "Lorena!" shouts Marakie. She can't fathom her guardian not coming to help her. Maybe he's drunk, sick? She looks around for cops on patrol. Vehicles are parked near the intersection, but there's not a person on foot except an old woman with anxious steps pushing a grocery basket past Cauldwell Avenue. Lorena is upstairs in her apartment above the bistro when she hears the screaming of her name.

Marakie turns and runs toward Lorena's Place and just makes it to a spot between the grocery store and the parked vehicles, but two men with nylon stockings over their heads and matching scarves in their back pockets crash out of the side cargo door of the van.

She snatches her cell phone out of her coat. Extreme anxiety interferes with her coordination. She fumbles and drops the phone on the pavement. She got to 91. She bends over, reaching her hand out, to press the final 1, while yelling for help, but one of the men wraps his arms around her thighs to lift her, while the other gets behind her and covers her mouth. She uses the leverage of the man holding her from behind, while she engages her strong hip extensors to push each foot down to the ground, then opens her mouth wide and chomps down. The man covering her mouth hears a crack and feels the splitting force of over 150 pounds, focused through sharp front teeth. The attacker in agony tries to pull his fingers out of her mouth. He's in more pain for trying. He smashes his knee into her back to get his bloody fingers from between her teeth. She opens her mouth, screaming. He yanks out his fingers, takes his scarf out and wraps them up.

Marakie slams her textbook against the head of the man trying to lift her. He stands up and waves his index finger at her. She spits out pieces of flesh. Lorena bursts open the front door and runs like a sprinter to save her friend, her breasts popping halfway out her tank dress. She's in army mode, high-tailing past the apartments and grocery store and with an angry *kiai!* She slams her fist against the bones of the thigh-grabber's left eye. The punch sounds like a fastball striking a catcher's mitt. Blunt. He staggers and drops to one knee. She punches him again and again in the same place. "Help. Help!" Marakie shouts. He manages to cover his head from the fourth blow, gets up off his knee, stumbles clumsily onto his feet and pushes her back. Now, with the first man's fingers crushed and bleeding, and the second man's blood trickling out through the nylon stocking from around the soft bone above his left eye, the two miscreants become enraged and bellow like animals.

Traffic on the main drag cannot see the assault behind the troop of parked vehicles. But the shouts reach an apartment building across the street, as well as the one just a few doors beyond the grocery store. Marakie regains her footing and she and Lorena run to the bistro. She feels relieved for a moment. Everything is going to be okay.

The assailants sprint after the women. They are too doped up on cocaine and adrenaline to care about their injuries. As they get closer, Lorena stops on a dime, turns and screams, while kicking wildly, she catches both men on their shins and knees. As they both hop on one foot, Marakie scratches through the nylon stocking over the bitten man's face like a cat fighting for its life. He covers his head as her nails come down in vertical curves.

Lorena lands a right cross against the same spot near the thigh grabber's left eye. Blood is pouring out through his eyehole. He laughs and puts his hand behind his back. Lorena sets up to kick him again but he pulls out his switchblade and slashes her tendon. She grabs the back of her ankle and lowers her body, while screaming out curses. He lands a roundhouse kick to the side of her head, sending her to the pavement.

A third assailant, watching from the half open side door and determined to end this quickly, jumps out of the van and races down the sidewalk. Lorena gets back up, breathing heavily. She's forgotten her tendon and wants to get back in the fight to protect Marakie, when the third assailant with lots of momentum tackles her, all 180 pounds of him. Lorena is lifted off her feet. Her yellow dress blooms upward as her back slams against the sidewalk. Her diaphragm spasms from the impact.

Now she's on her back; the lioness in her is subdued. The three men grab Lorena. She feels herself being raised off the ground. Marakie yells, "No, leave her alone!" Lorena, knowing what's about to happen, yanks her feet and hands to get free. The three men run sideways with her to the curb, swing her from side-to-side until her body reaches the height of their heads, then they let go and watch her body strike the edge of the curb.

They run back to Marakie who is covering her mouth and shaking her head. She cowers. The third man, the tackler, dives for her legs and slams her on her back. Marakie is stunned out of her mind. She is unable to continue resisting. Two men grab each foot and the third holds her under the armpits. They race to the van. They pass her cell phone. She reaches for it. The driver jumps out and holds the side door wide open. They toss her inside and then hop in one at a time.

Traffic halts. The driver jumps back inside, puts the van in gear and does a U-turn. The van swings around in a violent skid that tilts it off its long axis. Marakie, stays put. The three men in the cargo area, straining against inertia, all crawl to one side. The van is now moving on all four tires. The side cargo door slides on its track, and they struggle to slide it all the way closed. After the van fishtails, the momentum from the inertia helps to slam the side door shut. The driver hits the gas.

Several people inside the apartment near the grocery store heard the screams, rushed to their windows, and called 911. They saw Lorena being thrown to the curb and now not moving. Some ran out to help Lorena who had lost consciousness, her back badly bruised, maybe broken. Blood oozed from below her calf. People ran out from an apartment across the street. One of them, an old man and former cop, saw Marakie's books on the ground and her cell phone. He left them alone. It would be crime-scene evidence.

From Cauldwell Avenue, one block away, across an open area with green grass, the hitman watches from the Escalade. "Those freaking oafs," he mutters as he takes off after the beige van.

# 3

## Intersecting Currents

ACROSS TOWN AT MIDNIGHT, rookie cop Ford McCurdy is at the wheel heading east on Randall Avenue with his field training officer riding shotgun. McCurdy just put away his second cup of coffee.

"My spotlight's gone out. Turn on the *alley* to light those doors," the FTO said while pointing his finger out the window. His assignment was to train the rookie until a suitable replacement could be found. One FTO was on his scheduled day off, another was sick, and the rest were attending to fresh meat right out of the academy. It was a last-minute assignment for this FTO. He had a gold bar on each collar of his white shirt and his shield was bright gold with 12 points set in a blue background. His signet ring was like his shield, too. He wore it on his right index finger, the one he was pointing with.

"Yes, Lieutenant Jones. Turning on the alley light." McCurdy pressed the button on the instrument panel and applied more brake, bringing the police cruiser down to a crab's pace. Traffic on the two-lane was more circumspect due to the police presence. Minor pad and wheel noises had bounced off the walls and windows of storefronts and warehouses. Jones was tensed with alertness in the passenger seat because he knew this night would be more than dangerous, especially for the rookie. He had measured that possibility three days earlier.

Lieutenant Jones raises his hand. The cruiser stops. "There's something going down right here, McCurdy. Does that façade look strange to you?" he asks.

McCurdy is youthful and gullible to a certain extent. He bends forward. Jones pushes his extra weight against the seatback. McCurdy has a clear sightline to the brilliantly lit plexiglass doors. "Not to me, Lieutenant." The rookie, in his cleaned and starched uniform, wonders if his field trainer is just busting his balls.

About a mile to the west, the beige van holding Marakie Dewabuna, crosses under the Bruckner Boulevard Expressway heading east-south-east. The road ahead is clear for two lights. The driver is up to 40 mph. After passing the first light, the driver digs into his tight pocket, tugging at his phone. He can't get it out. His tugging movements jerk the van side-to-side. He regains control.

The rings and vibrations of the phone will stop soon. If the driver doesn't answer, he may have to give up some fingers or get no money for this caper. Or end up dead. Or all three—beginning with his fingers. The top of his phone is out. Red dots ahead are closing in fast. He digs deeper to get a good grip. One last pull. The van yaws to the right.

Three car lengths ahead, a chauffeur decides to step out of his limousine. From his wing mirror he catches sight of the outline of the van closing in and barely touching the vehicles behind him. His window is up. He panics to get it down in time to fold in the mirror. The van's headlights are on him. He quickly covers his head and angles his body to the right.

Marakie heard the huge sound of the van hitting the mirror. She thought the driver hit a person. The driver abruptly steers left. Tires screech as he veers back into his lane. The assailants shout out obscenities and the driver shouts back. The cargo space inside contains no cargo, just three men and their kidnappee. There's no padding, just an old rusted floor, and like a loudspeaker, the hollow space amplifies every sound. The radio is blasting. Marakie covers her ears.

The driver regains steering control. The wheels deliver a piercing sound as the van crashes to a stop behind the line of brake lights.

"Hello?"

A voice in a flat, unchanging tone asks, "Mr. Jiekang, do you have her?"

Relieved at not hearing *The Supervisor's* voice and talking very fast, the driver says, "Fuck, yeah, a couple of minutes ago. We grab her after she left the restaur—"

"Your radio is too loud, could you turn it down?" Jiekang turns the radio off.

"That is better, you were saying."

"My guys got injuries. She's a fucking handful. Time to get paid now?"

"Certainly, it is time for you and your crew to get paid. Proceed to the agreed-upon street," the flat voice said. "My courier is on his way. He will hand you the money in a silver-aluminum attaché case. It contains 50,000 U.S. dollars, in twelve stacks of twenty-dollar bills."

Jiekang pumped his fist. "Okay! Twenty minutes. Traffic tight." The flat voice on the other end said, "You make it there in ten," then abruptly ended the call.

"Hello, you there?" Jiekang asks. "Can't hear you." He looked at the screen. Sucked in air through his teeth and put the phone on the dash. In Mandarin he said, "Hey, keep it fucking quiet back there!"

The three men in the back shouted to Jiekang in Mandarin, "Are we there yet? You drive clumsy. My fingers are bleeding; need to go to hospital." Jiekang pounded the bottom of his fist against the bulkhead. The three men laughed like hyenas.

Jiekang, the driver, crossed Randall Avenue onto Truxton Street, passing several detached semi-trailers and low brick buildings with large rolling steel doors, all locked down for the night. He turned left at Oak Point Avenue, then turned around and saw his three partners through the perforated bulkhead snorting cocaine, and the huddled girl, his $50,000-dollar ticket. "This cat wants us there now. Make quick, okay?" Jiekang put his foot down. The ten-year-old rusty van sounded like its broken-down condition.

The lights were turning in his favor, "Hold on back there." He treads heavily on the accelerator, increasing his speed from 40 mph up to 75 for over eight blocks. The engine roars. It doesn't sound healthy. The quick acceleration pushes the three men against the rear doors. The one whom Marakie bit uses his bloodied hand to keep from banging into the inner door handle—a natural reflex. He slams it against the steel panel. Marakie is terrified at the sound he makes. It reminds her of the cries of animals being slaughtered.

The old engine thrummed richly as if *it* were high. The ride was bumpy and fast and the men in the back, experiencing cocaine intoxication, were exhilarated even more by the van's speed as it careened on the Peninsula in the South Bronx in the direction of the Bronx River near one of the largest food-distribution facilities in the world: *Hunts Point*. Jiekang was smoking a cigarette and in fantasyland about the payoff. The promise of an attaché case loaded with $50,000 and the threat from the hitman, who called himself *The Supervisor*, were enough motivation to heighten his alertness at the wheel and just enough for him to consider his options. He calculated 50,000 divided four ways. At the eighth block he slowed and took a sharp left on Faile Street.

Marakie, in her late twenties, was rolled up like a ball, in the corner behind the passenger seat. She had circled her arms around her shins, pushed her cheeks against her knees, her eyes peered over her upper arms at the men surrounding her, two with nylon stockings over their faces, taking in the white powder through tiny stained nose holes. She kept her eyes from look-ing at the face of the man she had bitten.

It was 12:05 am. Marakie's mouth was covered with duct tape. Her breathing was irregular. She fidgeted inside the dark rusty van. The men got quiet and looked at her. Marakie stopped fidgeting. The men's intentions were clear. There was no refuge and no one to help. No escape, she con-cluded, after reciting in her mind an impromptu mental litany of what could happen. She recalled her friend getting cut above her heel and then tossed up in the air to land on the street, back first. Was Lorena dead? No matter what, Marakie was not going to surrender what was meant for only one man—her body and soul. The dome light kept blinking on and off. Her cap-tors appeared, then became dark outlines and then reappeared—each time in a different part of the van.

A nightmare. She gazed behind them through the back window and saw buildings and street lamps passing by, shrinking and then moving out of frame. Her sight fixed itself on that window. Her awareness of the van's creak-ing and the occasional bumps were replaced by fleeting images parading in reverse. The three men looked at her, then turned and looked out the back window, too. Marakie looked further up in the distance to the mast of a col-orfully lit tower crane, and then, the blinking lights of the operator's cab. Be-yond the cab, she could make out a jet hurtling upward after takeoff, to reach cruising altitude. She wondered how she'd feel if she were inside that plane right now, going back to her home in Africa.

Four thousand three hundred and sixty miles away, at 5:06 in the morn-ing, the traffic is light on Route 21, in Tunisia's capital of Tunis. It is a vibrant spring day in Tunisia on the Mediterranean coast of northern Africa. The sky is a sparkling, clear blue. The first rays reach over limestone hills. The shoul-der of the highway is lined with small palm trees that look like large pineap-ples. They whiz by. Beyond the palms and underbrush on both sides of the highway are majestic white structures. The apartment buildings, businesses and mosques are all white with large, blue doors and windows. Some are de-signed with gently rounded corners. In the far distance is a white building with a large, sky-blue dome. After admiring the sun's play of light on these structures, a man inside a tan Mercedes, the one with the monotone voice, is heading to Aéroport Tunis-Carthage. He's about to place a call to Logan, the hitman in the South Bronx who is following the beige van.

Adlai Borg is a tall man, originally from Valletta, Malta. He is part British and part Maltese, with gray hair, stony eyes, overhanging brows, a square mesomorph's head and a sallow complexion. His white suit blends well with the local architecture.

Borg swallows a shot glass full of chilled *Bukha*, made from Mediter-ranean figs. Jessica, Borg's executive secretary and personal bodyguard, is a petite French woman in a red dress, nipped at the waistline. She is wearing a Tahitian pearl choker. She sports a curious smile that is seldom replaced by any other expression, especially in public. Borg hands her the shot glass. She reaches forward to the driver's back seat and drops it into the holder. Borg moves his left hand up and down her back. She leans against his left arm, then dials Logan's number and hands Borg the phone, but not before kissing it first. Borg directs a stern gaze at Jessica. She winks at him. Borg places his left hand on her knee and she runs both of her hands over his. Sunlight washes through the windows and augments the car's silk-beige interior.

"Logan, did you take care of the diplomatic escort?"

Logan, Borg's professional hitman with the battered face, says, "Yes. He's done."

"Charming. I do not want just the girl, but all of them, shall we say, liquidated. I just spoke to Jiekang. I told him that my courier was on his way and that he should be at the agreed-upon place in ten minutes."

"I comprehend, Mr. Borg. That will be a grand total of six kills within an hour. You're running a huge tab."

"You are terribly unaffected by the lives you take."

"Just unaffected. It's my business, a regular job."

"I see. I like your attitude."

# 4

## Weapons Drawn

LOGAN HEADS EAST ON OAK POINT, passing several women on *the night shift*, in garter belts, stilettoes, and curve-skimming minis. He can still see the van ahead. He then turns left on Faile and spots the van slipping into a space behind a flatbed near the corner of Randall Avenue, the approved spot for the payoff.

"Six kills?"

"That is correct, six. But I'll call in when they're all gone, Mr. Borg." I'm going to hit sixty kills tonight, getting closer, Logan muses.

"Right. We have entered the airport grounds. I should like to hear the news before we take off. It is a two-and-a-half-hour flight and I must nap before we land in Tüyap, Istanbul." Jessica sits up, assessing her surroundings.

Logan listens as he parks the Escalade in front of a building with a colorful, forty-foot banner displaying tomatoes and chili peppers wearing top hats and mustaches. He pulls his jacket sleeve back and tells Borg, "I see the van. They've got nine minutes. I'll do them all at a quarter after."

"That will be at 6:15 in the morning Tunisia time. Splendid. Ring me as soon as you have done with it." Borg ends the call and hands the cell to Jessica. As she's about to put it in her clutch, he grabs her choker and pulls her to him. Her smile doesn't change. The driver catches Borg's move from the rearview mirror, then immediately faces the road. "You are dangerously beautiful, are you not?"

Jessica caresses Borg's hand, which is still pulling the choker. Their noses touch.

"I can be one, or the other." She stares into his stony-gray eyes, then to his protruding eyebrows, then notices his whole face. She wants to be with someone, but it's not him, yet he's wealthy and pays her well, for *very* close personal protection.

Borg says, "Or both?"

"Yes, both, whatever you want me to be. You've got me by my collar. Do you want me to be just beautiful and your... play toy?" She takes her hand away and closes her eyes.

"We will be getting out soon. I have enemies. I want you to be dangerous. When I want you to be anything else, I will tell you. So, *do not* assume anything else."

She opens her eyes and says, "Then, you will unhand my $11,000 necklace. I earned it."


Logan slides his hands back into his pair of ultra-thin marksman gloves and then takes out his Walther from under his legs and another, an Iraqi Tariq semi-automatic, out of the glove box.

Back on Randall Avenue Jones says to McCurdy, "After our shift, fill out a requisition to get the pads and rotors checked. Get used to doing paperwork from the start."

"Yes, sir," the rookie replies. He sees a figure in his peripheral vision. He turns. Across the street, a petite, scantily clad woman with dark hair and a short orange skirt is climbing up the steps into the sleeper cabin of a custom semi rig. Such blatant disrespect for the law, McCurdy observes. "Sir, what about?"

"What about what?" Jones sees the woman closing the sleeper cab behind her.

"Should we issue a summons or make an arrest?"

"Par for the course, McCurdy. We'll attend to it after this."

"Yes, sir."

Second Lieutenant Ahmad Jones, in his clean, white shirt fitted perfectly over his vest, looked to his right and ran his eyes sideways, up and down through the plexiglass double-doors of Jenkins Auto Supply. He pulled in the latch and opened the car door.

Turning back to his partner, "McCurdy?"

"Yes, sir?"

"How does your setup feel?"

"Not tight... and not sagging sir. My Bat utility belt feels fine." Jones smiles and then notices McCurdy's duty-belt and his taser next to his firearm. "That's good, and that's an excellent company, too. Got my DB from them. But bring your CEW to your weak side. I assume you're right-handed?"

"Yes."

"Changing sides will prevent you from whipping out your taser when your firearm is required."

"Right, sir." Jones stepped out and faced his trainee from the sidewalk. "Consider drinking less coffee."

"Too much, sir?"

"Ask your bladder."

"Yes, sir. Should I get out with you?"

"Wait inside. Stay idle, in park, with your eyes and ears open." Jones shut the door.

"Sir, should I call this in?"

Jones swung around and cupped both palms on the cruiser's windowsill. "What do you think, McCurdy?" He paused a beat, sensing his trainee's mind searching for the answer, and then said, "You can follow my lead for now. Procedures, McCurdy, always follow procedures, but be willing to modify them within the law in the interest of saving lives, which we've taken an oath to protect. Cook your brain for your own answers, and when you've cooked it enough, if you are still uncertain, ask. If your FTOs just give you the answers to all your questions, it will go in one ear and out the other. But when you strive... dig to uncover the answers, through alertness, keen observation and study, then it becomes personal."

McCurdy, although confused, thoughtfully nods.

"Expect the unexpected, McCurdy. Nothing is always as it seems. Read Emerson's essay on self-reliance. Apply its overarching premise to your PSA.

"Do you know your 10 codes?"

"Not all of them, sir."

"I haven't met anyone yet who did."

"Do you know all the codes, sir?"

"I'm in the same boat as the rest of us."

"I've brushed up on tactical hand signals, just in case."

Jones nodded. "Good. So, what's a 10-75P?"

With a grin McCurdy says, "Park, walk and talk."

Jones directs his eyes and ears at the southwest corner to his right, listening to something faint. Still cupping the sill, he squats back down to talk to his partner. "That's good, rookie. Unless you or someone else is in mortal danger, especially during the first shift and on patrol in a high-risk area, never ever execute a 10-75P, when you're solo without a 10-85 to Dispatch."

"What's a 10-85?"

"Self-reliance, remember? Look it up."

"Yes, sir, Lieutenant Jones."

Jones turns to the corner again. "Something there is out of place... what I'm about to do isn't exactly by the book. Call it in, a 10-85."

McCurdy looked puzzled.

"The code for an additional unit. If Dispatch asks, say it's a 10-10. Add *possible prowler*—don't just say 10-10. Roll the cruiser down a car length." Jones took his palms off the windowsill as he pushed out of his squat and walked toward the plexiglass doors.

McCurdy heard muted voices and commotion coming from the semi's mobile apartment across the street. He moved the cruiser away from directly opposite the front doors of the building.

McCurdy watched his FTO turn around, gaze left and right, then walk up to the side of the front door of the block-long storefront. He veered off to the right of the double doors, making certain not to frame himself at the window, in case some bad guys had him in their sights. They could fire from behind the front counter. Jones examined the doors. He took out his tape, which he used to measure out collisions. He found out why those doors looked strange.

McCurdy reached for his shoulder holster unit. His thumb was on the transceiver button. Unsure of himself, he said, "Unit 525, over."

"Go ahead, 525?"

"*Ah*, ten-four, we're parked on Randall, between Coster and Faile. Random building check at Jenkins Auto Supply. 10-85, over."

"Copy that, 525. Reason?"

McCurdy froze. His heartbeat raced. "*Ah...* it's a 10-10."

"Say again, 525?"

"I mean, 10-10—possible prowler."

"Ten-four. 525 requires additional unit, possible prowler. Random building check, Jenkins Auto Supply, on Randall, middle of Coster and Faile."

McCurdy took a deep breath inside the idling, police-issue Ford Explorer and watched his field-training officer while monitoring the police radio. He turned on the overhead light and looked up some 10 codes. He then picked up the briefing report, as he listened to a call about a jumper—a man found dead on 149th Street, the gang of Asian kidnappers still at large, and a burglary suspect apprehended across town on Lafayette. There was extreme danger in the air and he was oblivious to its huge size.

Jones wasn't oblivious. At six feet, with eagle eyes and overweight, he stepped a few paces back and took in the overall sweep of the neon-orange-lit building. The retail structure brightened intermittently from the glare of passing headlights. He turned toward the street and looked to his right. He noticed a flatbed and the way the light of a high-beam from behind illumined the side of it. He noticed that the beams came from beyond the west wall around the corner on Faile about fifteen feet away from where he stood. It illumined floating particles and flies. Then he noticed the beams, the flies and the particles vanish.

Jones looked to his left, noticing the slew of retail stores about three-quarters of a mile to the west. There were two long rows of buildings that displayed colorful produce signs. From Jones' vantage point, the buildings merged to a point in the distance, lit by low-voltage street lamps. Beyond those structures, Jones took in the clear night sky. He listened to the sounds of the night beyond the normal street sounds. He slipped into a space of no thought. A moment later, he reached into his tactical cargo pocket and pulled out a cell-phone-sized, pre-programmed astronomic device, with past and future celestial positions of the nine celestial bodies. The data covered a span of 9,000 years, 5,000 years into the past and 4,000 years into the future. He entered the current date, place, and time.

A map of the heavens for 12:07a.m.appeared on his small screen. Jones took a general gander at it while maintaining awareness of the sounds and sights of the two-lane, the noisy escapades coming from the semi, the idling police cruiser, and the sidewalk near the flatbed. He checked out the Moon, which was nearing the zenith of the South Bronx. He looked up and to his right, toward the east. At that angle the Moon, (signifying the public), wielded a stronger pull, Jones thought. He checked the screen again. The Moon was passing through the constellation of Libra, indicative of warring factions and energy out-of-balance, in most cases.

Jones then considered the Moon's celestial position from the standpoint of *Jyotisha,* the Indian astrology system. It was passing through *Swati* (the Sword), a group of stars within Libra's constellation that is associated with the restless winds of the northwest. The wind speed was at 16 mph where Jones stood but was running toward the northeast. Jones was focusing more now on the restless winds of scattered and chaotic human energies bent on breaking the law. The group of stars on the local horizon of the South Bronx was *Mula*, represented by a plethora of entangled roots. Mula has an affinity with *Nirriti*, the goddess of destruction, which precedes a new creation. From its many meanings, Jones considered its association with butchers, cruelty—violence.

Jones directed his attention back to the patrol vehicle ahead. He considered the brake problem and the broken spotlight on the A panel right above the mirror. He redirected his gaze back to the information on his screen more specifically. The star Antares, known as Alpha Scorpii, the Red Giant, twelve times the mass of the Sun, was on the local horizon. His mentor, an old man living in Cádiz, Spain, once told him that this star, pertaining to his student, represented an extraordinarily all-embracing factor and influence that related to the lofty work of high initiates in both ancient and contemporary mystery schools.

His mentor also told him that, in general, the forces pertaining to this star implied that each growth of a person's spirit sometimes required a toughening of the steel of character through burdening circumstances. The significance of the Moon's position and Antares climbing above the eastern horizon, with Mula, were in sync with Jones' feeling of a huge threat about to precipitate on these streets near Hunts Point.

But maybe he was making too much of it, he thought. Jones put the device and tape measure back inside his cargo pocket and returned to the cruiser.

It was 48 degrees and the winds were down to a whisper. On the two-lane, vehicles whizzed past Unit 525 at an average of eight per minute. Jones walked back to the open passenger-side window and said, "Those commercial doors don't meet the International Building Code. That's why they pulled my focus."

"Building codes?"

"The doors don't meet the IBC codes for exit and egress. They don't exhibit the proper height or width. The Department of Buildings Violations will be notified. Just write it up as a Class 2 violation, along with the facts I just gave you." McCurdy put his briefing and 10-codes manual away, then wrote down the information as his FTO conveyed them.

"Saturday morning, now a little more than ten minutes old, and with a Full Moon is a measurement for trouble."

McCurdy finished writing then added, "Okay, sir, but Full Moon? I don't believe in that astrology stuff."

"Neither do I, because it isn't something to believe in. Yet, it is something to know a lot about."

Tickled by his trainer's reference to astrology, the weird IBC violation, and the notion that it was all part of a grand plan to get a rise out of him, Mc-Curdy said, "Okay, sir. I'll keep an eye out for random lunatic assholes."

With emphasis Jones said, "Keep your eyes in your head, your mouth shut and your ears open. Use them. Those are your tools to stay alert."

Jones studies the shimmering moon. The cruiser is still idling. Winds stir up again. He's a few feet away from the passenger door when he remembers several monographs from the JSTOR digital library he had read. They contained the real-world correlations that several police departments made regarding the Full Moon and the incidence of crimes. But Jones knows that the New or Full Moons aren't the only factors in high-volume police calls and interventions. In this instance there are a multitude of factors, including the Moon, the group of stars in Swati, Mula and Antares, which, when taken together, could coincide with extraordinary events. Those elements would *be* a factor during Jones' present tour.

Ford McCurdy had been with the 42nd Precinct since January. He'd been patrolling the Melrose section of the South Bronx, a predominately residential area. He'd gotten comfortable working the rectangular-shaped neighborhood. He spoke fluent Spanish, which was a plus in these parts. He learned the proper use of all the technical and manual equipment inside the patrol car, got acclimated to the routine, and initiated legitimate traffic stops on his own, under his other FTO's watchful eye. He took part in three arrests, displaying promise while still a rookie. He would surely move up the ranks of LE, his other FTO said. McCurdy, with his frank and open personality, was a quick study—but then he got transferred to the 41st Precinct.

Two hours earlier, just as Friday the 26th was nearing the cusp to Saturday and during the huddle in the briefing room at Longwood, located on the other side of the Bruckner Expressway, McCurdy, now transferred to the 41st, was handed a tour near Hunts Point. Now he was behind the wheel and new to this police service area, trying to find logic between full moons and building-code violations. Then there's the prostitution happening under his nose across the street. McCurdy wasn't sure whether his trainer may be seeing stars of his own. His bladder was pushing from all that coffee—his FTO got that part right. His inner belt, which keeps his pants up and where his duty belt is attached, was feeling tighter. For a few seconds, Jones, about to get back in the cruiser, considered the recent question he had asked himself.

It was almost four days ago, on the 23rd, while he was reading in his den that the question arose spontaneously from his mind. He laid the book he was reading on his desk, which he had built out of bird's-eye maple. It was sturdy and wide, one that could accommodate the thirty-odd books that were lined up in military fashion, arranged from smallest to tallest, along the broad surface. On the top right near the edge stood a thirty-inch acupuncture model, along with books on pressure points, Jujitsu and Chin Na, Jujitsu's Chinese equivalent, weapons and other rare books on the fighting arts. He inserted Octavia Butler's *Parable of the Talents* back into the empty space between a book of Paul Laurence Dunbar's poetry and Lee Child's latest thriller, *Without Fail*. Jones had consulted the digital clock to his right and recorded the time of his question.

At the far left of the desk nearer the door, Jones pulled out three books: Neil Michelsen's *American Ephemeris for the 21st Century*, a table of diurnal proportionate logarithms, and a book of longitudes and latitudes for the U.S. Then he placed his pen against the paper and made some initial calculations pertaining to time. He was rendering an astronomic map of the heavens. He applied simple addition and subtraction to relate the place of the question (the longitude of the South Bronx) to the nearest Prime Meridian. He corrected clock time to Local Mean Time and then calculated the interval between it and the previous Noon.

Jones then heard sounds of paws striking the hallway floor. His Siberian husky, as if cued by Jones' calculations, sauntered into the study and halted a few feet from the doorway, waiting for permission.

"Skippy, I'm erecting a map of the heavens for this moment in time." The Sibe's breathing quickened; its eyes danced. It stood up straighter, wagging its heavily furred tail. It sauntered closer to lay its head on Jones' thigh. Jones petted Skippy's head and massaged his neck. The Sibe looked at him. *How present were those eyes*, Jones thought. He listened to the cycles of Skippy's breathing. Its sound and rhythm took him to another place in his mind.

He considered his own breath, of how it slowed whenever he silenced his mind, or gazed at certain stars at night, or when he directed his attention to his Source. He contemplated whether the Earth, the planets, or the stars breathed, and if so, of how long it took the Sun to complete one cycle of breathing. Was it months, years, decades, centuries or millennia? Jones came back to himself and looked at Skippy, who seemed to smile and then turned around and swaggered toward the doorway.

Jones, in a short afro, was wearing an extra-large blue jersey, numbered 16 for the NY Giants quarterback, Kerry Collins. He talked to his dog, "I'm converting longitude into time. Now, I'm adding a ten-second correction for Equivalent Greenwich Mean Time and another ten-second correction for Local Mean Time." Skippy wags and smiles, then suddenly arches downward, stretching out his paws, and after a deep and sonorous yawn, stands up straight again.

"Almost done, Skip. I'll take you out shortly. I'm factoring the sidereal time for tonight, April 23, 2002, at 9:35 pm, correcting for EDT, and now I've gotten my adjusted sidereal time." Jones took off his glasses and looked at his friend, "Get me *Campanus Table of Houses*, please." Skippy ambled to the front of the maple desk and looked up to find the general position of the thin goldenrod-colored book. He secured his paws on the edge of the desk and thrust his nose against the book's spine, pushing it toward his master without disturbing any other books. Jones, sitting high at his desk, pulled the book the rest of the way out. "Thanks, buddy." Skippy was excited, looked sideways, and took his paws off the desk. He paced around to where Jones was working. Jones stopped what he was doing to pet and massage his canine pal again. Its grey and white fur glistened under the full-spectrum desk lamp. After that, Skippy stepped backwards a few paces, then moved in a circle and lowered his body onto the warm Chinese-red carpet.

Jones leafed through *Campanus Table of Houses* for the latitude of the South Bronx. He used 40 degrees and 51 minutes. He jotted down the degrees and minutes of the twelve cuspal signs on a legal pad. Once he completed the initial calculations, he examined the data. Then he corrected the planets' celestial positions for the time in question. He measured out the longitudinal passage of the nine celestial bodies: The Sun and Moon and the planets from Mercury to Pluto.

"Cancer is on the horizon of the South Bronx at one degree and fifty-one minutes of arc. Venus is conjunct the fixed star Caput Algol. What do you think, Skip?" The dog stood and barked three times, and then lowered his white underbelly to the carpet again.

"The chart says that my question is premature, as referenced by the early degree of Cancer. And with the Moon in Virgo, conjunct Delta Leonis, which is more than fifty light years away, then I would agree that my question may be a bit unseasonable." Skippy rolled over to his right side. He spread his fore and hind legs out and dropped his grey-white head to mingle with the bright-red carpet. His eyes, one brown and the other blue, were directed to his master.

"Venus is in trouble. She's in a late degree and so close to Caput Algol, plus she's hidden away in the Twelfth House of confinement. Skip, it looks like my simple question is overshadowed by trouble." Jones continued to study the chart the way his father Robert Jones had taught him, when rendering a map of the heavens to reflect a specific moment in time.

Skippy stood up and yawned again, then turned and lowered his body. His eyes darted to his master, then to the window to Jones' right—about ten feet from the acupuncture model, then behind him at the entrance to the hallway and his leash hanging around the doorknob.

"The Moon is near the star Delta Leonis. *Hmm,* it's associated with a girdle, the back of something, and the ribs. It's fifteen degrees from an exact meeting with Venus. Could be fifteen days, or fifteen weeks—"

Skippy barked.

"You say months?"

Skippy barked again.

"But fifteen years, Skippy? As rule, a horary chart doesn't plot that far ahead in time."

Jones looks at his friend, "To a novice, that information would be quite perplexing, huh, Skippy?" The Sibe scrambled to his feet and moved leisurely past the maple desk to the window. He barked and turned.

"Coming right over." Jones hurriedly drew a circle with a compass, on a sheet of white construction paper, and then, with a straightedge, he inserted six lines, passing from one side of the circle through the center to the other side—twelve sections sliced like a pizza. He rechecked his math, and then placed the corrected degrees and minutes of celestial longitude of the planets and the Sun and Moon into some of the sections, called Houses. He took an overall look at the chart for more details about his question. Jones meets Skippy's eyes and in a less playful tone, Jones says, "*Hmmm,* four days. It says that in four days, me and the full-blown outcome of my question will connect in time."

Jones' question was one that most men and women ask themselves several times a day. Skippy looked away, then back at him, then away and back. Skippy wanted tons of exercise—all Sibes do.

Jones got up from his chair, feeling stiff. Before he erected his chart, he had been sitting at his desk reading Octavia Butler's novel for almost three hours. He stretched his hands up toward the ceiling to loosen his back, and then walked to the window facing the street. He raised it up as the waves of hustle and bustle rippled in, followed by a drift of crisp fresh air. Skippy looked up at his master. Jones looked down, "Okay, Skip, let's get out and walk through the neighborhood under this clear night sky."

Now, four days later, Jones was on patrol duty early Saturday morning with rookie officer Ford McCurdy whom he had first met at the briefing before they hit the streets. Facing away from the plexiglass double doors under a bejeweled sky, Jones ponders whether his own expectations related to his question will weave themselves into the prosecution of his civil duty.

*The time frame of the chart points to tonight and probably within the hour*, he thought. He sensed the approaching confluence of question and answer: of his duty to protect and serve, of his and McCurdy's teamwork and more—all entangled with every other event in all of space and time. It is because of this confluence that Jones won't comprehend the form his answer assumes when it is finally put before him; neither will he understand its deeper portents pertaining to the *fifteenth year* from now.

Jones remembered the horoscope data that pointed to a probable interference pattern or state of mind that would be just enough to cloud his recognition of the question's outcome. That interference could blend with the first shift of the night, the graveyard shift, and present a complex array of intersecting forces—a scenario many layers deep. It was already coming to a head where he stood between the cruiser and the double doors.

McCurdy, *the new rookie*, couldn't stop thinking that a joke was about to fall like a boulder—on him. He had to go to the bathroom but was nervous about telling his FTO. Jones opened the squad-car door to get back in and continue their patrol.

"All appears to be in order. We can move on. Cancel the 10-85." McCurdy was about to transmit when Jones felt an urge to look ahead in the direction of the southwest corner from where the high beams and the flies appeared. "No, wait!" he said.

The street lamp at the southwest corner just blew out.


Inside the beige van, the second man, the one whom Lorena punched in the head, moved closer. Marakie breathed anxiously. He yanked off the duct tape. She couldn't see his face, just his dead eyes and the bloody gash on the side of his head where the bone above his eye pierced the skin. Her anxiety turned into hyperventilation. The van's brittle rust was the dominant smell, in addition to the amalgam of body odor that suffused the air. The tackler also moved closer and covered her mouth with his hand. Her eyes darted from side to side. She reached out to push the hand away. Water from her eyes streamed out through the corners and onto her cheeks. She knocked the tackler's palm off her mouth for dear life. The tackler swung his hand to his opposite shoulder as if he were about to slap her. His eyes looked more sinister. Now, she heaved her breaths. Her eyes widened.

The man with the gash pulled the blade from his back pocket and pointed it toward her left eye. "Don't say a word," he whispered in Mandarin. She got the essence of what those foreign words meant. The one whose fingers Marakie bit also came closer. Now there were three smelly guys on cocaine surrounding her, one on each side and the one with the switchblade just a few inches from her face. She turned away, trying to think straight. Her hands were still free. She wondered if she could get away by grabbing the knife and stabbing her way to safety. The thought and the action were worlds apart. The man holding the blade replaced the tape. All three pulled away from her toward the cargo door. She felt relieved but knew it wasn't over. Jiekang left the keys in the ignition and got out of the van.

Jones, whose left foot was already inside the cruiser, on the footwell, heard the heavy breathing from around the corner and then a door open and close. He said, "Cancel that call." McCurdy took his hand away from the transceiver. "There's something behind that wall... it's a 10-5, for the 10-85." Jones lifted his foot out and quietly closed the passenger door. McCurdy was about to rotate the spotlight on his side toward the corner but called it in first.

"Dispatch, Unit 525, on Randall between Coster and Faile. I repeat: we require another unit."

"Copy that, 525. Uniformed officers require another unit on Randall, middle of Coster and Faile Streets," McCurdy turned to Jones.

"Way to go, McCurdy." Jones whispered, "Turn your radio down."

"Unit 525, Unit 6 is the closest and is en route to you. Heading north on Barretto, a mile from Oak Point Avenue. Couple of minutes."

Jones heard the reply and responded in low tones, "Unit 6, turn right at Oak Point Avenue, turn left on Faile, the threat is on Faile." McCurdy climbed out of the patrol car and looked around, then glanced over the car roof at Jones who was about to rush to the south wall of the building. After hearing so many stories, McCurdy was still not convinced that this wasn't a joke. A measured tempo and rhythm of groaning and moaning sounds, combined with irregular breathing, came from the semi across the street. McCurdy turned back around to face Jones. He said, "What are you... what are we doing, sir? Shouldn't we continue to follow procedures—you know, *wait* for backup?"

Jones spoke over the roof at McCurdy, pointing to him and then to himself, "I am your backup. You are my backup. Adjust to whatever this is."

"Whatever *what* is, sir?"

"Exactly." Jones walked briskly with definite steps toward the edge of the wall of the auto store and pushed his upper arm against it as he advanced to the corner.

"Fuck," McCurdy mutters as he half-slides back inside the cruiser. He reaches the instrument armrest and flips the switch for the bar lights. Red and blue flashes bounce off the apartment across the street as well as the semi, while giving the neon-orange auto store a nightclub appearance. Mc-

Curdy wipes sweat off his face and dries his hand on his pants leg before he swivels the spotlight forty-five degrees to his right, past the south wall to the flatbed and ahead of Jones who is now less than ten feet from the southwest corner. McCurdy hits the newly issued touchscreen under the mobile laptop for the in-car video camera. He trains the camera angle on Jones and to a wide sweep on either side of him. He weighs whether to drive the cruiser diagonally into the intersection of Randall and Faile but decides against it. Instead, he quietly closes the door and darts behind the cruiser and over to the south wall behind Jones.

McCurdy pulls out his duty pistol, a Glock 19, and wraps his right hand around the grip, extending his index finger along the barrel and cupping his left hand around the right hand, thumbs forward, with his forearms bent downward and to the left, away from his body and the back of his FTO. He had never withdrawn his weapon on patrol before. Before Jones reaches an arm's length from where the two edges of the building meet, he withdraws his sidearm, a SIG Sauer P226 Equinox, recently approved for NYPD cops. He turns down the volume some more on the radio nested in his duty belt by his left side. Six-and-a-half years of police work take over, but he overrides the unconscious impulse and carefully reholsters his firearm until he hears it click. Instead, he withdraws his ASP expandable baton and snaps it downward.

Jiekang sees the flashing lights and the spotlight reflecting off the flatbed. He figures he's being set up in some sort of operation. If it's an operation, then that woman in the back is part of it. Maybe she's a police officer with a pistol—a fleeting thought—but to believe that also includes the fact that he's never going to see that $50,000. He wants to believe in the money even if, at some level, he's already determined that he's not going to get it. He decides that his cut of $12,050 isn't worth confronting what lies on the other side of that wall—BUT $50,000 IS—so Jiekang opts not to share it. His accomplices are all coked up anyway and he's the mastermind of this operation. He takes one more bite from his chicken and tosses it on the street near the flatbed. He licks his fingers and wipes them on his pants. He pulls a nylon stocking over his face. He can't call the courier who is bringing the money; he can only wait for his call. He assumes he must be around the corner with the cash, hiding from the cops. He pulls a switchblade out of his pocket. He wants to get a look. Maybe it's just a traffic stop. A ticket is being issued. It'll be all over quick and soon. Jiekang inches his way to the edge of the wall less than ten feet from Jones and McCurdy.

Logan, the hitman, steps out of the Escalade and onto the street at the other end of the block and takes refuge in the shadows, staring at the bright intersection of Faile and Randall. He crosses over to the sidewalk, stays close to the walls and windows of storefronts. His movements stimulate muscle memories of years in other countries maneuvering through layers of deadly hostiles that showed up as men, woman and children on streets and in villages. They move like ghosts across his mind. Is he still keen to his surroundings? Does he still have that bite, that superiority, in hand-to-hand? Can he still detect adversarial eyes staring at the back of his head from fifty feet? Logan keeps hidden as he answers these questions, emerging as reflexes from his unconscious. He measures each step toward the lighted crossroad.

# 5

## Ninety Seconds of Terror

"LIEUTENANT, WHAT AM I DOING HERE?" Jones turns around and spots his partner's back against the wall.

Jones raises his finger to his lips, then lifts his hand to his ear, then pats the top of his head and points his index finger to his chest. McCurdy gets it. Jones commanded him to shut up, listen and to cover him. Jones puts his back against the wall and shakes his head sideways. He turns with his arm against the wall, and raises and lowers his head. McCurdy remembers to turn his body armor toward Jones' back. He remembers all the coffee he drank. He is more conscious of his bladder.

Jones hears moaning from around the corner and then a muffled scream. In the distance both officers hear the faint sound of a police siren and sub-dued chatter from the radios on their belts.

Jones holds his position at an arm's length from the wall's edge. Jiekang swings his arm in an arc around the wall without exposing too much of his body. Jones snaps back faster than a reflex, barely escaping the point of a blade coming around the wall's edge toward his left ear. The blade dings against the bricks.

Jiekang steps out into the open. He's five-eight, wearing jeans, a black t-shirt and a black stocking over his head. Muscles and blood vessels push against the skin of his arms. He's built, stocky and fleet of foot. Keyed up with high expectations of living large with $50,000, his determination to get paid is white-hot.

Jones walks toward Jiekang with his ASP trailing behind his thigh. Jiekang backs up toward the flatbed. "I'm a police officer. Put down your weapon." Jones passes the beam of the spotlight and cuts across to his left. Jiekang faces him, looks around at McCurdy, who is shouting commands and pointing his pistol, then looks past him to the end of the block. There's no courier. Maybe he *was* being set up.

*"Fuuuuck!"*

The three men inside the van surround Marakie again. They mock her, pulling her blouse, popping buttons. Her screams are muffled by the duct tape. She regrets even thinking about being on her own and imagines Frank Scudder tearing open the doors to save her.

Jiekang bounds forward, making violent stabbing attempts at Jones' thighs and body. All miss by a few inches. He slashes the air in figure-eights. Vehicles slow down on the two-lane. Drivers gape in wonder and then hit the gas. Jones evades. The attacker is bewildered. McCurdy points, gives more commands, but doesn't shoot. Jones gauges the continuous pattern of the blade. Both sides of the knife are sharpened. He anticipates the direction of the next downward arc. It comes. He steps left then strikes the back of the knife hand with his baton. The *pop!* sound the strike makes and the knife bouncing off the ground are followed by another even louder *Fuuuuck!* from Jiekang. His hand is dead on his wrist. He whistles loud enough for the other three to hear. The one with the gash and the one with the bloody fingers jump out of the van. The one who tackled Lorena stays behind and circles the roll of tape around Marakie's ankles and wrists. He hops out and slams the doors behind him.

Halfway down the street, Logan speed-dials his boss and says, "Mr. Borg, I make out at least one police patrol car at the exchange point. The group you hired is engaging a police unit. What are your orders?"

Holding another shot glass of Bhuka between his fingers, Borg asks, "Can you get to the girl?"

Logan steps off the sidewalk and into a dark spot in the middle of the street. "Yes, I know where she is. I can get to her. But I will have to eliminate everyone before any extra help arrives—no charge for the extra ammo."

Mr. Adlai Borg looks out the window. Not a cloud anywhere. The driver curves around a bend in the road, bringing direct sunlight again, into the car. Jessica is being dangerous, keeping her eyes on and off the road. Watching for any markers that pull her attention. A dozen red flags appear from poles 25 meters tall. Planes descend in the far distance.

"You know the rules."

Logan hastens his stride. A street lamp lights his black leather jacket, his shiny nickel-plated pistol and his battle-worn face. He walks out of the light and back onto the sidewalk. The next street lamp is fifty feet from the back of the van. "If you want the girl and those fuckups to stop breathing, this is the best plan."

"I am reconsidering my objective here. No policemen, unless they are antithetical to our plans."

Logan says, "Sir, you wanted me to take out the girl and her abductors and make it look like a botched kidnapping. It's logical. Perfect. They're coke-heads, which adds to the illusion. They'd be blamed for the murder of the DSS Agent Frank Scudder, too. One of them will have the Walther in his dead hand, after the girl gets it. This won't look like an assassination, but a frenzy caused by coke, munchies and fried chicken. So far, we're on track, but there's little time. It appears, sir, that these cops *are* antithetical."

Waiting for a response, Logan tightens his lips and shrugs his massive shoulders. He tilts his huge head side-to-side, slipping his neck bones back in place. He continues to take measured steps. He sees Jiekang and a cop. He keeps out of the storefront lights. He quickens his pace and determines how much time he has before he must piece together another plan of attack.

In Tunisia, the driver of the Mercedes parks at the departure entrance of Aéroport Tunis-Carthage amidst a platoon of yellow cabs. Jessica gets out first. Puts on her shades, then walks to the other side. Her every step is a mantra, composed of two contradictory phrases: *I'm beautiful, and move out of my way or I'll kill you.* The driver takes one suitcase out of the trunk and then moves around to the passenger side. He walks up to the curbside check-in and hands over the luggage, for Borg, then gets back into the Mercedes. Jessica looks around and then opens the back-passenger door. The rippling sounds of twelve red flags situated high up in front of the entrance provide a sense of the intensity of the operation that the man from Malta is quarter-backing.

Borg steps out of the luxury car in a state of serious thought. Jessica hands him an earpiece. He's confident of the new course. He's carrying nothing and looks like he's talking to himself. "We will leverage her, Logan. Dewabuna will do what we tell him if we show him we have her." The Mercedes pulls away, and Borg and Jessica walk between two large potted plants toward the airport's sliding doors.

Logan questions, "Then you want her alive?"

The doors open. Borg with Jessica enter the spacious public hall. They are met by the standard ambient music, elegant yet easily forgotten. There are the smells of sweet Tunisian doughnuts, called *bambalouni*, the sounds of last calls for boarding, and the sights of *Al Jazeera* broadcasting with breaking news on wide screens. The architecture is clean and simple, combining modern and Islamic architecture. Borg's arms don't swing as he heads to a bright corner, near the entrance to the AVS VIP service lounge to finish the call. He stands erect. Although his features are unremarkable, his taste in clothing isn't. His white, three-piece suit with navy-blue tie and matching handkerchief and his light blue shirt are the expected attire for a man with his global clout. From the cut of his suit to the polish of his shoes, and with Jessica by his side in her red sheath dress, they draw looks of admiration from the public.

Borg's eyes narrow, "I did not bloody say I want her alive, either!" The furrow above the bridge of his nose deepens. The hairs on his overhanging brows pop out. Billions of dollars are at stake. He's weighing whether the young woman is worth more alive.

In the darkness, Logan asks, "What is it then?"

Silence.

"Sir. Mr. Borg?" Logan's tally will be sixty contract kills if he gets the green light from Borg. It's important to him. He wants to act now but is compelled to wait.

In the airport hall there's an update through the PA system in German about a flight to Dusseldorf. Borg then hears the announcement of his flight to Istanbul, makes up his mind, while within earshot of people speaking Tunisian Arabic and French. His furrow shallows. He says, "Logan, it is simpler to leverage Marakie Dewabuna than to groom someone to take the place of her father as president. This is a snatch-and-grab and it equals a huge ransom. Take out the gang and get her out of there and back to the Queen's City into safekeeping. I'll arrange for a flight out of Westchester County Airport to Northbolt. That is my final decision. Ring me when you have secured the president's daughter." Jessica points to her watch. "Right. Logan we are walking to the escalator."

"Sir, take it from someone who's been a key player in reengineering several African governments. Africa is loaded with hungry politicians who will do anything for power. My tradecraft there has proven very useful for decades. Seen it all. This chick's a loose end that needs to be ended. Tonight."

Growing impatient yet keeping his voice flat, Borg says, "The salient point here, Logan, is that if Dewabuna's daughter is dead, he has no heir. The lineage is broken and whomever we control in that country's highest office will help us to chop up Afarland into little pieces. We send in our equipment and it is the score of a millennium."

"So, I eliminate her?"

"Bloody No! Dismantling the culture to that extent will create chaos. The people, yes, the people of Afarland must exist under the *illusion* of leadership, not chaos. I have heard your arguments and told you already what I want." Borg with even tones but louder, drives home his point: "ABSCOND WITH THE BITCH AND GET HER INTO SAFEKEEPING!"

Logan was pacing in step with the verbal exchange. He hears shouting and a police siren. He hears two now, one from behind him and another ahead of him behind buildings. He carries his pistol with the barrel pointed to the ground and continues walking toward the van. He considers the possibility of having to reload during a gun battle. To steal the girl, he will have to shoot at police. The shouting and the sirens get louder. He pulls a double stack out of his left jacket pocket as he watches the driver of the van trying to stab the cop in the white shirt.

He shakes his head, "Amateurish!"

"What?"

"Nothing, sir. It's that gang. They're real amateurs. More cover for us. Cops shouldn't investigate too far. Yes sir, I'll get her into the safehouse in New Rochelle." Three steps are all Logan takes for him to release the old magazine, index a fresh one, and pull the slide.

Angered at his employee's questions but hiding it, Borg whispers, "Right. Logan, do I need to remind you that you are tactically the best I have? A trained bloody assassin, an expert marksman, and a strategist—with thirty-one years killing and playing political chess. Nothing and no one can get in your way. So, get the bloody job done. And Logan, not all African politicians are power-hungry, because if they were, we would have no resistance doing business with them. Cheers."

He hits the button on his earpiece. Jessica takes out the boarding passes from her clutch and they step off the escalator onto the second floor and proceed to the first check point and the departure gate.

"Cheers, Mr. Borg." After hearing the outcue, Logan places a call. "Marcus," he says, "Are you docked?"

"Since a half hour ago. Why?"

"Change of plans. Detach and throttle up now."

"Been doing that for the last hour."

"Well, get rid of her. I may be coming in hot, and heavy one passenger. Borg wants the girl alive." Logan ends the call. He continues to walk up Faile Street and notices the developing confrontation in front of him. He wonders why the cop in the white shirt doesn't draw his firearm, is surprised at how he handled the first knife attack without being cut and is incredulous as to how this cop is going to handle three more men with knives while his weapon is still holstered.

McCurdy repeats his commands to Jiekang with one good arm and another blade. "Police! Drop your weapon. I said drop your weapon NOW! Put your hand behind your head."

Two more attackers come from behind the van, out of the darkness into the spotlight, bounding toward Jones—the one with a scarf around his bloody fingers and the one with a gash on his head. The Tackler waits behind the van.

"Police! Drop your weapons now!" Jones commands again. The echo from his voice bounces off several buildings. There is an intangible current of force from his words that slows them down for a second. Even Logan, still getting closer, feels an unexplainable sensation from the command's impact. Maybe it's the cop's voice, deep, almost baritone. From across the street, lights turn off. The people in the apartment are smart enough to look at violence from the window, without exposing themselves. Shades lift halfway up and dozens of pairs of eyes peer out windows to see the mayhem starting. McCurdy catches his breath, keeps his pistol on target and rushes in a slant behind Jones, past the front edge of the building and the spotlight, to the lamp post with the broken light.

Across the street from Unit 525, the woman in the short orange skirt and her john inside the semi can hear the commotion. The dangerous situation just excites them more.

McCurdy's face is flushed. Can't hear too well either. His bladder is pushing. He clutches his transceiver and pours his physical anxiety into the call: "This is 525... Send all you've got." McCurdy gulps down more saliva, "Randall... and Faile. Send backup. More... I count two or three perps with knives."

Jiekang needs to see better. With his good hand he yanks off his stocking. The other two follow his lead.

"Asian. They're Asian, that, that gang; mid-to-late twenties, all you got." He stops transmitting. *"Shit, what the fuck?* Police! I said don't move! Put your weapons down or you'll be shot!"

The response from headquarters in Longwood: "Unit 525, Unit 6 is a half mile from you. Units 511 and 574 are also en route. Backup is coming. Three units are heading toward you."

"Ten-four." Disoriented, McCurdy backs against a garbage can at the street corner. He has a long view of Faile Street, of Jones and the first attacker. Behind the three men, he makes out a silhouetted figure halfway up Faile. Logan stops moving, as the other cop stares in his direction. McCurdy thinks it could be an innocent bystander. He shifts his attention and sinks his hips down until his knees drop a little, then inclines slightly forward on his toes into a shooting stance. He's about to discharge his weapon on men with knives threatening his trainer.

But he won't shoot. Lieutenant Jones is too close to them, plus if he misses, he could hit that person, whose outline just appeared less than halfway up the street. But what if it's another attacker? Would it matter?

McCurdy isn't sure if his trainer's vest can protect him from a stab wound. He wants to stop them, without hitting his FTO. "I said drop your weapons, now, assholes. You are all under arrest." McCurdy knows that his commands have little influence. Now, The Tackler steps out of the darkness and into part of the spotlight. McCurdy is terrified, his voice rises an octave, "*SHIT, FOUR!* Police! Put down your weapons. Show me your hands." He knows that Jones is outnumbered but is still evading jabs and slashing arcs from the first attacker's only good hand. The other three take turns jabbing their weapons at his partner. McCurdy thinks he can't isolate Jones far enough away to get a clear shot.

McCurdy knows he is lying to himself.

Jiekang lunges at Jones, who steps out of the line of attack and strikes the elbow with the rigid piece of black polycarbonate, then jabs the point of the baton directly on the nerve near Jiekang's armpit. He wobbles near the edge of the wall. Jones' tactics were executed within one second of time: the step, the strike and the jab. Jiekang has no feeling in his arm. *Clunk* goes the second knife as his arm goes limp.

"*Zhua Zhu Ta!*" Get him, he yells. Without the use of his arm its movement resembles that of a zombie or a chimpanzee.

"You've been warned. Now drop your weapons," Jones commands; his firearm is still holstered.

Logan steps off the sidewalk into the middle of the street. He's 40 feet away from the back of the van.

The Tackler leaps toward McCurdy who is standing within 21 feet of him. Jones sees the intent of the attacker running around his left flank between him and the flatbed. Jones waits until he's about to pass him, then pivots around with his baton and strikes the nerve directly above The Tackler's left hipbone. He stops instantly. His body seizes as if it's receiving an electric shock. He loses the feeling of connection between his upper and lower halves. The speed of his precipitation against the concrete follows a momentary suspension in time as if his body, like a puppet, is held erect by strings and the strings are summarily cut. He lies helpless and feels like his body is broken in two.

Jones hears another muffled scream from inside the beige Ford Econoline. He springs toward the van when the other two come at him. Jones' back is against the spotlight as he advances. The third attacker, with the gash, feints the point of his blade to Jones' abdomen, but Jones knows he's going to move from low to high and go for his head. He does, and Jones sidesteps to Gash's left and surgically thrusts the end of his baton into the nerve near his left cheekbone. Gash doubles over with an attack of nausea. His arms dangle. Queasiness zaps his capacity to move his fingers. Like an old western where the gunfighter was too slow on the draw and doesn't hit the dirt right away, the third attacker has no energy except just enough to beat his heart. The knife drops first. What suspense! Then finally, after many seconds and like a balloon with no air, he falls.

The last one, Bloody Fingers, grabs the knives belonging to his fallen comrades. Jones steps back away out of the spotlight toward the garbage can at the corner, near the lamp post, while evading, slipping and sidestepping his attacker. McCurdy moves away from the can toward the right, into the beam of the spotlight, watching this thrilling action sequence. He isn't certain what to do next. Obviously, his FTO has this situation under control but he wants to help, to contribute something. He's now more interested in this display of good police tactics than his need to relieve himself.

Years of combat training, taught to him by his father, increase Jones' ability to listen and interpret where the energy will go next. Jones' actions are executed in advance of each of the attackers' moves. The last attacker, Bloody Fingers, more buff than Jiekang, holds a knife by the blade tip and throws it at Jones' head. Jones ducks the moment before it leaves the attacker's hand. It misses. Jones walks forward, forcing him backward toward the edge of the neon building and into the spotlight.

McCurdy is near the grill of the cruiser and partially blocks the spotlight, he's breathing through his mouth. The knife had banged against the garbage can. He doesn't hear the police siren. "Where's our backup?" he asks out loud. He's hysterical. "Shoot 'em, Lieutenant. Shoot 'em. There could be more." Amidst the horrible sounds of three hurt attackers, the partial light casts hard shadows on the fourth attacker's face. He's about to throw another knife at Jones. The attacker is isolated.

"Shoot them, Lieutenant... You are within your right." McCurdy moves away from the cruiser several feet behind Jones' back to get a clear shot.

He can use his pistol now. He can help his FTO. He can shoot if he wants to, but he must consider the ramifications of his actions.

His legal mindset comes out of some deeply cavernous left field. Each cartridge has an attorney attached to it. That thought stops him cold. Paperwork will be demanded for each cartridge discharged. Investigations. Internal Affairs. He is more concerned about being wrong than acting. He considers whether the law will be on his side, the media, or the crowd of people gathering at the windows.

Jones presses forward with no thought, just pure actions appropriate to the angles of attack. It's a ballet, a balancing polarity of slashes and misses, of lunges and jabs that hit nothing but the atmosphere around Jones, of overhead knife strikes that slice through space, but propel Bloody Fingers' upper arm almost out of its socket. Bloody Fingers is tired. Jones, who is overweight at two hundred pounds can move like someone who weighs only a hundred and thirty. The knife-wielding man is spent, frustrated. He can't touch Jones. "I am a police officer," Jones says, in Mandarin, "Put it down."

But Bloody Fingers is still too high on cocaine to appreciate the commands of the Mandarin-speaking, black police officer. The other three crawl on the ground and are unable to get up. One is nauseous; another has lost all tangible connection between his upper and lower halves; Jiekang's arm is useless and the back of his other hand feels like a wrecking ball fell on it.

Bloody Fingers is bent over, catching his breath. McCurdy steps to the left of the spotlight toward Jones. "It's okay now, partner," he says. "No, it isn't," Jones says, pointing. Gash, who is still nauseous, grabs a knife, forces himself up and moves closer behind Bloody Fingers.

Bloody Fingers goes for Jones again. He cocks his knife like he's going to try an overhead strike, in a move of blind fury. Jones steps back and to the side, just missing the knife-point. The attacker's shoulder partially dislocates. The blade's momentum continues arcing backwards, then bites deep into Gash's flesh, through his upper thigh, as he was faltering less than a foot behind Bloody Fingers.

"Serves you right. DROP YOUR WEAPONS. GET ON THE GROUND!" McCurdy says.

Blood gushes out of his artery like beer out of a punctured can. The victim is now one big scream, in Mandarin—baffled, amazed and shocked. As if he woke up from a dream, he covers the geyser with his hands as primal sounds rise from his diaphragm through his throat and out his mouth.

After seeing the dark fluid shooting out of the perp's thigh, McCurdy is reminded of all the Samurai movies that he'd seen, like *Yojimbo* and *The Seven Samurai,* where this very thing was portrayed. Now he realizes that blood could have easily been his or his trainer's. His initial reptilian-brain response is to run. The scene just got more real.

Bloody Fingers is still not down. He moves toward Jones, who slides his baton into its scabbard on his utility belt.

McCurdy's breathing speeds up. His vision narrows more. He can hear his heart pounding. The wide-angled spotlight from his unit, and the red and blue flashing lights disorient him more. The whole scene: the spotlight in the foreground, the highlighted flies and dust, the low light in the background, fear of more assailants emerging from the darkness, up Faile, the uncertainty that his partner may get stabbed at any moment, and that he may have to kill someone tonight, paralyzes his capacity to act.

He imagines his wife, Susan, and Marie, the name they chose for their baby girl on the way, and himself having to skip town. While on probation he could be fired without an explanation, plus he could face criminal or civil charges at both state and federal levels—worse, he would go out with the stigma of not defending his partner.

The three downed attackers are still crawling, cursing and attempting to get on their feet. With less energy McCurdy says, "Where's our fucking backup?" He doesn't realize that only a minute had passed since everything got crazy. "Why don't you shoot, Lieutenant?" McCurdy is puzzled as to why his FTO doesn't present his firearm at the attackers. They most assuredly would drop their weapons and raise their hands. Wouldn't they?

Could it be for the same reason as his? McCurdy hears cursing, criticism and condemnation bouncing off the wall of nearby buildings. They're coming from behind, from both sides, from out of the darkness up ahead—out of windows, through doors. He thinks he hears someone with a firearm behind him from across the street. He turns around and points his weapon. With tunnel vision he still turns around slowly and checks off everything within his purview as he continues to swivel his head in a circle. His hears his heart pounding but he still can't tell which direction the harsh words, the sounds of windows and doors, or the cocking of the firearm is coming from.

He runs the statistics through his mind of numerous cop shootings, the public's outrage, and his family's protection against repercussions. He's got to do something more than just watch. He sees the last knife-wielding assailant about to attack Lieutenant Jones. No, his FTO's vest won't protect him from a successful knife attack. McCurdy fumbles his Glock into his holster. By now he realizes that his trainer knows what he's doing.

McCurdy reaches into his bat belt for his flashlight.

# 6

## The Fight After the Fight, Part One

MCCURDY AIMS THE FLASHLIGHT'S BEAM into Bloody Fingers' eyes. His sight is muddled but he moves steadily on, shouting and speeding toward where he thinks Jones' head may be. Jones casually takes one step back. The attacker stops short on his left foot and swings his right arm backwards, up, over, and down, in a vertical circle, like a cricket bowler. He misses Jones' head and body by a few inches.

Still dazed by the sudden blast of light, in addition to his cocaine high, Bloody Fingers swings his knife point past the horizontal line. Now, Jones steps onto his right flank, seizes the attacker's wrist, twists it, and brings his palm to an area above the elbow, guiding the momentum to the right and toward the ground.

Not far from the van now, Logan can see that the cop in the white shirt is commanding the situation. He crosses his arms as he looks back toward the Escalade and both sidewalks, then back to the fight. He is temporarily interested in what this cop does next. Now, Logan is concerned. If this cop can do more damage than what he's witnessing, then he will have no choice. He will have to shoot that cop against Borg's orders.

Bloody Fingers, who is more horizontal than vertical, is pulled around Jones' axis, until Jones reverses direction and redirects his attacker's momentum in the opposite direction, by applying torque to the wrist.

Bloody Fingers' body flips to the left and his feet hit the side of the flatbed.

Jones slams the base of his palm at a point outside Bloody Fingers' right eyebrow.

Logan shakes his head and uncrosses his arms.

Bloody Fingers crashes against the pavement.

Jones turns the unconscious Bloody Fingers to the prone position, lifts out a pair of cuffs and restrains him—the fourth and last assailant of the infamous kidnapping ring. Jones slides the unconscious body across the sidewalk and up against the wall.

McCurdy reholsters his flashlight and withdraws his firearm. Excited, he stumbles back across the spotlight and braces on up against the west side of the neon wall, "Way to go, sir! Shit!"

"*Tingzhi...* Stop!" Jones' attention goes back to the four men on the ground. They did stop. Jones turns to his partner whose weapon is pointed at the attackers. Jones, standing a yard from the wall opposite the flatbed, can hear McCurdy's excitement through his erratic breathing. He gestures at McCurdy with the back of his hand, inviting him to move closer.

"Are you breathing, Officer McCurdy? Those lawbreakers on the pavement don't present a threat but be vigilant just the same." McCurdy lowers his weapon while keeping his eyes on them. But Jones isn't completely certain of his own words—the part about not presenting a threat. Current astronomic configurations suggest that there's more stuff coming.

McCurdy steps closer to Jones and holsters his weapon. Jones extends his hand with the palm up. "Ford, here. Feel my pulse."

Jones puts his partner's fingers an inch below the fleshy mass at the base of his thumb. The sirens are several blocks away. McCurdy's pulse is still racing. Jones' pulse is normal. In less than ten seconds, McCurdy's pulse is the same as his FTO's.

"Our pulses have entrained," Jones says. "They share a common pattern of ease and energy-in-balance. Your body will learn to maintain this state, even as you are engaged in police work and on the razor's edge of a life-threatening encounter." McCurdy's tunnel vision widens to normal, and his breath becomes more stable and rhythmic. He takes his fingers off his field training officer's wrist.

Jones remembered the chart he calculated, while standing in front of Jenkins Auto supply. Of how the group of stars called Swati, The Sword, related to the attackers brandishing knives. But he knew that there was more to it, and that he had to generate more presence for what was to come—from out of the unknown, the indeterminate—into time and space.

Inside the semi, the sounds of two adults moving nearer heaven is loud and just the comic distraction McCurdy needed. The silence moved upon the heels of primal utterances.

McCurdy grips his duty belt with both hands. "I don't know what you did, sir. Everything was a blur." McCurdy wipes his forehead with the back of his hand and looks his FTO in the eye, embarrassed.

"Sir, they were all around you. I didn't dare—"

Offering encouragement, for now, Jones looks eye-to-eye at his partner. "You had a dilemma, officer. You wouldn't shoot without chancing friendly fire. We were facing an extreme situation. They, including me, were moving targets, linked together under horrible lighting." McCurdy lowered his head, his hands grabbing his utility belt.

Jones knew the real reason why McCurdy didn't shoot but used another approach.

"You acted on the information reporting to your senses. You are not a seasoned police officer yet but you will be. There are statistics about line-of-duty friendly fire. Tonight, you could have increased that statistic but you didn't. You exhibited thoughtfulness and restraint."

Jones looks around and sees outlines of people behind windows and motorists driving past the scene.

"And your flashlight maneuver was apt. I presume that the reason you made that choice was because you saw that I was bringing the situation under control. A way through your dark dilemma was presented, and you were present enough to seize the *light* and you used it. I believe that all humans are both each other's teachers and students all at the same time. Yet I was operating as your field-training officer. I was engaged in training for you, while you played the role of student. And yet, Officer McCurdy, the roles could have easily been reversed."

"I am confused."

"Confusion is a spur to catapult you to another level of skill. Every time we sally forth, even me as a Second Lieutenant, it's another cycle of training."

Across the street, a car stops in front of the semi, a young kid gets out and throws a beer bottle.

"Look out!" Jones jerks McCurdy back. The bottle breaks on the side door of the flatbed, followed by the word *PIG!* Jones steps to the edge and into the spotlight and stares at the kid who rushes into his car and drives off like a scared rabbit, fearing the stare of a cop because that means he could be identified sooner than later. Jones faces his trainee, "Stay alert, McCurdy."

McCurdy thought that he was anything but apt. He justified his decision not to act on the imaginative basis of a thousand-and-one legal things that could have befallen him. But Lieutenant Jones could have been killed in the line of duty and he, the trainee and partner, could've been the one to prevent it. So, McCurdy didn't feel deserving of any compliment. But he was a rookie and that thought gave him some relief. He was determined to get his cop-craft in order. Maybe Jones was right after all about the spur to move to new levels of his craft.

As if in suspended animation, McCurdy's awareness suddenly fell on the blood still pouring out of the nauseated attacker's thigh. McCurdy pulled out sanitary gloves from the compartment in the back of his duty belt. Went to his unit, put the car in gear and drove diagonally onto Randall and Faile. Jones had put his gloves on, too. He removed his tourniquet from the front of his belt.

Still in training mode, Jones said, "Officer McCurdy, throw me some gauze, lots of it." McCurdy felt better, when his field trainer added "officer" in front of his surname.

He smooths his hand over his red hair, then around the back of his neck, to his mouth. He replays the events for future reference, for the incident report and for legal reasons. He must stay clear, lucid. He remembers his trainer's words to him at the passenger window: "Expect the unexpected." He opens the trauma kit and takes out several gauze packs, opens them halfway and runs to the stab victim. Together he and Jones apply wads of gauze and put lots of pressure on the gushing hole at Gash's upper thigh.

Jones positions the tourniquet, pulls it tight, then turns the windlass to compress the arteries above the heap of strategically placed cotton squares. "Get me a Sharpie."

"Sir," McCurdy says, "I've got to go somewhere and take a piss."

"I need you here. This is not over. What time do you have?"

"Twelve eleven, sir. But, sir." McCurdy pulls a Sharpie from his lapel pocket. Jones writes down the time he put the tourniquet around Gash's thigh. Then he goes over to Jiekang.

"You'll get feeling in that arm in a few minutes," Jones says as he puts the stainless-steel cuffs on Jiekang's wrists. McCurdy squeezes the button on his transceiver, "Unit 525. Have managed to control the threat. Need an EMS ASAP at Randall and Faile. A kid's been cut near the femoral artery. Is stabilized. Administered a tourniquet to slow the bleeding."

Jones goes to The Tackler who had slithered his way from the wall. "McCurdy throw me a cuff." Jones catches it. "*Kao zai qiang shaàng...*" Jones commands, which translates to "Go against the wall!" The Tackler snakes his way back to the brick face. Jones cuffs him.

All during the ninety-second encounter, scores of vehicles passed the scene on Faile and Randall. Traffic kept right on moving. Some slowed down wanting to see cops in action but feared that they could be the victims of stray bullets. Traffic flowed. Most people wanted nothing to do with cops doing their duty that late at night.

Logan reaches the back of the van and pulls the door handle. Marakie's muscles tense up. The beam from the spotlight and car lights shines through the holes of the driver's side partition against the inside doors. The first thing Marakie sees when the door opens is a hulking figure with a scary face. Her screams come with a sharpened edge, like a squeal. He points his pistol at her. He's not going to get her to the safehouse—can't without executing police trying to do it—something that Borg didn't authorize. He can kill the girl and eliminate the problem. Mr. Borg will understand. He puts his finger on the trigger. The suppressor is still warm. He is about to pull.

But Logan remembers what Borg said—that he was *tactically* the best he had, *a trained bloody assassin*, and an expert *strategist*. Pride and respect in his skills from his boss convinces Logan to take his finger off the trigger. Plan B. He pushes the door with his thumb on the handle. It locks without an audible click. Logan darts past the right taillight.

Jones hears the scream and moves past the flatbed, to the van's side-cargo door. It's locked. He edges his way toward the back. Logan crouches. Jones comes carefully around, withdrawing his firearm.

Logan stays low, creeping steadily along the van on the street side.

On Faile and Oakpoint where the Escalade is parked, light coalesces on the banner with the tomatoes and hat-wearing chili peppers. A police vehicle will turn onto Faile any second now. Logan has one chance to make good on his promise to his employer. He has never failed a mission.

Jones comes around the left taillight. From inside he hears another squeal and moves to that point between the rear doors. A car is coming up the street. Not a patrol car, but its lights expose Logan's position.

Jones turns to the west wall and asks Jiekang, in Mandarin: *"Is anyone else inside besides the girl?"*

"No!" Jiekang said; he wasn't surprised at all that the cop spoke his language.

"This is the police. I am going to open the rear door." Jones takes hold of the handle. The car from up the street passes. As its light shines on him, Logan pretends he's inserting his key into the passenger door lock. Jones pulls the handle back. The door creaks and yawns on its hinges. He sees some light streaming out the perforated driver's side of the bulkhead. He moves the points of his pistol and flashlight throughout the interior. The flashlight beam reveals a young woman slumped on the cargo floor.

He sees her eyes for the first time. They are charged with fear. They close. Jones remembers the streetwalker with the puny orange skirt getting into the semi. The girl's blouse is red, and open halfway. *Is she a lady of the evening?* Jones asks himself. No, he thinks. He moves the light away from the passenger side of the bulkhead that she's leaning up on, but its lumens still allow him to notice her eyes. The fright in them, quickly softens into a precarious state of relief. She blinks a few times, and then drops her head down slowly.

"You are safe now, miss."

Logan opens the passenger door and slides over the bench to the driver's side. The keys are in the ignition. Jones opens the other door. Marakie lifts her head to size up her knight in shining armor, her James Bond. She recalls his voice commands when he was fighting those thugs. He must have handled them all by himself. Tall, well groomed, neat in his uniform, a little over-weight, that's okay—a little exercise will do the trick—and resourceful-looking with knowing eyes.

"Ma'am, I'll get you out of these fetters." Marakie remembers Lorena's words about people calling her ma'am. *Ma'am* and *fetters*, she ponders. How differently this policeman spoke. Maybe they all speak that way, respectfully. She never had a policeman speak to her as one in need of help.

The light that shines from outside and through the perforated partition is blocked. Logan takes a deep breath. Jones sees the large body eclipse the light. Maybe a fifth member of the gang? Marakie waits for her James Bond to cut her free. Jones whispers, "Stay down," and sends a message through his transceiver, "McCurdy, 10-10 P in the driver's seat."

McCurdy hears the code, *an unidentified person,* in the driver's seat. "Copy that." He turns from the four kidnappers and catches sight of the barrel pointing out the window.

Jiekang, cuffed from behind, had his head down. But through his peripheral vision he saw movement inside his van. He looked up at the driver's side window. The muzzle of a pistol was trained at his head. He lifted the sole of his foot, *"Fuuuck!"* The Tackler, Bloody Fingers, who just woke up, and Gash, also spotted the man with the pistol. Gash tried to crawl under the flatbed. The others squirmed, trying to block getting shot in the face. They lifted their feet up and then their knees, screamed, cursed, pushed their backs against the wall and turned their heads to the side.

McCurdy steps behind the wall's edge for cover. He bops his head out while aiming his pistol. "Police, put your weapon—" A piece of the wall's edge, above McCurdy's head, shatters from the two rounds.

Logan didn't wait to hear the end of the cop's command. Breathing fast, McCurdy pins his back to the south wall. He'd never been shot at before now. Jones heard suppressed gunfire. Six shots hitting doomed kidnappers and brick.

The atmosphere is solid. Tight. The commotion stops. A dead silence follows. Unit 574 skids to a halt an inch from the curb, across the intersection, across from McCurdy. Officers jump out, hear McCurdy's voice and get into position. Logan starts the van, shifts gears and releases the brake. The new officers on the scene hurry to the passenger-side window. Jones steps halfway inside to grab the girl. Logan backs up from the flatbed, switches gears and then takes off, crashing into the right-front fender of Unit 525. Somehow the collision jimmy-rigs Jones' spotlight. It blinks on. Logan just plows through, pushing the unit out of his way. The sudden inertia from the van's collision knocks Jones off the cargo floor, out of the van, and onto his back.

# 7

## The Fight After the Fight, Part Two

THE VAN TURNS LEFT HEADING WEST, with Marakie in tow, back doors swinging.

"Oh... shit!" McCurdy yells. "Dispatch. 525, 10-10—shots fired. Men down. A shooter got away heading westbound on Randall. Four men are dead."

Jones sits up and says, "McCurdy, stay here and wait for more backup." The two cops rush to Jones, who gets to his feet and runs toward their unit, 574.

"Officers, I'm commandeering your vehicle." An officer digs for the keys, "Yes, sir, Lieutenant."

Jones slams the door and pulls out with siren and bar lights. "Dispatch, Lieutenant Jones pursuing suspect driving a tan Ford Econoline. Empire blue and white plate, Foxtrot, Alpha, Whiskey, niner, one eight six. The shooter's driving and a woman, a victim, is in the cargo area against the bulkhead. I just passed Barretto Street. The shooter looks like he's about to turn left on Tiffany."

Logan, with a two-block head start, turns left on Tiffany Street and gives the old van the gas.

"We've got three units: two heading westbound on East Bay and a third on Ryawa."

The van's red lights are three blocks away. "Have Ryawa get on Viele and Tiffany and head northbound to meet the two from East Bay. Then continue northbound for the intercept, joining into a rolling roadblock. If the block is good and the shooter maintains his course, his only option is to turn around."

"Copy that, Lieutenant. Advising the three units to head northbound on Tiffany to seal off suspect's route."

"I'm heading southbound, right behind. There's nothing but the waterway ahead. Dispatch, possibly a getaway boat at the pier near Barretto Point Park. Alert the Coast Guard in case there is, and suspect slips out from our sandwich."

"Copy that. Calling CG sector New York."

Logan is a block from East Bay Avenue when two squad cars scramble onto Tiffany and set up a roadblock. The third unit hasn't yet gotten to Viele Avenue, which is perpendicular to Tiffany and a block away from East Bay. Logan reaches 90 mph not far from the roadblock. Officers jump out of their cars, pull their pistols and take cover behind open doors. Logan tightens his jaw. Bullets are zinging at him. One cracks the windshield; another takes out the right headlight. They aim at the tires. No time to stop the van's momentum by shooting at tires. They jump back. He slams the van into the two cruisers that formed the point of the V. Police don't shoot at the back of the van. Logan redials his friend at the pier.

Underneath the bow of a 34-foot, cruiser-class boat, Marcus, a long-time associate of Logan, was looking at the bright moon through the skylight and enjoying the smooth strands of long, chestnut hair, moving rhythmically and plunging up and down over his face. "I'm at the controls," he says and ends the call.

"Yes, you are... at... *my* controls." She bends downward, vibrating, covering some of his body with all of hers. Marcus thinks her lips are sweet, like syrup. They move to a few inches from his right ear. He's excited by the sensation she gives, the thrill of a woman in total surrender.

Below deck, the cabin is roomy. She's comfortable. Marcus rolls left until he's on top of her. The moonlight exposes her tender skin, even pinker now, below her neck. *Every bulge in the right place,* he thinks. *Voluptuous. Thin at the waist and a rounded backside equals an hourglass figure,* he thinks. His mental measurements of her excite him more.

"Aren't you glad you called our service and got me and not that street trash?" she asks. He just wished she didn't talk.

Next to her, the light on his cell comes on. He pushes up off her body and steps out of the V-berth onto the cabin floor. Pulls on his pants.

"Ye*ah,* whatever you say..."

She smooths her hair back. "Rhonda. My name is Rhonda." Marcus pulls his t-shirt over him and grabs his phone. "Whatever. Time to go." He watches her turn onto her right side, sporting her long, glamorous hair all sprawled on the pillow and partially concealing her breast, also pink and exquisitely shaped, stunning in the moonlight. Unlike in ordinary hotels, Rhonda hadn't served a customer on a watercraft, she mused, and in such a cozy, little environment. She felt comfortable there. A finished cabin with burl-orange mahogany, wood flooring, a 19" TV, and a shower.

Rhonda sits up and finger combs her hair, then pushes of the bed. The moonlight streams through the skylight. Marcus thinks that her curves and silky and sensuous body are even more provocative from a few feet away. She closes the distance. Marcus stares as one hypnotized.

She pushes her warm body against his. He fondles her breast. Lusty sentiments pour through her eyes. But they also look sweet and innocent. Something Marcus had never seen in the women he's known. Hers is a real smile, with dimples and all, with high cheekbones and a pleasing jawline.

He fights the impulse. She says, "Honey, you paid for three hours, you have an hour to go. Don't you want to—"

She spoiled the moment again. Her voice was unnerving—nothing like her looks. She was all woman, though, no doubt. Her pitch was just too low. Too deep for his sensibilities.

"You have to go now." He takes her clothing off the hanger and tosses it on the trapezoid-shaped mattress, then he climbs up the steps to the deck and heads for the cockpit. Not a cloud anywhere. He stands before the controls, which are backlit in cobalt-blue light. He turns the blower on, and then goes to the ignition switches. He fires up the starboard engine, checks the status, and then fires up the port engine. Checks his RPMs. Puts the controls in neutral as he activates the digital anchor. He jumps onto the pier and detaches the fore and aft cleat hitches. Starboard side. A couple of minutes later, the escort pops up on the galley in shapely, beige dress slacks, a white lace top and a coral blazer.

Marcus extends a hand and helps her onto the pier deck. She digs into her clutch and pulls out a cigarette case, tamps one and lights it. Rhonda wants to get out of New York and see the world. Maybe he's the ticket. A man of means. She remembers hearing stories of high-class call girls that were paid thousands of dollars to travel with rich guys to remote parts of the world. Maybe Marcus *is* rich; maybe he is just what she needs.

"Bye, Marcus. I hope to see you again soon. Do you fly a plane?"

Marcus flashed back to times when he piloted bush planes and attack helicopters in Africa: on water, on land, day or night, during civil wars and putsches, and in areas with no infrastructure. His mind flashes to narrow escapes and being shot down.

Marcus' thought returns to the pier deck. The engine murmurs. He secures the lines around the boat cleats, Rhonda ambles toward him; he can feel her heat more than a foot away. She picks at the hairs protruding above the neckline of his t-shirt. Marcus, a sucker for beautiful women, yet compelled to search for their slightest imperfections, thinks she is fine, and though she doesn't sound like Betty Boop, he is growing less mindful of her low register.

"As a matter of fact, I do fly." Rhonda's eyes brighten. She takes a puff, and then does something off-putting—blows smoke out of both nostrils, which breaks the sexy spell.

Marcus steps back on deck. "If you stole anything, I'll come back here, I'll find you, and I *will* take you for a ride."

Rhonda's imagined future of emotional and financial security drained out of her. She was hurt by that remark. "I don't work like that, I mean, is it my voice?"

"Something like that."

"*Menopausal Voice Syndrome* affected my pharyngeal resonator. It came early for me. That's what they said. It's irreversible. Don't worry, I don't steal, and I don't have a contagious disease."

"That's the reason, huh, why your voice is so low?"

She nodded.

She let loose a soft plea, which raised the tone of her voice, "Call me again, please? I left my card on the bed."

Rhonda got jittery and threw her cigarette into the water. She rubbed her upper arms with her hands. She felt cold—in more ways than one. She felt his coldness. He could turn it on and off. Marcus watched her walk away, watched the way she held her purse in her carefully manicured hand. He took in the happy swagger of her hips. Her movements were all sexy and sophisticated. She turned and waved. Marcus just stood on the deck. She walked backwards a few steps then turned away. Her swagger was gone. He watched her stop a few times to adjust her high heels and expensive pantsuit.

He steps down into the cockpit and waits. And Rhonda steps off the pier entrance. Logan skids to a stop about three van-lengths from her. She hurries onto Viele Avenue where her car is parked. Quickly enters it and drives off. Logan jumps out and runs around to the back. Jones passes around the two police cruisers on East Bay and Tiffany. He's at 100 mph. He sees the suspect opening the rear doors. Now, he's inside with his head ducked. Jones is a block away; now a half block. He starts braking. Marakie struggles with her abductor as he lifts her up and keeps his upper body bent forward. He jumps onto the pavement, like King Kong did atop the Empire State Building with Fay Wray in his massive hands. He carries Marakie past the sliding cargo door toward the pier entrance.

Marcus goes to the cabin to grab his pistol. Jones passes Ryawa and fishtails against the back of the van's right-rear overhang. Its front left-side pitches sharply left. Logan, barely clearing the left front, is knocked onto his left side. Marakie falls with him. He breaks her fall to the ground. He pushes her off and gets to his feet, picks her up again and runs toward the pier entrance.

"FREEZE." Logan has twenty more feet to go. "Put your hands up." He hears the cop moving closer. He knows where his pistol is. He's been in worse predicaments. He looks for Marcus. Stays close to Marakie. He figures this cop won't shoot at him if he's holding her. With his back toward Jones, and one hand holding Marakie, he quickly pulls his Walther out of his holster and shoots. Jones takes cover behind the van. Logan can't make it to the boat with Marakie unless he gets the cop out of the way first. Borg didn't say anything about beating a cop almost to death with his bare hands.

Logan looks up and sees the boat but not Marcus. "Hey, cop, I'm unarmed." Logan turns around, slowly walks counterclockwise past the pier entrance, to a patch of grass and puts Marakie down, then engages the safety and skims the gun toward the van. He still has the other pistol, the Iraqi Tariq semi-automatic, on him. He raises his hands again and walks in a wide circle toward the cop. Jones again says, "Freeze." Jones moves to the side of the van and steps slowly forward. Logan, stepping back, while thinking of a way out, says, "Been squatting behind a desk, have you? I'm a man. Why don't you show the bitch over there that you're not just a pencil-pushing, overweight motherfucking bum with a badge?"

Marakie looks left toward her abductor, then forward at the officer, who holsters his weapon. Her eyes are saying why doesn't he shoot the guy?

"Say anything you want about me." Jones walks to within a few feet and points to her. "She is a lady and you will swallow those words."

Logan springs forward, like a pass-rusher, lifting Jones off the ground and flinging him over ten feet, until he rams Jones' back into the van. No reverberating echo, just a muffled crash. But Jones' excess weight, muscular back, plus his vest, keep him from being entered on the injured list.

Logan's upper back is two-and-a half feet wide, and between his shoulders and neck are a bundle of muscles half the size of tennis balls. Natural body armor. Marcus gets on the pier deck. Recalling Borg's orders about cops, Logan picks up the suppressor end of the Walther and uses his mighty arms to pistol whip Jones in his ribs with the butt, then goes for the side of his head. Jones strike-blocks a point located a hand's width from the wrist of the gun hand. It's all over. *He should not be able to continue to fight*, Jones thinks. But he's still standing. Logan rears back for a head butt. Jones pulls power from the ground and through his legs and lands a right uppercut against Logan's nose as his head moves forward and slightly down. The man is taller than Jones and husky and the cracking sound is unsettling for Marakie. She heard it from fifteen feet away.

Logan's head snaps up and back but his neck is strong. Blood drops from his nostrils. He feels tired, and now dazed. Jones' surgical strike-block plus the uppercut is working. Logan drops to one knee momentarily. Never bested before in hand-to-hand, except by one man, he stumbles back on his feet like he's drunk.

Marcus is two-thirds closer to the pier entrance. Two of Jones' ribs are cracked. He struggles to get his breath on track, then remembers to stop struggling with his body. The impact from hitting the van moved through his back to the front.

Marcus is at the pier entrance with his pistol. Logan wipes blood away from his eyes, doubles back more and drops on his butt. Jones clambers forward. Marcus can't believe his eyes, he doesn't want to injure Logan's ego by taking out the cop, not just yet. He thinks Logan will get the upper hand. He keeps the muzzle down. Logan says, "What did you do to me... cop?"

Jones lifts part of Logan's upper body, from his jacket collar. "Apologize to this lady." Then he cocks his hand back. He wants the man to see his palm coming from far away. Jones slides to the pavement as he wallops Logan's bloody face on his way down. The sound of the palm hitting the left side of the face was like the sound of goulashes splashing against a big puddle of water. The right side of Logan's head strikes pebbles on the asphalt. He's down but not unconscious. Jones holds his left side; his ribs aren't just cracked—they're broken. He will die if a jagged edge punctures an internal organ. He gets to his feet.

Marcus stepped off the pier entrance and onto the street. Straight ahead, on Tiffany Street, he sees the swirling lights of a patrol unit and hears it swerving. Jones gets up and looks for a pair of cuffs. He withdraws his firearm. In soft words, Jones says, "Police. You are under arrest. Turn on your stomach with your hands behind your head." Logan complies. Jones keeps his voice down. He's about to check for weapons as he begins to Mirandize him. He can't find an extra pair of cuffs, so with his right hand he lifts the top of the shooter's jacket, up, over and down over his upper arms. Jones steps back. Marakie tries to get out of her duck-tape restraints. Jones looks over at her.

Marcus is shocked to see his associate slapped across his face and now prone and with a cop standing over him, reading him his rights. He got a good look at that cop. Two streetlamps lit up the scene. Marcus could get off a clean shot. Marcus, a former mercenary at six-two aims. The police cruiser slides to a stop behind Jones' cruiser. Marcus says, "Hey, you!"

63

Logan, with his chin on the ground, turns to his right. He sees Marcus. "Kill him! It's self-defense." Jones turns to Logan then at the pier. Marcus fires, hitting Jones, center mass, twice. He bends over and then falls on both knees with his left palm on his eighth and ninth ribs and his right palm on his chest. He looks toward the young woman. Sees a sparkle in her eyes, then sees the ground moving closer, then nothing. His shoulders hit the asphalt first, then the side of his head.

Marakie Dewabuna stares at Jones' body, looking for any sign of movement. For Marakie, the pace of time de-escalates... stops. For her, the strength and resolve of this cop, checked as it was by two bullets, was the end of all time—as if Jones were time itself and had stopped like a clock and had halted everything else in the world, too.

He's still not moving. Neither is she. Of all the thoughts of James Bond and his resources that Marakie projected onto this cop, and with all his daring in protecting her and getting her to safety, Marakie understood that he was still a man, with strengths and weaknesses and instabilities. Yet, with all her conclusions, she tells herself:

"This man is the man I've been searching for!"

Her abduction, Frank Scudder's murder, Lorena's injuries, and the horrible men trying to rape her, the bumpy ride, and the huge scary man, the gunshots, still bound by duct tape, and now her Bond shot to death were all Marakie's nerves could handle. She swooned against the patch of grass, near the pier, on Tiffany Street.

# 8

## The Party Crashers

MCCURDY DASHES OUT OF THE CRUISER. He doesn't yell *Police!* but takes aim. He's going to make up for his clumsy responses. He just saw his partner get shot. He shoots Marcus in the shoulder, gun side. The second and third ones miss. McCurdy takes cover, but Marcus is ambidextrous, "Logan, I will cover you." Marcus switches hands and returns fire, splattering bullets at the van. Logan feels weak as he rolls over onto his back and then to his feet. Giddy, he wiggles out of his jacket, then puts it on again.

He takes his Iraqi Tariq pistol out of his deep pocket and points it at Jones' prone body. "Okay, cop, this is still self-defense."

McCurdy pops his head from behind the van. "Stop! Police!" He pulls twice at the shooter but misses. The third shot hits Logan's calf. Marcus points near McCurdy's foot. He fires and keeps firing. McCurdy takes cover again. Marcus is out of ammunition. Then Logan points at the door of McCurdy's patrol car and uses up his double stack while lurching violently to the pier entrance. He and Marcus keep the pressure on as they make it down the pier and into the boat.

McCurdy comes from behind the patrol car and over some pebbled grass to the pavement. He kneels over his partner. "Dispatch, Unit 525 officer down, at Tiffany Street pier. Repeat, Lieutenant Jones is down. Tiffany Street pier. There's a woman, possible victim, also down. Can't tell if she's been shot." McCurdy is blaming himself. He feels an ever-growing knot, a vortex of dread, in his gut. "Two shooters are getting into a boat, maybe heading southbound in the direction of Rikers Island." He looks down at his trainer. His voice sounds like it is filled with marbles; he can feel the pink heat in his face. He wants to say that he badly wounded them, but instead he tells the truth. "I shot the Lieutenant's shooter in the shoulder and another shooter who was about to shoot the Lieutenant. I shot him in the leg."

"Okay, 525. Stay calm. Say again."

McCurdy yells into his transceiver: "I hit one suspect in the shoulder and another suspect in the leg. Both are white, about six-two or taller; one is wearing a black leather jacket, white hair, mustache, large head, bloody nose. The other is clean-shaven, earrings both sides, with maybe black hair, wearing white pants, and t-shirt, and chest hair like a bear. Need medical assistance for the lieutenant and the victim, ASAP."

The dispatcher inside the office, in a calm and understanding voice, says, "Ten-four. All right, you did well, officer. We've already notified CG about a possible getaway boat. Assume your partner is still alive and administer first aid. We're sending more units and emergency vehicles."

McCurdy takes his hand off the transceiver. Jones told him, "It isn't over." How did Jones know?

The rounds had hit Jones' trauma plate, neatly placed in a compartment in his vest, but the bullets' impact altered his field of reality. Getting shot at center mass on a vest, while not fatal, can feel like you've been hit on your chest with a sledge hammer.

Lolling unconscious on the ground, but still able to hear everything around him, Jones has a tangible feeling of traveling through space. Jutting above dense clouds he sees the summit of a mountain and a woman in a bright red garment standing on it.

*She is gracefully slim, has a long, regal neck and beauty that is impeccable and otherworldly—even perfect. Her eyes are like starlight—distant and remote—as if she is seeing hundreds of years into the past. Or the future. Hers is a face of pain. A moment afterwards, her expression changes into a glow, which imparts an inner smile to her delicate features. Her hooded down jacket and matching pants seemingly protect the woman from the cold. The outfit's bright ruby color adds to the warm feeling. She moves uphill over the uneven high ground with ease and silence—controlled dynamism. She saunters purposefully, drinking in each step. She reveres this part of the mountain.*

*Suddenly, 40-to-50-mph gusts bustle horizontally toward her at sub-zero temperatures. Cold air at such heights is denser, thicker and heavier. With these qualities combined, the snap and rapidity of the wind can easily overturn anything not firmly rooted to the ground. But the onrush of violent wind and freezing cold is gradually weakening as it comes hurtling toward the woman. Its punch is mitigated by the barrier that surrounds her for miles. Her field of pres-*

*ence becomes the slender, secondary barrier to the winds coming from the In-*
*dian Ocean that sweep upward along the primary wind barrier—the giant*
*mountain itself, fifty times the area of Manhattan. The wind impediment she*
*projects is an atmosphere of pure spiritual light and power that flows out from*
*her stillness. It is a presence that intelligently checks the wind and bends it, al-*
*tering its trajectory so it moves around her, while she remains composed and*
*unflappable in its center. The woman's gaze is directed toward Jones' inner eye.*

*The scene gets smaller as Jones moves back through space. He has the feel-*
*ing of being tucked back inside the center of his chest.*

The getaway boat, a Sea Ray Sundancer, changed its course from south
to west in the direction of Long Island Sound.

Unit 6, a black Crown Victoria, careens past the two busted cruisers.

Jones opens his eyes. McCurdy is hovering over him, excited and scared.
Jones hears nothing. He notices the rookie cop's lips moving. He feels altogether balanced, calm and powerful. He sees the young woman. Maybe she
was shot, too? He rotates himself on his back. She's lying on her side. No
blood from gunfire. She's out cold.

Jones feels no pain or discomfort of any kind. Strange. He sits up. His
hearing returns. He yanks his transceiver and says, "Dispatch, Lieutenant
Jones. I'm all right. I can continue my police duties." McCurdy sees the flattened cartridges on Jones' vest. Pointing to the pier, McCurdy says, "The
shooters got away, sir."

"Copy that, officer."

"You still need to get checked out." Jones, following procedure as well as
setting an example, says, "Copy that." Jones grabs McCurdy's hand and stands
up. They look toward the pier. It's high tide, on the East River.

"McCurdy."

"Sir?"

"You shot the shooter in the shoulder?"

McCurdy laughed, "But I did not shoot the deputy." He hears water. He
can't hold it anymore.

"That's the spirit, officer. Good cops have a sense of humor."

"You like Eric Clapton, Lieutenant?"

"Of course, after Prince and Jimi Hendrix. Masters, all of them."

"The two shooters got away."

"Well, you got past all that legal wrangling in your mind, right? You acted resolutely."

"How'd you know that—? Well, sir, I have a date with them bushes over there."

"Wait, I have something to tell you." McCurdy feels disagreeable. If he doesn't go now... Jones put his hand on McCurdy's left shoulder.

"Officer McCurdy, back at Randall and Faile, your confusion about what action to take could have gotten me killed—never mind that I was able to handle it. If you're going to be concerned about being prosecuted, this is not the job for you."

McCurdy was so off-balanced by what his FTO said that nothing else mattered, not even what felt like a quart of urine in his bladder that was just about to soak his pants down to his socks, before it could merge with 'them bushes.'

"The time you spent at the academy was the time for working out these legal points, as well as your private ideas about life, but not during your tour and not the first shift and, most especially, not during a deadly encounter."

Jones conveyed the seriousness of police work to his trainee. Had to lock it into McCurdy as a man, moreover as a *policeman*. What he did next was a dramatic scene. There was no anger, just a desire to reach the young rookie. Jones looked around to make sure no one could hear him. He looked sternly into McCurdy's eyes. He squeezed his shoulder.

"If you had done what you did tonight with another cop, you'd be fucking thrown out on your face, with no recourse for appeal, because you would be a piece of shit, not worthy of the uniform. Worse, you both could have been killed." McCurdy's forehead wrinkled, and his reddish eyebrows came together. He gripped his duty belt but wasn't sure if that was where he should put his hands. The expression on his face was just one, long, frown.

Now Jones applied a balm for the wounds he had just inflicted. He relaxed his hand and patted McCurdy on the shoulder, "Know what you believe, Officer McCurdy, because what you believe determines what you will do on these streets. Go to the range often. Become an expert in hand-to-hand, hand-to-knife, and knife-to-knife, with your duty weapon, and at using an ASP or baton. Your options become numerous when you are an adept in all of these. And, thank you, Officer McCurdy, for standing between me and those two fuckers." Jones' stern face relaxed into a real smile. "You did some good work tonight. You know you have to account for every spent cartridge in your incident report."

"Yes, sir."

The sound of a few yelps and more bar lights. The Crown Vic screeches to a halt at the side of Unit 525. The two front grills of Unit 6 and theirs form the letter V. Two detectives, Mitch Phelps, the driver, and Daniel Raye jump out past the side of the van. "Talk to them, McCurdy."

McCurdy first ran to the bundle of large stones near the edge of the street. He felt better about his future as an officer. Jones turned to the young woman who was out cold.

The last thing he remembers is telling the big man in the black leather jacket to apologize to her, then slapping the big man with all his might, then reading him his rights, looking for cuffs, then looking south toward the pier, and the flash. Then a mountaintop and a woman dressed in red.

Marakie, in the fetal position, starts moving and opens her eyes, seeing Jones. Just the sight of him alive makes her relax a bit more. Her blouse is torn. Her mouth and limbs are taped.

Her feet are bare. Dried tears sparkle on her face like stars. Can she be? Segments of ballads from groups like the Delfonics and the Intruders and Arthur Prysock move through Jones' mind as he looks at her. Could she be her? The thought disappears. Jones places her origin near Africa's eastern edge. He drinks in her eyes for a few seconds, her slender and regal neck, her smile appearing. More than enough time for him to never forget them. Jones would gaze into those same eyes years later, under a different sky, standing on a different region of Earth. Breathing different air.

Now, they are both under moonlight and opposite flashing lights, and waves crashing into breakwater.

"Miss, may I remove the tape from your mouth, please?" Her face is riddled with red and blue light. She nods. McCurdy points to the pier, the detectives walk toward it. "Officer McCurdy."

"Yes, sir. Coming, sir. I was talking to the detectives about the incident."

"You and I will have lots of paperwork to get done." McCurdy sees the young woman awake. "Officer McCurdy, would you get me a pair of scissors and a blanket?"

"Yes, sir." Jones talks to her while moving close enough to take the tape from her mouth. "My partner and I were doing a random building search when we heard the van." He peers into her eyes. She peers back. He says, "I heard you, too. The tape looks like it will come off easy. It's loaded with air. Here we go," Jones takes one side and lifts it, moves it halfway, then the other end, moving both toward the middle. He pulls the two ends. "There."

Her eyes stayed on the eyes of the police officer then moved to his service patch, then to the glint of his badge and the name: Lieutenant Jones. The last name has one syllable, like Bond and it begins with a J, like James. Compact. Solid. Like the officer before her. "Miss, you are safe now. Emergency Medical Services are coming. They will see to you. The men that abducted you are—" Jones decides to keep their execution to himself. "My partner has gone to get you—"

"Pair of scissors and a blanket," she says.

"Right." Jones sees a torch symbol on her collar. "Are you a student at NYU?"

"Yes," flustered by the man before her, she asks, "did you go there?" Jones was angry, blood-boiling angry, at himself for tending to that thug with the stab wound and not getting her out of that van earlier.

"My sister did. I graduated from Cornell in Upstate New York." McCurdy had hurried to his unit, popped open the trunk, and pulled out an emergency-vehicle blanket and a pair of scissors from the trauma kit. He ran back.

"Here you are, sir."

"Thank you." The young woman pushed her bound hands forward. Jones cut between her wrists as she pulled them apart to make space. He did the same for her ankles. He let her peel off the tape pieces herself and draped the blanket over her. He pushed off the ground into a half-kneeling position and then stood erect.

"Thank you, Officer Jones."

"You're welcome." He stood up and stepped back out and away from her, far enough not to be overheard. "Unit 525, possible rape victim, mid-to-late twenties, notify paramedics."

"Copy that, 525. Paramedics already en route to the Tiffany Street pier. Will convey victim's information now." Jones walked back to her. She moved involuntarily. Jones saw signs of shock and thought of what he could do to calm her. He knew the body very well, knew what points would help, but he had to allow the paramedics to do their work.

Jones pulls out a small pad and pen from his duty belt. "What is your name?" Besides just getting her name, Jones said this to put her mind on something different.

"My name is Marakie Dewabuna."

He writes it down, "Pleased to make your acquaintance, Miss Dewabuna. I am Lieutenant Jones, Ahmad Jones, 41st Precinct." Her last name is familiar to Jones. He runs a list of questions through his mind:

*Who is she and why are four men dead? Why did their killer abduct her? Was he in the van all along in the passenger seat or did he come from somewhere else? Why didn't he join the other four knife-wielding assailants in fighting me? What does she know?*

She sat up straight, tidying up what she could of her blouse and hair. She couldn't resist thinking of 007.

By then, there were more yelps. The siren of an approaching emergency vehicle broke the air and easily dominated all other sounds. Jones just stayed with Marakie. That was all he did. There's a silence. It's palpable. There's a lull in the chaos where he and Marakie are. Jones is completely present. His ribs are fine and he is feeling strong. He projects strength to her.

"Thank you, Officer Jones, Ahmad, for the blanket." Jones thinks her voice is beautiful. It is rich and full of life. Cultivated. There is something else about its tone that has a magical effect.

"You are welcome. Paramedics are here for you." Through the white shirt, Marakie can see part of the vest underneath the two flattened rounds. She lifts her hand. Jones follows it as her fingertips touch his chest. "You did get shot, Ahmad. I'm sorry."

"Yes, but my body armor protected me."

"Just like you protected me." She pulled her hand away, gently. She got quiet, getting snugger under the blanket. She nodded her head forward and backward. Her eyes darted in several directions.

"Something bad happened to my driver. He works for the Diplomatic Security Service. The last I saw of him was when he was in his car, slumped over."

"Where?"

"On 149th Street and Trinity Avenue, where I was taken by those thugs." She wipes new tears off her cheeks.

"You say that your driver is a DSS agent and is slumped over in his car on 149th and Trinity."

Sobbing, "Yes."

"Was it an SUV?"

"It was a Lincoln Continental."

"A Lincoln Continental."

"Blue."

"The agent's name."

"Agent Frank Scudder."

Jones was shaken by that news. He knew Scudder. "I'll call it in, Miss De-wabuna. Dispatch, 525, I was informed by the vic—her name is Miss Marakie Dewabuna, that DSS Agent Frank Scudder, was in a Lincoln Continental, on 149th and Trinity. Something may have happened to him." He looked at her. "He *is* Miss Dewabuna's designated security driver, over." She nodded yes.

"Copy that, 525. Detectives are already at the scene. He was fatally shot. The glove box was open. Possible robbery. We've notified the Fort Lee office."

Marakie overhears. Her body trembles. Her mouth opens. No sound is forthcoming. Seconds shoot by. Still nothing is heard but vehicle noises and the frolicking waves beyond the asphalt and breakers. Jones reluctantly steps back. She requires time and space to digest this new information, and a shoulder to lean on, and medical care. All three. Jones looks around for the paramedics and for a professional to comfort her. Marakie calls to him holding out her arms. She's isolated, in tears. She drops her arms in defeat. She looks both right and left like a child who is lost and searching for her parents. She wipes her eyes with the backs of her hands.

Jones goes to her and kneels. She reaches out. He wraps his arms around her. She drops her arms against his back. She roars her cry. Jones holds her up while on his right knee. Her chin rests on his left shoulder. He takes a deep breath and lets it out. Hers is fast and irregular. He slows his breathing. Her breathing slows; she stops crying. He continues to breathe slowly in and out. She feels an electrifying sensation all around her.

The pain in her lower back, caused by The Tackler who knocked her down, and Bloody Fingers' knee strike, left her body. Paramedics show up. McCurdy talks to them. Jones speaks softly, "Miss Dewabuna, first responders are here to see about you. I won't be far, okay?" Jones hears them coming from behind him. He stands as he lifts her, bringing her to her feet. She's standing upright for the first time since she was tossed into the beige van. She holds his upper arm loosely. The detectives return from the pier. Jones walks slowly toward them. His arm to the tips of his fingers slides on through Marakie's hand. Her eyes never leave him. Paramedics are a few yards away. Jones decides to talk with them. After a minute, Jones walks straight toward the van.

The paramedics take over. Speaking gently yet firmly, "Miss, my name is Annie, and my partner here is Tom. We're going to take very good care of you." Tom returns to the emergency vehicle for the stretcher. Annie asks for Marakie's name. She takes the stethoscope from around her neck and inserts the buds into her ears. "How old are you, Miss Dewabuna?"

"Twenty-five." Annie places the disk over Marakie's heart. The stretcher arrives. "Your heartbeat is normal. That's very good. Can you tell me what happened?" Marakie tells them everything.

The two paramedics help her onto the stretcher. "You're in no immediate danger, and, because of your ordeal, we're going to gradually strap you onto the gurney, Miss Dewabuna. We're going to make you comfortable inside and take you to Lincoln Memorial's Level 2 Trauma Unit. They're on standby."

The detectives are getting a few facts from McCurdy and taking notes. Mitch Phelps, a Lieutenant Detective, leaves his partner with McCurdy, and straightens his previously loose tie as he walks toward the van.

Jones looks over Phelps' shoulder at the paramedic, a noticeably physically fit woman. She and her partner are about to lift the gurney into the vehicle. They say *one, two, three* and heave the gurney into the truck. The sound of the emergency vehicle at idle is the loudest of all. Its engine sounds like a small factory. The lapping waves of the East River on the nearby shore run a close second. Jones watches from a short distance. Miss Dewabuna's eyes are still on him. Then the red doors are swung shut and the truck yelps. The siren takes over and Jones watches the ambulance speed up Tiffany Street until its bright lights and noise are gone.

Acting as if he owns the ground he walks on, Phelps asks, "You okay, Lieutenant Jones?"

"I suppose, Detective Phelps. No, not yet. I heard four shots, then I was thrown three feet from the air onto my back. Then, I saw four dead men, shot in the head. They were all fucked. I didn't process the viciousness of that scene. Then, I got into the cruiser, chasing the shooter, and then I got shot twice. Then I learned that a friend of mine, a friend of the precinct was killed.

"You mean Frank, Phelps says, with definiteness.

"Besides that... I'm okay."

Phelps notices Jones' hand over his left side and the two rounds that had bored into his vest. "Any serious injuries?"

"What are you, a paramedic?"

"Just worried about you, that's all."

"I had a few broken ribs from the butt of a pistol."

"Had?"

Jones is torn by an impulse to follow the emergency medical truck, or to stay put and answer questions. "What do you need, Phelps?"

"I see you took two on your plate. What luck! Though I'm shocked that you are not sure if you're okay."

"I suppose. I said I suppose."

"Are you really, okay? Tonight has been a blood bath—five homicides in less than an hour."

Jones expects him to get to the question. Phelps turns to the empty space, where the EMS vehicle was parked alongside his unit. "Did the victim say anything?" Jones doesn't answer that question but answers the unformed question before it.

"I cut them some slack."

"Them?"

"Stop your bottlenecking, Phelps"

"The four kidnappers. Oh, and the one with the cut?"

"One of their own did that, a friendly knifing, trying to get to me."

"Your partner said that you singlehandedly made four men with edged weapons look like pantywaists, without firing a single shot." He pulls at his mustache. "A friendly knifing, huh?" Phelps shakes his head after adding up McCurdy's and Jones' story.

"I was within my right to use my firearm but I didn't. I knew I didn't have to. I was going to do my job without it. They were cuffed and ready for the front desk. Then some guy shows up."

"McCurdy says a white man with a large face like rubber and grayish white hair shot the four perps?"

Jones looks at Phelps' ride.

"And I broke his nose before he got away."

Jones says, "That's a classy P71 Crown Vic." Phelps, following, plays along. He looks at it, too. He's proud of it. "Yep, may they never stop making 'em. Got it a few weeks ago," he turns left, looking at Jones, "Well, Ahmad, you started the party without us. The second time this week, and with fresh meat this time."

Detective Phelps, a member of the 41st Precinct, leans his back and the sole of his shoe against the side cargo door of the beige van. Jones does the same. They are side-to-side. More red and blue lights from several patrol cars, SUV headlights and spotlights wash over Barretto Point Park and the pier.

Jones says, "It's the other way around. The party started before us. Fresh meat and I crashed it."

"You're telling me—and no one got killed by us, thank God." Jones is silent and so is Phelps for a beat, "But Ahmad, this is the second time in one week that you called for backup and then literally jumped the gun. I know you're just trying to give these new recruits a *get-up-to-snuff* on their field training and the benefit of your experience, but you have to set an example."

Jones faces Phelps, recalling the four attackers, the bloody leg, their mysterious execution, McCurdy's trial-by-fire, two holes in his vest, his previously broken eighth and ninth rib, his dead friend and the traumatized woman and replies, "You weren't there when this shit started."

Phelps looks toward the river, then down. "No, I wasn't."

Stressing each word with quiet authority, Jones says, "Set an example? This, Detective Phelps, could not wait. Procedures were honored. Called it in. Our actions moments after were commensurate with the speed of unfolding events. McCurdy acted well under the circumstances—stellar actually. He wounded the man who shot me. An example *was set*—TO PROTECT AND SERVE."

Phelps pondered, "And the other man who was about to do you?"

Jones pointed toward McCurdy who was seated in the cruiser beginning the incident report. "Under the pressure of strangers bent on killing me *and* him tonight, that rookie has been through hell. He made his bones."

"I guess the new ball-bag is on track to complete his two-year probation."

"I know so, detective."

Both Phelps and Jones were Lieutenants, but Phelps was also a Detective Second Grade and felt he had a tad more authority.

He didn't—except at a crime scene.

"For you and the PPO's sake, both your reports better reflect the cold facts." Phelps uncrossed his arms and rested his elbow on his wrist while pulling at his mustache. His arms were as aligned as a carpenter's square.

"Not because I don't believe you, but because there can be no doubt that members of the New York City Police Department weren't the shooters. Sometimes even the public won't accept the truth. So, your stories—I mean your accounts—must ring true, even though they are true. I'm on your side, Jones. Trying to help you out, that's all."

Phelps put the sole of his foot down and patted down his freshly coiffed dark hair. He looked more like a movie star than a cop. "Daniel and I will get back to work, at Randall and Faile. We need you both there. Place is taped. CSU is helping us process the homicides at 149th and the ones on Randall and Faile." Phelps shakes his head. "Shit, it looks like another long graveyard shift." He starts for his partner.

"Phelps?"

Without turning, "Jones?"

"Why do you and Daniel get to wear a mustache, while the rest of us in uniform can't?" Phelps shakes his head again, "A note from my commanding officer says I can," and turns back around. "You want facial hair? Join the detective squad."

Laughing himself out of his contemplation, Jones says, "Why did you answer my rhetorical question... you stupid fuck?"

Without turning, Phelps slaps the wind in response.

"Hey, Phelps."

"What, Jones?"

"Frank was the victim's driver. The victim is a relative or maybe even the daughter of the president of Afarland. She is a foreign diplomat. Those four dead boys had her in their van, before the suspect whose nose I busted up shot them and took off with her. He's probably Frank's shooter. This feels a lot bigger than just an abduction."

Phelps turns around and takes a few paces toward Jones. "Thanks, Lieutenant. The information from that is solid. Part of your story checks out with what McCurdy already told us, but not that. McCurdy said he heard a woman screaming. He thought she was just another hooker that got in over her head."

Phelps was about to go further along that same line. Suddenly, winds blew in from the southwest. The rolling swell of the water broke into a huge violent pattern that reached a foot high. The salty waters of the East River submerged the rocky breakwater near Tiffany Street. A thin film streamed across the pavement some twenty feet away from the two men.

"She's no hooker, but a frightened young girl who was kidnapped, maybe molested, and kidnapped again." Phelps quickly changed his mind, patted his hair and said, "Lieutenant Jones, I have to go to Lincoln Memorial and ask her some tough questions to find the truth. Why are five people dead in less than an hour? And why is another woman, a Lorena Saint Jacques, who was seen with this alleged diplomat, in the hospital with a fractured cervical disk?"

"Don't know anything about another woman."

"Well, that woman in the EMS truck, she's the only one, for now, who can give us more information to heat up this investigation."

"Do what you have to do, Phelps, and do it with dignity." Jones walks to his unit.

"I need you and your partner at the crime scene, ASAP."

Jones shuts the door as McCurdy starts the engine. "Back to Randall and Faile?" asks McCurdy.

Jones directs his attention to the Tiffany Street Pier: the asphalt, the pebbled grass. He recalls the words of the shooter about sitting behind a desk.

McCurdy said, "Sir? Waiting for your orders."

Silence. McCurdy moved the gear all the way to the left and set the brake. The cruiser idled. The two officers took a much-needed breather.

Jones felt the wound near his right kneecap where Jiekang's blade had actually landed. He kept the incident to himself. He had gotten careless, he surmised, because of too much time spent at the precinct. There was too much energy directed to the supervising of daily activity reports, accidents, and crimes—too many administrative duties, such as arranging officer deployment for his service area. Someone else could do it. He had to get back to the streets.

Jones listened to the engine and the waves. Two worlds—the great expanse of river just beyond the asphalt and the pier deck and the limited space inside his patrol unit. He opted for the great expanse of patrolling the streets. He thought, *What if I had shown up after the crime of kidnapping was committed to coordinate various departmental entities and fill out a report for my captain's approval?*

He felt more blood trickling down his inside thigh. His ribs were fine, but his knife injury wasn't.

"Odd."

"What's that, sir?"

"Yes, McCurdy, we'll head back to Randall and Faile and finish up." McCurdy backs up and swings the front of the unit.

They head north on Tiffany.


"The Coast Guard is not far behind." Marcus got up from the helm seat and looked behind him. He slid the throttle forward to the end for top speed.

"Ditch the boat," Logan said.

"Okay, coming up on 132nd Street. Ready for a speed dock." Marcus throttled back, angled the boat sideways, brought the twin throttles together and cut the engine. He wiped the controls. The sound of the pursuing Coast Guard boat was getting louder. Any minute now, they'd be listening to someone on a bull horn: *This is the United States Coast Guard...* The two men arrived at Stoney Point and hightailed it out of the boat and into the shallow water, then crawled up garbage, dirt, huge rocks, and debris to level ground. Logan, with a gunshot to his calf, and Marcus, shot in the shoulder, didn't think about pain.

They stepped onto part of a wooden deck, and then veered to their right toward a fence and large stones. A dark-blue station wagon was against the fence. The rays of the moon bounced off its sides. Marcus picked up a large stone and broke the driver's-side glass, got in, and proceeded to hotwire it. They were behind a road sign, just a few feet away from the remaining deck. The sign read "DEAD END." The Coast guard light got brighter. It was half a mile to the east.

"What's wrong?" Logan asked.

"Battery is dead." Marcus and Logan ran up 132nd Street. Logan was hopping, not running. They hailed down a pickup. The driver, having been robbed before at gunpoint, reached for his pistol but not before Logan fired a shot at the door handle. The man shoved his hands up.

Logan hopped over to the driver, pointing his pistol with the intent to fire. "Get the fuck out and give me that hat." The man, about average height, took off his wide-brimmed, high-crowned hat.

"Slowly now."

He opened the door and climbed down onto the running board and got his feet to the ground. The man was wearing a wedding ring. Logan took the hat from the man, who then shoved his hands back up. Logan put it on.

"Got kids?"

"Yes."

"You want to go home to them?"

The man nods.

"There's a boat down there. You will move like the wind over dirt, rocks, and garbage and get into that boat, now." Logan pointed south. The man kept his hands up and headed to the section of the pier, looking down at the boat. He turned to Logan, who then gestured with his pistol.

The boat was floating away from the shore. "Better hurry."

Logan watched the man's head disappear below the pier section. Marcus ran to the edge of the section. He saw the man climbing down the side and into the water. Marcus rushed back. Logan climbed into the truck's cab and opened the passenger door. Marcus got in. Logan headed west and then north toward 278 and Manhattan, then to New Rochelle.

Over five years passed before Ahmad Jones and Marakie Dewabuna met again on a beach in a suburb of Cape Town, South Africa. It was on Thursday, the 25th of September of 2008, the day after Thabo Mbeki resigned as president.

Jones locked the door to his apartment across the street and walked to the beach. Marakie was watching the play of white sand on her toes, while moving casually along False Bay's eastern edge near the shoreline. Jones made it across the road with a friend when he caught sight of the woman strolling, alone on the beach.

He didn't recognize her at first. Her hair was shorter than before, on the day he last saw her. The ends of her natural curls stopped at her jawline, revealing her beautiful neck, which was slender, not long, but not short either. It held her head, pretty and upright, with an understated majesty.

The air was sensational. The sun was caressingly warm, and the woman was getting more beautiful as Jones and his friend got closer to the shore. He imagined that the sounds of the waves crashing were a soundtrack for the actions of what Jones had named the super-fine woman on the beach.

The couple, that was not yet a couple, headed toward similar points on Earth's grid, but, in a way, they *were* also those points and that grid. They approached a singular spot from perpendicular angles. Marakie was moving westward along the shore and Jones was heading south toward the shore.

There were whales in False Bay, including the Orca and the Humpback. The Humpback is known as a singer among whales. It would play a peculiar part in the next few minutes. The soon-to-be couple's meeting place was held in time by nature's wisdom. Long ago, its latitude and longitude were well established in the memory tablet, the memory of things to come; of a strange and wondrous alchemy between kindred spirits. Even Jones couldn't chart the exact coordinates of what would become a profound love. His method wasn't refined enough for this reality—although it was more than enough for the mundane things. There were even greater methods to the madness in his celestial work, which he would come to know soon.

Marakie noticed Ahmad approaching and knew right away who he was—the man of her deepest longings. He, too, would have seen her for what she was—his lady love. But on that night several years ago, he was called upon to absorb so much violence that it obscured his ability to glimpse the tracings of the woman he'd longed to meet since then. The responsibility was his for not seeing in her his own reflection. The connection with his deeper desires was lost because he was saving lives. It was a noble thing—Jones considered the needs of others first.

Now here he was, after five-plus years, at the exact place and time for a second meeting with her—a meeting without the baggage of discord. What was moving along the shore now had been there all along, even on that night in 2002, represented by ancient symbols on his bird's eye maple desk—a higher astrology that could only have been revealed through the eyes of the heart.

Marakie had just finished lunch across the road at *Ben's on the Beach*, a popular eatery in *The Strand*. Jones had planned to eat something later. Marakie wore a silk, lily-white, one-shoulder kaftan. Jones wore white Swedish knits and an extra-large, Cleveland Browns football jersey, orange with the white number 32. Suddenly, a gentle wind came in from the south, over False Bay, and pushed up against her garment like soft hands, revealing the outlines of valleys and protuberances, previously hidden shapes of her body. Jones was proportioned in his build. The same gentle breeze abated and then ran up against him. In Marakie's delicate left hand were the straps of her sandals, which swayed gracefully with each step. She was on her own now. There were no diplomatic security personnel directly around her. But they were around. Somewhere.

A wave flowed in, met the shore, and flowed back out, then their eyes met as if False Bay, playing matchmaker, performed the introduction.

*Her eyes are like the sparkle of a star. I do recall seeing those eyes somewhere. Her dress moves with the sounds of the bay. Her scent fills the air with fragrant flowers.* Jones said these words to himself. But he still did not recognize her.

In May of the previous year, Marakie had graduated from LUC (Loyola University Chicago) with a degree in Mechanical Engineering. She was celebrating her years of dedicated work by vacationing in South Africa, not far from her homeland. Jones had come to Cape Town from Moshi, in Tanzania, two months before. He rented a beachfront flat across the street from the bay. He was reporting on the transition of power from Mbeki to Jacob Zuma, freelancing as a foreign correspondent, under the pen name of Steve Watson. He freelanced for a small newspaper concern headquartered in New York.

Jones thought of Marakie for several years. He realized that he loved her from the start. Was certain that it was she that his chart had predicted. But he didn't see it then. When he first saw her that night, in the South Bronx, he loved everything about her: her oval face and her bright, expressive eyes. When she gave her statement, at Detective Phelps' office, at Longwood, Jones saw her under the bright light. He loved the twining movements of her long, brown hair against her bosom. He loved everything else, too—her soul, her spirit, the life that moved through her. He loved that moment in time, when he opened the back door of the beige van and shined the light on her. It was at that instant, that Jones' heart was captured, for the first time in many years. But that changed, after he boarded the van and was subsequently catapulted out of it and his pristine moment.

It must have been amnesia. He was an officer, professional, and didn't feel it was right to pursue her, under the circumstances. The deck was stacked in his favor. A cop saves a damsel in distress. Damsel falls in love with the cop. The chart also revealed that there was a need for distance in time. Jones wasn't ready for her, but she was ready for him.

Marakie knelt to pick up some sand. She was serene, ethereal in her mannerisms, admiring the water and the beach. The bay was on her left. She turned to her right and saw him. There was a palpable connection, within the field of space, between them—the kind of connection one encounters when the north end of one magnet and the south end of another magnet are sufficiently apart to produce a polarity, a calm field-of-attraction. He was the North Pole and she the South Pole. The magnetic field that formed between them had changed their lives, in the blink of an eye. Their hearts talked. In some well-documented studies, the heart was shown to emit fifty times more electricity than the human brain. Their meeting *was* electric.

Marakie had never forgotten Lieutenant Ahmad Jones. She took in his fine looks and presence. She liked that he had lost some weight. He was more muscular. He was nimble and tall. In no time, Marakie was certain that she had found the man whom she had sensed many times before, in her dreams, when she was a teenager.

Jones' friend had left him a few moments ago and veered off in the direction opposite the one that Marakie was traveling.

She stops, grabs some more sand and lets it flow through her open fingers. Jones takes off his sandals, to feel the warmth of the beach. They move closer, like two lodestones. They face each other, from a short distance.

Jones brings the tips of his fingers together. "Nice air," Jones says.

Marakie looks at the air, showing several angles of her face. "Yes," Marakie says, "I am liking this air, too, yes, it is—*much* nicer, right now." Every word she speaks, contains the voice of a smile, "And you look familiar. Have I ever seen you before now?"

More than five years of waiting, waiting for someone that she was sure she'd see again; their chemistry was apparent, not blatant. There was a courtliness and a gallantry in the space that was around them and was them. To Marakie, the two words: "Nice air" that Jones said were simple and brilliant.

Jones beheld the child-like manner her arms had spread out as she breathed in a deep breath. He felt as if she were breathing not just air, but the essences of sweet thoughts now streaming through his mind, about her.

"You have almost *taken* my line word-for-word," Jones said. "Truth is, you've taken much more!"

"Oh! *Hwhhhaat?*" she exclaimed.

When Marakie asked, "What?" her voice sounded as if she were blowing a piece of dust from his eye or the flame from a candle. The first two letters were reversed—the H sound came before the W.

"Correction, you *gave* me something. Something I may have forgotten, to see with the eyes of my heart."

Marakie said, "And I... *gave* you, as you say, this?"

Ahmad realized who the woman was that stood before him. "Yes. Yes. You and I are here, and... *how* I've missed you. I've waited a long time to share this air with you."

"Ahmad, I have felt your strength with me, in my study hall, in my breaks between classes, at Loyola, at the dinner table in the Presidential Palace. Ahmad, you've always been with me."

She held her sandal straps with both hands. She nodded, and Jones stepped closer, to within a yard. Her eyes followed him all the way.

Her voice changed to a whisper, "Well... my love. What will you do with it, this, with me... your new heart-eyes?"

A splash on the bay called their attention waterward. The white under-belly of a Humpback whale had shimmered for a moment. Then its mottled black body was swallowed up by the salty water. The bay got quiet.

Marakie let go of her sandals and leaped into Ahmad's arms. The waters had reached his feet. He held her. Softly. She wrapped her thighs above his waist. Her body, energy, and the fragrance she gave off was magnificent. This was the icing, for he had already been captured by something more substan-tial a few moments ago—her heart. They kissed, for an eternity of two straight minutes, and with no interruptions from DSS special agents, who were watching them, from some distance away.

"I never forgot you." She took her head off his shoulder and looked into his eyes. "Mr. Jones. Mr. Jones. Mr. Jones. I am liking your name and calling you Mr. Jones. Its sound is exciting—like we're going to search for the Ark, or a lost city, or—"

"A new life together?" He felt his head for an imaginary hat, while holding her against his body with the other. "I'll remember my Fedora next time." She uncurled her legs and put her feet down on the mushy sand. Looked up at him.

"I think a Stetson would look better on you." They walked some ways from the shore. She placed her sandals on dry sand and covered her eyes.

"I'm imagining you in a Stetson when we meet again," Marakie laughed. "You saved my life, oh my, close to six years ago." She uncovered her eyes and he laughed. They laughed like old friends laugh upon meeting after a long separation.

"Let's walk together," Jones offered. He was nearer to the water. She was next to his left shoulder. They held hands and were silent. After ten minutes, Jones turned his body away from the shore and faced her. Their heart-connection was exhilarating. After they were far enough away from the bay, so they sat. Marakie laid her ear against Jones' shoulder. Jones' friend sauntered toward them.

"Whose number is that?"

"Jim Brown, from the Cleveland Browns."

"Have you played many sports?" Marakie asked.

"Football, Gymnastics... and you?"

"Volleyball."

"Volleyball, now there's an exciting sport."

"Do you have a favorite football team?"

"Yes, the Seattle Seahawks."

"Then why are you wearing a Cleveland Browns shirt?"

"Well, because Jim Brown was an extraordinary player of the game. Which is your favorite?"

"I loved 'da Bears when I lived in the Midwest. Now, I'm a Seattle Seahawks fan."

"Is that right? Well, Marakie, I have a new team now." He moved his lips until they reached her ear.

"A team of two," he whispered.

When Marakie giggled and looked away to the water, her eyes reflected the movement of the bay. Jones' heart *led* him to say one more thing.

"Just a small space between our togetherness. There will always be that space, in our space."

Marakie turned to face him. False Bay started its song and dance again, this time even louder.

"I want you to meet my father, Ahmad."

"I'd be honored to meet him."

"Hello, and who are you?" Skippy had knelt at Marakie's feet, rolled on his back, then stood up and went to Jones and sat on his hind legs.

"Skippy, he's been with me, almost seven years now."

"Skippy, would you be my dog, too?" Skippy looked at Jones and then at Marakie, He stepped in between them, then moved in a circle toward the bed of sand and plopped himself down. Like a child lying between his parents.

# 9

## Defining an Enigma

IN TRIPOLI, LOGAN EXECUTES A SHARP RIGHT off Shari Al-Kubra Street. He lopes south past the mosque on the corner, drives three-quarters of the way down the back road, and then slows to a crawl.

"He's just one guy," Marcus, in the passenger seat says. Logan considers his partner's remark. His meticulous mind measures its worth against what he had learned from his encounter with the guy eight years ago in 2002, and his case file less than eighteen hours ago.

The crawl becomes a full stop. Logan recounts all the facts of the target, including his first impressions from the target's photograph. The crowd disperses around the sleek BMW in early morning sunlight. The car resumes its slow roll. Logan says, "For me to look at him as just one guy, would be to look at him wrong. I say he's a freaking squad, a platoon, a company. That's what he is until we prove otherwise. A bomb is a bomb until it is diffused, or until it is deemed not to be a bomb. So, for now, he is our most powerful—"

"Fucking b—"

"You got it! But he's in between us and our dough. But we assume until we have proof."

"Of what?"

"Turn right in point thirty kilometers." The navigation voice plays over the radio broadcast. The back road is clear. There's a short burst of acceleration. The state-run broadcast resumes. "Freaking propaganda!" Logan says, and turns the radio off.

"If he's not, then it's an easy 22 million euros. Okay?"

Marcus says, "Got it; he is a bomb until we prove he is not a bomb; only four radio stations in a country of over six million, eh? Are you going to finish the story?" Marcus asks.

Near the last quarter of the block, Logan executes another right turn onto the apron. He takes a hand off the steering wheel, lowers it to the controller knob at the center console. He turns it a bit and watches the GPS screen options, while keeping track of the curved wall of sandblasted security barricades directly ahead of him. He selects *Stop Guidance,* before the terse unemotional feminine voice prompt tells him what he already knows.

Logan, less weather-beaten and with a nose job, is white-haired and six-two and bearishly built. He obeys the signs in front of the concrete blocks and eases the wheel slightly left. The car rolls past the barricades toward the far end of the crowded lot. Along the way he drives between two lines of Salvage cars, mostly imported from Florida, which had been rebuilt, or had arrived slightly damaged, per the buyer's request.

Sunlight streamed into the car from the veteran hitman's left. The temperature had reached 62 degrees by 5:00 am, two-and-a-half hours earlier. It would get up to 83 by two in the afternoon, accompanied by the Ajaj, a dust storm.

Logan finds a space, near the end of the lot, which is made up of another wall of beige-colored concrete. He inches the imported BMW in between the lines, depresses the brake and pushes in the start button. At his left is a palm tree over 70 feet tall. Ten feet further is the barricade. The tree is directly across from the left front fender. At his right is a sparkly-blue Toyota Hilux.

"This is as good a cover as any, around here," Logan says. Marcus scans what's in front of him. Logan digs into the cup holder for the pack of cigarettes known throughout Libya as "Illicit Whites." He leans against the seatback, glides a cigarette out of the pack, takes the lighter from its port and heats the tobacco. Draws smoke into his mouth. He and Marcus watch several men roaming about the rear of the four-star hotel.

Logan and Marcus, his clean-shaven partner, with diamond studs on his ear lobes, similar in build, but an inch shorter, were mercenaries in bygone days. Skilled operatives. They neither left a target alive that was contracted to be killed, nor did they render a target dead that was supposed to remain alive. This mission was their first major one outside of occasional contract jobs, in five years. They were in their early fifties. Their target was Ahmad Jones, who was born and raised in the south side of Chicago. The mission's designation was indicated as: *High-value target. Terminate only if out of options.*

The two men were hired as civilian contractors, by a private concern the day before. This was Logan's and Marcus' second job with them. The two men were in that lot for one reason: make enough dough to retire. But they received a bonus—their last real *fix* because they were addicted to the adrenaline rush. But now, one of them was much more addicted to his body's own drug, than the other.

Logan, smooth and urbane, and Marcus, a bit of a romantic, lean against the leather seat sizing up the cadre of men.

"Which story, Marcus? I've got hundreds and between us we've got several hundred."

"The one you started telling, before you turned on the radio, the one about Angola."

After another puff, Logan, who is too health-conscious to drag the smoke into his lungs, flicks his ash out the top of the barely open window. He tells his story with the cadence of someone narrating a documentary. Just the facts.

"Well, I'm slithering on my stomach into deep shit," he says, "wiggling underneath twisted barbs and over the deep gouge I had dug in the rain. But I'm turning my body and arching my back like a porpoise, to get my ninety-two freaking kilograms to the other side of the fence, making sure my bare feet don't get snagged. The rain is hammering down on my back, like soft pebbles. Cold pebbles. But after I collect my weapons I slide over to the other side, I sneak on through the loyalists' camp. It's winter and I'm wearing my shorts, my safari hat, a Z-88—that I seized from an enemy combatant, who pointed it at me from a foot away, just a minute before I made it to the fence— my knife, and the 4.8 kilos of my cold *FN FAL* slung around my bare back—"

"Logan," Marcus interrupted, "I heard that story before, and the last time, you said it was a Vector 4. So, which is it, eh?" Logan blows smoke. He says. "Marcus. It was freaking winter. Middle of June in Africa—and the rainiest. But I was digging a hole in the ground like a freaking scent hound."

"You mean, like a dirty dog," Marcus said. He coughs and lowers the window a few inches. They look at the men drifting back and forth, along the hotel's rear entrance.

"Your guess." Logan blows smoke again, while looking for markers, those telltale signs that can reveal useful information about the weapons those men may have tucked underneath their clothing.

"My guess is that they're Internal Security Agents with Zastavas."

"Semi's, huh?"

"From Yugoslavia, or M9s. Yes, I'd guess M9s." Logan takes in another puff, holds it in a few seconds, then blows it out in a burst. "And no, I dug that hole, in my shorts, like a scent hound, but I was hauling my FN FAL, instead of a South African battle rifle. Anyhow, I triple-tap the target with my newly acquired Z-88, with suppressor attached and all, while he is still sleeping. Poor fucker. There were seventy, maybe eighty men in that camp. Probably a whole company, but I didn't give a fuck. I waited for the opportunity, when they were sleeping. They were all dead to the world. There wasn't even a watch. But I waited 'til the target's chest stopped going up and down, then I went back the way I came, under the barbs and over the hole, and past the guy I shot with his own pistol. My thirty-ninth kill."

"You up to what—"

"Ninety-one, and when I get to a hundred... it's the *end*. Not doing it anymore."

"You said the same thing when you hit fifty."

Logan reflected for a beat, then shook his head as he looked at the armed men, who now appeared to be moving with a purpose and not haphazardly.

"Shit, I did all of that in a Southern African winter-rainy wonderland," Logan said.

"And you are lucky it was raining hard, eh, to loosen up the dirt and provide enough noise to drown out any sounds you made, or you surely would have been a *dead* freaking scent hound and I would be in this Beemer about to engage this one guy, or platoon, with some dip-shit partner whom I suspect would not have a thumbnail of your tactical skills."

"You said 'eh' again, twice." Logan said.

"I did not."

"Right, Marcus."

"He's a goddamn bomb," Logan said. "But, I like dog-of-war, but I dig scent hound for a moniker, and *merci pour le compliment*. But that fucker is not just one guy."

"You win Logan, you win. He's a high-value target, maybe a Claymore, with one hundred fucking steel balls, about to kill us. Not just *one* guy. But don't forget, I shot him and he went down." They continue to conduct surveillance from their vantage point at the back-left corner of the rectangular parking lot, while engaging in their ritual of putdowns, banter, and smoke.

Logan reaches behind his seat and grabs a green binder. "I'm ready," he says. Marcus nods. Logan says, "We complete this job, collect another 11 million, and get back to Kamloops, eh? By way of London."

Marcus pulls out an Illicit White and lights it. "Now, *you* said 'eh.'"

Logan says, "I meant to." Marcus shakes his head.

"Unlike you, Logan, I do not just puff smoke into my mouth, I drag it into my lungs. They institute a ban on cigarette smoking in public places and I may be the only asshole probably in all of Tripoli to jettison smoke rings out of a car window near a bunch of armed nationals. World Health Organization shit."

"Indeed, Marcus, I need a good smoke, before a major op, and this *is* a major one, I feel it. And, by the way, as I see it, the way I smoke, I've got at least another twenty years. You, if you're lucky, may get five. I would hate to see an X-ray of those bellows of yours."

"Really, Logan? Thanks a lot for those thoughtful words. One day you may just eat them. Glad Bilal kept his promise, eh, and put a pack inside. And he came through beautifully with the 1911s we asked for. Let us hope he is as good at logistics as he is with contraband and micro pistols." Marcus looks down and gestures with his hands. "And, by-the-way, what the, Bilal gets us a beautiful ride with clean beige bucket seats and no freaking belts."

"He's from eastern Libya; belts are not compulsory there. A habit, so we can fit in."

"Fit freaking in, we are from Canada and there, in Canada, we wear seat-freaking-belts. Belts save lives."

"But who are you to be talking about saving lives? Have you tallied the number of lives you've unsaved?"

"Business. Just business. That is the only thing I can say against this Bloke, Bilal. He got everything right, the car, the cigs, the ten-ring ammo, but we could have been taken out by another car, before lighting up, or checking our hardware. Can you picture that, two professionals like us, thirty years in the shit, buying it, because some asshole who cannot drive straight, crashes into us with his family car? Be a shame to leave like that. Better be worth it, sure hope executing this Jones is not our only option. But if it has to be, I won't shoot at his vest this time."

"Up to us."

"No Logan, it is up to him. It would mean that we do not get the 22 million euros—if he chooses to not play along and we must, as they say in America, whack him."

"It has always been up to us. Borg gave us the op with that in mind. We'll make Jones see it our way."

Both men, now worked up and motivated, put their cigarettes out in the tray, take a few moments to check their pistols again, where their extra mags are and then reholster their subcompacts inside their slim pancakes at the small of their backs. They get set, then exit the BMW, sporting battleship-gray suits, charcoal-colored string ties, and dark glasses, but lacking the true art of ceremonial figureheads. They button their specially made suits, a precaution. Their intention of comporting themselves like important men, like, how heads of state act and move when departing airplanes or getting in and out of limousines, is stopped by a sudden dusting of red-brown sand from the frontier out of the southwest. Marcus, who spent some time in Qatar, was no stranger to sand storms, and got back into the car with Logan just in time to evade a direct hit from the thin blanket of sand dune in the air. "Ajaj came early," Marcus said.

The winds that brought it had originated from Libya's Marzuq Sand Sea, about 700 miles west of Tripoli. It lost momentum, though, by the time it reached the back lot and four-square miles of the city. It covered all the windows. Logan started the car to use the wipers. Outside looked like a dense fog. Ahead of them and on the other side of the hotel, traffic slowed down, and wipers and water were the only things that kept traffic moving. Still, the flow of traffic stayed almost the same.

With the sandy element to contend with, the third leading cause of death in Libya was traffic accidents, involving both pedestrians and drivers.

Now, the Jerez Black BMW, known for its deep-blue metallic hue, looked like every other car in the lot, dusted with a thin film of reddish-brown sand. The tall palm tree shaped like a giant vase, with long, wide leaves, partly shielded the car. For them, even the winds originating as far away as the nations of Algeria and Niger, arrived earlier, and appeared to rebuke their airs.

A strong local wind, coming from over the Mediterranean, sends the dust southward, clearing away the fog.

The two still had an edge in their early fifties but weren't as flexible. They were frozen in time. They were still the best, so they thought, and they were right, but only at certain things, like training defense forces, providing intelligence for coup plotters, arranging assassinations, blowing up rebel strongholds, and engineering regime change. But they hadn't taken any jobs for the last three big-ticket items since Nelson Mandela took the oath of office in May of 1994. Instead, they made their money doing contract kills.

Logan and Marcus lived off their earnings, until they ran out in 2005, which is when they retired from retirement, and reentered the marketplace—two decommissioned guns for hire. Their reputations preceded them. If there were a draft for former mercenaries with superlative credentials, they would be number one picks in the first round. Since 1980, they ate with, drank with, strategized with, and on several occasions, were involved with assassinations of local chiefs—who had too much political leverage—presidents and revolutionaries. They had been in the game up to their necks in several African countries.

They were two contradictions in their expensive attire. Inside, whatever spark of conscience or soul they possessed had all but entirely gone out. They created more terror in ten minutes than most humans could bear if those minutes were spread out over ten years.

With thirty years of violent memories and habits toward people and nations swimming around like sharks in their subconscious, they confirm that the men who are moving about the rear of the hotel, dusting sand off chairs and each other, are indeed Libyan Internal Security forces, checking vehicles, watching patrons enter and exit, and sharing information with each other. They're dressed in street clothes, sport jackets, and t-shirts—no uniforms, so average persons, especially visitors from other countries, can't tell.

Still inside the BMW, they notice up to a dozen palm trees spread haphazardly around the parking lot, and two that frame the door of the rear entrance. The trees remind them of Namibia, Guinea-Bissau, Burkina Faso—places they were sent to ply their tradecraft. They open the car doors, step out and walk diagonally toward the entrance on the thin film of sand and meander between bumpers and grills belonging to Toyotas, Kias, Hondas, Jeeps, and BMWs. At 7:38, they hear a loud thud from the other side of the hotel, an accident, which breaks their nostalgic reverie.

They reach the point between the lot and the rear entrance. Logan bends over and scoops up a clump of sand at the base of a palm tree. He considers the distance it traveled to arrive at that spot, and how it altered the color of most things in its path in less than a minute. He lifts it to his nose.

Marcus looks down at his partner in crime. "My adrenaline is pumping. Smells like the old times, eh, Logan?"

He nods while gradually opening his hand and looks him in the eye, "No, Marcus. We crossed the Mediterranean to do a job. It smells like new times. A life of leisure. Ahmad Jones is twelve floors up on the northeast end of that building. He's our ticket out of putting ourselves in danger to make a buck. A 22-million-euro ticket if we take him alive. I could finish my quota in my own time.

"As they say in America, 'get out of town,' Logan. When we were out the first time, we had fucking money, fucking... gorgeous women, and still had..."

"I know, *freaking nightmares*. Would you take it easy with the language?> It's making my head ache. Sure, we had money, but not 22 million euros—more like a million. You are having second thoughts." Logan stands up and slaps his hands together, alternating them up and down like brass cymbals, while the green book he took from the backseat is tucked in between his upper arm and body.

Marcus steps closer and whispers, "Living that life of leisure? Maybe we were both miserable. I am no psychiatrist, but maybe we ran through that money so fast, so we could get back into the shit. *This* is our life. Look—you were all pumped up telling that story in the car about the guy you triple-tapped—the asshole whose pistol you confiscated and then used on him. We have demons that have demons—and we have orders to kill that guy Jones on the twelfth floor, if he says no. It is up to him."

"For 22 million, divided in half? But you can stay in the game, poor? I'm running this op. It is up to us to make him see the wisdom of doing what we ask. Remember that." Logan's gray eyes are pointed at Marcus' blue.

"After this job, we'll discuss retirement, when we get back to Kamloops. I've nine more kills and I'm finished. It's the only thing I'm good at doing—killing. Millionaires. But even so, our target, Ahmad Jones and us, we met him near that pier eight years ago. He landed one, broke my nose, and you double-tapped him, center mass. I wanted you to kill him, and after you shot him, something told me that the guy was wearing an extra piece of metal under his vest. I admit it, you stopped him from getting the better of me."

"Well, does he know who you are?"

"I was gone before he could get a bead on me. He may have heard you call my name."

"What about that other business, did you—"

"You and I both heard that stuff about Jones, for the first time. Anyhow, as impressive as his dossier sounds, we will take him back to Borg, because though he may be a bomb, he is still, as you would say, just one guy."

# 10

## Jones' Dossier

LOGAN, A DEADLY RASCAL IN A SUIT, is professional-looking, with his neatly combed and trimmed white hair and mustache. He could be the archetype for an old-time train conductor. Marcus, of the same breed of rascal as Logan, is also neat and tidy. Logan squeezes the green binder, with the government seal, between his upper arm and body. The armed security force catches a glimpse of the seal and stands at attention, when the two men arrive at the rear entrance. The security force nods as a group, and Logan and Marcus return the gesture. Inside the binder is an official-looking document with a forged signature expertly written. They face the automatic doors and step closer to the sensor. The doors spread open and the two men walk into an air-conditioned lobby.

The binder includes a photograph of Ahmad Jones clipped to the top-right corner. The photo is a full-body shot of Jones, wearing a white tunic over white pants, being embraced by members of the Dogon, in a remote village, in Mali, West Africa. It immediately conveys a feeling of quiet power.

Before Logan and Marcus landed in Tripoli, their boss, Mr. Borg, having flown them in to West London from Western Canada, invited them into his cigar-smoke-ridden office to give them, by way of introduction, a verbal dossier on their target:

"I watched this man for over four years, after he foiled my attempt to get a foothold in Afarland. Then, he disappeared leaving no digital prints for several more years. Right, well, Mr. Ahmad Jones, our target, has reappeared. He is a *Horary Astrologist*. Do either of you know what that is?"

Logan and Marcus turn to each other while astride their yellow buoy seats. It was windy at two o'clock, with two hours to go before sunset.

Light from the setting sun coming through the window hits their eyeballs. After the wind dies down, a thick branch from a sycamore tree returns to block the sun. They stop squinting. The window takes up the whole west wall—no blinds or shades, just six large rectangular sections through which to view the estate grounds. Men and women comprising security are milling around outside. They are casually attired and act like residents enjoying the grounds around the stone mansion. While relishing the rich blend of Cuban tobacco wafting in the bright, twenty-by-twenty, sky blue office, Logan and Marcus reach back into their professional histories, attempting with no success to conjure an image of a Horary Astrologist.

After scratching his beard, Logan says, "No, Mr. Borg, I've never heard of one. What about you, Marcus?"

"No, neither have I, but we have heard of astrology."

"I see. The *torcedores* of Cuba are highly skilled at hand-rolling tobacco leaves."

"Yes, Mr. Borg," Logan says, trying to read the man, and determine where this is going.

"And Ahmad Jones is a highly skilled Horary Astrologist."

With surprise, "Certainly, Mr. Borg. Who is Ahmad Jones? But what is that word, *horary*?"

Borg, seated behind his fancy mahogany desk, enjoyed another puff. He was wearing a tailored, bulletproof English suit, dark-gray and double-breasted. Always dapper, Borg's head was coiffed, dark-brown hair, dyed, and a pale, almost anemic complexion. Borg drew the smoke to the back of his throat, expelled the last mouthful, then placed the half-smoked cigar into the platinum-plated, tobacco-leaf ashtray to burn out and die.

Logan had never met Borg before—they did all of their dealings by phone and a personal server. He figured that Borg was about six-two or three, because he sat high in his chair. As a connoisseur of fine clothes, Logan admired Borg's deep-purple tie and how it blended well with the rest of his ensemble. He figured he was just as meticulous with his business dealings as he was with his threads. Logan felt that he could count on this quality in Borg, and concluded that he and Marcus would be compensated for their services in a timely manner. He watched Borg's complexion change from pale to pink when he mentioned Jones.

"Ahmad Jones is an exceptional man, with an extraordinary talent in astrology. Among his many skills, we especially like his acumen pertaining to acquiring valuable information only minutes after constructing a horoscope for an event, or the birth of a person, a business, or the time a question is asked."

The former mercenaries listened, their hands involuntarily feeling for a non-existent armrest on their canister-shaped seats—uncomfortable and diminutive—Borg's idea, to keep his employees literally and figuratively off balance.

"Gentlemen, a Horary Astrologist, with horary meaning hour, just like the word horoscope means the view or scope of the hour, is a person who can take the time of an event, or a question, and find out, locate, and even predict things. For example, they can locate missing people or people who go missing on purpose. Predict the time something is to occur, down to the day. They can also locate missing objects, large or small. William Lilly, one of astrology's gifted minds, was born in Leicestershire, about 255 kilometers northwest of here. It was he who developed many of the modern rules of this art in the 17th century.

"Here's an example. Do either of you like dogs?"

Logan nods, while Marcus refuses to answer.

"Right. If you asked me where your lost beagle was, I, as a horary astrologist would record the time of your question, consult a nautical almanac or an ephemeris, which contains the midnight or noon positions for the known planets of our solar system including the Sun and Moon for an entire year. I would perform mathematical calculations that would relate their current celestial positions with the terrestrial time and place of the question."

Logan was scratching his beard again.

"Do you follow me so far, gentlemen?"

"Yes, with you, so far," Logan said.

"It would perhaps take an expert in this branch of astrology fifteen minutes to a half hour to ascertain the beagle's whereabouts and condition, and render a conclusion, but for Ahmad Jones it would require less than three minutes after the chart was cast."

Marcus folded his arms. "Got it, Mr. Borg."

"Right. As for the missing beagle, I would measure the distances—of the Sun, Moon, or planet, representing the asker of the question—from the one representing the beagle, as each would be represented by a planet, the Sun, or the Moon. I would convert their degrees of celestial distance, or angles of separation, into kilometers. For example, if the Sun and Mercury, representing the questioner and the beagle respectively were nine degrees apart, that would equal nine kilometers. I would adjust that relative distance, separating you and the beagle, to half the kilometers, or double the kilometers, or leave the full nine kilometers, according to the degrees of Mercury's distance north or south of the celestial equator. The Sun is always at zero declination—"

"Sounds technical. What do you want us to do, Mr. Borg?" Logan interrupted. Borg caught himself engaging in an awkward display of hero worship. He pulled open the bottom right-hand drawer and took out a manila folder and withdrew a page from it. Borg stood up. Logan felt he was correct about his height.

Borg went on, "From 2004 to 2005, Mr. Jones has helped solve 53 cases for several law enforcement agencies using this and other astronomic formulas and systems, one of which I have greatly oversimplified in this instance. Jones was especially adept at finding bank robbers, fugitives, and the headquarters of illegal drug rings. He even helped the FBI's Human Smuggling and Trafficking Center while on a job in Ohio, in America's Midwest. When he came on board, the Bureau found the location of the smugglers who had been operating for a few years under the radar."

Borg finishes paraphrasing the document and puts the folder down. He walks to the piecrust table and lifts a tall bronze pot. He holds the lid as he pours fragrant black coffee into his cup. Logan is anxious.

"Do you think Ahmad Jones is after you?" Borg ponders the question, while lifting a sugar cube out of a dainty crystal bowl. He studies its shape and color, drops it in, then watches it drift below the black surface to the bottom of the cup. He stares over his right shoulder at Logan.

"No, Logan. At present, I do not believe he is." Borg places the sugar cube tongs back on the table. "But I, that is, we, *The Consortium*, want you two to scoop him up for us. We know where he is." Borg adds warm frothy cream, watching it neutralize some of the rich black coffee color, and stirs.

Finally, Logan thought, Borg has ceased with the foreplay.

"Would you two like some coffee?"

"No thanks, Mr. Borg. So, you're paying Marcus and I to scoop—but then what, take him out?"

"You said it with a nonchalance as if you were saying, 'Should I wear this tie, or should I take my shoes off?' So matter-of-factly. I know, you *are* unaffected, as you told me." Borg sips his coffee.

"We believe that every man has his price. No, we do not want him bloody *taken out*; The Consortium wants him as a salaried employee." He returned to his chair.

"How?"

"Negotiate; you two sit him down and negotiate. You can do that, right?

Get him to acquiesce to the offer of a lifetime. My secretary, Jessica, will provide you with specifics of the offer."

"Okay, then, where is he?" Marcus asked.

After another sip of his drink, Borg returns the cup to its saucer, and clears his throat.

"Are you sure I cannot offer you something, gentlemen? What about some tea? I can have Jessica bring in Lapsang Souchong, imported straight from the Wuyi Mountains."

Becoming irritated with Borg's distractions, Logan said, "No, thank you, sir. We would like to get to work."

"Very well. Right. You must know where Jones is. Well, Jones is near the southern boundary of the Mediterranean on the shores of North Africa."

"Libya, Egypt, Morocco? Where?"

"Libya."

"Libya?"

Borg said, "How's your Libyan Arabic?" Logan always had minor trouble with some of the nuances of the Libyan dialect. But he didn't convey that. He lifted his thumb straight up. Marcus did the same.

"We still got it. Where exactly, and when do we leave?"

Borg gestured to Logan, who was relieved to stand and walk to the right side of Borg's desk. "At the Africa Nova Hotel, between Shari Al Kubra Street and Omar Almukhtar Street. We will relay his room number to Bilal, before you arrive. The GPS will be preprogramed to take you there. Watch the speed limit, it is just 40 kilometers; do not smoke anything, as Libya's policymakers banned illegally produced cigarettes that are still being smuggled in. Tomorrow, at 3:30 am, is your early morning flight. My private jet will take you to Tripoli International Airport." Borg, seated in his high-back executive chair, opened the middle drawer and withdrew a green leather binder. He handed it to Logan, who opened it and checked out Jones' picture. Marcus got up, too, and stood beside Logan.

When the men saw the picture, they were surprised to see the cop they encountered several years earlier. They felt that their target was formidable but they didn't telegraph that first impression to Borg. Logan had no idea that the man he confronted at the Tiffany Street Pier was so accomplished.

To them, Jones looked self-aware. They caught that immediately. Tall, muscular, handsome, and not haughty. Nothing about him stood out—that is, out-of-proportion. Here was a man, in their estimation, who was together.

"Looks American," Marcus said.

"Right, he is originally from the Midwestern United States. Chicago."

Logan and Marcus sat back down. They find the recessed handles on the sides of their buoy seat.

"Bilal will be waiting outside TIP, to take you to your vehicle. He will have deposited pistols and suppressors of your choice under the seats. You three will stay in close contact, during this operation."

"Operation? Which returns me to my previous question. What, specifically, besides scooping him up, and negotiating, do you want us to do?"

"Jessica will give you the details."

"I want to know now, negotiate what?"

Outside the wind blew the leaves on that same sycamore branch over to the left, and sunlight poured into the office again. Logan and Marcus couldn't see Borg without squinting, so they put their left hands against their foreheads.

"We want you to bring Jones back here. Do whatever you must do. Just be careful with him."

While Logan was looking over the green notebook, Marcus said, "Mr. Borg, some brainiac wiz-kid hora... horar—"

"It is Horary Astrologist."

"Right. He won't be a problem for us."

"Ahmad Jones was a cop, patrolled tough neighborhoods, in New York's South Bronx. From his file, it appears that Jones could handle hardened criminals." Borg sipped some more coffee. "Including you."

Logan scratched his beard. "Several, by himself, without even drawing his pistol; see, he is much more than an astrologist—we can use him in lots of ways."

"Mr. Borg, we are seasoned, professional game changers, instrumental in altering the course of many sovereign nations, and assassins, not hardened criminals. There is a big difference between big time and small time, and we are the former. Marcus and I have always completed our jobs."

"What about the job in the South Bronx?"

"Cops showed up and you said not to kill any—"

Borg had heard tough guys set themselves up in a class of their own. Many of them didn't measure up. He knew that Logan spoke the truth, based on his order not to kill any cops, but he had to keep him off-center, so he visibly dismissed Logan's remark.

"I said, unless they were antithetical to our mission." Borg changed the subject.

"It is written here in several incident reports from the 41st Precinct in New York, that on many occasions, before backup arrived, Mr. Jones had already handled the situation, without shots being fired," Borg continued to read.

"Okay, the man has some street smarts," Marcus added.

"No, this man is more than smart; he is a smart man's smart man, which is the reason why we have got to have him. We need his astrology skills for The Consortium. We have projects all over the world where this species of information-gathering can trump our competition. Moreover, an astrologist, an exceptional one like Jones, can find the weak points in a nation or in an organization or group—their vulnerabilities—even when, in the flow of time, a weakness can be exploited. He can accomplish those feats with a sheet of paper, a pencil, a nautical almanac, or ephemeris, a table of sectors, called *Houses*, and a list of world longitudes and latitudes. Jones can even look at his watch and narrow down the constellation presently on the eastern horizon and still get a bead on what is going on. We are beta-testing its use, in America.

"Now, if you have any problems..." Borg hesitated, like he didn't want to say what was on his mind.

"If we have any problems, sir?"

Borg rubbed his forehead, his pink face turned pale. He continued looking at Logan, "If you have a real problem getting Ahmad Jones back here, then he could have a deleterious influence on our international business affairs—if he is anywhere on this earth and not working for us." Borg, relit and took a puff on his cigar, leaning back. The setting sun moved below the thick Sycamore branch and brightened the room once more. Logan and Marcus, each took out a pair of sunglasses. They figured that Borg wouldn't take it as a sign of disrespect. Borg, as if reconciled with his thought, sat up.

"If getting him to board that jet is impossible..." Borg got up and paced behind his desk, nervously buttoning and unbuttoning his jacket, then rubbed the back of his neck. He turned, took a few steps to the sterling silver tea service, turned toward the window to look at the mansion across the street, while running his fingers over the scalloped molding of the piecrust table, then shifted his eyes to the two men. A whole minute elapsed before he would finish the incomplete sentence, "If getting Ahmad Jones to board that jet is not possible, then your orders are to terminate him."

Borg sat down as if he had the wind knocked out of him. He sipped some more coffee.

"The CIA tried to recruit him, as did the FBI, which is good for us. Even so, if he's not working for *our* interests, he is working *against* our interests."

"Understood," both men said.

Borg became more reconciled to Jones' fate.

"Do everything you can to get him here alive. Negotiate. The Consortium will give him a blank check. Tell him so, and after talking with him, well, if that does not work, try drugging him and get him on that jet. And if you cannot do that, then wipe him off the face of the earth."

"Only execute him as a last resort. Understood," Logan said.

Marcus asked, "Will that be all, Mr. Borg?"

"You will each get 11 million if you bring him back, but if you fail to do so and terminate him, then you will be left with 22,000, to be divided between the both of you. I trust this will furnish you with enough of an impetus to return here with him. Have a productive trip, gentlemen. I will have Jessica arrange for you to be fitted with new suits and for the car to take you to Northbolt."

"New suits?"

"Yes, and these are special."

"Well, thank you, but as a gesture of good faith," Logan said, "we want an initial balloon payment. Marcus barely shook his head in surprise; then Logan added, "We now have new Swiss bank accounts and want five-and-a-half million each." Borg filled his mouth and blew out a few smoke rings.

"I will do 11,000 each, but gentlemen, 11 million? How do you figure that we are going to spot you 11 million?"

"Because you know what we are capable of. You know our qualifications, or you wouldn't have flown us here. We have never failed to complete a job, except the one in New York, based on *your* orders, which gave us no option but to stand down. That was your SOP. We followed it." Logan told Marcus to kill the cop, but Marcus shot him in his vest. Logan kept that part to himself, to protect his partner.

"I couldn't understand why you wanted the DSS agent dead but not cops, they're both law enforcement." Borg rubbed his neck.

"Plus, we were both shot, trying to follow your instructions; we wouldn't have made it to the boat with the girl. I wanted the cop wasted but there was no time."

"Jones, indeed, was antithetical to the mission. Yet, if you had succeeded we would not be here discussing the capture of a great asset, or a great problem for The Consortium. You both probably have a grudge to settle with Jones, and that's why I sent for you."

"Well, Mr. Borg, you want Ahmad Jones? We will bring back your Horary Astrologist, here to this office. Then you can plop him down on one of these fancy, uncomfortable seats you had us sit on."

Borg twirled his cigar between his lips, before drawing more smoke into his mouth.

"11 million is enough of an impetus for us. So, killing him is *not* an option." Marcus looked at Logan, then at Borg.

Borg blew out some more rings. "Right, I, we do want Jones, alive, but only if he is here and nowhere else. You have negotiated well; do the same with Jones. Bring him here to me. I will arrange for five-and-a half million to be wired to each of your accounts now." Borg picked up the phone, "Jessica, get me Jim at Alpha on Cannon."

"Yes sir." Borg put the call on speaker.

"Alpha Bank on Cannon Street. Jim Progl speaking."

"Jim, this is Adlai. I have two employees on contract."

"International wire transfer, hold please. Zurich, Geneva, or Basel?"

"Where is their primary account held?" Borg looked up and waited for their answer.

"Geneva," Logan said. Jim Progl heard Geneva.

"One moment, how much Mr. Borg?"

"Five-and-a half million euros in each account."

"Thank you, sir. Full names and IBANs."

"Gentlemen, Jim requires the names on your accounts and your international bank account numbers." Logan and Marcus supply their names and account numbers.


Logan and Marcus had landed fifty minutes ago at Tripoli International Airport. They had cruised just under the speed of sound for 1,600 miles in a blue and white Cessna Citation. Their assignment, per Mr. Borg, the boss of a private paramilitary concern, The Consortium, was to spend ten crucial minutes at work inside the hotel, by taking Jones into their control, driving another 18 miles back to the airport, and then reboarding the jet for the three-hour flight back to a private airstrip near London—Northbolt. They planned on this being their last assignment. They were smart enough to know that they had to quit before pressing their luck. At least one of them was—more than the other.

Bilal, the North African contact, pulls off the ramp, from Almukhtar Road onto Azzayadi Street. He's driving a recently dune-dusted Toyota Land Cruiser that's been completely armored, from top to bottom. He's a hundred yards east of the hotel. Bilal swerves around a pickup truck, passes an accident scene to his left, and angles into the space, away from the corner. His assignment is to manage the success of the operation. If all goes as planned, Bilal gets two million. With that money, he is going to take his wife and daughter away, to live in Palm Beach, Florida. Bilal glances at a manhole cover on the sidewalk to his right.

At 7:41, the automatic doors slide apart. Logan and Marcus, with dusty shoes and some sand grains clinging to their suits, swagger toward the centerpiece of the hotel lobby. To the right, at the far edge of the long counter, Logan gestures to the clerk, like he's giving him a command.

The clerk responds quickly. He's five-four, with flawless attire and a huge smile, "Welcome to the Africa Nova. How may I help you, sirs?"

Logan opens the green binder and asks, "This, man, here?" He hands the binder to the clerk, who lays it on the desk in a flat, open position, looks at the picture and the official document, laden with an embossed government seal and signature, which no one would question. After acknowledging the man in the photo, the clerk says, "Yes," then closes the binder and hands it back to Logan. The clerk waits.

"You must do something else for me, something technical. So, if you can't do it, I need someone who can." The clerk squints his eyes. Logan's dialect is unclear. The clerk is looking to understand the request. Marcus is nervous, mostly about his money.

"What is it, sir, this technical point?" Logan leans over the counter and talks to the clerk who then excuses himself. He walks a few paces behind the counter to the central door. It has an electronic, keyless lock. The clerk wavers, then jabs the bright green numbers on the touch screen, opens the door, and disappears into the IT closet.

Logan checks his watch, then glances over to the dining area at the far left behind a large window. Several guests are moving along the line at the buffet; a few of them notice the well-dressed gentlemen at the front desk. A middle-aged, full-figured woman meets Marcus' eyes and quickly turns away. He stares at her for a moment then shakes his head. He has no time, he concludes. Logan thinks about his life of leisure and it is looking more promising by the second. After a minute, the clerk returns from the closet. "It is done," he says, and then withdraws two fresh keycards from the drawer, swipes the cards, and hands them to Logan. Then with another bout of hesitation the clerk says, "Suite 1264." Logan responds with a nod, and then nods to Marcus, who is reimagining life with 11 million in exchange for ten minutes of tough negotiating.

The men take long steps along the curved contours of the front desk to between the dining area and the counter's edge. The spacious lobby carries the sounds of their hard-soled Ferragamos as they strike marble. They stride up a slightly inclined, winding staircase that leads to three elevators on the mezzanine. Several nervous guests at the buffet furtively follow the men with their eyes, as the two reach the landing and step out of sight. Logan presses the call button. They take a few moments to check their appearance, as they stand opposite the silvery, mirror-like elevator doors, framed in bronze. The chandelier above them shines brightly on their rugged faces. The middle door opens from left to right. They step inside. Logan selects the number twelve.

"We bring Jones to the war room on Level B, convince him to ride back with us to TIP, then get back to London, eh?" Logan says.

"Wicked, man! Back to London, then Kamloops," Marcus says.

"Check. We finish this in ten, like we planned."

Inside the elevator cab they stare up at the floor indicator light, as it moves uninterrupted through the numbered circles. The time is 7:42 am.

# 11

## Line of Scrimmage

THREE MINUTES BEFORE, at 7:39 a.m., on the busy corner of Omar Al-mukhtar Road and Khalifa Azzaydi, an orange minivan had T-boned a white sedan. The driver of the sedan turned out of the side street onto the main road, but didn't yield right of way to the minivan, which smacked into him from his left, after a long screech, at thirty miles per hour. The sedan's driver-side airbag didn't inflate. The minivan's steering wheel didn't have one. The front of the struck car, facing an imaginary twelve o'clock, was turned away upon impact from that direction to almost three o'clock. The sedan pivoted around its back wheels, which angled it almost parallel with the minivan.

Logan and Marcus had heard that screech and the inevitable crash from the back of the hotel, as they were staring at palm trees. With the front side fender lightly crumpled, the driver of the white sedan, a botany student from Italy, who installed his own seatbelts, climbs out. He is not hurt, so he digs his right hand into his pocket while asking the other driver if he's okay. He starts computing the damage to his own left-front fender and tire, the top of which is bent inward close to twenty degrees. The rim bent inward and slashed the tire. The hissing sound was less loud as most of the air came out about a minute after impact. The driver of the orange minivan points an accusing finger.

A family man, he says. "You could have been killed. My young son is in the back seat surrounded by bags of fish. *He* could have been killed, and I could have been hit from behind, and killed."

"I am sorry. I should have not made the turn." The student was respectful, but was more concerned about transportation, of getting back to Msallata, 67 miles east of Tripoli, where he is staying to complete his olive tree research. On Omar Almukhtar, motor vehicles have barely enough road to pass around the accident scene, which juts out two-thirds into the flow of traffic. The honking continues. They turn around and notice a white SUV pulling up along the curb of the side street.

The drift of honking morning traffic, like an old snake, curved around the accident scene. The minivan driver, well known for bringing in the freshest fish, studied the long line of traffic immediately ahead, and far up Omar Almukhtar Road. He rubbed his palm across his wide forehead, worried that his fresh kingfish and huge prawns wouldn't be fit to sell by the time he got to *Souk*, the Arabian market. He thought of Libyan dinars wasted. No return on his investment, but worse, his reputation.

The driver of the sedan started photographing the angles and the proximity of both vehicles. He noticed two patrol cars coming toward him from the other side of the road. The minivan driver tended to his son, in the backseat. He saw the police just as he was about to park on Khalifa Azzaydi, the side street off the main drag. He shut the door and walked toward the other driver. The patrol cars waited at the median before crossing. A moment later, the two drivers forgot their accident and watched the traffic, remembering those times when they had driven past fatal vehicular collisions, grateful to God that it wasn't them. They felt lucky that they weren't dead. Then, they looked behind them, at the Toyota Land Cruiser. They knew that enforcers of the regime drove the same model of SUV. They panicked.

In the same instance, across the street and twelve stories up, Ahmad Jones awakens and raises his eyelids halfway as trouble scurries nearer. The centers of his hands feel full, like the pressure of moving water running through a fire hose. They are warm, too. He lies across the long backless sofa inside his suite. These sensations are new for Jones, maybe an urgent signal from his body that a substantial charge of energy resources is now on tap to meet a crisis. At age 42, and awake with his eyes closed, Jones feels an inner strength that he has never felt before.

Jones—to put it as Octavia Butler did in one of her novels—is a "black wall of a man." A big cat that arches its back, extends its forepaws on the grass and stretches out its powerful arms and legs. They dangle over the sofa's edges while he stretches a little, before the peril that he feels shows up. Several of his vertebrae pop as they loosen.

In an understated way, his opposites are in dynamic balance. He is muscular and agile, supple and hard, deadly and calm. His face has an openness, like a clear glass with an inner light pouring out with a dark-mystic quality. Jones lifts his head. The sparkle from some region beyond his dark-brown eyes shoots out northward between the open drapes to a crystalline blue sky, the first thing he sees when he opens his eyes.

In the hallway, some four hundred feet away, a ding goes off, as the elevator door opens along its track. Logan and Marcus step out onto the twelfth-floor hallway. It is barren of people, who are mostly downstairs at the buffet. They notice that the long corridor gets brighter every couple of seconds. They observe the growing intensity of sunlight; it acts like a pointing finger, as it moves imperceptibly upward, illumining the wall after streaming through several large windows, each one separated by four feet. The hallway is alive with light. Logan thinks of old westerns where gunfights took place at sunrise. He wonders how many duels occurred at high noon. Logan says, "We're on Jones' floor now. Any changes? Do we proceed?"

"Borg says to get it done." At street level, Bilal, parked in the Land Cruiser, on Khalifa Azzaydi, takes his cell away from his ear. He is eager to smoke a cigarette but doesn't want to attract attention. He imagines life in Palm Beach, while watching the aftermath of the collision.

The minivan driver holds his hands out in front of him while verbally making his case and gesturing to the sedan, instead of its driver standing before him; then he gestures back to his own vehicle, to illustrate the damage to his grill. The flow of traffic, already slowing, due to the accident, comes to a halt two blocks ahead as the state militia arrives in white SUVs. They start vectoring traffic two blocks up onto Shawqy Street.

After stopping traffic enough to cross the median, the two black-and-white patrol cars arrive at the accident scene. The police both park on the right of the sedan, near the curb and away from the intersection. They exit their vehicles. The sedan driver complains to the minivan driver about the blind spot created by a beat-up pickup truck parked at the corner. The officers look around the area of the accident to get the complete picture. Facing south they spot the pickup truck, then notice the Toyota Land Cruiser to the left. They look at each other and then back at the two men. For once they're not first responders to a death scene. They walk closer to listen to the two men, not as cops as much as two human beings.

Each party to the accident explains his side, and then the officers point out the fact that their vehicles are blocking the morning commute. They stand back and take several pictures in less than a minute, then tell the men to park their vehicles on Khalifa Azzaydi, the side street. The owner of the sedan can't start his car. The owner of the minivan cranks his up and parks alongside the curb on the side street, a few car lengths behind Bilal's Land Cruiser. The minivan owner crosses the street and in less than a minute the cops and the owner of the minivan push the broken sedan with the owner at the wheel off the main road about two car lengths.

The wake-up music in Jones' headphones begins precisely at sunrise as his feet flatten against the textured carpet. It's 7:43 am. While hearing a favorite piece of music, he visualizes the composer in his mind's eye—a lean, courtly gentleman wearing black-rimmed glasses, and hair, short and gray that is thinner at the top than at the sides. The gentleman is standing. Tall. He is ramrod straight. Still standing in an atmosphere of generous applause, he plays the first melodic strains of a jazz classic, before he takes his seat. Once seated, he continues playing with majestic precision born of complete dedication to his art. His broad smile is genuine. Majestic. He turns to his players and they smile back to him to return the current. Jones remembers this scene well, when he watched the lean, courtly gentleman in Paris.

The scene riffles across Jones' mind in less than a second.

Jones steps to the window to acknowledge the beauty and elemental power of the Mediterranean, and then glances at the rubbernecking traffic, the back and forth of windshield wipers and the dusty remnant of the Ajaj. He notices an orange minivan pulling away just a few feet from a parked Toyota Land Cruiser. He also checks out four police vehicles. He shifts back to the Mediterranean, zeroing in on the contrast of color between the dark seaweed beneath the surface of the water close to Tripoli's shore and the sea's aqua blue. After another stretch reaching toward the ceiling, as more bones crack with relief, Jones feels coherent, like a laser beam.

The landline rings. Jones steps from the window to the night table a few feet behind and to his left. He sits on the bed, lets it ring a few more times, then picks it up. He pulls his headphones off, and places them on the bed. Speaking in Libyan Arabic, the man says, "Mr. Jones, Mohammed here, from the front desk. Two men are on their way to your suite. They *claim* to be *Mukhabarat el-Jamahiriya* national intelligence. I hope you secured the safety latch because they have a keycard, two to be exact. They shoved an official document in my face. I was forced by the authority of its signature to give them the cards."

Silence.

"Mr. Jones. Mr. Jones. They showed me official documents but I feel something is amiss. I just know it. Please be careful."

Replying, in Mohammed's native language, Jones then says, "Thanks, Mohammed, for your concern about my welfare."

"You're welcome, Mr. Jones."

"Call me, Ahmad."

"Yes, Ahmad."

In the twelfth-floor hallway, a barrage of reverberations course throughout, faintly, at first. The pace of Logan's and Marcus' stride is insistent. Staggered. Energetically off-key.

The melodic jazz still pours out of the device. Jones puts the telephone handset back on its base and gets off the bed. He moves quietly, listening, between the bed and the sofa, through the very short hallway where the only light source is from the large window, now behind him. He turns around to catch another glimpse of the sky and then faces ahead and continues pacing through the hall, turning left at the wall's edge.

Jones strides past the kitchen, to the archway that is shaped like an old-fashioned master keyhole. He stands in the middle of that huge keyhole shape, extends both hands sideways, grabs the gold-platted edge-pulls, and drags the sliding doors out from inside the walls. He turns around to see the doors meet and click shut. The light from the outside that was coming through his bedroom window illumining the hall and some of the living area is now cut off. He turns and faces the front door as he moves quietly into the airy living room.

He stands in semidarkness. Sunshine gathers behind the drawn maroon curtains at the far end to the north. He slips on his beige khakis, pulls the zipper, buckles his belt, and slides two toes into a pair of caramel-colored flip-flops. He watches light in front of him, coming through the gap at the bottom of the door.

In his mind, Jones sheds anticipations and expectations of the men coming down the hall. It is one of his ways of responding to events; freely and without the constraints of preconceived notions. It worked when he was a cop. Jones is at-the-ready for whatever shows on the other side of the door.

Now, he remembers something his teacher had shared with him two months ago, while they sat together eating a cold snack of mixed olives and cheese at *Restaurante El Faro de Cádiz*, in Spain. His teacher said: *At the approach of danger, encircle yourself with an awareness of personal invulnerability.*

A little less than ten hours before, Ahmad Jones had strolled into the Africa Nova Hotel after his twenty-four-hour flight and slow taxi-ride, on Airport Way—a long, neatly laid, curvilinear stretch of road, dotted with olive trees. Mohammed, at the front desk, had just started his shift when he met Jones for the first time. They chatted in Arabic, about ancient statesmen like Marcus Aurelius, Patrice Lumumba, Akbar, and great poets like Rumi, Omar Khayyam, and more recent greats like Khalil Gibran and Maya Angelou. Mohammed had a high regard for Jones.

Upon his arrival at the hotel in Tripoli, Jones remembered not to insult the bellhop by tipping him—a custom not acceptable to Libyans. The bellhop, an old man, and very robust with a barrel chest, carried his luggage up the winding stairs to one of three elevators at the mezzanine, stepped inside the middle one, got out on the twelfth floor and carried Jones' bags through the long hallway, and into his suite. Jones shook his hand and thanked him After bolting the door and applying the latch, he inserted his passport, wallet and laptop inside the hotel room's electronic wall safe. Watching it automatically shut Jones turned off the lamp, ambled through the large keyhole arch, then passed the kitchen, through the short hall and into the master bedroom.

The light in the bedroom was on when Jones arrived. He removed clothing every step along the way, except for his boxers and his bright green, blue and silver football jersey. The suite had a faint smell of aromatic spices, which floated up from the lobby. The atmosphere in the suite was light and comfortable. Instead of using the bed, Jones climbed onto a deep-red backless sofa with his Bose headphones already adjusted for proper fit. He turned the lamp off. Through the window, Jones gazed at an orange star, called *Deneb Kaitos*, located in the tail of the whale in the constellation of *Cetus*. It was very bright that night and easy for him to spot. The constellation was close to Tripoli's meridian, at 10:30. Ahmad Jones was invited to an event, to be held at the Corinthia Hotel, by invitation, to give a talk on the impact of astronomic cycles on international trade. The hotel is a few blocks east, on Al Kurnish Road, which runs parallel to Omar Almukhtar Road.

Claudius Ptolemy—the second-century mathematician, geographer, astronomer, astrologer, and author of *The Almagest*, which dealt with the geocentric motion of stars and planets, wrote in his book, *Tetrabiblos,* that *Deneb Kaitos* was of the nature of Saturn. To Western and Indian astrologers, Saturn, with its rings, traditionally signifies boundaries, limitations and restrictions. It is a planet that both historically and statistically coincides with a difficult test.

While stargazing, Jones asked himself an open-ended question, "Why did I notice this star just now?" He accepted the idea that some faculty within himself had already provided the answer. He often received surprising responses, from within, to questions put forth in this manner, especially upon awakening. He didn't chart it using astrology—he was too tired from his trip. From his playlist he selected his favorite *Ahmad Jamal* version of *Poinciana* to play as he drifted off to sleep. This music reminded him of the Pershing Hotel in Chicago, where Jamal, recently honored with the title, *Master of Jazz*, played that piece in 1958. Jones' parents were in the lounge of the Pershing Hotel, when Jamal recorded *But Not for Me* on a Thursday night in January. Jones grew up in Kaskaskia, Illinois, 14 miles north of Chicago, where he was born. He desired to remind himself of his parents and his American roots as he lay across the sofa under the Libyan sky. He programmed that musical selection to awaken him at sunrise.

Still poised in the semi-dark living room, in his football jersey and khakis, Ahmad Jones hears the rat-a-tat of footsteps in the hallway. Logan and Marcus are within a hundred feet of the door. They are tightly organized. Their dissonant intentions—motivated by euros, their egos, and their futile psychological fortifications against mortality—run in opposition to the refined orchestrations of *Poinciana*, which Jones can still hear from his headset parked on the bed, even from behind the pocket doors. Low-pitched strings, percussion and muffled drums blend in. Even though the music is consigned to the background behind the sealed keyhole, as the danger inches nearer, the music unfurls out of the headphones, commingling with the atmosphere of peril as if to neutralize it as it gathers momentum, filling the space inside the executive suite. From Jones' position in the ever-shortening distance between him and the two-man unit, he remembers Deneb Kaitos, the star he noticed at Libya's meridian.

The march of each step is more jarring now. Jones listens with his whole body. His right hand is resting on a red easy chair, one of two; the other chair is across from the coffee table, about fourteen feet away near the maroon curtains to the north. On the other side of the door, the bright, sun-infused hallway is long and sinuous, luxurious and uncarpeted. The hard leather soles intermittently strike the polished marble in a love-hate dynamic, a continuous marriage and divorce of small impacts.

The menacing reverberations remind Jones of when he was a young teenager crossing the tracks from school, in Kaskaskia, stopping to put his ear to the steel alloy, knowing that sound would soon appear around the curved tracks as a locomotive. It was inevitable. From his railroad-track-crossing experiences, Jones had unwittingly trained himself to hear at a distance.

Ostensibly, this is not a covert assignment. Logan, the lead man of the op, doesn't care if the man he's after hears him and Marcus coming. They are armed with 1911 Colt subcompacts. They didn't let on, when Borg mentioned Jones' prowess, that they were curious about his present capabilities. Logan remembers the picture, taken of Jones in Mali, of how Jones was thinner and powerful looking. Could Jones still defeat multiple attackers, is he better at combat, now, since that night in the South Bronx, eight years ago?

Could Logan handle Jones?

Logan and Marcus have been trained under severe and grueling conditions. Each man's body had been toughened by the pressures of other climes, deserts, winters, mountains, and torrential rainforests. And three decades. They still didn't register pain like ordinary mortals—no expression on their saturnine faces. There is no easily perceptible light behind their eyes, except that of a cold determination appearing in contrast to the hot, rust color of Libya's dunes when seen from satellite images. Like the planet Saturn, their assignment was to follow the plan to the letter, and in an organized manner. Like Mars, their intent was to administer violence if called for. They were still in the mode of remembering a foiled assignment from years past.

Jones had been trained, too, but under a different set of severe conditions—formally, by his father Robert and on the streets. By 2001, before making Second Lieutenant, Jones was used to interacting with some of the meanest, toughest, and most innovative criminals. Handling these situations had become second nature, as if he were enjoying a ball game with his buddies. On his beat, Jones was respected, not feared, which is how he desired it to be. No one who knew Lieutenant Jones ever committed a crime in his presence.

Jones' football jersey is numbered 84 for the Seattle Seahawks' wide receiver Sam McCullum, a master of the game who put himself in the most opportune positions, to receive Jim Zorn's passes. In the field that is off the field, Jones empowers himself to do like-wise—to always be in the optimal place in his mind and heart and soul. Like McCullum, Jones will be ready for the inevitable snap in the inevitable game about to start, regardless of whether the twists and turns of the next second translate into a deep ball, a bullet pass, or a handoff.

The cacophonous interplay of alternating steps and their echoes, shaped by the acoustics of the spacious serpentine corridor, have stopped. Logan and Marcus are five feet away now, behind the suite door that has become the common reference point for both them and Jones.

*The coin is tossed.*

*It's lifted into the upper air.*

*The fated sky—an invisible referee, influences the outcome.*

*The door, 35th yard line.*

*Kickoff.*

Jones unlatches the secondary. Whoever opens the door will kickoff new forces that won't be reconciled, until more than seven years have passed over these heads.

# 12

## Reunion

FOR AN EIGHTH OF A SECOND before that door opened, Jones' inner silence changed his experience of the stream of time. He stepped back next to the red easy chair, and noticed the light that seeped in, under the door. Parts of it were blocked out. For him, time had folded. He was in a pocket of timelessness, a zone, within the flow of time. In the zone he heard the word, "execute."

The eighth of a second will pass like a measured interval of silence in a piece of music. Logan and Marcus have orders to deliver Jones to Borg in London. Stakes are high, for them, but not for Jones. Ahmad Jones—4,650 miles from his home is an ex-cop, married, and a light sleeper, who less than a minute ago, was stretched out across the sofa with his namesake *Ahmad* Jamal and his music, echoing rhythms from far-off worlds. He is present and ready—yet for what? For anything.

The curtains to Jones' left, in the spacious living area are drawn; in some places, they overlap. Flickers of sunlight peer through parts of the irregular juxtaposition of each curtain. Light catches the dust silently swirling in the air. It illumines the carpet—as if a new reality, an option play, offers itself to Jones on the other side of the rich fabric. It reminds him of something he learned from the old man in Cádiz, that: "Everything in life is made of life." Jones applied that to the men behind the door. They are life and he is life.

Jones' living area is warm-toned. A breeze billows the drapes and the low light brings out a hue like maple syrup that colors the easy chairs and the rich, red-mahogany credenza against the wall to the left of the door. Pleasant smells, from the kitchen again, come into the living area replacing the smell of seaweed and salt water.

The distant sounds of piano, drums and bass fiddle pour out from behind the sealed archway. It's the first bridge to *Poinciana* that Jones can still hear as the curtains' balloon shape flattens and the voice of the south wind dwindles. The smell of bread being baked tumbles in with gentle breezes. Jones could get used to the smell of bread being baked underneath the hot Libyan sands. Unfortunately, he would awaken to it for the remainder of his stay.

Obeying an impulse, Jones opens the door to see Logan with the keycard in his hand almost frozen in the air, preparing to let himself in. Logan lowers his hand. Marcus is forty-five degrees behind Logan, and to his left.

The men's relative positions are meant to disorient and confuse Jones' perception of depth—a tactical configuration in the hallway to give the duo a psychological advantage in case they must get physical right out of the gate. Behind them is an aquarium-sized window where the deep electric-blue of the Mediterranean is clearly visible. Sunlight creates a corona around the perimeter of both men's heads, giving them an "angelic glow." Their black shoes are still covered in dust as old as Libya's sand dunes, and, like the desert, their faces are beaten and hard, yet still, Jones perceives in them the same light and life of God that is in him. It is there—beneath years of cumulative darkness, below their present capacity to feel it, to notice it. Jones perceives it as the flaming force of the spirit of brotherhood that exists beyond distinctions and labels.

Jones does a quick read, like a quarterback before the defense. He senses the pistols behind them, the heavy metal, under their suit jackets. The men exude something that conveys the impression that they're used to getting what they demand. They bring with them the atmosphere of menace, like a Lawrence Taylor pass rush toward a quarterback, who is hurriedly forced to rid himself of the ball or get knocked down—hard. Jones felt that atmosphere while still in the zone, in his pocket of no time. Now he has the ball, that powerful energy still pouring through his hands, and he will do with it what he pleases, and when he pleases. He will remain a brother at the soul level and yet provide an exacting lesson, like the planets Saturn and Mars combined— an *organized whipping* that will bring his two guests to their knees, or worse if negotiations travel too far south. Jones will decide what play to make. It is up to him. Up to the life in him, to act.

Logan can sense Jones. He is no pushover. He felt it when his nose was busted that night. This man standing in his football jersey has masked his physical dynamism behind a quiet visage, he thinks. Logan perceives a quality in Jones, an elemental power like a seven-foot leaping panther compressed inside a docile lamb. Jones' inner being, by intimation, says: *Do no harm.*

Logan, steps toward the doorway a mere two feet away from Jones. "We are with the *Mukhabarat el-Jamahiriya*. We have held you under surveillance since you left the TIP and have been investigating you."

Just then Jones notices Marcus' hands dropping to his side and the nuances of Logan's speech. There is a trace of a French accent. It has a well-modulated timbre, thoughtful, the work of many years of speaking English, French and Arabic. *His voice would sound great on the radio*, Jones muses. Logan also says, "We know that you have been invited to speak at the *3rd Africa EU Summit* today at the Corinthia by a couple of important people in the membership of the *Economic Council of West African States*."

No question was asked. A silence ensues until Logan closes the composition book he was reading. Logan continues, "Our investigations lead us to believe that you are here for other reasons. Are you a spy, perhaps, Mr. Jones?"

"Yes. I... am here for the summit but am I... what?"

"Here for other reasons?"

"It is as you said."

"You are here for other—"

"As you first stated, I am here because I was invited to speak at the summit."

Logan steps diagonally, between the wide doorway and Jones' right side, until he is behind him, scanning for any telltale reactions of recognition. Jones just looks ahead. Marcus moves to within two feet of Jones. He doesn't look at Marcus, though, but around his head, at the sea, through the window behind him. Marcus turns around, wondering what Jones is looking at.

Standing behind Jones, Logan reads from the composition book again: "You are an American citizen now living in Afarland. But you do what, astrology? *Hmm*, tell me, Mr. Jones, did you see this coming? But if you did know in advance, why would you be here now? You do not need to answer. But there will be time for that."

Jones felt the muzzle of the subcompact against his floating ribs.

"You will not attend that summit, *but* you will come with us now. You can ride in our BMW. It has a new-car smell, *but* it may be the first of new car smells for you, but maybe the last smell period, unless you cooperate."

Jones remembers the voice. Still looking around Marcus at the hall window, Jones says, "I know that you are not who you say you are. You are not with Libyan Intelligence. If I dealt with you now, there would be no repercussions from the government. You would be operating surreptitiously inside a foreign power without permission. If anyone is going to have a last smell, gentlemen, it will be you two, for attempting to impersonate intelligence officers, and to *attempt* to do harm to an invited guest and speaker at the summit."

With levity, Jones turns to Logan, with his back to Marcus. Logan's upper arms are quite thick, eleven inches wide, more than Marcus', and his wrists are thick, too. Intimidating, but somehow familiar. Whenever Jones had encountered men with this type of build back east, it still never ended well for them.

"I wonder if you are capable of giving fair use to some of the *other* conjunctions in the English language, *but* I may be wrong."

"So, you understand the trouble you are in?" Logan says.

"There you go," Jones replies. Looking Logan in the eye, "Now, what do you want?"

Bilal has the muted cell on speaker, on the seat. He hears the exchange and wonders out loud in Arabic, "Why doesn't Logan stop talking and take Jones to the war room? Stupid men!"

Jones had gotten Logan to change his speech pattern without asking him to and he made Marcus turn around. They were both taken off guard.

Logan cocks his weapon. "Mr. Jones, we have a business proposition to present to you. You will go with us and we will explain the details."

"Where?"

Jones turns around, Marcus crosses the doorway and seizes Jones' right arm. Logan screws on his silencer. Jones relaxes. What happens next puzzles them. As Marcus turns to take Jones out into the hall, the force used to pull him out reverses and Marcus is yanked back inside, like an animal harnessed to a short chain, which when extended to its limits, stops short, and by an equal and opposite force, brings the animal backwards. Jones doesn't budge but glances toward the safe inside the wall to his left and to the right of the maroon drapes. Marcus tries to pull him off his spot; his face grimaces and becomes distorted but still, Jones doesn't budge.

"What is going on, eh?"

Still on mute, "Yes, what *is* going on, Logan?" Bilal in the SUV asks. Bilal, the lone man at the wheel who put the plan's logistics together, checks his watch. More than ten minutes have passed. Logan turns off his Bluetooth as he pushes against Jones' back while Marcus pulls. Meanwhile, Jones literally and figuratively, stands his ground.

Jones learned how to drop his center, to become as stable as the Earth, many years back. He learned some other methods of directing the energy flowing through his own body, from his teacher in Cádiz, as well as other methods he picked up in times spent camping, in some of the highest mountains of the world.

Jones gets another intimation, through a biblical verse: *"Resist not evil."* Logan brings his pistol to Jones' head. Jones releases his energetic anchor to the floor and steps forward, pulling Marcus over the plane of the suite door. Jones and the two men are now standing in the brightly lit corridor of the twelfth floor.

"Now what?" Jones asks.

Marcus doesn't know what to do with Jones. He draws his pistol and points it at him.

Logan holsters his and walks back into the suite to the double doors and separates them. The doors crash to a stop inside the walls. He goes to the bedroom looking for something. He sees the headset and hears the music. He comes back out and looks toward the safe. He crosses past the red easy chair to the front of the coffee table, to the north part of the suite and opens the drapes. The warm tones vanish. The mellow, maple-syrup color is now flat and one-dimensional. Logan opens the safe and seizes Jones' laptop, wallet, keycard, and passport. From the main floor console at the front desk, Mohammed had remotely unlocked the combination to the electronic safe so Logan could extract its contents. Jones faces down the corridor. Logan holds Jones' belongings while closing the door behind him.

"Now what?" Logan asks. "What you call, in America, a 'road trip.' This way."


When Jones checked his charts before leaving his wife in Afarland, a country off the East African coast, he studied the crisis points. The trip involved some risk, but Jones understood that the tablet of the true astrologist is not like a dried skeleton, as his father Robert once said, to be used by dilettantes. Even the most severe configurations in a chart show a way through, a way out. Jones' way out would come by surrendering the last vestiges of his desire to control the outcome of events. Do nothing. It was a test of Saturn, which in his astrology, had just entered the Seventh House, the sector of open confrontations. He had made this measurement weeks beforehand, along with two other supporting measurements that pointed to the same probable condition: crossing paths with international power players and their enforcers. The bright orange star that Jones saw last night was a reminder that there would be hard lessons (Saturn) to learn.

Jones still felt he would get to speak at the 3rd Africa EU Summit. Still, he didn't know how it would come about, being that he was scheduled to appear in three hours. He was humble enough to be neutral—even with his astrological know-how, worldly experience, his double master's degree from Cornell, and his work in law enforcement and with international political entities—Jones surrendered the human need to know the reasons why he was where he was.

As they walk, the sounds of four hard-leather soles and two flip-flops echo in slow tempo through the spacious corridor of the hotel. Ahmad Jones, husband, astrologist, ex-cop, and a man of peace, glances to his right. The sparkle in his eye careens through the window to the sky, then the sea. He takes in the rhythm of the aqua-teal waves, the flight of birds, and the sunlight—a type of spiritual food for him. From his suite, number 1246, the footsteps grow fainter, a dissonant ending to a dissonant strain. Back in the master bedroom, Ahmad Jamal and his jazz trio finish the final section. Halfway to the elevators, Jones thinks he hears applause. As he nears the doors, he notices the elevator light, on the far left, passing 8, then 9, then 10, and with that, a mounting tension. The elevator to the left opens. Five members of an elite paramilitary unit storm out into the hallway, brandishing gas-operated assault rifles.

# 13

## Interference

THEIR INSIGNIAS SURPRISE LOGAN AND MARCUS, more so than the unit's AKMs, pointed at just their heads. Still, the former mercenaries hold stern faces to conceal their apprehension. The unit surrounds all three men, each has a plug in their left ear.

"Don't make a move," the leader says quickly and with a heavy guttural accent. His insignia is two golden stars below the *Hawk of Quraish*, on a tan background.

"I'm Colonial Talil. Who are you and what are you doing in this hotel?"

No answer.

Four men point their weapons, while a fifth one steps to Logan and adjusts the carry strap on his rifle sling. He takes Jones' laptop, wallet, keycard, and passport from Logan, and then steps back. Another elite member pats him and Marcus down, then takes away their pistols and Logan's green binder.

The colonial opens it, looks over the signature and says, "Where did you get that document?"

No answer.

"This man is a guest in our country. As far as detaining him, we know of no order coming through Libyan Intelligence such as contained in this document, which you presented to the front desk. The signature was forged."

The colonial watches body language; sees nothing but two calm faces of hard defiance.

"Who do you work for?"

No answer.

Disgusted that the two men didn't say one word, and thereby silently challenged his authority in front of his men, he issues an ultimatum. "You will step into that elevator with us. In the War Room, below this hotel, you *will* give me the answers to my questions."

Logan uncrosses his hands. "You obviously are unaware of who we are." Colonial Talil's men shift their eyes from the sights of their weapons to him, watching for their cue. What if these two men are conducting a legitimate operation, under the orders of their nation's leader? Did this man outrank their colonial, a Brigadier perhaps?

"We are aware. As they say in the west, you are walking dead men."

In clear Libyan Arabic, Marcus says, "That is dead men walking, asshole. And no, that is not who we are." After the men heard that challenge, their eyes twitch, their legs convulse. Now, it is Logan's turn to say something, in their language. "But, it is you who are dead." They adjust their side stance, leaning forward on their right legs, waiting for their colonial's command to shoot them where they stand. Tensions, born of the unexpected, grow, as if two hands with an infinite rope had tied a knot around the air. The elite men wondered what that could mean, as the two men have no weapons, and it is five against two.

Talking their language, Logan said, "Inside, you are dead inside," to confuse them.

"Now, put your hands behind your head. Get into that elevator," Talil said. Logan still has a keycard in his pocket. Talil slings his weapon around and takes Jones' personal effects from one of his men and hands them over to Jones. Logan and Marcus, masters of strategy, follow orders and interlace their hands, in front of them and bring them up and around, to the back of their heads. The elite group follows their moves with their muzzles. They walk into the elevator facing two officers, who are backing into the cabin, while they are followed in by the remaining three.

Jones watches Logan and Marcus turn clockwise to face the closing elevator door. They didn't look intimidated, Jones thinks; yet, four members of the group did. Inside, the leader presses the letter B, for the War Room, a floor with several interrogation chambers. Besides basic hotel security, these men, if called by a member of the hotel staff, are supposed to handle a real terrorist threat to hotel guests and staff. Jones heads back to his suite. As he walks along the corridor, his adrenaline is still pumping in earnest, and then it drops precipitously.

He is losing consciousness. He lifts his wrist to check his pulse. He drops his keycard. His pulse is thin and jumpy. He takes several steps. He slows his breathing. He lays his things on the marble floor and locates specific points on the side of the arch above each eye to keep himself from losing consciousness.

Nothing works; he *will* collapse.

He grabs his stuff and summons enough strength to walk further. A few yards from his door his legs give out. He leans against the large window and stares at the sea. He sees his wife in his inner eye, feels his head against her warm breasts, as he had rested it there countless times. He sends pure feelings of love to her. There's a weak sensation in the pit of his stomach. His heart gallops; he hears it beating. It's all he hears now.

Something different is happening to Jones. His body slides along the window; he doesn't hear his laptop crashing against the marble floor. He wouldn't care if he did. His body and head follow.

Flashes of a goalpost and crossbar, television cameras, and a bejeweled ring flow across his mind. Then, passes the silhouettes that he knows belongs to his two pals that were forced into the elevator. As for the last few minutes, Jones had obeyed his gut feeling. He had done nothing to Logan and Marcus. And something unexpected happened. They were benched. So was he. *But for how long?"*

# 14

## A Pair of Old Pros

LOGAN BERNARD AND MARCUS DUBOIS step into an elevator with members of an elite paramilitary unit; they are pinned into the back-right corner. There is no chance of them getting away, with five AKMs, a lighter version of Kalashnikov's AK-47, now trained at their chests.

The hotel's six elevators are standard size: six-and-a-half feet wide and seven-feet deep. The elite squad members wear body armor but are not aware that the two men in the back corner are experienced assassins.

Marcus said, "If you want to go home to your families, then put your weapons down and we will go finish our business."

"You give orders to us; we land on B level, we will see who gives us orders." Each man had a knife on the left side, where the thigh joins the hip. Logan and Marcus were close enough. They were a foot-and-a-half from the lead man, Talil. The average height of the men in the unit was five-ten, with their combat boots. Logan and Marcus had the height advantage by four inches. It was an even matchup just the same. The unit had firearms, okay for close quarter shooting, but they were shorter in height than Logan and Marcus, who had none, but were taller and more experienced in the craft of terror. But the elevator wasn't moving. That was good for the old pros because, once they got to B level, they would lose their present close-quarter option. The unit would put more space between them, which would lower the odds against them of staying alive. They had to take this unit out immediately.

Jones snapped out of his torpor and got back on his feet. He picked up his things and proceeded to his suite. He needed water. Couldn't locate his keycard. Was on his way to the concierge to get a replacement. Jones headed to the staircase, diagonally across from the elevators.

Talil turned a key that was already inserted into a panel, then pressed B. The elevator moved and the mercenaries acted quickly within the small space. They noticed that each man was exposed from the neck up to the crown of his head. Their hands weren't covered either. They should have been, due to the heat the firearm released when fired. Logan slipped forward and down. He pushed Talil's Kalashnikov upward with his left hand then withdrew his combat knife and rammed it sideways into both kidneys, like a shish kabob. Logan was good at this attack and could always feel when he hit his mark. Talil, dead on his feet, plummeted down to his knees, but didn't quite make it to the floor. Logan held him up for a shield, as he pivoted right and stabbed the next nearest man, at Talil's right flank, sending the four-inch serrated edge through his kneecap. The man's scream was quickly silenced, as Logan took the knife out and attacked his neck, then his head. Some blood streamed from the second man onto Logan's jacket.

Logan and Marcus were bent on preventing shots being fired in the elevator. They already had more then they wished to handle even though they did it with ease. If the sound of a AKM was heard outside, those men in the rear lot would come running. Plus, they still wanted to take Jones, so, any interference now would prevent their successful operation, which meant that they would have to give their deposit back.

Marcus snatched up Talil's weapon and aimed it at the remaining three men. They put up their hands, their weapons suspended on their slings. The elevator stopped and opened at B level. In front of them was a long corridor, the size of a New York City block. There were several doors that were spaced nearly twenty feet apart, staggered from one side to the other. Each door was massive, with no spaces underneath, up top, or anywhere else. They looked watertight. Marcus pitched his head to the right and the three men walked out. Logan stepped over Talil and the second man, then turned around to make sure they weren't breathing. He dragged each one out, while Marcus pressed the button to hold the elevator, still pointing the weapon at the three men. Logan cut out a piece of clothing off Talil and used it to clean traces of blood inside the elevator.

"What will you do with us?"

"That is up to you. What is behind these doors?" Marcus asked.

"They are offices. For enemies of the Libyan people, we question them; they are suspects, sometimes members of rebel groups."

"Interrogation rooms, for people like me?"

"Yes. No."

"Just messing with you. Well, I am interrogating you now. You have keys?"

"Yes, we all do."

"I just need yours, show it to me." The man fumbled through his clothing. His hands were shaking. He lifted the Velcro flap over his thigh pocket and took out a keycard, about two square inches.

"At least you are telling the truth. Take the key, open the first door on the right and file in." The men went to the first door; it was the size of two standard doors combined. Solid. The other two men were even more nervous as they watched their comrade press the keycard against the sensor by the door handle and pull. The door didn't budge. The heat from the desert floor had caused the metal door to expand into the surrounding wall. The man kept pulling. The other two were relieved. They felt they were on borrowed time. Once that door was opened, if they went in, they knew they would never come out.

"You two, help your brother," Marcus said.

Reluctantly, the remaining members of the unit each took turns. The door started to pry open. It sounded like a heavy file cabinet being pushed or pulled along a marble floor. When it opened, the dank smell inside flooded the corridor. The room was pitch black. There was no flooring. There was a light bulb in the center of the room. A chain was suspended from it. Trying to be obedient, the man with the keycard went in and pulled on it. The faint light flickered, revealing a desk and two chairs.

The three men coughed. Marcus covered his nose with the crease of his elbow. By then, Logan had dragged his two victims, one at a time, through the doorway into the center of the room, in front of the desk. "Are there any more like you, sneaking around elevators, or in these offices?"

"No."

"Better not be. Get in," Marcus said. Once inside, Marcus pulled the heavy metal door behind him. Logan went back to the elevator. He heard a muffled six shots and empty shell casings hitting the metal door. Marcus opened the door. "It was getting hot after three shots," Marcus said. It was smoking. "I thought I was going to need a shooting glove."

Logan said, "Let's get back to the twelfth floor." They retrieved their subcompacts, and then leaned against the door, pushing against resistance, until it was shut.

"Wait, I have to go back in there," Logan said. They both wrested open the door, which was easer then before. Logan looked at the five dead men inside, rolled one of the men over to his right side and slid the combat knife out of its scabbard. Afterwards, he closed the door. The two men stepped back into the elevator. Logan said, "We'll get Jones to the lift at the far end."

Marcus said, "I do not want to remain in this country another minute." Logan turned his Bluetooth back on, "Bilal, this is Logan."

"What are you doing?"

"The Job we were hired to do. We'll get back to you with an update."

Bilal said, "Logan, traffic is thick, are you in the corridor?"

"Yes, but we don't have Jones."

"Shit."

"Keep it together, Bilal."

"I'm parked near the removable plate. The lift for the manhole is five-hundred feet from the elevator. Traffic is being diverted. Change of plans. Leave the car."

"Marcus' assignment was to follow us."

"Too risky, I'm taking all of you to the airport. My vehicle is official, your BMW is not."

"Copy that." Logan finished the call.

"Let's get Jones. We're leaving the BMW." He and Marcus got back into the elevator.


Jones was about to take the stairs to the first floor, when he heard movement in the elevator. He walked over to the elevator door and waited.

# 15

## Second Verse, Same as the First

THE DOOR OPENS. Logan and Marcus nearly freeze where they stand as Jones steps inside the elevator, shortening the distance between them. He steps to within three feet of Logan who is poised near the back corner. Marcus circles to Jones' right with his weapon drawn.

"Who sent you?" Jones asks. Logan reaches for the key, which is still inserted into the panel. He turns it and presses B. The door closes, and the cab begins its descent to the War Room.

"Who sent you?"

"Mr. Jones, you've thinned out since we last met, but I'll ask the questions."

"You have ten seconds to tell me something real." The opposite door opens, closest to Logan and Marcus. They step backwards into the corridor. "Mr. Jones, this is not Tiffany Street, so step out of the elevator, and we'll answer the best we can."

Jones walks through the elevator, from the opposite side. Logan is directly in front and Marcus is to his right.

"All right answer my question, the best you can." Marcus brings his weapon down. The elevator door is closing. Jones steps out onto the dirt-floor corridor. Logan notices Jones' football jersey. "How about those Seahawks?" Logan exclaims.

"Yes, how about the Seattle Seahawks. They're my team."

Logan swings his hand behind his jacket and stows his weapon into his pancake holster. "We are here to make you an offer in exchange for your expertise in Horary Astrology."

"Oh? How much?"

"Whatever."

"Whatever. You mean I have a blank check?" Jones looks at his watch. Logan and Marcus look at each other, nodding, then focus on their target.

"So, what do you want me to do?" Marcus puts his palms against his head, expecting Jones to comply. He's going to be rich.

"First and foremost, we want you to come with us to London. There's a private jet at TIP that will take us to our boss, the one who will answer any questions you have."

Jones lowers his eyes and sees drops of blood leading from the elevator to the huge metal door, at his right He looks, first at Marcus, then at Logan. He shakes his head. "No, I will stay here, and *you* will return to London. All by yourselves."

Marcus's smile drops. He says to Logan, "Like I said, it is up to him." Jones steps out of his flip-flops. Marcus reaches for his pistol. Logan puts his hand out, for Marcus to stop. Jones sidesteps to his right, into a leap, and lands the edge of his right foot on Marcus' chest. The inertia of Marcus' body makes him absorb the full force of the powerful kick. Marcus' back slams against the metal door. Jones lands another kick to his face, at the button of his jaw. The back of his head strikes the wall with a snap. Marcus is out cold and starts to fall. Logan withdraws his weapon, aims and shoots, but not before Jones grabs the lapels of Marcus' jacket and pulls him around as a shield for Logan's bullet, which strikes Marcus' back.

Jones pushes Marcus into Logan who is slammed to the wall. Logan lifts his pistol from behind Marcus, but Jones grabs the barrel while Logan's finger is still inside the trigger-guard. Jones flicks it up, bending Logan's finger, backwards. Without thinking, Logan lets go of Marcus who drops to the floor, along with the weapon. Logan straightens his dislocated finger and steps over his partner; Jones rushes forward. Logan reaches to the ground, grabs sand, and throws it into Jones' eyes, lands a palm strike to Jones' head, then an elbow strike against his jaw. Jones is dazed. Logan lands several kicks against his knees, body and head, to bring him to the ground. Jones' arms dangle and he can no longer defend himself. Logan pulls Jones' jersey and head-butts him. Jones stumbles backwards and falls on the dirt floor.

While half-awake and half-unconscious, Jones feels strong currents of energy moving through his body, like he did upon awakening in his hotel suite. He *listens* for Logan's next move. Logan grabs the combat knife he took from one of the members of the paramilitary group. He lifts it up with both hands. The point is aimed toward Jones' heart. He can end it now, as payback for Jones dislocating his forefinger, and settle for 11,000 euros, or get Jones on that jet. Jones stays on his back. Listening. Logan puts the knife away, and, instead, is about to knock Jones out with a kick to the side of his head. Jones turns. Logan's size twelve is about to connect. Jones grabs the foot and twists it, first one way, in a short arc, then the other way, in a longer arc. Tendons and ligaments ripple and tear.

Jones' eyes are still closed, as he turns his body, using his back as an axis to sweep Logan's other leg from under him. His body lifts horizontally in the air. He lands on the dirt floor and the dust balloons out from under him. Logan can't get up. Marcus is still knocked out or dead. Jones rubs his hands together to get the dirt off, and then wipes around his eyes. He opens them. Logan's eyes meet Jones', who picks up Logan's pistol, takes out the magazine, removes the extra cartridge and throws them on the dirt floor.

"Eight years ago, you murdered four people in cold blood back in New York."

"I know what I did. Because I did it, asshole."

Jones grabs Logan's jacket lapels and pulls. "You stole the life of DSS Agent Frank Scudder. You made his wife a widow."

"I was doing my job," Logan says and spits in Jones' face.

Jones holds one lapel with his left hand and smashes his fist into Logan's nose. Jones lets go of the lapel, so Logan's head can bounce against the floor.

"They were friends of the 41st Precinct, you piece of shit."

Jones' words kept rising an octave, with each indictment.

"You murdered someone who served his country honorably."

Logan is mad and frustrated, as he looks at Jones, who is circling him.

"So, why should you live to kill again?" Jones wipes the spit off his face.

Logan wipes the blood from his nose, looks at it and then stares at Jones. He lifts his head and drops it again. "It isn't in you to kill me in cold blood."

"In your line of work, you are trained to never underestimate anybody. That's contract killing 101."

"I can't move. What did you do to me... this time?"

"Tell me your name first." Logan is more frustrated, weak and mad about being bested by the same guy a second time. "Logan—Logan Bernard."

Jones is more composed. "Struck a point near your Achilles tendon to slow you down. I know these points blindfolded. You know, we may look and act like two disparate characters but, Mr. Bernard, we have one thing in common."

"Yeah... what, the fuck, is that?" Jones takes Logan's belt and ties his hands. He does the same to Marcus.

"We are both humans; therefore, we are not disparate, but one. You still have an opportunity to transform your life."

"I knew... you wouldn't kill me."

Jones turns to look at Marcus. "Your friend isn't dead. When I grabbed his jacket, I felt the material. Tough and bulletproof. The Libyan authorities will take over from here. I'm going to the front desk. You will go back to where you came from. Remember my warning."

Jones walks to the elevator, steps into his flip-flops, presses the button, then turns.

"Who sent you, Mr. Logan?" He waits for the answer. Because of Jones, Logan had to get a nose job, now his nose is broken again, his right forefinger is dislocated, and the sinews of his right leg are traumatized. Logan tries to lift his head up but can't. His face turns red with defiance. There is the sound of people talking and after a moment of bizarre tension, the door opens. Four members of the security detail at the back of the hotel are in the elevator. They pull out their weapons.

Logan thinks: *I'll tell security that this man may have killed my partner and was about to kill me. He's a former cop and he killed some men and left them in that room.* Still unable to move, Logan mentally checks for Jones' second keycard, to set him up.

In concert, the security detail says to Jones, "Put your hands up."

# 16

## Aries

AHMAD JONES AWOKE AT 2:59 AM, at his home in Incalzael, the capital of Afarland. Seven years had passed since his encounter with Logan and Marcus, in Tripoli. His cell phone sounded a minute later. He turned toward the bedside table, to his right, grabbed the phone and brought it to his ear.

"Yes."

"I have another assignment for you, Ahmad."

He rolled onto his back and whispered, "What service may I render, teacher?" Jones' wife turned to him, while she yawned, blinked several times, and moved her soft fingertips up and down his chest while her eyes were still closed.

"Chart the call to figure it out. Details in person, like always. If you are of a salt, which I know you are, then you won't require me to tell you."

Jones wiped his eyes and checked the time of the call.

"You will absorb all expenses for the trip. You will meet me in Cádiz, in two days, on Wednesday, March 15th, at 3 p.m. sharp, at the park at the intersection of Juan Carlos and Calle Alcalde Blázquez."

Jones' eyes adapt to the dark, he can make out his wife's lovely face even better.

"I also have something to show you. You will come across the smell of honey when you come to within one hundred feet of the park. I will be at the start of an arrangement of small white-marble benches, oblong in shape and arranged in a half-circle facing south. On each bench is an elaborately carved relief depicting one of the Twelve Labors of Hercules. A piece of molding has broken off along with the lower half of the recessed apron on the first bench, which represents the first labor, in the sign of Aries, where Hercules rescues the land of Diomedes, the son of Mars, by capturing the wild horses and mares of war, who had ravaged the countryside and killed many of its inhabitants.

"The bench with the missing piece of molding is the spot where I will be seated when you arrive. The benches are situated inside a living wall made up of several species of shrubs and trees—palm, olive and purple jacaranda, even almond trees."

Jones' wife moved her fingertips further down, while drawing her body closer, the caller could hear her breathing heavily.

"Ahmad, my son."

"Yes, teacher." Upon hearing those two words, Jones' wife took her hand away.

"Ahmad, have you updated the national horoscope of Afarland?"

Keeping his voice down, "No, I hadn't." Jones felt an uneasy silence after his reply. Jones looked at Marakie, his wife. Marakie could make out the silent mouthing of: "I love you." She returned the sentiment. The two lovers were like spectral figures to each other. Jones pressed a button on his hand-held remote control device. The shade to the skylight retracted, allowing more light to fill the bedroom.

The silence broke after a full minute had passed.

"Well, now is a good time. Ahmad. I suspect that the chart rendering of Afarland's position with respect to her 30-year cycle, will be an occasion for a plan, a strategic one, to be worked out, especially when you add to it the other corroborating measurements. You must be at the cabinet meeting on the 21st. For now, I expect you to be at our trysting place on time. Our meeting must start then. Be careful."

"About?"

"Distractions." The call ended and Jones turned his cell off and put it back on the bedside table. "Baby, good morning."

Marakie beamed. "Come to me, baby." Jones slid over, put his arms around her and they kissed, richly and long. Then Jones got out of bed and slipped into his robe and turned on the light, whose base, the color of teal is shaped like a gourd. Marakie turned on the teal gourd light on her side of the bed, too.

"I didn't remember to remove my earrings, honey, we got to bed so early." Marakie puts her robe on and steps into her dainty little house shoes. She seats herself in front of the vanity and takes off her earrings. She turns to her husband, who's gazing back at her, smiling knowingly.

"Ahmad. I know that look. You're going to work. Before you leave me, read to me."

"Read, baby?"

"Your manuscript. Just a couple of pages... I want something of yours to send me off to sleep; your manuscript will be sort of my bedtime story. Darling." She looked at him, longingly, as she put her earrings into her jewelry box. She put her hands on her lap. Jones walked over, knelt, and put his hands on hers. There was still that dynamic tension between them, drawing them together like two magnets. Jones got up.

"Well, do it, and then hurry back to bed, after you finish working, and wake me up with your kiss and love me back to sleep." Jones knelt by Marakie again and they both looked at each other's reflection in the vanity. Jones kissed her and stood. She looked up at him with eyes filled with dignified surrender.

"I'll get the manuscript." Jones went to his bedside table and picked up his handwritten manuscript. His wife rose from her vanity bench and sashayed to the bed. Jones put the manuscript on the table and stood behind her and helped her disrobe. He moved both hands down the sides of her neck, shoulders, arms, and elbows, then clasped her hands. She tilted her head back. She let in his kiss. He then picked her up. She wrapped her arms around his neck, as he lowered her body onto the satin sheet. Its ruby color picked up the glow of the ruby around her ring finger. Jones sat up beside her and began to read.

"Several months ago, in November, I was out of sight of my home, which was many thousands of miles to the east. I was searching out new information on an old topic. I was in north central New Jersey, called Middlesex County—which, I realized, is a name apropos to its geographical placement—yet, I will not comment on any other meanings which can be culled from it, or associated with it, without digressing from my account."

Marakie turned to Jones and smiled. "Middlesex County?" She and Jones shared a laugh. Jones continued:

"I pulled out of the left lane and slipped into the middle. I passed the Rite Aid truck because I could no longer depend on the driver, who broke eight minutes of constant speed, to lag under its limit. Maybe it was the thin film of watery oil and grease on the road, after the rain. Or maybe the driver felt that I was tailing him. Cruise control wasn't working in my rental. I relied on the big rig, which I just maneuvered behind. It maintained a dependable, 66 miles per hour.

Behind the wheel of a black Dodge Charger, I was enjoying every moment in this super-cool ride—indeed one that handled so smoothly that I could do 80 without feeling the car-speed increase in an appreciable manner. Especially being mostly unconscious, which is the only way to drive. The trip was uneventful, and the ride was so comfortable on the way to the pizza shop on Sicard Street, near the Rutgers University campus. My immediate requirement was to arrive there on time without succumbing to that feel of 66 while going 86—in other words, without being stopped by a State Trooper and ticketed for speeding. My meeting was at 3:00 in the afternoon. The big rig carried the name of that Danish conglomerate, *Maersk,* written on its cargo section. Stable company. Stable driver. I kept two car lengths behind it. Chargers are popular law-enforcement patrol vehicles, and I assured myself that my new foil didn't interpret my presence as a tail either, or as a cop, and slow down. But if a Trooper pegged me as one of his own, well, I guess any speed would suffice, as my vehicle would be rendered, in a way, invisible."

"Baby, that's sexy."

"And you're sleepy?"

"Some more please."

"I was enjoying part of that iconic stretch of highway, *The Turnpike*— 123 miles long, from the George Washington Bridge to the Delaware Memorial—its length *shaped* like a mathematical curve that moved through the state credited with hosting the first football game ever. It was 2:35 and I was making good on the time when the clouds cleared up and I noticed the exit for New Brunswick.

"There it was, Exit 9 for Rutgers University. I moved to the 12-foot lane as I pondered the date of New Jersey's founding. It was Tuesday, 18 December 1787. It was born in the sign associated with institutions of higher education and sports: *Sagittarius.* It is said that the 26th degree of Sagittarius is where the galactic center is located. Well, when New Jersey was founded, the Sun's position was at the 26th degree. Some astronomers have speculated that not only does it contain millions of suns, but a Black Hole also exists there. This could explain the sucking effect that American football has on so many people, who are drawn magnetically into the vortices of the sport. The fact of the Sagittarian Sun of New Jersey may account for Rutgers and Princeton being perfect for this celestial signature of higher education and sports.

"There was something prophetic in this arrangement—of Sagittarius, the Black Hole and American Football—that was to literally play itself out on a plot of land, or a theater of battle, a piece of earth between College Avenue and Sicard Street, less than a quarter mile from the snake-like Raritan River, and across the street from the pizza shop I was bound for—strong enough to stay fastened to the ground even though it was situated just across the street from that Black Hole."

Marakie yawned while clasping Jones' upper arm and leaning her head against it.

"After paying the toll, I came closer to the site of the burning ground underneath the College Avenue gymnasium. I call the field of play the burning ground because the fiery sign of Aries had appeared on the eastern horizon when the first intercollegiate football game began. So, if the players and onlookers had faced the east at the horizon line before the game commenced at 3:00 p.m., on 6 November 1869, they would have been facing the mathematical section of the sky called *Aries*, which happened to be occupying the constellation of Pisces, whose anatomical correspondence are the feet.

"More on that later but the tropical sign of Aries was the dynamic spark, like a kickoff that coincided with the beginning of the thing. The field was approximately 'three hundred feet wide,' according to the journalist on hand at the time—where fifty men saturated the field of space with their striving and all-out competitiveness and, thus, engendered a morphic field of kicking, making goals, forming human wedges, knocking down fences, making mass plays that promised collisions, pain and injuries. This morphic field became a gigantic thought-form that we call *American Football*, and has a unique astronomic position, based on the time and place that the teams began to mix it up on College Field.

"Now, Jupiter, the planet that is associated with Sagittarius—called its *ruler*—and Pluto, which wouldn't be discovered until 41 years later, had formed a conjunction, at five minutes past noon, on 29 October 1869. Jupiter and Pluto conjoined in the sign of Taurus. Jupiter, representing learning, and Pluto, the perspective of mass influence, and Taurus, the earth-field, announced, through their relative positions, an unusual admixture of academia, sports and power—even destructive power—long before the time that the Tufts-Harvard game was played on Jarvis Field in 1875. That game, many believe, was the first *real* American Football contest. The sign of Aries was on *its* horizon, at Cambridge, Massachusetts, as well, at kickoff. More on *that* later, too.

"*The Daily Targum,* on page five, did a spread on the Princeton-Rutgers game, titled *The Football Match.* Before the Boston Rules of the Tufts-Harvard game were deployed, was not Aries, perched on New Brunswick's horizon, representative of the fiery leadoff? And was not the initial spark created by the first mount, a la Princeton, the beginning of a new thing in the earth?"

"Ahmad," Marakie said.

"I have some work to do. I'll meet you in bed in fifty-eight minutes,

Marakie my love, *and don't you go nowhere."* They both laughed.

"You can take the whole hour." She paused, to put her feelings into words. "Baby, love you, and love your story, so far." She pulled the sheets back over her. Jones leaned over and kissed both her eyes.

He put his manuscript on his writing desk across from the foot of the bed, took his laptop and left the bedroom. He crossed the center of the house to the back door and stepped outside under a stellar canopy. The sounds of crickets were omnipresent, the moon was descending and he could make out the silhouette of Afar Mountain ahead. He heard the faint sound of the ocean, just behind the large mountain, situated directly across the water from Tanzania's Mount Kilimanjaro. The two structures—the former, a standalone mountain; the latter, a stratovolcano—were like lovers separated by hundreds of miles, who'd never know each other's touch.

Jones had set his laptop on the footstool in front of him. His outdoor chair was a square bamboo frame with a high back and firm cushion. He saw the computer screen prompt, entered his password, and then accessed his professional astrology program.

Jones updated Afarland's horoscope, saved it, and then brought up the event chart, or horoscope, for his teacher's call. Jones looked over the event chart on the laptop monitor. It supplied levels of information far deeper than the little bit his teacher shared.

Afarland's cabinet meeting in six days was at the beginning of the Spring Equinox, which occurs in Aries. Three o'clock, the time of Jones' meeting with his teacher, is known as the hour of Aries in some circles. The designated bench as described by his teacher depicts Hercules' first labor in the sign of Aries and Jones was also born in that sign. And yet, this was not all. Afarland, the country off the eastern coast where his wife Marakie was born, joined the family of nations, in the sign of Aries. And Jones' teacher called him at roughly three in the morning.

These correspondences were not without their meaning, Jones surmised. The time was five to four, and Jones would keep his promise to his wife. He took time to scan Afarland's national horoscope and noticed something very strange. Afarland, like the broken piece on the bench, was heading into a crisis, a potential breakdown of civil services, a coup d'état. Ahmad Jones, under the alias Steve Watson, went online and booked a flight to Jerez Airport near Cádiz. He would have to board three different planes.

After he purchases the tickets he comes back inside, locks the doors, and walks thoughtfully back across the center of the house. He puts his equipment on the desk, disrobes, and switches off the light. He crawls underneath the bed covers like the big cat he is and awakens his wife with a kiss.

Two days later, Jones caught the floral, honey-like smell coming from the almond trees as his bus rolled into its designated stop. His teacher was meticulous with the smelly details, Jones thought. He sat on the right side of the bus and peered out the left window, looking at the park, over several talking heads. The park was beautiful, with magnificent colors and fragrances, and, more importantly, there were no smart-surveillance cameras or CCTVs.

Jones was skimming through a Cádizian newspaper. He finished reading the latest news about Spain's Prime Minister, and last year's foreclosures, and expats retiring to Cádiz from Britain. Since his days as a beat cop in New York, Jones' Spanish was still good.

Several passengers, women mostly, eyed Jones, as he was the only black American among the passengers. They noticed how graceful and economical his movements were. He appeared to be a man of culture. One woman, wearing a floral-pink gypsy dress with a red rose resting atop her long and full, dark-brown hair said to her companion. *"Alto, moreno y guapo,"* which means tall, dark and handsome. Afterwards they laughed. When he stood up, the woman with the red rose followed his every move. She smiled to her companion sitting next to her, nodded, then looked at Jones some more.

The men on the bus were tired from work, mostly blue-collar. They didn't pay much attention, as they've seen Africans before from parts of the Spanish-speaking central African country, Equatorial Guinea. Jones refolded the current *Olive Press* newspaper and left it where he found it on the bright-green seat to his right, the only empty seat on the bus. Sunlight came in from the west through the sparkling-clean windows. The bus stopped at the corner of Avenida de Juan Carlos 1 and Calle Alcalde Blázquez. The driver applied the emergency brake, doors opened and Jones stepped out through the rear. A stream of passengers flowed out behind him. He was the first one to step onto the sidewalk on Blázquez. Jones' watch read 2:58 pm.

The two gypsies stepped off the bus. They were both beautiful women. The one who was admiring Jones spoke to him from behind. Her voice was soft and musical, "Are you, um, from Africa?"

Jones turned around while others were still stepping off the bus, passing around him and the two women. He noticed her pink outfit, the red rose, gently and diagonally inserted into her swirling updo and how she carefully joined her fingertips. She was about five-three, in her early thirties, with steady dark-brown eyes, that looked at him amorously. The average human would have been taken off-guard by that look. Jones wasn't average. Her companion was the same height, wearing a rosy-red dress, with those same expressive eyes. They were both poised as they waited for him to speak. Jones remembered what his teacher said about distractions.

"Yes, I am," Jones said.

The woman spoke slowly, measuring each word for accuracy. "Welcome.... to... Cádiz. Maybe we meet in the future sometime? I do *Astrología*.

My name is Valentina. Please, my English is not so good. *"Hablas español?"*

Jones looked at his watch, looked around her to the wall of trees and hedging across the street. "Just a little—*un poco.*"

With the same cautious, measured tempo, Valentina said, "This is my sister Luciana, and, you?"

Always the gentleman, Jones said, *"Valentina y Luciana, Yo soy un amigo."*

*"Un amigo!"* The women bent their knees and bowed their heads, and laughed, blushingly. "Would you like to walk with us, Amigo?"

Valentina pointed her forefinger over his head. Jones stepped to his right and turned slightly left and up while keeping a vigilant eye on his surroundings. He saw the sign: *Astrología.* It was wedged into the right corner at the bottom of a second-floor apartment window. He turned back around and gave Valentina a friendly smile.

"Thanks for the invitation. *Vaya con dios,* ladies." Valentina locked arms with Luciana and smiled back.

*"Tu también."*


Jones surmised that Valentina and Luciana were the minor distractions his teacher talked to him about, less than 48 hours ago.

He checked his watch. It was 2:59. The park was behind the bus to the west. The density of passengers and pedestrians disappeared around street corners, into restaurants and apartment complexes. After the new passengers hurried into the bus, the driver tested the air-brake pressure at pre-start and then turned the key. Jones faced the park where his teacher had arranged the meeting. Once the light turned and the bus took off, Jones crossed the street. The smell of honey was stronger now. He replayed in his mind the contents of his teacher's call, which again had somehow bypassed all the barriers Jones erected to prevent anyone from locating him at all.

Jones once owned forty cell phones. He purchased a new one and destroyed one every three months during the ten years he had been using cell phones without adding any personal identity markers, and living and doing business under an assumed name. Each phone was equipped with a virtual private network and high-level encryption. Jones didn't desire any members of the FBI or other law-enforcement agencies to get a bead on him. He preferred it the other way around. Yet, Jones never called his friends at the Bureau, USMS, SWAT or any of the state and local agencies. Rather, he sent them his best thoughts and sentiments. He had helped them enough while in the states. Jones laughed every time his teacher called him on his new private number, since after he left America in 2009. How did he hone in on Jones'

41<sup>st</sup> phone?

"Ahmad, come and sit by me." Jones stepped in between two jacaranda trees and sat on the first bench, by his teacher.

With a big smile, the teacher said, "How is your manuscript getting along, my son?"

"Well, my teacher, it is getting along well." The teacher was silent as a breeze came through the enclosure and with it a butterfly, a monarch.

"Get it done sooner than later."

"Yes, may I ask why?"

The teacher wore a grave expression, "You will need that book, for another reason, besides sales. I will tell you nothing else; yet, when a situation presents itself, then you will realize the book's dual purpose."

Jones looked left at the gently curved line of benches. "My son, you are here because these twelve labors attributed to Hercules and represented by each bench are to be undertaken... by you." The teacher waited for his student to digest his words, before saying more.

"I gather that you have examined the chart of Afarland, and advanced the positions of the planets, the Ascendant and Midheaven?"

"I have."

"Is there a way through, a door in time and space, for Afarland to not fall under the weight of its cyclic challenge?"

"Yes... I can only affirm it, yet as to how, it is too early for me to fathom."

"If you believe what you just stated, then it *is* too early. Your perception of time and space is a construct that you have used because the routine of acknowledging them has been part of your life-condition. In that vein, what do you think about astrology, is it a construct?"

"Yes, and a useful one."

"It is useful, like a hammer is to a nail, when constructing a frame-structure for a new house; or buckets to hold water, which are carried to a small plot of land where an entire family can drink; or a mathematical construct used to fashion a measurement tool that can be used to determine the effects of wind vortices on tall buildings. And yet, my son, they are all constructs. All made up of the same cosmic stuff. Like this butterfly, whose species traveled a vast distance and now takes up residence here."

The monarch alighted on the golden handle of the teacher's frosted-crystal walking stick. Jones watched as the delicate creature's tawny-colored upper wings fluttered, slowly.

The teacher beamed a smile at the butterfly, then faced his student.

He said, "The math was created to solve a problem. Astrology's foundation, a la the horoscope, is mathematical, as you know. I am preaching to the choir. Yet, putting the notion of constructs, which are useful to the average person, aside, I will ask again. Is there a way out that you can discern in Afarland's chart, to keep its government from being torn asunder under the pressure of its first major challenge since its official membership in the United Nations?"

Ahmad took out Afarland's chart, from his jacket pocket.

"The shortest distance between two points, my son, is the assumption of a virtue, even if you deny, or do not sense that you possess that virtue. Therefore, assume that you know—play, pretend." The teacher's eyes sparkled.

Jones said, "Aries is the lead-taker, the forceful drive from the scrimmage line, one who breaks through the defense, burning a hole through opposition, to the light of day."

"You know what the stakes are," the teacher said.

Jones noticed a way through. "I see it—it's a reversal; that's it, a reversal, a play-action pass, a big play."

The monarch took off and alighted on the twelfth bench.

"See? 'Assume a virtue if you have it not,' so said Hamlet. You did and you've engendered a useful construction that wasn't *too early* to fathom. So, what is your reversal based on?"

"The two planets, which are each in the other's natural sign, the mutual reception. It is the way out, of Afarland's coup d'état. And I can see a way to help Afarland's ship-of-state to stay seaworthy, during the hard times."

"Splendid, my son. Now, I asked you here to convey an important teaching, for without it, your reversal would collapse. It is this: you must keep your energy balanced, harmonious; that is, allow nothing to upset your equilibrium. For without conformity to the principle of balance, Ahmad, the butterfly of state can only fly on one wing.

"Ahmad, during the season of summer, in North America, several attempts will be made against you, do not succumb to anger, because anger is a fire-extinguisher. It will rob you of the fire of life, which is your energy. What goes around, also comes around. It is the law of the circle. Defend yourself and anyone who requires it, but do it dispassionately, without qualification."

"I will, my teacher."

"Can you feel within you the balanced force inside this natural enclosure?"

"Yes, I can."

"Take that feeling, of nature's balance, with you. Breathe in that balance, Ahmad, my son. This test is the first of twelve-major tests. The butterfly has landed on the final bench, your last test.

"So, to paraphrase an ancient teacher, pass through this first gate, Aries; complete your task and climb the great mountain to Uhuru, after successfully performing your first act of service."

"Uhuru?"

"I and another will meet you there."

"In six days, at the cabinet meeting in Afarland's capital. I will inform a select number of that cabinet of the danger that approaches, after arranging a sit-down with the Interior and Defense ministers first. I see clearly what has to be done."

"Then, go and do it. *Adieu*, not goodbye."

*"Adieu."* Jones stood. His teacher, a native of Afarland, was dressed in a silken-white, two-piece suit with matching sandals and a pink, Mandarin collar shirt. He stood six-three; he was muscular—an older gentleman, but with the appearance of a man in his twenties.

"Ahmad, Valentina and Luciana, well, they are my daughters."

Ahmad smiled. The teacher strolled between the jacaranda trees and crossed the street. Jones sat on the bench, quietly mulling over all that his teacher had said to him. The monarch flew high above the trees and out of sight.

# 17

## The Configuration of a Nation

ON MONDAY, MARCH 20th, Ahmad and Marakie arrived at the Defense Minister's home on Ruby Street, 15 miles north of the Presidential Palace. It was 11:17 am. The meeting was to begin at 11:27 sharp. The Defense Minister's home had peach outer walls, woodland-green trim, and a gabled, teal roof. There was an outgrowth of colorful tropical plants and numerous palms. The house was situated on an inclined plane with the highest part at the back. Behind the house, the land flattened out as the slight incline leveled off. On a misty day, if you stood out back and looked to the northeast, you would see Afar Mountain—almost half the size of Mount Kilimanjaro—appearing and disappearing behind the haze like a foundering boat. On a clear day, it glistened with the colors of seashells. Afar Mountain defined the northeastern edge of Afarland.

The driver opened the back door. Jones stepped out of the SUV and noticed the top part of Afar Mountain towering behind the teal roof. It appeared to be right behind the house, due to its immense size, but it was scores of miles away. Marakie slid over and Jones took her hand. The sound of the driver gently closing the door followed behind the couple as they strolled to the front door, taking the serpentine pathway that led to it from the curb. They talked and laughed, quietly. The pathway was composed of black obsidian rock, four-feet across. It was shaped like a wide, elongated S. Jones and Marakie enjoyed the short walk between the exotic color palette of reds, yellows, and bright purples. The border of white sand on each side of the obsidian path was flush with the short, finely textured grass, reminiscent of a putter's green, beyond the border.

A man opened the front door. He was wearing a teal-colored butler outfit, minus the bow tie. He had a solid frame, was a few inches shorter than

Jones, bald, with a round head and an intrinsically happy manner. His feet were perfectly spaced apart and exactly three inches from the entrance. He looked at them in turn and then bowed.

"Mr. and Mrs. Jones, welcome. Mr. Whallun knows of your arrival and I am honored to receive you."

"Thank you," the Joneses said.

The butler stepped back and Mr. Whallun, the Defense Minister, appeared.

"Ahmad... Marakie, you both grace my house."

"Thank you for giving my husband a few minutes of your time."

"Indeed! Well, it is I who am grateful for any time your husband can give to me. Please come in."

Marakie entered first, admiring the soft light in the vestibule that led into the spacious living room. She stepped through a doorway to the left and into a parlor. Alexander Whallun looked Jones in the eye.

"Ahmad," he said, "our Minister of the Interior is out back. Please, follow me." Turning then to Jones' wife who was already comfortable on the settee, he said, "Marakie, my wife, is on her way downstairs to visit with you in the parlor."

"Your hospitality is most gracious. You have a lovely home."

"You're too kind, Marakie."

The two men walked in a straight line from the front door to the rear of the house. There were few walls, just a spacious living and dining room and lots of windows for the sun to stream in. Jones and Whallun went to the back of the house through the half-open French doors at the rear. They alighted onto the back porch, between two cylindrical pillars. Each pillar was nine-and-a-half feet high and set ten feet apart from the other. The pillars were decorated all around with one-inch-square tiles colored white, sky-blue, dark-blue, aqua, and teal. Jones and Whallun looked across the grass to the man standing at the far end of the garden pond bridge. They beheld Afar Mountain, which stood majestically in the culminating sun. The Minister of the Interior was leaning over the rail watching the fish swimming in the pond.

The Jones' escort, charged with their protection—and who barely spoke a word—and who had followed behind them in silence as they strolled up the S-shaped pathway, kept watch outside the Whalluns' front door. In the parlor, Marakie heard muffled footsteps on the second floor, and then Mrs. Whallun came down the stairs. She was wearing a lavender-dyed maxi dress with ancient symbols of Afarland's past. Her garment was shaped like a long Dashiki, but with short, billowing armholes. She wore 24-karat gold bangles on her wrists.

Mrs. Jones stood. "Marakie, how nice to see you!" Ethel Whallun said, while taking her guest's hands in hers. They hugged. "I haven't seen you in such a long while. You are everything your name implies—charming and beautiful."

Blushing, she said, "Oh, thank you and yes, it has been a long time, and you look lovely, and your home, Mrs. Whallun…"

"Oh, stop! I'm just Ethel. And, Alexander and I do the best we can with this place." She let go of her hands and stepped back a few feet.

"Let me look at you, my, you are stunning in your white Kaftan; there's even a hint of pink! My, how wonderfully you've grown up. You have a glow." Ethel heard talking out back. "And your husband, you must tell me how you came to meet him. I imagine you're very happy in your new home in Incalzael. Do you still have a residence in South Africa? Come upstairs and tell me all about it. Tea and pastries are on their way up. Come, we have lots to catch up on."

The two crossed the entranceway and walked up the short flight of stairs.

Whallun said, "Our Interior Minister is on his way over. How's our time, Ahmad?"

"We have a minute to go, to begin at 11:27, Mr. Defense Minister."

"Just this once, I'll let you off the hook, but from now on, I'm Alex."

"Very well, Alex."

Whallun raised his hand for the Interior Minister to speed things up. The man waddled over. He was of medium height, about five-eight, and had a pot-belly, a recent attribute of many Afarlanders. He was astute and published, with degrees in engineering and chemistry. He stepped off the grass and onto the marble floor, and turned around to look at Mount Afar, then turned back while walking and almost lost his balance, and finally greeted Jones between the pillars with a handshake. All three then proceeded to the spacious sun shelter.

"Ahmad, please sit at the head," requested Whallun. "Traditional Afarland culture always invites an important guest to sit at the head." The time had arrived for the meeting to begin. Matters of state. Jones spotted his chair and walked confidently to it. He pulled it out, quietly, stood in front of it, hitched his trousers and sat down. The ministers both took their seats after Jones took his, around the brown, oval table.

"Sirs, I have good and bad news." Jones was upright in his chair, wearing a navy-blue jacket with no buttons, and matching pants. His white shirt was Mandarin-collared like his jacket. He wore a fleur-de-lis near his heart with three plumes that were the same colors as the clock in the Presidential Palace: blue, yellow, and pink. The two ministers looked at one another for a beat, and then directed their full attention to Jones.

"The government of Afarland has four months to ensure that an egregious attempt at power does not succeed on Saturday, 29 July."

Whallun rubbed his forehead then the back of his neck. He had no expression on his face. He asked, "You are predicting that there will be a coup attempt, on that date?"

Jones said, "Gentlemen, more than that. It may actually succeed but won't last longer than approximately seven hours."

Ali Filbert, the Interior Minister, leaned back in his chair, stretched out his legs and crossed his arms. Suddenly he sat up and leaned forward. His usually restless eyes were steady. "With all due respect to the president and his daughter, who is your beautiful wife, and to our host here, Mr. Jones, how in heaven's name did you come into that way of thinking?"

Whallun turned to Filbert. "This man has advised over 17 international entities, maybe more. Let's suspend judgment until we have all of the facts."

Filbert breathed a sigh and nodded—Whallun had just put his credibility on the line with Filbert. Whallun said, "Do proceed, Ahmad."

"Your question, Minister Filbert, is apropos to my answer, for it was in fact by heaven that the configurations pointing to a putsch were first confirmed. In my work abroad I've seen hundreds of these types of trends in the life-cycles of businesses and political entities."

Filbert countered as he sat up, "Yes, but what about a country of over five-and-a half million people?"

"Size is never an issue, Minister. Everything has a cycle and all cycles can be measured and illustrated by planetary geometry. The cycle for Afarland as a political entity began when she was recognized as a member state; hence, part of an international organization. Before that time, there was no confirmed beginning of Afarland upon which your local historians could agree. I used the time when Afarland was admitted to the International Organization of Sovereign States."

"When was that, Ahmad? But before you answer, would anyone like some refreshments? I know you would, Filbert."

"Yes, certainly!" Filbert responded.

"Just a glass of water for me, thank you, and it was 25 March 1996, at 3:01 pm," Ahmad said.

The butler appeared in the doorway. Whallun gave him a signal and the butler vanished as quickly as he appeared.

"The date when the General Assembly of the United Nations, by more than two-thirds, voted in favor of Afarland's admission is recognized as her natal birth. I've constructed a visual flowchart of Afarland's government structure, using concurrent astronomic data. Four months from the nation's recent birthdate, by which the chart was calculated, there are indicators pointing to a potential coup, although it was calculated only a few days ago.

"When I saw the progressed Moon in the Tenth Sector of the Executive Branch, ruling the Eighth Sector of the cabinet, the initial scheme suggested an entanglement with the president and his cabinet. When I saw that the Moon, symbol of the rank-and-file Afarlander, was at an angle of ninety degrees to transiting Pluto, a hard angle to a planet historically correlated with extreme tension, death and destruction, and Saturn opposed to the executive branch, my initial read took on more of the same theme, but this time a more serious tone—the end of Afarland."

"You say, the *end* of Afarland?" Whallun asked.

"As you have known it all of your life. The Moon was in the Tenth Sector, the rulers of Afarland, and Pluto was in the Second Sector of the wealth of the country. The geometry of the planets illustrated the underlying motive for the coup—to kill for wealth. Millions of Afarlanders will be adversely influenced by the forced political shift if this is not mitigated. Political intrigue and the machinations of deceit are connected to the land of Afarland in the Fourth Sector, representing opposition elements that are mutually incompatible to the president and his administration. These configurations, taken together, show an approaching structure of wealth that is appropriated through obliteration."

"Wealth—for whom?" Filbert interjected.

Jones paused to weigh the consequence of his answer.

"Wealth for the highest-ranking commissioned officer in Afarland's Army."

"And obliteration?"

Jones, with passion in his voice, uttered, "The obliteration of Afarland's constitution, prepared by the old Afarlanders, the real constitution, not the one submitted for approval by the body of nations, which is more standardized. No, the obliteration of recognition of the laws of life, the principles of spiritual balance and the spirit of brother-sisterhood that have been the warp and woof, the cornerstone of a people who acknowledged their Source, their Life, as the principal foundation of Afarland society."

"So, what you are telling us is that our highest-ranking officer, General Garaka, is going to seize power so that he can become wealthy?"

With less passion and more gravity, Jones says, "Negative, but to become popular, by his wealth—a means to an end. And to influence an entire people with his charisma, the wrong kind, of which he possesses an abundance. His mindset, devoid of heart, this thought-form of selfishness, is already a gathering cloud over the population. The worst case, of a cult of personality, gentlemen, you can't imagine. Creating chaos, confusion, and violence never seen before.

"The president will be deposed and General Garaka will move in to take his place as Head of State. The General may not even know about this very far in advance. Also, there is a group of the wealthy elite who are focused on Afarland. Foreigners. They are going to approach him with a plan to obtain more wealth through the land."

"And you gleaned all of that from your astrology charts?" Filbert asked while crossing his arms over his rotund belly.

"Plus, my years of experience unified with my knowledge of political science and government. Now, I am specifically unaware, at this moment, of specific intrinsic wealth pertaining to the land, except fish and textiles. Yet, there is a chance that there are diamonds, copper, silver, and gold, underneath Afarland's capital."

Whallun and Filbert looked at each other and nodded.

Jones stood, and quietly pushed his seat back. Filbert sat up more. "I attest, based on my initial examination of Afarland's chart, and your confirmation, that the land conceals massive wealth beneath the ground. This group knows about it or they will soon come to know. The clincher is this—the group and the general may not even be aware of what I have just stated."

Whallun and Filbert stared at one another again.

"But they will be. Gentlemen, please keep this quiet until I vet the rest of the cabinet. The lives of all cabinet members will be in jeopardy, before or on that day.

"There is a window in time that I located in the horoscope. It is a window that will open and close seven days before the coup. When looking at a horoscope, there is always a way out, through or around the worst of predictions. I have given you ample warning. I have more information, which I'll share tomorrow with the invited members of the president's cabinet. You have my resume outlining the international governments I have advised, so please consider my warning today with the gravest of seriousness."

The ministers rose from their seats.

"If General Garaka is going to try to take over our country, we should just arrest him for attempted treason, take him to the shore of the Bay of Teal, and shoot him!" Filbert said.

"The coup attempt will occur with or without the general. Taking pre-emptive action by executing him won't stop anything. This is a test for the entire nation, and The General is just the trigger. No, we must allow events to unfold. After all, gentlemen, you have advance intelligence of a certain turning point in Afarland's course. Please await my more detailed report at the meeting."

# 18

## Afarland's Cabinet Assembles

"WITH DEEP EMOTION, LADIES AND GENTLEMEN, I must tell you that a coup d'état is heading to Afarland like a falling star. It is scheduled to hit us four months from now—in late July." Ahmad Jones, the newest cabinet member, sits down. His five minutes are up.

"You say in late July... a coup d'état?" Clarise Ajanlekoko, the Minister of Finance, turns right, then left, then at the man across from her. She uses gestures calculated to disarm him mentally, to suck out his spirit through his eyes.

"Precisely," Jones says. Clarise interlocks her fingers on her lap then pounds them on the table like a gavel striking a sounding block. "You've stated everything except the date and time, Councilmember Jones. Surely you can be more precise than that."

All the cabinet men agree that Clarise is as beautiful as a dream with her curves and slender figure and her short elegant bob framing her oval head and playing against her fierce eyes and exotic cheekbones.

Jones says, "29 July, before sunrise." He is the calm weather in the eye of a cyclone surrounded by towering thunderstorms. The finance minister is that swirling mass sitting across from him.

"And late-July trip destinations for thousands of tourists, Councilmember Jones? Are these not also headed, like a falling star, to use your words, for long vacations to our hotels?" She separates her hands to the armrests while snuggling her body against the comfortable, high-back chair. A few of the male cabinet men notice the sinuous movements of her body and are taken off road.

147

Clarise says, "Why can't you predict something that doesn't negatively impact our nation's international revenue?"

"You talk as if you're scolding a child and making him take his toys outside to play," Abdu Khamisi, the Minister of Security, interrupts. Jones' focus is to maintain poise, to keep the meeting respectable.

The temperature in the oblong meeting room is still climbing. Outside, the sky is blue. All members except Jones are unnerved because of the dizzying heat, and the shocking news they just heard. The smell of salt water is strong in the air. The variously colored hand fans the members are using to cool off are a kaleidoscope of irritated butterflies.

Clarise fine-tunes her hair—primping up before the kill. She picks up the revenue projections for Afarland's tourist season. She smiles to herself as she leafs through the fourteen-page document, held together by a surgically placed staple. She pries open her designer reading glasses and moves the sides of her head into the temple tips. Every move she makes is sheer drama—captivating, alluring.

Jones, however, is not captivated. His only job is to maintain poise.

She rises, all five-four of her. Jones can see the paper's reflection on her tinted lenses. The throwback of that image gives Clarise's eyes a machine-like appearance, which lends a sinister aspect to her smile. Jones realizes that she must be dramatic—it's part of her makeup. She enjoys keeping her peers enthralled.

The noisy waves breaking over the stone wall behind the Presidential Palace where the cabinet meeting was held, were the only sounds heard in the room before Clarise spoke.

"Gentlemen and ladies, I have compiled the appraisal for this year, based on statistical facts, projection metrics, and the past year's tourism revenue, and on the revised tourism laws of Afarland's Tourism Act of 2016, which *I* helped to design. I and the tourism board used revenue estimates and specialized assumptions founded on definite formulas. In my experienced judgment, we shall meet and exceed even last year's financial numbers, come this summer." She puts the document on the table.

"So, what evidence, Councilmember Jones, do you have that our country will suffer a coup, other than your charts?"

He gracefully rises from his chair as Clarise returns to hers.

"As a precursor to my answer to your question, Councilmember Ajanlekoko, I used specialized formulas, too, based on thousands of years of observation, and established rules of interpretation developed by astrologers, many of which, were astronomers, mathematicians and even physicians. Such was the role of the astrologer in past ages who reckoned with celestial motions and configurations that coincided with wars, the rise and fall of nations, plagues, and today, even bull and bear markets, and coups d'état. My calculations are founded on specific indicators that have shown up during most of the coups that have occurred on the African continent. Those indicators, along with specific measurements, such as progressions and transits over the next year, have yielded critically important information, leading to a startling conclusion, through a process of astrological deduction that cannot be ignored or taken lightly without grave errors in judgment."

Ahmad Jones' attention was not in his head; there was no mental chatter there. The part of his body he was most aware of was the area around his heart. Three months earlier, in Cádiz, Spain, his teacher had shown him how to enter an even deeper field of presence and poise through becoming more aware of his heart and speaking from its center. Combined with the effects of Marakie's companionship and the love they shared, Jones emanated a huge field of poise throughout the room. He remembered what his teacher said about balance.

Clarise, unaffected, shot up, "I asked you what evidence you had."

Clarise removed her glasses as if she had landed a right cross on the tip of Jones' chin. She pulled her seat against her calves and sat down, then touched the sides of her hair again.

Still in the eye of the cyclone, Jones said, "The evidence, Councilmember Ajanlekoko, is all in the math, like your actuarial report."

The other cabinet members were at once pleased and energized by his repartee. Members on both sides of Jones and Ajanlekoko were facing the middle of the long table where an exciting exchange was about to get more exciting.

"You have asked me what evidence I have, other than my charts. It is this—that the two are the same—that is, the evidence is in the charts, from which the facts have been culled. The charts represent several streams of data—facts, mostly mathematical; some based on past performances of planetary periods expressed in astronomical and nautical terms—that coincided with political upset, and the rest is culled from my experience and expertise in this vein. I have used the same formulas of analysis in my consultations with over 17 other nations, mostly African, some European, and a few Caribbean. I speak to this august body from the vantage point of practical knowledge; I see all the indicators of a coup, just as you see the trends of this summer's tourism estimates."

Jones paused. The waves from the Indian Ocean, boisterous before, became calmer. The sound of men and women breathing could be heard for a moment. He gave the cabinet time to digest his words.

"The financial estimates, mathematically derived, must also be considered, within the context of the time frame that I presented to you a few minutes ago, obtained by the application of my definite rules," said Clarise, furiously as she leaned forward. Jones' demeanor was cool and refreshing, in the intense heat.

Ali Filbert, the Minister of the Interior, was restless. He sat to Clarise's right. He said, "Point of information! Your statement involves Afarland's security, which is my domain. I haven't noticed any signs of a coup and neither have any members of my policing and national-security staff. What you have predicted will be devastating, by and large. But how can you be so sure? I mean, in your councils with other states, have your charts, or you, ever been wrong, Councilmember Jones?"

All eyes went from Filbert back to Jones. His answer came after a few seconds of pregnant silence.

"No."

The returning sound of violent breaking waves against the stone wall was comparable to the dire projection outlined in Jones' charts in opposition to the misguided optimism for Afarland's tourism numbers. The cabinet's reaction—to the factual way that Jones said no—took the form of a noteworthy silence. Anticipation grew, rapidly, throughout the room. What more would the newbie show for this pronouncement of national proportions?

Cabinet members sent surprised looks at one another's faces from side to side and across the table to try to get a read on what the other was thinking. After less than a minute of these jerky movements, low murmurings, and the activity of mentally digesting Jones' prosaic *no*, the cabinet's attention returned to the astrologist. There was resistance; Jones expected some at first and not because of what he said, but the cabinet's concern as to how he arrived at his conclusion. His next duty was to show why and how a coup could happen, whose immediate references were astronomic charts, keyed to past cycles in the politics of nations.

The flow of Jones' presence, one of respect and honor, helped to maintain his equipoise while the emotional gravity in the meeting room intensified and the temperature still rose unchecked. Because of last night's lightning storm, which knocked out the thermal power station, the capital's supplier of electricity, no air-conditioning units or ceiling fans operated inside the Presidential Palace. This was a magnificently built, asymmetrical structure that partly jutted over what Afarlanders called the Bay of Teal and Aqua, where waters from the Indian Ocean ebb and flow.

Everyone in the meeting room was uncomfortable in the 96-degree heat wave, and consequently, the cabinet's thoughts naturally assembled around the dire realty of coups and the historical evidence that they never end well. Economies and infrastructures are destroyed and people get killed during coups—and not just the citizens who get caught up in the disarray and mayhem, but, more specifically, the members of an ousted leader's inner circle, which the men and women squirming around this long table were. Hence, their suspension of belief in the inevitable coup was understandable—it acted as a mental and emotional sedative.

Jones lifts the crystal pitcher that sits between him and Clarise and pours out another glass of water. The sound of iced water against glass is cooling, in a way, to the group. Each one in succession now pours and drinks. The four pitchers are passed around until their last remnants are consumed. Jones places his glass down carefully.

"Addressing your point of information, cabinet member Filbert, a severe challenge is approaching Afarland that is no different from what any other nation has faced that has experienced one or several coups d'état on this Earth. And yet, like several Privy Councils and cabinets that I have advised, you have advance knowledge of it—not from rumors, a disgruntled army, or mercenaries within our borders, or other telltale signs. No, we possess an itemized timeline, with a specific focal point, which in this case is called: Afarland's *points of crisis*."

Jones stood on the east side of the oval, onyx conference table in full view of his peers. He was ramrod straight, not stiff or slouching, just natural. He was poised in his body, all six feet of the man, wearing number 24 on his extra-large Nike-gray Seahawks' home jersey. In front of him and behind the members on the other side of the table was a wall mural of a map of Africa's political world. Above it was a surreal depiction of a golden-yellow sun sending its light rays into every one of Africa's States.

As for Jones, still standing, something went out of him like a virtue, inexplicable, which each cabinet member experienced according to his own mental and emotional composition. Nevertheless, a spirit of brotherhood engulfed the meeting room. The wind changed course.

The scent of pine trees mixed with the salty sea air and flowed into the large room. It refreshed the atmosphere inside and delayed, somewhat, the kneejerk reactions of the group. The average height of the cabinet members was five-eight. Jones was the tallest of them all.

"Our military is well paid and there are no complaints from our officers," said Abdu Khamisi, the Minister of Security, sitting across the table near the Interior Minister. He didn't look at Jones but looked to his right at the president. His spectacles conveyed a look rather than a need. He possessed several degrees—one in international law; the others in sociology and philosophy. His voice was an octave higher than most. "I see no signs of a putsch, Mr. President—no security issues, no communications from our neighbors: Comoros, Madagascar, Mauritius, or any other African state—warning us of such a violent event." He sucked air in through his teeth and tilted his head back, sniffed, then turned to face Jones, "Nothing in this salty air, our Afarland air, smells like the makings of a coup."

Jones acknowledged Afarland's president at the far end to his left and was about to convey a more moving tone through his next remark to obliterate an atmosphere of indifference and light-mindedness. Then he remembered that compulsion is no way to convince anyone.

Taking a breath, Jones said, "The perpetrators are not outwardly aware of their future treason. The coup d'état is not timed to expose itself until several weeks before."

"Then, if the alleged perpetrators don't know that they are going to stage a coup, how can they stage one? Sounds like the last supper," the security minister said.

"We never know what we are capable of until we are motivated to a given extent. The perpetrators will be motivated with sufficient force to launch a coup. They will know in time, Security Minister Khamisi."

The president, whose bloodline reaches back to Afarland's ancient spiritual rulers, had both palms face down on the table. The ring of state, one of two ever crafted, sparkled. He listened to all the speakers and their arguments, weighing the words he had heard thus far.

Khamisi said, "Your timetable is too precise. Maybe you're involved?"

"Involved? What is wrong with precision, brother security minister? I'd like to hear more," said Alexander Whallun, the Minister of Defense who sat to Clarise's left. An older man in his mid-sixties, he was robust and shrewd, with a keen expression of interest.

"Show me the math and any factual data," Clarise said, after taking a deep breath.

Jones briefly directed his attention to the far ends of the table as he panned his gaze first right, then left, like Clarise had, yet not with the same intent. He repeated this panning as he spoke, "We are fortunate to know beforehand the likelihood of this putsch, which gives us one hundred and twenty-one days to tack the ship of state onto a truer direction."

"The attack on the Twin Towers. What about that?" asked Khamisi. "Did you see that before it happened?"

The entire cabinet felt Jones' emotional response to the question. "Only in hindsight, a day or so after it occurred." Jones took a second to remember that moment when he checked the inception-chart of the United States. "I updated the horoscope for the Declaration of Independence. Eleven days before the attack, Saturn had returned to the place it occupied on 4 July 1776."

"Saturn's revolution around the Sun is approximately twenty-nine-and-a-half years. It is an essential timer of coups. If there's time, I will elaborate."

The people in the room all looked glassy-eyed at Jones.

"Also, someone had predicted 911 more than a couple of years in advance."

"Who?" Sophi, the Prime Minister, asked. He sat to Jones' right at the other end of the table.

Jones turned, "An astrologer, Latinist, and medieval scholar named Robert Zoller did, Mr. Prime Minister, a native New Yorker. It all began with the total solar eclipse of 11 August 1999, to which Zoller issued three warnings, in his magazine *Nuntius*. He was very specific about from where the attacks would come. He said the critical point in time, for the United States would be the month of September of 2001."

"That seems somewhat precise," Khamisi the security minister said. He leaned forward, as did the lovely Minister of Agriculture, Faika Desta, to his right.

"That last prediction came one year before the attack," Jones said, then continued, "Honorable members of Afarland's cabinet, it is well documented and dated. My detailed reports, based on my experience of watching the correlations of history and planetary cycles and the fact that I have studied your national horoscope, may assist you in giving me some consideration as I illustrate further the veracity of my submission. It is my national horoscope, too, for I am a son of Afarland."

"You are also a Chicagoan, an American by birth."

"Yes, he is both. Do they say anything—your charts, to be exact—about any destruction of our capability to continue exporting of our crops?" Desta asked.

"Yes. What about our industries?" interjected Aziza Jengo, the Minister of Industry, Trade and Investment. There was a knock on the main door behind Clarise. Khamisi got up and answered it, then sat down.

The cabinet was more excited to hear, out of curiosity, Jones' illustrations. Desta and Jengo were fanning themselves wildly as the heat continued to take its toll; empty pitchers were being filled with ice water by two helpers from the palace kitchen. When they left, Khamisi locked the doors and the meeting restarted. The ministers of industry and agriculture listened to what Jones had to report. Both had sweet, open-minded dispositions.

Their questions were motivated by a desire to understand what was predicted to happen in their land.

"Our land and infrastructure will remain intact," Jones said.

"Doesn't sound like a coup then; sounds like an attempted coup," Khamisi said.

Jones continued to stand, bringing his fingertips together. "Well, my experience with several heads of state—analyzing their horoscopes and, to my chagrin, being correct in my assertions 99% percent of the time—has informed me that this is more than an attempted coup that will just fizzle out like a flash in a pan. Lives could be lost. The heart-set of Afarlanders can be skewed. Of these incontrovertible facts—based on several hours examining the mathematics of planetary geometry in Afarland's national horoscope and comparing it with thirty other coup charts—Afarland is indeed headed towards a dark cycle, as all things that have a beginning and an end, eventually do. But you, we, have the light of foreknowledge to get through it."

"You're an American by birth, you are indoctrinated to be optimistic," Clarise said.

"I thank God that I was born and raised in America, and now I share with you all the same optimism. No, even better, I share with you all a cosmic optimism." He turned to the security minister, "Mr. Khamisi, to me, when you can anticipate the trend of a future event, that is a good reason to cultivate optimism, backed by hard work and intelligence. It is as plain as the gold-rimmed spectacles perched on your nose."

"Lives will be lost?" the Prime Minister asked.

"Yes, Prime Minister Sophi, lives will be lost."

Silence filled the room again.

President Dewabuna said, "If you please, Mr. Jones, share with us more particulars in your charts." Clarise glanced at the president with a half-smile, her fierce eyes softened when she looked at him.

"Yes, Mr. President, I will, and plainly, while occasionally using certain terms of which you may not have an immediate grasp, yet which I will use to clarify certain points. Then, I will share with you all a solution, outlining three priorities that will indeed minimize the loss of life both within this cabinet and among our five-and-a-half million Afarlanders, before, during, and after this critical point in time."

The cabinet fidgeted a little. The president gestured with his hand to proceed.

"Thank you, sir. To elaborate on what Saturn's transit means, in West Africa, you have Benin's chart with transiting Saturn moving to conjunct its own natal position, forming a Saturn Return on 12 December. In that same month, of the year 1989, the Marist-Leninist regime of President Mathieu Kerekou ended."

"But ours is not a regime like his was," Clarise interrupted.

"Yes, yet, I never stated that it was, Madame finance minister."

Silence.

"I merely state this fact of history, to show the astronomic correlations with major shifts in political entities. Now, pertaining to political entities, Saturn symbolizes the structure of a government, its constitution, and its executive branch. Whenever it cycles to form certain angles, expressed by degrees of celestial longitude, in relation to the place it occupied at the nation's birth, along with other supporting planetary positions, political shifts tend to occur."

"But, was that repeatable? Did it happen more than once?" Khamisi asked.

"Yes, I will illustrate this. The long dynasty of Muhammad Ali-Pasha, an Albanian soldier under the Sultan of Ottoman, in Turkey, which lasted from 1805 to 1952, ended when Anwar al-Sadat announced over the radio the takeover of the Faruq I government. On Wednesday, 23 July 1952, at 7:00 am, in Cairo, Egypt, Saturn returned or moved to its natal place at just two degrees from exact in the nominal independence chart of Egypt for 28 February 1922. Here, we see the government of King Faruq I, represented by Saturn, come to an end when Saturn returned to the place it occupied approximately thirty years before. President Anwar Sadat's assassination and Hosni Mubarak's ouster—both occurred during a Saturn return."

Clarise cleared her throat as she put her pen down on the table and sat back. She turned to see the president gazing at her. He had wooly, gray hair and beard. He is president only in name, to emulate most countries. He is really the last surviving member of the Royal House of Afarland, who took office after the *Council of Twelve* left the country. In its first modern election, Afarlanders elected him because of his tie to their ancient past.

Jones continued, "Now, consider that Zimbabwe had its first Saturn Return on Monday, 26 January 2009. Sixteen days later, the Movement for Democratic Change leader, Morgan Tsvangari, was sworn in and he and Robert Mugabe, shared power for four years—at least in appearance. BBC writer Joseph Winter said of President Mugabe, 'He will only step down when his revolution is complete.' That statement was an uncanny reference to the revolution of Saturn. Winter's comment was amazingly on point."

"When will Zimbabwe's next Saturn Return occur?" Khamisi asked.

"Twenty-eight September 2038, but Mugabe's personal Saturn Return, based on his presidency from 1987, occurs in October-November, of 2017."

Khamisi removed his glasses and propped his underarm over the toprail of his seat. Each chair was the color of teal; its cushions were made of soft, kidskin leather. He said, "It appears that Saturn has a qualitative and quantitative value in your calculations of predictions."

"Yes, Saturn, from the standpoint of astrology, represents an expression of energy. And yes, it is a recurring quality in the horoscopes of coups. Yet, it does not mean that a coup will occur just because it shows up. There are usually other factors that, taken together, point to the same thing. Here's another example of a repeatable occurrence with Saturn as a key factor."

The cabinet didn't give the rising temperature as much attention now, for they were both intrigued and frightened at Jones' account. The more accurate statistics he gave, the more apprehensive they became. For them, specificity always trumped ambiguity.

"For Mozambique, your closest neighbor on the mainland, I observed an instance of transiting Saturn opposite to where it stood on its natal day. Usually Saturn takes 14 years to travel halfway around the Sun. The halfway point is called the *Opposition* as it is opposite to where it was at birth. It is an opportunity for any government to look at itself. Oppositions allow governments to be more objective.

"Marxist collectivism had dominated life in Mozambique from its day of independence, which began on Wednesday, 25 June 1975. In mid-October to early November of 1990, Saturn opposed its natal position. The government changed its constitution, which is related to Saturn, on Sunday, 30 November, allowing for more privatization and new freedoms. I will get to Afarland and how these cycles pertain to her, and—"

"Does this Saturn phenomena only affect African countries?" Khamisi asked.

"That's right, what about, *uh*, Spain," asked Sefu Tendaji, the Minister of Education, "when Francisco Franco died in office?"

Jones looked out the window at the great baobab trees that lined the main road from the Presidential Palace. He remembered what he studied about the end of Franco and the beginning of Juan Carlos. *Did Saturn play a role in the transition?* he asked himself. He recalled that it did.

"Yes, it did, though it was not by returning to its birth position. The day that Francisco Franco died and Juan Carlos assumed leadership, Spain's planet Saturn was squared by Jupiter in the same degree. It represented a critical point in Spain's political trajectory.

"Also, there's enough evidence to show that when another planet such as Uranus is a certain number of degrees from Saturn, government reforms are usually swift and sudden. Uranus suggests revolutionary change, a break in the status quo, and reforms. For example, in Mozambique, by the time Uranus had completed a transit of the Sun in January of 1989, President Joaquim Chissano, who was Samora Machal's successor, no longer supported state socialism as the principal form of government. The Sun governs the leaders of nations, be they presidents, emperors or kings."

"What about the chaos in Libya in 2011?"

It was the second time the president spoke. Jones bowed his head again, and said, "Sir, Saturn returned to its position on 21 August 2011, the same position it occupied when Libyan independence from Italy was declared under King Idris 1, on 24 December 1951. Regarding the NATO strikes in Libya, militia groups, and civil unrest in 2011, Saturn returned two months before Muammar Qaddafi was killed. Also, the planet Uranus (eliminator of the status quo) squared the Sun, representing the Libyan leader precisely on 20 October, the day he was killed."

The cabinet's attitude had entirely changed to one of thoughtful consideration at the credibility of Jones' assertions based on his examples.

"Please remember, distinguished council, that God is the master of all time, space and cycles. And this is just such a period and cycle—an opportunity for something different and beautiful to emerge on Afarland's horizon. I ask that each one of you repeat nothing that you have heard today, to anyone but yourselves, and, even then, with the utmost care. Also, the minutes of this meeting should be kept under lock and key or destroyed. Jones turned to the president at his far left.

President Dewabuna stood up and walked over to Jones. Clarise followed him with her eyes. "We will take an hour to cool off and for our afternoon repast. Please return at ten minutes after two, to hear what our Minister of Astrology has in mind, to meet this challenge ahead of time."

# 19

## First Interview

THURSDAY, 20 JULY, NINE DAYS BEFORE the predicted coup, some three months after the cabinet meeting, Jones was eating the last morsel of his well-done steak. He blotted the corners of his mouth with the half-folded napkin, pinched the stem of his glass and drank the rest of his mellow red wine. It was vintage, 1976 Rioja Gran Reserva from Barcelona. The rioja paired well with his Mediterranean salad. Its year also paired well with the year that the Seattle Seahawks played their first preseason game.

Jones breathed a deep, energizing breath from the belly upwards. He pressed his back against his seat a bit and closed his eyes for a short while, directing no attention to his upcoming interviews, his talks and book signings, or his overarching commitment. He considered his teacher's remark, about his book's dual purpose.

The atmosphere in this space was light and clean. The décor was smart, efficient and economical—as it should be. The noise was low and monotonous, but tolerable. Although not full, the overall space was long and wide and high. It could house up to a 150 people. Jones still had privacy, despite the size; it was cozy and comfortable.

Jones had napped before his meal. Marakie, his wife of almost eight years, had left him a few hours earlier to attend an online meeting. There was no clutter anywhere and the solitary red rose on the windowsill added a fragrant accent to the Zen-like ambience. Jones needed time to himself.

The gold-plated cutlery he had used reflected the last of the tiny flashes of light streaming through the windows and onto the tray, glassware, china, an unused buttonhole napkin, and the few crumbs left behind.

Jones moved these to the small adjacent table, located the laptop sleeve near his seat, and pulled out his tablet. He took it out of sleep mode and accessed Excel. The spreadsheet contained the speaking schedule that his publicist had prepared and sent to him earlier in the month. Jones had started the first leg of a barnstorming tour for his latest book, and his first phone interview, a cameo, was going to take place in a couple of minutes. He stared out the window and took note of his speed, watching wispy cloud formations zip by. He heard, as if for the first time, the long, continuous, and regular sounds of the huge machine interacting with the air outside. It was an unmistakable reminder of where he was. Now, the sun was gone. He felt a tiny yaw, the twist and oscillations around the long axis of the plane.

The flight attendant approached and said, "Mr. Jones, we'll be starting our initial descent into Chicago shortly, but you still have time for dessert. May I bring you something?"

"Certainly! What's good on the menu?"

With four fingers the woman slicked back strands of her auburn hair, around her left ear. "Ah! Well, we have a chocolate mousse layered with fruit and cream."

"May I have two, to go, for my wife and me?" He pointed toward the lower deck where Marakie was working. The couple had seats in business class, the hump section of the 747 Jumbo. Jones sat on the upper deck in the first row while his wife was working, below.

Carol, the flight attendant said, "Yes, indeed, Mr. Jones, with pleasure. We'll have it ready for you when you disembark."

The attendant walked toward the galley while checking her watch and the unlit no-smoking and fasten-seatbelt signs. She halted, turned clockwise around, and returned to Jones' row. She moved with elegance and poise, always with a smile, which was not a pasted-on smile but one of inner confidence, of powerful, stored resources. It was the spontaneous smile of meeting new and fascinating people, and of living her dream of being chief purser, salaried high like the sky.

She oversaw the cabin crew, was competent and seasoned, with many years of moving through Earth's upper atmosphere. Her shoes were polished up to a simple satin sheen; her company uniform was well cleaned and pressed. There was nothing ostentatious about her hair, nails, makeup or jewelry—nor about her crew. These simple accoutrements represented her and the flight attendants. As all flight attendants must master certain personal protection skills, and with all her years of experience, Jones could sense an enormous field of force around her—behind all the poise and etiquette displayed in the delicate gesture of sweeping the hair behind her ear—which would be an asset in an emergency. She was like a character in a spy film, an asset indeed—deadly, yet sweet.

Carol said, "Mr. Jones, I forgot to mention that you still have some time yet to finish your work before you and your wife have to stow your laptops in preparation for landing."

"How much time?"

"My educated guess is fifteen minutes. When you hear the double-ding, the captain will give the inflight announcement."

"Would you please tell my wife about the time, too? Thank you."

"Yes, I will, and you're most certainly welcome, Mr. Jones! In a few moments, I'll clear the center table for you. May I get you something for now?"

"I would like to have two bottled waters, please. Thank you."

"You're welcome." Just then, Jones' phone rang. He put on his headset, adjusted his mic and said, "Ahmad Jones."

"Mr. Jones, hi, I'm Ron the engineer, calling you before we go live. Are you ready?"

"Yes, Ron."

"Great, sorry to cut it so close. I'll patch you in to the studio; the next voice you'll hear will be the host. We're on in 10."

This was it. Jones thought of his wife, his teacher, and his forthcoming work in the U.S.

"You're listening to Nelson Thomas, host of *Astro-Talk* at KJRT in Philadelphia. My guest today is Astrologist Ahmad Jones. Mr. Jones how are you today?"

"Alive and well, Nelson. Thank you for having me on as your guest."

"Thank you, Mr. Jones! And congratulations to you for the increasing success of *Football's Astrological Measurements*. We've sold over three hundred copies over the past couple of days on our website store alone. We've ordered more books."

"That's great news. And call me Ahmad, if you will. I am also grateful to all the people who've purchased my book and to *Astro-Talk* and KJRT for promoting it. I am sorry for the background noise, as I am still up in the air in flight."

"It's not bad and I'm sure our audience will understand." Nelson said, "So, let's begin with what made you write a book that relates football to astrology. I read in the acknowledgements about your dad and how he was influential in your desire to study astrology."

"Yes, he was. My father, Robert Jones, had great depth of being and so did my mother. I was home-schooled by them. Robert was an Army vet and built the house where we lived. Leah was a schoolteacher who earned a degree in liberal arts with a major in history from Spelman College in Atlanta.

"Once a week, my dad took me to Patriots Park, south of Northwestern University's campus and close to the shores of Lake Michigan. Most times, the western horizon was clear, and my dad would show me principles of celestial navigation, such as how to measure the altitude of the sun with a sextant, and the procedure for using a nautical almanac, and logarithms."

"So, you were gaining a solid foundation in celestial navigation?" Nelson asked.

"Right, and land surveying, which required lots of math. At night, he showed me how to measure the altitude of the Moon and certain fixed stars, like Sirius, the brightest star in the heavens, Alderbaran, the brightest in the constellation of Taurus, and Betelgeuse, another bright star that lies to the upper left of Orion's Belt. Dad instructed me with a solid brass Vernier sextant that was given to him while overseas. I remember him saying, on one Saturday afternoon as we crossed Davis Street and Forest Avenue on our way to the park: 'Ahmad, in life you should always know where you are—your position in the scheme of things and your direction. You are a citizen of a larger town than Kaskaskia, or of America, or even of the world. You are a citizen of this solar system, this galaxy and this universe! Learn to co-measure yourself with these.' My dad's words made deep impressions on my young heart."

Nelson Thomas asked, "And, how did football make its way into your life and your book? Did your dad influence you to take up the sport?"

"Yes, my father did. Even as I say this, I feel his heart. Dad was all heart, born in Leo, the sign of the heart. In his spare time, he correlated the stars in their courses with world events. He loved history and constructed the chart for the beginning of the Civil War, after he discovered the time when confederate soldiers first fired on Fort Sumter in South Carolina, on 12 April 1861, at half-past four. He also charted big football games, the most memorable ones, like the Giants and Colts in '58, and the Harvard-Yale game of '68."

"Sounds like he was quite a man. How did he see football?"

"He made symbolic references about football as being compelling to watch, while at some other level it was a metaphor for treading a path that leads from one point to another point—from ignorance to enlightenment, for instance. He would say that to know one's self was to discover the path to daylight—like advancing the ball into the end zone. It could take several downs, years or decades, to accomplish, or it could happen in the time it takes to blink. He would say that to strive amidst opposition during a point of crisis—to find the gap, the hole, in the defense, or to outperform defensive tackles, corners and safeties—to see a worthy objective and goal and to move toward it with dexterity of spirit was to transform into a spiritual athlete. He taught me that my greatest adversaries were within my own mind—within the house of thought and feeling. To outmaneuver and transform them all was to experience a new kick-off—a new beginning in the game... of life."

"And on that note, we must take a brief time out for a commercial break. Stay tuned for a new kick-off with Ahmad Jones, author of *Football's Astronomic Measurements.*"

Nelson said, "Okay Ahmad, we're off the air. I've heard a lot of coaches talk about football, but none of them ever put it in those terms. That's awesome! It will be a good teaser for our audience to buy your book. I could stay on this topic for the remainder, but that might not satisfy our listeners, probably just me. In any case, we're on the air again in 3, 2... Hello again! Nelson Thomas here and welcome back to *Astro-Talk* based in Philadelphia. I'm talking with author Ahmad Jones about his book, *Football's Astrological Measurements*, which is out in bookstores now. And we're selling signed copies on our website. So, Ahmad, how did you find the time to sign over four hundred books?"

"They were published in South Africa. I spread it out over about two weeks, about forty a day, to get them all signed."

"Do you think that American football is the most popular sport in the states, and if yes, then why?"

"The Super Bowl is a good gauge to its popularity around the world. To me, there are many dimensions to it, which I do expound upon in my book, through astrology. For example, draw the number eleven, either on paper or in your mind. Next, draw two horizontal lines to connect the two vertical lines. This is the symbol for the astrological sign of Gemini. Now, if you look carefully you can see the gridiron as the top and bottom horizontal lines are the end zones and the vertical ones are the sidelines. Of course, a real field does not have the overlapping, yet, you can draw the comparisons."

"One of my producers just brought up the symbol for Gemini. For those of you watching our podcast, via our website, it has just appeared on the lower-right-hand corner. Okay, Ahmad, now what?"

Jones noticed the illuminated fasten-seatbelt sign and as he did so, he flashed a thought to Marakie.

"If you watch any football game—high school, college, or pros—there's one thing always present—adaptation to change. Those words are at the core meaning of Gemini. There is one thing that is ubiquitous throughout the game of football—at any moment an action can occur that requires everyone to adapt and change, to react and realign in a different way. You see it after a change in the game plan, for a new quarter, after a down or a tactic or a play, after a new read by the quarterback or by the defense. Physical and mental flexibility is the key to playing the game. Brett Starr, along with Lombardi, changed the Wedge into a Quarterback Sneak and thereby won their third championship in 1967. If something wasn't working, then there was something else that could work."

"Are you saying that, as in football, so in life, Ahmad?"

"Football as life is a type of short story, with drama, thrills, suspense, heroes and antiheros—performed for huge segments of the population, between August and February. It's a game for men who think big."

"I don't want to belabor the point, but why do you think that is so?"

"Being open to other useful possibilities is what football conveys—both in this instant and at this level of our conversation. In the month before a new season, a mutable sign represents the field of space through which the Sun transits. A mutable sign is always adaptive, like a revolving door. When one season rolls into another, there's a flexible and changeable quality in the air that allows for a new frequency, a new season, to emerge. Gemini, Virgo, Sagittarius and Pisces are the four signs that precede each season. They form a cross, a Mutable Cross in astrology, representing a coterie of forces associated with varied experiences and constant changes, and these attributes can also typify life.

"It's amazing to watch how an interception, by a safety or a cornerback, followed by a touchdown, can demoralize an opponent, while at the same instant, increase the morale of the other team. Yet, this can also be reversed in an instant. This dynamic also operates off the field.

"Gemini is the quintessential sign of change, showing the continuous shifting between the pairs of opposites in nature—breathing in and out, night and day, the waxing and waning of the Moon, birth and death, etc. One who observes life carefully can govern or command these opposing forces because they can transcend them and not be swayed by them. Thus, when a football team commands the field, the tendency for that team to fumble, get intercepted, incur penalties, etc., is much lower because the team operates beyond the pull of the swing of the pendulum. Do you understand?"

"Yes, Ahmad, I do. A team can push the envelope to such an extent that they can operate from the center of the pendulum and not be jostled to one side or the other."

"Right, like when the losing side never loses its poise. This is one message that is clear in any game of football. If you look at it, there's a lot of the Gemini force at work. You have two groups of eleven men facing off. Eleven, by its shape, with two vertical lines, illustrates the two teams, where each is represented by one line. In the middle of the two lines is the neutral zone. So, there you have it, but also, Gemini's opposite sign is Sagittarius, the sign of one-pointedness, focus and accuracy. These two signs and the energies they represent work as a unit, not separately. One is constant change and the other is focus and they work best when blended together as a single entity."

"Are you saying then, Ahmad, that when using the two signs as a unit, if a team is losing, they must adapt to their opponent's game?"

"Coherence is the key. Real coherence in a team allows the eleven on either side of the ball to command the field every time. When coherence is lost and not regained quickly, then momentum shifts, turnovers, fumbles, incomplete passes occur until energetic coherence is regained. But I may be getting off on a tangent..."

"Oh, no. What you say is interesting. Please continue."

"I am saying that opposing dualities and conflict, collisions and grand tackles and spectacularly long touchdown runs characterize this game. Duality reigns supreme. I said before that football is high drama—during any good play where one team wants something bad and the other team is attempting to thwart it from happening. All great drama is based on this and so it is with football. A quarterback attempts a pass play but a pass rusher will see to it that the quarterback ends up hitting the turf first. It's the same at the other end of that pass, if not successful.

"Now, in reverse, the pass rusher attempts to tackle the quarterback on that pass play, but the quarterback prevents him from achieving his desire by getting rid of the ball in under two seconds with a stellar pass—very dramatic. So, that's the game and it's the same in life. There is no difference between football and life. It's all life expressed on the field and off. There's always a field, a space where we do things in different ways."

"*Uh huh...*" said Nelson, "So, someone like the Seahawks' Marshawn Lynch, who played running back, or other great ones of yesteryear, like Red Grange, at certain times must have been, as you say, energetically coherent on the field to—in Lynch's case—outmaneuver five or six defenders, like he did when he ran those 67 yards for that touchdown."

Ahmad reflected deeply on Nelson's mention of Marshawn Lynch. "In that moment, yes, he was the master of the field, and of the pull of opposites. To command the shift in a football game is to hold the pairs of opposites in check—the pendulum does not swing to the other side. To transcend duality and to operate beyond the game and still be in it, is exciting. Most players do it all the time, maybe not consistently, yet all players, in this and other sports, get beyond the field of play into the zone. That's the thrill of it. Because anything can happen that breaks the status quo. This game is where the four forces provide the lesson. As these four signs represent the countless, varied experiences that we all encounter, they help us to become self-aware. In life, some experiences just wake us up; they point out things. A person becomes more alert and less prone to make the same errors..."

The double-ding sounded again, accompanied by the plane's slight attitude nose-down.

"Nelson, I've been instructed to stow my laptop in preparation for landing. I have a couple of minutes left."

"Ahmad, I'd like to invite you back on, and talk more about these astrological details, especially concerning the fact that you give more weight, in your book, to the charts of the teams as entities, and less to the charts of the players. Can we start with this as the initial topic, that is, the general influence of a team chart, at another time?"

"Certainly, Nelson, and I enjoyed being your guest on *Astro-Talk*."

"Have a safe landing and we'll catch you later, okay? Thanks for your time!"

"You're welcome."


After Carol bussed the table, she went to the lower level. Five minutes later, Marakie came up the stairs with her Mac and headset. Jones helped her stow her electronic gadgets in the overhead compartment. She kept her laptop with her as she got into her comfy seat and breathed a sigh.

"Did you rest?" she asked.

"Yes, my love, I rested well and had time for a brief interview. I'm ready." He tilted left and planted a gentle kiss on her right cheek. Marakie in turn kissed his left cheek and as she moved back, she saw a small fragment of cashew butter on the widest part of his ruby-colored silk tie.

"Oh, honey," she said, "your beautiful tie!" She spotted the unused napkin, the one with the buttonhole that was left behind when the tray items were taken. She unraveled part of it. Carol, the flight attendant assigned to them, approached as if cued to appear at that moment.

"Mr. and Mrs. Jones."

Marakie looked up.

"Is there anything I can help you with?"

"Yes, please. May I have a bottle of seltzer water?"

"Certainly, I'll get it immediately."

She arrived in an instant with Schweppes on a small, round tray. This was not the kind of emergency that Jones had in mind when he measured the flight attendant's skill-set in meeting a serious problem. Marakie thanked her and placed the bottle of club soda on the table in the middle of the two seats, then folded back a corner of the napkin and dipped a tiny portion of it into the sparkling liquid. Someone had pressed Carol's call button and she excused herself to answer it. Marakie had placed the fingers of her left hand behind the tie.

"I should have seen that stain a mile away. After all, I am an astrologist." Marakie was amused but held back her laugh so she could concentrate on getting out any trace of that spot. The semi-wet point of the napkin and tie had barely touched. The speck was gone. All that was left was the slowly evaporating fizzy-water, which took any food residue with it. She blew at it. Her hot breath accelerated the speed at which the stain that almost was, was now gone.

She petted the tie, moved her soft hand up the silk material to the knot at his neck, straightened it, and then with a look of both amusement and concern said, "There, all clear."

Jones kissed her cheek, then said, "I did a partial tie-tuck, even covered it with one hand... Didn't work? All right, when I'm eating during my tour, I'll make the buttonhole bib my first order of business."

"I'll hold you to your promise, dear." Jones put his tablet back to sleep and stowed it.

"Darling," Jones asked, "how did your conference go?"

# 20

## Four Stars Behind Bars

FRIDAY, JULY 28TH, ONE DAY BEFORE the predicted coup, Mike Cappello, had an hour to go before hitting retirement age and was en route to oversee his last assignment, in the field.

"Lake is coming up on the right, a good fly-fishing spot," Cappello says.

"Yeah, heard about the rainbow trout there," his partner Mark Reese says.

"Brown trout, too. Shame." Cappello says.

"Yep, got to throw back those salmonids."

"Negative, it's the worms. Up to thirty-five bucks for the red ones." Cappello saw the pier coming up on the right. "There's the boat launch... and the staging area."

"I suppose you don't leave your worm-ends free, then," Reese says.

"The smart fish—and they're all relatively smart—nibble at the ends without hooking. Me, I spear the worm at least three or four times and leave a tiny piece hanging. I don't lose any worms without gaining a catch, especially from March 'til June."

"I guess you'll be baiting red worms a lot now," Reese says.

Cappello's belly laugh came on. He would've laughed more, but for the important job ahead. It did help dissipate some, but not all, of his pent-up energy.

"Well," Cappello said, "just be careful *you* don't get hooked during this op. Let's gear up and get to work."

Reese made a sharp right off State Route 20 and turned into the gravel lot near the lake's edge. Thick darkness was all around the two agents, so they sat in the car, waiting for their eyes to adjust. The lot sloped down towards the lake to the right where several small boats were moored. On the left there were over ten nondescript vehicles near the crest of the slope. Beyond the row of vehicles was a mobile office trailer like the ones you see on construction sites. It was long and wide, and propped up on cinder blocks. It blended well with the landscape. Specially constructed shades prevented its bright indoor lighting from bleeding out, except for the door opening and closing.

Cappello and Reese exited their decoy vehicle, a moss-green Mini Cooper Convertible, and after stretching out their arms, they slid on the raid jackets over their Kevlar vests and walked past the vehicles up to level ground, then up a few wobbly steps to the door of the mobile trailer.

Cappello called out in the darkness, "Case Agent Mike Cappello and my partner, Mark Reese, arriving for duty. May we come in?"

"Yes, sir. Everyone is inside, sir," the guard said.

Like the gatekeeper outside a lodge meeting, the armed guard opened the door.

Cappello said, "Loosen up, Officer LaPorte. What do you think this is, the civil service?"

"Yes, sir. Loosen up, sir," LaPorte said with more enthusiasm.

"Okay, now... that's better. You've earned your hazard pay this month." Cappello shook his head.

Cappello and Reese stroll in. LaPorte closes the door behind them and stays within earshot. Inside are 29 men and women in tactical gear discussing an operation around a large desk made up of three white, polyurethane folding tables. Each one is six feet long and three feet wide. On it is placed an enlarged street map of Deception Pass Bridge and the immediate surrounding area. Everyone is talking. Voices are merged into a sea of sound. Several officers from different agencies notice Cappello and go to greet him. Just then the SWAT Commander rushes over.

"Mike. Big fucking night for you," he said, while they shook hands.

"Yeah, more ways than one, but not too big I hope." Cappello whispered, "No, Jones' intel's solid and I am 99% certain of it. We're gonna clean up early and get these folks back to their families, girlfriends, boyfriends, in one fucking piece. My gut tells me that all we'll need is an entry team."

The Tactical Commander said, "Your gut, huh?"

"My gut."

"Okay, you give me the green light and I'll rally everyone. Your decision. But since you have experience with this sort of thing, if we must execute with more personnel, then you tell me when and we'll take it from there."

Smith, nicknamed "Smitty," the SWAT Commander, six-three, has ponderous eyes, a deep voice that carries well, and facial expressions that are animated with tons of life. There is something electric and vital about him. Smith places his hand on Cappello's shoulder.

"Mike, I'm certain you know what you're doing. Got complete confidence in you, buddy."

But Cappello was nervous and emotional.

"Yeah, thanks, Smitty." Cappello glanced at the map of positions to be covered by SWAT, U.S. Marshalls, State Police, and FBI units. Cappello was the case agent for the whole operation. He stood to the side of the center door and nodded to Smith who stood a couple of feet to his left.

"Okay, let's huddle up," Smith said. "Mike Cappello, as some of you are aware, is our Incident Commander. What he says next will determine how we make use of our adrenaline tonight."

Laughter.

"Okay, everyone, gentlemen and ladies, Commander Smith and I have consulted about this op and many of you have provided valuable input, even when not knowing all the particulars." Cappello scratched the back of his head while deciding how much information he was going to reveal about the operation. Looked over at the men and women standing before him, with their eyes glued on him. He went with telling them the essentials.

"Anyway, we talked earlier in considerable detail about why this must go down after midnight instead of as a predawn raid. As you can see, all the tasks on the backward planning schedule are done, which brings us to this point here." He aimed his forefinger on a section of the large piece of drawing paper on the east wall near the side-door entrance. Reese stood a few yards to his right.

"This is the centerpiece, the drop-dead window, of this op."

There wasn't a peep in the trailer. Cappello had the floor. He was a highly regarded agent. But if he told these 29 men and women all the *particulars*, they'd conclude that he was bereft of his senses. As of now, they respected him and Cappello intended to maintain that status. Cappello wanted to leave law enforcement on top, like Peyton Manning after Super Bowl 50.

Speaking with the cadence of a preacher, and with the added dramatic flair of Rod Serling, Cappello said, "Folks, you all know what your assignments are. There isn't much here to go over, just a few things. So, from O-fifteen to O-twenty-one, we may be on the fucking-fly during that time. Yet, all I know is that those four felons are gonna be driving on that bridge inside that window."

LaPorte could hear Cappello, from behind the door. He clenched his fist in agreement.

"Let me put it this way: those guys are gonna try and won't succeed in getting themselves across that bridge; so, I ask all of you to be flexible. We're gonna catch those four felons as a team—a team composed of men and women across four law-enforcement agencies, working together."

LaPorte did an uppercut gesture, like Tiger Woods would sometimes do, after an Eagle shot, or a Birdie. The spark of excitement shook the trailer on cinderblocks; everybody was feeling ready, were indeed, flexible and alert. There was enough enthusiasm to knock the mobile office on its side.

"Okay," Smith said, "let's save our enthusiasm. Channel it for the work that's in front of us." Smith nodded at Cappello.

"We don't know, exactly, where the suspects are right now, but fuck, we do know that they are on this island and we have precise, quantifiable intel as to when and where these... miscreants will cross that bridge. And so we're going to be at that bridge because it's the last fucking bridge they will ever cross as free men. It must happen and it will happen, tonight."

There was razor-sharp tension in the mobile office while Cappello paused, considering the stakes of this op, his career, the lives of these lion-hearted men and women, but most of all, the credibility of his source.

"Again, our drop-dead time is within a six-minute window. Are you ready?"

"YES!"

Some of the officers adjusted their helmets and throat microphones.

"You have the green light! It's a go! It's show time! So, take up your positions, practice radio silence until you hear from me. That is all."

Smith said, "You heard him. Proceed to your assigned positions. It's exactly 2300."

"Smitty," Cappello said, "I'll see you at the staging area, wherever that will be. When I know it, you will, too, in less than a blink."

"Let's get 'em Mike."

Cappello and Reese made a straight line for the door. LaPorte anticipated their approach and opened it.

LaPorte said, "I liked your talk, sir. We'll get 'em... *Hmm,* fuck-en-fly!" Cappello and Reese walked down those wobbly stairs, down the hill, past the row of vehicles, and into their decoy car. "Let's get to the food mart ASAP," Cappello said.

Reese angled into the driver's seat and got back on Route 20, continuing in the same direction.


Eight days ago, Special Agent Cappello was presented with the Meritorious Achievement Award along with two other agents at a special Honorary Medals Ceremony in D.C. The award was well deserved but far too late in coming, according to a number of agents and workers on the administrative side of the 56 field offices, including many resident agencies and even a legat, a legal attaché, or two on foreign soil.

Special Agent Cappello had a 91% clearance rate. If he and his team were given a murder or kidnapping or robbery to solve, the case got solved and was never left open. This was due to Cappello's far-out, unconventional way of getting to the bottom of cases. It was what uniquely qualified him to be given that award and to be the leader of his division. Some toyed with the notion that he solved cases more bizarrely than all the field agents in the Bureau, which may have been a stretch; and yet, his record showed that for the last eight years, all of his cases ended extremely hot, and with enough evidence for the attorney general to submit those coveted search and arrest warrants, which got the felons convicted, and hence, deposited in a cell somewhere. It was Cappello's oblique and unorthodox, but down-to-earth, solutions to federal cases that had never allowed any one of his to wind up in the cold-case cemetery since 2009, the year Ahmad Jones left the U.S. to live in Africa.

Tonight would be Cappello's last operation in the field, and the end of his career in the Bureau. His solution mindset was curious to his colleagues. But he had help from Ahmad Jones.


As Cappello and Reese crossed the south ramp onto Deception Pass Bridge in their specially equipped convertible, Cappello, now almost at the mandatory retirement age, pondered his perilous yet exciting professional career as an FBI special agent. He was seated on the passenger side, and extremely aware of low-channel noise on the two-way radio. He, in a manner of speaking, time-traveled in his imagination to a week earlier when he was back in his office listening to Jones' voice in his earpiece.

In his vivid imagination, he could feel the resistance of the carpeted floor against the soles of his medium-brown Oxford wingtips. He could even smell the new leather as he paced, in his mind, back and forth from the doorway to the huge tinted square of glass on the west side of his spacious government office in Seattle. He remembered the stacks of folders that lay at strategic locations on the blue, fitted carpet, and how he didn't just walk on it but used it as a makeshift desk. He remembered how all the paperwork in those folders was getting him nowhere. To him, the men he was looking to bring to justice were clever, as most felons are, but these men were uncannily clever—almost supernatural in the way they operated. He had a suspicion but filed it away in his mind until the opportunity that he sensed would soon arrive and present itself—like the empty space on a puzzle where he could insert the final missing piece.

Cappello's time was running out. It was his case and the robbers were still out there and were still free to commit more bank robberies across state lines. To him, to get an award for helping to solve eight years of cases, only to leave one undone on his way out, would be like receiving a standing ovation after giving an emotionally rousing speech and then tripping over a wire and falling off the stage.

Reese sped along the overpass. Cappello experienced that feeling of height on the bridge. His nerves were a few feet from the edge of a precipice with a long, steep drop, which was a good sign that his body was preparing itself for what loomed ahead. He didn't see the bay under the bridge but could sense its enormous elemental force as an inexplicable sensation of pressure against his body, which, when joined with his kinesthetic awareness of elevation, gave him a supercharge, one might say, of something invigorating. It was as if the elements themselves were at his aid and assisting the team he had mustered for tonight's op.

His attention returned to his office and how he left off the search for meaning in the piles of investigative documents on his blue carpet-desk. He remembered looking out for several miles toward the shipping channels and wharves of Puget Sound, remembered the exhilaration of the moment when he answered the phone and listened as he got up and meandered around his office, upbraiding the tender carpet fibers. He remembered how he started walking in a circle, unconsciously keeping step with the rhythm of words coming through his earpiece that rounded off with precise information, describing an astonishing scenario with a weighted probability that it would play out a week later.

Now, it's a week later. They cross the northern ramp of the bridge into heavy darkness, save for an approaching vehicle or two. Mike Cappello is about to finish his 39-year career—with epic and dramatic moves leading to a grand finale—because Mike Cappello should end his career as the head of this team after solving every case for eight years.

"There, behind the flatbed," Cappello said, after passing over the ramp. Reese had cut the car's speed in half. Cappello had pointed at the swaying pines that screened off the back of the lot. The retaining wall behind those conifers was four feet high with a trench depth of ten inches. Reese, still driving over 25 mph, turned into the lot.

"Slow down, Nascar! Eight paces beyond those evergreens is a wall and behind that wall, is nothing."

Reese glanced at his superior, then returned to his driving.

"It's a weak wall," Cappello said.

Reese wanted to make a good showing, so he kept his cool.

Cappello was still tiptoeing on that edge, listening to his ego tell him how humiliated he would be if he left the Bureau with an unsolved case on his watch. The ponderous mini-convertible slowed to ten, plodding over water, uneven surface cracks, and chunks of petroleum-based flatop.

"This lot, Reese, is chunky like it was jackhammered," Cappello said.

"So, how do you feel?"

"Like I am going to be jackhammered!"

"About getting that new badge next Tuesday."

"Yes, I'm talking about the same thing; I'm still processing it, Reese."

Silence.

Reese thought, *what's there to process*, but he didn't say it.

"How far down is that drop?" Reese asked, pointing at the screen of pines to their left.

"Two hundred feet, approximately. Parts of the earth's strata protrude at the bottom."

The lot had no municipal lighting. The whole area was without power, as planned. Cappello looked out his side window at the vehicle stream on Route 20. He listened to them whizzing in both directions. Stuck his head out. Saw the beaten ground below with the aid of the faint light from the food mart twenty yards ahead. He assessed the effects of years of sun, rain, wind and heavy machines.

"Wow, this pavement looks how I feel. Raveled out." He stuck his head back inside, pressed the window button, and listened to the sounds of the street diminish.

Reese grabbed his beard. "Well, you'll find something to keep busy when it's over."

Cappello noticed his partner grab his beard for the second time. He took on the role of the wise teacher.

"Listen, I know you're stuck at a desk for now, but cut that beard, man. In close quarters, your enemies will use it against you. Okay? Move into position."

Reese felt around his beard and jawline.

"What about stubble?" Reese pondered.

"That's tactical."

Reese, sitting low in his seat, depressed the clutch and adjusted the stick. He eased the Cooper convertible back a few feet toward the flatbed's gooseneck hitch. The armored convertible was jet black and weighed 3,076 pounds. The supercharged engine went silent.

"It's now 11:15. We'll tarry here 'til half-past midnight." Cappello felt his creds and badge, to remind himself that he was a highly qualified special agent of the Federal Bureau of Investigation. In another pocket, he moved his fingers over his meritorious achievement medal.

"This is gonna be the biggest collar of my career. My swan song."

Cappello thought about what he had just said. *Was it to be his biggest collar?* Cappello sipped his coffee, which was an hour old. The two agents kept a weather eye on the man standing to the left of the central register at the back of the food mart. He was of medium height and stout, with black hair. He billowed his red-plaid shirt below his belt-line. The man lifted his head toward the front of the store after he proved-out the register and left the next day's cash in the drawer.

"What's he looking at?" Reese asked.

"He's not looking; he's thinking. So it ain't us."

The man faced down again, opened the moneybag and loaded the cash, checks, and credit card receipts into it. He removed his glasses for the last time, folded them and slipped them into his shirt pocket, then zipped up the bag and walked through the doorway behind the counter to the store safe.

Cappello said, "No customers. Stay alert, in case this guy has a dilemma, one we don't know of."

"But we're not here for him."

"We're getting close to a critical moment in time. Anything can happen or won't. I've learned to expect the unexpected, which is a valuable skill to acquire in this field."

Cappello and Reese watched the lights turn off in succession: first the ones at the ice-cream section at the back end, then the deli lights to the right, then the ones above the food and dry-goods aisles on the other side. The light up front stayed on, for the cops. The heavy rain had filled several small cracks in the pavement between the storefront and the Cooper.

"I hope this isn't his flatbed; it's good camouflage," Reese said.

Cappello jutted forward. "He doesn't drive. On foot. What the hell is he holding?"

"Looks like part of a pallet of paper towels."

The stout man tossed the package on the bench near the entrance. Upon entering, the lot, Cappello had numbered the sides of the small structure with the aid of the headlights, just in case. He'd know if something was false. Thirty-nine years of meticulous observation had taught him the skill of looking. Cappello had sharp eyes that didn't narrow under an adrenaline rush. He was experienced in that way. The store owner whistled as he selected one of the many keys attached to his belt rig to lock up.

"Still think that ain't his truck behind us? He's going to load that stuff onto it," Reese said.

Cappello whispered, "No, he's not. Here he comes. What the hell is that?"

"Could be the theme from *Star Wars*. Not up on this week's top-10 whistle tunes."

The food mart owner dummied past them. His eyes were fastened only on what was in front him. His small flashlight was aimed low. He continued over to the lot's entrance and disappeared on the side of the road, heading north.

"Superman. The one with Christopher Reeve. He's whistling that tune," Cappello said as he gulped down more coffee. Reese reached on the dash for his Red Bull.

"This is a good position despite the uneven surface," Cappello said. "We'll mark anyone or anything fore and aft." Cappello felt around his go vest. He said. "It's cool, around 60 degrees. Comm protocols coming up soon. I have a good feeling about the whole job. Look around, Reese. Our units have melded behind trees and shrubs like some creepy *Night of the Living Dead*, or that new series. I can't see any tell on our units, can't hear 'em or smell 'em, and, most of all, I don't sense 'em."

"Unseen, the walking dead would tell. Probably would smell like they look—like crap, if they were nearby. Sorry, off on a tangent. Like you said, it's a good field position."

"Handed over to us—date, approximate time and place. All we have to do is execute."

The two men had a straight diagonal line of sight from the lot, on the east side near the wall of evergreens to the pedestrians on the north entrance of the bridge and to those down its length, to where it veers left over Pass Island.

"Check our special team of backpackers and tourists taking selfies. They even look nerdy. God, this is a great op. Like extras in a movie. And us? Far enough away to watch the action on that bridge with glasses. This op is gonna come off great."

"Hope so," Reese said.

"It ain't about hope, Agent Reese. It's all about timing."

A couple of pairs of bright headlights approached the end of the bridge. Two silver trucks filled with aircraft diesel fuel crumpled over the last few feet of the bridge. Cappello followed the noise of the trucks for several blocks.

The bridge was the focal point of the joint operation. Deception Pass Bridge, completed in July of 1935, was 28 feet wide, a two-lane, almost 1,500 feet in length and a bewildering 200 feet above the bay at low tide.

"Not a Crown Vic, Tahoe, Caprice, or high-performance prowler in sight. Just plain looking vehicles." Cappello said, "Players... report in." As he put the radio back in its cradle, the low channel noise remained. "My neck is on the line here, Reese. Operation Four Stars Behind Bars has kicked off."

The interagency task force, known as The Three Four, was to be embedded in a cloak of invisibility until called out, between 12:15 and 12:21 am.

"We'll make it happen," Reese said.

The first response of two clicks broke the squelch on the radio.

"That's unit one," Cappello said.

Four more double clicks came in succession.

"All five units are in place. Now, we wait. This is a huge deployment of human resources, Reese."

"I copy. As you said, this op is all about timing."

Agent Reese was a put-in at the last minute. Cappello had borrowed him from Cyber Division. They continued to monitor the ramp to the lighted truss bridge and all vehicles that passed them in both directions.

Cappello checked the time again.

"Soon, they'll be heading south past us and onto that connector where we'll put the choke on them."

Reese scratched the back of his head, nervously. "I heard some astrologer provided the intel. Is that true?"

"We call him an astrologist and that's correct, last week."

"I'm not too sanguine about this. What, what if he's flat-out wrong? He could be, you know. If he is, then we've wasted time and taxpayer money and we—no, you—won't come out well on this one if it flops. Your swan song will be the blues." Cappello listened, letting his partner have his say.

"There may not be a collar for you to ride off into the sunset with. There it is. The bad guys evade justice for the fifth time. Heck, they could be near, or on the right coast: Boston, New York, Pittsburgh, where they could get lost in millions of people. Why would they come here with, *uh,* what is it, only 58,000 people? It doesn't add up."

"Copy that, Reese. The intel is accurate, the Deception Pass Bridge will be their biggest mistake."

Silence.

Cappello leaned forward, looking at the sky toward the southwest. He pointed. "There goes Mars and Saturn in their descent. The stars shine brightly in Wyoming. That's where you're from, right?"

"Correct. Laramie." Reese was anxious about what Cappello was about to say next.

"I spent some time in Cheyenne before I married. Vacation. Met a girl. We'd look up at the Milky Way, from the backyard of her house. Then one day she laid it on me."

"Please, no details. I grew up fifty miles west of Cheyenne."

"She laid this quote on me. She said, 'If the celestial bodies are placed by God where they stand in their signs, they must necessarily have a meaning especially for mankind, on whose behalf they were chiefly created.' After she said that, we saw a meteor, a shooting star they call it, enter the atmosphere. It was some night. Made her my wife not long afterwards."

Reese pulled the tab on his drink. "When were you in Wyoming?"

"Summer of '94. Anyway, Tycho Brahe, the astronomer, is the one she quoted. My astrologist friend hasn't gotten it wrong since we met some years back."

"If this op goes bust, his blunder will explode through the bureau—and on your lap."

"You just joined the Bureau. The astrologist's countless hits are classified, so you couldn't possibly be able to gauge this thing."

"Well, I have a right to voice my opinion."

"Noted, we are in the middle of an important operation; and we are moving that six-minute window to the end. Regardless of what you feel about the source or the form of that intel, just pretend it's the best possible intel you've ever acted on. If anything goes wrong, it will indeed fall on my lap. And you, well, you'll be able to tell the story of my blunder."

Cappello grabbed his binoculars from the dash. The units were in their assigned positions. Cappello, a six-foot-one former cop, detective, and star high-school basketball player, with square head and chiseled features, did what any lawman would do during a stakeout.

"Let's lighten the mood a little, Reese?" he said, while looking through his binoculars and talking at the same time.

"You know, Reese, you're a... you're a Seahawks fan, right? I vividly recall the Seahawks' preseason game in 1976—their first game ever. I was there. I was eighteen. Was there. Yeah, I was there on King Street in the dome not far from the end zone. I remember drinking Coke out of a large cup."

"Okay, drinking Coke out of a large cup? The way you said that sounded weird."

Cappello put the binoculars down. "No, Reese, the way you said it was weird." Cappello lifted the binoculars again. "Never did powder. What's eating you?"

Reese said nothing. He was visibly putting two and two together.

Reese said, "I was around two then."

"When?"

"In '76, and you don't look your age. That Dick Tracy cut and the few gray streaks put you in your mid-thirties."

"I don't feel thirty."

Reese put the Red Bull on the dash. He rolled some peanuts in his hand like dice and popped them in.

"Yep, those four bank robbers were lucky enough to elude the law for almost two years. Been hiding out in northern Puget Sound for several weeks."

Now, it was Reese's turn to lighten the mood. "Back in the huddle, did you notice Smith's star when he sneezed? The thing sparkled when he lifted his arm."

"Did you know that Smitty was invited to the Met to train for six weeks?" Cappello asked.

"Really, the Met? Whhoot? Unbelievable!"

"So is that pabulum about his star."

"You're saying that he wasn't invited to Scotland Yard?"

"He trained with them after the Commissioner and City Hall dropped the funds. He's the best they come, for a SWAT Commander. I'm checking out that caravan of high beams and rear-end lights floating across the bridge."

"You think our guys are there? If they were, they would be early, and your intel would be off by forty minutes."

"My friend hasn't been wrong yet." Cappello put the glasses on the dash. "I guess you think you're helping me to see the light. I got a whole lot riding on this. I can't have you second-guessing me. Messes up my timing, my edge." Cappello took another gulp of his coffee.

"Players," Cappello said. In the huddle before the op, Cappello's comm protocols were one click, which stood for: not them. The procession of five clicks ensued.

Cappello put his styrofoam cup into the holder inside the console.

"You know, Reese, this cup reminds me of the old days, when I was a cop on stakeout taking the edge off. When I was four years active, I enlisted in the Navy Reserve. One afternoon, when I came on deck from the mess, a military working dog, a Belgian Malinois ambled my way. He had an aggressive, mean streak—you know, looked like it was going to leap at my face, bite out my left eye."

Reese, playing along, with low enthusiasm asked, "Did the dog have a rank?"

"Funny you'd ask that—it did. It was an MWD dog, no kidding. It was a Lieutenant. Me, I was a Petty Officer Third Class; had a rank. So, his handler says that 'the Lieutenant,' nodding to the Malinois, 'expects you,' meaning me, 'to salute him.'

"I said, 'We're at sea, land is back there, over 320 Clicks. We're working.' The dog, I mean the Officer, growled and eyeballed me." Cappello lowered his window halfway. The sounds of traffic and the smell of rainwater added some excitement to the story. He continued, "The Lieutenant took a slow step forward. The next step, his paw was still in the air, a few inches off the deck. That was when the handler told me to salute him now or suffer the consequences."

Reese got pulled into the story. He knew that MWDs were highly trained.

"We had put out for five weeks. Nimitz-class super carrier. I was surrounded by ocean and just staving off nausea, so my indignation and imagination took off in several directions. The threat was too ambiguous. So, I stood erect and square and smartly lifted my hand up and saluted the little feller. Guess what the dog did."

"You mean the Lieutenant."

"Affirmative."

"Saluted?"

"No, man. That Belgian Malinois turned to his handler as if to say that MF better have saluted me, then swaggered past me, like it was chow time."

"Are you teasing me?"

"God's truth. That animal took a gander at my left upper sleeve, saw my single red chevron and eagle. Discerned my rank—I mean it was probably trained to identify all sorts of shit. Somehow it identified me as a PO3 and barked. I'll never forget it."

"What was it, Cappello, a dog or a lieutenant?"

"Exactly."

Reese laughed, cautiously. He pulled more peanuts from his slash pocket and popped them in, to check the jitters. Underneath, Cappello was fuming about what Reese had said earlier.

"Mid-thirties? Gray streaks? Is that right? Tell that to the system that's forcing me to retire. I've got plenty of years left to nail bad guys—been playing this game for a while now. I've honed my investigative skills."

"Easy, brother. Cappello, a few seconds ago, you're telling me about a dog that—"

"That dog, I mean, shit, the Lieutenant was a dog! I've got to hand in my badge in three months. The stakes are too high on this op."

Reese was apprehensive.

"I put too much into my career. It has gotten to me, Reese... Reese—my wife and I haven't had sex in over a month."

Reese scratched the back of his head. "That's not my business."

"Just venting. She thinks it's her. I tell her, 'No honey, it's my job.' Then she says, 'Well, when you retire, it will be different. You'll make more time for me.' Reese, this op has got to be perfect. No mistakes. If this should blow up—I just can't go out that way, so, sport, I'd be the worm on the hook for the rest of my life. It would be embossed in the annals of the FBI. Cappello put his hand on Reese's shoulder and stared him in the eye.

"I need you to be behind this op one hundred and ten percent. Okay? So, I can enjoy my wife again."

Reese softened up. "And how does a black dude end up with a name like Cappello?"

"Long story."

"You've been sharing stories, two, so far. I like stories."

"It's gonna have to wait."

Reese checked out the ramp beyond the blanket of dirt and fresh grass that reached beyond the asphalt to the street. The directional lights on the bridge provided additional lighting. Cappello fell into a nostalgic dream.

"Last stakeout, Reese. I'll spend the next three months using up my vacation time. The Seattle Seahawks. That's when my career began—39 years in law enforcement, Reese—39. Weren't many of us in this field in this part of the world when I started. That Sunday, the day before I took the police exam, the Imperial Bridge in Austria collapsed at five in the morning. One driver didn't make it. An employee of the Vienna Transport Company had crashed along with the bridge into the Danube. But he did make it."

The sounds of traffic died down.

"The driver climbed to the top of the empty bus and remained until help arrived. It was the beginning of a shit storm of a day, because nine hours and twenty minutes later, Niki Lauda, the reigning world champion Formula One driver, from Austria no less, was taking his second lap in the Grand Prix at the Nürburgring Racetrack in Germany. Lauda crashed his Ferrari into an embankment and almost burned to death."

"I saw the crash depicted in that movie, *Rush*," Reese said. "When I was sixteen, I wanted to be a racecar driver. Figured I could meet girls that way. I didn't have a car to take a girl anywhere, so I went out for football."

Cappello took his glasses off the dash again. "What side of the ball?"

"Safety; I was a Safety."

"Well, I played basketball. Guess you tackled that problem, you know, women. From what I learned of your driving skills at the academy, you might have gotten somewhere. So, yeah, 1 August 1976, started out bad—bad—with the bridge and the crash, but that afternoon the Seattle Seahawks took the field for the first time, about nine hours later. They electrified that gridiron; brought some light on a horrific day that started in Austria. The horror ended in Seattle when Coach Patera put Jim Zorn in at the third. Zorn was my hero; he still is. I am Jim Zorn tonight. Plunkett and his 49ers were two seconds away from a tie. Tonight, those bank robbers won't know what hit 'em—Jim Zorn style."

"Yeah," Reese said. Cappello was on a roll.

"That Monday after the game, I took the civil-service exam at Saint Germain High. I was eighteen at the time."

"No kidding," Reese said.

"Perfect score. A couple of weeks go by, so I scoot over to the Seattle PD, fill out the application, and I'm on the streets fourteen weeks later, getting the required field training. Got a detective slot in '84. Lucky for me that Seattle had a big department. Did homicide for three, rotated into auto. No choice. Didn't like it, so I applied to the FBI in '86. Got in. Was a special agent by '87, when Otto was Director. Now, I'm getting eighty-sixed... shit-canned into civilian life—no choice there, either."

Reese got used to Cappello's abrupt changes of topic and demeanor. He checked his sports watch. 23:51. Cappello's attention returned to the food mart, and then to a splash of light across the street.

"Should've paid my water bill while the place was open; coffee's giving me a turgid bladder." Cappello opened the door, waited a beat, then pulled it back shut.

"I'll retire with accolades or resign in failure after tonight. My legacy—Special Agent in Charge of the FBI's Seattle Field Office—hinges on what will or won't happen on a short section of road between 0-fifteen hours, and a small window of just six minutes." Cappello got pensive as he sipped some more coffee.

"Hey, Cappello?"

"What?"

"How'd you get that last name, and what about your turgid bladder, and do you really believe that music coming out of your mouth? If you do, then what are we—"

Cappello spoke over his partner again. "Ahmad Jones still had access to the NCIC. He saw the data on our four, soon-to-be-captured notorious thieves. He called me late, last Friday."

Cappello positioned his body diagonally, between the inside door and seatback.

"I hadn't seen or heard from Ahmad since 2006, after learning that he's married and living in South Africa, and with a book out. So, I ask him, 'We've had several robberies, four men. Some local agencies are looking to us for help. They've eluded us. It's uncanny, like they know when and where and how to lose us. When will I catch 'em?' Jones says he'll have an answer for me in an hour. A question... that's all that my friend Jones required was a question. He used the moment I asked the question, and the coordinates of the place where he was when I asked it, which was somewhere in the mid-west. Ten minutes later, he notified me at the office, at around ten. He had calculated the date and place where the robbers were going to be, their direction of travel, and the approximate time they would be in cuffs. So, I made some calls. Ahmad Jones had erected a special astrological chart, called a *Horary Chart*. It's a horoscope set up to answer a specific question asked at a specific time and place. He said that the men on the lam were represented by the sign of Pisces, on the cusp of the Seventh Sector of the chart."

"You can't be serious..."

Cappello's tone deepened.

"Take this seriously whether you believe it or not. We have 29 men and women out there because of this intel. You want to steer clear of desk work for the rest of your probation? If anyone can make that change, I can. And you can fast track to something field-related."

Reese lit up with renewed vigor. "Our thieves? Seventh Sector?"

"Precisely, and Pisces' opposing sign, Virgo, was on the cusp of the First Sector, representing me, the asker of the question. It also included the inter-agency task force. These sectors, otherwise known as *Houses*, are opposite each other; the first sector or house, is in the same relative position as nine is opposite three on a clock. Me, you, and the rest of this task force are on the 9 o'clock line."

"The 9 o'clock line? I don't understand but it sounds real cool."

"Just think of any horizon as being represented by a horizontal line, with nine on the left and three on the right, okay?"

"I follow."

"Reese, this op is based on what Jones provided and even if you don't understand it, our tactical plan is still a go."

"What else did he say?"

Cappello relaxed in his seat. He was getting through to his new put-in partner.

"That Jupiter, the planet of fortune, and what some call luck, was placed in the First Sector; that is, the left side of the horizontal line where nine would go on the clock face."

"Yeah, Mike, I got that part."

"Well, Jupiter happens to be the robbers' ruling planet, but it's placed in our sector. This configuration is like enemy combatants placed behind enemy lines because their ruling planet, also representing them, landed in our sector of the horoscope."

"Let me get this straight. You, me and all five units are represented by the First Sector. Do I have the language right?" Reese turned his whole body toward Cappello for the first time. "Cappello, is this another one of your stories, like the Belgian Malinois, the MWD?"

Cappello kept talking, "Now, Jones said that Jupiter, the robber's ruling planet, is weak in the sign opposite the one it governs—meaning Virgo, which is to say that the robbers are out of luck, because the beneficial qualities of Jupiter don't express well in Virgo and that planet, their ruling planet, is on our turf, so they're fucked."

"Sounds like double jeopardy, for their ruling planet."

"We're on a dangerous op. I'm amped up. Talking about this helps me to even out. Now, here's where law enforcement comes into the horary chart more precisely."

"I'm listening."

Rain pattered the windshield and roof.

"Now, the planet Saturn, in this case, represents the law. When I asked Jones the question, Saturn was in a certain geometrical angle in space to Neptune, as observed from Earth. This angle is called a square, an angle of ninety degrees. When the planets represented are at right angles, they are at cross-purposes, so we look for a buildup of tension that relates to the meanings of the planets involved. Saturn, the law, puts pressure on Neptune, representing the bad guys, and it is the only planet inside the robber's Seventh Sector, which Jones said is the co-ruler of Pisces, their ruling sign."

"So, the two planets are squaring off—the law and the four robbers."

"Right."

"Okay."

"Those are two astronomic angles that are testimonies against the robbers' escape from the law this time. They have no luck with their ruling planet, Jupiter, because it's bound up with all the red tape and ramifications of the analytical sign, Virgo, and with Saturn's energy limits and strictures, which represents us, authorized to enforce federal laws."

"Us?"

"Now, you're catching on."

Trying to sound affable, Reese says, "I'm doing my best to keep up."

"Right, now whoever leads the op is ruled by the Tenth Sector, which is equivalent to the high-noon position on a standard clock face. The pattern of the modern western horoscope is just like a clock in some respects, even though Sector One starts on the 9 o'clock line and two at 8 o'clock. Anyway, the Tenth Sector represents the leader, the boss of this op, which is me and, to a degree Smitty, the SWAT Commander."

"You? Wouldn't Cummings be the boss?"

"It was through Cummings that I got the assignment but I'm the case agent and incident commander running it, like most owners or general managers would hire a coach. There's a difference, and my boss would come under a different sector."

"Which one?"

"You would count Ten Sectors counter-clockwise from the Tenth Sector, which means that the new Tenth Sector, stands for my boss, who is, to put it another way, the boss of me that is the boss of this op. There are 144 basic Sector structures to reading any astrological chart."

Reese was rubbing the top of his head. "I don't understand one iota of what any of that means. And how do you know so much about astrology, anyway?"

"After working with Ahmad Jones on some cold cases, which heated up, when we took him on, he trained me just enough to understand the signs of the Zodiac—the Houses and the planets' geometric relationships to each other. Want to know how this op is going to end?"

"What do you think? My life and the lives of fellow officers are at stake on this. So, right now, I'm a captive audience." Reese finished his Red Bull.

"Jones said that the outcome of the op for us is represented by the Fourth Sector, which is located where six o'clock would be. Again, Jupiter is the governing planet of that sector, too, because its sign, Sagittarius, governs it. Jupiter, again, is positioned in our First Sector, so they end up with us—under arrest. Also, the outcome for our four robbers is ruled by Gemini in their own Fourth Sector, which is the end for them. Now, Mercury, Gemini's ruling planet, is in the Twelfth Sector of prisons."

Reese pulled at his beard.

"Listen Reese, none of this astrology stuff would have gotten this far in our field office unless me and a few others had studied it sufficiently enough to understand its basic SOP. And, by the way, seen it in action when working countless cases. Once we grasped the rules, we've benefited from it, together with all the FBI's other practical sciences and tools.

"Lastly, Reese, the felons' ruling sign, Pisces, as a water sign rules large bodies of water, which in this case, is Deception Pass and the Skagit Bay area. This, as you know, is the sign of their Seventh Sector and Gemini, the end of the matter for them, rules bridges. Now, their Fourth Sector is also my Tenth Sector and this is another clue that they will fall into our hands. The bridge and law enforcement are being brought together in time. This clinched Jones' analysis for me. There are more than these indicators that point to them getting apprehended. If, after this operation, you want to know the rest, just ask. When you return to Cyber, it may be useful to you. But if you do well, and I put in a good word, you may have some wiggle room."

"So, he got all of that from a *hor-or-ary* chart, huh? Did you share these details with the other agencies of this taskforce?"

"The main ones I shared it with are Smitty and the Assistant Deputy Director in D.C."

"The ADD of the FBI? He's on board?"

"Both men know of Jones and have firsthand experience of his valuable contributions to the Bureau, to this country. All my boss wanted to know was the result. When I told him that Jones provided the intel, he used his clout with the AG to get us the green light. Ahmad Jones has a perfect track record and these bureaucrats know it, even if they don't fully understand it. Yep, feels like old times. After this, it will be all over."

"Well, you've got 'til February. You'll receive a beautiful retirement badge, and they look even better than the standard issue service ones."

Cappello shook his head as he squeezed the bridge of his nose. "I've got three months' vacation that I never took. I'm gonna take it after this is over. The Mrs. will be thrilled."

"I know just the place for your vacation, Johnston's Bait and Tackle—all kinds of crap pinned to your bucket hat, being that you know so much about worms."

"Yeah, look at me—hooking big fish instead of big criminals."

The temperature dropped enough to affect the windshield. Reese wiped the accumulated condensation off the inside.

He said, "Weeks, months, sometimes years of tactical and strategic preparation are required to catch hardened criminals. Well, my friend Ahmad took the weeks, months and even years of finding these guys out of the equation. Result? We stepped up our prep time; we're well-oiled, low-life catchers right now. He gave the Bureau actionable intel in less than fifteen minutes, just one week ago."

Cappello shook his head again.

"What have I been doing for the past 39 years to deserve forced retirement?"

Reese searched all his pockets for more nuts but came up empty. "You kept living and got old, Cappello. Age limits—it's the system."

"I know that, Reese. I wasn't asking a freaking question."

The streetlights were out for a quarter mile. A faint light shone from a couple of windows across the street. Their eyes were well adjusted by now. TacOps agents notified their contact on the island to disable targeted streetlights that morning and to delay attempts by personnel to assess any damage and to not act on any calls from homeowners until the next morning, Friday, the 29th of July.

Cappello pulled out the felony warrant from the glove compartment. He waved it a couple of times.

The faint light went off from those windows across the street. A moment later, Cappello saw a bright disc moving along the sidewalk through his side window. A woman, about 40, was on the same side of the street as the house that went dark. She was returning home holding a short leash with a Chihuahua attached to it and a plastic bag. Cappello watched her. She was slim, wearing a close-fitting, one-piece, magenta sports garment. Cappello had noticed her when she first left her house several minutes earlier. He had noticed how the headlights illumined her shape from several angles. She walked toward the last house across the street. The dog halted and flinched, barking in Cappello's direction.

"You suppose that nervous rodent is talking to us? Aye, Cappello, maybe it's expecting a salute?"

"Quiet."

The dog found a spot and the woman stood, waiting. She thought she heard talking from the parking lot, then silence, while watching a pair of faint headlights, coming from the other end of the bridge. She turned toward the origin of the voices she heard and spotted the Cooper and the outline of the police bumper-grill guards. She bent over, pointed her light near the dog to see where to close the jaws of her pooper-scooper; sealed the plastic bag, picked up her pet and turned toward her house, then back at the Cooper. She walked away, keeping her flashlight down.

Cappello said, "I suppose that animal wouldn't be worth a dime if it didn't bark. It neglected to when she walked by the first time. It had other matters more pressing, maybe like my turgid bladder."

While he said these things, Cappello recalled the sequence of the woman's movements: first the Cooper, then the house and then back to the Cooper.

"She made us," Cappello said.

"Not because of me."

"No blame, and don't call it a rodent—my wife Josephine loves them and I got her one for her last birthday." Cappello played that scene over. "Do you think that woman and the dog know the suspects? If she and it does, she could tip them off, right? It may be a long shot."

"That's one hell of a long shot."

"Maybe we should check her out. See if she's got a Facebook page."

"You're the boss."

Cappello played the scene over and over.

"Did you notice, Reese, the way she looked at the passenger-side window, toward us? I did—of the thoughtful way she took in the house, and then, as if she were adding up all these facts, how she looked one more time in our direction. It all boils down to something."

Cappello brought the window down and took a long breath. "Check her for wants."

Reese pulled out the mobile data unit from a compartment in the middle of the convertible. He opened the federal database while Cappello brought up a satellite map on his cell. He dropped to street level and found the house number and gave it to Reese.

After a minute, Reese added, "NCIC says a Jenifer Stevens lives there."

"Description."

"Oceanian American, five-seven, 138, brunette with brown eyes."

"And?"

"She got a speeding ticket in 2007 on Route 26, in Portland. That's it."

"What about wants? And, that ticket. How fast was she going?"

"Eighty-three and no wants."

"Nothing else?"

"Negative. Anybody who picks up after a Chihuahua in this bosky neighborhood... Ms. Stevens is either very clean or very not clean."

"You saw her turn away, then turn back?"

"No."

"Well, I got to where I am because I notice the details. If you want to stay out of Cyber, you got to do better at noticing the details, too."

# 21

## The Stakeout on the Edge of Forever

CAPPELLO STILL THOUGHT THAT JENIFER STEVENS WAS A PERSON OF IN-TEREST because of something that Jones had told him. He watched the new cycle of lights and moving vehicles, while doing what experience had taught him to do.

Reese said, "I just looked up Ahmad Jones. It says here that he went missing during Super Bowl 40 and hadn't been stateside until last Thursday. He was in some country, South Africa, then Afarland, off the coast of East Africa."

"Yes, I know all about it. Jenifer... Stevens, Mark?"

Reese knew something was different. Cappello hadn't called him by his first name since they met a few weeks prior.

"Michael?" Reese countered.

"Jones wrote in his report that there was a chance the robbers would change their plans, due to a third party's involvement at the last minute. He called it a *Translation of Light.*"

"A translation of light?"

"In that chart, the Moon, allegedly Jenifer Stevens, in its transit through the Zodiac, forms a square with one planet, then conjoins a second planet. So, the light of the first planet, in this case Saturn (our joint task force), gets entangled with the second planet, Neptune (the bank robbers), by the Moon's motion. The Moon's movement is an indicator of how a thing develops—it's a timing device, like the minute hand on a clock face. The two planets show the types of conditions we can expect to encounter before we nab these bastards. Jones said to be prepared for a new player at the last minute who would lead us to them. He also said the robbers would certainly pass over that bridge but maybe not the way we'd expect them to."

"How else?"

"In the horary chart, the Moon would first square Saturn in the Tenth—that's the law. The way I figure, Jenifer, who is represented by the Moon and who just saw our federal vehicle, may be pointing us out to the robbers, as represented by the conjunction to the second planet, Neptune, the planet of deception. If you remember, it's the co-ruler of the robber's Seventh House."

"What the, what? This op is going to go bust and me with it—"

Cappello talks over his partner, slowly, "Everything Jenifer did when she showed up with that dog has meaning, for me, in the context of the astrological chart."

"But—"

"SHE'S—she's, going to lead us to them!"

Silence.

"A light had gone off in her house and she wasn't in it, which means that someone, or more than one person is inside. Jones said that a third party may enter the picture—a woman because the Moon rules women—and the Moon does form an angle with Saturn. That's us, the law, and then it moves forward in the Zodiac to conjoin Neptune, bringing us and them together, entanglement, on this day, around this time. Reese, this is it."

Reese took a deep breath.

"Do you like *Star Trek*?"

"Are you?... Of course! I'm a Trekkie"

"Do you remember the show about Edith Keeler?"

"You mean, *uh,* the one called, *The City on the Edge of Forever*"?

"That's the one! All right then. McCoy goes through the time portal ahead of Kirk and Spock. They meet Edith Keeler who acts, in astrological terms, as a Translator of Light because she first meets Kirk and Spock, then McCoy. In Quantum Physics, she's about to engineer a type of quantum entanglement, joining all three together."

"Yeah."

"So, at the time, Edith never mentions to Kirk that she met McCoy. In

191

other words, she didn't translate the light yet, until when she and Kirk are on their way to the movies, which is when she mentions McCoy to Kirk."

With verve, Reese chimes in, "Then Spock appears and then McCoy shows up from across the street."

"Bad-ass right. You see, she was like the Moon that brought Kirk, Spock and McCoy together by contacting each one in their turn. So, the Moon (Jenifer) in Jones' horary chart first contacts Saturn (us) by transit and then to Neptune (the robbers)."

Reese reaches for his drink and realizes he finished it. "Okay but doesn't Edith Keeler die in the end?"

"Nobody is going to die on this op. Plus Jones didn't mention anything about a casualty, or casualties."

"So, Jenifer Stevens is like Edith Keeler, bringing us to the bank robbers?"

Cappello used the glasses to study the house that Jenifer Stevens entered.

"You really think she's involved? There are thousands of women on this island."

"Well, in the short time Jones has been around, he's gotten us to this stage in the game of cops and robbers."

"But we're not cops."

"Mark, I play the role of your superior. I have shared the facts with you, observable facts, I may add. You play the role of my partner. Now, just cut me some slack."

"Okay. What do you mean by this stage in the game? I haven't seen any indication that your intel is sound. The FBI uses science to catch the bad guys, just saying."

"We've got lots of manpower out there, Reese."

Reese rubbed his beard and pulled at his mustache. "What if this is nothing but blue smoke? This guy, sir, I mean, shit, come on."

Reese checked his watch again. Cappello drank the last of his coffee and leaned against the front seat cushion.

"I can't piss and I'm reaching my rambling limit."

"Rambling?"

Cappello said, "Are you listening?"

"Sir?"

"I asked you here for critical support on this one, because you're good."

Cappello waited for that last comment to sink in and paused until Reese, a newbie, appeared satisfied with himself. Cappello, after all, was a veteran law enforcement professional who had directed FBI field offices in three states: New York, Ohio, and now, Washington.

"Really," Cappello said, "you indeed have the physique of a Safety and you know how to tactically drive a car, but my partner is sick. He's built like Dick Butkus and he has brains as well, ready to learn new things. If you're biased against new ideas, then maybe you should've chosen racecar driving. An agent must have an open mind to test out theories and unusual domains of information-gathering over several years and be willing to embrace new paradigms if they are viable, and especially when they have a history of success, and if they lead to captures. Jones' intel has those attributes. That's all."

Cappello never looked at Reese while he spoke but kept his eyes between the bridge and the house.

"My glutes need a break. And I've gotta pay my water bill. Oh, God." Cappello lifted his dark-blue dockers and stepped out into the quiet drizzle. He left for two reasons. One was to empty his bladder, which would allow him to stretch; the other was to give himself and his partner a few moments alone.

He walked back from the wall of evergreens, stepped in and shut the door.

"My grandfather was Italian and my grandmother was from Addis Ababa in Ethiopia. They fell in love while he and his unit set up shop there in her country from 1936 to 1941. No one knew about the affair until they fled Ethiopia, when the emperor, Haile Selassie I, returned. In all the excitement they managed to make it to the states, to New York. Anyway, that's how I got my last name."

Reese stared at Cappello. "Okay, it's your show."

"As I'm quarterbacking this drive, I expect to absorb all responsibility for the outcome. It's 12:10. Put your mind on this game. Let's exit the Cooper, make it to that freaking house and see what the hell Ms. Stevens is up to."

Reese's breathing accelerated.

"All units: quarterback's in shotgun." Cappello said.

Cappello and Reese exited the Cooper with a splash into the water and onto the deteriorating asphalt, the grass, and the dirt. They moved north along the side of the road in the same direction the store owner had taken. After fifty feet they waited until the road was empty, then sprinted across Route 20 donning their FBI jackets—an apt symbol for the planet Saturn. They drew their weapons. Jenifer Stevens' house was a dark-blue, one-story with white window panes and shutters. The Chihuahua started barking long before they came within two hundred feet of the house.

Reese was more relaxed now that he was moving. "Did the astrologer say anything about dogs?"

"No. Quiet."

Reese moved close to Cappello and whispered, "That's how I even out. I'll head west between these two sets of pines and clear the back."

Cappello looked at him sternly. "Head on a swivel. No one gets hurt on this op."

Jenifer Stevens' house was separated from another ranch house, to its left, by a line of pine trees. Cappello ran across Stevens' lawn, crouched and looked inside the left-front window through a space underneath the lowered shade. Inside, the living room had dark hardwood floors. Cappello followed a patch of light all the way to a barely opened door, then checked out the kitchen island to the right. He looked at his watch as two bulging eyes suddenly peered through the space under the shade. Cappello's startle reflex ended in the same second it started. Someone called the dog. Its big eyes withdrew as it scampered along the patch of light and disappeared.

Reese kept his weapon close to his torso, took deliberate steps, conscious of each one. His heart felt like it was smacking blood through his arteries. He had mastered building-clearance tactics at the Training Academy. His movements were honed to the point where he could execute them unconsciously, but his extremities were weakening, making him unstable. He noticed the open garage attached to the house. The door was open.

*Was it an invitation? Maybe Jenifer Stevens left it open or opened it. Or maybe the bank robbers did it, whom Jenifer could have forewarned. But why would they do that? What if this was all wrong and Cappello's intel was inaccurate? But what if whoever was inside, knew that scores of law enforcement personnel would be coming. Maybe Jenifer did leave it open.*

These thoughts plagued Reese but he moved through them, testing their logic. He had no more time to equivocate.

Reese noticed the garage's entry door leading to the inside. He ducked in and walked sideways. He got to the window of a black Ford SUV. Looked inside. The engine was cold. He cleared it. When he got to the back door that led into the house, he put his ear to it. He heard several male voices coming from his right. He turned around to look out through the garage-door opening in case someone followed him inside. The dog was still on edge. Reese didn't hear Jenifer's voice. He tried the doorknob. It wasn't locked. The sound of drizzle faded as he went in.

Cappello saw Reese's silhouette as he was crossing the plane between the kitchen and the living room. As Reese got closer, he heard the men talk of crossing the bridge and leaving Washington. A mirror was across the floor, inside the bathroom. He stayed concealed, using the mirror's reflection to see into the room. He also heard the word *elections* coming from a stout man with freckles. The presidential elections took place last November. But why would these dangerous characters mention an election now? Reese's mind was racing. He saw the empty space near the window shade, figured Cappello was looking at him, and circled his raised fist.

Outside, and crouching against the house in the light rain, Cappello says, "Commander Smith, four stars are at the north end, inside the first house on State Route 20, a ranch, dark blue with white shutters."

In less than three minutes, two SWAT units of five men armed with assault rifles appeared out of the darkness. They rallied around Cappello. Smith arrived and signaled for the units to circle around to the back of the house. He then kneeled to Cappello's left, who kept his eyes on Reese.

"Special Agent Reese is our point," Cappello whispered, "He's inside wearing his jacket."

"Copy," Smith said sub-vocally. He was ready for Cappello to give the go-ahead.

Reese saw four men reflected off the bathroom mirror, which was diagonally opposite the kitchen and to the right of the inside front entrance. The four men were holed up. White, average height, early thirties, clean-shaven and well-groomed. Not your average-looking felons. They were checking the sights and the mags of their weapons, while they waited for a certain time to exit the house.

"Good work," the stout man with freckles said.

They were organized and moved in a regimented way. They had changed their appearance. When they robbed the last time they all had facial hair. Jenifer was sitting in a chair at the far corner of the bedroom opposite a window, holding the Chihuahua. She was reading something. The mirror also reflected her position off to the left. Reese could make out all five people in that one room. Jenifer was away from the kill zone.

"Stand by."

The SWAT team commander waited for Cappello to give the final go-ahead. Cappello pulled the warrant out of one of his leg pockets. Reese waited for the dog to start barking. When it did, he waved his hand forward and walked across the floor. The rain had stopped a minute before. Reese opened the front door, just a crack. Cappello saw the door move and nodded at the SWAT commander.

"This is Smitty," he whispered, "all units to the first house on State Route 20, at the north end. Suspects are inside. This is what we trained up for."

The two units moved around the back and entered single-file like a snake and took positions. Armed and ready, one unit went through the garage doorway to the back and cleared the rooms. The other unit moved through the kitchen and entered the living room, where Reese was standing. The units waited for the raid order. Everyone had an earpiece. No words were spoken, just hand signals. The robbers weren't aware of anyone inside. The dog kept barking.

On the Whidbey Island side, state and local police, along with SWAT, converged on the house. There were no lights and no sirens. Others sped across the bridge from the Fidalgo Island side, the undercover tourists and backpackers, too.

Two other SWAT units entered through the garage. Still, the felons were too busy talking, and not aware of what had gathered just a few feet beyond the doorway. There were at least 17 men inside the house, behind the interior wall of the bedroom. They took up all the space in the living room like a crowded elevator. They had on masks and goggles.

One SWAT unit, some Fed agents and U.S. Marshals filed underneath the south bedroom window, which was diagonally across from where Jenifer Stevens was seated.

Next came the bullhorn's ear-piercing sound: "DEAR BANK ROBBERS, YOU ARE SURROUNDED BY FIFTY OFFICERS OF THE FBI, SWAT AND UNITED STATES MARSHALS."

The SWAT unit threw a flash-bang into the bedroom as they breached the door. The announcer kept talking in real time while SWAT was bursting in: "HANDS UP! DROP TO YOUR KNEES. THERE ARE FIFTY OF US AND FOUR OF YOU. DON'T PLAY THE PERCENTAGES. YOU'LL LOSE." Then the sirens and flashing lights were heard and seen all around the house for added effect.

The four felons obeyed. Immediately. They each put their Smith & Wesson M&P on the bed, before compliance. The U.S. Marshals could see everything through the blinds. Jenifer Stevens and the Chihuahua got on the ground. She was hysterical with tears. The Chihuahua was running but wasn't getting anywhere while she was holding it. It was now a bundle of highly agitated nerves, on top of its natural nervous tendencies.

"GET ON THE FLOOR NOW!"

"ON THE FLOOR! HANDS. SHOW ME YOUR HANDS BEHIND YOUR HEAD. DO IT NOW!"

"DON'T MOVE! Commander, the four stars are in custody. The four stars are in custody."

Cappello checked his watch. It was 12:13. The four robbers and Stevens were cuffed and pulled out of the house. A white bus pulled into the driveway to the left of it. Several pictures were taken of the four men in custody. Lots of officers wanted to be included but Cappello wanted to wrap this up, so the men were marched outside and shoved into the white bus. Stevens, the last one to board, was held by the elbow.

Cappello shouted, "Smitty?"

"Yeah, Cap?"

"I need a word with this suspect, alone."

"Sure thing, Cap." Smith led her out of the bus and met Cappello near the front door.

"Hey, good job, Cap."

"Thanks."

Cappello looked at his watch, then at her. Like the NCIC database stated, she was a brunette, about 5'7". Cappello thought she was Hawaiian.

"I won't beat around the bush, so how old are you, Ms. Stevens?"

She was still wearing her Magenta outfit. "Thirty-three."

"Where were you born?" He knew the answer, based on the information from the NCIC. It was a lie-detector question to set up a baseline for other questions. Plus, he liked the sound of her voice. It was even and soft. The huge lights, powerful luminescence, revealed an attractive woman.

"In Portland."

"Portland, what?"

"Oregon."

"What about your parents?"

"My parents are from Maui."

Cappello proceeded to the important question: "What were those men doing in your house?"

She moved her hands, slowly, like pistons, looked at her handcuffs, sobbing. Cappello waited for her to respond as the drizzle started again and upgraded to rain.

"Damn it, Washington, enough with the rain already," Cappello said. It looked like Christmas came early. Over 15 cars and SUVs were scattered along the road, with the white bus in the driveway. A long line of vehicles, formed on each side of the bridge. Deception Pass Bridge was inoperable.

Stevens said, "They came in this morning and took over my house. They told me to do what I usually do so no one would suspect anything. I saw your car but they said that they would have a gun on me. I wanted to run to it. You must have been in it. I figured the law was inside but I was scared. They'd been watching me and 'knew my routine,' they said."

"What is your routine?" Stevens took a beat to answer.

"I'm a Travel Agent, I have a home-based business. I walk my dog at specific times but am inside most of the time—"

"Jenifer—Ms. Stevens—I suspect you're not involved with those guys. Now, look me in the eye and tell me you weren't." Cappello looked into her olive-brown eyes.

"No, I wasn't."

"You'll be asked many questions by a specialist. Just explain what happened, the way you did to me. Keep it simple, just the facts. Okay. Just a precaution, we'll secure a warrant to search your house, in case those bad guys left something that we could use: like a schedule of bank heists, or names and addresses of associates, fingerprints, you know, usual incriminating stuff." He was watching her movements as he talked. Her eyes darted at the mention of each item.

"Okay. What is your name again?"

"Mike Cappello. I'm a special agent for the FBI. By the way, do you have a Facebook account?" Just then the Chihuahua ran through the legs of law enforcement personnel to its owner. She smiled and Cappello grabbed up the dog.

"Her name is Selena."

"Selena?"

"Yes. The Greek word for the Moon."

Cappello said nothing, for a beat. He had a feeling about her.

"Would you like me to take care of Selena 'til you come back? My wife has a Chihuahua."

"That would be nice, Mr. Cappello and... no, I don't have a Facebook account."

Cappello wasn't taken in by her voice anymore; now, with Selena on the scene, he knew that she played a role with the four felons.

"No Facebook, well, that's too bad. I'll see you when you've been debriefed. If everything checks out, you'll be able to return to your home by early morning. Here's my card."

'Thank you."

"Commander Smith will escort you into the bus. Smith, who heard everything, walked up to Stevens. "This way Miss."

Cappello looked at his watch again as the SWAT truck rolled out of the driveway and headed south over the bridge. The time was 12:21 a.m. He nodded at Smith who was coming toward him.

"Smitty? Will you please get the team to search every inch of that house. I'll get the AG to email a warrant, in the next hour or two. Anything unusual, call me."

"Copy that."

"When the warrant arrives, have your team look for any books on astrology. Not the sensational stuff; I mean books with complex mathematical techniques, election charts, horary charts, astrocartography, etc."

Reese had walked out the front door and stood with Cappello, while he and Smith talked. He was breathing heavily. He was shaken and attempting to hide it.

Smith said, "Okay, Cap." Turning to Reese, "Good job Mark. Cap, I'll notify you if we see anything fitting that description."

"Tell you what, tape it up. No one in. I'll be back in a couple with my partner and we'll check it ourselves. Orders to not touch anything until I arrive."

"Okay, Cap."

Reese said, "What are election charts?"

"Where did you hear that, Reese?"

"When you said it to Smitty, I heard the word *election* used by one of those men, the one with apparent UV exposure. You were right."

"An election chart is cast for a moment in time that is considered propitious enough to begin something. The suspect could have plotted the timing of those bank heists beforehand. Thanks, Reese. What you just said to me may get us to the bottom of this case, quick. Jones was right. Those men were going to go south on Deception Pass Bridge, just like he said they would. Let's get back to Seattle and to our wives. By the way, Reese, you were correct."

"What?"

"Dogs; the Moon represented an animal—in addition to the woman suspect—the third part, the translation-of-light. Its name is Selena, which is Greek for the Moon."

"Damn."

Cappello holds Selena. He feels the quickness of her breath. He knows there is something else about Jenifer Stevens. He has one day left, before his three-month vacation and retirement, to find out more. The two agents walk off the lawn, across Route 20, dirt, grass and deteriorating asphalt, and get inside the Cooper.

Reese shuts the door. "I'd like to meet this astrologist."

Selena barked, wagged her tail, and then got quiet on Cappello's lap.

"Now, you've got two. Why are you holding it for her?"

Silence.

"So, what else besides *election* did you hear?" Cappello asked.

"Just something about crossing the bridge and elections, and about leaving Washington. Also, she was looking at a paper."

"Elections? You mean the midterm elections?"

"I don't know, I just heard the word *election*."

"Plural or singular?"

"Plural. Why?"

"Reese, there's more to Jenifer Stevens and I know she's dirty. What paper?"

"I couldn't tell; it should be inside. So, you're certain, huh?" Reese started the car.

"Very... Shit, my three-month vacation was supposed to start tomorrow... I have to talk to Jones; we may have a suspect that uses the stars to aid crooks."

200

# 22

## Reemergence

WHEN AHMAD JONES LANDED AT CHICAGO O'HARE, early Thursday morning on the 20th, his presence in cyberspace sent a wave of strange excitement throughout the federal law enforcement community. Since February of 2006, much of the usual Bureau gossip had centered around finding the answer to what had happened to him—whether he was dead or alive. Bureau personnel pitched the question in many of the nation's field offices, resident agencies, and some legal attaché offices around the world, too.

In the backyard of a house near Brentwood Court in South Bend, Indiana, a special agent from the FBI's violent crimes division of the CID positions some more hot dogs on his charcoal grill with a pair of tongs. Joking with his fellow agents he says, "Maybe Ahmad Jones had secreted himself away, inside some African hotbed, getting a depth-analysis of the political scene, using the stars."

A Tactical Intelligence Analyst from the FBI's Cyber Division lab in San Francisco was a few yards from his workstation. He was facing the ocean. He had just finished a threat assessment and was on a break. A cobalt-blue color permeated the large room of over fifty people. There were several door-sized windows, with slightly tinted views of the outside; there were plasma screens, huge monitors, and scores of computers. The FBI's seal was visible on all four of the TIA's monitors. He walked to a colleague, who was standing in front of one of the door-sized windows, sipping coffee and admiring the sparkling waters of the ocean.

She asked, "Hey Charlie, what about Jones appearing all over the Internet? Where could he have been for so long?"

In a sarcastic tone, he said, *"Ah...* him. It's anyone's guess. Probably retired to some small settlement near a sacred lake in a far-western mountain village near the tower of Chun. Didn't like retirement and decided to get back into the shit."

She almost spilled her coffee while laughing. The TIA unscrewed the cap on his water bottle while looking through the plexiglass at the bridge a half-mile away.

A Deputy Special Agent in Charge from Central Texas left her office to chair a meeting, two flights up. She overheard the question concerning Jones while charging through the narrow-angled hallway behind two other female agents. Reflective warm-beige floors, several large cherrywood doors, bright wall sconces, and northern lighting also coming from the ceiling reduced that feeling of moving through a cold and impersonal government installation. Concerning Jones, the DSAC said, with a purposely exaggerated dialect, "Dang! Are y'all kiddin' me? Don't you know he'd set up residence stateside—right here under y'all's noses, since 2006, which means you two have come up short, real short." She walked in-between the two women as they quickened their pace through the hallway. Her high heels added a staccato beat to her step. The two agents kept up and all three powered-through the corridor.

The DSAC turns to both women in succession. "And y'all call yourselves intelligence analysts, special agents? Can we move on to more important stuff?"

She picked up speed and left them. The elevator was a few feet past J. Edgar Hoover's portrait. The doors parted and the DSAC stepped inside and picked up on an old discussion with one of her peers. The rest of the small crowd in the elevator stood straighter. The two bemused agents held back their guffawing as they neared the elevator until the doors closed and the next two floor numbers lit up.

The nation's Federal Domestic Intelligence and Security Service had no papers on Jones' eleven-year disappearance, which a few close friends of his called a deliberate concealment. They were correct in their assessment. Jones accomplished it with 41 cell phones, an alias, and probably luck. Two days earlier, on July 18, no present-day electronic resources could turn up a digital ID on him. The most current information was eleven years old, which was when Jones disappeared from Ford Field while under surveillance.

The agents that were stationed at Ford Field during Super Bowl 40 couldn't explain what they saw or didn't see. Some of them retired; others turned in their gold badges and ended up in the private sector. Some did consulting work, executive protection—the usual stuff. A few wrote books about their work in the Bureau. Nowadays, most divisions wouldn't spare time or human resources to analyze Jones' file. But there was one out of thousands of agents who had a mild obsession with him. She was the head of the Resident Agency in Kaskaskia, Illinois. She still wondered how he had managed to slip out of sight in front of federal agents. But there were caseloads requiring active investigation. Evidentiary consequences led special agents on trips to the AG's office, especially the big cases—a "special" that gets bumped to the top of the heap.

Jones' file wasn't that special anymore. It had descended far below the summit of cases. No more could intelligence analysts and special agents use up office time to ferret out the appearance of a new lead, inspect old information, or question the agents at the scene for new information. They would use The Astrologist as a foil if it elevated the mood. The signs of the times, including a budget north of eight billion, has since directed Bureau personnel to concentrate more on actionable intelligence, to *check* and *mate* more criminals before new federal crimes, attacks on U.S. soil, or major altercations on the world stage could happen. The 2016 elections engendered a flood of information.

There was one special agent from a field office on the west coast who was frustrated by the endless array of caseloads. "There are crimes, death and ultimatums," he said, "approaching us from every angle of the compass. They're just suspended in a solution, enveloping the globe. Every particle is a potential flashpoint!" The agent loosened his tie in front of his co-workers. He snapped up from the light-metal chair and ran out of the cafeteria. His three fellow agents, seated at a round metal table, acknowledged the truthfulness of his explosion. They hurried after him. They all had been there. What he felt wasn't burnout; it was the perceived conclusion that there's no end in sight for the need for law enforcement, with lots of perceived futility sprinkled on it. His request for a leave of absence for the remainder of his shift, though, was denied. For him, a little bantering about The Astrologist would've been a welcome diversion.

With tons of pressure from the growing wave of threats facing the United States, including investigations into government corruption, Russia, North Korea, Syria, private server security and emails—the novel assumptions surrounding The Astrologist and his whereabouts after eleven years were still a theme of discussion for professional agents, even some trainers at Quantico—that is, until Ahmad Jones landed in Chicago.

Infused with an atmosphere of thick secrecy around him, Jones appeared on every major intelligence database in the law enforcement universe: U.S. CUSTOMS AND BORDER PROTECTION, the OFFICE OF BIOMETRIC IDENTITY MANAGEMENT, and the U.S. EMBASSY AND CONSULATE, to name a few. He had two major reasons for coming into the United States. During an interrogation, an FBI special agent would learn the first reason. Then, after a shooting, would learn part of the second.

If federal law enforcement personnel were eager to rehash the story of The Astrologist's disappearance, but advised to lay off the subject, what would those same men and women do upon hearing of his reappearance? The question would be answered soon.

When the second reason got out in the open, a couple of FBI Special Agents from Ohio would become aware for the first time that the reason Jones was here and what he was about to do would affect international relations, as well as generate a reassessment of the SOPs of all major U.S. intelligence agencies. Also, adjustments in U.S. foreign policy to the nation of Afarland would occur. Now, nine days later, on Saturday, July 29th, nothing short of a sensation would be presented in front of scores of millions of people, tonight at 7:00 pm EDT.

A special agent of the Bureau's Ohio Field Office informed the Special Agent in Charge of the Kaskaskia Resident Agency that he received unconfirmed intel of Ahmad Jones' whereabouts. Jones was at Mangala Park. He was wearing red sneakers, a white polo shirt, and beige khakis. Other details were provided.

The information he shared was designated actionable. The park was in a county under the SAC's jurisdiction. She assembled five out of her thirteen-person team to intercept him. Compared to some, hers was a relatively large resident agency; some RA's only have four or five staff members. She borrowed two from the fugitive squad and two from tactical; her partner made five. All the others were itching to get out of the office. The team of five was determined to take selfies with Jones—hard evidence—proof that they had discovered him first after more than a decade.

But the Kaskaskia RA had competitors who also caught Jones' blip on their radar.

# 23

## Huddle

NICK MARSHALL WAITED FOR THE RED VIPER to pull out. He eased the Caprice into the empty space under the shade and cut the ignition.

"It's 1251 hours," Marshall said to the three men inside. "Stay loose."

A shiny black Tesla Model S was parked behind them. In front, the men in the Caprice watched the taillights of a black Mercedes C350 backing in. The rear half of its front-left tire angled out and then gradually turned in. As Marshall and the men were checking their weapons, they heard the gear click; a few watched the Mercedes nudge forward and after it rolled ahead a bit, the Mercedes' tri-star trunk emblem grew larger by the second as its rear-end backed in to within a foot. A couple of the men checked the safeties on their pistols and secreted them into their nylon holsters at the ankle and small of the back. Marshall holstered his pistol in a specially crafted pants pocket. He checked the park grounds at his right, then looked at a picture that he'd taped to his dashboard.

The C350 had a wet mirror finish—its rear-end reflected the Caprice's grill and headlights. Two young men exited the car. They were tall, agile teenagers, wearing basketball shorts and sleeveless t-shirts. They ran past the Caprice toward the basketball court near the intersection. Flashing vehicle lights and key-fob chirping sounds followed. The line of all three black cars looked like the start of a funeral procession.

Jones is strolling down Mangala Park toward Treefold Avenue, talking on his cell phone. Marshall tightens the focus on his binoculars.

"Show time!" Marshall said. "There's our target. The op, is green." The men climb out of the vehicle at the park's south side. They adjust their clothing. Jones is leaving the park, heading toward the sidewalk. He glances to his right to take in the information presented by the Caprice, the black finish, the tinted windows, and the serious men getting out of it. He walks down the slope across the park at an even pace.

Jones listens to the heavy clunks of the sedan's steel doors being shut; first one, then two, then one-two. The four thuds carry a tone of inevitable threat, a percussive effect—plain metal on metal—stark, blunt and unambiguous. Not poetic, just menacing prose.

The four men divide themselves into two units. The first unit is comprised of three men: Marshall, the leader, is a former army sergeant. He is over six-two, at two-fifty—robust, all muscle, thick-necked, wearing mirror-coated sunglasses like highway patrolmen do.

Drew, a hippy-looking club bouncer from Austin, Texas, is of average height, with a wide goatee, steady light-brown eyes, and jet-black one-word tattoos over his huge biceps and triceps. His right bicep says, *Don't*, the left says, *Fuck*, the right tricep says, *With*, and the left one says, *Me and My Tats*. Hung, who is five-ten, is former Taiwan Special Forces. Each operative of the Alpha Unit weighs in at a minimum of two-forty, and wears magni-grip football gloves.

The second unit is one man, Peter, an Albanian, who is taller and bigger than the other three.

He wears black, which syncs up perfectly with the three black cars. He is motionless and ready, in his muscle t-shirt and slacks. He watches the whole park from the Caprice. His demeanor is like Robert De Niro's character, Neil McCauley, in the movie *Heat*. Serious as death. His presence and look are menacing. Drew and Hung are intimidated by him. Peter's job is, like an office manager's, to ensure that the op runs successfully.

Marshall, Drew and Hung move at a brisk pace onto the park grounds. Drew shoves his long hair away from his eyes. He traps a football between his torso and his left bicep. Their brisk pace becomes a stride. Hung, who is built like a Bolo tank, strides at Drew's left, carrying a small syringe hidden in his left palm. The protective cover is still on. Marshall, with the pocket holster, wears a black t-shirt, relaxed-fit jeans and a white Kangal cap. He's dressed like a golfer, casual, with his white Lugz sneakers. The three men start jogging toward the northeast to where Jones will be if he follows his present course.

Like a scene from an old Akira Kurosawa film, the sun overhead dims. There is thick cloud cover. Mars, the planet statistically biased toward force, severity and firearms, is conjoined Kaskaskia's meridian. A stern breeze sends a folded sheet of colored construction paper skittering over the grass.

# 24

## Boisterous Elements

MANGALA PARK'S NORTH SIDE WAS CUT OFF by an old chain-link fence. The fence was set between the park and a newly stamped gravel driveway. Both the fence and driveway ran parallel to each other for three blocks. The driveway was a rear-access service road for a line of stores and restaurants arranged along its east-west axis. At 12:56, a flashing blue light appeared behind the windshield of a black SUV after it turned left onto the gravel road three blocks west of the park. It traveled eastward at a stealthy 10 mph.

Beyond the line of stores and eateries were several blocks of townhouses, continuing northbound, from the fence. A concrete L-shaped walkway framed-off the park's south and east sides. A platoon of white ash trees framed the west. Behind the trees were two giant sandboxes, playground equipment, and close to a dozen kids under supervision. Some parents played with their children, making mud pies together, spotting them on the jungle gym, and pushing them on swings; some grownups just sat on the grass in the shade fooling with their electronic devices; others were sharing the latest gossip. The grounds of the planted space slanted upward to the west and the top of the slope.

Jones' feet hammered the hot and dry grass that crunched under his steps. The grass had been mowed that morning, was dew-moist, dark-green and fresh but now the green scent of all its organic compounds had evaporated off. It was stiff, and the smell of death scented the air. The clouds finished their pass over the sun, which sent a sheet of light over the scene. A kid snatched the meandering colored paper and folded it into an airplane. He took off, lifting it above his head as he ran to his playmates.

A huge flood of adrenaline poured into Jones' bloodstream, just as it did in the corridor of the Libyan hotel seven years ago. He was facing another spell of weak legs and unconsciousness, so he had to act. His clothing would keep his movements unrestricted, loose and agile. Jones was more than midway from the edge of the park grounds from two points: where the old chain-link fence was at his left to the north, and the same distance from Treefold Avenue, the main drag, ahead of him to the east.

A drunk couple sat on a dark-green bench a short distance from the row of ash trees at the crest of the hill. The drunken man, almost six feet, with a grizzled beard, and wearing a long, black windbreaker, spotted the four characters getting out of the car. He pegged them as civilian contractors, a hit squad that was after the man with the red sneakers, white polo and beige khakis. The drunk peeled himself off the bench while his girlfriend, who was leaning on his left shoulder, stretched out her petite body.

"Hey! You mens... ya butter leave that dude feller alone!"

Marshall, Hung, and Drew all turn at once without a break in their jogging pace. They move like a flock of birds, as one, when changing course. Peter, the Albanian, keeping watch by the Caprice, unfolds his arms and straightens to attention. He hears the derelict and keeps his eyes on him. He puts his fingers to his earpiece, expecting to hear updates from Marshall.

"Yeah, I'm yaking at choo! You, ya hear me? Hey, fellas... any of you spare some change? My old lady's hungra... er, sick. HEY, I'MMM GOIN'T' call the coppers. Got any weed?"

The drunk got set into a wide stance. He swayed back and forth and dug into his coat pocket for his cell. He rummaged around in the greasy left pocket, yanking the lining inside out. Underneath his coat, the waistline was bulky. He withdrew nothing but the flap with pulverized potato chips compressed into its inner seams, some of which sprinkled onto the grass. Ravens made a shrill sound when those chips landed—there were no worms or grasshoppers in sight. A few ravens landed nearby, edging closer to the food, like the three men closing in on their target. The drunk felt inside the other pocket, clutched his phone and pointed it at the hit squad, as if the act of pointing started the recording option.

"Focus on the target," Marshall said. The squad tried to appear natural. Drew donned a Chicago Cubs hat, and Hung wore the Bulls to match his shirt. Their intent was to dress casually but there was nothing casual about them. Their movements were too deliberate and intentional, a sharp contrast to the kids at play. Whatever their outfits were supposed to suggest was cancelled out by their demeanor. And so, the old proverb still stands—clothes don't make the man.

They passed the football back and forth while jogging past the middle of the park to where Jones would soon be. They had tactical wear underneath their outfits to reduce the imprint of their weapons.

Their assignment was to procure Jones, move him to the basement of an empty two-story building with a *For Lease* sign on the second-floor window, some 30 miles west of there, and to interrogate him. Upon acquiring satisfactory answers, they were then to dispose of him.

Marshall flanks to Jones' right. His strategy is to catch the ball and then throw it to Jones while rushing him, as if Jones is part of a drive. He expects the ball to hit him unprepared, to distract him, but if he catches it, he will sack him as if he were the quarterback, giving Hung enough time to use his syringe.

Several miles to the east, the rumbling engines of a jumbo jet get louder as it approaches the space above the park. It's heading west, inbound for final approach.

In addition to his height, Marshall is built like a left tackle, with broad shoulders, huge pecs and legs like tree trunks. He can move like Aaron Donald, the defensive tackle, can move. Fast and accurate. His momentum times his mass can certainly knock his target to the ground—hard. Hung is closing in fast behind. His assignment after the tackle is to shoot up Jones with a tranquilizer. Hung's red-and-black-plaid shirt is open down the middle; a silver crucifix hangs between his two tattoos. His left pec has a red dragon breathing golden fire toward the right pec, which displays a map of the Chinese mainland.

Drew's assignment is to grab the ball after Jones is down, throw it up, catch it, and throw it up again and catch it, in a repeating cycle. To onlookers, the scene will look like the man with the red sneakers sustained a minor injury, a sprained ankle maybe, or had the wind knocked out of him. That image will satisfy anyone as being the result of a football accident. "People get hurt playing football all the time—concussions and what have you, don't ya think?" That should be the reaction of the spectators in the park. Marshall and Hung, after the injection, will each place one of Jones' arms around their shoulders and drag him off to the car and Peter. No one will suspect foul play.

There are millions of dollars invested in this op. If they fall short of their objective, the people who hired them will give them nothing—part of the agreement. The people who hired them would put a foreign assassination team on it to make up for lost time—a more expensive option. They have international connections. The men of the first unit were each promised 1,150,000 dollars. The second unit, comprising Peter, gets 250,000 dollars. The men were admonished not to tell the others what their cut was. These were rugged men for hire. Jones was only six feet, with no chance against a single, let alone a four-man group, two of which are former military men. They were extremely motivated by the multi-million-dollar payday, making for the dangerous duo of a high-stakes payoff and tactically trained killers. Two-thirds of all these men's professional lives had been invested in hurting, maiming, or killing. In some jobs, the third option came first.

As the three men close in on their target, the wail of the jumbo jet's four engines fills the sky. On the gravel access road, the SUV sits low and steady, accelerating through the back lot. Its blue light pulsates, framed around by tinted windows. About 11 miles to the southwest at Park Avenue Beach on Chicago's south side, an unprecedented 25-foot wave comes in from Lake Michigan, smashing against the shoreline. It pounds parked cars and sets off alarms.

High winds, high waves, and even a jumbo jet reflect the violence that is about to drop down on the park grass.

# 25

## The Snap

DREW IS 45 DEGREES BEHIND JONES' RIGHT. Marshall is ahead of Jones, at 45 degrees to Jones' front right. Drew pitches the ball to Marshall who then throws a bullet pass to the target. Jones is at the apex of a wide triangle, with Marshall and Drew forming the base. When Marshall knocks him over, the whole thing will look like a tackle being made. The ball will be in plain sight.

Nice trick.

Moving from a jog to a sprint toward Jones, Marshall's molded cleats rack off patches of grass. But what Marshall hadn't anticipated, which will cost his team $3,700,000 plus new assignments, is that Jones played football.

Jones watches the crosshairs of the ball as he absorbs Marshall's bullet pass with his fingers. He pivots left and turns 180 degrees to the west, facing uphill to the platoon of ash trees. He grips the laces of the ball with his ring and pinky fingers and heaves it above his shoulder. He takes a hard step forward and squares his shoulders and body toward Hung. He releases the ball after bringing initial power from the ground through his pivot foot, which transfers through his thigh, which is then regulated by the torque coming from his waist, until it finally passes through his throwing arm, on down to the snap of his wrist.

There was a space of seven feet between the ball and Hung's head. The last thing he saw with his left eye was the crosshairs of a football, screening out everything in sight but itself.

*Crunch!* The football's pointed end plows through Hung's left eyeball, forcing it back into its socket. The ball bounces about four feet off the bones around the eye and the bridge of his nose. The weight of his falling body onto his knees is poignant. Final. One man down and on the disabled list—two men left in the game. Drew grunts in anger.

Before the men had gotten out of the Caprice, Marshall said to Drew sitting on the back seat, "Here's a rubber band. Tie your hair with it and tuck it under your cap. Just a suggestion."

"A suggestion, huh?" Drew never liked to take orders. Hated authority. "He was born recalcitrant," his parents told police, after he was arrested at age ten, for stabbing his teacher. His hair was below shoulder-length. He took the band and put it in his pocket. Marshall shook his head and didn't push the issue.

Drew, now facing Jones, rushed his front-left side. Jones back-pedaled and cut left toward Marshall who was closing in. He executed a slant right across Drew's own left side, grabbed and held onto his hair from the nape with his left hand, and with the other took a handful of skin under Drew's underarm and shoulder blade. Jones gripped, pinched and squeezed, crushing capillaries underneath Drew's flesh.

Drew squealed like a hamster; he was immobilized by pain and the threat of more if he tried to get away. If he moved his arms forward or moved his torso while his skin was compressed, it would be like pulling his skin away from a tightly closed vice. Jones clutched Drew's brown, wavy hair near the soft skin at the base of the neck, and with his forearm resting on the top of Drew's head, which he used as a fulcrum, he pulled. Another squeal became a blood-curdling scream.

Jones recalled his teacher's warning about anger, but these men were extremely dangerous professionals, so he could not be lenient. He would dispatch them impartially, however. Jones used Drew's hair and skin as handles and his body as a tackling sled and quickly closed the distance with Marshall.

Jones rammed Drew's body-sled into Marshall's chest. The pistol that was holstered on the small of Drew's back struck Marshall's solar plexus and dropped on the grass. The impact zapped the wind out of Marshall who doubled over on top of Drew. Hung had been screaming for some time now; blood spilled from his eye and nose.

The shadow of the jet's underbelly passed over the park grass and the fallen men. The waters of Lake Michigan calmed. The driver of the SUV with the blue light halted over the gravel, kicking up a bit of dirt underneath. The driver peered through the windshield and the chain-link fence at the three men crawling on the grass. Peter meandered near the edge of the park grounds.

"Red sneakers, beige khakis and white shirt heading due east. Also, add three men on the scene. Appears to have been trouble, some football game maybe," the driver of the SUV said.

"Copy that, Sparks. I'm two blocks away."

"Copy that, Agent Nolan."

Peter stared at Hung writhing on the grass. He had no reference to process what he had just seen. Jones never launched a punch or a kick. Peter tried to get enough momentum with his huge body to run fast enough to grab Jones, expecting to collect 250,000. Peter, though formidable, was just too slow. But he was going to salvage his cut. His intent was to singlehandedly capture Jones. The time was 12:58.

# 26

## Interception by an SSAC

PETER THOUGHT, AS HE RAN TO THE SCENE, *What a clumsy setup, a mock football game with meager tactical advantage. I would have just clobbered the target and brought him to the car. They should have left that play to the pros on the field.*

Peter stopped short. Jones was disoriented and a few feet from the sidewalk. A flashing blue light hit his eyes. It was heading south toward the park. No sirens, just a two-second wail. Hung was still screaming. Peter also saw the car that came with that blue light. It was a federal vehicle. He also saw several park patrons getting a fix on Hung.

The guardians of the kids on the swings and jungle gym heard the wail and stopped what they were doing. Marshall, still winded, looked back to the drunken man with the cell phone. He got to one knee and holstered Drew's weapon for him. He then withdrew his G19.

From the other side of the fence, FBI Special Agent Liam Sparks couldn't see Marshall's weapon from his angle; he just noticed the man with the Kangol hat on one knee, lifting his left arm and holding it steady. He didn't see his other arm or the Glock 19 in his right hand.

Marshall acquired his target. He had Jones in his sights and all he had left to do was pull, and his employer's problem would be over. But that was a last resort, and worth nothing if he didn't take Jones alive.

"Possible weapon being drawn. What are your orders?" Sparks asked.

Marshall aimed at the back of Jones' right knee. Considered his two associates' inability to quickly make it back off the park grounds and into the Caprice.

"Are you certain?" Agent Nolan responded.

Marshall lowered his weapon. He also considered the payoff if he wounded Jones and got him into the car. He raised his weapon a second time. Heard the two-second wail. He weighed the odds, was frustrated, then lowered and holstered his weapon.

"Negative." Sparks said.

"What's happening now?" Agent Nolan asked.

"That creep couldn't have called the FBI," Marshall said. He was mad as he lifted his sunglasses and stood up.

"Get up, Drew." Marshall pulled at his belt. Drew was dazed, the back of his neck was red. He got to all fours with Marshall pulling the back of his belt. He finally got on two feet, wobbly, like a baby just learning to walk. Peter arrived, and he and Marshall went to Hung. They each took an arm, dragging him back to the Caprice. Drew collected the ball.

Sparks said, "There's no threat. I can see his hands. Looks like they were playing a game of ball."

"Copy that."

A black, unmarked Crown Victoria with government plates pulled in on the south side across the street from where the black Caprice was parked. The scene was looking more and more like a funeral procession getting underway. But there would be no corpse. The men inside heard Nolan and Sparks on the radio and were ready.

Marshall staggered to the car. Hung was complaining in Taiwanese. The tinted window of the Crown Vic slid down. Hung's angry words carried to the adults near the sandbox.

The man behind the wheel of the Crown Vic asked, "Is he all right?"

Marshall said, "He'll be okay. He had a football accident." Drew lifted the football so the men in the car could see it. The window slid back up.

"Shut up, Hung! You're attracting too much attention. Man up!" Marshall said. Peter opened the door and he and Marshall shoved Hung inside.

Sparks and his partner remained parked along the rear access road on the north side of the fence. They observed the civilians in the park, looking out for their safety. The last vehicle, a black Charger, the one with the flashing blue light and wail sound, came up along the curb after cutting in front of a parked minivan. It skidded a bit then stopped in front of Jones. The people in the park were acutely aware of all the black vehicles. Tensions grew. Parents collected their children off the swings and jungle gym and rushed to their cars. Some hurried out the gate, crossing in front of the parked SUV, on the gravel back lot to their homes. Everybody saw the man with the red sneakers stumbling to the car. They suspected that the stumbling man's civil rights were about to be breached. Cell phones, many of them, started recording.

Jones is a stone's throw from curious motorists slowing down to catch a peep before moving past the small crowd. There is a fleet of spectators with their cell phones out and Jones hears the noise of subdued but somewhat discernable comments.

"That guy beat up those men in seconds—that was really something! I saw the whole thing," an Indian man said on his phone. A few onlookers turned around and nodded. One of them, a mild-mannered guy, with long blond hair, standing beside the Indian man said, "I'd remain silent about that if I were you, unless you want to be questioned as a witness." The man continued his account in his native Tamil.

"He's handsome," a thirty-something woman said. A dirty-blonde with a tattoo of a pink heart on her left foot and a flaming arrow on the other. "He could just take me out anytime!"

Jones clambered his exhausted body to the curb, out of the hot sun, away from the litany of speculation, and stood before the standard-issue government vehicle. He had handled three men inside the park—one was probably maimed for life.

The public green area was peppered with four menacing black vehicles—three of them with oscillating blue eyes, chrome grills for mouths, and federal tags. Their appearance was contrary to the park's serenity and community health objectives, funded by ballot measures and private/public partnerships—tax dollars.

The passenger-side window of the black Charger came down revealing an attractive woman with captivating blue-gray eyes. Jones saw her eyes first. She had on dark-blue cargo pants and a short-sleeved, black-flannel shirt. Her duty weapon was holstered below her right shoulder. He guessed that she had a connection to eastern Europe, maybe Russia, maybe the Ukraine. He also noticed an African connection. Jones got all that information after a few seconds. He tried to get a look at the driver. Her driver wore a sleeveless athletic shirt and tactical pants. He was talking to the agents in the other vehicles, advising them to maintain their positions. He had a look of haste. Something happened here, but what? He thought that the surveillance camera at the corner of Treefold and South Boulevard would furnish enough information about it.

The woman spoke with a brisk pace, bathed in soft, yet firm tones, "What is your name, sir?"

"Ahmad Jones, ma'am."

"Mr. Jones, please get in."

Jones opened the back door and climbed in. Agent Nolan got out, closed the door after him, and stepped back in. The driver pulled away from the curb, executed a U-turn, and sped away north. The crowd with the cell phones couldn't make out what they just captured. The man wasn't cuffed or manhandled or outnumbered but climbed into the back seat all by himself.

Jones is getting weaker and colder. He stops trying to place the driver's origin. The AC switch is bumped up to max. The frigid temperature inside the sedan mingles with the blended odor of leather holsters and gun oil. It is a grave smell for a grave moment. The temperature outside is north of 86. Jones went from one extreme to another.

Nolan swiveled counter-clockwise to face the man she had heard stories about. Jones slid over behind the driver.

"I'm Senior Special Agent Brenda Nolan and my partner here is Special Agent Alejandro Dumont. We're from the Kaskaskia Resident Agency."

Dumont got a quick glimpse of Jones through the rearview mirror. Sunshine streamed into the car in flashes. "It's a pleasure to meet you, sir," Dumont said. Nolan looked at her partner with no expression on her face.

"A friend of yours, Special Agent Jack Peterson, called me there. He requested us to pick you up. We should debrief you."

Jones voice was weakening. "Thank you, Agents Nolan and Dumont... I have a flight in a couple of hours. I should get to my hotel to gather my personal effects... Radisson, near the airport, please."

"Okay, we can do the debrief after you collect your things. It won't take long. Dumont, let's take Mr. Jones to his hotel."

Jones leans heavily on the backrest. Electrical output from his brain reduces to less than half; his self-awareness recedes. The world outside is staying outside. His body-engine cranks a little, then tentatively, like the clicking sounds of a weak battery. Then Jones' senses finally flip inward.

"Are you all right, Mr. Jones? You look ex—haus—ted." That is the last word Jones hears. His torso follows the tilt of his head, which slams onto the bench seat. His last thought, with little electronic power, still makes it across the abyss of awareness. He whispers, "Marakie... have to reach, Ohi... O..."

His arms and legs dangle over the edge of the seat's leather welting. The ring on his right forefinger has the center stone facing palm side. It is a ring of unusual craft and style—a thick, red-gold band with panels of yellow diamonds.

There's a group of stars, called Chitra, in the constellation of Libra. Its symbol is a brilliant jewel, fashioned by the celestial architect—according to the old Sanskrit writings. The star group's meaning relates to the planet Mars and stands for the warrior endowed with grand resources. That portion of the sky was on Kaskaskia's local horizon when Jones, wearing a brilliantly tooled ring, had pressed into service a minute part of his combative talent. It was 12:59.

Six agents had canvassed Mangala Park's north, east and south sides—seeing to it that the man, known in certain circles as The Astrologist, would be secured as he stepped out of the park onto the pedestrian path on Treefold Avenue.

Agent Nolan, born of a Russian father and African-American mother, is five-ten with rich, dark-brown hair. Her dreamy eyes and soft features convey the look of a supermodel—with a badge and pistol. A police lieutenant from Chicago's Cook County encountered her during a sting operation. He called her (off the record) the quintessential man-magnet and said (on the record) that Nolan was a highly skilled law enforcement officer. Today was her twelfth day as Supervisory Special Agent in Charge of the Bureau's Resident Agency in Kaskaskia, Illinois, just three miles north of Mangala's Park. Eleven months earlier, she was serving as Special Operations Supervisor for U.S. Customs and Border Patrol Protection in Texas.

Three women, all mothers, left through the gate with their kids. One of them, who was expecting, said, "Did you see those two drunks near those trees? They've been engaged in such depravity for the last two weeks." The other two women turned to catch a glimpse of the couple.

She said, "I've called the police and they haven't lifted a finger to see about those two. You'd think these cops at the park would take advantage of a two-for-one deal and arrest those drunks.

One woman, a retired banker with her grandkids, said, "They're FBI—not cops."

The drunken man in the windbreaker meandered back to the dark-green bench and his girlfriend, still lying on it, near the row of Ash trees, and fell onto the end of the bench. In a clear lucid voice, he asked the woman lying there, "What just happened? What was the FBI doing here and who were those men? We weren't briefed about anything that I heard of. Who was that guy getting into that Charger?" The woman, his partner, wearing a frazzled dirty-blond wig, said, "Beats me, honey. Spot any drug-pushers? Any action for us to call in?"

"Negative, looked like a crime in progress, a 10-31, and 10-32 and 33, man with a gun and an emergency. The Bureau's here; they're on it."

"That's just dandy. How much time left for this shift to be over? If there's any damn paperwork to fill out, we're off the hook. The Feds will do it."

# 27

## Interrogation

"STOP THE CAR HERE," Agent Nolan demanded. Agent Dumont pulled over to the curb, about a block past the rear-access driveway of the first townhouse. Dumont unlocked all the doors and rolled down the windows. Nolan hopped out. She opened the passenger door carefully. Jones' arms and legs were hanging over the edge of the bench seat, and his head rested right-side-down. He lay like an injured animal, with the crown of his head against the armrest.

"Should I call an ambulance?" Dumont asked.

"Dumont, there should be a diagnostic penlight in the medical kit inside the glove box. Get it for me, please, and a wipe and a pair of nitrile gloves." Agent Dumont stuck the gear in park and set the e-brake. He disengaged his latch plate and buckle and reached over to open the glove box. The red medical bag sat on top of the vehicle owner's manual. Dumont unzipped the kit and searched around scissors, tweezers, cotton balls, swabs, duct tape and the first aid manual. He spotted the white penlight in an interior compartment, grabbed a wipe, and pulled out a pair of gloves from his thigh pocket.

He reached in between the two front-seat headrests. "Here you go."

"Thanks," Nolan crouched down on the sidewalk. She wiped her hands with the sanitizer, eased on the lavender gloves, and placed two fingers on the side of Jones' neck at the carotid artery. She felt a normal pulse. "Still receiving blood to his brain; there are no visible or palpable signs of any obstruction," Nolan said.

Just then, Marshall and his men had driven past Nolan and continued north. The two other FBI vehicles that followed from the park had pulled over and waited behind.

Nolan switched the penlight on. She opened one of Jones' eyelids, shined the light on his eyeball, and then did the other. "His pupils are dilated. Ahmad Jones, Ahmad Jones! Can you hear me?" Just then Jones took a deep breath. "Mr. Jones are you all right?"

Jones opened and closed his eyes several times. Nolan saw his pupils return to normal after a few seconds. Jones first saw the back of the passenger bucket seat, all hazy at first. And then, after it came into focus he looked up at Agent Nolan.

"We were concerned about you, Mr. Jones," Dumont said.

"Yes, Mr. Jones," Nolan said. "Do you know where you are?"

Jones slowly sat up in the seat and looked at his red sneakers, then slightly behind to his left at the red brick house across the street. Jones said, "Yes, I'm about a hundred yards from Mangala Park in a black Dodge charger with two FBI Special Agents, Nolan and Dumont, from the Kaskaskia Resident Agency."

One agent from each of the other two vehicles had arrived in time to see Ahmad Jones sit up in the back seat. (They decided against asking to take a selfie just then.)

"We're five-by-five; no problem here," Nolan said. "Copy that," Sparks said. They walked back to their idling vehicles and turned around a few times to get a sense of the man they've heard fantastic stories about. Nolan shut the back door and plopped onto the passenger seat. She placed the penlight in the medical kit and shoved it back into the glove box. "Let's go to the Radisson. Shall we?"

Jones latched his seatbelt. The car rolled out into the scant flow of traffic and kept at 40 mph. "So," Nolan asked, "if it wasn't epilepsy or a brain injury... or drug abuse, then what was it?" Nolan observed Jones' eyes through the rearview mirror as she mentioned each of the three medical conditions, especially the last one. She was looking for any indication of drug use in his reactions. She took nothing for granted; she was an agent, doing her job and wasn't about to let any hype about Jones cast a veil over her eyes.

Jones thought well about his answer. No one knew about his problem, except his wife, Marakie. A couple of years back, Jones had developed this condition of whiteouts when too much adrenaline pumped into his blood, due to extreme circumstances. He can have the strength of ten when there's a violent threat, but after the threat is over, adrenaline output drops so fast that he gets nauseous, dizzy, sees white and passes out. It takes him a few minutes to return to consciousness. If he didn't tell her the truth, he couldn't justify a previous call asking them to pick him up.

"Could you open my window halfway, please?"

Agent Dumont lowered the window and Jones took a deep breath, holding the air in for eight seconds, then letting it out easy.

"My body reaches very high levels of coherence," Jones continued. "It wasn't always the case, until the fall of 2010 in Libya, when I collapsed in a hotel corridor."

Still looking at him through the rearview mirror, Nolan asked, "Libya! What were you doing in Libya?"

"I was invited to speak at a summit of African and European leaders. That morning some trouble showed up at the door of my hotel suite, but I didn't use my standard resources to correct it. At first."

"What standard resources?"

"Safety skills."

"Defensive tactics?"

"I prefer to use the word *safety*. For me, this word touches many worlds." Nolan looked away from the mirror and drew up her shoulders. Jones looked out the window at the unpaved road, blurring under him at 40 mph.

She turned to the mirror again. "Granted, you didn't use your standard safety skills. Then what?"

"I allowed a different option to come into play. The thing just worked itself out, and without me having to fall into automatic safety mode. So, I did virtually nothing, and my fight-or-flight energy had nowhere to go. I couldn't tolerate the extra load of energy resources and fell unconscious."

Nolan continued watching Jones' eyes and body language.

"Then there was the winter of 2011, when I collapsed a second time. I was in Cape Town, South Africa, on my way up Table Mountain in the aerial cable-way. Do you have any bottled water, Agent Nolan?"

She hesitated, before answering, watching his every move. "Yes, look under the driver's seat. There should be two or three there."

Jones uncoupled his safety harness and bent forward and down. He slipped his hand under the seat and pulled out a liter of spring water, then reattached the harness. He broke the seal and drank down a third, then resealed it and put it between his knees. "In the tram was a wild bunch of tourists, about five or six guys from Eastern Europe. I could tell from their language. They were reckless and bullying some of the other tramsters."

"Tramsters?" Nolan said, with a smirk.

"Yes, that's what I call them, me included. So, we're three minutes into the trip, about two thousand feet and climbing. I can see that some of the women are in distress, and I ask these boys to please conduct themselves with proper decorum. 'There are ladies and young children in the tram,' I said."

"The biggest one, about six-six, says to me, 'I am going to fix you. We are going to fix you!' The head guy didn't know what hit him."

Nolan tosses her shiny hair back. Jones looks past her to the yellow light up ahead. "I'll venture a guess that you saved the day, with your safety skills."

"Not quite as simple as that. I move to a corner, to keep the tramster crowd from danger. I am alone at the far side of the cable car. They spread out toward me. There are about thirty people inside. That's half the tram's capacity. I have lots of room to move around."

Dumont brought the Charger to a stop for the first time. The other two government vehicles followed behind. The light changed and the Charger continued up Treefold Avenue.

"What did you do next?"

"The centerline of the body is the weakest. Many vital organs and pressure points are there, as you all should know from your defensive-tactics training at Quantico. I decided to strike each one in a weak area, for the sake of brevity.

"The big guy grabs my lapels and twists his closed fist so his knuckles can press into the muscles of my neck, my windpipe. Then he lifts me off the metal floor."

"Why did you allow him to manhandle you?"

"By doing so he would commit himself."

"Commit himself?"

"Once he had me in his clutches, I also had him in mine. On his centerline his throat was unprotected, so I just grabbed his hair with my left hand, upon which he attempted to lessen the pain by shoving his head back, which is what I expected him to do. This opened the space, between his flexed arms and his Suprasternal Notch. I jabbed my right index into and down that notch. I dropped to my feet, while he grabbed his throat, choked, and forgot all about me."

"How much force did you use?"

"Very little, my moves were in harmony with the severity of the threat. As a habit, I consider the return current of my thoughts, feelings, and actions to others."

Jones unscrews the cap and takes in more water, then continues, "He comes at me again and so, I flick the back of my fingers like a whip against his trachea with very little force to stun him and he goes down like a barbell plate. He clutches his throat, which is a natural reaction to that kind of hit.

"The crowd of people wedged themselves into one side of the tram. They were putting their hands out, gesturing for everyone to stop. There hands were on their mouths in surprise. They were frightened. They thought the big guy was about to drop dead near Table Mountain, inside the cable car. I turned around to reassure them that he was just knocked out. In that instant, I miscalculated my footing, slipped and banged the floor with my back. After looking at what happened to their friend, the other four or five guys landed on me like metal filings drawn to a magnet. They kicked me, stomped me and kicked me some more."

Agent Nolan's smirk turned into a grimace, but she knew the effect a story could have on the human psyche. So, she exercised caution. Was he telling the truth or was he hiding something?

"What happened next was outside the lines of human reason," Jones said. Despite her efforts of extreme caution, Agent Nolan's ears perked up with anticipation. She and Dumont were both captured by Jones' telling. She turned in her seat to look straight at him. She felt that Jones' position behind Dumont was an invitation for her to look at him eye-to-eye, and at a more convenient angle than directly behind her. She had keen senses, always ready to learn something new about people—that's how she was trained, to keep learning. The Charger purred up Treefold as the two enthralled agents listened. Their speed was now 50 mph. Jones took in some more water.

"My hands and feet and the center of my chest, near my heart, got very warm, then full."

"Full, of what?"

"The best way to describe my feeling would be to imagine a fireman's hose between both your hands, when the line is fully open. Well, the center of my body was the main line and the soles of my feet and my two palms made four additional lines. Something that felt like water but was really an extraordinary current of energy came through all five points. I didn't feel the kicks and stomps after a few seconds. I was aware of looking down at my body from about twelve feet up. The tram roof didn't obstruct my vision. I saw right through the roof at my body lying there as it was getting pounded by size tens and elevens." Dumont turned to look at Nolan, and then faced forward. Nolan didn't look at Dumont, who was feeling left out. He was getting jealous of Jones' reputation and the possible effect it could have on his partner.

"I saw the other people, most of them locals, all squeezed together, diagonally across from me, gesturing with their hands to stop. I saw and heard an old white man on his cell phone calling for assistance in Afrikaans. I saw and understood a little boy and his mother speaking Xhosa, pleading with them to stop kicking me. Language was no barrier in my state at that moment. I saw an elderly South African woman get on her knees, lift her hands and ask Jesus to deliver me, and to keep this incident from harming race relations. And I saw a strapping white South African man who wanted to help me. I could sense his thoughts and emotions taking form: 'I should help him but if I do, they will hurt me too, even though I'm white.'"

"Some of the people grabbed their own heads while they were screaming at my attackers. The biggest one, recovering from the hit, struggled up and leaned against the wall, cupping his neck with his big hand. He was limp and out of gas. I watched with no hatred or anger. I was composed, calm and unconcerned—nonchalant even. In my physical body, I had reached an extremity. My whole being was like a taut, violin string. There was no place for the powerful energies moving through my body to go. My awareness went beyond my physical form—no limits. I registered no sense of time or space because I had no concept of them in my present reality. I saw the tram door open and other people coming in to stop the guys still beating on my body. They were pulled off me. (I mean my body, because I wasn't in it—I was observing it.) The lady with her hands up in the air said, 'Jesus! Thank you, Jesus!'"

"Then, in a blink, I was behind my eyes again. I didn't feel a thing except stronger integration within. I felt more connected inside; I felt whole energetically. I was better attuned with all parts of myself. Of course, I then began to feel the pain of the abuse I had taken, but it wasn't overwhelming. So, now, if I should handle attackers, my energy levels peak, providing me with an extraordinary supply of coherence, but after it's over, I hit bottom quickly."

"How many times has this happened since 2010?" Dumont asked.

Special Agent Alejandro Dumont was born and raised in the city of San Miguel, El Salvador. He lived more than 9 miles from Volcán Chaparrastique, the stratovolcano that dominates the landscape toward the southwest. While hearing Jones, he remembered days when his parents appeared to be sleeping. His grandmother Vania forbade young Alejandro from disturbing them. When he was sixteen he said to her, "But they look funny sleeping during the day." Vania, a wise old woman, who was four-nine with large, brown eyes and long, black hair reaching to her ankles, said, "They're not sleeping, Alejandro darling, they're working outside their bodies on the volcano." This was on Tuesday, January 1st, 2002, just 15 days before it erupted. There was very little damage. Because of this memory, Dumont could make some sense out of Jones' story, even though he didn't believe in such things anymore.

"This makes the third time. I never look for fights."

Nolan recounted to Jones, "You were a New York City cop for five or six years and your last PSA was Hunts Point in the South Bronx. I presume you were mixing it up quite a bit: Locking people up, doing the paperwork, then getting back out on the street, I would say about two hours later."

Jones smiled and said, "And?"

"Why would a guy who never looks for trouble work in an environment where, at that time, confrontation was as inevitable as the sound of a subway car? You could've asked for another beat."

"Though it was challenging, it wasn't as bad as the stories you hear—at least after the whole Fort Apache era. There were some dangerous moments, but altogether I learned a lot about people. I became a cop because I knew from experiences with my father how to relate to people," Jones smiled as he reflected. Nolan noticed it when he got to the subject of people. She looked past Jones, at a commercial vehicle out of the rear window, then back to him.

Jones could see his father in his mind's eye. After looking in the direction of passing cars, he then turned back to Nolan. "I had the graveyard at first, from eleven to nine in the morning. As you are aware, most crimes are committed between ten at night and three in the morning. Well, the problems I faced during the early hours were of the vehicular nature—accidents in my presence and not in my presence. Some ladies of the evening. Collisions were a serious thorn, though, because of the reports I had to fill out for the insurance companies—the paperwork was dreadful." Jones paused for a beat, then shook his head.

"I almost get a whiteout right now thinking about it—that would have been my fourth one!"

Dumont smiled and looked at Nolan, who again didn't return the gesture. She just frowned through her smile.

"Then," Jones continued, "there was directing traffic during endless construction. Overall, I didn't mix it up that much."

"Mr. Jones, why did you have us come to pick you up? You know your reputation precedes you or you wouldn't have felt inclined. You must have been certain that we would want to help you. I have to be objective about this and your reasons for coming here, after eleven years with no intel on your location—"

"Yes, you are correct about my reasons for contacting the Bureau. Some men were about to dish out an order of trouble."

"One of my men said he thought he saw someone draw a pistol at the park, and something about a ball game, was that connected to you?"

"Yes."

"Who are they?"

"Not sure, but I could already feel a rush. So, I called my sister in New York and asked her to contact Special Agent Peterson, and for him to contact a unit close by. If you hadn't come when you did, I would have been in a bind. I had my safety skills, but it was afterwards when I whited out that posed a problem."

"Well, you could have vacated your body again, right?" Nolan said, as if everything he just told her and her partner was bullshit.

After her sarcastic remark, Jones looked directly into her eyes. Nolan felt a current of force, carried through Jones' warm smile. It reminded her of her father, who worked as a maker and repairer of fine furniture. He was a skilled artisan, meticulous in his craftsmanship, humble, respected by their neighbors. He and her mother, who was born and raised in Upstate New York, carried themselves with dignity and kindliness, always saying something pleasant to the people they encountered, when they went out for walks, sometimes during very cold afternoons. Nolan remembered how during walks in the cold temperatures of Kharkiv, in Ukraine, even in January, the coldest month, she and her two brothers always felt warm and comfortable. A warmth that was palpable and not imaginary, radiated from their father's heart. She wondered what her father, whose middle name, Igor, which means protected, really knew about life.

After all these years, she remembered that one thing, when Ahmad Jones looked into her eyes. Dumont drove through a construction site. A lady with a sign turned it from slow to stop. He braked, while a dump truck, hauling dirt and huge rocks, rolled less than 10 mph, across the street.

After Nolan's vivid recollection, she said, "I am sorry, I didn't mean... what about the police? You could have dialed 911. They would have arrived faster."

"True, but they don't know me like the Bureau does."

"You could've name-dropped the FBI and we would've vouched for you."

The lady turned the sign back around to slow. The Charger rode over a couple of loose and slightly warped, metal construction slabs, and continued north on Treefold.

"Yes, and they would be asking more questions than you are right now. And the police would have been right; they would have discovered that I had just returned to the U.S. and had not been active in any way that they could give an accounting for since 2006. Again, the police would have been right. They would have considered the possibility that I may have radicalized, was a terrorist, or a spy, or anything. They would have been right again, as pertaining to the limited amount of information available, to think that way, before more information was available to them, like me waking up."

Dumont looked at Nolan, as if to say, "maybe he's right."

"So, Special Agent Nolan, you can see by the evidence that I had to have you here first to get me out of trouble. I don't think the local authorities would've understood as quickly—especially about my whiteouts. If I was a Kaskaskia cop, having seen me a few moments ago, a multitude of red flags would have been raised. I would've looked suspicious. Maybe with time, yes, Kaskaskia PD would've seen a different picture, but my history with the Bureau was my best play. If I had lost consciousness in police custody, there's no telling where I'd be now."

"But you were a cop, so why wouldn't they have given you the benefit of the doubt?"

"Agent Nolan, I felt you," (Nolan was taken by surprise the way Jones said, *You*.) "You and your team of special agents were my absolute best prospect, given the time frame I had to work with, which was less than four minutes, and not KPD. My history with the Bureau is why you came. I understand the need for answers—it's the nature of your job. Nothing is as it seems on the surface."

The Charger pulled in under the outside ceiling of the Radisson Hotel. Dumont kept foot pressure on the brake. Nolan turned back around and faced front. She said, "Well, Mr. Jones, that's some problem and some story you have. I'm glad we were here to help you out. We're at the Radisson and I debriefed you, so you don't have to come in to our office. If you ever require anything from us again, don't hesitate." Agent Nolan got the card out of her pocket and handed it to Jones. Besides a number and email address, it read: U.S. Department of Justice, Federal Bureau of Investigation, Special Agent Brenda Nolan, Intelligence Branch, FBI Resident Agency, Kaskaskia, Illinois.

"Thanks, Agents Nolan and Dumont. I owe you one."

Agent Dumont set the brake, stepped out and opened the door for Jones. He got out and walked around the back. Nolan stepped out, too, and extended her hand to Jones, who helped her out. "I am honored to have met you, Mr. Jones."

"Call me Ahmad."

Not jealous anymore, Dumont asked, "Can we take a selfie with you, Mr. Jones?"

"Certainly! And please, Ahmad."

Sparks who had pulled up said to McNulty, his partner, "Hey, what are we, chopped liver? That's Ahmad Jones over there!" He picked up his radio and said, "Agent Nolan, we're coming over."

She waved at them, including Williams and Frazier in the other vehicle. The drivers turned their machines off, their doors slammed one after the other in measured four-four time, one, two, three, and four. They hurried over to meet Jones, like young kids running after an ice cream truck.

Agent Nolan said, "Agents McNulty, Williams, Frazier and Sparks, I'd like to present Mr. Ahmad Jones."

"You can call me Ahmad."

Sparks put his hand out to clasp Jones' hand. He looked Jones in the eyes unabashed and said, "Glad to meet you, sir!"

"Agent Sparks, the pleasure is mine. Agents McNulty, Frazier and Williams, I'd be honored to press your hands." The agents stood in a line and came up one-by-one.

Dumont placed his phone on a makeshift holder on top of the Charger and set it for ten seconds. All seven of them lined up in front of the Radisson's lobby. Flash!

"Take care, Mr. Jones," they said, while walking back to their vehicles. Dumont got in. Jones opened Nolan's door for her. "Ahmad," she said, "I'm happy you weren't dead."

"Oh, thanks!"

"There were rumors floating around the community. How can I—we—contact you if we need your services?"

Jones studied her question, balancing his decision to stay clear of the Bureau. He'd already helped Special Agent Mike Cappello with a case in Seattle. Today, six special agents came to his aid in his time of need, including Special Agent Peterson, who must have still considered Jones his friend. Jones decided then and there that he would help them if he could. He removed a thin notebook with a pen attached from his back pocket and jotted down his cell number.

Just then, a van with a defibrillator-service logo pulled into the parking space directly across from the hotel's entrance. A tall man with wide shoulders, thick wrists, and trained muscles got out holding a scanner and a metallic clipboard. He passed in front of Jones, Dumont, and Nolan, and entered the hotel. Nolan remembered seeing that van out the back window when she was debriefing Jones. The man looked at his phone, being careful not to meet anyone's eyes. Jones looked at the man like he knew something, then checked his watch. Nolan caught his glance and spoke to Dumont with her eyes.

Jones held the paper in front of him. He said, "Give this number to no one unless you get permission from me. As of now, you are the only one permitted to contact me. Do you comprehend?"

Agent Nolan considered his request and said, "You have my word. By the way, why are you here, Ahmad?"

"To promote my new book."

"And, how did you break surveillance at the stadium?" She half-smiled at Jones. She liked him, but couldn't tell if she was attracted to him, or just attracted to the stories, and the idea of such a man. But what difference would it make, either way, she thought.

Jones' eyes sparkled as the corners of his mouth lifted a bit. He knew she was still interrogating him. He felt that she wanted him to know that she was still doing just that.

He said, "Do magicians ever reveal their secrets?"

"Are there secrets? And are you a magician, Mr. Jones?"

Jones smiled. Nolan crossed her arms and said, "I'd like to know how you did it."

Dumont was feeling uncomfortable with Nolan's bantering.

"I walked out of the stadium, that's all I did. It was the easiest, most profound action I'd ever done up to that point in time. When I walked out of that stadium, my life changed. Two years later, I found the love of my life, by an African shore. Then another two years later, I was about to give into the thought of never seeing her again, while sitting in a Libyan jail. Then, my life took another turn when I watched a halfback shed more than five or six tackles, and run 67 yards, before landing in the end zone."

Jones handed Nolan the notebook. They shook hands again. Then Jones walked toward the hotel lobby.

Nolan got halfway into the car, then turned and watched Jones pass between the hotel's automatic doors. She waited. She noticed the military-style cadence, his command of his own body, his seasoned gait. She waited until the doors came together behind him. Nolan climbed in the rest of the way and engaged her lap-shoulder belt.

"Out of 56 field offices and over 200 RAs, we got to Ahmad Jones first," Dumont said.

Nolan kept her own counsel. She knew Ahmad Jones had some other reason for being in Kaskaskia, besides his book—it was something big. She said, "Dumont, I hope you're hungry."

"Yes, I am, but I'll be digesting more than food. This last thirty minutes was most interesting. I love my job!"

"That makes two of us. But I'm starved."


Sparks and the rest of the agents were bound for the RA. Jones headed to his third-floor suite. He had one hundred minutes to go before catching the 3:17 flight to Ohio. While in the air, he would examine the astronomic significance of a strange woman in an orange car doing a burnout, less than an hour before his attackers and Nolan arrived.

# 28

## The Strange Woman in the Orange Car

AT 12:02, FIFTY-SEVEN MINUTES before Jones lost consciousness in the FBI vehicle, a car skidded diagonally toward the curb on Treefold Avenue, the place where Nolan and Dumont picked up Jones. The driver stomped on the brakes. She was going to hit the sidewall of the right-front tire where all those symbols and alphanumeric data were engraved. The resulting tire, wheel, and suspension damage would be significant even though she was only skidding rightward at 20 mph toward the six-inch curb.

There were no parked vehicles ahead and the one behind the woman was a velvet-red Chrysler Mini, ninety feet away. The woman had all the space she needed for her convertible to crash against the embankment without banging into another vehicle. The inevitable collision with the curb, never happened.

Instead, the woman released her brake pedal and freed the wheels. They moved the car's weight forward. She used the momentum and turned into the curb and the easement. The tires made impressions on the grass. She pushed her left foot down while moving the stick to the right and back, gave it some gas and backed off the easement. To a few onlookers, what the woman did next was both impressive and strange.

Like lightning, she let out the clutch, stepped on the gas, and shifted to second gear. The engine revved up to 6,000 RPMs. The woman then popped it and turned the wheel, which sent the car away from the curb. Then she pressed down on the brake for five seconds while still giving it the gas. The whole scene stole the attention of all the park patrons as a thick, asphalt-filled vapor coalesced around the front tires like a dense mound of cumulus clouds. The car's rear end swerved until the orange car was parallel parked. After the third second, she killed the ignition.

The woman, still inside, had voluminous red hair, with retro curls trained to fall full over her left shoulder, and deer-shaped eyes. Her irises were filled with a vintage blend of brown and green with a touch of blue. The sun had climbed to its highest point in the day. She wore Swarovski champagne-crystal drop earrings that reflected the sunlight and an expensive Tahitian pearl choker. She possessed an old-world charm with her finely chiseled jawline and full lips. She was dangerously beautiful.

From the basketball court across the street, young men stopped playing on the porous green asphalt to catch the aftermath of the spectacle. The drop-dead gorgeous redhead, inside a convertible. When they had set up again, a college senior with a high free-throw percentage had seen enough. He was the driver of the Mercedes C350. He was six-two and bounced the ball and bent his knees three times. He paused after he put a precision finish on his shot. The ball passed through the hoop in almost total silence for the second point. The kid who fouled him and his teammates lost the opportunity for the rebound. They paid the price for divided focus.

The redhead commanded just about everyone's attention. The near collision and burnout appeared natural—it was, to all who heard or saw it, a flawless execution of a complex maneuver.

"Actual events are seductively plausible," wrote Thomas Williams, and that event was natural, plausible, and seductive to all—except Ahmad Jones.

The woman had driven past a man running southbound on the grass, at the edge of Mangala Park, about thirty feet from the intersection. He was running, with his head turned sideways, in the same direction as her convertible, toward a large ash tree rooted on the corner of Treefold and South Boulevard.

The ball arched downwards and landed into the man's curved fingers. The sound it made proclaimed him as a pro. He turned and jogged to the car, the source of the smoke and smell of hot, gooey pitch. The man, a fan of burnout competitions, scanned the car's candy-orange outer body. He crossed the sidewalk to the easement and bent over and peered through the passenger window at the chick behind all the commotion. She brought the power window down.

With a tone of indifference, he said, "You look okay. But are you okay in there?"

"Yes," she said, "I... the road was slippery. I don't know what possessed me."

"You controlled a skid."

He straightened up while he caught the football in one hand and handed it off to the other hand.

As if on cue, the wind blew as the rest of the Audi's windows dropped down halfway—the convertible top lifted, and the back window and frame clicked into position before sliding down into the rear deck. The woman's hazel eyes were more easily discernable as the air between her and the man with the football, was still clearing the space of dust and smoke residue.

The gust also wind-swept her hair. After a few seconds, her curls settled back in front of her left shoulder. The car's tires didn't bite well upon braking. The final tack coat, applied over the new road just after midnight twelve hours before, hadn't cured. It was now a hot and humid summer afternoon and the new road's condition made skids more possible, but for some peculiar reason, the road passed the inspection and was open to traffic.

With no friction, her front tires locked, packing into its treads the gummy emulsion of tacky asphalt. The car had slid and yawed for three feet, and not far from the ash tree at the corner. The road's top layer of skin hadn't interlocked with the bottom skin layer, which had already cured with the main bed of asphalt. This wasn't a cosmetic job; the road had been milled beforehand. The final sealing coat was mixed too thick and the temperature was 83 degrees and climbing. So, the smell of hot-mix asphalt, reacting to the ambient temperature and the high heat from the friction of tires and road, had spread fast.

The undercover twosome sitting on the park bench near the scene of the skid had pinched their nostrils. The couple stopped messing around when the ruckus occurred. They were a husband-and-wife team who agreed to take the dangerous job. They liked their assignment—the edgy, exhibitionist, role-play added a dynamic element to their marriage. They were paid to frolic while conducting surveillance. Sam was burning up in his old, beat-up coat; other than that, he was okay with his role. Sam and his wife, Beth Ann, ambled westward together to the empty bench fifty yards away at the other side of the park, near the crest. For them, an easy ten minutes of ambling.

Jones and his friend, Ray Simmons, saw the bright car slip on the road while they sat in the middle of the park, due west. Jones noticed the drunken couple heading toward him, toward another bench, further up the slope. Like the uncured road surface, Jones couldn't get any traction on what he just saw. There was something more to it. He checked the time: 12:05. Something wasn't as straightforward as the car's straightforward-looking skid and spinning tires. Add to that the convertible's performance of the folding top and the whole scene was lopsided, off balance, askew, awry—*ah,* on purpose. There were more bits of information registering somewhere in a realm beyond the threshold of those visible facts.

# 29

## Unheeded Warning

IT WAS 12:25 PM IN KASKASKIA, 23 minutes after that car jumped the curb. At the same moment in time, a regime change was in progress 8,820 miles away, off the eastern coast of Africa. It was happening eight hours ahead, at 10:25 pm.

In grand pain, on his knees, the small man proclaimed, "As sure as the sun will rise tomorrow, you will answer for the crime of treason against our person and the sovereign state of Afarland... *ahhh!*"

The big man said, "Quit your yelping, old man. You, sir, may not be alive to *see* the sunrise tomorrow." He *was* big, trained in combat tactics and special military operations—a giant at six-seven, dressed in black fatigues, with a small head that was out of proportion to his height and build, growling those words with his deep voice.

Za Dewabuna, the President of Afarland, only five-nine, tried to evoke some dignity from his captor with his plea/decree. He looked up at the big man's full cheeks, square jaw and wide head, then looked toward the central window in the east. To look at any part of his punisher brought on a profound spasm of dread in the old man. The big man's growls were even more alarming.

The periodic blasts of wind came about nine seconds apart now, as if a giant being were outside breathing in and out through the window at regular intervals. Silk golden-yellow curtains rose to an angle of nearly 40 degrees and like the undulating curtains, Dewabuna's thin locks ruffled vigorously. He shut his eyes from the dust that blew in with the warm air. The curtains fell back in slow motion like two parachutes toward the aqua-colored wall.

At each gust, the golden-yellow curtains parted open floating up and away from the wall, revealing the moon, rising in the east—also the direction in which Afarland's main road, *Le Coeur* (The Heart), was laid out. Za Dewabuna recalled his place of birth several kilometers up Le Coeur, a road aligned with the rising sun and stars. Majestic baobab trees lined each side of the road, escorting vehicles to and from the Presidential Palace in the nation's capital—Incalzael. The name of this capital, in some respects, is like the ancient name for the Sun from the days of Atlantis, as described by Phylos the Thibetan in *A Dweller on Two Planets.*

There were bodies scattered over the zebrawood floor. The president had been dealt a severe beating. Afterwards, he had spoken whatever paltry confidence he had left in a series of huffs, lisps and whispers, without moving his lips or his jaw, which was slightly unhinged on the left side. Only his tongue moved a bit, which altogether made him seem like a ventriloquist. There was something strangely familiar about this scene, about what was happening to him, he thought. He made certain not to use grammatical contractions, for these were too painful to say under the circumstances.

The big man, The General, swaggered several steps backward and dropped his two-hundred-and-thirty-six-pound mass onto an antique armchair, ripping through the middle of the hand-woven cane. The kidney-shaped French writing desk before him, with metallic edges leafed in pale gold, contrasted with The General's black boots, pants and short-sleeved shirt. Even his watchband was black but his eyes were light brown. If The General could have acquired black sclera contacts, his black motif would be complete.

There were bright, happy colors all over the room except for The General. His black beret and sunglasses made the whole scene look both comical and bleak when viewed from across the room. That was how the old man saw it, like he was looking through the other end of a pair of binoculars. He had been beaten into another world, both unreal and real. His breathing was still rapid, his field-of-vision narrowed. He was both on the outside looking in and still on the inside looking out. The reception room was a seven-sided structure. Its accoutrements, in contrast with the greasy general, were out of place with each other like two incompatible chemicals exploding when brought together. The old man kneeling with an almost busted jaw was facing his usurper, who now propped his army boots atop the vintage desk, distressing its hand-rubbed finish.

Remembering something important, The General took his boots off the table, then sat straight in the delicate chair. He turned it to face the middle of the desk and on his first try, pulled open the right middle drawer and grabbed a bottle of Drambuie liqueur, his Commander-in-Chief's favorite brand. The bottle was less than half full. He lifted it and gestured with the bottle to the old man and then slammed its concave base onto the desktop.

The rich finish took on disfigurement like the old man. Next, he rummaged through the bottom drawer and found two old-fashioned glasses, pouring an ounce in one and three in the other. He drained the glass with the ounce, paused, then burped. He slammed the empty glass's open end on the desk, then picked up the other glass and strutted past the window and golden-yellow curtains, to his captive.

"This is for the pain, old man," The General said. Then, he grabbed the man's neck, the way Popeye's nemeses Bluto would grab Olive Oil's stringy neck, and forced the Drambuie into his mouth. The old man coughed out much of it onto his white shirt and pants, doubting that his jaw would ever be right again.

The old man's pain was both physical and psychological. He was on the edge of shock, but he was once a strong man—strong in his heart. His pain was like a tiny earthquake on the left side of his jaw. The General held the old man up and paused to look behind him at the framed picture on the west wall. The scene showed the helpless old man, many years previous, in a scrum, in forward position, at the Rugby World Cup in New Zealand in 1987. Then, The General took in the wall-to-wall, pale-gold streaks alternating with brown-to-black streaks of the hardwood floor imported from Gabon.

The phone rang. The General took his big hand from around the president's neck and jogged to the desk. Everything shook, including the picture on the west wall and the windows when he did that. He scooped off his beret and wiped sweat off his face with it. Took a deep breath then picked up. The old man slouched forward, helpless and pitiful.

"General Garaka, we will soon have Ahmad Jones at hand. And his wife very soon."

"That's great news, Mr. Borg."

"Is the ring-of-state, safe?"

The General muted the call.

He whispered, "Where is the ring?"

The old man hesitated.

"Where, is the ring? I won't ask again."

With a lisp, he replied, "Behind me, in the safe, behind the picture."

"Yes, sir, the ring-of-state is secure."

"Are you in total control of communications?"

"Yes, sir, like clockwork, all communications in and out are under my control. The airport and communication networks have been secured by my men. The country is blind and deaf and our neighbors to the west and south will not interfere, *nor know* of what is happening here, for some time. Then it will be too late."

Despite it all, President Za Dewabuna hadn't lost his sense of humor or his intelligence as he attempted to smirk at the general's grammatical error.

# 30

## The Neglected Redhead

BACK IN KASKASKIA, at Mangala Park at 12:35, Ray Simmons, a muscular fire-engine operator of medium height and a year from early retirement, asked, "What, Jones, did you make of *that* burnout?"

Jones said, "On the surface, an unconscious reaction to a celebrity?"

"QB... celebrity? *Ha ha ha!* Man, maybe four years ago, but even then, he hadn't seen much action on the gridiron. Well, he's holdin' the rock now, so I'm goin' ta cop a squat on this here grass, while QB gets his rap on. Watch the action the way QB used to—from the sidelines. This could take a while—that chick is hot, man! So that's all, ya reckon, Mr. FBI?"

"Consulted for them; been out for some time now."

"Man, I knowed that, but that ain't stoppin' that mind o' yours. I can hear your brain cells popping over something. I wanna hear 'bout what you thinkin'... One of your crime stories in progress? Come on man, before Amy calls. I just know she's fixin' to ask me t' come home and do some chores. Man, *ha ha ha!*"

"Ray, do you talk like that around ranking officers?"

"Who... Cap'n? No man, just around my army buddies and a few folks at the barber shop. If he heard my ain'ts and hear-bouts and fixins, man! Those insignia and badges would peel off his dress uniform, every one of them—and his toupee, too! He'd swear I was speaking another language, wondering who this FEO is. Nope, Captain is as straight-up-and-down as those bugles on his collar. Think they'd let me chauffeur a hook and ladder and operate the pump and all? I'd get the hook all right. Yeah, I gets my syntax together when I has to, on the job."

"What about your wife?"

"Amy? Man, she loves it when I talk that way. Says it reminds her of one of her favorite comedians, Stu Gilliam—and she right, *ha ha ha!* She majored in English, man. Did you know that? Yep, helps me stay loose, man. Those 56-hour tours are murder. But now, I don't have to sleep at the station for another two days, man!"

"Still on call, though?" Jones asked.

"You know, us firefighters have shorter lifespans than most people—even people like you, when you were active, that is. That's why I'm gettin' out at 51." Ray crossed his fingers. "I'll have done my twenty by next year. Helped many people and saved a lot of property. But now it's time to book, man. By the way, who's your barber, man—who did you up?"

"Lonnie, over on Maple Ave. I stopped by yesterday."

"Lonnie, yeah, man, I know her. She's good and very pretty, too. Amy don't want me being faded by no woman, though. She's seen Lonnie, with her slamming body, barbering dude's heads—case closed! But damn, Jones, she hooked you up a dope recon!"

"Williams is good, too. I saw him do a precision cut, even better than the one I have. You might try him."

Ray passed his hand over his own hair, "Well, ain't the same thing as having a woman like Lonnie fussin' over your hair for a half hour, doin' her precision stuff. Jones, how long you gonna keep stretchin' out them shoulders, man?"

"I'm finished now." Jones sat beside Ray on the grass. "So, Ray, getting back to your question about what I make of that event with QB and the girl, here's something hypothetical. Let's say that it's the off-season and you're driving home from work and you roll past Russell Wilson or Donovan McNabb or Ben Roethlisberger playing catch with their buddies, throwing the rock from one side of the road to the other. You say, "That's! whoever! No one's behind you and you're just a couple of yards away from an NFL quarterback."

"Man! Yeah, but you lost me with Wilson, McNabb and Roethlisberger because QB wasn't no starter."

"Stay with my narrative for another moment and think of me as your cap'n, because your syntax is gettin' to me, man!"

"Alright, *ha ha!* You got jokes!"

"So, you slam the brakes and pray you can clasp his hand and get an autograph, or get out and play catch, to throw a few with him and, if fortunate catch a few, and then get back in after you've taken a picture or two or three. Then you go home and tell the greatest story ever around the dinner table."

So, what's your point, Jones?"

"We read the world around us in the same way we've set up our personal preferences, which most times is accepting what we see out there without hesitation. The more often we see something, anything, and accept it, the more it becomes part of our reality. It will continue to show up unquestioned until—"

"Until someone like you questions it."

"A question that's never been asked. That woman saw a somewhat famous athlete. That appeared to be the case when she skidded. Before she came along, that drunken couple who just staggered past us were carrying on something fierce on that bench." Jones whispered, "By the way, those drunks are cops."

"Say, what? You must be on soapsuds man! Cops? Okay, what makes you say that, Ahmad?"

"Markers, for one. His trouser legs are extra-long and wide. Plus, when he passed us, I saw an imprint on it, probably a Glock 22. As a cop impersonating a drunk, he favors his right foot on purpose because it helps him to handle the discomfort of almost three extra pounds, including the rig. That's one typical marker of an ankle holster. Anyway, those two weren't paying any attention to QB, and neither was anyone else in this park. There are at least thirty people here. So, that redhead notices QB's slicked-back hair, mustache and beard—those weren't his signature looks when he was in the league. How did she know it was him? I think she found the man that she was ordered to find—only it's not QB."

"What, ordered to find? What you sayin', Ahmad?"

"You asked me to tell you one of my stories. The thing is, QB loves the game of football more than a pretty face and an expensive car. He's obsessive that way."

Jones stood and joined his two thumbs and held his palms open. "Hold on a second," Jones said.

*THUMP!*

"You still got it, Jones. Good catch. Just like in high school. Now, explain to me—"

"I'm just talking. Pay me no mind."

The intersection of Treefold and South Boulevard in Kaskaskia was busy with the sounds of young girls and boys screaming and running from one another, of older kids playing with remote-operated drones, and a couple of Frisbees sailing by.

The tops of the trees on each side of Treefold bend toward each other forming an archway for several blocks. The sun flickers through gaps in the moving leaves, through the windshield and onto the soft, cream interior of the convertible, over the redhead's maroon skirt and lemon-yellow blouse. She's inside the car with its engine running—and apparently hers is, too! Perfect timing, she thinks. She rolls back to where the sun isn't so strong, keeping pace with QB as he walks from the tree. The former NFL player is within an arm's reach.

"Aren't you the quarterback from the—"

"Not anymore," he interrupted. "Excuse me, please." QB guided his fingers into position to meet the oncoming football.

*THUMP!*

"Nice spiral, Jones," QB shouted. Jones took a bow.

"Wow!" she said, "fine catch. *Hmm,* you've got strong-looking hands."

She extends her upper body over to the passenger side; relaxing her arms and hands around the leather seat. She wants him to feel that she is comfortable with him. The more she leans over, the more QB notices her breast. She lifts her head and looks him in the eye. The whole scene is one of desperation.

"What else do you catch?" She asked, still leaning her body over the passenger's side.

QB leaned against the hot car. He said, "Baseballs, fish, Sometimes I catch hell!"

She said, in quiet tones, "*Hmm,* you're so crazy. I mean *what else,* darling? I was just on my way home. Had to get out and do something." She pushed her lips forward, pouting. "Then I slid on this road gunk." She stopped pouting and wore a serious face. "I was bored, still am!"

"Did more than slid; it burned!"

"It did. Didn't it?"

A black Chevy Caprice with four men in it came to a stop at the corner, diagonally across from the basketball courts, facing east on South Boulevard. It stopped before turning left to head north.

# 31

## Cold Streets

THE REDHEAD GOT QUIET after she spotted the black car. She looked further up the park grounds, at Ray, then at Jones as he threw the ball.

She said, "Are your friends over there your teammates?"

*THUMP!* QB caught the ball and tucked it.

"They're just some guys who throw with me every now and then," he said as he tilted his head to the side.

The Caprice turned and passed her. She noticed it from the corner of her left eye.

"Hey, why are you looking at me that way?"

"You remind me of that poster of Raquel Welch, when she starred in *One Million Years B.C.* in 1967."

She watched the Caprice in her rearview mirror for any deviation in its direction. The Caprice continued north until it got real tiny after a few minutes. She pretended to adjust her hair a bit and then resumed the conversation. She wrapped her arms around the passenger seat again. Nine young men had been watching from the basketball court, missing shots and not guarding their men. Players weren't manning their positions too well. A player, the owner of the Mercedes, was frustrated by their lack of discipline.

She turned up the charm on her mark, "Right. I remind you of Rachel Welch, huh? Well, I'm flattered. She is still a beautiful woman. I hope to look as good as she does when I'm 75. *Ah,* I would love to have your autograph and I would like you to imagine just where I'm going to keep it!"

"Get ready," Ray said, "he's pumpin' it. You gonna needs some extra yardage, man!"

"Go long. The winds are north," QB shouted.

*THUMP!* "Ahmad, that was your best catch yet," Ray said.

The redhead covered her ears, "Instead of shouting and paying attention to that ball, pay some to me. Will you, please? So you, you remind me of a young William Shatner, as Captain Byers in *Judgment at Nuremberg.* Here— you can write your autograph in my little book. There, on the inside-back-cover." She dug into her bag and handed him a Parker luxury pen.

"I have a collection of these," QB remarked. "To whom do I make it out?"

"Patricia—Patricia Larkin."

"I think I hear an accent. Where are you from?"

"*Ah,* I'm from, New Jersey—New Brunswick."

"Jersey, huh? Okay. *To Patricia, Patricia Larkin. So nice I wrote it twice. You look great for a million-year-old babe! Love, QB.*"

"My, you have a very light touch, don't you? You write very fast and pretty," she said. She read it through and smiled to herself. "Love, QB! Here, take this. It's my number."

"True, I can write fast and legible, but not pretty; that's for the ladies."

"Oh, then how about appealingly?" she teased.

Jones, in the middle of the park, forty yards from QB, noted the time she handed his friend the sticky note. He imagined the approximate geocentric positions of the planets based on what he remembered of their degrees when he last looked at the ephemeris.

Jones' buddy, Ray, jogged over.

"Did you see how QB let loose that deep ball with an extra flourish of his fingers on the finish?" Ray asked.

"I did. QB was one of the best at it."

Jones concluded that Mars very was close to the meridian of Kaskaskia, directly overhead—Mars being a planet associated with crashes, burns, and violence, within the context of the car's small jump over the curb and the heat generated by the spinning tires. He also felt that Uranus, associated with sudden and bizarre happenings, was on the local horizon due west. These two planets, with their volatile natures, would exercise a considerable confluence with that skid, but alone, they wouldn't explain the woman's amorous behavior at the scene.

"When you call me, then I'll drive back here," she said. "You and I can enjoy a hot night out on the town—or a night in. It's your call, baby. I'll be what you want. I'll just play along."

*THUMP!*

"I'd be happy to, Patricia, but right now, I'm playing with the guys. It's guy stuff, catching up with a good friend who just returned. I may be a couple of hours. I'll have to call you later. You have gorgeous eyes, but they look angry."

She turned her head right and looked over the green bench to the field, to Ray and Jones, then left to the digital clock, and back to QB like a whiplash. Her long, full, well-cropped hair was obedient and as red as her temper.

"Oh, the guys, you say! The ones you just throw with every now and then? When an opportunity like me comes around. Take it!"

QB had come across these kinds of opportunities before, when he was on his team's roster, but not this type of reaction.

Patricia, that is Jessica, overreacted. She'd had enough of Borg, and decided she was going to stay in the U.S. She liked QB, but his game came first and not her. She slid all ten fingers through her hair, from front to back, and then adjusted both sides of her blouse, then spoke in an ever-increasing pitch. "Okay, well, QB, you have an open invitation. If I don't hear from you in an hour, I'll take this million-year-old body to bed—to nap, alone! I will assume you don't want any of this, any of me."

She sobbed as she spoke, "And you can *tear up* my number. Don't put it in your cell unless you're going to use it—this afternoon. Thanks for your autograph. You've got great Spencerian penmanship. And if your lovemaking is anything like your writing, then you don't want to miss out on an equally *good...* writer!"

She slid back, secured herself in her seat and drove off. After a hundred feet, she considered stopping the car and turning back to try a new angle but that would look too much like stalking. Funny that her face, hair, body and confidence couldn't pull this man away. She kept moving south until she reached Oakton Street and a red light. She retrieved her ringing cell from the saddlebag on the passenger floor. It was encrypted end-to-end.

"Yes?"

"Jessica, have you taken QB out of the equation?" the voice asked.

The sound of traffic swishing by on both sides, along with this man's cold, calculating voice, mesmerized Jessica into a flashback. With her deadliness, able to kill with one strike, which she has done several times, she couldn't resist Borg's unusual control over her emotions. She remembered those sounds from the late 1990s, when she lived on the street near the London Bridge station. No one cared about her then and she didn't care about anyone now—just herself, just surviving.

She remembered when she was eight when her father had scolded her after his wife, her mother, died. How he shoved her away when she wanted to hug him to dissolve his pain through loving affection. How he ordered her to sit down in a seat near strangers across the aisle in the bus. As she paused at the red light in her orange convertible, Jessica remembered her father's pain but not his love.

She went back to that vivid feeling of rejection, when she slung her toy pocketbook with its long black strap over her shoulder. The passengers had stared briefly at her, and then back at him. She recalled that they were stone-faced—even they were no consolation. The bus was cold and her father was colder. Everyone was icy cold.

When Jessica was much older, she was destitute and couldn't pay her way. She would wake up near the station and then drift back to sleep again to the sounds of the street. In her present state of mind, she never wanted to hear sounds that way again. She was emotionally out-of-balance, and their connotation made her feel helpless, without resources, cold and unloved, with no way out. Borg had replaced her father, the only type of men to which she could relate and understand. She felt trapped. QB was different, somehow. He went against all her previous programing about men. He didn't fall for her. He challenged her to look at life from a new angle. He did that in a few minutes. Not even beauty, a perfect figure, sensuality and her promise of a generous sharing of her body were able to lure her star athlete.

*Maybe QB doesn't like women*, she said to herself.

"Negative, sir, he is still in. No chuff. I am close, though. Sorry, sir. My cellphone signal is getting weak... Okay, that's better."

Borg said, "Your compensation of 50,000 is waiting for you but you will receive nothing if you don't draw QB out of that park Do you understand, Jessica?"

"Yes, sir."

"Did you see Ahmad Jones?"

No answer. She took the phone away from her ear and detached the headset.

"Jessica, did you see Ahmad Jones?"

"Yes."

"What time do you estimate that my men can procure him?"

She hadn't thought out a contingency plan—not a complete one, just bits and pieces. She sat waiting for the left turn signal. She had nothing.

"Give me twenty minutes to craft a new plan. I will call you then."

"Did Jones appear suspicious?"

"I could not tell. He was too far away. I caught him looking over at me, though. I think he was checking me out."

"He probably was, but not the way you think. Ahmad Jones is very perceptive."

"Just give me fifteen minutes, and yes, I will acquire the mark. I will call you right back."

"Jessica."

"Sir?"

"Ahmad is a world-class astrologist."

"I do not care if he can read my palm! I am sorry."

"You sound unsettled. Have you eaten? You know what occurs when you do not eat."

"No, I have not—not since last night; had a stomach ache. I am better now."

"Well, I said *astrologist*, not *palm reader*. The two are as diverse as *The Ritz London* and a fleabag motel. Do you understand my meaning, Jessica?"

She again flashed back to the feeling of cold concrete bleeding through cardboard, of waking up in a tent, wondering what she was going to eat and where to wash herself without being labeled. She relived that feeling of dread, of apprehension at night, of police and strangers. She could feel the knot below her ribcage tightening. She was feeling sorry for herself, which was just what Borg wanted her to feel. It had worked on her so many times before. Jessica was not the captain of her soul; the man on the other end of the cell phone was—or seemed to be.

"Sir, I understand, sir."

"Jessica, the private councils of 17 nations had enlisted Jones as a confidential advisor."

"If it is confidential, then how do *you* know?"

Silence.

"It is my job to know. Do not get sassy with me. Remember who you were and who you are now. And do not forget who I am. These nations paid him very handsomely to plot out the social, political, and economic courses of their governments. The Sovereign Republic of Afarland on the Indian Ocean was one such nation. We received word just two days ago from our people inside Dewabuna's regime that back in March of this year Jones had warned of a putsch happening this month, on this day. This is July, Jessica. We came up with the plan for the coup just last June with General Garaka, before we found out that Jones had already plotted it. We had not heard a peep from him since 2010. We only recently discovered that he was bound for O'Hare."

"Really?" Jessica remarked.

"Right, and this job is no ordinary one. Our man gained access to the minutes of a secret meeting during which President Dewabuna was briefed with members of his cabinet, on March 21st. They were warned of the putsch based on Jones' astrological analysis. General Garaka was not made aware of this meeting and the members were sworn to secrecy, but he got wind of it and got one member to talk. Jess, we have interests at stake in Afarland— *huge* interests! I sent two special men to deliver him to me, back in 2010. Even they came up short. This thing with Jones is what I was afraid of. Jess, we have to assume that Jones knows much more of the ramifications involved, which could interfere with billions.

"We just want to have a conversation with him in a private setting. Jones probably knows what you are going to do next. If he suspects anything, all he will require is the time of day and he will figure out your next move before you do. Also, he has friends in law enforcement at the federal level and virtually unlimited avenues to trace you to us."

Jessica was agitated over his last four words: *trace you to us*. The threat was not well hidden.

"You said I will not be paid until I get QB away from Jones. Well, I want to get paid. And his other friend, Ray, should be out of there by now. Geoffrey was just inside Ray's house. Fifty percent of my mission is completed. I *will* finish at one hundred percent."

"Yeah, baby, what's up?" Ray answered his phone.

"Where you at, honey dude?"

"Hey, who's this? Amy? Baby, don't scare me like that! You can let me talk all cockeyed but don't *you* do it!"

"I want to have a little fun with my baby. I don't get to spend weekends with you for weeks at a time. Also..."

Ray pointed to the phone and nodded to Jones. "Here it comes," he whispered.

"Listen, I need you to fix the seat on my rowing machine. It feels off-center. Okay, honey. Hurry back. I love you!"

Ray put his head between his hands, stood up and wiped the grass from the back of his pants. "I've got to go, Ahmad. Take care, buddy. Nice to see you."

"The pleasure was mine, Ray. Say hi to Amy and the kids."

Jones watched Ray run over to QB, shake hands and then get into his fire-engine-red Viper on South Boulevard. A black Caprice was behind Ray as he crawled out of his spot and drove off. The Caprice settled in and waited, then a Mercedes backed in, in front of the Caprice.

Probably a police service area, or something more, Jones thought. He remembered how the Caprice lingered when the redhead was talking to QB and the curious way she watched it.


"Jessica, after listening to you and considering what is at stake here, my associates and I have decided to take you off this assignment, directly. I will let my men handle both Jones and QB. You have tried and failed. We will arrange a jet for your return. I gave you a direct order. I will find another job for you."

"But I cannot—"

"I said that I will find you another assignment. I want you Jess, back here with me."

In a submissive tone, as if under a spell, she said, "Well, when you say it *that* way, Adlai."

# 32

## Key Players

BORG ENDED THE CALL WITH JESSICA. A group of NSA personnel had recorded their entire conversation.

"General Garaka, do accept my apology for the momentary interruption. An urgent call. We are presently all assembled."

"Yes, sirs!"

The General stood at attention to give some token of deference to Borg, as if the Maltese man were standing a couple of feet away. Dewabuna looked up at the big man, wondering how the hypocrisy of such a boisterous character like General Garaka could have gone undetected.

An attack on the Presidential Palace, the coup d'état, had occurred on the day Ahmad Jones predicted. Dewabuna, panned right-to-left over the barely recognizable corpses of Clarise Ajanlekoko, his Minister of Finance and his Minister of Security, Abdu Khamisi. They were shot dead and propped up under the window to the east. Each time the wind billowed the golden curtains their bodies appeared. When the wind ceased, the curtains covered them again. Dewabuna noted the other casualties. Every other member that attended the meeting last March, except Ahmad Jones, and the Prime Minster, who left Afarland the week before, was dead.

The Minister of Police, who was invited to the initial meeting but was too busy to attend, lay next to the president. The rest of the cabinet were several feet behind him—some spread out underneath the rugby picture and some in the vestibule, shot before they could escape. There were no bullet holes in any structure of the palace—each projectile forced its way into its human target. The General was a marksman. He had received his logistics and marksmanship training in Angola and Djibouti.

The president wondered whether these dead cabinet members were honorable or were in bed with Garaka, but could not be trusted, hence murdered?" "No," he thought, "they were honorable because they were present at the meeting. They were the ones that Jones warned to leave Afarland." After the cabinet returned from their afternoon break at the cabinet meeting, Jones suggested that they leave under the guise of a government recess. But the cabinet did not heed Jones' life-saving suggestion. They stayed in Afarland and will now remain—and so it is with me, Dewabuna thought. Jones also arranged for Afarland to join the African Union at a specific time, which happened without The General's knowledge. Jones' connections with heads of state, along with President Dewabuna's approval, enabled this secret membership to occur. The news would be kept under wraps, at the AU headquarters in Addis Ababa, Ethiopia until further notice. At one point as he scanned the mayhem, Dewabuna thought he saw an eye open and close, but he discounted it, thinking that Drambuie and his beating had affected his senses.

Adlai Borg, on speaker, continued, "Right, so let us review the action items from the previous meeting, to be certain that you have carried them out to the finest detail and that sufficient progress has been made. The signature event is that you will be installed as the new head of state, which is by your laws allowable if there is no heir apparent to take the reins of political power. Yours is a peculiar blend of presidential monarchy. For the aforementioned event to take place, you should have accomplished the following three things:

"First, we must procure Dewabuna's signature on a duly arranged resignation letter. Remember, General, his signature will preclude any debate at your National Assembly. Your Government Secretary should also have signed it. There will be no Constitutional Court judgment regarding Dewabuna's stepping down and handing power over to you, for there will be nothing to debate."

"Yes, Mr. Borg, I have the resignation document in my possession."

"Very good, General Garaka. Your Lieutenant General LaBrahm will be held accountable for the assassination of the cabinet and will be executed for murder and treason. This would be according to your laws. Dewabuna will resign after he announces to the people of Afarland that he was corrupt and behind the attempt to mine the gold under *Le Coeur,* using an unregulated private Canadian gold mining concern, for his own greed—to the cabinet's displeasure. It will be Dewabuna who gave LaBrahm the order to execute your cabinet. He will give that speech at sunrise tomorrow on *Afarland News.* The BBC, Al Jazeera and CNN will broadcast it around the world, among others. He will give you the implement of office as he is taken away to be executed. A rogue Afarland national will kill his only child while she is in the U.S. There will never be a Dewabuna in office, ever again. We are taking care of that. It should have been taken care of a long time ago."

"I understand, Mr. Borg. All is being arranged for tomorrow."

"Secondly, have you procured the mandate signed by the cabinet on your behalf and signed by Dewabuna? The citizens of Afarland will expect you to show it."

General Garaka hadn't remembered that detail and didn't recall what was done with the mandate after it was signed. He pressed mute.

"Where is the mandate?" he glared and snarled at Dewabuna. The president looked down at the distressed Cabriole legs of the writing desk. The light in his eyes got dimmer. Everything he heard was so airtight and thought-out—even his own upcoming execution. He was crestfallen, broken. He looked up at the general and tilted his head toward the safe. He thought that they didn't have to die; they all signed the mandate, under great duress, and he himself had signed it. The president looked down again.

The general unmuted the phone. "Yes, sir, I am in possession of the mandate."

"Very good. That is fine, right! Now, *'oil'* ask you the final question."

On Baxter Street in West, London, the other seven men in the room all stared at Borg after his strong native accent slipped through. Borg was born and raised in Birmingham in the West Midlands. When he graduated from Cambridge, he learned to speak with the typically British accent used by news reporters and political office-holders.

"Sorry, *I will* ask the final question now."

General Garaka turned off the speaker and picked up the handheld.

"Thirdly, Garaka, are all members of the Cabinet, with the exception of one, deceased?"

"Yes."

"That went satisfactorily well. Good, I have marked these off. We can move forward then with our agenda—I mean *your* agenda. That is, I mean to say, we are here to assist you in your—"

"Mr. Borg," Garaka interrupted, "I will see to it that the transition is smooth."

It was Borg who now put the call on mute. He said, "Garaka calls murdering cabinet members a smooth transition." The men saw the humor in that statement but didn't laugh. They continued to stare at the groomed lawn and artistically manicured landscape through the vapor and smoke-filled air.

Borg, the chairman of this audio conference, glances at his agenda and at his partners. He unmutes and says, "Good, very good. I suppose we can proceed."

Borg's partners are all dressed in dark-gray business suits. Five are sitting in red-velvet chairs around a hexagonal table. The table is cut out in the middle. The room is built like a racquetball court with a giant window where the main wall would be. It is similar to, but larger than, Borg's office, with no blinds or shades. Borg is seated at the table directly opposite the window. It is also divided down the middle with six rectangular sections on each side. It is inside a mansion in Hampstead. The wall-to-wall carpet is a brilliant vermillion red. There are glasses filled and half-filled with spirits. Two men are smoking at the middle of the window. Borg's Cuban cigar smolders in a glass dish next to him.

The eight men all nod. On the table in front of Borg is a charcoal-black conference phone. It is shaped like a stealth bomber sitting on a low tripod with a keypad extending from its nose.

"Do not take anything for granted," Borg warned Garaka. "You have 72 hours to concentrate and solidify your authority. Because your country is not a member of the African Union, there will be no serious problems in that part of the world. The African Union is a joke, anyway."

General Garaka was a complex man, which The Consortium was about to find out, "You little fucker! We are doing business and this isn't personal, so keep your opinions about my continent to yourself."

One of the two men standing at the middle of the window and looking at the fine-trimmed grass turned and stormed over to Borg.

"Excuse me, Garaka, but what continent?" Lekha Hanson, the chairman of The Consortium in its present chairmanship rotation and now Borg's boss said as he sat down at the table near the stealth bomber. "If I remember Africa's geography, Afarland isn't even located on the continent but is an island in the Indian Ocean. Granted, you may be part of the East African Region. And yet, there were never any indigenous Africans on your land until your people arrived. Seems to me that your ancestors assumed ownership over it when there was no one there to challenge them."

The General is silent.

"Hello? Garaka, are you still with us?"

General Garaka felt like giving Hanson a piece of his mind after that remark.

Hanson continued, "Why give a damn about the African continent? After this is over, they will surely give a damn about Afarland. We all stand to gain if you fulfill your part. Was it a ruse, your willing cooperation with us?"

Hanson didn't wait for an answer. "Dewabuna opposed your plans to mine the gold ore stored under the heart of your country and he has let his people down. With him out of your way and with our help, every citizen of Afarland will be wealthy. And you even more so. No man, woman or child will want for anything. That is all for now." *Click.*

"Yes, sirs. Very good, sirs!" General Garaka put the phone back in its cradle with care, playing off his blunder of flying off the handle with The Consortium for the president.

Dewabuna, after having swallowed the rich Scotch whiskey moments ago, smiled. He looked straight into General Garaka's right eye. He felt different now. He felt flippant and defiant. He was warm inside his body and could now tolerate the pain in his jaw and on his knees.

He said, "The correct word is *or.*"

General Garaka swaggered toward the president and said, "What did you say to me, Za?"

The president spoke very slow, with irony—despite the pain each word brought on his jaw. He slurred, "It... is '*or* what is happening here' not *nor*. If you... plan to, seize my country and, run it, you will not... hold power past seven hours, let alone seventy-two, if you do not know how to use those tiny words properly in a sentence."

General Garaka lifted his right hand and was about to whip it across Dewabuna's broken jaw. He remembered that Dewabuna had to give a speech the next day and he could not do it if he could not speak. He wondered how Dewabuna heard Borg's mention of 72 hours, from so far away, when it was not on speaker. But recalled that most coups leaders took at least three days to tighten their control.

Outside the palace lightning came from the northeast; intermittent flashes lit up a section of the nearby baobab trees, giving them the haunting appearance of gigantic human hulks. The company under the general's command that was stationed outside saw this play of light and shadow. They were a special mercenary group, in addition to Afarland's army, that took up positions around the palace. They were imported from Central Africa and prepared to drop any loyal Afarlanders who might appear, upon getting wind of the silent takeover.

A thunderclap arrived a second after the lightning, which struck terror into the minds of these newly arrived imported fighters. The thunder

sounded like a charge and the baobabs appeared like two long lines of soldiers on each side of *Le Coeur*, the only road leading to and from the Presidential Palace. If you counted them, as far as you could see in the dark, they
would number fifty or sixty on each side of the road. The mercenaries were
fierce, accustomed to violence and indoctrinated to fear nothing, but they
had never experienced such a seizure of limb-shaking fright from the combination of thunderclaps, lightning flashes, and baobab trees before. Something supernatural was at play. They stared at one another with bizarre
expressions. The sound of thumb safeties became a concert of clicks.

The position of the palace, perched on a low hill, called *The Royal
Promontory*, made it easy for the men to see down to the bottom of the hill,
at the lines of baobabs. Behind the palace were the bay and the ocean.

General Garaka drifted back into the president's busted chair, fuming to
himself, for not putting Hanson in his place. He removed his sunglasses and
howled, exposing his pearly-white teeth. His brown eyes glistened as the
doleful sound changed to bombastic laughter. The sound bounced off the
walls as the curtains rose again, uncovering Clarise, who was also Dewabuna's mistress, and Khamisi beside her. Another strong wind blew from
the east. The president squinted again, as more dirt hit his eyes.

The General said, "You dare to correct my English? I know more than
you think, old devil. No more talk. You and your regime. You had your chance."

The General looked around, first to the well-apportioned dining table
made of red mahogany polished to a high-gloss finish, then to the Louis XV
rattan chair made of ebony wood, covered in gold-leaf, and signs of more af-
fluence.

The president had been propped back on his knees by The General and
was stock-still. His eyes went to the velvet chairs surrounding the dining
table.

The general said, "I am a man of action. This country needs a man who
acts, not a man who just move his lips like a cow and buys fine furniture. You
were once a lion. You played a lion's game." He poured himself another glass
and gestured toward the rugby picture. "Now look at you." He gulped down
the liquor in one swallow. "You just chew your cud and pretend to be the lion,
the president. Me? I am the lion now!"

The coup leader bolted over, pressing the muzzle of his Browning semi-
automatic handgun against the president's left temple. He then turned to the
white mantel and the clock to the south. The clock was shaped like a human
heart and was encased within a fleur-de-lis made of several metal alloys and
overlaid with 24-karat gold. One plume was cobalt blue; the middle was
golden yellow; the last one to the right was a rich pink.

General Garaka was supposed to do a better job of running the country.
But he and his men would soon discover that they made a tactical error based

on incomplete information about the timing of their coup d'état—according to Ahmad Jones. The apprehension felt by the more than one hundred men stationed outside was the beginning—a foreshadowing—of their end.

The General said, "You will give that speech tomorrow, in pain, and then be executed. And, your daughter?"

Za Dewabuna's serenity was broken but his eyes didn't betray it. The liquor acted as a temporary shield, giving a surcease from the mental and emotional impact of his psychotic foe.

"Yes, my people are overshadowing her. She's all the family you have left. We know where she is—right now—in a hotel in *Owhieeoh*."

Dewabuna thought to himself: *That's Ohio, you imbecile!*

"I leave you with your ministers who are no more."

General Garaka took the muzzle of the semi-automatic from the president's temple and strutted to the wall in the west. He lifted the rugby picture off its hooks and opened the safe. He checked to see if the signet ring and mandate were there. The mandate was in a teal-colored envelope. He took it out and unfolded it. The signatures of the now-dead cabinet members were somewhat clear and visible—then he examined the resignation letter. There was something missing in the letter, which in his drunken conceit the General hadn't noticed—it was the most important feature, and therefore had political importance. Garaka placed the ring and documents back inside the safe. Before closing it, he took out the crystal case that housed the ring of state. He reexamined all twelve jewels encircling the center stone, then put the ring back in its case. He closed the safe. To him, his scheme was moving smoothly.

General Garaka laughed in a deranged way. He replaced the picture. He stepped over the corpses as he neared the hallway and vestibule. He pulled open the glass doors leading to the outside. He listened to the waters behind the palace and the lowered voices of his men who surrounded the Presidential Palace.

The muzzle imprint remained on Dewabuna's temple. General Garaka left the old man with several bodies of people with whom he had once talked and laughed. The silence around him was that peculiar atmosphere, beyond explanation, when a presence can still be discerned around a body when the life has withdrawn. Nine men and three women lay still around the main parlor and corridor. The remains of the president's most senior advisers reminded him that he would share their fate; moreover, that his daughter would be assassinated.

The president murmured to himself, his face wet with tears. He looked around at his cabinet and lamented in whispers, "Ahmad, you warned us about this moment in time. We all saw it—the handwriting on the wall and the betrayal. Ahmad—*Mar... a... kie*—I love you!"

The president, *with tied wrists and ankles,* rolled like a tumbleweed, on the wood floor, wishing to die. The whiskey made him less afraid but he had to live on through his suffering, taking personal responsibility for the putsch.

Dewabuna puts his ear to the floor. He hears the ocean waters breaking against the rocks underneath his home, for the palace was constructed above the narrow inlet that the people call the *Bay of Teal and Aqua,* which flows out to the Indian Ocean. Dewabuna catches the smell of saltwater, which gives him hope. His olfactory sense still works, despite damage to his nose and mouth. He looks at his chair and writing desk, then upward at the window as the next gust comes in. He sees the bodies below and is reminded of the love he was planning to share with Clarise as his wife.

President Dewabuna would close his eyes—for sleep, he thought—and be reawakened to face humiliation, sorrow and death. Lying on the floor, in and out of consciousness, he is stirred by a familiar voice.

"President Dewabuna." The president opened his eyes.

"Sir, Mr. President!" The whisper was coming from across the room, near the writing desk. Dewabuna thought that the whiskey was causing him to *hear* voices, but he had swallowed only half a glass. Still, he rotated his body to the right where he could see his old rugby picture, until he landed on his left side, where he beheld his Minister of Defense—alive!

"Whallun, you're, *ughhhh...* alive?" Dewabuna breathed hard. He was off-guard and used a contraction, which placed too much tension on his fractured temporomandibular joint.

"Mr. President, are you okay, sir?"

"Ye... yes. Do you know where my daughter is?"

"Yes, Mr. President. We've been keeping tabs on her as you requested. She's en route to Ohio in the United States. She might be there already. And your son-in-law is in Illinois. Sir, my wounds are serious. I'm losing blood. I don't know how long I've got. I may be playing dead—but this time for real."

"Do you know what for?"

"Sir! You know where she is and why she's—"

"WHAT are Ahmad and Marakie there *for*?"

"Sorry, sir, something about football."

"What? The World Cup? That's, *ughhh...* in Brazil in two years."

"Sir, not association football—American football. He's got that book published about American football. Don't you remember the plan?"

Whallun only knew half of the plan.

"Ahmad," said the president in a whisper, "will take care of her."


An unmanned aerial vehicle, launched from a naval base at Camp Lemonnier in Djibouti, had focused its bright lights to illuminate parts of *Le Coeur* and the upper landscape near the palace. Moments before, the lights had appeared as lightning due to the special cameras and new equipment—a cloaking distraction. On the last hour of a 12-hour routine surveillance run, it had switched to special night-sensors that canvassed the quarter-mile near the Presidential Palace. The computer screens of the remote drone operator showed the heat signatures of a company of soldiers.

Bowmen Hicks and the *senser* or camera operator, Lieutenant Rose Bailey, were manning the surveillance. Hicks called his superiors.

# 33

## A Football for a New Life

TWO MINUTES LATER, back in Kaskaskia, Jessica sat in her car with her hands on the wheel. Her arms were stiff. The cars behind her continued honking; some drove around her. The signal was red again for the second time. She blinked faster and rolled her eyes until the tears came. She considered her predicament. When the light changed, she turned left at the southeast corner onto Parker Street and then turned right into a gas station. She made a half-circle rightward until she crossed the apron leading onto the east side of Treefold Avenue. She doubled back, heading north toward Mangala Park.

Jessica braked and pushed in the red triangles to activate her hazard lights. She depressed another switch and watched the deck lid open and the convertible top come out. When the top closed and the windows rolled up, she took off her red wig.

Her dirty-blond pageboy cut was asymmetrical, with clean lines. Jessica was a beauty even without the red wig. She shook her head and ruffled her hair, combing it with her fingers. She made a U-turn and continued in the other direction for three miles to the pancake house on Treefold and Howard. Memories of past nights on the street with no food stirred her appetite.

QB loved football and kept women at a distance—the length of a football field—during preseason and regular season. Now retired, he spent his days and nights discussing games past with his buddies—those deep-throwing game-changers, interceptions reintercepted, fumbles recovered, sacks that came when he didn't even have the ball and his fondness of the sport. His personal relationships followed the pattern of his career—short, with rare moments of action, and in a way, still unfinished. This last interaction, with a gorgeous woman though, stirred up something different in him. He wasn't sure what.

Jessica sped toward Howard Street in her sports car.

Jones rushed to the ash tree.

"That lady came out of the void and ended up giving you a piece of paper. Nice work my friend."

QB was scratching his cheek. "Yeah, the paper, Ahmad? That's a negative on the paper, my friend. Women! I explained that I was throwing with my friends and she blew a gasket; she was damn gorgeous, too. She said if I didn't call her by one o'clock, then not to call."

"*Hmm*, it's just about one now. Her ultimatum is very specific. What's next?"

QB ripped up the sticky note. "I'm not too good at this anymore," he said. "Nah, she's not for me. I was curious, though, to see how far she was gonna go," QB said.

"If Ray had just heard you, he'd probably say, 'since when is a beautiful, intelligent and self-supportin' chick not your type, man? A chick like her comes to you? Man! When was the last time a fine woman stopped to give you her number? You oughta count your blessings…' or something to that effect."

"Sounds funny, Jones, expressions like that coming from you."

"What was your take on that skid, burning rubber, the girl, those sorts of things, because from what I remember about your career, you never had facial hair, 'til now, and you kept your butt on the bench for three years and only filled in once or twice."

"I don't know what you're trying to get at."

"I'm saying, not trying! Something isn't right, because you scored only two deep TD passes in three seasons. Most times, you pitched to your backs and several of your passes were incomplete. Your stats didn't show lots of yardage. Plus, one time you were even booed. Of course, you could play your assets off in college. That's why you were the first pick in the sixth round. The ACL injury stultified your chances. But, to your credit, QB, you never threw an interception; maybe that's why the GM didn't cut you off the team."

"So, what of it?"

"And how could she tell that was you, with your beard and long hair? You've stayed out of the spotlight. Did she call you QB?"

"Yes, she did. She recognized me."

"While driving like that up onto the curb? Strange."

"What?"

"Nothing, I guess." Jones knew the lady was a plant but didn't tell his friend. Because there was more to this woman showing up now, than appeared on the surface.

"I think the girl likes you, needs you. Maybe she's like you in some way, where something didn't go as planned in her life. Something didn't quite make it or was deferred, strategically delayed, maybe until today."

"Hey, yah! Going all Langston Hughes, on me. Huh, Ahmad?"

Under the ash tree, Jones stuck out his hands and QB handed him the ball. Jones held it in the middle, between his fingers and spun the ball on its axis end-to-end. They looked across the street at a young man running, passing the basketball, getting into a three-point position, catching a pass, ducking, dribbling, then shooting a perfect three. The wind rustled the leaves of trees all around. A couple of ravens flew inside the tree's leafy enclosure to some branches inside. The smell of asphalt hadn't completely gone away; neither had Jessica's perfume.

Jones said, "I think you have a golden opportunity to have a nice woman in your world—cultivating your throwing arm—you know what I mean. Maybe this is someone who needs love and wants to give it, too. Who's to say where she and you go from there?"

Jones put his arm around his buddy's shoulder. He spoke like an older brother.

"Dude, you could reconsider giving her a call. You've been out of practice with the ladies. Maybe now's the time to get back into playing—catch the girl instead of catching that ball. She skidded into your life. What do you think Joy would say if her death made you shun another woman's affection, out of fear of being unfaithful to her?"

Jones walked a few paces with the ball. QB stared at Jones, then they both checked out the basketball game. After some thirty seconds, he said, "I don't know, Ahmad. She was a little pushy and unpredictable. Something was off."

"You remember the other day when I shared a few things about your horoscope?"

"*Ah... yes.*"

"I said that near the last of July, or early August, you would meet a woman. She would come out of—"

"Nowhere. That's right. Out of nowhere," QB interjected.

"Right, and suddenly, as your progressed Venus conjoined your natal Moon in the Seventh House of personal relationships—and transiting Uranus, the unexpected, entered your Fifth House of romance to conjoin your natal Venus, which is the planet most associated with relating socially with others, especially women."

"Yeah, Ahmad, but you said she would be a blond and this girl's a red-head."

"Well, does she fit any criteria besides her hair color? Be more direct but in a caring way and be the gentlemen that you already are. You've got two college degrees, plus your other skills. All I'm saying is, you may have the time of your life, like winning a Super Bowl all by yourself—and instead of a Lombardi, you get her. By the way, did she tell you her name?"

The words *Super Bowl* and *her* combined had a peculiar effect. QB assembled the sticky-note fragments.

"Patricia. She's from Jersey."

Jones considered his last comment. "She told you that?" Jones tossed the ball.

QB tucked the football under his arm and looked at the tire tracks on the easement.

"How else? Yes, she told me."

"She said the word *Jersey*, without anything attached to it? One thing, my good friend, give me the details. How did she say that she was from there?"

QB picked up the last piece of the sticky note and stood up. "I asked her where she was from and she said, 'New Jersey,' then 'New Brunswick,' okay?" Jones saw the big picture, while QB began dialing the number.

"New Jersey? Not just plain Jersey?" Jones thought a bit. Something was false and yet, this woman drove into his friend's life as he predicted.

"Okay, Ahmad, you sold me. I've dialed her number. I owe you one."

"It's your show, my friend."

Jessica had placed her order two minutes earlier when her other cell phone rang.

"Hello?"

"Hi, Patricia. This is QB."

Jessica's hand trembled. This was the pivot-point in her life. She would have to leave Borg now and not look back. One day she would tell QB about her past. She took a deep breath and said, "QB! I'm surprised to hear you! And excited to hear from you. Would... would you hold on for a minute— honey?" She muted the call.

"Sure."

Jessica took her encrypted phone out of her bag and speed-dialed. If she didn't do something now, then Borg's men would.

"Yes?" Borg answered.

"Sir, Jessica speaking. QB just called me. He wants to see me. What are my orders?"

"Are you sure? Our men are watching them now. They were about to go in for QB *and* Jones."

The Caprice was parked across the street on the east side, three car lengths from the intersection near the basketball courts.

"Pick him up and keep him until you hear from me. And Jessica, Jones may have put him up to it. Be careful. I'll notify Marshall."

"I understand."

Her order of sausage and buttermilk pancakes had arrived, but she was too excited to eat. She paid for her order and left it on the table.

"Where are you?" QB asked.

No reply.

"Patricia?"

"I'm sorry, I must have forgotten to unmute. I'm in my car now."

"I'm here at the park looking at your tire marks. I can play catch any day."

Jessica put her red wig back on and pulled the latch to lower the convertible top—all was as QB would remember it. She could sense the presence of money and a chance to begin a new life—without Adlai Borg breathing down her neck. She would take QB out of harm's way, until she could think of something.

Jessica asked, "What made you change your mind so fast?"

"My friend hurt his fingers."

"So, you are saying you don't have anyone to play with you? How convenient!"

"No, I don't mean that. Not at all."

Jones was making rapid, vertical circles with his hand.

"I don't want to go straight home, I mean. I can't play football all the time. Understand?"

Jones lifted his thumb and nodded *yes*.

"I think I understand. I'll see you in less than five minutes," she said.

"Okay Ahmad, it's done. She sounded really excited."

"You sounded like you were reading a script, but you did all right. Just remember her loveliness and you'll be fine, pal. I'm catching the 3:17 flight to Ohio to promote my book. My wife's already there."

"Guess this is bye for now, old friend, and thank you for your helpful comments." For the first time in a long time QB smiled from ear to ear. He respected his friend.

Jones eyed the Caprice as he walked with QB to where the tire marks were. The candy-orange Audi appeared a half-mile up. The men followed the car's progress as it neared the intersection.

"I don't know what the hell I'm getting into but Patricia is a fine woman."

"Patricia. How cool. Nice name," Jones said. She pulled up across the street in front of the courts. She got out and all eyes from the basketball court got a closer look as she sauntered from across the street to meet QB. She stopped ten feet away with her hands on her hips.

"You ready, QB?" she teased.

QB opened his hands and Jones tossed him back his ball. "See you, Jones."

"I'll see you the next time I'm in town, my friend."

QB went to the car, talked with Patricia for a moment, and then walked her around to the passenger side and opened the door. She looked at him for a beat then sashayed to the door and got in. He continued around the back until he reached the driver's side, dropping the ball in the small space behind the seat.

He shouted, "Ahmad, I'll tune in to *The End Zone*, tonight."

"Thanks, QB."

"I'm starved. Let's get something to eat, baby," she said. "How do pancakes sound to you?"

QB made a U-turn and headed south, waving. Jones watched the red hair blowing back as she cuddled up closer to her new friend.

Jones started walking west toward the couple on the bench. He thought about having those undercover cops call in a 10-37 for a suspicious vehicle. He decided against it. He knew that whoever was in that Caprice with tinted windows would make a move any time now. He had another idea and took out his cell.

# 34

**Disappearance at 40**

"CHEYANNE, IT'S AHMAD. I'm in the Midwest."

"We haven't heard from you in months," Cheyanne said. "Guess you don't need to use an encrypted phone anymore. You're all over the Internet. Rakesh asked about you just last night; saw your book for sale online. Football? You didn't tell us about it."

"No time to explain, sis. Would you make an urgent call for me?"

She picked up one of three cellular phones on the desk.

"Okay. Who to?"

"Please notify Special Agent Jack Peterson at the FBI field office in Cleveland.

"Tell him that his friend Ahmad Jones is in a situation, one against four, and for him to contact his buddies in Kaskaskia to pick him up—now. I'm at Mangala Park on Treefold and South Boulevard. Cheyanne, you'll have to call Peterson, I've just texted you his private cell."

"Got it. I'll call now."

"Thanks, sis."

"Get back to us when you get this straightened out. You hear?"

"Sure, later. My best to Rakesh."

Cheyanne dialed and hit speaker.

Two hundred and forty miles southeast of Kaskaskia, two FBI special agents are barreling to the airport on I-77 in their brown Chevy Tahoe. They're discussing a former independent contractor who resurfaced about a week ago.

"The last time I saw Ahmad Jones was in Detroit at Super Bowl 40 when he disappeared," the man with the cigarette said. He sat on the passenger side. After he answered his partner's question, the once lean and now over-weight agent, whose bright-yellow tie appeared to be choking him, took another long drag from his 6-minute-old Chesterfield. He wanted to feel useful again. He felt hampered by routine.

Each time his team presented the hard evidence to the AG for criminal prosecutions that landed several *model citizens* into federal prison, another company of bad guys appeared. *What's the use?* he often thought.

"I miss my hometown of Tuckahoe, Virginia," he said. "That's why I enjoy Chesterfields."

The towns of Tuckahoe and Chesterfield were about sixty miles apart. Peterson drew a peculiar comfort from each drag.

"Can you elaborate? What do you mean, Jones disappeared?" the other man asked.

The G-man's lips parted and the semi-perfect rings that shot out in slow motion were sucked out through the window of the SUV as it accelerated another ten miles, in addition to the 68 it had already done. The agent watched his smoke vanish. He was reminded of how his work and talent was just like that smoke. Fleeting. He cocked his head to his partner at the wheel.

"Jones was sitting in the end zone, Seahawks' side. We were watching him and a lot of good *that* did."

"Why? What happened?"

"We lost him—our monitoring game was over. I see Jones looking at his watch, when a moment later, the Steelers' Michael Boulware intercepts Ben Roethlisberger's play-action pass to Antwaan Randle El. Then the flurry of Pittsburgh's Terrible Towels is swinging all around the joint. I turn back and *SHAZAM!* No more Jones."

"What do you mean, no more Jones?"

"I mean that Jones was no longer in our sights. Game over! That was it. We—I had arranged to talk to him. You know, to make him an offer on behalf of the Bureau: advisor to a new forensic special sector of certain eligible DOI personnel.

"You meant to hire Jones? Bring him through the back door to work for the FBI—at the Super Bowl?"

"Pitch. I was going to *pitch* the idea, with *creds* and all. I sent agents to inform Jones that I had to meet with him. You know, guys he knew. After that Seahawks' interception, they lost track of him."

"So, Jones does the rabbit and he's—"

"It wasn't like that. See?"

"But he's surrounded by a hierarchy of the nation's best government agents, and state and local law enforcement. They have him under their noses and he executes a David Copperfield?"

"He executed an Ahmad Jones! There was no blue smoke and no secret doors. He was in plain sight."

Peterson started puffing faster. When he felt more composed, he said, "He must have left and somehow got through the perimeter. None of our guys, not a one, saw what he did or when he could have done whatever he did; neither could they deduce how he could have done—whatever!"

"Got any *the-o-rees*?" asked his partner.

"My rational mind says that it was during the commotion over the interception. Jones' whole section stood up. He must have used that as an opportunity. But exactly what he did, I haven't worked it out to this day. There were several of our guys inside and a plethora of street agents."

"*Plethora*? Haven't heard that word in a while. Why do you use big words when you get anxious?"

"I'm not prevaricating—but what do you mean by big words? Well, we had 'em out there, see, on Brush and Beacon, even on Madison Street. There was a cordon of National Security special-events personnel. I furnished a platoon of them with Jones' description: *African American, age about 30, clean-shaven, about six feet, one-eighty pounds, with a well-groomed and short afro, muscular, wearing a vintage Seahawks' blue satin jacket*—bright blue and hard to miss. It stood out against the sea of Pittsburgh yellow. Still, Jones had vanished like my cig smoke—now you see him... So, I informed my men to detain him and notify me. It may have seemed an improper use of manpower, depending on your take.

"Who did you tell them Jones was?"

"I referenced the fact that he was a guy who helped the Bureau tremendously. You know, helping us, and special agents like Mike Cappello from Seattle, to get hard evidence to put several criminals behind bars and that we had lost contact with him several months ago. You know, O'Donnell, when Jones helped me out, those criminals stayed behind bars."

"Did you mention that he *wasn't* an informant?"

"No, because if I had stated what he wasn't, it could've stuck in some agent's mind, I mean, the ones who didn't know Jones. What if several devices, or just one, had a battery that malfunctioned, or a weak signal, someone could have heard the word *informant*, but not that he wasn't one. You see? In the back of their minds they would factor in that informants weren't always friends of the law before they became informants—even after. So those two words, *detain* and *informant*, in the same message, could've been misheard. And if an agent saw him, there's no telling what could've happened."

"To Ahmad?"

"To the agent. Ahmad put two of our agents in cuffs, no kidding. He was pumping gas and two of our men were investigating the string of gas-station robberies at gunpoint. So, one of our men man-handled Jones and got put into a wrist lock. Then his partner tried to pry him loose."

O'Donnell reached 80 mph.

"Hey partner, slow down."

"Sorry but this story is giving me an adrenaline rush."

"So, Jones locks both agents' wrists, bone against bone. They can't break loose, because Jones has the leverage to bring them to the ground."

"Fucking kidding me?"

"Jones has them pinned in the parking lot; with little more than a couple of ounces of force, he reaches for the cuffs."

"I never heard any of this."

"Then he calls HQ. One of our men says, "Please, Ahmad, don't hurt our men, teach them a lesson, only. So Bob and I show up—we all had a laugh. When the two agents were free, and Bob and I explained who Jones was to the Bureau, we all went to the tavern and had the time of our life."

"Charges?"

"Nope. Anyway, at Ford Field, I knew that if I failed to talk to Jones that day, I'd never see him again—I just had a feeling. Anyway, the agents would treat him with respect, being that he helped the Bureau. I figured Jones would understand and go with it. It was a million-to-one shot that he and I were there at the same time. I hadn't talked with him, really talked that is, since he'd lectured in Virginia and that was in 2005. So, one of ours IDs him, see?

"At the entrance on Marsh Street. He remembers Jones from a short time before, so he notifies me. I advise the agent to keep several pairs of eyeballs on him and communicate this to the rest of our unit, to say that Jack's good friend is in the stands and he wants to say *hi*, and then I'd decide when it was a good time to run down and see him or to send my guys to collect him. They track him to his seat in the end zone."

"Weird!" O'Donnell says.

"I figured the whole thing sounded weird to them, too, that I was using federal manpower to send him a message. You see, I didn't want Jones to be the victim of a misunderstanding, a suspect, a person of interest, or worse. You know that Super Bowls are big targets and if incomplete information got out about him, he could've been in danger. Jones wasn't the type to take anything lying down and I was afraid that he would attempt to do to our men what he did at the gas station, if anyone laid a hand on him.

"I assured myself that I could get to talk with him without putting him in harm's way. I was justified in playing it like I did."

"How's that?"

"Because the whole thing was green-lit by my field office supervisor.

"I had about 21 agents on all points of the lower-level end zones. He should not have gotten out of there unseen. My men were tasked with other duties there and I couldn't get to him right away. Heck, since the DHS designated the Super Bowl an NSSE, all the headaches from coordinating with near sixty law-enforcement agencies made it impossible for me to concentrate *only* on Jones. For the big game I was one of three leads for coordinating intelligence in the stadium, personnel, and special circumstances. Anyway, as I said, the field office asked me to reach out to Jones when I informed them of his whereabouts. That was sufficient for a call to action. We were going to recruit Jones. We were going to offer him a GS-11 pay grade with all the benefits, somewhere near the 50-yard line."

"You're joking! That's a lot more than a new hire would get. Did this guy possess the required four-year degree, two languages, and the twenty weeks of training that they made *me* go through to get this job?"

"O'Donnell, the answer is *yes*, except the twenty weeks. Jones earned two degrees from Cornell."

"What? A Bachelor's?"

"He holds a master's in *poli-sci* with the same in government. Speaks Hindi, Chinese, Swahili, and some Russian, in dialect. He could run a country, this guy. His thesis related astronomical events to political events, especially of the type where large groups of people are impacted, and when the leadership changes by death, or assassination, or a coup or public uprising. He plotted these for several nations and showed their direct correspondence with planetary cycles. His book is required reading in one of our divisions since it gives the rules for anticipating political upheavals in any country. We passed it on to our friends in Fairfax. We could gather intelligence about governments and hand it off to our attachés around the globe before governments knew what was going on. When Jones left us, we were beta testing it."

"Shit!" O'Donnell said. Peterson said, "One reason why the Bureau wanted him, and still does, is that he can provide us with reasonable anticipation of probable national and foreign political changes that may have world consequences. What he does can be measured, and so it fits the general designation of a science."

"That's a lot to consider, Jack."

"I know. He was a ghost for more than a year until that game, then... Shit, did you see what that man did in that truck? He's lucky we've got some other place to go."

"I saw it coming," O'Donnell said.

"So, anyway, Jones became a ghost again during that game."

Peterson lifted the ringing phone from the holder in the center console, put out his cigarette, and answered, "This is Special Agent Peterson speaking."

"Special Agent Peterson, my name is Cheyanne. I'm calling on behalf of Ahmad Jones."

Peterson pulled the phone from his ear like it was a Taser about to shock him.

Special Agent Mason O'Donnell saw Peterson jerk the phone from his ear. "Is there a problem?" he asked.

Peterson nodded. "You say you're calling on behalf of Ahmad Jones?"

O'Donnell's double-take almost caused him to swerve into the right lane into a cement truck. He quickly got back in the passing lane. Peterson was too shocked to notice.

"What can I do for you, Ms. Jones?"

"My last name isn't Jones, but this is urgent. Ahmad is in big trouble and asks that you call your federal friends in Kaskaskia, Illinois, to bring him in. This must be done *yesterday*. He's got maybe three or four minutes, tops. Please hurry, he's my brother."

Peterson put the phone back in the holder and on speaker. He took his notepad from his inside pocket and clicked the nub on his fountain pen. "Give me his location, Ms."

"Call me Cheyanne. He's on the northeast corner of Treefold Avenue and South Boulevard in Kaskaskia, in front of the basketball court, wearing..."

"I'll make the call now. Tell him to sit tight. Thank you, Ms., *uh,* Cheyanne. What's your last name?"

"Pradesh."

"Thanks Ms. Pradesh." Peterson ended the call and dialed the local switchboard. "Tony, this is Peterson, and this is urgent—can you get me through to Napoleon Davis in Kaskaskia, please?" O'Donnell looked at Peterson. He'd never seen his partner with such a look of concern.

"You look like your dog just died."

"Dialing Agent Davis," Tony said on speaker.

"You have reached FBI Special Agent Napoleon Davis, I'm on vacation. If this is urgent, contact Brenda Nolan at..." Peterson dialed the number without writing it down.

"Special Agent Brenda Nolan speaking."

"Agent Nolan, Jack Peterson, Cleveland Field Office. I have an urgent request, we have an important asset, *ah,* an independent contractor, named Ahmad Jones."

"Did you say Ahmad Jones? The guy who—"

"Yes, him. I need you to collect him right now. He's in over his head. Black man, about six-one, or thereabouts, early forties, wearing a white polo shirt, beige khakis, and red sneaks. Short hair, classic military style."

"I'm leaving now. Will notify you when we've picked him up. I'm looking forward to meeting him," Nolan said.

"Agent Nolan, he's also my friend," Peterson added.

"I appreciate that, Agent Peterson. We'll bring him in safe." Nolan hung up. She couldn't believe the call she just got. She picked up the landline and pressed the numbers *eight* and *one*.

"Sparks, McNulty, Frazier, Williams and Dumont: meet me in the conference room. This is Priority One." The woman and four men heard the request over the intercom. The boardroom was at the end of the hall. The agents hurried to the plexiglass boardroom door located at the middle of the conference room. In the center of the north wall at the far end was a map of Illinois with pushpins on the primary cities in the counties the RA served. To the right of the map were the pictures of the President, the U.S. Attorney General and the FBI Director. They formed a triangle with the president at the apex. On the west wall across from the middle door was a framed copy of the Declaration of Independence.

The cities with the red pins were the high-crime areas. There was lots of red. The windows on the west wall, on both sides of the framed document, were tinted. Every wall was light gray. The lighting was standard ceiling fluorescent, which took away most of the warm tones. The only thing in the room with some warmth was the large walnut-brown conference table. There were 14 wheeled, ergonomic, gray chairs. The carpet was wall-to-wall presidential blue. Laptops were set up, all around the desk. For security purposes the laptops were locked, showing the Department of Justice seal, on the splash page.

The five agents file in. Special Agent Nolan stands in front of the three pictures at the north end of the table with one hand on the top rail of a chair. She's the Supervisory Agent in Charge (SAC) of the RA.

"Ahmad Jones has been identified. He's at Mangala Park and in some danger."

"Ahmad Jones? You're kidding!" Liam Sparks exclaimed. Sparks was former Navy Intelligence who had decided against going into the CIA. As part of the Tactical Squad, he wanted to be able to take bad guys into custody. He was five-eleven, clean-shaven, with dark hair cut to precise specifications.

"Forget the stories you've heard. He's in trouble and we're the closest to him."

"What about the Kaskaskia police department? I mean, why us? I want to meet this guy, but their house is a mile from the park and we're three miles away," said Annette Williams, a CPA, five-ten, with a law degree from Hunter College and a member of the Fugitive Squad.

"I need you all to meet me in the garage in one minute. That is all."

# 35

## Astrologist on the Brain

"JONES ARRIVED IN THE U.S. on the same day his book was released. What's he doing in Kaskaskia?" Peterson wondered out loud to O'Donnell. "It's been ten years—ten years—since I've talked with that son of a gun!"

"The way you describe him, Jones sounds like a resourceful guy," O'Donnell said. "It's possible that he didn't do a rabbit—maybe he was hiding in Ford Field."

"Rabbit? Hiding? *Please!* Jones and Rabbit in the same sentence, just doesn't add up. He would never do that—run away or hide in a stadium like a criminal—he had no reason to. Besides, he's always been an up-front guy. He's not the sneaky type. That wasn't the way Jones conducted himself."

Peterson sat upright on the Tahoe's passenger seat, blowing smoke every 30 seconds against the sagging flexible fabric of the headliner board. Gravity had coaxed its beige-colored vinyl material into the shape of an upside-down triangle, exposing the foam underneath, and Peterson used it for a target. He was breaking protocol for the first time in his 20-year career as an FBI agent: Never smoke on the job. It was unprofessional. Hoover's rules.

"One of the facts of life, Jack, is breathing," O'Donnell admonished, "Me, I'm trying to quit but I have enough will power not to smoke while I'm on the job."

Peterson said, "I get you, you're right. I haven't touched a square in years; this is my first pack. So, before we lost track of Jones, my plan was to take him out for a bite at *Fu Lin's* on Blaine Street, about six miles north of Ford Field. He got to the stadium at 5:27 pm, about an hour before Seattle and

Pittsburgh tossed that coin. I remember the time they gave me like it was yesterday. His $800 seat lined up with the first letter **E** in Seattle painted on the end zone. That reference point made it easier for our people to keep up surveillance. And being on the upper-level sidelines, as well, gave us the height advantage. Still, a lot of good *that* did!"

Peterson sucked in another mouthful of smoke. After that, he changed topic. "You know, that Ahmad Jones was some kind of man. He often used to quote from Emerson who said that, 'Astrology is astronomy brought to earth and applied to the affairs of men.' He said that was what he did."

"Sounds like astrology to me," O'Donnell said.

"True but he used it well; provided relevant data for local and state police endeavors. I liked Jones. We solved many cases in unusual ways."

"Liked?" O'Donnell inquired.

"Even if I tried, I couldn't be mad at Jones—even if he *did* the rabbit."

"You just said that Jones wouldn't—"

"I can't believe I said it but look—any reasonable guy would conclude that there was no other way to get lost in a stadium. The lady I talk to said I should pay attention to my feelings. People in our profession tend to sweep shit under the rug. Then, when you're not looking, it creeps up on you. She said I should be like an observer from the outside, you know, like a witness."

O'Donnell asked, "Doris, right? You've been in therapy with Doris?"

"I've got to stop defending Ahmad. She said that it was about my self-worth. I don't know why I'm telling you this."

"I can forget what I hear very easily."

"Jones knew I wanted to talk to him. He must've sensed it. He's the only person who understood where I was coming from." For a moment, Peterson was lost in thought. The two men were quiet enough to hear traffic noises again.

"One day, my ex-wife and I hiked up Rattlesnake Ledge in North Bend, Washington. Jones led the way, and instead of talking all the way up, that son-a-of gun didn't say one word.

"So, Stacy and I followed suit. We didn't say a word, either. The hush around us was calming, except for people jabbering on the way down past us, and those getting ahead of us. My ex and I had never experienced quiet to that degree, ever. We felt at peace, really at peace up there with Ahmad. Stacy and I felt closer as a couple. The week after, my ex and I were still experiencing the quiet, the stillness. We were unconditionally happy for the first time, in five years of marriage. Yep."

The sounds of traffic on I-77 grew louder. Peterson was self-absorbed.

"Yep," Peterson said, "the thing about Ahmad was that when you were around him, you could be sure some new angle on life would unfold before your eyes. In my case, ears. I miss that."

Peterson flicked his cigarette out the window. "I thought we were friends but after a year or so, Jones wanted nothing more to do with the Bureau. We all felt it was because he was just a contractor and that he wanted more money, so we acted on that assumption. The last time I saw him was when we all went to Seattle to watch the Seahawks play the Dallas Cowboys. It was a close game. That was late in October in 2005. After we left Qwest Field, we went to a restaurant. Jones had finished eating a Mediterranean salad. I told him that the FBI could use his help, and not as a contractor. We had a plethora of cold cases and he said, now get this, he said that if we wanted to prevent, not just solve, but prevent problems of terrorism, at home or anywhere else, that it had to start with self."

"What the hell was in his salad?" O'Donnell remarked.

"Yep, should have had forensics analyze it for their *unknown chemical evaluation* test." Peterson laughs, O'Donnell joins in and they laugh hysterically.

"I'm at a loss to solve that one."

"Preaching to the choir there, O'Donnell. Jones said that all the world's problems start from the inside and work their way out. Then he got up, put a sawbuck on the table and excused himself. He was cordial and respectful, always a gentleman you know."

Peterson pulled his tie from side to side. "He never came back. That was a week after Stacy filed for divorce. The peace on that ledge wore off. In a way Ahmad vanished two times; the first was at the restaurant and the second at Ford Field. I lost a real friend. Soon after, my wife and I were legally divorced. So, he left that night, in 2005, when a bunch of us were at this Italian restaurant on Bellevue Way and 8th. I can't remember the name; just that the food and service was great, and it was above ground level. You lived in Seattle once, so you—"

"Maggiano's—you were at Maggiano's, right?"

"Right!"

"Bellevue. It's in Bellevue."

"I'm a federal agent and Jones, he's a free-agent. I respect that lifestyle—even envy the guy. When he disappeared in Detroit without talking to me, though, I took it personally, in the gut. The things we could have accomplished with Jones onboard. We've got some other astrologist in there now, but he can't do it like Jones could—you know, seat-of-the-pants. He doesn't have that. He's too rigid in his thinking and interpretation. Not Ahmad Jones. Hadn't heard from him in ten or eleven years—but that's water under the old bridge," Peterson mused.

O'Donnell said, "Are you certain of that? Well, I consulted an astrologist once when I lived in Boston. My older brother taught me to learn about anything and everything. I grew up with that inclination, that mindset. You know? So, I was interested. You wanna know what the astrologist asked me? He asked me if I ever considered a career in law enforcement. He said it was something about my Moon and Mars' conjunction in the Tenth House in Scorpio. He said I had a great facility for getting to the bottom of things and how that quality would make me an excellent detective. He said that the conditions would be just right for me to make a career change around the month of December of my 28th year. He called it my Saturn Return or something. I listened to the tape of that reading a few weeks ago. Anyway, I made a career decision around late November, in my 28th year. I left investigative journalism and took the exam for the Boston PD!"

Peterson tamped his pack and took out another cigarette.

"I entered the academy, was a patrolman for five, then became detective-third-class in my sixth year. Got second-class two years later. I got out before applying for my gold badge. Now I'm driving this SUV while you talk about this astrologist who may, I suspect, have been a central figure, like my older brother, to you. But, listen, you must admit that if Jones called you, he must think of you as a friend."

"I never had a truer friend. There were people I've known from high school, through college, to now. At best they're fine acquaintances. No disrespect, O'Donnell."

"None taken."

"You're my partner. How many fine acquaintances put their lives on the line for their partners?"

"Novel question."

"My job is my friend, a weird one, but still my friend. Every day, something new, unexpected and exhilarating. Always there to do things with."

"Jones isn't tied down to a career like you or me. We're government men with a mandate of fidelity, bravery and integrity. And Jones, well, he can take off whenever it suits him. I'm no psychologist, but I think that Jones' freedom is what's got you blowing smoke at that makeshift target, not his magic act."

"I thought he was my friend," Peterson said.

"You just said that you never had a *truer* friend."

"O'Donnell, you're a well-trained agent, but I did not need a word-for-word playback of what I just said. For now, let our conversation be free and unhampered from the shackles of precision."

After a couple of minutes of tense silence, Peterson said, "Almost at the airport."

"Just a couple of miles."

Like a veil was lifted, Peterson put the cigarette back inside the pack. He said. "When I learned of his new book two days ago—*Football's Astrological Measurements*—I skimmed through some of it. He wrote about the San Fran 49ers, when they played Seattle at the Kingdome in 1976. He wrote, and I can only paraphrase, that when the game began at 1:06 or 1:07 pm, I'm not sure which, the constellation on Seattle's local horizon was called *Swati*, a group of stars in the constellation of Libra, according to Indian Astrology. Well, it turns out that this group of stars contains an attribute related to the Hawks and the 49ers. They're called the *Lords of the Northwest* and there are 49 of them, called the *49 Winds*!"

"I wonder how he trawled that one out."

"But there's more."

"We're at Arrivals now."

"Just listen to this—it's the clincher. Jones wrote that the game took place in the sun sign of Leo. You know, it's the sign for late July and most of August. And that the Sun, which is associated with Leo, is related historically to gold, as well as to kings, queens, and royalty. So, the 49ers name ties into the gold rush of 1849, and that game was played in the *King*dome."

"Okay, that's pretty good. But do you think we can concentrate on our assignment now? Ruderman's planet, I mean *plane*, may arrive early. Enough of this astrology stuff, please!"

Peterson pulls out a Chesterfield while going back in time. He takes several puffs and sends his ash out the half-inch space between the window and the doorframe. He sucks in another mouthful and notices the other end turning bright orange. He hits the vinyl again and looks ahead, watches the future running at him at 78 miles an hour, on I-77 in Akron, Ohio. The air traffic control tower at CAK grows nearer.

"Jones was a special type of intelligence analyst. Back in 2003, you may have read about that human trafficking market that was operating here in the state. Well, I was in Seattle when an agent from the Cleveland Field Office contacted us, so we brought Jones in to do his thing. We had the agents from Cleveland on loudspeaker when one of them said, 'If we only knew their whereabouts.'

"Jones constructed a few different charts using Cleveland's coordinates for that oblique question. About ten minutes later, he asked for a street map for Cuyahoga Falls. We printed one out, tacked it on the corkboard, and he circled a three-square block, *chunk!* We advised our fellow agents to put surveillance on that chunk for three months. They got together a task force of U.S. Marshalls, along with the local police and the ATF. FBI ran the investigative op. Then, we got the hard evidence. Went to the AG with it. Secured the warrant and brought that place down. We got a hit. Ahmad Jones demonstrated a method that, in addition to our other evidence-gathering strategies, helped another FO, by locating the headquarters of a human-trafficking market. *I kid you not!*"

"You have case files? Show me. I'd like to see that hard evidence for myself. I know I'm just a newbie, almost ten months now, but this sounds like some *Philip K. Dipshit, Minority Report!* What you've just told me about the 49ers is something I can conceive. It's the random stuff that's hard to track. Back East, I worked one of the most violent counties where aggravated assault, rapes and robberies occurred almost every day. The feeling was that the crimes weren't planned, just on the fly. They just happened out of the blue. Just like that, with no warning. Do you think Jones' skills could provide advanced intel on random stuff like that?"

"If anyone could create a method to plot random, he could," Peterson said. "Someone asked that at Quantico and Jones said that nothing that appears to be random is actually random—that there was no such thing as an accident. He said that an accident is another name for a law in nature that isn't understood yet!"

"No accidents, huh? Tell that to my wife when the cabin belonging to an 18-wheeler rammed into our parked minivan that she had just exited. The guy was drunk and lost control. It smashed into the driver's side and reached the passenger's side, pushing the mini up against a brick building seconds after she got out to get her nails done across the street!"

Peterson listened and then said, "I know all this sounds crazy, but Jones is the genuine article."

"A few moments ago, you said that Doris, your shrink, told you to own up to your feelings. I can't believe I'm saying this—and not to make excuses for Jones—but you just did it again. Maybe he is and maybe he isn't. Anyway, some of his alleged exploits sound like elements of modern folklore. Sorry about my precision, but that's how I'm wired."

"I'm retiring after this is over."

"After *what* is over?" O'Donnell asked as he pulled into the Arrivals entrance of the Akron-Canton Airport. They drove up to Delta.

"You haven't been fully briefed. I'll inform you after—later—but I'm leaving because of something Jones told me over ten years ago. Here we are."

"You've got Jones on the brain, pal!"

"Guess I do! Now we wait for Ruderman."

# 36

## Marshall's Contingency Plan

AFTER JONES SAID GOODBYE to Nolan and his new FBI friends, at the entrance of the hotel, he withdrew the keycard, moved carefully into his suite, and inspected each room. He had tucked himself into a hotel, near the edge of town, and 5.3 miles from Mangala Park. Of the three basic room categories, Jones picked the executive suite. Because of its space and location at the end of the hall, it presented more mobility options. It was the size of a micro-apartment. Jones pulled out his cell to call Marakie. The guest-phone rang. It was 1:30 pm. Jones put his cell on the table in front of the south wall, where a picture of Lake Tahoe was hung.

"Yes?"

"Mr. Jones? Hi, I'm Mason Holmes in Seattle. I sincerely hope we're still on for the interview?"

Jones hadn't remembered the interview his publicist had arranged with the Seattle-based radio show.

"Yes, Mason, we are." Jones stood on one leg each time he untied and pulled off a sneaker.

"That's good. I called a couple of times before, and I really prayed that you would answer. I just finished with my first guest and talked you up. We go on the air after the commercial in, say, 40 seconds. How's the weather where you are, in Kaskaskia?"

"Hot, Mason, pretty hot."

Jones relaxed onto the armchair. He heard the commercial being played, then silence. The intro was a jazzy prelude on the piano.

"Welcome to the second half of *Mason Holmes with the Stars*. My guest is Ahmad Jones, astrologist and author of *Football's Astrological Measurements.* We are delighted to have him on the show. Ahmad, you just arrived in the states from Afarland. Is that right?"

"Yes, Mason, I wrote my book there."

After waking from a long sleep, Marakie Jones opened her laptop and typed: masonholmestars.com. She had checked into the Peregrine Hotel, in Peregrine, Ohio at 6:18 am. The waiter had just brought up her late, late breakfast. Mrs. Jones propped up two standing pillows against the headboard and leaned back. She stretched her legs out on the king-size bed and tucked a short-rolled, decorative pillow under her knees. She balanced the tray on her lap.

On the tray were plain Greek yogurt, fresh strawberries, toasted sourdough bread, a pot of fragrant black coffee, and a small pitcher of real cream. After a short, solemn prayer of gratitude, she turned on the flat screen and paired the website. Marakie caught the music intro for the show, a few bars from Ahmad Jamal's *Poinciana*. She smiled as she listened to the fanfare of Jamal's piano artistry, then the brilliant rhythm section of bass and drums. For those few seconds, the trio's orchestration was familiar and comforting. She felt closer to her husband, as they had enjoyed hearing Jamal in person in Chicago. She hadn't seen her husband since Monday. They were a time zone away. The numbers on the digital clock on the night table changed to 2:30 inside suite number A359.

Marakie flashed a smile after hearing her husband's voice on the radiocast. She poured some coffee, then skated her thumb to the up arrow on the remote and applied just enough force for the volume slider to move four lines to the right. She was set on hearing every word, in case the chewing vibrations inside her head muffled any voices. Marakie picked up a slice of sourdough, brought the knife down on the edge of the short stick of butter and took up a thin square. The day was already underway and a soft, solar warmth filled the room. Mrs. Jones was happy and proud of her husband. He was a guest on a national radio program. And she was also pleased that their *plan* was working. She rubbed the butter on a triangle of warm toast as she listened to the conversation.

"Afarland, how cool!" Holmes said, "They're in mid-winter there, yes?"

"That's right, Mason. Winters are not as cold there as they are here in the states, but you still have to bundle up. I was glad to move from winter into summer in a matter of hours. Now that's cool."

"Cool? That's how I'd like to feel right now as we move through the dog days of summer. So, Ahmad, please tell us about the Seattle Seahawks in '76, as it related to the astrology of their first game. I think our Seahawks fans, the 12s, would be thrilled to know."

"Well, first off, the Seattle Seahawks were conceived long before that first-ever game, when they took to the field to do battle with another NFL team. All that had come before, for example, the franchise award of 1974, the new franchise name, Seattle Seahawks, the draft, building a coterie of solid players, the practices and drills, the relationships between players, coaching staff, management and owners—all that came into being to create a coherent, professional football team that elected to receive when the San Francisco 49ers put the ball in the air at 1:06 pm, on Sunday, 1 August 1976.

"At that moment, the game clock and the astrological clock started ticking and the beginning of the Hawks' life-cycle started. In any horoscope of a game between two teams, the sign on the eastern horizon represents the home team and the sign on the western horizon represents the visiting team. So, the Hawks' Ascendant is the last degree of Libra. They were born on the edge of two signs and that's how they play—with an edge, meaning that they're on fire. To be on the edge is to strain your energies to their limits. When you do that, wild things can happen. Their horoscope is front-loaded with fire—five planets in fire signs—including the cusp of the Tenth House of status and reputation. All fire!"

"Ahmad, that explains a lot. I've never heard of the Seahawks lacking enthusiasm or spirit—never, even when they've lost."

"You probably never will, because the nature of fire is to rise, illumine and expand."

"And for those who are just joining us, author and astrologer Ahmad Jones is with us talking about his new book, *Football's Astrological Measurements.* We have autographed copies available for purchase from our website."

While Mason apprised newcomers about the show, Jones scribbled a name on his legal pad. The name was Ralph E. Hay. He tore the page with Hay's name on it and placed it near the base of the lamp, at the edge of the table. He swiveled his high-backed chair toward the door after hearing movement in the corridor. It wasn't guests, or housekeeping, or any other hotel staff. It was something else. He put his attention on the other side of that door to listen, like he used to do when putting his ear to the tracks listening for the approach of locomotives. Jones' father had taught him that the most expeditious way of intercepting a potential threat was to anticipate it beforehand and thus, reduce the element of surprise.

"Ahmad, what did the Seahawks' horoscope have to say about the matchup?"

Jones swiveled back toward the south wall. "As the constellation of the scales rose past the Earth's skyline, so did those scales signify that the two teams looked unbalanced. One franchise was 30 years old; and the home team wasn't even an hour old yet, on the field—if you don't include practices with real NFL teams. San Francisco's plate was apparently tipped in their favor.

"The 49ers would naturally *outweigh* the other team because of their age and their experience at winning games. They would conduct a master class saturated with teachable moments for the new expansion franchise. Yet, there would be many experienced players with the Seattle Seahawks who dealt out several teachable moments to the 49ers that day. They had winners, also. They would just about tip the plate in their favor and almost break the scales beyond measure.

"The symbol of gold was flying high at the zenith. Four celestial bodies were in the sign of Leo, which is associated with gold, because it is ruled by the Sun. It is the sign of steady fire, illumination, of intense solar power, and of unassailable light. So, the sparks of fire emanating from the Seahawks that day reflected off the faces and minds of the fans who witnessed that spectacle. Leo symbolism filtered through *both* teams. Being born in the sign of Leo attuned the Seahawks to fire and spirit. Having their Ascendant near the planet Uranus, which is statistically biased toward the unorthodox, sudden shifts of conditions and is known as an electrifier—this team was and still is equipped to achieve anything."

"I can feel that fire as you describe it, and not just the heat of summer!" Mason said.

"Yes, Mason, and it was a grand matchup. Uranus, the planet of unusual outcomes was just about 16 minutes away from meeting Seattle's local horizon, and in a way, spreading its vibrations on the field.

"Ahmad, I attended that game at the Kingdome and to hear you talk about what was happening, per your charting of the event, is intriguing. What else can you tell us about it?"

"Quite a bit, Mason. Right-handed quarterback Steve Graf was taken out of play a little into the third quarter and replaced by left-handed quarterback Jim Zorn, which turned things around—just like Uranus, which had risen above the horizon a half hour after kickoff. The gold rush began and ended with gold for both teams and not *that* much more for the winning team, because reversals were to come, as was indicated by the sign and constellation of Libra. In the context of the game, this sign heralded a faceoff—the dynamic equation of the human struggle for victory, between the teams. It also symbolized the 180-degree shifts in direction and fortune that would come when the lessons of experience on the field, were learned and a new door for the players appeared, was opened and entered."


Jones sat before a wide dark-walnut desk. The desk was flush with the wall and had a rich, cream matte finish. There was a picture of a pier on Lake Tahoe facing him, centered a few feet above the desk that faced the picture. Its frame was chrome molding, of simple construction and with a high gloss. Its POV was compelling, as if you were standing on warm teak wood in your bare feet and peering as far as the eyes of your imagination could see. There was aloneness conveyed by the water around the pier, and silence, even. Jones could relate.


"The Seattle Seahawks had picked up a new tempo-rhythm after Jim Zorn warmed up his arm and stepped onto the grid. He, along with wide receiver Sam McCullum, had blown open that door with nine others and vanished into a zone. They came out on the other end of that hole with three TDs and with Zorn stopped just two seconds short of scoring another touchdown in the 4th quarter."


Sunlight flowed into the suite. Through the cotton-lace curtains on the two windows, rays of light presented a soft ambience. A thin line of sunlight had shown through a gap between one pair of curtains, up near the rod. Like a laser beam, it struck just above the spyhole on the door. Jones sat at the west side of the room, ten feet away from the door, on the topmost floor of the building. Behind him, to the north, was more living space, with a connecting door directly opposite Lake Tahoe. The legal pad lay on the desk in front of him, to his right, with a few notes previously jotted down to refer to during the call. The spacious living room led to a kitchenette behind the south wall, and a king-sized bed in the master bedroom was situated out back toward the southeast. Housekeeping had put their finishing touches on it. The scent of oranges was still in the air.


"Uranus arrived to coach 'em up, landing in the Seahawks' First House and very near the line of Seattle's horizon. Being placed in the house of the Hawks, this planet and its meaning is front and center as their primary paradigm."

"And what is that?"

"The unexpected! Uranus, in a way, defines the Seattle Seahawks and yet, I use the word with caution because once you define something, you can only see your own definition of it and miss important information about the thing itself. Hence, you can impose limits on your own perception. Because Uranus is associated with things that defy definition, it can't be pinned down. I felt the connection was good, in a loose way. So, to me, the Hawks always have pluck and are full of astonishing turnarounds. They are intense and fun. If one were to ascribe a metaphor for Uranus, in terms of that football game, Uranus would be the QB, Jim Zorn. He had set a new tone, from the 3rd to the last quarter. Uranus, the planet of surprises, stands at 3 degrees and 59 minutes of arc from Seattle's Ascendant degree."

Mason said, "I remember Carl Jung saying, *Whatever happens in a moment of time has the qualities of that moment of time.*"

"Indeed, and what better example than to move from zero, in their first preseason game, after five minutes into the 3rd quarter, to 24 at the end of the 4th, in answer to the winning team's 27?"

"I get that you're referencing Zorn and McCullum," Mason said.

"They made big plays, together with the other nine men, clearing the path, turning darkness into light, making things happen. When Jim Zorn stepped onto the field, I felt that he brought with him a heart and mindset that glimpsed beyond the appearance of the 24–0 lead by the opposing team."

"I too, think he saw the equation in a unique way," Mason said.

"That's right, and he transformed the momentum and velocity of the game. The soon-to-be 12s watched and participated in that quantum wave of possibilities and were behind the team. Zorn led his men to engage a set of solutions, on the fly, which turned the 49ers' possible shutout—inside out!"

"Do you think an astrologer, or astrologers back then, charted the game time?" Mason asked.

"Probably, and astrologers back in 1976, who charted the game beforehand, would have anticipated the *quantum* feature and dimension that overshadowed the Seattle Seahawks then."

"I'd like to hear their take on that game; guess I'll have to contact some of my colleagues."

"I'd be excited to hear about that," Jones said. "I know of one person who did, who was not an astrologer. I can say that the journalist Julie Nelson wrote that Jim Zorn, 'Handled quarterbacking differently than most players.' That is one-way Uranus presents itself in the Seahawks' chart. Not just doing it smarter or better, they do it differently. To me, at 6'2" and 250 pounds, Zorn mirrored the essence of that moment. I mean, the qualities of the celestial scheme at that time were indicative of the unorthodox and terrific potential of the new team."

Jones had to convince certain listeners that the reason he was in the states was just to promote his book. He knew that the people who plotted against Afarland were listening in. It was an opportunity for Jones to use some misdirection, like a play-action-fake, in American football. His love of the game buttressed his enthusiasm on the air, which could help to cloak his main objective.

"Seattle received the ball at 1:06 pm, when the game clock started on Sunday, 1 August, at their first preseason game. At that time, with broken cloud cover and a temperature of 67 degrees inside the stadium, the Seattle Seahawks began their interrelationship with the current astronomical configurations. Nelson's statement reflected the significance and meanings empirically associated with the planet Uranus: different, unpredictable, noteworthy, unexpected, and unusual."

"I concur, Ahmad. In my astrology work, I have seen conditions change, swiftly, when Uranus was prominent in some way, among other corroborating astrological indicators."

"Good point, and in connection with that, the conditions that Jim Zorn's presence on the field had changed and the progress he helped to accomplish, in the one-and-a-half quarters he played, was daring and unpredictable and memorable and exhilarating to the fans who were privileged to be at that game. You know because you were there."

"Boy, was I!"

"The Sun was in the precise section of the sky known as *Leo*. As a part of our cosmic landscape, it is historically related to the concentration and expression of intense solar power. In the royal courts of the East and Asia Minor, this concentration was portrayed in social terms by the charisma and leadership of kings, queens, emperors and rulers. Today's presidents, prime ministers, general managers and CEOs are a more contemporary fit."

Jones had a saddle-colored duffle bag with several small compartments and a garment bag of the same color. Inside the duffle bag was a small aluminum briefcase. Inside of that was a secret government document, among other highly significant items, which Jones would require before the day ended. His two pieces of carry-on luggage lay against the closet near the entry. He was going to leave the hotel for the airport right after the interview, and yet, in the back of his mind, he was anticipating another roadblock.

"Ahmad," Mason continued, "I was intrigued by the numeric relationships that you mention in your book. Of course, I am aware that it isn't about numerology; yet, you do sight a few interesting relationships. Would you speak about some of those?"

"Of course, the name *Seattle Seahawks* is composed of 15 letters. During the preseason period of 1976, they played six games in which they won one and lost five. They were 1–5."

"Anything else?"

"Both the names *Seattle Seahawks* and *CenturyLink Field* reduce to the double-digit number 16, when you add the numerical equivalents of each letter. This is further reduced to the mystic number 7."

"Fascinating, go on." Mason said."

"In connection with 7, this may be even more interesting when you add the price tag of Seattle's football franchise from back in 1974. It was $16 million, most of which was paid by Lloyd Nordstrom and family. And, the start of their first game was at 1:06 pm."

"Ahmad, that's got to be more than coincidence and it's immediately verifiable. What about the team itself?"

"At preseason week one, on that Sunday, 1 August, it was time for a public display of the personal and group resources that were hammered, honed and ready. It was a time for the grand test in front of tens of thousands of Washingtonians. It was a time of physical, mental and spiritual exposition—a showcase and demonstration of hitherto unproven skill. And it was the time for a major reversal, a momentum shift, a la Seattle, under the concrete *dome of kings*—and beneath the greater dome of heaven's planets, stars and constellations unseen."

"You're describing conditions that I had witnessed but had no concept of at the time. What else?"

"Well, as the earth rotated around its axis, four celestial bodies had culminated and rallied close to Seattle's local meridian. If the Kingdome had no roof, and if day had turned into night, the 60,825 fans in attendance could have looked up to see Mercury, Venus and Saturn with their naked eyes. The Sun was there, too, and yet it was the middle of the day and no planets could be seen—and no sun even, for the fans were inside under the dome, where 11 men were poised together to breathe their first breaths as a team."

"Those statements are pretty lyrical, Ahmad!" Mason said. "I'd like to move on to a more general football theme for those football enthusiasts who like other teams in the NFL. Would you talk to us about the origin of the NFL from an astronomic angle?"

"Certainly. There's a 96-year-old document on display at the Football Hall of Fame in Canton, Ohio. It records 8:15 p.m. as the start of a meeting that led to the formation of the *American Professional Football Association*. That name was changed on 24 June 1922, to the *National Football League*. There's little time for me to delve into this completely, so I'll present just a few salient points."

Jones read the name he had written on the legal pad, "Does the name Ralph E. Hay ring a bell for you, Mason?"

"No, Ahmad, not just yet."

"Mr. Hay convened the meeting with the owners of 11 pro football teams to discuss the formation of a league. He was the owner of an automobile concern and he was good at it—a superb salesman. He had the common touch, was well organized in his business affairs, and he loved football. In fact, he was the owner of the Canton Bulldogs. Before there was a National Football League, there were several local leagues and the Bulldogs were members of the Ohio league."

"I think I've heard that name before, now that you mention it."

"Well, then I used Mr. Hay's date of birth, which I gathered from my research, to render a basic chart. He was born in the tropical sign of Capricorn and had an Aquarian Moon. These, along with the rest of his stellar alignments, in my opinion, possessed the right celestial chemistry at that moment in history to get the ball rolling."

"To get the *ball rolling—ha haaaa...* Good one, Ahmad!"

Outside Jones' suite, a man was filling out a service record of inspection. The hotel had installed Automated External Defibrillators (AEDs) on each of its eight floors. The inspector, the same man who Nolan had seen through the back window and that passed her and Jones in front of the hotel, was from Senegal. He was six-three and a champion wrestler, back home. He was Marshall's third unit, *the contingency plan*, and was to be paid by Marshall. He had on a pair of black Dockers and a white button-down shirt with a company name on his left lapel. The company makes periodic checks of its defibrillators to ascertain, among other things, the device's capacity to give off a correct charge when attempting to restart a heart. The technician who does the check may or may not have to replace the lithium battery, or the pads, or both. After a thorough scan, the technician writes down the date of the inspection on a service card with an adhesive backing and places that card on the side of the metal cabinet containing the AED.

The man checked his watch, 1344 hours. He assumed that the security latch was engaged on Jones' door. He would wait until Jones opened it to make his move, or pretend to be room service. But there were other options. His apparent job, checking the defibrillators, allowed him to circulate through the premises without suspicion. The imposter was now at the end of the hall, near the AED cabinet across from Jones' suite.

# 37

## The Killer Behind the Door

JONES CONTINUED, "RALPH HAY'S INNATE AFFINITY with order, system, and management (Capricorn) and his ability to contribute something socially by bringing several clubs together under one umbrella (his Aquarian Moon) were useful tools for laying the foundation upon which the superstructure of today's NFL now sits."

"Okay, Ahmad, would you tell our listeners what that foundation was?"

Jones was more aware of a presence lurking behind the door as he was talking. He kept up the dialogue so as not to tip off whoever was on the other side. He felt a current of force. It emanated through his hands and body.

Jones said, "Hay proposed a more disciplined and coherent structure for the sport of football, which it did not possess at the time. Players could jump around from one team to another, asking for more pay. Team owners could recruit college students to play games. There was no set system of account-ability or regulation. Hay saw that as a problem, as did *Papa Bear*, the late George Halas, founder and owner of the NFL's Chicago Bears. So, Hay, as a professional in his own right, being the head of a car dealership, having an unprecedented aptitude for selling, and owning a football team as well, used his natural talents of creating order and efficiency, along with his social skills, to further sell his ideas for forming a league. This fulfilled Hays' natural Capri-cornian tendency to organize and manage effectively and his Aquarian need to bring people together in a spirit of cooperation, friendship and unity. I make these points because I have looked at his basic chart within the context of his sharp business sense and his love of football and people."

"Ahmad," Mason asked, "would you explain how Capricorn, Ralph Hay, and the NFL relate to each other?"

"Yes! Others at the meeting probably had planets or points in Capricorn, or even had been born under that sign, yet when the meeting began at 8:15 pm, the 22nd degree of Capricorn was on the geographic coordinate of longitude for Canton, Ohio."

"Ahmad, at the beginning of that meeting, Capricorn at 22 degrees was passing over the sky above Canton?"

"Correct, and Ralph Hay's birth occurred when the Sun transited that same degree of Capricorn."

"That fits, when one recalls that the key phrases for Capricorn are *I Use* or *I Manage*."

"Right, and when looking at the Tenth House cusp in the horoscope of that meeting, being aware that it signifies the head, leader, or manager of something—one who officiates, or who calls the shots—it resonated with Hay who hosted the meeting and helped to manage its operation for those two hours."

"What about George Halas? He was there. Was his astrology significant in any way?"

"Certainly! Maybe even more so than Ralph Hay's—in this wise: George Halas played and coached football and is credited in some circles with founding the league. There are many opinions on this, yet I see both men as playing significant roles at that one meeting.

"Halas' Moon, his habitual response tendencies, and his Mars, the action planet, are in conjunction in the First House of the APFA chart, which is the house of the APFA, itself, as a whole entity. His Saturn is conjunct the cusp of the Seventh House in Scorpio. Halas' influence as one of the APFA's founders is made plain in the chart. Saturn brings rules, laws and restrictions, just as Hay's Sun in Capricorn brings the same types of elements as we mentioned, such as order, management and organization. Now, Hay's Saturn, at birth, had traveled completely around the Zodiac and returned to the same degree of Virgo in the birth chart of the APFA. This is a very precise position of Saturn, the maker of rules and regulations. So, both these men's planetary influencers were positioned in the APFA horoscope, in sectors or houses of significant importance."

"Do we know what Halas' or Hay's Ascendants are?"

"No, I don't have their birth times, but someone out there may know. Yet, look at the fact that the last names of both these men begin with the letter H. In numerology, the letter H is associated with none other than Saturn itself. Getting back to what Hay did for football, as the owner of the Canton Bulldogs and in his own life as a business owner, his portrait says volumes about him. It shows a man who is confident in his suit and tie, with his cigar and a real smile, caught from a 45-degree angle. Hay knew what success was and he exemplified it."

"I see," Mason said. "Astrology and football are a big deal today. More people are learning how the game is played. They understand it better than before and it's exciting to watch. My engineer has just handed me your book with some of Ralph E. Hay's astrology in it. You said that at the time of the meeting, Saturn was *in confluence* with Ralph Hay's Saturn in his personal astrology. You write here that it was: *germane to Hay's calling of both meetings, which led to better organization and rules for the bourgeoning sport of American professional football.* Would you talk about the cycle of Saturn and that second meeting that took place at his showroom on Cleveland Avenue and Second Street in Canton, Ohio?"

"Yes, Mason. Ralph Hay was experiencing his first Saturn Return. On Friday evening, 20 August 1920, the American Professional Football Conference was born. That was their first meeting. He was 29 at the time. In astrology, the Saturn Return is an important measurement and is grounded as an observable astronomic cycle—as all cycles are. Hay's life condition was moving into a new gear and he was ready to bring to fruition what a few men had suggested (one of them being Jim Thorpe), a new paradigm in American football—the organizing of a national league."

"Just to make it clear for our audience, Ralph Hay's Saturn Return was operating during the second meeting?" Mason asked.

"At both the first and second meetings, actually. When the APFA was formed on 17 September 1920, Hay was still in the cycle of his Saturn Return. Whenever Saturn makes a complete circle around the Sun, based on where it was in its travels at the time of birth, and arrives at the same relative position that it occupied at that birth, it denotes a significant opportunity to move in a new direction. It also suggests a potential departure from the status quo, or if stubbornness prevails, it will signify the digging in of one's heels to keep things as they are. It indicates the inculcation of a different point of view— the asking of new questions never asked before."

"So," Mason asked, "the shift of pro football into a more codified sport was in tandem with the shift in the direction of Hay's thinking about the game, and in tandem with his Saturn Return?"

"Precisely, and we can include Halas, because his natal Saturn was on a major axis of the APFA chart. Hay wasn't the only man there making significant adjustments to how teams would organize and how games would be conducted."

"Your examination of Ralph Hay's birth chart was calculated for January 12th, 1891. You used a solar chart, where the Sun is placed on the horizon—one of two kinds of default charts when the moment of birth is unknown, correct?"

"Yes, indeed," Jones said. "Now, Hay's Moon and his Jupiter were in the sign of Aquarius, the sign of brotherhood, associations, and groups of like-minded folks who have collective goals. Hay's natal Moon in Aquarius signi-fied his need to identify with the group dynamic, and his Jupiter signified how he attempted to reach out to others through friendship and the contri-bution of something that he felt was socially, organizationally and, of course, financially important. Yet, Halas was born in the sign of Aquarius, and it was very close, just 4 degrees away from Hay's Jupiter in Aquarius."

"One could say, Ahmad, that their Aquarian energies, which were con-joined by aspects like the conjunction, helped to intensify the goal-fitting na-ture of that meeting, including reaching out to other teams to play together as part of a league of pro-football clubs."

"Indeed."

Mason said, "There was another individual that you mentioned, who greatly influenced the way the game is played. Would that be Hugh 'Shorty' Ray?"

"Yes! In the section of my book that you reference, I used the horoscope of the NFL as the main chart for the league. It is based on the date, time, and place for the second meeting in 1920. The name *National Football League*, coined in 1922, was a name change, but still, the earlier horoscope is the pri-mary chart. And yes, Shorty Ray figures precisely in *that* league chart. From the standpoint of the geometric relationships of the planets, when the NFL hired Ray, there was a *Geometry of Meaning*, to use Arthur M. Young's book title. In 1937 and throughout 1938, the planet of innovation, science and technical prowess—Uranus—crossed the NFL's Taurus Ascendant on Thurs-day, 29 April 1937. Then it continued to stay in the NFL's chart's First House, which denotes the league.

"On December of that same year, Uranus was retrograde; that is, it ap-peared to move backwards against the Zodiac, moving clockwise to the same degree of the APFA's Ascendant, at 9 degrees of Taurus on the 24th. In Janu-ary of 1938, Uranus was already moving forward (counterclockwise) again in the Zodiac and was still in that 9th degree until 12 February. I preface these next remarks with this, because 1938 was the year that the League made the quantum leap in its rules and its officiating to bring in a more scientific ap-proach. So, 1938 was a watershed moment for the organization, based on the cycle of Uranus around the Ascendant, which, as mentioned, represents the League.

"Shorty Ray was a technical advisor and this title wasn't loosely given because he knew the rules in three sports and made them better. One more thing: Ray's planet Mercury, which indicates his general thought processes, was in the sign of Virgo (detail, specificity and a systematic approach to the rules), which was conjunct the NFL's natal Sun in Virgo, the sign in which the second meeting occurred. Ray's Uranus, planet of innovation, is close to his Mercury and the NFL's Sun. His energy, represented in his basic chart, had a lot to convey, which accelerated the transformation of the League's rulebook. Also, Ray's Saturn is square the NFL's Sun at the exact degree. To put it another way, the NFL was in a cycle where an upgrade was possible and Ray was the primary agent of change for that upgrade to occur. This relationship is highlighted in the chart and shows how Ray and the NFL collaborated in a very specific way, which led to the technical improvements made to the game."

"Astounding facts, Ahmad, and, unfortunately, that's all the time we have left. I wish to thank you for being my guest on *Mason Holmes with the Stars*. I look forward to having you on again soon."

"Mason, the pleasure was mine. Thank you for inviting me."

The outcue music was the same as the intro and then the music tapered off into dead air. While Jones was about to call Marakie, Marshall's third unit had just sneaked into the adjoining suite.

Jones put the phone back in its cradle. He heard a woman's voice telling listeners how to acquire a transcript. He zeroed in on something from behind the connecting door. He walked over to it. Up to now, Jones was somewhat laid back about these deadly attempts to get to him. He had anticipated them, as he had seen the possibilities for interference in his own chart. He wasn't certain, though, if the powers that be, or that *were*, knew the real reason why he was in the states. The force moving through his hands had diminished and he was feeling at low ebb. He remembered a discourse given by his teacher, while sitting on the grass, at an altitude of 3,000 feet, in the Province of Cádiz.

The sun had just risen. The teacher and Jones peered into it. They stood there for 15 minutes, allowing sunlight to enter their bodies through their eyes.

The teacher was stoic, as always, and yet the love of his giant soul poured out to Jones. His every move was a gesture filled with love, wisdom and power. He pointed his forefinger toward the Strait of Gibraltar. "My son, the power of love is the supreme power. Like the sun, it is selfless in its conveyance of warmth and vitality and during these safe periods of gazing at it, you can feel its sparkling coherence and stability. Ahmad, be like the sun always, and use your *guns of love*."

The teacher turned to his smiling student.

"*Guns of love*, I like that."

"Liking it is sufficient; yet being It, is more useful." After their sun-gazing session, Jones felt enormous vitality move through his mind and body.

"Mirador del Estrecho, is a terrific vantage point to see a part of Africa, remember your task for Afarland."

"Yes, we leave on the 20th."

"I saw in you many lifetimes of violent recklessness. You've conquered much of that in this life. Your energy is your resource. Protect it from lack of self-control. You know how a wrecker ball slowly destroys the outer walls of a solid structure through repeated impacts, and so, the substance of the nerves is disturbed, subtlety eaten away by the emotional wreaking ball of anger. Hence, you can expose yourself to the lowest conditions and outcomes. Irritation and its allies are energy vampires." Both men took their seats on the warm grass.

"What if my life or my loved ones' lives are in danger?"

"Always do what is timely and appropriate in the moment, my son. Protect yourself and them. Just refrain from pouring any destructive mental baggage that might remain—in you—into it."


Jones received a notification on his cell, an alarm set to go off the moment that the critical point of Afarland's astrology was due. He suspected that there would be a media blackout. The country could now be in disarray, he thought, if the necessary steps to prevent it were not implemented, as Jones himself had urged back in March. If Afarland was in the midst of a putsch, Jones was equipped to take immediate action in the states. He had everything required to be successful. There was nothing on the news about his father-in-law or Afarland.

What if the coup were in progress? Jones didn't want it to be but he felt that it was. The chart was clear. There was no room for mincing the data to reflect new hopes or happier outcomes. It explained why people were after him. Jones had enemies from when he was a contractor for the FBI and when he was a cop, and his classified work with 17 nations, where he provided them with practical intelligence to avoid political reengineering. There were many reasons why a clandestine group of people would want to get rid of him. He was considered dangerous to the criminal element. He was an astrological private eye, with two degrees and spiritual insight, who got to the core of things in minutes. That was too much power for one man to have— power to see the development of things in advance and to do something to change it.

Yet, Jones was aware that these skills and capabilities were loaned to him by God, his Source, to use judiciously.

The timing of the attack at the park was consistent with Afarland's timeline of anticipated events. If I am being tracked, he thought, then my wife and perhaps my sister may be as well. They could already be in danger. Jones was two states away, from Marakie. Flying time was an hour and seventeen minutes. Marakie and Cheyanne needed protection now. Jack Peterson, he thought, could look after his wife until he arrived. He pulled out agent Nolan's calling card and dialed.

"Kaskaskia FBI, Special Agent Nolan speaking."

"Agent Nolan, this is Ahmad."

Nolan got a little flustered upon hearing his voice. She and Dumont had ordered turkey sandwiches to go and were eating in the Charger.

"Just a moment." Nolan pointed to the napkins, which were out of her reach. "How may we help you, Mr. Jones?"

"Please, call me Ahmad. I will be with my wife only several hours from now. There may be a coup in progress. I haven't heard anything yet and my wife is the daughter of President Za Dewabuna of Afarland. There's someone here at the hotel, too. He's wearing a white button-down shirt and black Dockers work pants. Agent Nolan, I have something important to accomplish at 7:00 pm, something in Ohio. I cannot be late. I require your immediate assistance."

"Mr. Jones, we're eating lunch outside your hotel now. Yes, I remember the man entering the hotel and I saw your expression. We pulled back around and took up shop here for a while in case you needed our help. What can we do?"

"Notify Agent Peterson and request a security unit to protect my wife. She is the only child of a sovereign leader and she would be the next in line to succeed as the head of the country."

"Would be, Ahmad?"

"There are people who want both my wife and me dead."

"I'm making the call now, Ahmad. Where is she staying?"

# 38

## 9,800.92

AT THAT SAME MOMENT, one state away, Peterson said, while powering down his window halfway, "I was at the Seattle Field Office around three in the afternoon back in 2004," Peterson began. "I was filling out some paperwork on a case I was involved in when this guy calls me."

"Was it Jones?" O'Donnell asked.

"Who else! We'd been struggling with this case, see? Both local and state. A bank robber was operating close by but kept putting distance between himself and us. It was uncanny; like the thief had a sixth sense of when LE was near. He had robbed three small community banks in a week in Olympia and Portland—in one week! The prick didn't have a pattern that we could pick up on, but we knew that was him and only him, no accomplices."

"How did you know that?" Reese asked.

"He was an egomaniac. The security cameras recorded a ton of footage. He didn't care that we had tape. He thought he was that good or he just didn't care. The papers made our whole task force look incompetent. No arrest and no hard leads, other than his face on tape and where he had last been. Nobody got hurt during the heists; he just did robberies. Still, the cops asked for support and we gave them the use of the local FBI's resources. We had to help them locate this criminal and fast. So I'm at my desk on the seventh floor and security calls me up about this guy who wants to see me. He says he has information about the thief that will quickly result in his capture."

"So, I pick up the phone. Probably some crank, I'm thinking, and ask him if he's talked to the local police."

"He says, 'Right now, I figure the FBI would be more open to hearing what I can provide to get this guy off the street. I'm sure I can help you. Is there a special agent with whom I can sit down for a chat?' Those were his exact words to me, 'With whom I can sit?' Now I'm thinking that maybe this guy could be a guy working for that guy, or maybe a guy who got cheated by that guy. So, I tell him yes, he can talk to us. There was something in his voice that convinced me that we had a possible lead that we couldn't take lightly. If we deemed it credible we would share with the local law."

O'Donnell said, "Something in his voice—you mean, you had a hunch?"

"That's not what I said. I said that his voice... Well, okay, it was a hunch. So, I bring him into a front-office situation and put him through the metal detector. I saw at first that he wasn't your run-of-the mill Joe. We did a short evaluation of his mental and emotional condition. After we patted, we chatted. Me, two other agents, and Bob Hollis, my partner who retired last year, we take this guy Jones upstairs. We assess him and conclude that he could be connected to the felon."

"Right," O'Donnell said, "How else could he know anything?"

"It seemed logical that he wanted to make a deal," Peterson said, "maybe turn him in because of a falling out with this guy. The U.S. Marshalls were in on this and there was a $10,000 bounty on him. If the guy was struggling to make his rent, we could draw a motive. We walked Jones up to the conference room on the fifth floor. That was the floor for Criminal Investigations at that time. We asked Jones for his name and address. He told us. We didn't shoot interrogation, of course, so we waited for him to talk to us. Jones said that we're an intelligence-gathering agency and that he had some intelligence about the bank robber at large. You'll never guess in a million years what Jones pitched to us first."

"What was his pitch?"

"At first, I didn't believe what I heard him say. He said that he had $9,800.92 in that bank and he wanted it back. That's what Jones said. Jones came to the FBI to ask for his money, like we were some deposit insurance safety net or something. We were doing 50-hour weeks because of terrorist leads we were investigating—over 40 of them at the time. We were all tired and frazzled, and our shift had just begun.

"Tassie Scott, one of my agents, told me afterwards that she thought he was a lunatic and that he should've been sent to a shrink, 'Because anyone coming to an FBI building asking for $9,800.92, with a straight face to boot, is probably suffering from a dissociative complex and could be a potential danger to us, himself and society.' She was freaking out when he said that, but he was serious about getting his money back. But as she listened to him, she realized that he was as sane as any of us in the room."

"Maybe he did it for shock value," O'Donnell offered.

"It worked. Jones had us thinking on a different frequency after he opened his mouth. Bob was the SSAC and the tallest, at six-four, so he took over, for *real* shock value. So, now Bob says, 'That bank is insured, Mr. Jones. You'll get your money back in a couple of weeks—at most, in three. You're a depositor and as a depositor the FDIC insures your checking, savings, business, joint and any other accounts. They've been around since 1933 and will make good on your funds. That's what the FDIC means: Federal Deposit Insurance Corporation. The keywords here, Mr. Jones, are deposit and insurance. Do you understand?'"

"Jones says that yes, he understands, but he requires his money now, that two weeks is too long. Bob's intimidation skills had been checked and mated. The only reason we didn't show Jones the door was that he could be a person of interest. We were checking up on him in real time in the back room—NCIC, everything.

"Bob says, 'Do you expect *us* to give *you* money?' and Jones answers, 'Yes.'"

"What? You're kidding. Jones was asking the FBI to give him money?"

"We all began thinking of our firearms," Peterson said.

O'Donnell restarted the engine, turned on the AC low and cracked his window. They were at the curb at the airport.

Peterson said, "So, we played along and I chimed in, like I was considering a way to bring him his money, so, I asked him how much money he lost again, and he answers, 'I lost nine-thousand eight-hundred dollars and ninety-two cents.'"

"Now Bob is asking, 'Mr. Jones, you said you can help us. How?'"

"Jones asks, 'Ever heard of Noreen Reiner?' So, I asked him, 'Who in the hell is Noreen Renier?' I look at Bob and Tassie. And Mike Cappello is there, too. They were part of the bank-robbery squad. Tassie and Mike threw their hands up, but Bob knew of the lady. He leaves the room for a minute and comes right back. Then Bob says, 'Yes, she taught at the FBI training facility in Quantico in the 1980s. What's she got to do with this?'

"Jones answers, 'Renier was able to heat up cases that went cold. I can help you keep this one from getting warm. These robberies are still hot cases and I know where this guy is going to be, tonight.'"

Peterson checks his cell.

"Ruderman has arrived. The rest of Jones' first job with us will have to wait."

# 39

## Friendly Meeting Between Agencies

THE BROWN TAHOE'S MOTOR WAS STILL RUNNING. O'Donnell pressed the ignition button to shut it off. The Ohio winds had kicked and howled their velocity, pushing against the line of moving vehicles and people, punching hats off, blasting parts of human anatomy that were unprotected or uncovered. The Tahoe's red-on-white government vehicle registration plates were a guarantee that the traffic officers patrolling the pickup section at the Canton-Akron Airport would bestow professional courtesy to the federal agents inside.

They were anxious men in that Tahoe. Thirty-four minutes earlier, Peterson had said, "I'll check the flight status," as their SUV turned left off Lauby Road and headed to the Arrivals entrance of the terminal. He had entered the current date and flight number on the app. The plane had been delayed due to hazardous crosswinds. The men had circled the length of the terminal several times, when finally, as they sat at the curb, they were notified that the plane had landed.

They didn't have to do that. They could've just sat where they were now, at the curb, and waited. But they kept circling and observing, alert for things that were out of place, refining their skills of observation and anticipation. Soon they would see just that—something out-of-place. Yet, they would not notice it—it would sneak into their consciousness later that day.

What the men saw was a piece of a puzzle. Later, they would remember what that piece was and where it had fit. But now, they were just two anxious and disciplined men in God's Army, watching the cycle of the flow of traffic, of drivers inching their vehicles between other vehicles, to park momentarily near or at curbside, exchange hugs and kisses, load up baggage, return to the driver's seat, then inch back out into the traffic stream. They took turns drinking coffee; first one then the other, like they rehearsed it—waiting near the curb with the winds kicking up again.

A Chevrolet Caprice with Ohio Highway Patrol plates came in from two lanes over and drove up parallel to the Tahoe. The state cop opened his passenger window, looked through it a little upward to the driver's window and over to the passenger side. He evaluated, then smiled in recognition, and then leaned to his right. O'Donnell lowered his window down halfway.

"Sir! You cannot wait here. There's a cell-phone lot parking area north of you, where you can communicate with your party when they land. This is a pickup-only area."

Incredulous, O'Donnell brought the rest of his window down. The state cop must have seen the mounted spotlights, the plates; overall, the official nature of the vehicle. The officer continued, while pointing, "Take Lauby Road, then your first left turn and signage will guide you the rest of the way—"

"You're joking!"

The state cop wore a serious face.

"He's just messing with you," Peterson said.

"How you doin', Fed?"

"How *you* doin', Dick? Made detective yet?"

"Is that why you called me Dick? Because you think I made detective?"

"No, because it's your name. You could never be a detective, but if by chance you did become one, you'd be Detective Dick and that would be meaningless, a double negative, because all detectives are dicks."

"I go by Richard, but you can call me Dick this time. And yes, I did, make detective 12 days ago."

"Congrats, Detective! As for me, this is another field-training day and as for us, we're hosting someone from *outside* the Beltway."

"Doesn't sound like fun. Anyone I know?"

"Odds are against it."

The detective looked at O'Donnell and said, "Peterson's a fine agent. My name is Williams. Nice to meet you."

"Likewise, O'Donnell. Special Agent O'Donnell."

"*Ah,* let's keep things informal. We're all family here," Peterson said.

"Then, just O'Donnell. Pleased to meet you, Williams."

"Same. Peterson has been up to his neck in crap—taking crap and dishing out crap—for a long time now. Sometimes he even looks like crap!"

"Don't let your gold badge go to your dick-head, Williams," Peterson countered.

Williams stops bantering to scan his surroundings. He looks behind him, then left, and lastly to the front. He doesn't notice anything, so he leans again toward the passenger window to resume the conversation, "Correction—he's been in the game long enough to make tough guys crawl into a corner and suck their thumbs. We get together now and then at Mulligans, on Belden Village Street, drinking, good food, and shooting the shit."

"I know the place—been there only a couple of times," O'Donnell said.

"Let's all meet there soon, sometime before the end of the third shift. Anyway, you guys are free to park here, under my jurisdiction."

"Juris what?" Peterson said, and pulled out a cigarette.

"Never seen you with a square, on the job."

"Just started, when you showed up."

"Right, I caught the smell as soon as my window went down."

"Then I guess you will make a good detective."

"Well, I'm buying," O'Donnell said.

"That's mighty nice of you, O'Donnell," Williams said. Then, looking at Peterson, he adds, "See you at my place for the Bengals/Vikings game?"

"About twelve days from now. I'll be there, Williams, and, *ah,* congrats on your promotion. You're already a fine detective... smelling smoke the way you just did."

"And Peterson," Williams makes a gesture, "bring Special Agent O'Donnell with you. You're into football, right?"

"Played on special teams in my junior year in high school."

"Groovy!"

"Thanks, Detective Williams, for the invite."

"Welcome. Just Williams. No State. Be careful out there."

Detective Williams released the brake. The Caprice rolled forward at about 10 mph, its passenger window closing in tandem with the car's speed. The new detective of the *State Police Investigative Division* checked out the crush of people getting in and out of cars. The ambient light streamed first over the hood and then flowed back off the trunk.

O'Donnell swiveled his head in a short arc side-to-side. He said, "Williams takes good care of his vehicle. What did he mean by *No State?*"

"No formality, statecraft, that sort of thing."

Peterson presses the green button on his ringing cell. "Agent Peterson speaking."

"Agent Peterson? Brenda Nolan, Kaskaskia FBI."

"You can call me Jack. What's up?" Peterson wanted to give a better impression to O'Donnell, "How can the Ohio Field Office be of service, Agent Nolan?"

"Call me Brenda. I have Ahmad Jones on the line with me. Go ahead."

"Jack, my friend!"

Peterson rubbed his forehead with his thumb and pinky, while holding his cigarette with his first and second fingers. For O'Donnell, the sounds of the wind and the procession of numberless vehicles on the active lane were no match for the deafening silence of Special Agent Jack Peterson at that moment. He tried to decipher Ahmad's voice; gauging it against everything he had heard. To him it was authentic and well modulated, like a singer's voice— deep, empathic, nuanced. He watched Peterson's reaction during the six seconds of silence before Peterson spoke, "Ahmad, great to know you're alive, dear friend. I was glad I could help you."

"You're the second person to tell me that today. Jack, my wife Marakie is in town. Would you see to her safety, as a precaution?"

"What's this about?"

"She's the daughter of President Za Dewabuna of Afarland. About the trouble you helped me with earlier, I'm certain that trouble was sent by the people who are behind the government takeover of Afarland."

Peterson said, "Ahmad, I don't doubt you're giving me facts, but I am curious, as I haven't seen or heard, through any international alerts, of a coup taking place in Afarland. So, how do *you* know that a takeover is going down now?"

"I charted Afarland's timeline back in March, met with their cabinet and explained the measurements and metrics. I gave them a very grounded heads-up about this day, a highly critical one for Afarland as a political entity. The plotters of it have already tried to stop me."

"From doing what?"

Jones heard movement behind the door that connected to the adjoining suite. He turned to face that door as he answered Peterson's question.

"From getting in their way. The president's daughter is my wife and I play a role in the administration's cabinet meetings."

"I see. Are you *getting* in their way? I mean, why are you here?"

"I'm on tour promoting my book. I'm scheduled to be interviewed on *The End Zone* sports program. These attacks are to stop me from appearing on that show. Think about it, Afarland is experiencing a coup, I'm a member of Afarland's cabinet, married to the daughter of the president and I'm about to appear on a syndicated program with a global viewership."

Peterson flicked his cigarette ash out the window. "Okay, Ahmad."

"The studio is in Peregrine. Jack, see to my wife's protection, until I arrive this evening?"

"Certainly, Ahmad, but if she's the daughter of a leader of a sovereign nation, there should be a diplomatic security service detail already assigned to her?

"We didn't initially secure a DSS detail on purpose Jack, my call."

"I assume being under less scrutiny is how you mean to play whatever hand you are playing."

"Jack, this is international chess, off the board and on the streets. Marakie could be exposed."

"This, I don't understand, but, you, I think I understand *you*, which is why I will do what I legally can to assist."

"I owe you Jack. The people behind this want to close any possible links with the current administration. And I mean, close them forever."

"Any names?"

"General Garaka, for one, and probably one other cabinet member. I also feel that my sister can use a layer of protection. They could use her, possibly, as leverage to influence me."

"Okay, first, where is your wife?"

"Jack, I'm texting you the information now."

"I see it, and your sister's location."

"Thanks, Jack."

A glossy black Mercedes angled in from O'Donnell's left flank, passing the Tahoe and pulling into the empty space two car lengths ahead. The taillights brightened towards the top as the brakes went on.

"Ahmad! Hold on a sec." Peterson squinted, while looking at the outline of the plates, then choked-out his cigarette and took a sip of his coffee. Something about the scene warranted a closer look.

Peterson snatched a pair of binoculars from the glove box and turned the focusing knob until the plates were sharply defined. He checked out the U.S. State Department seal at the upper left.

"Peterson?"

"One minute, Ahmad. Checking something out."

The driver, a thin man with wiry movements, wearing a black slim-fit suit and a white shirt with an ill-fitting collar rushed out. He hurried around the back to the passenger side and met a man and woman, coming out of the terminal. He shook hands with the taller, muscular man, also in a black suit, but with pants just an inch short of being high waters. The woman, older, matronly, overweight, and the same height as the driver, was nervous. She stood by the tall man's side, wearing a colorful merge of modern and traditional Afarland attire.

O'Donnell, a connoisseur of luxury cars, wore a look of envy. The driver of the Mercedes stepped aside and opened the right-back door for the woman. He held his right-hand palm-up, which the woman took in hers as she eased downward into the back seat, pulling in the remainder of her long garment. The tall, muscular man already walked around the back of the SUV, to the other side. The driver shut the door, yanked a black handkerchief from his inside jacket-pocket and cleaned off the door handle. He looked around the airport terminal and stopped turning when he noticed the brown Tahoe behind him. He saw two white men and the government plate when he executed his double-take. The thin, wiry man couldn't see much through the tinted windshield, except a little more than silhouettes of Peterson and O'Donnell.

He hurried around the back to the driver's side, where the tall man was, and repeated the ritual for him, except for holding his palm out.

He then stepped inside the idling black beauty. The two agents noticed the thin-bodied man's deference to the new arrivals and figured they were people who wielded some political clout.

"Nice wheels. Looks hot off this year's line, the new GLE class SUV, with its 7G-Tronic automatic trans with paddles," O'Donnell said with a tinge of envy.

Peterson was surprised. "You know your Mercedes. Can you make out the country code on the plate?" He offered his partner the binoculars, to which he gestured *not necessary*.

"Z L Afarland!" O'Donnell said. He finished his coffee and put the empty cup in the cradle. The Mercedes backed up a few feet then angled forward and was quick to lose itself in the parade of traffic.

"Repeat that," Peterson said. "Ahmad, what's the name of the country again?"

"Afarland. Why?"

"Because a brand-new Mercedes just pulled away from us, with diplomatic plates for Afarland. Ahmad, if you think that there is a *persona non grata* in our midst, I can't do anything about anybody without first contacting the Department of State. There's the Vienna Convention, Protection of Diplomats, diplomatic immunity, etcetera. If you've got any hard facts, I know someone who works with the Assistant Chief of Protocol for Diplomatic Affairs, there."

"I do, Jack, but this has to play out without their help."

"Okay, I trust your judgment. For now, my partner and I will collect your wife and take her to our field office and make a call for your sister, to make sure they're out of harm's way. Ahmad, if this backfires and people get hurt, I will be asked why I didn't apprise other agencies, like the DSS, and maybe the CIA, even my own superiors, about this situation, due to its international nature. My career could end, but not on my terms."

O'Donnell whispered, "Mine, too."

Jones considered his next few words. He understood the sacrifice his friend was making, including his partner. He felt in his body that everything he was about to do would work out in the end. At this time, Jones felt his strength returning. He felt all parts of his body merging together, conveying a feeling of energetic coherence and alignment with himself, such that he'd never experienced. It was during this feeling that Jones said, "Jack, don't worry about a thing."

"Ahmad, my faith in you and what you do, is why I will keep this among us. We're about three miles from the Fairlawn Hilton. We'll be there just as soon as we pick up a mover and shaker from D.C. Call your wife and tell her to get ready to leave. Don't worry."

Nolan said, "Ahmad, I'm still here. We will come up to your—"

Peterson, O'Donnell and Nolan hear a crash.

# 40

## Jones' Second Attack

THE DEFIBRILLATOR MAN BURST THE DOOR OPEN and stood toe-to-toe with Jones. Making each strike count, Jones hit the man's body with an uppercut to the pit of his stomach, then a kick to his right inside knee, followed by a reverse elbow strike to the man's head. Jones' efforts to unbalance his opponent were in vain. The man stood three inches taller and outweighed Jones. His shoulders rolled forward as his hand tightened around Jones' neck.

Jones attacked the pit of his throat with a finger jab.

Nothing. The man's hand and arm didn't break loose after that strike, which should have stopped him cold. Jones was suffocating. The attacker didn't speak. He growled, while looking into Jones' eyes. He didn't have much time to live. The man was sent to kill, only. Jones could bring him to death's door, with a certain strike near the angle of his jaw, close to the carotid artery. The man applied his other hand to Jones' neck. He controlled whether Jones would take another breath. With no ability to breath in, Jones wasn't at an angle to strike the jaw. The man shook Jones, pushing his huge thumbs further against his trachea. He noticed the attacker's prominent cheekbones. If he struck them just right, he could upset his entire energy system.

Jones smashed his right foot against the big man's left cheek the moment it left the ground. It elicited a dull sound. It should have knocked him over. Under extreme desperation Jones kicked him again and again, alternating his feet and smashing them against both sides of the face. The last one loosened his attacker's grip just enough for Jones to leap four inches upward, arc his inside arm around the back of the man's neck, land on his feet, and flip him over his hip.

There was a loud thud. Jones coughed several times. But just as soon as the man's back hit the floor, he was on his feet. Jones was still recovering from near strangulation when the man leapt at Jones and clutched his body around the waist. He lifted him, then twisted to the right and let go. Jones soared until he struck the wall. The man came steadily on. That part of the wall didn't give one bit because the stud was directly behind it. Jones ricocheted off the wall like a ragdoll, yet landed on his hands and feet. The assailant growled some more and reached out to grab Jones, who was still coughing but stayed low to the ground. They circled each other. Jones' back ended up facing the Lake Tahoe picture. He crouched low, took a long deep breath, and sprung out with both palms in a drive block, lifting the man off his feet. The north wall reverberated with the impact of the large man's body knocking into it.

Jones is already dizzy from the adrenaline rush. He cannot chance whiting out while this huge man is still able to dispense fatal damage.

The assailant shook his head side-to-side, pulled a claw-like karambit out of his long front pocket and rushed at Jones again, slashing left and then right. Jones feels like he is just about spent. Then, unbidden in his mind's eye, he sees an American football running back stiff-arm a tackle off his feet. This inspires him. The mental scene ends. Jones evades the knife attacks and then notices a medium-size hardwood table near the bottom of the lace curtains. It is two-and-a-half feet square with an artificial flower in a vase on top. Jones drops to one knee and lifts the table by one of its legs. The man keeps coming. Jones swings the dense wooden table against the closest knee. There's a crack, but it isn't bone. The table breaks into several pieces.

With only a table leg in his hand, Jones meets more oncoming slashing motions with a swing from his makeshift club to the back of the man's knife hand. The wallop is so loud that it echoes through the adjoining doorway into the other room. The karambit drops to the floor. The assailant doesn't react but keeps coming at Jones, whose vision starts blurring, while he is losing consciousness. He can't rely on Nolan to arrive in time. In one big burst of will, Jones jumps on the man's body and wraps his right arm around his neck, while both of his feet are off the floor. If the man doesn't go down this time, Jones will surely die.

Jones' head and shoulders are hanging over the assailants' upper back, while the assailant is still standing. The angle between Jones' forearm and bicep muscles shortens fast around the assailant's neck and throat. The man is about to fall backward. Then he rams his knee into the pit of the assailant's stomach while the back of his upper arm forces the assailant's head forward and down. His weight gets heavier as oxygen to his brain is being cut off. The big man falls to his knees.

Jones drags the man over the broken table pieces and drops him face down on the carpet. Jones' breathing is rapid, like an animal's. His instinct is to kill this man. He squeezes more and more as the muscles in his neck and jaw tighten to support the effort. Just as he's about to break the man's neck, he hears the words of his teacher, as if he were kneeling next to him and talking into both of Jones' ears.

*My son, is this man still a threat to you?*

Nolan and Dumont scramble to the left end of the hotel's reception desk. The elevators are directly across from the right side. Dumont presses the call button. The elevator indicator is lit on the third floor.

"Special Agent Nolan, Kaskaskia FBI," she flashes her credentials and badge. "Tell me which room Ahmad Jones is in and give me a master keycard—fast!"

"Oh, my!" the hotel manager says. "I just saw Mr. Jones...e's, *ah...* he's in suite, *ah...*"

The manager pulls a fresh keycard from underneath the counter and inserts it into the encoding machine while checking the guest manifest.

"Hurry, damn it!"

"On the third floor, end of the hall. Suite 318."

"Where's that keycard—"

"I'm getting it now—"

"Well, break out the card then, a man's life is at stake."

The manager swipes the card and hands it to Nolan. She snatches it and hurries to the elevator.

"Please don't lose that card or I'll have to rekey the entire hotel," he shouts.

Dumont paces by the elevators. When Nolan arrives, the elevator door opens and they rush inside.

"He's on the third floor, Room 318." Dumont presses the number on the control panel.

"Jones, we're on our way up. We're almost at your door. On our way, we'll be there."

Inside the SUV Peterson glances at O'Donnell while rubbing his hands on his head.

Jones couldn't hear anything. He was unconscious. The phone, still on speaker, had left Jones' hand when the assailant, an assassin, grabbed his neck. Nolan and Dumont get to the third floor and off the elevator. They run to the end of the hall, stick in the keycard, and take out their Glocks. They rush in when the little light turns green. They open from the left side. Nolan steps into the suite, moving ahead of Dumont, then Dumont ahead of Nolan.

They hold their pistols close to their bodies, pointing them down at 45 degrees. They pass the Lake Tahoe picture on the long wall to their left, and then reach the edge of the shorter wall to their right, clearing the hallway inside the suite. They look into the living room past the wall edge. . They see the pieces of the small table, Jones' cell, a cracked vase and an artificial rose.

Nolan asks, "Ahmad Jones, can you hear me?"

In the lobby, the floor manager called the Kaskaskia Police. Several guests heard the commotion and had also dialed 911.

Back in 318, both men were face down with Jones not moving. His arm was still under the man's neck. Dumont left the living room and crossed to the left side of the suite near the long wall. He checked beyond the Lake Tahoe picture into the kitchen and back rooms, and then came back and approached Nolan.

"All clear," he said. Nolan aimed her weapon at the assailant for a beat, until Dumont arrived. She deposited her weapon into the shoulder holster and knelt on her left knee. She felt Jones' neck. His pulse was as strong as it was the first time she'd checked it at Mangala Park.

Dumont reached into the assailant's pockets and body for weapons. He picked up the karambit with his pen and dropped it into the trash basket at the end of the short hallway behind him. The trash bag became an evidence bag, for now. Nolan knelt on her other knee and turned Jones over on his back. He appears to be sleeping, she thought, remembering Jones' explanation of his adrenaline whiteouts.

"Dumont, call 911 and check the suspect's pulse."

Dumont made the call, while placing his index and forefinger on the assailant's carotid artery. He found it.

"He's alive," Dumont said, with indifference.

*There's got to be more to Jones' story than this coup. Why would he be promoting a book right now?* Nolan thought.

"Hello, is anyone there? This is Peterson."

Nolan just remembered that Peterson was still on the line, when the commotion started. She lifted her cell from her thigh pocket.

"I guess you heard everything, Agent Peterson?"

"Is Ahmad okay?"

"Yes, but he's unconscious."

"What happened?"

"Can you see to Jones' wife and sister first? We've got a situation here. Peterson, I'll call you back when I have a few moments."

"Alright... copy that. I'll get back to you as soon as my partner and I are on our way to Marakie's hotel." Nolan thought she saw the assailant move. She drew her weapon and pointed it, waited, then she called to Jones, "Ahmad Jones, can you hear me?" She put her weapon back inside her holster, but not all the way in—she was too distracted. She put her phone away.

Dumont holstered his weapon. He surmised that a prone, unconscious man couldn't pose a credible threat as he brought his right hand around his side and lifted his cuffs out of their pouch on his utility belt. He simultaneously moved the assailant's left wrist to the small of his back, about to cuff it, along with the assailant's right wrist.

But both Nolan and Dumont had made a tactical error.

Nolan then noticed the muscled suspect's eyes open. She saw him wrap his left hand, like a snake, around her partner's left wrist as he lifted his head off the floor.

"Dumont!" Nolan shouted.

There was the sound of bone snapping. The assailant rolled his body from his stomach to his left side and then onto his back, while taking Dumont's wrist for the ride. Dumont's hand and half his forearm were now underneath the man's lower back. Nolan's weapon was in the holster under her armpit, with the bottom of the grip facing out. Jones' head was underneath it. His body was face-up on her lap. She braced her holster with her left hand, while pulling the grip out with the right, but only pulled it out a third of the way, before the assailant's next move put her in check.

She noticed the assailant's face, all black and blue. He pulled his hand from under his back and Dumont's wrist and grabbed Dumont's ear, jerking it down, which rolled his body to the left. The assailant switched hands, putting his right one under Dumont's left armpit and his left palm behind his neck. They both rolled leftward. As Dumont's body rotated, his legs made an arc in the air and crashed onto Nolan's shoulders. She buckled under the impact against her own shoulders, bending forward and downward.

The hired gun withdrew Dumont's duty weapon from his strong side with his right hand and gripped it from the draw stroke. He was a professional. Nolan and Dumont's heartbeats accelerated more with each passing second. He rolled the pistol into position and got set, but his trigger finger was extended as he pointed, first at Nolan, then Dumont, then Jones. Jones was the designated target. Jones was awake but somewhere else.

He was standing on the top of a great mountain, a few feet from a man over six-three and about 180 pounds. His garment was deep purple with gold trim. This man's skin was walnut brown with a subtle undertone of blue. His long locks were covered on top with a brilliant white turban that had a flawless 118-karat, heart-cut diamond in the center. One end of the turban reached to the man's fifth lumbar vertebra; the rest was wrapped in a design that crossed and re-crossed certain areas of his head. The man wasn't a Muslim, a Sikh, a Hindu, or a Zoroastrian; he was something else. The man seemed familiar. The scene changed.

Like an establishment shot in a movie, in his altered state, Jones saw general sweeps of barren land, dust and rocks—the permanently employed actors on a semi-desert stage. Their blocking could have been directed by powerful anti-tradewinds coming from the northeast, below-freezing temperatures, and a layer of frost down to three feet deep. It was the broad high-desert region connecting Tanzania's Mount Kilimanjaro's two main peaks, Mawenzi and Kibo.

Nolan sat still as she gently pleaded. "Why do you want to kill this man? We are federal agents and this man is a friend of the FBI. He is a part of our family of federal officers. Think. You pull that trigger, you will get the death penalty, I promise you," she said.

No answer.

"You will be charged with first-degree murder; it carries a felony charge. You will be guilty of malicious, premeditated intent to kill a federal—"

"Shut up!"

The hired gun growled and moved his finger to inside the trigger guard. From Nolan's perspective, his gesture heralded Jones' death. If the shot exited she would be wounded or dead, too, and then, her partner. Dumont's left shoulder was pinned under the assailant's knee, and his calves were still perched on Nolan's shoulders. It was an unusual configuration of bodies, and yet, it was the right configuration for something unusual to occur.

Nolan felt Jones shaking as he, emerging from his altered state, still felt the freezing nighttime temperatures of the region portrayed in his vision. As the American adventurer, Peter McQueen in 1908, described this region near Africa's largest mountain: *These rocks, hills and mountains are thrown together in dreadful confusion—the wreckage of a former world.*

The man with the turban appeared, smiled, pointed at Jones, and then said: *Return*. And so, he did. Then Jones saw night turn to day, reaching 100°F. At the same time, Nolan felt Jones' shaking stop.

The elapsed time was less than a second—from the moment the hired gun trained Dumont's pistol on Jones, through the surreal desert scenes and the turbaned man with his pointing finger—until he opened his eyes. Jones was now conscious of where he was and of his predicament. Before this, it was just like that time when he lost consciousness while riding the tram in South Africa, when he was free of the restriction of his physical body and the limited range of his senses—how he could observe his attackers and the frightened onlookers with an impartial, spherical awareness. Jones had measured the placement of Dumont, Nolan, the hired gun, and himself from outside his body, even before he got behind his eyes again.

# 41

## The Upside-Down Shot

AFTER LOCKING ONTO NOLAN'S EYES, then her weapon, and feeling her thighs against his upper back, her warm right palm under his neck, and her left hand supporting his right side—Jones knew that he had the leverage required to pull off a trick play. He had two choices—both were long shots. The first one was plausible and the second was downright crazy. Jones could draw the pistol from Nolan's holster in one sharp movement and stop the threat or he could stop it without drawing the pistol.

The second option could work, because the pistol was inserted two-thirds of the way in. Jones had a single opportunity to execute it flawlessly. It was an uncalculated risk. Jones knew, that is, something beyond him *and still him* knew, that the man with Dumont's pistol would not triumph. Jones understood pistols. The safety on Nolan's weapon was mounted on the trigger. He had to accurately get his finger in front of it and pull. Jones wasn't concerned about the success of this tactic.

He exhales. Nolan's pistol is less than twelve inches from Jones' gun hand. Instead of pulling the weapon and Nolan's upper body to him, he pushes the weapon away as he slips his forefinger through the trigger guard. Like a 180-pound rolling pin, he turns his torso counterclockwise on top of her knees, then over her waist and belly. Her lower and then her upper back press hard against the floor. Dumont's legs slip of off Nolan's shoulders and onto Jones. He continues to roll onto her chest with the pistol partially in its holster. Nolan grimaces.

He is now lower than the hired gun who is kneeling on his left knee and bearing down on Dumont's shoulder. Jones is in an awkward shooting position. He flips the barrel up. The muzzle is trained on the target at the end of

Jones' turn. He gets his other hand around the grip. Nolan is flat on her back with Jones' upper body on top. Nolan's thigh muscles are tightly compressed, while being stretched to their limits, and her heels are against her buttocks. The strong pull on her shoulder harness is even worse. She cannot move. Nolan's holstered weapon in Jones' hand is pointed upside-down at the target's forearm.

There were two slight bucks. The hot shell casings hit Nolan's torso. The gigantic booms of the pistol reverberated across the room.

# 42

## Mistaken Identity

IN THE LATE 19TH CENTURY, bullets were propelled down gun barrels by ignited, black gunpowder. The powder didn't explode, but instead caught fire quickly enough inside the tiny space to launch the projectile to its target. They made a loud enough pop that drew immediate attention, but most nearby ears could tolerate the sound and continue their business. Jones had fired a weapon whose projectiles reach speeds faster than 1,200 feet per second. The sound barrier at sea level, give or take small variations, is 761 mph. The hired gun from Senegal was hit with bullets moving at supersonic speed, in a place where the sound could only bounce off the walls, windows, and through the doorway leading into the next suite.

The two explosions that all four experienced in that small living room provided enough pressure to check the smooth functioning of their eardrums. Like watching a movie with no sound, the hired gun's screams of pain were inaudible, even to him. The bullets were lodged in his arm. With one of his senses gone, the others were sharper, especially his sense of touch. All four were deaf.

Jones' deafness went away almost as soon as it came. He lifted his body off Nolan, recovered Dumont's pistol that lay near the downed assailant. Dumont was busy getting on his feet, without the use of his left hand. His left shoulder was in pain too. Jones handed Dumont's pistol to him, handle first. Dumont received it with his non-dominant hand and nodded as he took his weapon. Because of his heightened coherence, Jones was the most able-bodied person to stand the shockwave. His adrenaline rush was enough to precipitate another whiteout, but this time it didn't. He had several times the energy and at long last he could command it.

"Agent Nolan, I'm sorry if I hurt you," but to Nolan, Jones' words were inaudible.

"You saved our lives!" When she spoke, her words vibrated inside her head, but Nolan's ears weren't as bad as Dumont's.

Nolan was reliving the facts of her life. It could have ended in those last few seconds. She didn't conclude that the hired gun was just going to do Jones. The scene kept replaying, with new scenes injected by her, where the hired gun shoots her and her partner, too. She was still supine on the floor.

"Are you all right?" Jones asked. Nolan was still replaying the tape in her mind. She sat up and saw the bloodstained carpet. The hired gun's mouth was open, but she didn't hear any sound. She watched him looking at his right arm. His eyes moved haphazardly. He used his left hand to stop the blood from pouring out of it. The hired gun was sitting upright. His head was tilted back in agony. Nolan took out her weapon and was about to shoot him again. She was not quite in the world that she knew and took for granted.

She pointed her weapon. Jones stood, between Dumont and the hired gun. "What did you do, Ahmad? He's still alive." The words still vibrated in her head.

Jones went to her side and slowly guided the muzzle downward. He turned to look at the hired gun who was still in shock and bleeding.

He stared intensely at Jones, then at his arm, then back to Jones, who ran into the kitchen, yanked a long, orange dishtowel off the hook and returned to the hired gun. He wrapped the towel around his lower arm near the elbow; it quickly absorbed the copious stream of blood. He loosened the man's belt, grabbed the buckle and slid it out through the loops. Dumont and Nolan both had their guns on the assailant as Jones secured the belt around the towel as a tourniquet.

"That should do, until…"

"What did you do?" Nolan asked again.

Jones turned as he went back to the kitchen to rinse the hired gun's blood off his hands. "Stopped the threat," he said as he wiped his hands and returned to Nolan.

"No, Ahmad. What did you *do*?"

"I shot the *flexor digitorum profundus*, the muscle that controls his trigger finger."

"What? What the—fuck?"

Jones extended his hand to Nolan. She kept eyeing the hired gun, and then looked at Jones' friendly, open palm. She secured her pistol, then clasped Jones' hand and pulled herself up. Dumont, in pain, kept his pistol pointed at the hired gun, while his left hand stayed parked next to his thigh.

Jones placed his palms over Nolan's ears while she looked around, still in a bit of a shock. The tiny bones in her inner ear were traumatized. After a minute, the ringing in her ears stopped.

Nolan felt different, as if awakening from sleep. She heard, as if she were incrementally increasing the volume of a radio or TV, the hideous sound of the hired gun's screams.

Like she was half asleep, she asked. "Where did you learn to shoot like that?"

"Never *learned* to shoot like that."

"Ahmad, the slide was facing down and the grip was facing up." Nolan turned to the hired gun and raised her voice. "WILL YOU SHUT UP? WE'LL GET TO YOU IN A MINUTE." Nolan turned back. With the voice and timbre of a child talking to a parent after being tucked into bed, she said, "I don't believe it. You got off two rounds with my Glock. It could have backfired."

Jones whispered, "Negative, the slide had room to slide and allow the empty shells to fall out. And your weapon wasn't fully holstered."

The hired gun kept his screaming down, per Nolan's angry outburst. The sounds were muffled, like a hurt dog. Dumont kept his pistol on him. Jones noticed a tear forming in Nolan's right eye. He separated his hands, as if a giant invisible balloon was inflating between them. She stepped closer to Jones, into his space, her trembling body pressed against his. Jones held her, making sure to place his heart over hers, while she was sobbing, instead of crying. Dumont looked at Nolan inside the circle of Jones' arms, then back at the hired gun. Dumont had a troubled look. Nolan's arms and hands lifted around his back. She had never trusted anyone so fully—it was an experience she had never had. Jones held her. Dumont couldn't hear anything.

Jones said, *"Vse budet horosho."* (Everything will be fine.)

Nolan stopped sobbing and looked up at Jones again.

"You speak my language?" she asked.

"*Nim noga*—a little," he said.

Jones went to the kitchen and brought back some tissues. Nolan wiped her face with them.

"Dumont, how is your hand and your wrist?" Nolan asked, pointing.

321

"YOU'RE ASKING HOW MY WRIST IS?"

Nolan nodded. Dumont spoke loudly—his ears were not yet normal.

"MY WRIST FEELS BROKEN," Dumont looked mentally exhausted.

Jones directed Dumont to sit down. Jones sat behind him. The hired gun lay on his back. Jones circled his legs around Dumont's waist. He lowered his weapon. Nolan went for her pistol again, covering the hired gun. Nolan could feel a little sunlight on her back.

Jones first placed his hands over Dumont's ears, allowing his heightened coherence to move through them and through Dumont's head. Nolan watched her partner move his jaw around. Dumont felt the pressure subside and the sound returning, like stopped ears becoming unstopped when chewing gum, minutes before an airplane touches down.

Jones checked Dumont's wrist, "Your wrist is a little hyper-flexed, not broken. I'm going to fix it for you. Okay?"

"Yes."

Jones put his thumb on top of his other thumb and pressed down on the injured part that was jutting outward due to dislocation and tissue damage. The move put the small bone back in place. Then he held a series of acupressure points around the wrist cuff while touching an area along his spine. He did the same for his left shoulder. Dumont could feel himself relaxing. After a minute, Jones stood up and went to the man he just shot.


Outside the hotel, four Kaskaskia Police patrol cars pulled up in front of the Radisson: one parked on the street, another prowled around to the back, and two stopped on a dime, in front of the main lobby doors. Four men and two women ran inside the lobby. The second 911 was for the shots that were heard. Another three cars showed up. All three parked on the main road, in front with the first car. After learning where the gunshots were fired, all four ran to the north side, where a cop from the first responders, let them in. The second set of officers ran up the stairwell to the second floor, then they carefully traversed one more floor to reach the third. There were six cops positioned between the door to Suite 318 and the AED box. Across from them, on the other side of the door to Jones' suite, the second unit of four officers showed up with their weapons drawn, awaiting orders from their sergeant. The cop nearest the door had three chevrons on his upper arm.

Sounds from police radios streamed into the rooms from the other end of the hallway. Guests stayed inside, looking through spy holes as they listened to commands and orders from people who spoke with authority. While inside, Jones, Nolan and Dumont heard a deep voice from behind the door.

"This is Sergeant Peabody of the Kaskaskia Police Department. I was informed that... FBI is in the house."

"Any more help may have to wait," Jones told the hired gun. His bleeding slowed, due to the tourniquet, but not enough. Jones got to his feet, and so did Dumont.

Dumont rubbed his wrist, "Thanks, Ahmad. It feels better."

"You're welcome."

Nolan began walking toward the door. "Yes, Special Agent Nolan and Special Agent Dumont are here from the Kaskaskia RA."

"Stay where you are for now. Okay, Agent Nolan?"

Nolan didn't take another step.

"What's going on, officer?"

"Just doing my due diligence, Agent Nolan. Now, Dispatch said that three guests at this hotel heard shots fired. Do you and your partner... do you have control of the situation, Agent Nolan?"

"Yes. The suspect was shot here. The weapon is secured."

"Copy that, Special Agent Nolan. Okay, so far. Now, I must satisfy myself that you are who you say you are before we go any further."

"Are you kidding?" She started for the door again. The sergeant was insistent.

"I can hear you coming closer. I said STAY where you are, didn't I? I need you two to toss your badges and IDs toward the door. I want to see them. Okay?" Turning to the officer next to him, Peabody points down the hall and says, "Officer Tan, I want them to get into 318 from 316."

Officer Tan relayed the message to the second unit that arrived. Two cops hurried down to the lobby to get a key for 316.

Nolan stepped back to the middle of the room and said, "Okay, Sergeant Peabody, we're sending them to you now."

Nolan and Dumont tossed their credentials and badges toward the door. One officer used the handle of a large mirror to scoop them up.

Peabody said, "Okay, we're going to push the door open a bit so we can get a better look. I want you to lay on the ground with your hands behind your head."

Nolan said, "You've got to be kidding!"

"Negative. I don't kid around with my life, or the lives of my officers."

"The suspect is already on the floor, but he can't put both hands behind his head because one of them was shot and he's still bleeding."

"You shot him?"

"Yes, no, but he was stopped, so we have an obligation not to let him bleed out. One of us must cover him in case he tries anything. We cannot all lie face down with him."

"I'll do it," Dumont said. With Jones help, he rolled the hired gun over on his stomach and placed his knee on his neck. Payback. He bent over his upper body, with his hands behind his head. Jones followed the sergeant's orders.

"I saw a federal vehicle out front, but you could have been compromised and you may be speaking under duress—or you may be one of the bad guys, or bad girls. So, just play along until I have verified the identity of the person with whom I am speaking—*ah,* I expect you to comply."

A mirror the size of a 12-inch pizza was angled in through the door into the room. The sergeant saw: Nolan's full head of hair to the far right, a conservatively cut black man in the middle wearing red sneakers, a larger black man face-down with a blood-stained, orange towel and brown belt around his right arm, and a light-skinned man wearing a t-shirt bending forward while kneeling on one knee and with his other knee on top of the suspect.

"*Ah,* Special Agents Nolan and Dumas, show me your faces."

"That's Dumont, sir."

Nolan and Dumont lifted their heads to stare into the mirror, positioned underneath the Lake Tahoe picture. Tan checked Nolan and Dumont's faces against the ID pictures. He nodded to Peabody.

"Who is that gent with the red sneaks lying near you, Special Agent Nolan?"

"Officer Peabody, that man is Ahmad Jones. May we get up please?"

"Well, I'll be! Ahmad Jones in the flesh, huh?" Peabody shook his head. "You say it like I'm supposed to know who the hell he is. Well, his name didn't come after the words officer or special agent. You can get up now. So, who in Sam Hill is he, the shooter?"

Nolan and Dumont stood up.

"Is he the shooter?"

"Yes, sir. He saved our lives. He stopped the suspect from probably shooting all three of us."

Peabody spoke into his transmitter. "Officer Lloyd, need you to look up a, excuse me Agent Nolan, give me that name again?"

"My name is Ahmad Jones: A-h-m-a-d, Jones."

"*Well, thank you,* Mr. Jones! Did you get that, Officer Lloyd?" Lloyd was in one of the patrol vehicles out front.

"Affirmative, sir. I'm on it."

"Now, I could've sworn, with no fear of contradiction, that I directed my inquiry to Special Agent Nolan. Mr. Jones, you don't speak unless I speak to you. Are we clear?"

Officer Tan, who was holding the mirror, angled it so the sergeant could see Jones' position on the carpet.

"Yes, Sergeant Peabody."

Peabody cocked his head right and left.

"It's all about respect," Peabody said.

Nolan turned to glance at Jones. She said, "Sergeant Peabody."

With an edge to his voice, "Yes, Special Agent Nolan, until I learn otherwise."

"Ahmad Jones used to help the Bureau, even state and local."

"Informant?"

"Consultant."

"You mean, he was an informant before he became a consultant?"

"Negative, sir. He came on," Nolan cleared her throat, "was invited by the Bureau *as* a consultant."

"Copy that. What about the man who was shot?"

"We don't know yet. He had seized my partner's weapon and was about to shoot Jones, but Jones stopped him."

"For the record, how did Mr. Jones *stop* him, Special Agent Nolan?" Peabody was still talking behind the door.

"He shot him."

"With his own weapon?"

"No, he didn't have a weapon. It was with mine. The suspect seized my partner's weapon and meant to shoot Jones, but Jones used my weapon to stop him."

"Used? Then you gave it to him."

"No, he had my weapon, did some unbelievable... damn it, he just had my weapon."

"Whew! This story is getting goofier and goofier. That's a doozy of a scenario! Let me see if I got this right: two FBI agents had their weapons taken from them. The suspect took one and a Mr. Ahmad Jones took the other? There are ten or eleven officers in this hallway and I can't vouch for their silence in this regard—in the locker room, at the dinner table, or on a stakeout."

The two officers returned with the keycard to 316. Officer Tan spotted them and went to meet them.

Tan said, "The Sergeant's been stalling so we could get into the other suite. One unit goes in on my mark."

The two officers nodded, went to the door, and withdrew their weapons.

"So, the good guy, who I reckon is Mr. Jones, used one agent's weapon to stop the other guy, who was using the other agent's weapon. Sounds like that sci-fi movie with Bruce Willis. You know the one, *Proxies*?"

The sergeant turned, searching for Officer Tan, who just came back to 318. The sergeant had a question in his eyes. Officer Tan lifted the handle of the mirror. EMT personnel had arrived at the south end of the hall.

Tan said, "You mean *Surrogates*," then whispered, "We have the keycard."

"That's right, *Surrogates*. That sounds about right, *ah,* Special Agent Nolan? Are these men surrogates?"

"What I said is the truth. And the suspect is bleeding."

"I can see that."

Tan was a movie aficionado. "Bruce Willis was an FBI agent in that movie."

"Thank you, Officer Tan. I'll remember to get my *surrogate* to enter it in my report."

Peabody listened to his shoulder holster's body transceiver.

"The agents' identities are confirmed by other federal agents who left the hotel about a half hour ago."

"Thank you, Officer Lloyd."

Officer Tan withdrew the mirror and nodded to Peabody, who signaled the men to enter 316. The sergeant opened the door more. He was a salt-and-pepper-haired, tall, rugged man in his late forties, black, and wearing glasses. He had his weapon close to his right side. He had the look of street smarts. Bright, piercing, dark-brown eyes, some furrows and bumps on his face, bushy eyebrows—most important, he had a knack for exploiting the absurd.

He whispered, "Petty and Daniels, let's cut some pie."

Officers Petty and Daniels entered suite 316, clearing all the rooms, and came into Jones' suite through the adjourning doorway. Peabody pushed the door open all the way. Sergeant Peabody cleared the plane of the doorway briskly, arching his way in. He gradually increased his field of view as he advanced along the wall, a small slice at a time, with his weapon in firing position. The other unit made its way in. Dumont and Nolan saw them enter. Jones was still. Once they cleared the door, they saw Jones, and the hired gun on the ground. Peabody pointed to the kitchen area. Daniels and Petty passed the broken table and the hired gun and made it to the south wall and the Lake Tahoe picture. They followed the same protocol when clearing the kitchen and the backroom.

"Okay, Mr. Jones, you can stand up. One of my officers just spoke to Special Agent McNulty at Kaskaskia RA. Said that they left you at the hotel. So, that part of the narrative checks out, and he mentioned Mr. Jones that you're some kind of hero."

Jones stood up. Nolan tried to help him up but was too late. "This is a crime scene now," Nolan whispered to Jones. "Kaskaskia PD will be all over here in a few minutes. Why are you really in the U.S.?"

"Not here," Jones whispered back.

Nolan's curiosity kept her going, "I'm still freaked about how you shot a man twice with my weapon still inside my holster, without getting a sight on the target, without the slider getting jammed and stabilizing the recoil. The gun was upside down."

Peabody noticed the paper on the desk with Ralph Hay's name written down.

"Who is Ralph Hay? Anyone."

"Never heard of him, Sergeant," Nolan said. Peabody looked at Jones.

"Hay is the guy who helped form the APFA, the precursor to the NFL."

Peabody pointed to the middle of the living room. "What does the NFL or this guy Hay have to do with that man being shot, by Mr. Jones, and you two feds here?"

"Nothing. I was doing a phone interview and Hay's name came up. This happened before the suspect on the floor crashed through that door from the next room."

The crime scene photographer came in. She had been taking pictures since arriving at the front of the hotel, and on up to inside the third-floor hallway. The officer at the door had her sign the notebook and checked her in. She came in through the other suite and went to work.

She was in her late thirties, a platinum blond with a reputation for accuracy and clarity.

"Officer Tan, you know the routine. Nobody comes in here unless they have a specific function to perform."

"Yes, sir."

"Here are your badges and IDs. I hear the feds are back to nine millimeters again. So, who's that perp?"

"No ID.

Excuse me, Sergeant Peabody. I have to talk with Jones for a minute."

Nolan motioned Jones to move closer to the curtains. Petty and Daniels stood near the opposite wall. The photographer took long shots from the corners of the room before focusing on more specific areas: the blood-stained carpet, the doorway between suites, the broken table and the artificial flower. She moved in and out, felinely, smoothly and gracefully.

Nolan glared at Jones, demanding an explanation. Jones began, "Agent Nolan, last March, I provided critical information to the governing body of Afarland, in Africa, using best practices as an astrologist. Based on my critical analysis of future trends related to the horoscopic flowchart of Afarland's progress over time, I predicted that an attempt to unlawfully seize power would likely happen on this very day. I am certain it is occurring as we speak. In anticipation of this, President Dewabuna amended the constitution which, until that time, had a clause inserted prohibiting anyone but a member of his family, meaning my wife, Marakie, from taking the leadership role in the event of either his death or his incapacity to lead. Marakie stated that she didn't wish to shoulder that responsibility. So, the amendment allowed for me to also assume leadership. I accepted the president's offer, which the cabinet supported, rather reluctantly. A constitutional review ensued to ensure there would be no breakdown of the laws of Afarland and the maintenance of good governance. I attended that meeting as an honorary member of the president's cabinet."

Nolan said, "So, Marakie, your wife, according to Afarland's constitution, is the next in line to lead should the president be removed from office—and you, per constitutional amendment, are also allowed to take on the role, which means that both you and your wife are targets. A more specific reason why you wanted Peterson to see after her."

Nolan felt good about herself. She was more informed and felt more in control of the situation.

The rest of the second unit remained outside 316, while two paramedics arrived and took over. Daniels and Petty watched from the east wall. Daniels graduated three years before Petty; both were close to six feet and experienced. The medical unit was told it was a Code 1, used for stabbings and gunshot wounds. One paramedic, named Fioritto, took the hired gun's distal pulse; it was weak. The hired gun was maneuvered off his stomach and onto his back. The other paramedic, Ting Wang, peeled back the orange towel. She noticed the bloodied rounds that were lodged in his flesh. Wang re-covered the wound with several sterile gauze pads, then wrapped a bandage around it, not too tightly. She checked his pulse.

The crime scene photographer noticed something against the east wall and said, "Officers, you're standing a foot away from two 9-millimeter casings." She had already photographed the shell casings near the bloodstain on the carpet. So far, the photographer had laid down four yellow evidence markers.

Petty and Daniels stepped away from them and repositioned near the doorway.

The manager of the Radisson attempted to come through Suite 316. He stuck his head inside.

"Sir, this suite is now part of a crime scene," Officer Tan said. "You cannot come in until all evidence has been documented." The manager was wearing a navy-blue jacket with a white shirt and a pink rose on his left lapel. He went back into the hallway.

"Oh, my!" he said. "This man was shot in my hotel. He was checking the defibrillators? Must be a new guy. I'd never seen him before today. Who did it—the man with the red sneakers?"

"You'll know everything when the police report is filed," Tan said.

"This one's to be taken to Kaskaskia Memorial, under guard," Sergeant Peabody said.

"Yes, sir," Fioritto said.

"Petty, Mirandize him." Nora Petty stepped from the doorway and over to the hired gun, to read him his rights.

As Jones and Nolan moved away from the curtains, Jones finished with, "—which is the reason that I can't miss my flight to Ohio."

Nolan walked over to Sergeant Peabody.

"Sir, my partner's wrist was injured during the incident."

The sergeant gestured to one of his officers who possessed a first aid kit. The paramedics were still getting the hired gun ready for the ride to the hospital. An officer named Parker, who had first aid training, checked Dumont's wrist and felt very little swelling.

"What is your name, sir?" Parker asked.

"Agent Dumont, Alejandro."

"Agent Dumont, can you squeeze my hand?"

"Yes, I can."

"Your wrist doesn't look bad, doesn't feel broken or even sprained. Do you want me to make a splint to minimize movement, or would you like a painkiller?" Dumont glanced at Nolan.

Moving it around, Dumont said, "No, thanks. My wrist is a little sore but it feels fine. Amazing!"

"Sergeant," Nolan said, "Mr. Jones has a plane to catch for Ohio. I should get him to the airport, so he can get to Peregrine and handle a crisis. I will answer any questions you have and Mr. Jones will be on call tomorrow to answer your questions."

Nolan looked at Jones. He nodded.

"Sergeant!" Peabody tapped his transceiver. "Yes, Lloyd. What do you have?"

"Mr. Ahmad Jones is wanted in three states for a capital offense. It was one of us, a woman officer. The NCIC database also says that he escaped capture by U.S. Marshalls in both Miami and New York eleven years ago, for another murder, a federal agent. He just turned up on their screens today."

Peabody rubbed his head from front to back. His brow tightened as he lifted his pistol and pointed it at Jones. He said in soft tones, holding back an angry outburst, "Freeze! Mr. Jones. Drop to your knees and interlace your fingers at the back of your head. DO IT NOW! I have issued you a command and a warning."

# 43

## Jurisdiction?

JONES COMPLIED BY SLOWLY LOWERING HIS KNEES to the floor. He lifted his hands and rotated his palms forward and backward, then interlaced his fingers and not for a second did he take his eyes off the Sergeant. Special Agent Nolan keenly observed Peabody's body mechanics. She had seen all the moves done hundreds of times by cops when practice shooting at the Maxon Range in Des Plaines: *disengage the safety, pull the slide back, hold both hands just right around the firearm with index finger extended before engaging the trigger.* She had watched him follow that familiar pattern, except for the scary fact that his index finger wasn't extended, but his thumbs were. Jones could be shot dead.

Nolan faced Peabody, her back against the curtains. The sun was descending. More light suffused the room. Peabody was in front of the Lake Tahoe picture, and in front of the writing desk. Fioritto and Wang were mostly in the line-of-fire. They were behind Jones' back, a few feet away. After some seconds of uncertainty, the two paramedics resumed their care for the wounded man. Their sudden movement distracted Nolan, who then turned back to Peabody.

Speaking softly now, she says, "Sergeant Peabody, why is your finger on that trigger of your weapon?"

Peabody was steady and careful. The muscles of his forearms were as taut as violin strings. They appeared to have been chiseled out of stone. He figured if Jones saw a cop's forefinger around the trigger, he would just stay put. Peabody answered, "You and every officer in here heard what I heard. Why is my finger on the trigger, you ask? I'm performing my sworn duty as a police officer serving my community." Turning to Officer Tan, he commanded, "Tan, I need four officers for backup."

"You mean witnesses," Nolan said.

"I'm not giving any quarter to chance." Sweat formed around Peabody's bushy eyebrows.

Tan, at five-seven, from Southern China, hastened out of Suite 318 into the hallway where the other officers were at the ready. Tan said, "I need four officers inside, two through each suite."

The hallway was well lit. The hotel guests continued to stay inside their rooms. Two officers remained in the hallway. The radio chatter was constant. One officer cordoned off Suite 316 with yellow tape. He angled the tape from the doorway to the opposite wall and around the underbelly of a credenza.

Two cops came in through Suite 316 and two others from 318. There were now eight cops inside Jones' suite. The crime scene photographer stood near the door of the adjoining suites. The two paramedics were focused on their job. Petty couldn't read the rights to the hired gun because he was unconscious.

"He's lost at least a liter of blood; our golden hour is running out," Fioritto said as he examined the puddle on the carpet.

Fioritto said, "Hold this, Wang, I'll get the—"

"Code 99," Wang said. She took the stethoscope away and administered CPR.

Fioritto said, "I'm bagging, you keep up the compressions." Fioritto placed a Bag Valve Mask over the hired gun's mouth, with one hand and squeezed the oval-shaped bag to force oxygen into his lungs.

Nolan looked at the scene and felt she was dreaming. "Sergeant, Ahmad is not a threat to LE..."

The sergeant turned toward the hired gun and asked Fioritto, "Is he going to make it?"

"His chances are good," Fioritto said.

Wang stopped CPR and took his pulse, then resumed chest compressions.

"What about fluids?"

"He has a better chance of surviving without them right now. He's still losing blood, and—"

"All the more reason to—"

"No, fluids would dilute whatever blood he has. No, we must get his pressure up and decrease more loss of blood."

Wang said, "His BP is almost normal."

Fioritto said, "Put two blankets on him to delay any onset of shock." He stood up.

"Copy that."

Fioritto rolls the gurney closer and collapses it down next to the left side of the hired gun. Ahmad Jones remembers his teacher's lessons and keeps his awareness around his heart, while a firearm is trained on him, a man is almost bleeding to death, an interagency feud is getting started, and eight sworn police officers, maybe even Dumont, think he is a cop killer. As the sun continues to set, more light streams in throughout the suite.

Still cool and careful, Peabody finally addressed Nolan's previous statement. "Jones? Oh, yes. He does pose a threat. Step away from him Agent Nolan, Daniels, Petty and you, too, Agent Dumont. I don't want this guy taking anybody's weapon, like he did yours, Agent Nolan, and shooting us with it. I have him in my sights and I don't miss."

Daniels and Petty pulled back toward the east wall, away from the yellow markers on the other side of the room, opposite the window, where Nolan and Dumont stood. The two cops at the adjoining doorway looked at the other two near the Lake Tahoe picture, just a few feet from Peabody. All four trained their weapons on Jones, from opposite sides of the room. They angled themselves away from the line of their colleague's fire. They were not certain what the play was. But Nolan stayed put.

Dumont moved to the side where Nolan was. Sylvia, the crime scene photographer, simply waited inside the adjoining suite until this show was over.

"This is my jurisdiction—federal. I'll stay right here." Dumont also stayed where he was.

"Oh, shit!" one of the four cops near the adjoining door said, under his breath. He had been involved in interagency battles before.

In his mind, the sergeant needed no justification, other than the alleged cop slayer before him, for pointing the muzzle of his Beretta at Jones' center mass.

"Quiet, Agent Nolan! He's mine now." Nolan forgot all about almost being fatally shot less than five minutes ago.

"Why are you pointing your firearm? That information can't be accurate. In my investigations of Mr. Jones, nothing of the kind ever showed."

"Don't speak, Nolan. Your *hero* is a cop slayer."

"Who are you to tell me not to speak? I'm a FUCKING... FEDERAL... OFFICER."

"If you don't keep quiet, you will be escorted out of here. Your Ahmad Jones is a wanted man." The other officers in the room felt the tension rise and were concerned for everyone's safety.

"No. No, he's not. He's not a wanted man. Please, sergeant, lower your weapon."

Dumont's heart raced and he was getting faint. If Peabody was deranged, out of his mind, then he could be shot, too. He was standing close to Jones. If Jones made a sudden move, he could get hit, perhaps in a spot unprotected by his vest in the event of a miss. Dumont imagined everything that could go wrong. But he was sure that Jones was capable of almost anything. He had shot the hired gun with a pistol that was inside a holster, upside-down, and hit the bad guy in a place that prevented him from pulling the trigger. More than just two precise shots, it was extraordinary. Jones had brought both his and Nolan's hearing back; he had unsprained his wrist. He had even won over Agent Nolan, whom *he* was going to ask out on a date when they left work. He was feeling sick of Jones, Jones, Jones! Dumont was suffering internally. Fioritto, who was the essence of cool and Wang, who wore her feelings in every facial expression, looked furtively around them while tending to the hired gun.

"BP is stabilized!" Wang said.

"Okay," Fioritto said, "let's get him on the gurney. I need two officers to help."

Fioritto and Wang each took one end of the hired gun. Daniels and Petty squatted down on one side, their hands underneath his lower back.

"One, two, and three." They lifted him a few feet and onto the mobile gurney.

"Start an infusion line," Fioritto said. He released a latch that allowed the gurney to lift. Wang took up an isotonic fluid bag while Fioritto inserted a winged needle into the hired gun's vein. Once the man was secured, Fioritto pulled the gurney away from the four officers and out the adjoining door. Wang held the bag. One officer lifted the yellow tape above their heads as they went out through Suite 316. Sylvia, the crime scene photographer, now stood at the doorway taking pictures of the empty space.

"Jones, get on your stomach. Officers." Jones flattened himself to the floor.

"For your sake, Jones, that man better not die. That'll be three," Sergeant Peabody said, as he still had his Beretta 9 mm trained on Jones, *the cop killer,* and blocked out any interference with his focus.

Peabody was a good shot. Petty and Daniels knew he was. In addition to his role as sergeant, Peabody was the chief firearms instructor and had won a first-place award at the National Police Shooting Championships in Albuquerque for hitting targets up to 50 yards—but that was five years ago, plus the targets weren't living, muscular felons.

So, Petty and Daniels, confident in their sergeant, were still being cautious, regardless of their boss' shooting record. Petty quickly went toward the window, after cuffing Jones. Nolan stood in front of Petty, and was an arm's length to Jones' right but she felt at ease near him. Jones was still centered in his heart.

With an ironic tone, Peabody said, "Well, Mr. Jones, I'm afraid you're going to miss your flight. NCIC data reports that you are a felon—wanted for killing a police officer in the performance of her duty *and* for killing a federal agent."

Nolan kept her tones respectful, "Sergeant Peabody, this has to be a mistake."

"We'll be going downtown. You can come along and see for yourself."

Dumont was shocked by what he had heard; then he was sad. *If Ahmad Jones could do this,* he thought, *then there's no hope for this world.* Peabody didn't want to believe it either. He saw in Ahmad Jones something different, but the recent news brought him down to earth.

Peabody continued, "Jones was also involved in a shooting at this hotel. That bleeding man may be the victim, for all we know. You two agents had the wool pulled over your eyes. Jones has been captured by members of the Kaskaskia PD. Let's make sure to execute this by the book. Daniels, make sure to read him his rights."

The other officers in the room had their pistols lowered near their torsos. Daniels said, "You have the right to remain silent. Anything you say can and will..."

"A felon?" Nolan knelt and whispered to Jones as Daniels was finishing his rights. "I don't understand what just happened, but if you *can* disappear, like I heard you did at Super Bowl 40, this would be as good a time as any."

Jones, self-possessed, said to her, "In the next moment, this will all be different." Officer Petty, still completing her field training under Officer Daniels' had heard Nolan's remark.

# 44

## Center of Gravity

"SPECIAL AGENT NOLAN, STEP AWAY from the suspect now!"

Nolan stood her lawful ground, "Sergeant Peabody, I could make this a federal matter and have *you* removed." Petty moved to Jones' left elbow. Dumont looked on. He thought about the first time he saw Jones at the park, the whiteout in the car, rushing with Nolan to get to his suite, the close call with the gunman, his wrist, a man wanted for murder, and Peabody's stance—now Nolan's. The crime scene photographer was still taking pictures. The hallway was still filled with two-way radio chatter and Kaskaskia's finest.

"Brenda," Dumont says. Nolan meets Dumont's eyes, and then she turns back to Jones.

Peabody says, "No, you can't make this a federal case."

"But." Nolan tries to interrupt.

"Agent Nolan, please step away from the suspect," Peabody insists.

"Agent Nolan," Petty confirms, "please step away."

Nolan turns to face Peabody, "No! This is my jurisdiction. I can obtain a warrant for your arrest for obstruction. I am within my rights."

Peabody's weapon was still drawn, "Now... step... away from... the suspect."

"*FUCK... YOU!*"

Petty and Daniels look at each other, then at Peabody, then at Nolan.

Jones turns to Nolan. "Brenda!" he says. Nolan turns. She gets on one knee to hear him.

Peabody observes the rapport between Jones and Nolan, but especially Nolan.

*"Ple pozhaluysta, osta aytes' spokoyny me."* Jones told Nolan to "Please, stay calm," in Russian.

With sarcasm in his voice, Peabody said, "What did you say, Mr. Jones? What did he say, Agent Nolan?"

Nolan, calmer than seconds ago, turns to Peabody, and stands up. "Sergeant, Ahmad Jones isn't a killer. There's got to be some mistake. Please, check your sources again."

"Officer Daniels, Officer Petty," Peabody says, and nodding to the two officers at the far wall near the adjoining door, "Reynolds, you, too. Hanson, take this scum out of my sight. LOCK HIM UP!"

Nolan steps to the side as Daniels and Petty attempt to lift Jones up off the floor, but something happens. The feeling in the room changes—tensions de-escalate, ease and dissolve. Once Jones is on his feet, Petty and Daniels attempt to move Jones out the door but they can't budge him.

"What's up, Daniels? Is this guy making you nervous?" Hanson asks.

"No," Daniels says. "You two are welcome to try. I don't know what's happening anymore."

"Let's go downtown, Jones," Hanson says as he and Reynolds, both taller and more robust than Jones, tug at his belt to move him from his core. Daniels and Petty take his arms.

Peabody removes his glasses, "What's the matter, officers? Escort, pull, or YANK Mr. Jones and get him out of here—out of my sight... WILL YA?"

All four try to move him again. Then, the other two officers near Lake Tahoe see a challenge. One of them, Officer MacDonald, is the department's Aikido instructor. He knows how to drop his center and make himself immovable, too. MacDonald theorizes that this must be what Jones is up to.

But Jones had directed his attention to his heart. His teacher in Cádiz told him. "Love is the solution to every problem, my son. When you allow the great love of The I AM of all creation to pour through you, anything less than *THAT* love is neutralized. Certain saints had this ability, germane to love. Accepting divine love as being present, where you are, opens the door to more of its flow."

The teacher was one of the few thousand Afarlanders who had sustained his attunement with the higher, ethereal world. He had shown Jones how to allow that higher love to move through the field from around his heart, through his body, and out from him. The old man had explained that unconditional love was everywhere present, like the warmth of the sun, and that through this practice, instantaneous change could come about, and nothing outside of love could ever do harm.

"We need help," Daniels said. "We can't move this guy. It's like he's nailed to the floor!"

"Let me help," Tan said as he scooted over to where they were. Now, Officers Petty, Daniels, Tan, Reynolds, Hanson, and Macdonald, six duly sworn men and woman of KPD's finest, got nowhere in their pushes and pulls. Sylvia took several pictures. Officer Parker, fresh out of the academy and still on probation, stood next to Peabody.

Nolan and Dumont were confused. "What is happening here?" Nolan asked Dumont, rhetorically.

"I don't know, but in light of what I've experienced since Ahmad got into our car, I'm baffled out of my mind."

"Do you think he is guilty?"

Dumont points to the cadre of officers, pushing, pulling, even leaning against him and using their bodies to deliver on Peabody's orders.

"Does it look like it matters what I think?"

"Sergeant, Lloyd here." Peabody's was surprised that his officers could not take command of this one man. He tilted his head left to listen.

"Go ahead."

"Sir, I've heard mention of Ahmad Jones from some buddies of mine in the Bureau and decided to look further. I contacted the New York District Office of the USMS to verify the reports. Officer Mitchell of Fugitive Operations said there was no outstanding homicide warrant issued for Ahmad Jones for the murder of a Policewoman Grace Giraud, for the date I gave him. He confirmed that no such event occurred at that time, eleven years ago. And the woman who was supposed to have been murdered, she, not a cop, has been dead since 1979. I also checked the New York State Division of Criminal Justice, to cross-reference it with the NCIC and nothing showed up. The screen was blank. Your call, sir."

Everyone in the room had heard what Peabody heard. Nolan covered her face, relieved. Dumont felt disappointed now that Jones was being exonerated. And yet, he was remembering his healed wrist, and Jones' quick, selfless responses to save him and Nolan from death by a bullet. The officers stopped trying to tackle Jones to the floor, which had been MacDonald's idea.

Lloyd continued from over the radio, "Sergeant, Mitchell also said that he met Mr. Jones and knew that there had to be a mistake. Mitchell put me on hold while he contacted the Miami District Office, and Deputy Marshall Burke said the same thing. He had only heard of Jones through his FBI buddies, who said he was *a stand-up guy*—his words. No man named Ahmad Jones has committed any capital offense—only helped to bring many capital offenders to justice. That's the record for Ahmad Jones."

"You're, you're stating for the record. None of this shit happened?"

Nolan smiled while trying to hold back a flood of emotions.

"Yes sir, and sir, Burke said that just a few hours ago, the NCIC was hacked and IT personnel have been working to fix the database. Their contact at NSA said it originated in China, but they think there may be a link to the UK, West London."

"Repeat what you just said?"

"I repeat. The NCIC was hacked. NSA traced it to China, with another connection to the UK. What's going on up there, anyway?"

"Just that you saved me a ton of paperwork. Everything is copacetic. This new information was timely. It's good. Thank you for your due diligence, Officer Lloyd." Peabody tilted his head back, swiped his right thumb downward to engage the safety and holstered his sidearm.

All within the room felt more at ease, including the cops in the hallway. The officers looked at him. He nodded. Officer Petty removed the universal handcuff key from her utility belt and unlatched Jones' restraints.

Peabody walked over to the window, to Nolan, who was looking between the curtains at the sun. He had been glued to one spot for 20 minutes. "Agent Nolan, you spoke out of line a minute ago."

"Yes, I did, Sergeant Peabody, and I am sorry for swearing at you. I was trained better. If you ever require our assistance, for anything—"

"Right, Special Agent Nolan."

As his adrenaline was winding down, Peabody was feeling conflicted. He'd been policing for 22 years. He felt like he'd won a pennant, or a gold medal, and was now ready to hang it up over the mantle in his home. He didn't care to do this work anymore. He wanted what Jones had but wasn't sure what that was.

"Officers, I've still got paperwork to do. Secure the scene. Nobody in except..." Peabody turned to Nolan. "I won't ever need Kaskaskia FBI... but give me your card and I'll pass it on to my peers, as a direct contact."

Nolan felt like Jones had just walked on water; she also experienced feelings coming from somewhere. She felt like she fell in love with Jones. It was bitter and sweet all at once. She couldn't reveal her desire for him. She was confused by the events of the last 20 minutes. Her training aided her in being able to define suspects through interrogation. She was good at figuring out what made people tick—but not him. Not Ahmad Jones. He didn't fit into any mold. She was scared and fascinated. She couldn't put him into a neat box, a slot or category. She wasn't used to anyone who couldn't be typed, figured out. Still, Nolan would keep a respectable distance. She saw Jones' wedding band. *She could almost see her, Jones' wife,* she thought, *through his eyes.*

Peabody walked away from the curtains over to the dark-walnut desk, in front of Lake Tahoe. Then he went to the center of the room to Jones and said, "Mr. Jones, I now see that the Kaskaskia Police Department, and particularly me, owes you an apology. Do you wish to file a complaint against me or any other officer?"

The sergeant stood a couple of feet in front of Jones. He looked around, stopping at each point of interest. His fellow officers were looking at him. He noticed a dent on the east wall, pieces of a broken table, and the blood-stained carpet. Then glanced at Jones and said, "Mr. Jones, you can call the Office of Professional Conduct in—."

"Sir, I don't require OPC—."

Peabody said, "If you wish to file—."

"Negative, Sergeant Peabody. You and your fine officers were doing your duty based on the information you had received."

"Mr. Jones. Go catch your plane. Officer Petty will get you to O'Hare pronto. Please leave your contact info with Petty in case we need to call on you about anything."

Peabody extended his hand and Jones his. They looked at each other, eye to eye, with respect.

Nolan put her hand on Jones' shoulder, as Peabody with a look of remorse, gently tapped Jones' left arm and walked out the door of suite 318.

"Ahmad, Dumont and I will stay here and brief Sergeant Peabody."

"Thank you, Agent Nolan, for everything." Jones took her by the arm, gently, and walked a few paces toward the adjoining door to 316. He whispered. "Trust that circumstances can shift at any time."

Nolan tried to maintain that *respectable distance* but her words were picked out very specifically. "Call me... Brenda?"

"Okay, Brenda." Jones let go and walked toward Lake Tahoe.

Jones picked up the paper with Ralph Hay's name on it, then put it in his pocket. Got one more look at the painting and was about to leave. Jones felt strange—like something had happened to him since the incident at the park, the fight in his suite, and the case of mistaken identity. The effect of whiplash isn't always felt immediately, but afterwards. Jones felt the spiritual equivalent of whiplash and his body was bending under the pressure.

He grabbed his two packed bags and walked out the door through the throng of officers from other units who had come. Petty, with pride, followed behind him. Nolan also followed Jones.

The sergeant took out a handkerchief to wipe the sweat off his brow, and then put his glasses back on.

Jones and Petty were halfway down the hall. Nolan stopped following and watched them get into the elevator. She returned to Suite 318 to have a talk with Dumont.

Jones got to the front counter and turned in his keycard. Officer Petty led the way to the squad car and opened the passenger door for him. Once inside, Jones took out his cell and called Marakie. The time was 2:34 p.m. CDT.

# 45

## Federal Etiquette

DUMONT AND NOLAN MET AT THE SOUTH END OF THE HALLWAY past the elevators. They stood near the stairwell away from earshot. Dumont asked, "What would you have done if Kaskaskia PD had taken Ahmad out of that room?"

Nolan said, "From what I saw, that couldn't have happened but if it could've, Peabody wouldn't have gotten past the doorway with him. I had two plays that I was saving in case I needed them, but as luck would have it, I didn't."

Dumont took a deep breath; his hand was on his wrist. He lifted his left hand and looked at it, front and back. "No pain, Nolan. Like that giant prick never landed on my wrist. It even feels stronger than before."

Dumont put his hands on his waist and asked her, "So, what were those plays?"

Nolan turned away from watching two men, one in a soft-gray summer suit and the other in a charcoal-black outfit. "Kaskaskia Detectives," Dumont said.

They both saw them emerge from the other end of the hallway, sign the crime scene logbook handed to them by Officer Daniels stationed at the door, and then duck underneath the yellow tape and disappear into the suite. She turned back to Dumont.

"I could have made Jones a federal witness against the shooter in the room. He had you and me, and Jones saw—preempted—the whole thing.

Peabody would've been tampering with a federal investigation."

"Pretty good. And?"

"That reminds me, we've got Sparks and McNulty working undercover on that fraud case in Skokie. This morning and after two months of video surveillance, the judge issued the search warrant. Forgot to mention it. It happened just before I received that call about Jones at Mangala. We have a short time frame to execute."

"How short?"

Nolan raised her hand with a quarter-inch between her thumb and forefinger. She said, "Let's hope that the suspect is home so we can serve him.

"We'll go in now. If he's not, maybe he'll get sloppy and go down in a traffic stop."

As if a light flashed inside Nolan's head, she said, "Dumont, we've just survived being on the business end of a pistol—mine—held by a killer. We should be out on administrative leave to process all of this, which would be my call, but I don't feel any of the effects—no trauma, nerves, nothing."

"Neither do I."

Nolan took her hair and smoothed it back from her occipital bone, then wrapped a hair tie around it. "That feels better." Then she related to Dumont the other piece to the puzzle, "Anyway, to answer the other part of your question, Jones is married to the daughter of a foreign president. That makes him a foreign diplomat through marriage."

"So, Jones has immunity? Think he is aware of that fact?"

"Of course. He didn't *make use* of it though."

Dumont looked at the cops at the end of the hall, then turned to Nolan. "You like Jones. Don't you?"

"Where'd that come from?"

Silence. Dumont spread his hands out, as if to say, *just asking.*

"What are you getting at, Agent Dumont?"

Dumont looked into her eyes, as if to say, *Come on, you and me both know that you're feeling some romance for Jones.* Nolan looked into his eyes, as if to say, *What, Jones? I'm a federal officer and I don't get romantically involved... with married men.*

She said, "Despite the no-trauma thing, I'm feeling pretty vulnerable right now, Alejandro."

Dumont looked away for a beat. For the last couple of minutes, Kaskaskia PD personnel were passing them in the hallway from both directions. Dumont still regretted that he hadn't stood up for a good guy like Jones—and that Nolan may resent him for that. He turned back to her and said, "Me, too, partner. If you're up to it, we'll check with McNulty and Sparks about that case."

"First," Nolan said, "we go back in there and talk to those detectives, then back to the car, I'm feeling hungry and still got half a turkey sandwich left."

Sunlight shone through the doors of the two crime scene suites and onto the east wall of the hallway. The two agents made their way back to the first suite, temporarily blocking out the light coming through 316. Nolan and Dumont signed the logbook that Daniel's held and ducked underneath the yellow barricade tape.

# 46

## Saving Mrs. Jones

DARLING, I AM SO HAPPY TO HEAR YOUR VOICE—not just on radio but to me, my love," Marakie said.

"Honey, the sound of your loving words just gave me what I required: the strength to press on. I have that meet-and-greet and book signing at the store as soon as I land. I'll be with you in a few hours and we'll connect at the TV station. One other thing, an FBI agent named *Jack Peterson* and his partner are going to pick you up and take you to their field office. Go with them. You know what I'm going to do. You'll be safe there. I'm certain they know where you are. Yet, as I promised you before we came to the states, no harm will come to you. So, please, be ready for those agents. A DSS detail will pick you up at FBI headquarters."

"Yes, Ahmad, my dear, I'll be ready."

Three days before Alexander Whallun, Afarland's Minister of Defense, was wounded during the murder of 14 cabinet members, he had requested that a trusted man, and ex-secret service agent, from Dewabuna's secret service detail, go to Akron, Ohio, to undertake *a mission* because he could be trusted to do the *job* perfectly. Whallun explained that this was a mission of life and death, in more ways than one, and unlike any other.

President Dewabuna's family was targeted for death. Whallun had sent *the agent* without the president's knowledge. Marakie was the president's only child and she would be the regent lineage bearer until she bore a son. So far, she and Ahmad had no children. If she died, the lineage would end.

The brand-new Mercedes with Afarland diplomatic plates was parked on the side of the back lot of Marakie's hotel. Now, standing inside a semi-dark living room, was the former secret service agent. He was the tall, muscular man with the short pants that Peterson and O'Donnell saw at the airport. He peered into the bedroom. The thin, wiry chauffeur was further behind him. The door was a few inches ajar. He saw bare feet, he heard talking from the TV, and he smelled the rich coffee. He heard a lady laughing and it wasn't from the TV.

Marakie was twirling her hair. "I'll be ready for the agents. I love you honey. Okay, bye for now."

The agent reminded himself about the reason why he was at that hotel and now in that room, and why he had to do what he was going to do. People were coming to kill his president's daughter. He had met Marakie, months before, but she wouldn't recognize him or trust him right off.

What if she didn't want to go with him and his helpers? What if she called the cops? He could have some problems. He had no real diplomatic clout because he was no longer part of President Dewabuna's entourage. He was a former agent because the president had fired him, for impropriety—so no immunity if he failed this mission. He was advised to do everything to ensure that she was *secured*, even if it meant taking her from the hotel against her will.

Kidnapping was a felony and if he was charged, he could get twenty years. The president wouldn't vouch for him. He had to use a soft approach to get her out of the hotel. Jones told Marakie that she would not be harmed, and now two strange men, not the FBI, were in her suite.

The former agent had graduated from college in London with a degree in international law. He was smart, able-bodied, and highly qualified to protect those under his charge, but here, he couldn't protect himself if his mission got away from him. The soft light emitting from the upper walls of the hallway reminded him of the luxurious hotels where he sometimes spent weekends in that far-flung country, of Afarland. And now, he could never go back there if he failed to accomplish the goal of this mission.

As lookout, the older woman dressed in colorful Afarland garb, waited in the hallway near the elevator. It was 97 feet from Suite A359. What was supposed to happen had to happen before any housekeepers, guests or hotel security saw them. There was a convention in one of the banquet halls on the ground floor and all the rooms on the third floor were sold to convention participants except for Marakie's suite. The chatty guests were eating a boxed lunch as part of their afternoon kickoff. None of the rooms was going back-on-the-market that day. It was quiet on the floor. There were no windows at either end of the hall. There was no general lighting on the ceiling, just the decorative wall sconces presenting a soft and mellow ambience. The diminutive lighting provided some cover for the operation.

The men were in the last room, which was on the odd-numbered side of the corridor in the A-section of the hotel facing Market Street, the main drag. The stayovers' rooms required 15 minutes, tops, to clean. The cleaning and staging had already been done except for the room the two men had entered—Marakie's suite. That one would take 30 minutes because it was bigger. No one from housekeeping was expected back because Marakie had asked them to return in two hours, but the housemaid got the time wrong and was, at present, on her way up. The men didn't know that but, because of the convention, they had a green light and acted with urgency.

Marakie heard movement from the living room. She thought it was housekeeping coming in to replenish the terry and change the bedding. They would be an hour earlier than she had requested. Marakie wasn't a stranger to various hotel policies. In her travels abroad with her husband, maids and even bellmen would enter their room without knocking. She hadn't remembered to engage the chain latch after her late breakfast had arrived and the room-service waiter had departed.

The ex-agent from Afarland rapped on the inside of her open bedroom door.

"Ma'am! No time to explain. You are in danger. So, please come with us."

The agent appeared out of the semi-dark living room. He was now standing about eight feet from Marakie. He spoke with authority, using short, commanding sentences. Marakie flew off the bed to the far corner of the room as if her entire body were a reflex. She held her upper arms with opposite hands as if she were cold. She was wearing only a black silk chemise. She returned to the bed and grabbed a butter knife.

"Who are you?"

The agent said, "Please, put the knife down."

Marakie didn't know right away if the men were cops or hotel personnel, or if they were part of the protection that Ahmad said was coming. Her arms were stiff as well as the rest of her body. She laid the butter knife on the windowsill and put her hands back on opposite shoulders.

Marakie responded with calm words, "Are you with the FBI?"

"No, ma'am. I am not."

Impatiently she asked, "Then say who you are, please, and spare me the need to question you. You're obviously not hotel security or the police. DSS?"

"Secret Service, ma'am."

"Now we're moving along. Secret Service, but for whom? You mean Diplomatic Security, don't you? Either way, the U.S. State Department hasn't provided security services for me. Show me your ID."

The chauffeur now piped in, "Secret Service, ma'am, sent by Alexander Whallun, Afarland's Minister of Defense, under grave circumstances. You have to trust us."

Marakie heard the other man but could only see the silhouette in the outer room. The shade was down in there. His wraith-like image startled her.

"Is my father, alive?"

"Yes, he is," the agent said.

"Thank God! Is he safe?"

"All I know is that General Garaka has him quarantined in the Presidential Palace."

"Do you know Ethel? Are she and Alex all right?" She took slow, deep breaths.

The agent explained, "Ma'am, I'm sorry to say that many members of your father's cabinet were murdered, with some of their family members, too. I cannot tell you if the Whalluns are still alive, ma'am."

"Murdered! Murdered! Oh, my God. How?"

Marakie sobbed. She remembered the time she was with Ethel, trying on beautiful garments, imported from France and South Africa. She recalled Ethel's round face and how it seemed to glow when she wore just the right earrings, and the string of pearls around her neck. The agent said that she was in danger. And to come with him. They were there to protect her; her husband said no harm would come to her. Marakie believed him, still. Now, it was time to think about her next move.

"Stop calling me ma'am! Mrs. Jones will do. What is your name?"

"My name is Rex. Ma'a... *ah...* Mrs. Jones. Please, we may be running out of time. I need you to put on street clothes and gather up your belongings— NOW! I am to take you to a safehouse until the coup in Afarland gets resolved, by order of Defense Minister Whallun."

"*The* coup? It happened?"

"Is happening."

The lookout by the elevator heard the shouting of NOW and cringed. She checked around, hoping no doors would open and no calls would be made to the front office. Marakie was quite upset by the idea that her father, Alexander Whallun, and his wife Ethel may be dead. And that the coup had gotten underway. She attempted to wrap her mind around the news. Rex looked her in the eye, pronouncing each verb with deliberation and stress.

Vexed by the delays, Rex said, "Please, *put* something on. We *must go* now."

The man in the living room said, "Yes, and gather up your belongings."

Rex turned to look at the chauffeur with a hint of intolerance. He turned back around and forced air out of his mouth.

Marakie walked over to the couch and opened her leather travel bag. She pulled out a long-sleeve, peach-colored blouse, matching pants, stockings, and other undergarments and walked into the bathroom. Two minutes later she came out and removed a pair of Merrell Verandas from the same bag and laid them side-by-side on the floor. She picked up her purse from the couch, looked at the clock's digital readout, then took out some money, counted it and put it on the table below where the flat screen was. It amounted to $3.37.

"What are you doing?"

"I'm leaving a tip."

She was leaving a real *tip*—a message that, she thought, only her husband would be able to interpret. Rex said, "Is that all you're going to take? We won't be coming back here."

"Yes, take everything," the chauffeur repeated from the other room.

Rex said, "I got this, Khaput. Okay?"

Khaput said, "Ma'am, you have ten seconds to step over the sill of that door with us, or we may all get... broken!"

"I said I have got this—Khaput. *CAPEESH?*" Rex said and then went silent but his patience with the interference of this man newly exposed to English was waning.

*"Capeesh?"*

"I'm coming!" Marakie slipped on a pair of sneakers. She stuffed all her clothing, including her Merrell Verandas, into the large suitcase. Her light jacket was in the living room. She put it on. Khaput walked in toward the bed and grabbed her laptop. Rex put on a pair of black-leather gloves and then searched her bag for the cell phone. He cracked open the back cover and removed the battery, and then put the phone back in her bag. This was going to be an operation within an operation that no one was to know about.

Rex said, "So you can't be tracked. Let's go! First, I need you out of here. Then I'll tell you what I know."

# 47

## Bad People

THE OLD WOMAN AT THE ELEVATOR WAS RELIEVED upon seeing Marakie, Rex and Khaput, the chauffeur, leave the suite. All three rushed to the stairwell. The older woman hurried to them and all four left together.

They exited the hotel through the side entrance. In the parking lot was a gray Mercedes Benz SLS AMG two-seater. It was empty and running, with locked doors. Rex pressed the wireless key fob and the gullwing doors lifted open. The trunk opened and as Marakie was placing her luggage inside, she wondered, *What if these were the people who meant to do me harm? What if these people were, themselves, the danger?* The lookout lady turned left and right and, as if she heard a sound she didn't trust, she tried to maneuver Marakie into the Mercedes but Marakie resisted.

She yanked her elbow away. "You've got crummy manners for people trying to help me!"

Rex put his hand up to the old woman and nodded his head. "Mrs. Jones, we're going now," Rex said. The older woman who spoke Zulu said, *"Hamba kahle."* (Goodbye.) Rex nodded.

Rex closed the trunk and said, "They're here, Mrs. Jones. Please get into the car. I'll explain when we're out of here!"

"Who's here?"

"The bad people, Mrs. Jones. The bad people."

Marakie climbed into the front passenger seat. Khaput and the woman got into the other Mercedes, the one with the diplomatic plates, and were the first to exit the lot. Marakie watched them leave. Rex started the car and turned to Marakie. "You cannot call your husband right now. Your phone was being monitored and I had to deactivate it. He cannot know, through that medium, that you are not where he expects you to be. I saw the message you had left, using your money to tell him the time you left. He would construct a chart of that time and attempt to find you."

Marakie said, "Very perceptive of you to notice that."

"Mrs. Jones don't worry about the message. If he shows up, he'll see it and know what to do. He has to do that TV interview and he can't be distracted from what he's about to say—more importantly, what he will show."

Rex was expecting her to say something. Marakie remained silent. Rex attempted to extract information out of her for the men listening in. Adlai Borg and his posse think they know Ahmad Jones' plan.

Rex put the car in gear and rolled out of the lot and onto Market Street. They headed due west toward I-77. The other car went east.

# 48

## The Mysterious NSA Agent

BACK AT THE AKRON-CANTON AIRPORT, it is 3:39 EDT. Peterson said. "No baggage. Our guest should be out by now."

Peterson turned just in time to see a woman strutting toward the Tahoe. She was five-ten, just an inch away from rivaling his height. Just then a strong gust of wind blew, which did not alter her swagger. Her movements were controlled and brisk, like a professional runner. Her demeanor? Intense, with a calculated focus in her eyes, which were beautifully crafted—eyes that spoke subliminally, without her having to speak. She was wearing a dark-navy skirt-suit with a crisp white shirt and was pulling a matching dark-navy roller bag. Everything about her said: organized, efficient and competent beyond the norm. If she were at an interview, her initial presentation, manner, and attire would account for 90% of the *yes*.

"Is *she* our guest?" O'Donnell asked.

"Yep, that's her." Peterson popped out of the car, swept the area, and opened the back door.

She stopped sharply, within two feet, and extended her hand, "Hello! I am Agent Ruderman."

Her long arm was suspended straight out like a wooden pole. The gesture was meant to keep Peterson at a distance, off-kilter—maybe both. Peterson clasped her hand.

"Agent Ruderman, Special Agent Peterson, nice to meet you and welcome to the Buckeye State."

"Thanks. Well, I grew up in Cleveland."

"Then, well, welcome home!" Rudderman didn't respond.

Peterson felt the tension mounting. She was going to be a handful.

Ruderman collapsed the handle until it clicked and placed her bag on the driver's side floor mat in the back. She undid two of the three buttons of her jacket and got in. Her movements were smart, deft and precise—cold, even. Peterson shut the door, stepped onto the running board and ducked in. Ruderman sat behind Peterson.

"I thought we were keeping it informal," O'Donnell said.

"Okay, O'Donnell, meet Ruderman."

He turned around and put his hand out. Ruderman squeezed and jerked his hand once.

"Gentlemen, what I'm about to tell you cannot go beyond us three. I have orders to see that Mrs. Marakie Jones is escorted from her hotel to a secure location."

"What? I don't understand. Our *Cybercrime Summit* has you as the keynote speaker. You're on at 4:30. We're here to escort you to the field office, that's all." Peterson spoke as he turned to face Ruderman.

"Our agency's priorities. I was sent new orders while in the air. I retrieved them minutes before I came out of the terminal, and confirmed them with my boss."

"Boy, you NSA people work fast. I have to clear this with *my* boss."

"Didn't I *say* that what I have to say cannot go further than us three? You will not clear anything. A new type of drone was flying over the Indian Ocean African nations—first Madagascar, Seychelles, Comoros, and, lastly, Afarland. Its infrared thermal imaging picked up a large group of heat signatures in a configuration that looked to be a military exercise. Upon further investigation, the technician, U.S. Air Force Pilot Bowman Hicks, out of Camp Lemonnier in Djibouti, saw several dead bodies inside Afarland's Presidential Palace. We concluded that a coup d'état had occurred. It is still happening. No doubt the communications networks and the airport have been commandeered—the usual coup stuff. The Internet service there has been shut down, as well as the wireless phone netw—"

"But why would the NSA send an agent to pick up Mrs. Jones to move her? That is not NSA's wheelhouse. Besides, that's what we were about to do, but we had to wait for you. You see, in a way, our orders changed, too, before we picked you up."

Silence.

"What does this have to do with Ahmad Jones?"

Silence. The Tahoe was still parked. "Okay, this all makes perfect freaking sense. The NSA wants to use her as leverage. Ahmad is my friend." Peterson turned and faced front. O'Donnell looked at him. Not a word was spoken.

"I'm calling my supervisor."

"Agent Peterson, your supervisor won't understand and we don't have time."

"Understand? What is your mandate, Ruderman?"

"We've tracked a group operating out of West London. We believe they're financing the coup. There's mounting evidence that they're running things from there. China may be involved. What's more is that Ahmad Jones predicted, some three months ago, that this coup would occur. Today. We monitored a conversation between a man named *Borg* and a woman named *Jessica*. We traced it from a call to Afarland, to a General Garaka, the man who is carrying out the coup.

"The group in London just found out a few days ago that Jones was aware of the coup, even before they had planned it.

"We listened in on their chit-chat. They were dumbfounded that an astrologer could figure out their move before they even conceived of it. That's like a chess player thinking ahead more than ten moves when just three or four is enough to have the advantage. That, gentlemen, is the reason why I've been sent to pick up Marakie Jones."

"You haven't said squat to us."

"We're—"

"No. You're being peripheral. That's not the only reason Ruderman. What's your mandate after Marakie is safe? What do you need us for? You've got access to the most advanced technology on the planet. What's an NSA agent doing in the field, in our Tahoe, anyway? Shouldn't you be monitoring phone calls?"

"We were and we're beta-testing."

"That's a catch phrase for anything and everything. You must think I'm a dick-head. Try again."

O'Donnell was tense, upon hearing the harsh exchange.

Ruderman wasn't going to get over on Peterson. "Jack—may I call you Jack?" Peterson said nothing. "I've been authorized to conduct a special field test for a new intelligence-gathering module. It is part of a new way to gain advanced warning of an imminent threat, big or small."

"Now, the plot gets thinner—by the mile. So, what does Marakie have to do with it?"

"We want you to let Jones know that you didn't get there in time. In the interim, we'll convince her to come with us by letting her in on the field test. After all, Jones called her and said that you'd come and offer her protection."

"So, you're taking advantage of the situation. I would be betraying Jones; I'd be part of your hypocrisy."

"Agent Peterson—Jack—the president has authorized this through the DoD. We have one shot at it. If it doesn't work and the president has gone out on a limb on this one, there will be no second attempt. Therefore, if both the FBI and NSA get a hit on this, it's good for both of us. Imagine the FBI and NSA collaborating and stopping terrorist attacks by having countermeasures in place before an attack would even get off the ground. This situation puts Ahmad Jones in the center because his natural response will be to locate his wife and he will probably lead us to her. If he is willing to help us, then all of his work will also be spontaneous. You see? That's why we will use this situation. Jones finds his wife and proves to certain members, in the Pentagon, that the use of astrology opens up new possibilities for counter-military action."

Ruderman's last words hit Peterson hard. He was conflicted. He was Jones' friend. He could also maintain a legacy after he leaves the Bureau. The only way he could live with himself is if Marakie went along with it, which means he would have to go along with Ruderman's plan. Peterson nodded to his partner.

O'Donnell started the Tahoe and pulled out of the airport onto Lauby Road, heading to the Interstate. He turned right, heading north. Peterson settled back in his seat.

"Don't you have better things to do than listen in on our conversations? You want to test his skill as an astrologist—by the way, that's what we call him, an astrologist—to determine if he can find his wife? Do you think he'll trust you after using Mrs. Jones as bait?"

"If he can do this, then we will approach him with an offer at a very high pay grade."

"Like what, an E-9?"

"All I can say is that the price of his technical skills will be, in our estimation, commensurate with a pay scale of what a warrant officer, at W-5 with

20 years, would get—only doubled. Jones can see what all the monitoring devises in the world can't. That especially is why his skills are useful. Street cameras can't track everything, at least not yet.

Peterson turned around. "You're kidding!"

"Do you realize what a talent like Jones could accomplish, with his skills and our military technology and intelligence? On top of our worldwide monitoring, there's no terrorist group in the world that could plan an attack without us knowing, anticipating and squelching it beforehand. As research, two of our analysts read his new book, *Football's Astrological Measurements*. They were intrigued and determined that there were concepts in the book that could be adapted—"

"Weaponized, you mean. You're looking to create a new position, a *black ops* astrologist."

"We *can't let* a talent like his disappear again—we *won't*."

"So, you're going to use Ahmad's wife as cannon fodder to make him play your war games? You don't know who you're dealing with, Agent Ruderman. I'm getting an uncomfortable feeling that you and your pals are behind this coup—more war games."

She brushed his last remark aside.

"So, do you think he'll work with us?" she asked.

Peterson was playing along as if she got to him. He was really starting to feel like a hypocrite on this one. Peterson said, "You're making him an offer that he can't refuse. He's got no choice. He's enlisted in the Wars of Cupid, just like all of us, including you, Ruderman."

She rolled her eyes, then said, "Yes, we are going to have something he wants. She looked out the window. There was silence for a moment, then she said—someone he loves. What you have to do now is show your face and Mrs. Jones will get comfortable."

"Hey! Stay left for 77," Peterson said.

Both men went silent for a beat. They passed the overhead signs and crossed the overpass. The sky was blue, and they could see for miles. There wasn't a building in sight through the rearview except for air traffic control. It looked like a small apartment with the glass-walled room atop the tower on the right side. It was off-center by design—the same as Ruderman's plan. In front, they could see a water tower several miles away as the road banked left, then straightened out and merged onto Interstate 77.

"Step on it, hard! We gotta get off at Exit 137A and we're at 113. That's about 24 miles. If we don't get what he's gonna want, then he ain't gonna want it back, and he won't attempt to recover what ain't missing," Peterson continued to play along.

"You got it." Ruderman said.

O'Donnell turned to Peterson, "If Jones is what you say he is, then he'll see right through these plans."

"I've read and heard scores of accounts. We've estimated Jones' skills on a sliding scale, with three for unassailable and one for excellent. We consulted our data of sealed intel from 17 countries and ended up with a number—two for supreme excellence. Jones isn't unassailable, and this op *is* several layers deep. As much as I would want him to succeed in seeing through it and tell us to turn her over, I'd like to see him get to the bottom of this rabbit hole and find her, but he won't. I don't believe astrology can aid him to get that far."

At the mention of the word *rabbit*, Peterson looked at O'Donnell, remembering their earlier conversation about Jones' disappearance.

"If you don't believe in him, then why are you in our vehicle and moving forward with this?"

"Because I want to be proven wrong."

"Now, you're rambling—one contradiction after another, Ruderman!"

Ruderman laughed, "Just factoring in all the angles. If Jones plays by the rules of human nature, we'll have what we want and he'll come to us. He'll have to help us by finding her. Then we'll see for ourselves if he's a three, that is, unassailable."

O'Donnell looked at Peterson, then in front.

"What if he doesn't do it?" he asked.

Peterson said, "What if he does? If he tries and fails, then case closed."

"But if he succeeds, case open."

"Then *he* makes the final decision."

"I know one thing—you boys have got to stop that Abbott and Costello back-and-forth. You're giving me a headache. No more, please! Time to put our game faces on."

Ruderman was hunched in the back seat.

"Like you, I'm looking at this from different angles," Peterson said.

"This is a very specific operation, with one goal. We don't need any more angles."

"Is this assignment *that* mission-critical?"

Ruderman leaned forward from the middle of the seat. She placed her elbows on the tops of the driver and passenger seats. She laid down an oblique stare at Peterson. Her bob-style, smooth blond hair tilted forward, her bangs inched out a little, revealing soft-angled eyebrows, a counterpoint to the determination in her blue eyes. A scent of perfume, hardly noticeable, reached Peterson's olfactory sense. He appeared to like it. He swung his head to get a look at her. Again, he was just playing along with her tricks.

"Let's get serious now, Peterson. I have a special dispensation authorized by the Secretary of Defense."

He turned his body toward her and spoke almost in a whisper. She moved closer. "Granted, I swore an oath to serve my country. So, you've got orders from my commander-in-chief." He firmly set his jaw and stared dead into her pretty eyes; her mouth was twisting out of her self-assured grimace, as the words shot out. "By the way, Jones is at least a three and at best a five." She primped her hair and sat back. He faced front and sat comfortably in his seat. He knew he had her. All was quiet for close to four minutes. Then that icy atmosphere began to thaw.

# 49

## Six-Two or Five-Nine?

"THERE IT IS, BEYOND THE OVERPASS," Ruderman said.

Peterson looked at his watch, "Nice going. We're ahead of schedule."

O'Donnell slowed, took Exit 137A, and circled rightward on the cloverleaf to merge with the traffic on Medina Road, which was also Route 18 in Akron. Medina was tree-laden and frontloaded with scores of places to shop. They passed Golf Galaxy to their right, then a BP station on Rothrock Loop. All three hadn't eaten for several hours. They drove by Chili's Grill & Bar, Applebee's, Olive Garden, and then Chipotle Mexican Grill. Everyone was hungry, but the mission was the thing. Medina Road turned into West Market. They stayed on it for several blocks.

"If we do this right, this will expand the parameters of intelligence-gathering."

"That's bullshit. My friend Ahmad Jones already expanded it. Where were you, Ruderman?" Peterson said, only partly playing at being peeved.

"Maybe so, but he did it without including us." Ruderman said. After crossing Morewood Road, they came to a slew of stores at the Summit Mall to their left, after which O'Donnell turned right on Market and crossed the apron into the hotel's parking lot.

Ruderman said, "The circulation geometry is easy to navigate. There's lots of space for this vehicle. Drive straight down the eastern flank toward the southern boundary."

There were no cars for three spaces. Mobility was the objective.

Peterson said, "You do know your way around here. Let's back into that first space. We need a clear view of our egress for a quick start if we're drawn into a chase." O'Donnell followed Peterson's orders.

Ruderman kept her cool. O'Donnell backed into the space and killed the engine, realizing that he was the foil for Ruderman's and Peterson's silent battle.

They got out, looked around first, and then strode to the side entrance. A couple with their children came out the side door. Ruderman caught the otherwise-locked door after the last person went out. She stared at the couple, the little boy and girl, and gathered that they were happy. She held the door open.

"Marakie is in Suite A359."

The third floor had sage-green walls with gold-trimmed baseboards and pale gold wall-sconce candelabras. The lighting was sparse—as it had been for Rex, less than an hour earlier. The corridor had a remote, far-flung feel— isolated compared to the busy commerce outside. Peterson, O'Donnell, and Ruderman passed through the doorway to the third-floor suite.

Peterson knocks. No answer. A second knock. No answer.

Peterson and Ruderman trade swift glances. She appears distracted. He looks around for a way in. Midway down the hall, to their right, an elevator door opens. A young woman dressed in a ruby-belted skirt-dress gets out. She's five-two with short black hair.

The young woman walks past several doors to the far end of the hall. The agents observe her. She unlocks the storage room. Goes in. After a minute, the storage door opens. The woman returns with her cart of cleaning supplies and rolls it to where the agents are.

"Good afternoon. Please excuse me, I have to clean this room."

The agents step back to give her space.

She knocks once and then turns around, glancing at the three strangers. She smiles.

Turning back around she says, "Mrs. Jones? Housekeeping," she performs the same ritual for a second and third time. No answer, then she inserts the keycard.

"Are you waiting for Mrs. Jones? She maybe, is gone out?"

The young woman enters the room and first off, turns on every light.

Peterson calls to the maid, "Yes, we're friends of hers. Can you please let us know if she's in?"

"Okay, I'll check for you."

Peterson's cell phone rings, "This is Peterson."

"Jack, this is Sanborn. What's your twenty?"

"We're on Market."

"Expecting you to bring Ruderman here on time."

"So far, so good," Peterson says, flashing a look at Ruderman, then to his partner.

"She's not here," the maid says. Peterson nods to the young woman.

Overhearing, Sanborn asks, "Who's not where? Where are you, Jack?"

"We're on our way."

Peterson recruited Jeff Sanborn, his boss, in the winter of 2011, after he graduated from St. Petersburg College of Business. Sanborn owned an insurance company that had gone south. Peterson had been a client of Sanborn and told him that if he wanted to help *ensure* Americans' and America's safety, he could find him a job with the Bureau. Sanborn called not long afterwards. Now, Peterson answers to him.

"Ruderman's tough. Isn't she? Don't compete; just keep the peace. Make the Bureau proud."

"I will."

"And, if you've got any ideas, then don't get any *more* ideas. I remember that Stacy was *a tall blonde*, too. Sorry, Peterson, I didn't mean. That remark got away from me."

Peterson flashes a different look at Ruderman now. She is panning around the room from the doorway.

"Yes, sir. Please explain."

"Explain what?"

"The last thing you said." Ruderman's blonde hair swivels and bounces when she turns to look at Peterson.

"What, about Ruderman? About getting ideas?"

"No, after that."

"The tall blond thing? She and I met in a meeting at the DoD last week. I was mesmerized by her height—six-two. Smart as a whip, also. And as I'm sure you've noticed, that beautiful long blonde hair sets her apart. Her height may be off-putting at first, so try not to feel intimidated."

Peterson smiles and nods *yes* while sizing-up Ruderman.

Peterson does the calculations: Ruderman is five-ten—Sanborn says she's six-two. That leaves four inches. Plus, her hair is blonde, but long and Ruderman's is a short bob. Maybe she cut it since last week. Peterson loosens his tie. He improvises.

"Yes, I was a little surprised. Listen, can I get back to you?"

"Get her here, fast." Sanborn says, before he ends the call.


At CAK airport, a random traveler walks into the women's bathroom. She opens one of the stalls. Screams. The traveler runs out into the concourse and hails a female TSA officer with the DHS. The officer enters the bathroom where she sees a tall woman with long blonde hair, lying on her stomach next to the toilet—barely breathing. The officer yanks the two-way radio from the pocket of her chest harness.

# 50

## What Are Friends For?

"THAT WAS A CLOSE ONE, MR. JONES," Officer Petty said as she turned into CAK's Departure section. It was 3:01 CDT.

"Indeed, Officer Petty," Jones exhaled long, letting go of the strain in his shoulders, his whole back, and, more importantly, the mental strain. "Indeed," he said again. He rolled the window down and exhaled; during which time Petty turned to see his facial expression change from one of grounded inner confidence to a scowl.

Jones' whole being absorbed an avalanche of antipathy, violence, and ill will. While on the roadside of Terminal One, he was cut-to-the quick. It was then that Jones felt a presence, the presence of something that seemed to know exactly the right time to launch an attack, an attack of evil will.

Jones had been on autopilot since the situation in the park, up 'til now. He fled for refuge into the space of his heart and felt a dynamo of fiery sparks burning away the particles of anti-love, vortices of anger and hatred, even jealousy. The space from inside the police unit began to feel lighter and more pleasant. That malefic presence receded.

Jones inhaled slowly and held the breath inside. Petty continued watching and saw, as Jones exhaled again, that the light of confidence in his face was returning. Petty had felt a tiny percentage of Jones' paradoxical dread and exhilaration.

"I can get out here, thanks." Jones opened the door and stepped out, stretched his hands upward and lifted up on his toes. People wondered at the scene: A police woman and a man, who wasn't wearing a badge, engaging in a bit of exercise, right outside the patrol unit's door.

Jones finished his stretch and walked along the side of the car to the back. The trunk opened automatically. He saw a couple of shotguns on a vehicle rack, a first aid kit and then his two pieces of luggage.

"Again, thanks for everything," Jones said, as he pulled the trunk lid down.

Petty, a middle-aged woman, divorced with two teenage boys, who'd been an officer for a year-and-a-half, said, "Mr. Jones? Just curious—I heard Agent Nolan say that this would be a good time to disappear. What did she mean, and what happened at Super Bowl 40?"

A State Trooper was coming up to and about to pass Petty's patrol vehicle. He looked at her and the man talking to her. He swerved to the right while preparing to render assistance.

Jones answered, "Super Bowl 40 is an old chestnut, Officer Petty. Well, maybe the FBI has information. After all, there's a story that's been circulating around the Bureau nowadays."

Only partially satisfied with his answer, Petty smiled a partial smile. "Well, anyway, have a safe trip. And let us know when you're in town again. I think Officer MacDonald would like to talk to you; he's our Defensive Tactics Instructor."

"I will come to your station if I'm ever in Kaskaskia again." They shook hands. Jones watched her walk around the car and get in, then he ducked his head and waved, then turned toward the terminal's sliding doors. The State Trooper drove away.

Jones went inside the terminal and pulled out his card at the kiosk. After a few questions about checked baggage and waiting for a later plane with the promise of a free ticket lasting one year, Jones got his boarding pass and proceeded to the checkpoints. He was aware that he still had lots of opposition to handle before the day was over. He recalled Agent Nolan's words when they talked in the kitchen of his suite—before he was accused of murder.

"Well, I guess the next time I see you, I'll be calling you—"

"Wait and see what unfolds. Watch *The End Zone* tonight at 6:00, Central Time."

Jones passed through the security checkpoints and got onto the concourse to his gate just in time to get in line for the boarding of First Class.

Marshall was driving the black Caprice. He had followed Petty and Jones since they left the Radisson.

"Mr. Borg, Ahmad Jones is out of our reach. A cop drove him to O'Hare and my other man was brought out on a stretcher. I don't have another play left, sir."

"Really, Mr. Marshall? You say you saw Jones in a police unit? Strange."

"How so, Mr. Borg?"

"Jones should not be walking as a free man. He was wanted for murder—we saw to that—but, somehow, he got through the system. But yes, Mr. Marshall, you do have another play. Do something. You are ex-military, for goodness sake! Surprise me or say goodbye to your money. There is no second-place prize with us. We have some experience with the notion of second place. You either do the bloody job or you do not. Now, do you not see that you have a play?"

"I don't follow, Mr. Borg."

Marshall drove into the airport lot and parked. He and Drew were the only men inside. Before they got there, Marshall dropped Hung off at Presence Resurrection Medical Center, which was on the way, just 5 miles back. He left Hung with Peter, who would see to Hung's care. The blow to Hung's eye from that football was serious. Marshall had left Drew in the car, so he could talk to Borg alone. If Borg cut him loose, he would have to compensate his men from his own stash.

Borg said, "QB and Jessica are together at a hotel. Go there and squeeze him, then take him to the building we reserved and have him contact Jones. They are best friends. If Jones hears his friend is being tortured, it will slow him down."

"I don't agree, Mr. Borg. It won't work. But I may have an asset in Pennsylvania, near the border. He'll get to Jones sooner. I'll get back to you in a few hours."

"Jessica can feed QB to you."

"Jones is about to board a plane. It's too late for that. My contact is our last play."

Borg had him on speaker. The other men nodded—all granite faces, expressionless.

"Okay, Mr. Marshall. You've got a green light. Get Jones out of the way and there will be another million for you."

Borg looked up after hearing a finger snap. His boss, Lekha Hanson, raised two fingers.

"Excuse me, Mr. Marshall. That is another two million. For your information, you have some competition regarding Jones."

"Competition?"

"We have also hired men to intercept and take out Ahmad Jones, if you fail to complete your assignment."

"Men, competition?"

"Right. A precaution. If Jones gets by you, then the pros will handle it. They're dead-set on killing him. They will be paid, but you won't. I want you to succeed, Mr. Marshall."

Marshall hung up. He resented Borg and his ability to play with his mind. Marshall kept a poker face as he returned to his car.

Marshall said, "The rest of our assignment will be conducted from here."

"What do you want me to do?" Drew asked.

"Just sit tight for now."

"Fuck, that's what you said before. We didn't catch Jones. Remember? That football fiasco was some cool thinking on your part. My shoulder's stiff and I still feel his fingers on my back, squeezing my flesh with his Kung Fu grip. Probably looks like a freakin' hickey! My old lady will think I'm stepping out on her. Shit, she doesn't know what I do when I'm away. This better be worth it."

Marshall was so psyched about getting an extra two million that Drew's harsh talk and subtle ultimatum had no impact. He looked at Jones' itinerary that Borg just sent to his smartphone. When Jones lands he'll be heading to a bookstore in Akron. That's where he'll be caught, taken to be interrogated, and then put to sleep—for good. Marshall dialed his contact in Pennsylvania. They served together in Desert Storm as part of the coalition force during the ground assault.

"Yes?"

"Hey, Sloan! It's Marshall. Long time, hey, still a sucker for old westerns?"

"You remember that, huh? I watched Shane and Silverado, back-to-back, just the other day. Man, I'm glad to know you're okay. Marshall, haven't heard nary a peep out of you since around 2013. What's that, four, five years? What's up, buddy?"

"I got a job for you."

"Job?" When Sloan heard the word *job*, he pointed to the phone, while looking at his wife and walked out the front door onto the sun-porch. Peering through the sunroof into an overcast sky, Sloan whispered, "What kind of job, Marshall?"

Marshall opened the car door and stepped out again. Drew was anxious, so he stepped out, too. Marshall walked down a line of vehicles, in the cell phone lot, to a row of bushes and stood. He watched Drew light a cigarette.

"I need you to assemble a fire team to pick up a person of interest for me. He's landing in Akron at 4:55 today. He's black, mid-forties, with a recon cut, last seen wearing red sneakers, a white shirt, and beige pants. I need to ask him some questions."

Marshall heard the laughter of children in the background. It was a bitter pill for him, then bittersweet, then not bitter at all. Sloan went back inside. He watched his daughter sitting in the dining room with her pink party hat and tutu, surrounded by her little friends. His wife, a native of Pittsburgh, stood behind their daughter. She pointed to Sloan and the daughter waved at him to hurry up. He muted the phone.

"Honey, Sophia, I'll be there in just one minute. Daddy has to take this call."

"Hey, Marshall, it's my daughter's birthday today. She's three."

"You're married, huh?"

Marshall wiped his forehead. There was an elapsed time of five or six seconds.

"Sloan, can you help me out?"

"I can't, Marshall. I have a family now, and a regular job. IT consultant. Sorry. I don't know what to tell you. We were both technical specialists in the army. If you're looking, I might be able to find someone out here."

"No, I trust only you to run point on this. It's okay, Sloan. We had some fun. Time is short, I gotta go. Take care of that family of yours."

Marshall considered his own family, which he lost—his wife, two children, and Pug, his dog. Sloan's life was a stark reminder of the pain that Marshall chose not to feel.

"Marshall, you still there?"

Sloan looked at his cell. Marshall had ended the call. Sloan felt guilty.

Now, Marshall was in trouble. He had no means to capture Jones and his men wanted their money. Soon, they were gonna demand it. His trick to catch Jones in the park had backfired. He had nothing; moreover, his reputation would precede him from now on, in the clandestine world of international mercenaries and their bosses. He would be the man who commits one blunder after another—the man who doesn't deliver. Marshall returned to the car to tell Drew the bad news. Drew was leaning on the hood. Marshall had 11,000 dollars. He would have to split it with him and Peter. Hung's cut would have to wait.

"So, what's up, Marshall?" Drew asked.

"I've got some—"

Marshall's cell went off, then the connection was severed. A few seconds later, the prefix 814 appeared. He knew it was Sloan calling back.

"Yeah?"

"What are friends for? You pushed me out of the way of that sniper in 2001. I wouldn't be here; neither would my beautiful wife and daughter. I can't forget that. Give it to me straight."

Marshall walks back to the row of bushes, remembering how he had pushed Sloan out of the line of fire in Kabul, the month before they secured it from the Taliban as part of the group that supported the Northern Alliance.

He *did* do something right, once. Now, he was going to do something wrong to his pal. Images of Scott Sloan with his family appeared at the door of Marshall's conscience—but that little voice was too weak against inflated self-interest. Marshall lived to serve himself and that was his cold truth. His ex-wife knew it and so did he. He saw no other way to live. He believed that was who he was—and so, that was *who* he had become.

But he was Sloan's friend and a friend wouldn't expose another friend with a wife and young daughter to danger or imprisonment. Marshall listened to the soliloquy in his mind: *Scott knows how to take care of himself. He's a professional. He was in Desert Storm. Compared to that, this is a walk in the park. It's just one man. Ahmad fucking Jones. Compare that to $4 million dollars and then I'm out, for good!*

Self-justification always prevailed in Marshall's world.

Marshall stared at the line of vehicles and Drew. "Okay, Scott, here it is, straight. There's a bookstore on Medina Road, and this guy..."

# 51

## QB and the Redhead

JONES' UNITED FLIGHT DEPARTED CHICAGO O'HARE for Ohio at 3:19 pm, CDT. His scheduled stopover in Akron was a bookstore on Medina Road off Route 18. The bookstore was approximately four minutes from the hotel where Marakie had recently left with Rex in the fancy Mercedes-Benz with the gullwing doors.

He remembered that his friend, Jack Peterson, would see to his wife's protection, so he wouldn't need to go to the hotel to pick her up.

He would rent a car and drive to the bookstore. Then, after the book signing, leave his rent-a-car in the lot and take a cab to Peregrine for the big TV interview on *The End Zone*. Jones had his reasons for playing it that way. Peterson would bring Marakie to the FBI field office. They should be there now, he figured. DSS would arrive there, too. Jones was not allowed to use his phone during the short-haul flight. These were restrictions that hadn't occurred when Jones conducted the interview in business class inside that jumbo jet. Jones was gradually crossing from Central to Eastern Daylight time. Still in the air, he had a couple of minutes to do some astrology work.

He opened his laptop and entered all the pertinent data for Patricia's car performance on Treefold Avenue in Kaskaskia at 12:05 pm. He clicked *OK* on the astrology program. The chart appeared after a second. It was an event chart that could explain what Jones didn't see as the wheels spun up that cloud of smoke after it left the easement and stole everyone's attention at Mangala Park.

He saw Libra, a sign indicative of relationships, in the First House, which stood for Patricia, her car, and what she did in it. The chart also suggested someone who is caught between two points of view, two choices—the Libran scales—that can lead to an important decision in order to break a stalemate. He looked for Libra's planetary ruler, Venus, Goddess of Love, among other things. Venus was in the sign of Virgo. Jones thought of QB because Venus isn't only weakened in Virgo, it's also at its *lowest* strength. Patricia, a real beauty, indicative of Venus, in Virgo, must have been in trouble at the time, weakened, but in what way? Could QB be the one to break that stalemate? Did he represent a new choice for her, a way out of her dilemma, represented by the Libran scales?

Venus was in the Eleventh House, of associations, clubs and organizations. Perhaps Patricia is part of an organization and she is unhappy about it. Jones was right about Mars and Uranus when he was at the park. They represented the violent sound and incendiary nature of Patricia's stunt. Jones thought that *if Patricia*—he pondered whether that was even her real name—*is unhappy being part of an organization, then she, no doubt, is engaged in something that makes her feel trapped.*

Also, Venus appeared to travel backwards through the sky, giving more weight to the probability that she is not who she says she is. With the Moon as her co-ruler, applying to a conjunction with Pluto, the ruler of the underworld, she was probably in a bad way—isolated and scared. But what does QB have to do with it? Uranus, the planet of sudden and bizarre happenings, is on the cusp of the Seventh House. That would stand for QB and his unusual luck of having a strange, beautiful woman coming out of nowhere, wanting to be with him for the night.

The plane nosed down a bit. The double-ding sounded, and Jones was prepared to stow his laptop. He felt the nose drop, then the announcement of the plane's imminent arrival in Ohio. He had to gather more information fast. He had noticed that Aries, the sign of athletes and collision sports, was on the Seventh-House cusp as well. That was another indicator of QB, Patricia's mark. Jones had figured out some of it in the time he had. He had a general sense of the event-chart's meaning. He put together a summary of what he observed based on the measurements in the chart: *QB was drawn away from me by a strange woman working for an organization against her will. She must've been in on the coup because those men came after me not long afterward.*

Jones had told QB that he would meet a woman, but a blonde. Could this be her? Maybe QB would become her passport out of this organization. Maybe she really liked him as much as he did her—and *needs* him, also. She might learn to trust, to even love, him. What she didn't know about QB was that he was former *Special Forces Operational Detachment-Delta*—highly trained and highly classified. Even Patricia's handlers would have a hard time finding that out. She was in good hands. Jones laughed. He closed his laptop and settled back with his eyes shut.

# 52

## Jones in the Red Zone

AT 4:39 PM, THE BOOKSTORE IN AKRON IS FULL. Inside, a couple sits along the front window. The man holds the woman's left hand as she, with a beaming smile, admires the diamond's glitter on her ring finger. Behind them, also taking advantage of the sunlight, are three eager Bryant & Stratton students preparing for the fall semester. There are Internet-thirsty laptop owners extolling the benefit of the free Wi-Fi. There are showroomers, taking photos of book covers and barcodes, intending to buy them online at a better price. In the children's section at the back of the store, elementary school kids snatch brightly colored books off the shelves under the watchful eyes of their parents. Wayfarers stumble inside heading for the store's public restroom. Several patrons dance around each other at the sports magazine newsstand, and there's a suave-looking gentleman strategically parked in the women's interests section, lying in wait for his next romantic conquest. Many shoppers fill the three sections of New Age, History, and Sports.

For the occasion, bookshelf stylists are merchandizing titles, including shelf talkers, at eye level—the store's most valuable space. Jones' book appears on every bookseller's *New Books* page. Booksellers are eating it up. Every major store in the country wants in. Only a couple of days are required to get books from the distributor to the stores.

Crystal Simmons, the store manager, was perched on the second floor near the escalator, surveying the crowd. She visually measured how the occupant load factor in the store invited safety issues. *There were logistical matters to consider*, she thought. There was one main entrance and one emergency entrance. Evacuation would be lengthy in a crisis. Simmons checked her store manager's manual for the fire department's numbers. The building code for the square footage of her store required about another 50 people for any violation of OCCUPANCY LIMITS COMPLIANCE GUIDE-LINES to occur. That number was fast approaching.

Simmons had a keen mind and observant eye. She was five-nine, sporting a black pageboy and bright blue eyes. She had vibrant energy all about her. Had an innate skill for identifying potential problems—danger, even. She was good at interpreting signs, markers. She was also a fitness buff. She had a lean, toned build. She had come in second in her first figure competition. She had been a decorated cop and a sergeant for two-and-a-half of her five years of stellar service. She had practical experience managing crowds; particularly after controversial court decisions were made public, or when celebrations got out of control, such as right after a big win at a home game. She rode the escalator to the ground floor and rallied her assistant manager and other personnel into the customer service area. She impressed upon four store associates the need for solutions to get people what they wanted, faster.

"This is a simple case of osmosis," Simmons said. "We have to balance the occupancy-load factor on the other side of those wooden doors."

"I didn't get that," a cashier said. "The occupancy-load factor?"

Simmons was very clear in what she did and said, but she could sound too precise at times, too official, like a cop who could quote an ordinance or a law verbatim.

Simmons said, "Jennie, walk with me to the front door."

The two walked out of the enclosure and down the middle of the store, pushed open the inner front doors and stood to one side in the vestibule.

"Field trip, right?" Jennie giggled.

"I need you to help as many customers as you can. Inform the others that our store is getting too full. We're reaching our limits for the number of persons who can occupy it at one time. This is generally determined by the size of our building and the number of exits."

With her finger, Simmons pointed out parts of the store to Jennie.

"In an emergency, the number of customers able to leave in a timely manner may soon be a problem."

"I understand now. I'll speak to everyone on the floor."

"Good. We have to manage this as if we've already red-lined. Okay?"

"Okay."

Jennie, a junior at Bryant & Stratton College, had every available bookseller at the checkout counter to draw customers there and to cash them out. This worked somewhat, because many were not there for the main event and were happy that all stations were manned. Simmons had her staff at the information desk working faster to answer questions and search for titles. The quicker the resolution of customer needs, the more the flow of customers improved, reducing stagnation. Crystal Simmons had a facile way of organizing people.

At the further side of the store, beyond the flurry of people hotfooting it to the escalator, and others rushing pell-mell to clearance tables—beyond the din of noise and the disorganized movement of human bodies—ex-cop Simmons had identified a suspicious man. He was tall, clean-shaven and well dressed. *He appeared to be ex-military*, she thought. *He stood ramrod straight. But he was all-wrong*, she concluded. He was nestled within the store's gift card section, wearing a Bluetooth in his left ear.

There was a good reason for the crush of people cramming into a space that was getting tighter by the second. Jones had written one book several years back, and had just published a new one. He wrote the first one about astrology's role in African history and the second one was about astrology and football. The news of the book signing had attracted football and sports enthusiasts and political-science students, as well as amateur and professional historians—and skeptics. Perhaps, the book attracted superstitious football fans, too, who just had to know the secrets about why sports teams lose games, or why they win—why the Cubs hadn't won a World Series after 108 years until finally they did. Why the Green Bay Packers won three championship games consecutively. Was it their astrology, besides their top-draw skills and coaching, in confluence with their experience, as a franchise, as a team, at a given cycle in time?

What did Vince Lombardi's astrological measurements have to do with it? Could the astrological makeup of one man, Lombardi, affect an entire team enough for it to become world champion for three consecutive years? Did his persona, expressing his planetary geometry, work so much magic on the field that the NFL dedicated their iconic trophy in his name? Who knows?

Included in this mix were dilettantes of history, intrigued by the merging of these two subjects; political students searching for the X-factor or a missing link as to why or how nations rise and fall; professional historians who came to hear what Ahmad Jones had to say so they could ask double-barreled questions, or conversely, who sought some new paradigms to incorporate into their work. The book had a niche quality about it and, yet, it had a broad appeal.

The demographics were another factor in the turnout. Quantifiable characteristics of both history and football fans are huge. Then again, some people had just happened by because they saw the large crowd and thought that someone famous was there, signing books. Maybe they could get a peek at Stephen King, Toni Morrison, Lee Child, Dan Brown, or Walter Mosley, shake hands, and take a celebrity selfie?

Both sports and history had their devotees, and there was even a third demographic—astrologers. This study also had its adherents. Astrology was the main thematic line for both books and thus, the hundreds of people flooding into the store could be from either one, two, or all three of these areas. At instant reflection, American football was probably the most popular of the trio, and, yet, there was even a fourth genre—spirituality. Jones' books had a far-off-worlds tone underlying the other three genres. This tone gave his books a wider dimension, which could be perceived by some beyond the reading. The author's style carried much heart and soul; it wasn't didactic or preachy. With all of that, there was even a fifth element—curiosity.

Mismatches are always exciting, like David facing off with Goliath, or a 300-pound defensive end squaring off with a 195-pound quick-offensive tackle. You would be interested to learn, whether you like football or not, the fate of the smaller player after several snaps. Or perhaps the larger one? Here's another mismatch: a picture of a mouse standing next to an elephant. The incongruity of these two animals side by side elicits levity. Football, side by side with astrology, and astrology standing alongside history, are both mismatches. To the untrained eye, the combination seems offbeat, unscientific, unusual, bizarre, weird and surprisingly—maybe even funny.

Yet, what person wouldn't desire to know how these incongruous pairs sync up? How many would be eager to learn how they blend together? Enough to fill up a store to dangerous proportions? A throng of people, around 240, now filled the Akron bookstore. You'd think it was Black Friday or Halloween, when books about astrology are front-and-center. But, alas, it was currently late afternoon near the final month of summer on a Wednesday.

People brushed by, bumping and knocking against each other, without afterward checking the state of their valuables. *A pickpocket's dream!*


Jones was scheduled to talk from 5:45 to 6:00 EDT, then sign books for 30 minutes, and then he'd be off to the TV studio, three miles away, to appear on *The End Zone*. The end of his striving was near.

The hinges on the outer and inner wooden doors were pressed into constant service by half-dozens of people coming in every five or six minutes. Only a few people were moving those doors in the other direction. The word had gotten out all right. Advertising had done its job—too well, too. When would the tide go out? When would the people stop coming through those wooden doors? Would the throng of people become a swarm?

The first order of business was to snap up a copy of the new book and scramble to the meet-the-author section of the store. After you secured your copy, you'd meander through the smallest gaps between other patrons, like a running back, with your book held tight. You couldn't help but be lured by the smell of rich coffee on the way, which could divert you off your route. After you took the escalator to the second floor, showed your book receipt, and hurried to the far end of the store, were you likely to find a seat?

No virtually unknown author with two seemingly off-the-beaten-path books had ever attracted such an interest before. But this occasion was different because the guest of honor took an apparently improbable theme and wrote something astonishingly new about it. It got him to a national TV spot and that show would be picked up in many foreign countries including Afarland.

This was an oblique subject, historically shunned by *practical* and *reasonable* men and women, frowned upon by some scientifically inclined professionals, and taken only with a glib pinch of salt by the rest, like the morning horoscopes. Yet, it was the *way* this piece was written that relaxed those strained frown muscles that urged the practical to *be* practical by noticing what was different and useful, and alerted those *reasonable* people to investigate first before passing judgment. The author's years of search and research to get it right had convinced some that there might be something *to them stars!*

It was the data, along with the recorded, recurring patterns, that one could not fail to give credence to. In these things, the book and its author were like the bride at a wedding—the center of attention.

Jones was still in the air.

Among these restless fans of this new tome uniting football and astrology, and the previous one uniting astrology and history, Scott Sloan was standing by the gift cards section, away from that crush of people. He was compelled to be there because of his army buddy. Compelled by a sense of guilt and obligation but not because he wanted to be there, in that store, of his own will. He would rather have been home with his wife and daughter, celebrating. But Scott Sloan was Marshall's friend to the end. Marshall shoved Sloan away from the cross-hairs of a sniper, only to shove him back into a new set of cross-hairs.

Sloan had put together a simple plan. He was an improvised *fourth* team hired by Marshall to keep Ahmad Jones from reaching *The End Zone*. Sloan was another hired gun, a freelance assassin, the free-safety—the husband and dad out on a limb—on a blind date with fate.

# 53

**Will the Real Monica Ruderman...**

PETERSON HAD TO BE CERTAIN before he acted. Now, where was the real Agent Ruderman? If she wasn't in the room with him, then where was she?

"Marakie Jones' room is cleaned out; she's gone." Peterson said. He was looking around the place for clues. He looked out the window, and then he turned around to see Ruderman standing by the door, bewildered. She had a knockout body. But he flashed a stern look at her. He walked to the writing desk before him and considered the way the tip was arranged.

Ruderman was worried but she didn't show it. Her eyes darted from the flat screen above the tip, to the bed with the tray of uneaten food, and the headboard, and then panned right and straight up to the window. Her tidy plan was now out of her control. She wasn't her feisty, sardonic self anymore.

"Best laid plans, eh, Ruderman?"

"Excuse me please?" Ruderman said.

She stepped out of the doorway, and walked past O'Donnell, and through the exit door to the stairwell. Peterson watched her leave and heard the door to the stairwell slam shut. He went out of the room to where his partner was, along the opposite wall of the corridor. He had to be as far as he could from the stairwell so as not to raise suspicion from Ruderman—or whoever she was—but close enough. The housekeeper was collecting the trash in a circular fashion around the suite.

Peterson whispered, "Something's not right about our friend here. It just hit me like a turd in a punchbowl."

"Shit?"

"Exactly."

"No, your choice of metaphors. So?"

"The woman out there isn't who she says she is. I spoke to Sanborn and he said he met Ruderman at a meeting at the DoD." Peterson looked around. The housekeeper walked out of the room with the trash can and emptied the contents into a large bag hanging on the side of the cart.

"Sanborn said that Ruderman was six-two."

"He could have been wrong."

"No, he said that she was six-two in flat shoes. Ruderman is wearing high heels and—"

"I can see that, Jack. Listen." O'Donnell took a moment to look toward the exit. "Sanborn may have her mixed up with someone else he saw at that meeting. I mean, he *could have* met Ruderman. Ask her, I'll back you."

"I have to make some calls, starting with Sanborn. If she's an imposter, we've... we've got to keep our heads on a swivel. Understand?"

O'Donnell nodded.

"Follow my lead."

Peterson started coughing—loud and fast, long strings of coughs—and loosening his tie and rubbing his forehead. Ruderman heard the commotion, put her phone away, and stepped back into the hallway.

"What's going on? Are you okay, Peterson?"

"No, *aaaasthma*, attack... *Cough, wheeze, cough!*"

"Where's your inhaler?"

"He left it home, forgot to bring it," O'Donnell said. Peterson's face turned red. "Bathroom!" He took a winding, stumbling course into the bathroom inside Marakie's suite. The housekeeper began to pull off the bed linens. She looked at Peterson, then turned to O'Donnell outside the hall, asking, "He will be all right?"

"I'll go see. Excuse me, Ruderman."

"Okay."

O'Donnell closed the bathroom door and turned on the water. Peterson coughed and dialed Sanborn's number.

The housekeeper called downstairs, "There's a sick man in the bathroom in Suite A359."

"Sanborn speaking."

"This is Jack, sir. Are you sure about Ruderman's height?"

"What? Where are you? The noise is making it difficult to hear you."

Peterson turned the water down and lowered his voice.

"Ruderman's height. Are you sure? Is she... what's her height again, sir?"

"Six-foot-two inches. Why?"

"This woman who says she's Ruderman is an inch shorter than me and I'm five-eleven."

Sanborn was at his desk when an agent walked in and waited with his palm covering the back of his other hand. He stood at attention. Sanborn got up and walked out the door and the agent walked out behind him into the hallway.

"Where are you now?"

"At the Akron Fairlawn on Market."

"You're supposed to be coming here. The meeting's about to begin, I'm a few seconds from the conference room." Sanborn looked through the window into the conference room. "Why are you at the Fairlawn Hilton?"

"I spoke to Ahmad Jones today. He was in Chicago and is probably in the air on his way here, maybe already arrived.

"He said his wife, Marakie, was in danger and asked if we could see about her. Ruderman told us to go to the same hotel to pick up Jones' wife. Do you have any intel on that scheme?"

"No. Where is Ruderman now?"

"Outside the door. O'Donnell and I are in the bathroom inside Marakie's suite. Don't ask; I made it up. Marakie is gone and we don't know where to or with whom."

Sanborn noticed the conference attendees looking at him. He said, "Did you notice something near Ruderman's left cheek?"

Peterson turns to his partner, "O'Donnell, did you see anything on Ruderman's left—"

Ruderman knocks and asks, "Are you guys all right in there?"

"... Cheek. Look for anything on her left cheek. Better leave, buddy. I'll take it from here."

O'Donnell stepped out of the bathroom and shut the door.

"Is your friend okay?" the housekeeper asked.

"Yes, everything is okay."

"How is he?" Ruderman asked.

"He's doing a lot better. He's taking it slow and should be coming out any time now. Any leads on Marakie?"

"Nothing."

Peterson feigned a cough and said, "Sanborn, I don't recall seeing anything on her left cheek."

"She has a mole on it. Can't miss it—if it's her. Listen, I'm sending Travis and Dmitri, to the site." Sanborn looked up at Travis and nodded.

"Get your partner," Sanborn said.

"Peterson, I'm back in my office. Pulling up a picture of Ruderman and sending it to your phone now. There, sent it."

"Thanks, checking my cell," Peterson clicks *View*. The photo is of a blonde woman with high cheekbones and a mole along the crease near her upper lip.

Peterman whispers, "*This* Ruderman has hazel eyes and an oval face. *My* Ruderman has blue eyes, a wide forehead and no mole. Sir, the two don't match. Are you sure this photo and the woman you met at that meeting are the same?"

"Absolutely; no mistake."

"Thanks, sir."

"What are you going to do?"

"Sir, this woman may have gotten to the real Agent Ruderman in order to get to Marakie Jones. This is probably related to the coup in Afarland but, sir, Marakie Jones wasn't here when we arrived. I gave Ahmad my word that we would protect her."

"Arrest her, then, and bring her here. If she's guilty, we have grounds to convict her for felonious assault on NSA personnel. Hold on. I'm just seeing an incident report on the tracker here. It says that a TSA VIPR officer found someone fitting Ruderman's description in the women's bathroom at CAK. She's alive but critical."

Peterson heard muffled voices in the room. He wet his face with cold water and looked at the mirror. He grabbed a hand towel. He checked his pistol and came out. He noticed the housekeeper turning the seams of the lampshades toward the walls as he passed through the doorway and walked a few feet toward his right. *Ruderman* stood near a wall sconce between him and the stairway. She looked at the exit door and then at him.

"Are you all right, Agent Peterson?" Ruderman asked.

"Are you armed, Ruderman?"

"What?"

O'Donnell took a few steps near her. He made himself bigger by placing both hands against his hips, exposing his pistol and badge.

"Okay, lady. What did you do to Agent Ruderman?"

"What are you talking about? What's gotten into you?"

Peterson moved closer. O'Donnell walked behind Peterson and planted himself near the exit door. She had no place to go. The hallway on the other side was too long—no escape.

"Attempting to convince us that Ahmad Jones was the sole purpose of your visit and that you were going to lure his wife to test his ability. It was a compelling performance. I agreed with you that my friend has a rare talent and I still believe that. You're not Agent Ruderman. She was found at the airport in critical condition. Are you ARMED?"

"And your coughing scene, that *was* a performance. You may have missed your true mission in life. My answer is *no*."

Peterson said, "You are under arrest for assaulting a federal agent and for impersonating one in the presence of two federal agents—O'Donnell and myself. That's all I can think of now. If you're guilty of any other crimes, we'll insert them into the list. Whatever your name is, place your hands behind your back."

Silence.

"Well, you *do* have the right to remain silent. Anything..." Peterson finished reading her rights.

He nodded to O'Donnell who cuffed her wrists. Peterson thought about the arrangement of money on the dresser. Perhaps Marakie Jones was pulled off the bed by force, spilling the coffee she was drinking. He remembered the haphazard look of the room when he first arrived. He was minded to tell the housemaid to stop cleaning.

"Don't take your eyes off her."

Peterson walked back into the room while O'Donnell stayed with the prisoner by the wall sconce. He added up the money on the dresser. He looked at his watch. It was 40 minutes after four. The tip was $3.37.

Peterson walked out of the suite and stood less than a foot from Ruderman. "What do you know about the people who sent you? What are their plans?"

She stared into his eyes. "My job was to see that Marakie came to no harm."

"Bullshit!"

Peterson snapped forward and grabbed her chin. She kept her eyes on him, as she jerked it away.

"Who are you working for?"

She put her right foot out and dropped it on the rug. "Listen and listen carefully, Agent Peterson. If you were an enemy combatant—if you and I were enemies—you'd be dead this instant."

She turned to O'Donnell, "And you, too."

"So, now you're threatening federal officers? I'll add that to the list."

"We both work for Uncle. What I'm about to tell you is on a need-to-know basis."

Peterson stepped back and took a deep breath. He went for a cigarette but changed his mind.

"O'Donnell, give us a minute." He stepped out of hearing distance.

"Go on."

"The real Monica Ruderman was going to kill Mrs. Marakie Jones. Yes, she was an employee at NSA, but she had been approached and compromised by the elite group in West London. We were led to her by covert intelligence on a certain Alexander Whallun, the Minister of Defense of Afarland. He is the one pulling the strings behind the coup. General Garaka, who's taking over, is just a Bot. I took Ruderman out of the equation."

# 54

**Navy Intelligence**

"SO, *RUDERMAN*—OR WHOEVER YOU ARE—you came here to *protect* Ahmad's wife?" Peterson asked, with definite tones.

"It's complicated, but... *yes.*"

"How?"

"I'll attempt to explain."

"Don't attempt, just explain. O'Donnell, you need to hear this." O'Donnell took his place on the other side of the suspect.

"I was informed while in flight that one of our teams in Fort Meade intercepted a hacking operation on the NCIC a few hours ago. We've been aware of Monica Ruderman's clandestine activities for several weeks now. So, we let her alone, not divulging what we knew, and proceeded to shadow her. Then, I—"

The three had heard cups and silverware being handled behind the door of the suite next to Marakie's. A blonde-haired woman who had just woken up came part-way out of the door in a red cashmere robe. She held the tray at a tilt but managed to lower it to the carpet outside the door to her left without knocking anything off. Her robe was not well fastened and it started to open. She wasn't aware of the three people standing in her blind spot, behind her and to her right. She turned around and almost jumped out of her robe but caught each side in time. She turned and stared at the tray while running her hand through her hair, exposing her pretty nails. The snoring inside the room got louder and more unpleasant.

Without looking at them she said, "Good morning."

"Good afternoon," O'Donnell said.

"It's afternoon already?" she asked and stumbled back inside. The snoring sound got quieter as the heavy door slammed.

Peterson and O'Donnell put their attention back on the suspect. She rubbed her left cheek with her left hand. Her right hand, still cuffed, was close by. "That woman had a nice French manicure," she said.

The agents were not in a laughing mood.

She continued, "So, Ruderman was supposed to speak at your cyber-crime huddle, which was just a reason to come to Ohio. She was the one who suggested the thing in the first place under the guise of new information that must be shared ASAP with the FBI. She spoke to your boss only a week ago, after they had met at the DoD, right after the Joneses arrived in the states. She booked a room at the Fairlawn, where Marakie was staying. So, when we discovered that Ruderman was in bed with the group in West London, we tracked her itinerary and I took the assignment."

"What assignment?"

"To present at your huddle."

"You're right, this is complicated!"

"You heard me say that I'd 'attempt to explain.'

Right. Well, your boss Sanborn acted quickly and gave her the green light to come and give your agency the benefit of her so-called new information. I saw an opportunity because I know quite a lot about cybercrime. I figured I could help both Marakie and your field office since Ruderman and the people she's aligned with had an illegal right-of-entry into U.S. criminal-justice databases. Not good. And I had proof just a few hours old to share with your field office. I was freaking mad that Ruderman was compromised and had let these London assholes dictate her behavior and actions."

"She's a traitor," Peterson said.

"Yes, she is."

"But first, I had to eliminate the threat at the airport—Ruderman—then come here to get Marakie out of harm's way, too."

"I've never heard of an NSA agent out in the field doing—"

The suspect kept talking, "I then planned to take Ruderman's place and show up at your huddle, to tell the attendees what happened and how the

NSA could benefit the FBI in a closer context. We had discovered the NCIC hack before any other agency did and we took out the accomplice to a potential kidnapping and murder."

"Grandstanding a little here. Wouldn't you say?"

"I suppose I'm overzealous but what better way to present at your field office than by revealing our successes over the last few hours? You understand."

"Do I?" Peterson asked, with the same degree of definiteness.

The suspect, seeming a little nervous, said, "Listen, Jack, in my work, flexibility is everything and my role had changed—while I was in flight and you were on the ground. I came here to protect Marakie but found out about the hack on my way here. A lot can happen when you're in the air. Listen, I grew up watching the Cleveland Browns. Do you remember the playoffs in '88 with Oakland, when that pass-play *Red Slot Right* was called by Coach Rutigliano, and how Sipe's pass was snatched out of the air by Davis?"

"Yeah, I do. What's your point?"

"That moment has become a metaphor for me. It's now a way for me to meet every challenge. I play both passer and interceptor. Just like now—I'm supposed to be a presenter and instructor, a conductor of breakout sessions, and an interceptor of a plan to kidnap and murder a foreign diplomat. My role requires me to adapt quickly to changing conditions."

"Well, I heard about your recent interception. Sanborn is pissed, by the way. He didn't say so, but he is. You're supposed to be the primary speaker now and it's 40 minutes after, so you'll have to morph back into your 'passer' role. You can still get there. So, what's with all that stuff you were spouting about testing Ahmad? Was that just something you cooked up while in flight, too?"

"Yes. I suggested that we use this circumstance to gain useful information. I meant everything I said on the way over here."

"You're an opportunist."

"I'm expected to be exactly that—which is why my pay grade and status is higher than you can imagine."

"I gather that you're not with the NSA?" O'Donnell asked.

The suspect smiled, "Correct."

"An opportunist. Well, someone got to Marakie. Ahmad is my friend and his wife is my responsibility. He was attacked. TWICE, and she is missing—all of this in less than two hours. How can you be so CALLOUS?"

When Peterson raised his voice, the maid's shoulders lifted like a startled kitten. Just then, the manager stepped out of the elevator and saw a woman in handcuffs with a man on each side of her. Then he noticed the distressed housekeeper and the tray on the floor with half-eaten food. He swallowed and walked up to Peterson, on his right. His name badge read: Harrison.

"I'm the manager of this hotel. Reception just received a call that someone was sick up here."

Harrison's radio hissed. He was a few inches shorter than Peterson, late 30s, with a likeable expression. He was well groomed and attired in a light-burgundy jacket with gold buttons.

"Thank you for coming up, Mr., *uh*, Harrison, but it was a false alarm. It was discombobulated but now everything is okay."

Peterson presented his credentials and O'Donnell did the same. Peterson looked him over.

"I'm Special Agent Peterson and this is Special Agent O'Donnell." Peterson didn't introduce the woman that was Ruderman's imposter because she hadn't told him her real name. He continued, "Would you please escort the housekeeper away from here while we conclude our work?"

"No problem, Agent Peterson. I am here to help in any way."

Harrison went to the doorway of Marakie's suite and called to the housekeeper, who was anxiously removing the bed linens. She straightened her body, "Sí, Señor Harrison?"

*"Maria, por favor, ven conmigo mientras que la policía termine su trabajo."*

"FBI. This is an FBI matter," Peterson corrected, revealing his knowledge of Spanish.

"I apologize for my blunder, sir," Harrison said, apparently distracted by *Ruderman*'s appearance.

Maria went to the dresser and took the money, *"Si, señor."* She left the room and they both walked to the elevator.

Peterson watched them leave and then turned to O'Donnell. "I think Marakie left here around 3:37 pm."

"How do you know that?"

"A hunch."

The elevator doors opened. O'Donnell caught up with the manager. "Mr. Harrison," O'Donnell said, "we require access to your hotel-security surveillance for outside the right-side entrance. Your feed from this afternoon at 3:37 on will be of help to the FBI."

"Yes, sir! When you're ready, come down to the front desk and ask for me. I'll take you to the control room where you can review the feed on the consoles."

"Thanks."

"You're welcome."

Peterson watched another set of elevator doors open. Special Agents Travis and Dmitri exited.

The two were in street-agent attire, jeans and polo shirts. Travis, with boyish looks, was a broad-shouldered health fanatic. Dmitri, almost his partner's twin, had a tattoo on his right forearm. Both were about six-two.

They walked over to Peterson and O'Donnell, and scrutinized the handcuffed suspect. Dmitri said, "Jack, Mason, I guess you heard that Sanborn asked Travis and me to take your suspect with us." The suspect noticed Dmitri's tattoo as he shook hands with his colleagues.

"She is—*this is*—on a need-to-know basis for now," Peterson pointed to the elevator and motioned the two agents to follow him. Travis whispered, "She's the one with the missing mole. I get it." Peterson returned, "No, you don't, Travis. This shit is beyond our agency." He nodded to O'Donnell. "You can take off her restraints."

Peterson watched his partner approach the suspect with the key. She turned around and he unlocked them.

She rubbed her wrists.

Peterson motioned her toward the exit door and faced her, asking, "What do I call you?"

She looked away, then at him.

"Make it a good one," Peterson said.

"Call me Darlene."

"That's a sweet name," Peterson was reading her body language, "Is that your real one?"

Silence.

Peterson's phone rang, "This is Peterson."

"Peterson, Sanborn here. I want you and O'Donnell back on the Dayton case. We've got a lead on another shipment, through Eddie. If it's credible, you'll run the operation. I need you back here pronto. Also, the huddle has started and we're getting screwed."

"No, Ruderman—I mean NSA Agent Darlene—took out Ruderman, who was sent to kill Marakie Jones. She's clean. She knows cybercrime and is prepared to come there to be the replacement."

"Update Dmitri and Travis about her, then get her on over here."

"What about Ahmad's wife? I said I would look out for her."

"I gave you a direct order, Peterson. Jones' wife is not part of your caseload—that shipment is. The Bureau has been after this evidence for over six months. You know more about it than anyone. This is your baby, Peterson, and it's our priority."

Peterson rubbed his forehead, saying, "Yes, sir. We're on our way."

"Of course, you are! My office—as soon as you arrive... *Ugh!* Brief me on Jones' wife later. For now, I'll see who I can put on it."

"Yes, sir," Peterson was deep in thought as he put the cell into his pocket.

"You two can head back to the field office. O'Donnell and I will arrive shortly."

"What about her?" Dimitri asked.

"She's one of the good guys." Peterson motioned for her to follow him into the stairwell.

The three agents watched the exit door close behind them. "Who do you work for?" Peterson asked.

"Jack, first you grab my chin and Mirandize me, then you have your partner move out of distance from us, so you can talk to me in private. You ask me my name, then you have your partner remove the cuffs, and now you've lured me out here... into the stairwell—all-alone with you. I'm not certain what you've got in mind."

"Well, then," Peterson said. "If you don't know what *I've* got in mind, then you're not much of an agent."

Darlene brought her body closer. Peterson noticed her perfume again. She whispered some numbers into his right ear: "3, 23, 1882." Peterson knew their meaning. She took her lips away from his ear, until their noses were a few inches apart. Peterson looked through the window at the men, who were observing. She turned and looked, too. Took a deep breath and said, "See you around, Jack."

She swaggered into the hallway. Peterson thought about her numbers, 36—24—36, smiled, then shook his head, out of his reverie.

"That's the flux capacitor, right?" Darlene asked, as she walked toward Agent Travis and his tattoo.

"Right," Travis said, "We were sent here to take you for a ride in our De-Lorean."

Peterson noticed her perfect stride, this time from the rear. *She looked real cute in her navy-blue skirt and short blonde bob*, he thought. He was intrigued by the mystery of who she worked for, what her capabilities were, and how deadly she could be. He had noticed that she wasn't at all bothered by her restraints. After a few seconds, he went into the hallway and said, "We've got this under control—just a misunderstanding. Darlene's clear. Take her to the huddle. Sanborn is expecting her."

Peterson and O'Donnell walked out the exit door and down the stairwell. The other agents and Darlene followed. Once they left the side entrance, the winds stirred and the sun brightened. Peterson remembered about checking the feed inside the hotel.

Peterson watched Darlene get into the agents' SUV. Then she got back out after taking something from her carry-on. She hurried over to Peterson. He noticed her. His senses replayed the smell of her perfume when she had leaned over inside the SUV. Peterson reminded himself how lucky he was to have a career where he could meet beautiful women like Darlene and just be content to maintain a professional distance, but still acknowledge their beauty and be enriched by the experience. Darlene handed him a thin folder. Inside was a photograph attached with a paperclip.

"Peterson, this is Marakie Jones."

"Who's the old man with her?"

"That's her father, the President of Afarland."

"She's beautiful. Can I hold on to this?"

"You'll need it. Goodbye, Jack. And O'Donnell, you ought to be more assertive, you know. Find her; I ran interference for you!" Darlene got back into the car. Dmitri closed her door.

Peterson said, "O'Donnell, don't get any ideas; you're still on probation. Ahmad should be at CAK by now. This is cutting things too close. All right, let's check the feed."

Dmitri, Travis, and Darlene rolled out onto Market Street. Peterson and O'Donnell walked around to the front and caught up with Harrison in the lobby.

"Can you take us to the surveillance room now?" O'Donnell asked.

"Yes, come with me." The three men walked across the marble floor to the carpeted hallway after they passed the side of the long, front counter. They reached a side door with a red circle and slash in the middle of it. Harrison typed in the passcode and entered the video-surveillance control room situated behind the wall of the front counter. It had a clean, cherry wood floor. The temperature was exactly 65 degrees. Three yards from the entrance and to the left lay a medium-brown walnut table with no legs. The table was made of solid wood and attached to the brick wall with large metal brackets. Two hotel-security officers manned the electronic equipment—one of them had just bitten into a club sandwich.

He was an older man, mid-60s, and retired military. He didn't need this job because he was well pensioned but liked the action anyway. He wore a white button-down shirt with a blue tie and gray pants. A cup of black coffee and an old-fashioned plain donut was spread out on the table, away from the equipment. The man's partner, who was out of the room, was three minutes into his ten-minute break. Three feet in front of the hungry technician was a yellow brick wall. There were six wall-mounted monitors extending from the wall. Each displayed three camera angles.

"Meeks, these men are with the FBI. They'd like to see tape for today between the hours of 3:37 pm and now." Meeks was still chewing when he lifted his hand, palm out and pointed his right thumb to his mouth. Peterson and O'Donnell looked at Harrison.

Meeks said, with a mouth full of food, "Sure. You're with—"

"You can finish chewing, Meeks," Peterson said.

Meeks was anxious, "The FBI. Must be serious." Meeks slid back on the wheels, got up, and shook Peterson's hand.

"Is Meeks your first or last name?"

"Last, first name's Delton."

"Okay then, Meeks, we'd like a playback for the right-side entrance to this hotel."

Meeks sat down again and slid forward to the table.

"What are you looking for?"

The two agents looked at each other.

"We're not certain," Peterson said, "but it involves this woman." Peterson showed the picture Darlene had given him to O'Donnell, who placed it on the table.

Meeks looked at the picture. "Is she the one you're after? I did see her, but not the older guy. Who are they?"

Peterson thought of an answer that would drive home a sense of urgency and still keep him in the dark.

"A possible kidnapping victim."

"Both?"

"No, just her."

"Well, she left here a short while ago—I mean about an hour ago—with other people."

"It's 4:57 now. Go back to 3:37, no 3:30 and start there and speed up the time so we can get through this."

Harrison looked happy. He left the room to make the rounds and see to his staff.

"Here goes. So, I'll maximize the image for the southeast sector of the hotel, go to house local, then play back. Sorry, I work faster when I say what I'm doing, out loud."

"Not a problem if it helps you to access the feed faster," O'Donnell said. He stood to Meeks' right and Peterson to his left.

"We'll go to camera, *uh, damn!* Sorry, let's see... Camera 15. You want it for today, right?"

"Yes, today." Both agents uttered those words at the same time.

"Yesterday?"

"Not yesterday," Peterson said.

"Then when, today?"

Peterson figured that when he said the words *yes* and *today*, they were spoken too close together. "Correct—today," Peterson said.

"Okay then. I'll put in the start and end times. That's 15:30 to 16:57. Okay now. So, I'll click on 20 vids at a time for Camera 15. That means we'll view 20 three-minute segments at a time and they'll run in turn. Ready?"

"Proceed, Meeks!"

# 55

## The Traffic Cop

AT AN APARTMENT IN LONG ISLAND CITY, the three knocks were definite, yet, not boisterous. The voice was in the lower register, tough, yet, friendly, "Ms. Cheyanne Pradesh, FBI Special Agents Herbert and Johnson, from the Brooklyn-Queens Resident Agency. May my partner and I come in?"

"Two questions: why you are here and who sent you."

"Ma'am, Special Agent Jack Peterson from the Cleveland Field Office called our boss to ask us to check up on you. Our supervisor gave us the go-ahead."

Cheyanne picked up a cell phone off her desk and moved nearer to the door. She peered through the spyhole at the two men. They wore black badge ID holders on a neck chain. They noticed the spyhole darken. Herbert looked at his partner. They both brought their IDs to the level of the spyhole. Cheyanne called her husband, Rakesh.

*This is Lieutenant Rakesh Pradesh of the 41st Precinct. Please leave a message.*

"Honey, call me ASAP. Two men are here. They say they're FBI and that Agent Peterson, who called earlier today about my brother, sent them over to check on me. For what? I'm missing something. I'm going to call the Bureau to check their story. Call me." *Click.*

Cheyanne went to the door.

"Who's your boss?"

"Special Agent in Charge Saunders. That's S-a-u-n-d-e-r-s—Saunders, ma'am. We'll wait 'til you confirm our identities with him."

Cheyanne called the Resident Office and got the switchboard.

"Special Agent in Charge Saunders, please."

"This is Saunders. Ms. Pradesh?"

"Well, yeah. How did—?"

"Caller ID. I presume you're calling to confirm the two agents I sent to you. Yes, I gave them the assignment based on Agent Peterson's recommendation. You're in safe hands. Got to go, Mrs. Pradesh."

Agents Herbert and Johnson saw the spyhole darken again. Then the door opened.

"Come in. What's all this about?"

Agent Herbert took deliberate steps; his arms didn't swing freely. "Special Agent Peterson said you might be in some trouble, that your brother is Ahmad Jones, and that he needed a favor from us. He asked us to keep watch until he can acquire more information. So, Johnson and myself are your guests, at least for a couple of hours."

Johnson was more like a kid at heart, more playful. "Do you have any coffee?"

"Of course! Make yourself at home. You can park there in the living room. I'll put the coffee on."

Cheyanne went into the kitchen, which was the first right-hand door from the entrance, and started the coffee maker.

"How do you like your coffee?"

"Milk and three sugars for both of us," Herbert said.

"Coming up."

"Nice rug," Johnson said, "Persian. Can we sit on the couch?"

"Of course. Make yourselves comfortable."


Jones' plane was about to land in northwest Canton. It was 5:05. He had not checked any baggage. He would get out in a jiffy, secure his rent-a-car, and drive to the bookstore on Medina Road. Jones had been breaking tackles over the last four hours. He had good blockers, like Peterson and Nolan, Dumont and Reese, and others of which he was outwardly unaware. He had lots of help from people who respected him, as well as from some whom he'd just met, and some who knew him only by reputation.

Why was his book so important? Why did he write it? And, why would the public care about a book with such an incongruous mix of topics? Jones had only one motive for writing it and now, he's going to appear on national TV to present something on a sport that he respects, in order to present higher, more subjective realities, of which the outer game is but the outer symbol. And, per his teacher's suggestion, at the park, in March, he would use the book's popularity to give important information that would alter the trajectory of a country and its people. After that, his life would revolve around a wider center of responsibility.

Less than 500 feet from the ground and heading south toward runway one-niner, Jones looked out the left-side window at the iconic air traffic control tower. The landing was barely noticeable.

"— *Airlines would like to welcome you to Canton, Ohio where the local time is 5:06 pm.*

Jones took his cell off airplane mode and called Marakie. The call went straight to voice mail. He left a message: "I've just landed, sweetheart. I'll meet you at the TV station. I'm picking up a car to go to the bookstore. I love you."

Back at the Fairlawn, Peterson asked, "Still nothing, Meeks?"

"Listen, I'll keep... Oh, wait. There, that's her. Right? Lovely eyes, and very beautiful?"

"Yes, that's her."

"Jack, that's the trio we saw at CAK."

"What are they doing? She doesn't look like she's being kidnapped. Does she?"

"Hard to tell," O'Donnell said.

"Want to listen in?"

"Yep."

"I'll also send this to your office. Just give me an email address. This system is set up with an IP. Just give me the credit for helping the FBI. Anyway, when I noticed them earlier, I was suspicious, so I changed the camera's viewpoint and switched on the audio. Just listen." Meeks turned up the audio:

*"You've got crummy manners for people trying to help me."*

*"Mrs. Jones, we're going now."*

*"Hamba kahle."*

*"They're here, Mrs. Jones. Please get into the car. I'll explain when we're out of here!"*

*"Who's here?"*

*"The bad people, Ms. Jones, the bad people." Click! Click!*

Back in Afarland, General Garaka had stopped by several diplomatic missions, and embassies, including the British, Chinese, and the U.S. embassies. He was allowed quick access to all of them and addressed each embassy's Deputy Chief of Mission, to relay news of the coming shift-in-power about to occur. Garaka assured the Foreign Service Officers, Specialists, and other staff members that no harm would come to any foreign nationals during the change of leadership. That, if there was any misconduct by locals, it would be met with severe penalties.

This is what he shared with each embassy's Deputy Chief, with minor additions and omissions:

*"President Za Dewabuna has stepped down. Lieutenant General LaBrahm has confessed to the murder of the cabinet members. In four hours, Dewabuna will make an official statement denouncing LaBrahm's actions on Afarland television and handing the reins over to me."*

After making his rounds, General Garaka climbed into his chauffeur-driven jeep and headed back to the Presidential Palace. His cell phone rang, "This is The General." He was feeling powerful.

"General, this is Borg. We may have a problem. At present the Joneses are still a double threat. We know that Mr. Jones is in Ohio and on his way to a TV studio. He is to appear on a nationally syndicated sports program."

The General sucked at his teeth. "What? Do I need to worry about Ahmad Jones, Mr. Borg?"

"*Ah...* We do not believe so, General. But we learned that the cabinet had voted unanimously to elect Ahmad Jones as the interim president; you made sure that the mandate and ring were in the safe. So, let's say that if Mr. Jones has plans to announce a *de facto* presidency over the air, he must have the implements to show it. He doesn't. You can accuse him of being the master-mind behind the whole thing."

General Garaka visualized the ring and the mandate. He was sure they were in the safe.

"Jones doesn't have them, you do. The rest is academic."

"Right," General Garaka said.

"If he tries to leverage any authority, it won't matter. We have someone here who will go live and denounce Jones' claims to leadership as fraudulent. He is not part of the line of succession and, even if he was, he does not have the mandate or the ring to govern."

"So... I won't have any opposition from Jones."

"Our men in the states have tracked Jones to a bookstore in Akron, Ohio. They are attempting to procure him now."

"LOOK, dammit! Don't... *procure* him—get rid of that cockroach! And his cockroach wife, too! If she's breathing, my authority will be questioned."

"Well, General, the moment the deed is done, I will call and we can talk about sending our gold extraction teams over there. Your country will be the richest African country; richer in natural resources than Libya's and Nigeria's oil, and Botswana's diamonds, combined. All Afarlanders will benefit. There will be no more poverty. You will be worshiped in Afarland and the envy of all Africa."

"Even more than Nelson Mandela was?"

"Was his country free of poverty?"

"I will be expecting to hear from you soon, Mr. Borg. Cheers."

"Cheers... *Mr. President.*"


Peterson and O'Donnell are en route to the airport, expecting to meet Jones. Peterson's cell is on speaker. The time is 5:21.

"Agent Nolan, I need Ahmad's number."

"Hold on, Peterson." Nolan called Jones. No answer.

"What's wrong, Jack?"

"Well, Ahmad's wife is gone. I need to talk to him."

"Okay! Jack, I'll see if I can reach him. Stay on the line."

"Jack?"

"Speaking."

"It's me. Agent Nolan is also on the call."

"Ahmad, she was gone before we got to her. I'm sorry, but at exactly 3:37 pm, a tall black man in a dark suit took her in a gray Mercedes-Benz SLS; I saw it on CCTV. "

Jones checked the time. "Did you plate the vehicle for APD?"

"Yes, there's an APB in progress?"

"What about its tracking device?"

"It's being handled as we speak."

"Thanks, Jack, I'm assuming it's been dismantled. If they've gone to so much trouble, they're not going to get clumsy now.

Stay on while I call my sister, Cheyanne, for a four-way conversation."

The agents had just reached the airport. They were headed to the Arrivals section.

"We're here at CAK, Jones. Where are you?"

"I'm en route to the Fairlawn Hotel for now."

"What? We've just arrived at the airport."

"My plane touched down ten minutes early, I was in First Class and the first to walk through the jetway. I had a carry-on and a personal item, and no baggage to claim and my rental, a red Ford Focus was brought to me."

"Wow, that's efficient," Peterson said.

Cheyanne left the kitchen when she heard the first few bars of the *Star Trek* theme. She picked up the cell, with the iconic music, from the top of her workstation. Herbert was seated, while Johnson was at the window checking out the street, and the Empire State Building across the East River.

"Hello?"

"Cheyanne, it's me. Marakie's been taken. Local cops and the FBI are on it, and I need you to construct an event chart for 5:25 pm today for Akron, Ohio."

"But she was taken at 3:37."

"I know, Jack, but the time you brought this to my attention was 5:25. Cheyanne will render a chart as if she's in Akron, using its coordinates."

"Okay, give me a sec... Agents Herbert and Johnson, the coffee's ready. You'll have to pour it yourselves."

"No trouble, Ms... Cheyanne." Herbert and Johnson walked past her workstation and into the kitchen.

"Great, they're there," Peterson said, after pulling out another Chesterfield while O'Donnell put the Tahoe in park in front of the Arrivals section.

"Yes, they came to my door about ten minutes ago."

Jones was a couple of miles from an exit. He was driving a red Ford Focus.

Cheyanne said, "Scorpio Ascendant... 28 degrees, 21 minutes."

"Okay, Mars is in Cancer right now. That should put her in the Eighth House."

"Right, and Mars is intercepted."

No response.

"Ahmad," Cheyanne said. He stopped at a red light. He thought about the intercepted planet, which is a planet wedged between two signs, within a small Sector. Any planet so designated, represents something that is constricted, restricted, stuck, hampered.

"You say Scorpio is rising, huh? And Mars is intercepted, wedged between two signs, in the Eighth. That could mean that Marakie, the car, and whomever she's with are confined in some way."

"Couldn't there be more than one kidnapper?"

"Yes, if there are other planets in the First House, or if the ruling planet is not alone in the Eighth, or is in a double-bodied sign, like Gemini, Pisces, or Sagittarius. Does anything meet that criteria, Cheyanne?"

"No."

"One person, besides Marakie. Jack, you said there's an APB on the car and it is also being searched for, by tracking?"

"Yes, Ahmad, I notified the tracking response center that the car is classified as stolen, to move things along."

"How far along is it?"

"Was slow going, Ahmad. A police report had to be filed first."

"Was it?"

"Yes, then the response center has to verify the report's case number, then location information is gathered, which is where we should be right now, if it all worked smoothly."

"So, the response center could track it any minute now. That's helpful information, Jack. Chey, where's Saturn in the First?"

"Sitting on its cusp."

"That makes two indicators that they were not in-motion for a short time, at least driving; they may be near water. All right. Chey. What type of water does Scorpio govern?"

Cheyanne thought for a moment as Agents Herbert and Johnson walked in with their coffees and sat down. Peterson, Nolan, and O'Donnell were silent.

"Lakes, ponds, swamps—water that doesn't move... stagnant."

"Right, and the Eighth House runs west by southwest. What type of water does Cancer rule?"

"Rivers, lakes, ponds... reservoirs."

"Okay, a Scorpio ascendant with its ruler, Mars, in its Natural Eighth House in Cancer, the sign of its fall, is the third indicator that points to the same thing. Mars rules engines and Mars is weak and intercepted; yet, in its own natural house. They are parked, either forced to, or by design, near water. What decan is Mars in?"

"With the Ascendant at 28 degrees, it's in Cancer decanate. And oh, Ahmad, the end-of-the-matter, at the Fourth House cusp, has Pisces, another water sign."

"Good, Chey, we have four supporting measurements, all pointing to similar conditions. Cancer's direction is north, so, once we calculate the distance between the Seventh House ruler, which represents me, and Mars, we will have our initial conditions that we can build upon. I'm going to park, one moment."

"Okay, I'll find the celestial distance between Venus and Mars."

"There's one other detail that turns this apparent abduction inside out."

"Ahmad, the distance is 7 degrees, 1 minute. Where are you?"

Peterson was surprised that Jones called it an *apparent abduction*. It confirmed his perception that Marakie didn't look as if she were being taken against her will.

"With Pisces on the cusp of the Fourth House, the end-result house, I can say that the whole thing was staged, as both Scorpio and Pisces relate to high drama. Something is out of joint. Pisces says to look behind the appearance. And because of the late degree, it is too late to do anything because an action is already under way. The event is already in-progress."

"So, let me get this correct, Ahmad," Peterson said, "You're saying that Marakie is in no danger?"

"Yes, Jack. Chey, I'm turning into a parking lot off South Main Street, onto Firestone Boulevard."

"Ahmad, I'm confused."

Jones pulls into the lot. He's tired and spent. He keeps the engine running."

"Jack. Marakie may be surrounded by danger but..."

"But what?" Peterson asked.

"Chey, something about the Mars interception is becoming clearer."

Cheyanne asked, "What do you mean?"

"Mars rules incendiary substances, besides engines that run on fuel. Now, Uranus is in a square with Mars, and Uranus is associated with sophisticated technology."

"That would apply to the high-tech tracking device, right?"

"I don't know."

"You don't know?"

"Right, and it's bugging me."

Jones leaned back and shut his eyes.

In his mind he saw his wife when they met on the beach, when they made love for the first time, and on the day she introduced him to her father. Jones remembered the poignancy of his declaration to her, *Marakie, my love, you will be safe at every point of the circle, from the time we depart Afarland, until your return.* He showed how her horoscope and Ohio's and, more importantly, the City of Akron were congruent and played well together. Her updated chart was also clear of any danger to her person, but he didn't tell her that his own chart was highly stressed with multiple challenges.

Among all these things, Jones considered how the true astrologers of old were highly practical men who belonged to scientific circles—like Johann Kepler, for example. Jones mused on Kepler's remarks in 1601 that *the belief in the effects of the constellations derives in the first place from experience, which is so convincing that only those who have not examined it can deny it.*

Under the extreme pressure of his wife's abduction and reaching an impasse in his interpretation of the chart, Jones' years of experience reveal a different angle.

"Chey, the Moon's last conjunction was with Pluto and, like Mars, it tends to show up as destructive and rules explosives. Pluto is in a hard-geometric angle with Mercury, which has rulership over small vehicles."

"Ahmad, Mercury is also Combust the Sun."

"How many degrees of separation?"

"One degree and 12 minutes of arc."

"So, being so close to the Sun, Mercury's force, symbolically, is burnt up. Mercury rules automobiles, Chey."

"And Jupiter ruling the end-of-the-matter Fourth House in square to Saturn is the sign of major shit. Ahmad, this is very serious."

Jones must talk things out.

"Okay, add to this the square of Uranus, which has rulership over high-tech devices, to Mars, which rules internal combustion engines."

Cheyanne considered Jones' last words about engines, "No."

"Yes."

"Explosives? You think the car is loaded with explosives?"

"A high-tech explosive, Jack. This is based on the indicators in this chart."

"I'll notify Akron's bomb unit," said Peterson.

"Jack, as I stated, we're too late to do anything about this, because the situation has already been or is about to be concluded."

Jones said, "Chey, what's the basic distance?"

"The ephemeris says the latitude of Mars is north of the ecliptic."

"North?"

"Yes."

"So, we have a basic distance of two miles. How many degrees of arc is the Moon and Mars, regardless of distance by sign?"

"One, two, three... 8 degrees and 12 minutes."

"If we multiply that by the basic distance, we get 16 1/2 miles."

"That's right."

"Send the chart to my phone. Brenda, Jack, look at a map of Akron for any lakes or ponds that are 16 1/2 miles due west by southwest of the Fairlawn. As soon as you find something, I'm taking off."

"Hold on," Peterson said. He and O'Donnell were still parked in front of the airport's Arrivals section, in the same place they picked up Darlene. O'Donnell pulled up a map on the mobile console.

Peterson said, "There's Crystal Lakes, off... no that's east. Wait, there's a body of water near South Cleveland..."

"Yes," Nolan said, who was looking at her monitor from her office, in the Kaskaskia RA. "It's boxed inside Bay Hill, Torre Pines and August Drives."

"Sending chart now," Cheyanne said.

"Figuring out the distance from your location on Firestone Boulevard and South Main to Bay Hill," Nolan said.

"I'll notify APD to get over there," Peterson said.

Three minutes later, three Ohio State Highway Patrol vehicles were speeding west on Route 135, Vietnam Veterans Memorial Highway. They took the exit to South Cleveland-Massillon Road, heading north. They were driving parallel with Bay Hill to their left.

Meanwhile, the Akron Police, with sirens blaring and distractors distracting, came down from the north heading south down the same road. They turned right onto Rosemont and the three state patrol vehicles turned left onto the same road less than a minute after. Now, both sets of police were traveling west-southwest, skidding left into August Drive, then accelerating south to Bay Hill and Torre Pines, which encircles the lake. Meeks from the Fairlawn's surveillance team had sent both departments the picture of the gray Mercedes. Law enforcement had the coordinates that Peterson provided.

Sergeant Shulman of the Akron Police said, "Unit 436 on August Drive, over."

Dispatcher said, "Unit 436, what's your thirteen?"

No Mercedes, yet. Traveling east, about to turn north on Bay Hill."

"Copy that, 436."

Peterson listened. He was connected to Dispatch. Pulled out another Chesterfield. O'Donnell wasn't thinking about his job. Now, he was concerned for Marakie and Ahmad, whom he had never met.

As if coming back from a kind of limbo, Jones sat up in his car. He said, "All right, everyone. She's not there. She's further south. Instead of west-southwest, it's now east-northeast. Find a body of water 16 ½ miles from my location, and those compass directions.

"Jack, could the response center have employed a kill switch? Because the chart indicates the car is or will be unable to move."

"Possibly, Ahmad, I haven't heard from them yet. They have me and APD Dispatch on hold."

"All right, Jack. Do any rivers or reservoirs, anything like that, show up 16 ½ miles from me. COME ON!"

Peterson blurts out: "Barberton Reservoir."

"Agent Jack Peterson, this is the response center. We regret to inform you that the Telematics Control Unit on the Mercedes had been disconnected. We cannot locate the car."

"Ahmad, did you hear that?"

"Yes."

"You were right."

"I ask again: Any reservoirs within a circle of 16 ½ miles?"

"Barberton Reservoir, Ahmad. Check Barberton," Peterson said, "it's 17 miles from you and it's east-northeast."

A half-minute later, the dispatcher said, "Unit 436, Dispatch with updated information. The gray Mercedes is near Barberton Reservoir, possibly stranded, and may be wired to explode. Bomb unit en route. Take 21 to Minor Road."

"Copy. Where's this information coming from? Over."

"FBI."

"Copy that. Do we know what kind of explosive?"

"FBI says, it's enough to blow up a small vehicle."

"Leaving August Drive and taking Rosemont to South Cleveland-Massillon Road. Over."

"Unit 427, behind you, copy that."

"Copy that, this is 538. We could use aerial support."

"Captain Bridgewater has been notified."

"Copy that."

All three units made a counterclockwise circle. "We're taking a shortcut to Barberton Reservoir."


The three squad cars headed north, up August Drive, east on Rosemont, and then south down South Cleveland-Massillon Road to Minor Road and Summit Road.

"It will save us five minutes," Shulman, in the lead car, said, "Let's give God's Army the best we've got."


"My navigation isn't working. What's the quickest way to get to the reservoir from Firestone?" Ahmad asked.

Nolan said, "Take West Wilbeth Road to 17. That's ten minutes from you. Then get to 76, stay on 76 until you see a Budget Car Mart on your right. Then get off on that cloverleaf and head north on Barber Road. Turn left on Summit Road and on up to the reservoir."

"Copy that," Jones sped out of the parking lot and onto South Main, leaving a trail of smoke. In less than five minutes Jones had already turned onto West Wilbeth Road and was about to merge onto 17. An officer in a patrol vehicle saw Jones pass, doing 90 mph.

This is Unit 15 with a 10-38. Ford Focus, red, possibly a rental, heading east on 17. Suspect clocking 90 mph, 45 past the limit. In pursuit."

"Copy that, 15."

# 56

## The Safehouse

"I'VE DISMANTLED THE TRACKING DEVICE. There's no chance of anyone homing in on the car," Rex said.

"I have to call my husband," Marakie insisted.

"Good. He'll know you're safe and sound. Here," Rex handed her a special phone.

"Thank you," Marakie dialed but the call didn't get through.

"I cannot reach him. The reception is not good here."

"There is the safehouse, across the street. Come, let us get inside." Rex crossed the median and turned into the lot. They stepped out of the car and walked a couple of yards along an unpaved driveway. They stepped over puddles and walked between long patches of mud. The safehouse was a large, stone structure. It wasn't someone's home but appeared to house something important inside. It was more of an enclosure. There were no cars on the premises.

"What is this place?"

"The safehouse."

"No, I mean *what* is this place *used for*?"

"An old water-treatment facility. Abandoned. Whallun said to make sure you got here and to inform Ahmad of your location. We must step inside and wait for more orders."

"How can we do that if the phone's not working?"

"Maybe there is a phone inside, or better reception. Come, let us go in."

Marakie thought Rex's answer defied logic but went along with his theory. She was certain that she was in no danger because her husband had said so. Rex took out a key and unlocked the metal door to the safehouse. Rex entered first, then Marakie.

Inside was a long and wide single room. Its dimensions were framed by a wall-to-wall concrete floor, 30 feet long and 20 feet wide. Directly in front of them was a pool, 20 feet by 10 feet, filled with water that was 10 feet deep, pumped in from the reservoir for periodic checks. The water glistened in the semi-darkness. Residual water pressed through filtration pipes and infrequently dripped into the pool. The water droplets lent an eerie noise to the layout. The only light source was a 60-watt overhead bulb and the ambient light from the open door. The structure had no windows.

Marakie wondered how deep the water was. Rex switched on another light near the door to his left. The flickers lasted for a couple of seconds, then the fluorescent lights came on, but there were still dark corners. The whole place was about 60% illumined. Rex walked near the short concrete wall along the length of one side of the pool and then stepped to a small metal bridge that overlooked the pool and the filtration area of the treatment plant. A network of pipes ran along the length and width of the water. He was standing four feet above the middle of the pool. He placed both hands on the metal railing while looking at silent ripples made by bubbles coming from below. Rex looked as if he were at a podium about to give a speech. He looked conflicted. There were pipes that stretched across the pool and pipes that were nearer the water, lengthwise and crosswise from the inner side of the concrete wall that surrounded it.

"It smells nasty in here. How long before we can go?"

Rex checked something in his inner jacket pocket and then said, "As soon as we are in the clear." Rex took a deep breath, then stepped off the metal bridge and walked over to Marakie.

The police cruiser pulls in behind the Ford Focus, his front wheels facing left. There are 24 feet of highway between both vehicles—an all-too-common scene. The way the scenario should play out, if the actors execute their roles flawlessly, is that the officer calls the commands and the driver obeys all commands, while staying put in the vehicle, hands always visible, and the engine silent. For all to indeed go smoothly, that's how the scene must progress.

"Unit 15, stopped on Route 17 near mile-marker 10. The vehicle is a rental, engine turned off. What's the status on our database? Is it back online?"

"Negative, 15. IT is still troubleshooting the problem."

"Is ODOT affected?"

"Negative. You can run the license through ODOT."

"Copy that."

"Units 578 and 536, en route. Over."

"Copy that. Driver is still in the car, his interior light is on, and I can see his hands on the dashboard."

"Unit 578, Copy that. Watch your back."

"Copy that, 536. Just got on 17."

The officer steps out of his cruiser. He checks his body camera and dash-cam. The officer passes his patrol vehicle's front-left headlight. He crosses to the passenger side of the red car. He considers the meaning of the passenger side window, already down. Maybe the driver is used to being stopped, or maybe there's a weapon, or maybe the driver is attempting to make this traffic stop run smoothly, without a hitch. His final take on the man inside feels right to him. The officer angles his body behind the doorframe.

"Sir, do you know why I stopped you?"

"Yes, officer."

"Are there any other occupants in the car?"

"No, officer."

"Are there any weapons in this car, or on your person, sir?"

"No, officer."

"I clocked you doing 91—the speed limit is 45. Pass me your license, registration, and insurance, please. Slowly."

"Officer, here they are." Jones slowly lifts his hand horizontally, while keeping his left hand on the dashboard in full view. The officer takes the car-rental agreement and the license. He checks them and notices Jones' Department of State temporary driver's license.


"Okay, Mr. Jones. Just remain there while I check your ID and this car's rental package."

"Yes, officer."

He returns to his vehicle and runs Jones' license. Being a State Department issued license, the officer believes that Jones is accorded special permissions by the U.S. Government—one of which is a certain immunity, even from traffic infractions. Because the NCIC, the National Criminal Information Center database, is still down, the officer cannot see the citations for Jones' work with various law enforcement bodies around the country. After having no hits from the Ohio Department of Transportation database, the officer exits his vehicle and returns to Jones' vehicle, this time walking to the driver's side.

"Mr. Jones, why were you speeding?"

"I was on my way to Barberton Reservoir."

"What's there?"

"My wife."

"Is there an emergency?"

"Yes, she was taken from her hotel at 3:37 pm."

"Taken by whom?"

"We believe she was taken as a safety precaution."

"We? Who is we?"

"My contacts at the Bureau, officer."

"Mr. Jones, have you served?"

"Yes. But I am using my know-how as a former cop in connection with the feds to locate her." Jones reads the officer's name on his badge. We don't have time on our side, Officer Tate. I'd appreciate your help to find her before…" Jones got quiet. He considered the information the chart relayed.

"Sir, how do I know that you were a former cop and that you have contacts with the Bureau?"

"Officer Tate, please call Special Agent Jack Peterson, Cleveland Field Office. Here's his number."

Jones had already written the number down when he turned his car off.

"All right, just wait here."

Officer Tate returns to his unit and dials the number.

"Cleveland Field Office, front desk."

"Officer Tate, Akron PD. Would you put me in touch with a Special Agent Jack Peterson?"

"Certainly. Agent Peterson is out in the field. I will call him on his cell and bridge you in."

"Thank you."

Peterson takes the cigarette out of his mouth. "This is Peterson."

"Officer Tate, Akron PD. I have an Ahmad Jones here. Says he's working with you."

"Yes, that's correct," Peterson said. "Also on the line is Special Agent in Charge, Brenda Nolan, of Kaskaskia FBI. Mr. Jones' wife has been kidnapped, we believe. And he was on his way to the scene. The Bureau would be grateful if you could escort him to Barberton Reservoir, which is where we believe his wife and her kidnapper are. Ahmad is working with us."

"Is he paying some sort of ransom?"

"No, it's complicated. He's providing information to the Bureau that can be helpful. Is he all right? We lost contact a few minutes ago."

"Is he a suspect?"

"You've got to be kidding."

"Well, I pulled him over for speeding. He says he was a cop."

"Yes, a Second Lieutenant in New York City."

"Is that right?"

"Officer Tate, can you clear the way for him?"

"Certainly."

"Thank you, Officer Tate. Ahmad Jones is working with the FBI, and with state and local law enforcement."

Car 578 pulls up behind Jones' car. Its distractors are on. The cop gets out and notices Officer Tate walking to Jones' car toward the driver's side. The second officer walks up to the passenger-side window. Two sets of flashing red-and-blue lights are followed by another police cruiser's lights. There are two officers inside. They both stepped out of the police vehicle.

"Officers on the scene, this is Dispatch. The man in the car is Ahmad Jones; FBI vouches for him. Sergeant Shulman from State and two units are en route to Barberton Reservoir. NCIC is still down. ODOT is running fine."

After Officer Tate speaks to the second officer on the scene, "So, Mr. Jones here was doing 91 mph in a 45-mph zone to get to the reservoir to help find his wife?" the second officer asks.

He sees Jones through the passenger window. The second officer says to Jones, "You're part of that commotion." The second officer looks over the hood at Tate, "I heard Shulman, Harris and Gilroy on the radio." Again, the second officer peeks into the window at Jones. He looks at Tate. Officer Tate says, "Take these." Jones takes his IDs and rental package.

"Mr. Jones, follow me," Tate says. The other officers get into their cruisers and switch the sirens on, while Tate heads out in front of Jones.

The officers who got out of their unit notice the other officers getting into theirs. "This is Unit 536, what's your status?"

"We're escorting the man in the red Focus to Barberton, Dispatch. Units 15, 578 and 536 are en route to the reservoir."

"Copy that, units 15, 578 and 536 en route to Barberton Reservoir."

They pull out with sirens, lights, and speeds reaching 60, 65, 75 mph, along the shoulder of Highway 17. The red Ford Focus is sandwiched between 15 and 578.

The State units are two miles from Minor Road, which will take them to Summit, near the safehouse.


Rex looks at Marakie with cold eyes.

Marakie noticed something familiar about Rex. She remembered the time she and her husband were driven to Alexander Whallun's house on Ruby Avenue. She recalled that it was he who was the chosen driver, he who stood guard at the front door, and he who brought them back to the Presidential Palace. Then, she recalled, a week later he was permanently dismissed from secret service detail after news about him having an affair with a member of her father's cabinet was made known. Rex wore a beard at the time, which is why she didn't recognize him sooner, and during the trip to and from the Whallun's house, he hardly spoke. But she knew him by another name.

Marakie sensed something strange about Rex and wanted to clear the air, to bring whatever was going on out into the open. She asked, "Hasta, will the bad guys find us here?"

Standing a foot away from Marakie, Rex said, "You know me. I am sorry, Mrs. Jones, but I have been sent to kill you."

# 57

## Too Late to Alter Course

HASTA GRABS THE PISTOL FROM BEHIND HIS BACK and lifts a suppressor from his outer jacket pocket.

"Oh, my God!" Marakie steps backwards toward the doorway; she turns and is about to run out. Hasta catches her pants at the waist and pulls her back past the threshold. Marakie screams, as she pivots her body rightward. Hasta sees a flash as his knees buckle, after the bottom of Marakie's fist banged against his temple. She keeps on attacking.

Her scream, the sound of a *kiai*, precedes a solid kick to Hasta's testicles. He hunches forward, clutching.

*"Kiai!"*

Hasta, knowing that her battle sounds are followed by fierce attacks, grabs her other foot before it pounds the other side of his head. He pulls her leg, to upset her balance. Still dazed by the blow to the temple and reeling from the second strike, Hasta hobbles to his feet, with Marakie's left foot in his hand. She leaps and smashes his head with her other foot.

Hasta staggers. Marakie's is back on her feet. He grabs her shoulders.

*"Kiai."*

Her palm crashes into his nose. Hasta lets go. He brings his hands over his nose and holds it with one hand, squeezing it. He watches Marakie, while feeling behind him for his pistol, which is a yard behind him near the pool.

He feels for his weapon, grabs it, as another *Kiai* fills the room. She quickly closes the distance. He takes his other hand away from his nose. He steadies the pistol with both hands. He considers his attacker's eyes and concludes that she is mad enough to kill him. He points.

"Stop... now!"

Hasta limps over to her and covers her mouth with his right hand and shoves the pistol to her chest with the other. Marakie's breathing is deep against the muzzle. She knows that there is some mistake. She knows she is dreaming. Her faith in her husband's words keeps her calm. *Impossible,* she concludes. *My husband couldn't have been wrong about my safety.* As that thought passes through her mind, Marakie gets still and quiet. Hasta removes his hand and steps back a few paces.

With the gun on her, he tightens the suppressor as he looks into her eyes. He displays no emotion.

To her right, through the open doorway there is a wide expanse featuring acres of wet dirt, wild grasses, bushes with fresh raspberries, behind which is Barberton Reservoir. Hasta puts the tip of the suppressor against his upper lip. She looks at him as if asking, *What?*

Three hundred feet away a couple of young herring gulls circle the water. Hasta has one chance, two bullets to do the job, which is what Borg and his team of suits are expecting of him.

The young gulls with their brown bodies are easy to track. He pulls the slide, points the pistol between Marakie's eyes. "No!" she yells. He steps back next to the concrete border of the pool and takes careful aim with a tight, two-handed grip, then pulls twice. The two pieces of hot ejected brass casings cycle over his head and sizzle briefly as they hit the surface of the pool.

"Goodbye, Mrs. Jones."

# 58

## A Final Good Deed

HASTA TAKES OUT ANOTHER CELL PHONE, "It is done, Mr. Borg." He puts his forefinger to his lips, instructing Marakie to remain silent. She takes her hands away from her ears. The bullets had passed through the doorway. The two young gulls splashed the surface of the water.

"Well done, Hasta. Get back into your car and return to the meeting place."

He checked out the bag of chloride dioxide, used in some instances to disinfect pipes. With his groin still recovering from the impact of a well-placed kick, his nose busted and his head throbbing, he limped over to the doorway and dragged the 25-pound bag over to the pool, where he hoisted it over the side. It made a tiny splash.

"She's underwater. Won't be found here anytime soon. I'm going now."

"Good work, Hasta. She sounded like a wild animal."

Marakie was silent, a little in shock. He switched off his cell.

In a whisper, Hasta said, "I was sent by Alexander Whallun to make sure you were dead. I wouldn't do it. I used his trust to protect you."

"Alex... Wh...?" Marakie cried as she hugged him.

"Thank you. Thank you!"

"I have to leave you here. Ahmad will find you. I'm sure of that, but you must tell him to keep your status as dead. Please don't call out to me. My car is bugged."

"Where will you go?"

"Mrs. Jones, I have to get lost for a while, leave the country. I have friends in London. I can't go back to Afarland. Not yet. If I do, I hope I can be in the good graces of you, your father, and your husband."

Hasta goes silent and places his forefingers against the sides of his nose. He scrunches the bones in place. "Where did you learn to fight?"

"My husband."

"You were about to kill me."

Still breathing quickly. "I didn't know what your plan was. I am sorry."

"Please relax, Mrs. Jones. You are out of danger. Well, tell your husband he'll make a good president and that Alexander Whallun is a traitor. His wife, Ethel, doesn't know what he has done and has been doing."

"And what about my father? Do you know if he is alive?" Marakie asked.

"Like I said before, I just don't know. I haven't heard that he wasn't alive. Chances are he is alive. Goodbye for now." Hasta limps out of the treatment plant, through the muddy, unpaved driveway and slips into his car.

Back in West London, Borg said, "Gentlemen, Marakie Jones will not be around to continue to cause us problems just by being alive. We can move forward in earnest. I am expecting to hear from Marshall. It is almost three in the morning in Afarland. In one more hour, The General will make his announcement, and by then, we can begin to send in our excavating equipment." The men inside the racquetball-court-size room were pleased.

Borg said, "Gentlemen, do we have further need of Hasta, alias Rex?"

All in the room nod.

"Right!"

Hasta heard sirens in the distance. At least a couple of miles to the south. He turned the ignition, put the car in gear and drove out of the muddy driveway to the main road. He headed north on Summit.

A half-minute later, the right gullwing slams into a tree off the road. The air howls as the fire takes in more and more air. The blaze is instant. Smoke rises and can be seen by anyone within four square miles.

Marakie heard the explosion. She knows that it is Hasta's car. She could have died in that car with him. *Why didn't they do it then, after they left the hotel?* she thought. *Maybe an oversight; maybe they wanted her to share private information with him that they could use later.* She wept for Hasta.

Then her weeping turns into a good cry, in gratitude to Life, to God, and to her husband's understanding that led to his accurate assessment of her safety.

She cries, "Thank you... God, for the wisdom you have gifted to my husband."

# 59

## Running Point

THE POLICE INSIDE ALL NINE CRUISERS and Jones heard the explosion.

The sirens roared louder. Marakie got up and ran out the door to Summit Road. She waved her arms. Three State Patrol vehicles arrived first. One of them set a perimeter, a quarter-mile further down, to block traffic coming out of a side street. Once there, the officer angled his car with the passenger-side toward the wreckage. Shulman stopped ten feet in front of Marakie. He took out his sidearm.

"Ma'am, please stay where you are. Don't move. Let me see your hands." Shulman looked for signs of explosives on Marakie's body.

"Officers?"

"MA'AM, get on the ground face-down and put your hands behind your head. DO IT NOW!"

Marakie raised her hands as she got to her knees, then put her palms on the ground and laid her head on the backs of her hands.

"Ma'am, I ordered you to put your hands behind your—"

"I will not put my face on the ground, like some criminal." Shulman's adrenaline rush started to subside. He didn't appreciate his authority being questioned.

"Ma'am, did you cause that explosion?"

Crying, she said, "No! and stop calling me ma'am."

"Are there any more bombs set to go off?"

"I don't know anything about any bombs."

Shulman, thinking she is not a threat, decides to get even, "Now, *MA'AM,* are you wearing a suicide ve—"

"Of course not, no. *I AM* the victim here—"

"Just stay put, ma'am." He squeezes the transceiver button.

"Dispatch, 436 at the treatment plant. There's been an explosion north of it, on Summit, and a woman met us on the curb."

"Copy, 436."

"Dispatch, we need a positive ID on the kidnap victim, a picture. At this point we don't have enough information."

"Copy, sending picture of Marakie Jones from Agent Jack Peterson."

Shulman returns to his patrol car to check his mobile unit, while the other two State Police still have their pistols out, watching Marakie. The other three APD units show up. They rush to where Marakie is. Shulman brings up the picture of Marakie and her father. He gets out.

"Ma'am, what is your name?"

"My name is Marakie Serapher Jones... not ma'am."

"Mrs. Jones, please, get up slowly, lift your hands way up, and turn completely around three times. We have to be sure." The APD officers are ready with their hands on their holstered weapons.

"Yes, sir." Marakie rises to her feet. Her peach-colored pants and blouse are soiled. She turns her body around three times. The officers satisfy themselves that she isn't hiding any bombs or weapons.

"My name is Sergeant Shulman."

Marakie started crying. "Where is my husband?"

"Marakie Jones, we were told that you were kidnapped."

She wipes her tears. The other officers holster their weapons. "I was. Then my abductor got into his car and it blew up. He was sent to kill me, but instead he saved my life. He took me out of harm's way."

Marakie turned around to see the smoke down the road. The police Unit-blocked out the still-burning Mercedes. Shulman looked at the billowing smoke, then turned to Marakie.

"Do you require medical assistance, ma'am? *Ah,* sorry."

"I'm not hurt."

"Okay, but when the medics arrive, I suggest you let them look after you."

"Please, may I sit down?"

"Yes, Mrs. Jones, come right this way." Officer Shulman opened the back door of his Charger and helped her inside. He shut the door. It was quiet inside the cruiser. Marakie needed that quiet. She watched the officers speaking into their transceiver mics, getting into and out of their vehicles, and unraveling yellow tape from one tree to another. She thought, *Who is Borg?*

She had a name—maybe Borg is the orchestrator. Lots of thoughts and images bombarded her. She was relieved for the momentary quiet. The smell inside was fresh, like the police car was just cleaned. She looked through the windshield to the revolving red-and-blue lights of the cruiser blocking traffic. She couldn't see what was left of the car; all she could see was thick smoke, near the ground, becoming thinner as it rose. She imagined Hasta inside. She remembered the dark empty hole of the pistol pointing at her, imagined being killed, and dragged into the pool, without ever seeing Ahmad again.

She took a deep breath, then remembered her husband's meticulous combat training lessons he started giving her, since January of 2011 when he returned to her, from Libya, after an unexpected stayover. She smiled as she visualized some of what her husband had trained her to do. She felt sad that she almost killed the man who just died saving her life. She rubbed her hair, then her forehead, as she sobbed.

Officer Tate came up Summit Road with Jones following a close second. Marakie heard the sirens and turned around to see three more units and a red sedan. She knocked on the inside of the window. Shulman opened the door.

"Mrs. Jones?" Marakie stepped out.

Marakie didn't hear the officer because of that red car she saw. She knew her husband was driving it. It came to a stop a few car lengths behind. Jones got out and ran to her.

"Ahmad," she said, "You are here!"

Oh, my husband, you were right. You were right, darling. I love you so much." They embraced for over three minutes.

A few miles away, a helicopter approached from the south, with Captain Bridgewater at the controls. After feeling more centered, Marakie looked at her watch. "Honey," she gently said, while wiping her eyes, "you've got to get to the bookstore for your talk... I'm okay... now. I'll be at the station by seven. What you have to do is bigger than both of us."

"Nigerian troops and the AU Peacekeeping force should have arrived at Afarland by now. An African Union Commission representative from Washington, D.C. also should arrive at the TV station, as promised."

Marakie nodded.

"On my way here, I confirmed that a DSS detail will arrive at FBI headquarters and get you to the station by a quarter to seven." The couple turns as Officers Tate and Shulman approach them.

"I'm assuming you are Mr. Ahmad Jones?"

"Yes, Officer, I am."

"Mr. Jones," Sergeant Shulman said, "Special Agent Jack Peterson wants to talk with you. He asked if I could take your wife to their field office. I said *yes*." Tate and Shulman looked at each other for a beat, then Shulman handed the phone to Jones.

"Jack, my wife and I are fine. I'm heading to the bookstore on Medina. Thanks for your assistance."

"Anytime."

"Got to go. I'll call you later before my wife and I are about to return home. We'll have a much-needed drink, you and I, and will play catch up. We'll come back for the Super Bowl in Houston. It'll be me, Marakie, and you and Stacy.

Hesitantly and all choked up, Peterson said, "Stacy and me are... okay, pal."

"Talk to you later, Jack," Jones handed the phone back to the sergeant, who began coordinating more with other patrolmen in the area.

Marakie said, "You look handsome, my husband." She ran her hands down the sides of his arms, and then gently adjusted his tie. A helicopter and fire truck emerged into the foreground.

"Got to go."

"I love you, Ahmad."

Shulman intercepts Jones, near his rental. "Are you in law enforcement, Mr. Jones?"

"Used to be, Sergeant. Now, I just consult. Thank you for your service and for bringing my wife to the field office."

The fire engine passed the slew of patrol cars, then the parking lot of the water treatment facility. The officer in the lone patrol car put the gear in reverse and moved out of the middle of the road. After the fire truck passed around it, the officer moved back into position. The bright red engine proceeded a quarter mile down Summit Road. The police helicopter, equipped with fire hoses, came to within a couple of hundred feet from the burning car.

Brenda Nolan was in her office in Kaskaskia. Dumont slowly passed her doorway and stopped. "Dumont, Jones' wife is safe."

"That's great news!"

"Now, Alejandro, about the Skokie case."

Jones got into his car and went back the way he came. After a few minutes, Peterson called back. "Ahmad, what's your location?"

"Driving south on Summit on my way to Medina."

"Okay, I'll meet you there."

"No, Jack... I'll be all right. Got to do this alone. Also, my wife is safe. You needn't be worried about her. Please, you won't understand why, not now, but there's an important reason why I need to attend this talk on my own." Jones was looking out for his friend. "I'd be thankful if you met Marakie at the field office; State Police are escorting her there."

Peterson saw the iconic communications tower for the fourth time.

"All right, Ahmad. You're on your own."

"Thanks, Jack. We'll get together before I leave the country. That's my promise to you."

Peterson and his partner got on the cloverleaf and crossed over to the other side, going north on I-77 towards Medina Road.

Peterson turned to O'Donnell, who is now seated on the passenger side. "I've got to run point for Jones, the only real friend I have. Just trust me,

Mason. He can't see everything. I'm a trained agent. I know what I'm doing."

O'Donnell is silent, especially after hearing Peterson call him by his first name. The last four-to-five hours has been a non-stop spectacle, but there is something that O'Donnell was curious about, something that Peterson had said earlier, that took his mind off his possible reprimand for disobeying a direct order from Sanborn.

"What did Jones tell you ten years ago, Jack? In the car earlier, you told me that when this was over, you were going to tell me what Ahmad told you at that time. I brushed it off, but now I'd like to know. I mean, this is the tenth year, right?"

Reaching up to 80 mph, Peterson said, "Ahmad suggested that I switch divisions, spend some time working behind the scenes... coordinating resources, organizing intel, working with the intelligence analysts."

"Switch divisions, huh?"

"That's about the size of it... Yeah, to put field work on hold from the beginning of June to the end of August."

"Did he tell you why?"

Peterson recalled, in his mind, what Jones had told him:

*"You turn 56 in February of 2017. It is also the year of your second Saturn Return, along with several stressful planetary pictures, so take it easy from early June to the end of August. At the beginning of that year, request a division switch."*

*"Because?"*

*"Because you are my friend and the issues you confront behind a desk, on operational support, will be less dangerous to your person than the ones on the street."*

"He never told me why and I never asked. That was the day we were in Bellevue, Washington, at that restaurant when he left the twenty on the table. I never saw him again, except at the Super Bowl when he disappeared. I never put in for that transfer."

"Why are you out in the field then? If you believe in Jones, why would you not act on his recommendation? Do you think this exposes *your person* to some risk?"

"Whatever the risk, a friend... *my friend*, may be a target and I want my last deed to be a good one."

"Last deed, what? You are leaving this life, I mean... the law?"

As a special agent for the FBI, yes. It's time to go."

"Now, I get it—with all your smoking, breaking the rules and all. You don't care because you're on your way out. Does Sanborn know?"

"I filled out the papers a week ago. Sanborn will have them on his desk tomorrow."


Ten minutes later, Jones drives into the crowded parking lot of the bookstore, very near the side entrance. Scott Sloan notices a red car through the store's side-door window. He moves closer to the sports section to get a better look and selects a baseball magazine. He holds the magazine close to eye level. There are two spaces side-by-side. Jones already changed clothes in the men's room at CAK. He has on the tie his wife had cleaned inside the plane, nine days ago. He is wearing a dark-blue, two-piece suit, a solid white shirt, and a pair of dark-blue lizard-skin uppers. He exits the car and walks through the side-door entrance.

From the sports magazine section, Sloan sees Jones enter. He can tell it is him because his picture is at the front entrance on a tripod. His orders from Marshall are to take him out at any opportunity he has available. The crowded store would provide the best shield for his covert endeavor. His plan is to get close enough to use his knife.

# 60

## A Standoff

THE ATMOSPHERE GOT MORE ELECTRIC once Jones walked inside. He passed several people with his newest book in their hands. Their excitement charged the store's atmosphere. People looked at him and then at his picture on the back cover. They pointed. He headed straight to the customer service bar. The manager spotted him and left the small enclosure, opposite the side entrance, and walked to him.

She extended her hand. "Welcome, Mr. Jones. My name is Crystal Simmons, the store manager. As you can tell, your book, or I should say, your books have attracted an unprecedented turnout."

"I am delighted to meet you, and yes, this is quite a turnout. Well, where would you like me to begin?"

"Upstairs. Please follow me."

She asked him how his flight went and how he felt about the city as they went to the escalator. He noticed how Crystal took account of her surroundings. In half circles—first one arc to the left, then to the right. To him, she had a vigilant eye. Sloan, from the front of the store, watched Jones and Simmons reach the second floor and then disappear. He figured Jones drove a rent-a-car; *maybe it was the red one near the side door*, he thought. He went out to find it.

Jones saw the banner with the front cover near the podium to the right. There were over fifty people in seats and another thirty standing. Simmons went to the podium, clicked on the mic, and introduced Jones:

"Good evening, everyone. Welcome to our author event. Tonight, Mr. Ahmad Jones is here. Please welcome the author of *Football's Astrological Measurements*, Mr. Ahmad Jones." She stood sideways and clapped. The audience followed.

Sloan felt the engine hood for heat. The red Focus was hot, so he went looking for the barcode. He checked the window to the back seat and saw a pair of red sneakers in a clear plastic bag. Those sneakers fit Marshall's description. Sloan took out a slim jim and popped the lock. He had been a specialist in the Gulf War, fixing vehicles and other equipment. It was easy for him to install an explosive charge under the driver's seat. It took him a little over two minutes to set up the vehicle so that if he couldn't reach Jones, then when Jones started the car, it would catch fire and explode. The trick had come in handy during the war. Sloan kept his pistol in his ankle holster, just in case.

Sloan had driven like a daredevil from Meadville, the northwestern part of Pennsylvania. He had arrived ahead of Jones' plane. He made sure to put on Ohio plates before he left.

A few minutes after Sloan wired Jones' car to explode, Peterson and O'Donnell pulled into the bookstore parking lot, right next to Jones' car. Peterson knew it was his—he remembered Jones' description when they last talked. Sloan, now wearing a baseball cap, didn't know right away that the Tahoe was an FBI vehicle until he saw the spotlight and the three antennas along the spine of the roof.

"That man is not Jones." Sloan put the hood down. Peterson got out and walked along the attached side-entrance walkway toward Sloan who was at his twelve. O'Donnell shut the passenger door and moved 45 degrees behind Sloan and ten feet away.

"I'm Special Agent Jack Peterson, Cleveland FBI." Peterson flipped his badge and identification and pointed to O'Donnell, "My partner is behind you."

Sloan turned around and saw O'Donnell's FBI credentials. Both Sloan and Peterson were the same height. Sloan noticed Peterson's silvery-gray hair, and the way it framed his square head. He considered his chiseled jawline, light stubble and deep-set eyes, highly alert. He had a determined look.

Peterson said, "Are you a mechanic?"

"Yes."

Peterson thought he was right to tail Jones. "The car whose hood you just closed. We happen to know the renter of this car, so what were you doing beneath that hood?"

Sloan looked behind at O'Donnell, then turned to face Peterson. Sloan noticed the ring on Peterson's finger; it was familiar to him. Sloan was a member of a Masonic lodge and Peterson was wearing the ring of a Master Mason. Perhaps he could take advantage of the Masonic Code, which was to help *a Brother* in distress.

"There must be some mistake, Agent Peterson. I just rented this car and wanted to satisfy myself that there was enough oil in the tank. You see, I'm headed east to New York, and don't want any surprises." Sloan made sure that Peterson saw him look at his ring.

"You must have paid a hefty price for that ring. I don't know where mine is."

Sloan said it incorrectly on-purpose, so as not to betray any secret words or catch phrases to O'Donnell whom he thought to be a non-mason.

Peterson wasn't fooled. The man was messing with Jones' car. Sloan conveyed a gesture, which would reveal his Masonic affiliation without O'Donnell knowing. Peterson saw it and while he knew that this man was a lodge brother, his tampering with Jones' car abrogated any binding obligation to help him. Plus, Peterson took an oath to defend the Constitution that he, with right hand raised affirmed, as a new special agent of the Federal Bureau of Investigation, twenty years ago, and had sworn to defend.

Peterson chose his words, carefully. "You're not the man who owns this car."

"Owns? This is a rental. The barcode is on the window. What are you saying?"

Peterson looked him up and down and noticed the print of a pistol on his left ankle. Sloan wasn't thinking like a father and a husband anymore. He knelt to tie his shoe. O'Donnell reached for his weapon.

# 61

## Saving Peterson

JONES SAID, "AND IN CLOSING, I'LL SHARE A PIECE I wrote a couple of weeks ago, in Africa. The Seattle Seahawks inspired it, and yet I relate it to football in general. Instead of the obvious, please insert your favorite team. My original name for it was, *Spirit of Football*. For now, I'm naming it *The Game*. Crystal Simmons had watched this part of the talk from the top of the elevator next to the guardrail. She turned to look over the floor below, to see if that strange man was still near the magazine rack but he wasn't there.

Jones said, "Time is an unbiased witness of events—its cataloger *and* the event itself. Time tacks on significance with the coming-into-being of a *Hawk* flying in the *Sea* of boundless possibility. The stellar NFL team, at kickoff, the team's *first-breath moment* on the astroturf, lends itself to computation: local time, longitude and latitude... sidereal time...

"Energy, movement in time—time-energy becomes the huddle, the formation, the snap, the handoff, the scramble... a pitch to the right, the drive... the victorious outcome—the cheers, the recognition of fulfilled visions.

"Time is a portal where monumental plays are born, drawn out—a play called out of infinity—where from infinity that play flows down into the cosmos and time and onto the gridiron, coalescing around a certain constellation of eleven men, obedient to the demands of a game clock and their own timing as a team.

"Players elevate together, in time. They vibrate beyond it and form a field-beyond-the-field. They become sustained in a matrix of teamwork—a timeless quantum gridiron. They play differently, magically, in a state of no limitations, the state... of no pain. Centimeters extend to inches and inches into feet. Speed! Acceleration! More feet morph into more yards. Cut! Slant! Dodge... Open! Teamwork evokes mysterious heavenly alchemies. Yards convert into downs. Downs reappear again and again—out of and into time—from the quantum-wave-field of... a *team*.

"The wave collapses into 67 yards... Touchdown! Players move together—and alone—on the precipice of epoch-making events. Notable. One, two-point conversion. Easy! The quantum wave collapses again into particles of time and the eleven men have again fulfilled their assigned task.

"The magic of victory and magnificent accomplishment, through this level of play, comes crashing down and flows through the team prepared with the resources of grand timing, coherence, respect for each other and the game, for fans... for the life that is contained within an astronomic cycle: observed, measured, and rendered into the horoscope for a special team.

"Lighted bodies in far-off worlds look on. On the offense, quarterback, tight end, running back, guards, tackles, and wide receivers—other positions masterfully attended. Time: the post-season, the large undulating mass of feeling and confetti. Time: the award of a 7-pound, 22-inch iconic work named for a grand coach of *The Game*.

"Thank you."

Simmons raced to the podium. "And now Mr. Jones will sign copies of your book for the next half hour." During the clapping, Jones heard: *Pop, pop... pop!* So did Simmons and the people in the café.

"Please excuse me for a minute," Jones said. Simmons was on the escalator; Jones followed.

"Akron Police Department, Sergeant Wil—"

"Special Agent O'Donnell of the FBI."

"Not so formal, remember?" Peterson said. Then his heart stopped beating.

"What can I do for you, Special Agent O'Donnell?"

"I'm calling from the Brick n' Mortar Bookstore on Medina, on the west side of the building. Shots... were fired and my partner is down. The shooter is dead. Request a couple of units... here. And... and a bomb unit. I've already called for an emergency medical team."

"Right away, Special A—"

"Agent O'Donnell will do. Thanks."

Jones caught up with Simmons as they left through the front entrance.

Simmons, in police mode, only went as far as the edge of the wall, and then she stuck her head out and brought it back—enough time to see the federal vehicle and a man in a light gray suit leaning over an older looking man who was lying on the ground. The younger man was loosening the older man's tie. She saw blood on the ground near another man who was lying on his side, apparently dead.

She stepped from behind the wall's edge. Jones followed and stopped when he saw his friend Jack.

"Ma'am, I need you to stay back, for now."

"Sir, I'm the manager here and a former sergeant of APD. Can I be of assistance?"

Silence.

"Sir, I said I am a former police sergeant—"

"Not... now!" Simmons keeps talking above O'Donnell's shouting."

"... In these parts for eight years, and right now I'm the manager of this store, so tell me what the HELL happened."

"Ma'am..."

"Crystal Simmons."

"Okay, Miss Simmons," O'Donnell tore open Peterson's shirt and noticed the flattened cartridge on his vest. "The dead man opened fire on my partner and my partner got off one round, center mass, as he went down."

O'Donnell holds Peterson's wrist. Peterson isn't breathing. O'Donnell puts his ear to Peterson's chest; he places two fingers against his artery. He begins chest compressions, away from the flattened cartridge.

Lots of people gather at the side of the store.

Simmons moves to Scott Sloan's body. She is facing away from O'Donnell. "I recognize this man."

"Administering CPR. Stay with me," O'Donnell says.

Crystal Simmons says, "When I first saw him in the greeting card section, I knew there was something unsavory about him."

"Jack. Come on, Jack, not like this."

Simmons turns around and says, "Like he was waiting for someone..."

She watches O'Donnell trying to save his partner's life and feels responsible. *I could have prevented this with just one call. I knew he was bad,* she thinks.

"Push harder and faster," Simmons says.

Jones marches past Simmons to O'Donnell. He kneels on his left knee and calls to his friend.

"Jack."

# 62

## Taxi

O'DONNELL STARES AT THE MAN IN THE ARMANI SUIT and ruby-colored tie who called his partner's name. He stops administering CPR, takes his pulse, then puts his head on Peterson's chest. No pulse and no heartbeat. O'Donnell stumbles upward to his feet and bumps his back against the wall.

Jones watches O'Donnell rubbing his forehead from side to side. Jones makes eye contact with O'Donnell.

"You. Get behind Jack and put your thumb, index, and middle finger on the center of his forehead, near the bridge of his nose. Do it now."

O'Donnell pushes off the wall and moves around Peterson until he stands opposite the crown of his head.

Jones takes off Peterson's shoes.

O'Donnell's sits on his knees.

O'Donnell knows that the man in the suit is Ahmad Jones. Based on Jack's stories, who else but Jones would ask him to do such a peculiar thing at a time like this? He places his thumb and two fingers on his partner's forehead.

Simmons notices the increasing number of onlookers. She wants to help but has to attend to the crowd.

"Put your other palm over Jack's heart, gently." O'Donnell does as he is told.

Simmons attends to crowd control.

Jones makes a fist with his right hand and protrudes the knuckle of his middle finger, then pushes it into the arch of Peterson's left foot.

O'Donnell looks on, almost in a daze.

Jones moves his fist back, as if he is pulling the taut string of a bow. Then snap-punches the middle knuckle into the arch.

Peterson's body twitches. He's coughing. O'Donnell looks at his partner then at Jones. Peterson opens his eyes to see his partner's head above him.

Jones says, "Please, Jack, stay quiet. Emergency vehicles are just down the street. You're going to be all right. It has been eleven years; I had my reasons, personal, nothing to do with you."

Jones kneels by Peterson and clasps his right hand. Peterson smiles, then looks away from Jones. "Huh, you said... desk... duty. But I didn't care. You... were... in trouble."

Jones wipes water from his eyes. Jack, if I had remembered what I said to you, years ago, I wouldn't have gotten you into any of this. I am sorry."

O'Donnell looks across to Jones from Peterson's left side. "I wanted to meet you, sir. If you hadn't arrived, my partner—"

"Who knows what could have happened, officer..."

"O'Donnell, Mason."

Peterson says, "Not your fault, Ahmad. A friend in need is a friend indeed—whatever the hell the stars say."

Jones nods. The two men smiled. People congregate in the lot. Vehicles slow to get a peep; honking and profanity follows, causing small traffic jams. People are coming through those double wooden doors now, five or six at a time, and into the parking lot. The bookstore is no longer becoming an occupancy hazard. Simmons goes back to work like it is another day on the job.

"But my car is in the lot."

"I am sorry, ma'am, but you must wait now, until the scene is processed. Please, everyone, do not block this lot. Paramedics are on their way and we have an injured man. EMS is coming. There's nothing to see here... Please, step back fifty feet."

"EMS is here, Jack. You're going to be all right. Over here, over here! My partner was shot with his vest on. His heart stopped, *then* started."

"You said his heart stopped and then started?" a paramedic asked.

"Right."

Peterson summoned the strength to say, "Ahmad, no matter what, get to your interview."

"I will, Jack. You're going to be all right."

"Jack was talking about you all afternoon," O'Donnell said.

"Excuse me, sir," one of the paramedics said. Jones stepped back against the wall, to allow the medical team to do their work. He looked at Simmons, at O'Donnell and the crowd. He had to head for the studio.

"Thank you for saving my partner's life, Mr. Jones."

"It's Ahmad, and you're welcome, Mason. Jack, we're going to attend a game together. The season regular starts in just a little over a month."

"Ahmad, friend, okay." Peterson lifted his hand.

"Mr. Jones, the dead suspect over there put something in your hood, Bomb squad are on their way." O'Donnell said.

"Thanks, I'll contact APD for its status, later."

Jones walked through the crowed and out to Medina Road just as a *Ride 4 Less* dropped off a customer.

"Excuse me, would you give me a lift to the *Sports Phase TV* station in Peregrine?"

"Sure, baby," the woman said, "Hop in!" She called it in. "Only a couple of minutes from here. I'll get'cha there in no time. Wow, you look real spiffy. You an athlete or something?"

Jones, still getting himself together after almost losing his friend, noticed the driver's ID card on the glove box: Olivia Terrel. Jones said, "I was an athlete, in another life." He saw a line of three police cruisers careen past him, heard the sirens and yelps, and saw a fire truck—which also served as a rescue vehicle and an ambulance—pass by. He wondered, for a beat, if those two entities, the bravest and the finest, would ever combine into a single entity.

"What happened back there?"

"An officer, a friend of mine, was injured in the line of duty."

"Oh, how sad. That's a shame. There's too much violence. I hope they caught the person responsible."

Jones thought about Peterson putting his life on the line.

"Yes, they caught the man."

She changed the subject, while running lots of green lights at 45 mph.

"Another life, huh? I had another life once... Didn't work out."

"And how is your life now?"

"Better than it was, since you got into my cab, angel!"

Jones was silent. His thoughts went to his wife, his friend, Jack, who was looking out for him, and to Brenda Nolan and Alejandro Dumont, showing up during his most extreme moment. They were now his new buddies at the Bureau. O'Donnell, too. He considered the quickly earned trust given him by Sergeants Peabody and Shulman. Then his thoughts went to his friend Ray, QB, and his new girlfriend, and everyone who had involved themselves with his plight. He had just one last thing to accomplish—for his wife, and for a people, and for himself. He felt uneasy.

Three car lengths behind the cab a BMW accelerates at twice the speed limit. It has a classy Diamond Silver Metallic finish. There are a couple of men up front. Smoking cigarettes. The men are determined to revisit and complete an old assignment that went south, over six years ago.

# 63

## Jenifer Stevens

INSIDE FBI HEADQUARTERS ON SEATTLE'S THIRD AVENUE, Special Agent Mike Cappello walks into the interrogation room, holding a cup of coffee. A guard closes the door after him. Cappello passes his eyes lightly around the one-way glass at his right, then at the woman sitting at the table in front of him. He nods to the agents behind the glass. The woman turns to look at the glass, too. Cappello is dressed impeccably: A light-gray, pinstripe, two-piece suit; white shirt and dark-blue tie. He is dapper. His official insignia dangles on a neck hanger, on a gold chain; and his duty weapon is visible near his right hip. Cappello wants to wrap this up fast, so, he conveys his officialdom and public authority, through his attire—to make a strong impression. He has a standard manila folder pinned between his upper arm and torso. He puts the coffee on the table and drags out a seat, one of the two plain metal chairs available to him. On the other side of the table another chair is bolted to the floor. The woman sits on it. To her right is a window with venetian blinds. It is sunny outside but the blinds are shut. No light streams in. The room is nine feet square.

"Ms. Jenifer Stevens, I am Special Agent Mike Cappello. We talked yesterday while standing on wet grass after the raid."

"I remember you, and thank you for helping with Selena."

"Selena was right at home, barked up a hell of a lot with her new playmate, Void."

"Void?"

"Yes, Void, of course!" Stevens' face glared at the remark. Her body-hugging spandex jumpsuit revealed taut muscles underneath its magenta hue. This initial reaction was enough to convince the almost-retired special agent that he was right about her. But he required harder confirmations.

"I see you waived your sixth-amendment right to legal counsel."

Stevens tried to wipe her eyes but had forgotten about her handcuffs. "You thought you had played a good hand, Ms. Stevens, but you were out-trumped."

"I don't understand." The stainless-steel cuffs landed several times on the table, as Stevens tried to separate her hands to explain.

"Yes. You do understand. I examined every robbery that was committed by your friends—"

"Those men were not my friends—"

"Care to know what I discovered?"

"Discovered nothing, you discovered nothing—"

"I *discovered* that they committed their bank jobs when the Moon was Void of Course. That specific time in each month, where the Moon forms no Ptolemaic aspects to a planet before it leaves the sign it's in. It gave your friends sort of a cloaking device. You arranged the timing."

Stevens' face was turning red. Cappello still required concrete facts before time ran out and she would be set free.

"There's also a ton of books on horary and electional astrology. My agents counted 54, on everything from earthquake predictions to plotting the outcome of the races." Stevens kept shaking her head. Her face turned from red to pale while Cappello was laying out his evidence. The men behind the glass weren't satisfied and needed more.

Cappello sipped his coffee.

"You will be formally charged with planning, aiding, and abetting four of the most prolific bank robbers I've ever seen and will—I repeat *will face* —300 months in prison."

Stevens wipes her eyes again, while Cappello talks. She says, "How do you come up with these thi—"

"By the end of your sentence, your Selena will be in dog heaven, and you, well, you'll be too old to wear your purple outfit."

"It's magenta—"

"To any good effect. So, are you an entrepreneur, or do you have a boss?"

Silence.

"Did you come up with your modus operandi all by your lonesome?" She kept shaking her head.

Cappello changed tactics.

"Ms. Stevens, if you cooperate with the FBI, if you come clean with us, the sentence will be cut in half, maybe more than half. So, talk to us. This is all being recorded."

She cried for two minutes—all the while trying to think of a way out of her mess—then lifted her head from the table. Cappello took the handkerchief out of his jacket pocket and passed it to her and spoke in low tones. "If you play your cards right, we'll see to it that your sentence is cut down."

After a sniffle, Stevens said, "Special Agent Cappello I don't know what I'm accused of here. I don't know what you're talking about: Moon, void, astrology. These men invaded my house. That's all I know. Really. Those books you mentioned were stacked inside the guest-bedroom closet when I took over the house. I've been meaning to get rid of them. Plus, I'm a Christian and I don't believe in astrology."

She relaxed her back against the cold chair. Cappello slammed the manila folder against the table. Stevens' muscle tension showed through her outfit.

"You're not too bright, Jenifer." He opened the folder. Stevens' eyes were glazed over. Cappello pointed.

"Know what that is, right?"

Stevens shook her head like before.

"It's got your fingerprints on it; you were reading this before we stormed your bedroom." Cappello spoke slowly. "It is a fucking horoscope. I've got eyewitnesses to prove it." Cappello wanted her to believe that one of the four men gave her up but it was his partner, Reese, who saw her with the paper, through the living room mirror's reflection.

"What does that evidence say about your alleged belief?"

# 64

## One-Hundredth Kill

OLIVIA TERREL, THE CAB DRIVER, TURNED LEFT onto a private road, which is the beginning of a two-mile-long stretch between lines of tall pines, spaced 200 feet apart, and behind which are several acres of beautifully cut grass. As they were about to reach the halfway point, they came upon the sign: *Sports Phase 4 TV*, to their right. The sign was in the shape of an expensive gold picture frame, with Vince Lombardi's iconic smile and pointing finger. To its right was a waterfall with rocks laid out on a plot of sand like a Japanese garden.

About a mile beyond the sign is a football field. It was built because the owners seemed to think that they could draw professional football teams to their private field for an occasional practice during the off-season.

"I see why you like to drive through this area of town," Jones says. He rubs his neck and shoulders, as he relaxes into his seat.

"It's beautiful," the driver said. "Are you supposed to be on TV or something, mister?" Jones looks out the rear windshield and sees the BMW shadowing the cab, at four car lengths. He turns back around. Sits up straight. "Yes, I have a spot on *The End Zone* at seven."

The cab moves through the long, serpentine stretch of road. No buildings obstruct the view, on either side. She maintains a steady 40 mph.

"Oh yeah, I watch that new show sometimes, with that guy; he's so handsome and smart. What's his name... Buck, Bruce, and oh, Max, he's a fast talker. You gonna be on with him?"

Suddenly, the BMW darts into the left lane, flying past them. Jones catches a familiar sight: diamond earrings worn by the man sitting on the passenger side. After a few seconds, and 75 feet ahead, Logan swerves the BMW into the right lane. Olivia slams her foot down. The cab skids to a stop. Logan Bernard and Marcus Dubois fling out of the car, pointing their weapons.

The cab driver leans forward and reaches under the seat. The bullet crashes through the glass. No suppressor is used. The sound effect is trailed by another round. Both crackles collide, creating overtones.

"Lady at the wheel, don't do anything stupid, but we're here for your passenger.

"Don't. Olivia, keep your head down and put your hands up. Do what these men say. You will be safe. They're professional men. They're here for me."

"I can take care of myself. I was in the army. I've got a carrying permit and my weapon is underneath my—"

"Hey, asshole, this ain't Libya, so get out of the car with your hands up and get over here."

"Olivia, these are serious men."

"I've got it."

"Okay, then use your foot to slide it out the footwell. And keep your hands up. They took out five heavily armed members of a militia unit, in Libya, in an elevator—all by themselves. I know because I was there."

Jones opens the door and puts one foot on the pavement. Olivia rethinks her words to Jones, about being lucky, but has concluded that her passenger must be mixed up in some nasty business. Jones waits a beat, and then lays his other foot down. He leans forward, out of the doorway and stands with his hands up.

"Come to us."

Jones walks toward the nearest car door of the BMW, which is facing him. There isn't another moving vehicle, on the ground or in the air, in any direction, as far as one's eyes can normally see. There's a wind gust—just blew in—from the west, thick clouds form, then lightning. The tire marks on the road, courtesy of Logan, are a curious measure. It reminded Jones of that redhead, QB's new girl, who skidded into his life. Logan could've just popped Jones, like he did Scudder without stopping, but he had to settle a score— with himself. Logan hovered by Olivia's window, not taking his eyes from the sight of her hands.

Marcus opens the backseat door and says, "Get in."

Jones turns about, meeting Olivia's fearful stare, and smiles.

Logan grabs the keys out of Olivia's car and runs over to put his gun to Jones' head. Jones is glad Olivia is safe. Olivia gasps and puts her hand to her mouth.

Jones gets into the car and Marcus follows him inside, boring the muzzle of his pistol under Jones' arm and against his chest.

"What do you want?"

Logan said, "To retire, fucker; you were worth 11 million to us back in Libya."

"Now, you are worth 15 million euros," Marcus said.

Marcus shoved the muzzle into Jones side, with more force. Jones focused on Logan's face, in the rearview mirror.

"Were?"

"We got nothing."

"Your fault."

"And you're going to be my 100$^{th}$ kill. You stayed out of sight for seven years—*seven years*—but when you showed up on Big Brother, we figured we'd try you again, to settle the score with the man. The 15 million is up for grabs."

"Dead. The man wants you dead," Marcus said.

"But did you see this one coming, Mr. Astrologist?" Logan asked, rhetorically.

Jones considers his answer. He says, "Yes, I saw you coming, through the rear windshield."

Logan smirked.

He took the next right turn, into a private access road. A sign read: *Phase 4 Field.* Part of the access road was built with red-orange concrete paving stones. The rest was dirt. A work-in-progress. Olivia was inclined to follow the BMW but she had no keys. Her mind raced, digesting the facts of the last few minutes. She stayed parked on the roadside, leaned her forehead against the top of the steering wheel, hands on her head. She felt the air come through the fresh bullet-holes on the windshield, straightened up, picked up her phone to call the police, when she spotted an SUV with flashing blue lights, in her wing mirror.

"The field is ahead," Logan said. "We'll complete the job there, once and for all."

The dust the wheels had stirred up had covered the car, just like the Ajaj did, in Tripoli, behind the hotel but more so. Logan stopped short of the entrance, cut the engine, flew out and slammed the door. "Get out, now!"

Jones thought about what he was going to do, then stopped thinking about it. He felt Olivia's weapon, a Compact 1911, underneath his jacket. She had passed it to him, reluctantly. He stepped out onto the unfinished road. A few paces away was the edge of the field. About ten feet from the grill of the BMW was the golden crossbar. It glimmered as the last rays of the sun were replaced by storm clouds.

Logan gestured toward the field, Jones walked onto the turf, with his hands up. Lightning flashed, and a torrent followed. The winds blew his jacket open.

Logan yelled, "Marcus and I are going to beat you to death. That pressure-point shit is for faggots. Fight like a man, bitch, before you meet your maker. You are certainly dressed for it."

Jones' suit was drenched in seconds. He thought of Abishai, his teacher, when the two had conversed in Cádiz, inside the park, on the bench dedicated to Aries. He thought of the Labors of Hercules, of how he was supposed to capture the wild horses and bring them into the Holy Place. Of how Hercules' companion couldn't handle the horses' wild energy and was killed. These men were like the horses, wild and deadly. The sun was coming back out, but the clouds remained, and lightning could be seen in the distance. The mercenaries put their pistols away.

"Okay, no pressure-point shit." Jones stood near the goalpost that was closest to the grill of the car. The two mercenaries were six feet away.

Marcus rushed at Jones with a ferocious kick aimed at his groin. Jones stepped back just out-of-range. Marcus almost lost his balance. Another kick followed with the same result. Jones' back was a couple of yards from the nearest goalpost to the car. Logan ran around that goalpost.

Marcus followed up with a jumping back-fist to Jones' face. Both attacks met only the air. Logan was now behind Jones and a few feet away from the solid piece of gauge steel and aluminum. He punched the back of Jones' head, to which Jones warded off the force of the blow by deflecting it *with* his head. He continued turning his head and body, gaining a spiraling momentum, and came back around with a semi-circular kick, with the outside edge of his lizard-skin shoe, to the right side of Logan's head. The force slammed the other side of his head against the goalpost.

It was all over. The goalpost wasn't padded. Its diameter was five inches. The impact broke something inside Logan's skull. Jones continued turning and faced Marcus, who jumped at him with wild punches aimed at his face and gut. Jones slipped all but one, the one he allowed to connect with his gut. He seized the punch-hand and put Marcus' wrist into a lock by squeezing his palm toward his wrist, then locking the elbow into his body. Logan was going for his pistol. Marcus tried to punch Jones and kick him with his opposite hand and foot but the pain in his captured wrist, and immobilized elbow, denied him any reach at Jones' body. Reluctantly, Jones forced Marcus' palm toward his forearm. Marcus tried to pull away. Jones snapped Marcus' wrist and let him go. Marcus stepped back and went for his pistol. Jones rushed to close the distance, then jumped up and stomped his foot through Marcus' right thigh bone.

Marcus went down. The leg dangled by its flesh and sinews. Marcus looked in wonderment, grabbing his unattached leg and wishing he'd just shot Jones, instead of going toe-to-toe. Marcus, with his only hand took out his pistol and pulled the trigger, wildly. Jones pulled out Olivia's 1911.

Olivia heard the shots. She cried, thinking that her fare was killed.

"Shoot him, Marcus," Logan said, as he leaned against the post as a crutch, to push himself up, from off the turf. The clouds began to disperse.

"It's over. Put it down." Marcus saw Jones take aim and lowered his weapon but, like those wild horses in the tale, he tried to lift it again. Marcus took aim. Jones had no place to run for cover. He was left with no option. He gave him several chances to stop. His police training with firearms had surfaced. Another shot echoed through the field. Marcus' body shuddered. He wiped his blood-stained chest with his gun hand. He frowned.

Jones kept the pistol on him. Marcus tried to lift his head some more, then his whole body relaxed completely on the astroturf.

"You killed my partner, you son of a bitch. You broke something inside my head," Logan said. He lifted his pistol.

Jones shouted, "THERE'S A TIME TO WIN AND A TIME TO LOSE... YOU'VE LOST." Logan still leans his body against the goalpost for support. He's on his feet and takes one step forward. He is groggy and uncoordinated. Logan collapses.

"You shot my best friend, Ahmad. You shot my best friend."

"Why 100?"

"What?"

"Why do you have to kill 100 people?"

Logan's gun hand shook. The pistol felt very heavy. Jones took Logan's gun away. Slowly. Logan was visibly humiliated. He reached for the pistol. His hand was still suspended in the air, as if he were waiting for Jones to give it back.

"What's wrong with me?" Logan's hand plummets to the turf.

Jones kneels, knowing that Logan is dying. "Why 100 kills, Logan?"

"Trained... I trained in Savate in my teens—won several matches." Logan kept shutting his eyes and opening them, trying to make sense of why everything was a blur. "I killed someone near the Stalingrad, in Paris, when I was 19, some fruitcake."

"And?" Jones said.

"A recruiter from the FFL... saw it, the... whole thing. Blackmailed me into joining up. Was... gonna go tell the authorities if I refused... he was going to tell. Was the head of a special group that operated, layers deep, in the... FFL. I was recruited, trained to kill... sent to Africa, not long after."

Logan turned his head to look at his dead partner. The hard turf was uncomfortable against the right side of his face. He turned and gazed at the sky again.

"Killed good guys and bad guys, for a price. Was good, was the best. But I feared the man I met at Stalingrad. 'You're my most promising piece of work, Logan,' he says, 'and can only leave our ranks when you make 100 kills; not just anybody, unless they get in the way of a hit, or a negotiation. You kill who we tell you to.'"

"He was bigger and stronger than me. Had me cornered, pulled out a knife. 'You murdered a Police Nationale and will go to prison for the rest of your life, or die, here. Which will it be?' He took his knife from my throat. I nodded *yes*. I wanted out after that. I was scared. I killed because I wanted out; I was scared."

"Why didn't you *take* him out?"

"I don't know. But it would be different if I had it"—Logan's breathing was strained—"to do over."

"The way you took out those four boys in New York, were you scared then?"

"No, happy. Orders. Made my 58th that night. Forty-two left. But I heard that the man in Stalingrad died last year but his edict stuck with me. Maybe he told someone; don't know. It became my mission. I can't move Jones. You hurt me, really bad."

"You did it to yourself, out of your own words. I fought you, as you wanted, like a man. No pressure-point, faggot shit."

Logan and Jones laughed, together. He was bleeding internally, from his skull.

"Do you remember the War Room, when I said that you have an opportunity to transform your life? You're transforming now, this instant."

"I regret shooting your friend, now, because he was your friend; you know, the guy in the car."

"Yes, he was my friend, with a wife and a kid on the way. You were careless in your disrespect for human life. Honor life! Logan, in doing that, you honor your own and THAT LIFE which breathed ITSELF into you."

Logan pleaded, "I want to live, Ahmad. I feel life in my body, for the first time. Never noticed it but it was always there," Logan wipes rain from his face with the back of his hand. "But my life... it's going."

"Life is a continuum, Logan and you'll be glad to know that Frank Scudder's son is fifteen, and Frank's widow remarried."

Jones could feel a different atmosphere around the two of them. The sun had come back out.

"That's good. Now, I feel regret for the people I killed, good and bad. No hard feelings." Logan looked up at the sky. He reached out his hand. Jones took it and looked him in the eye.

"I'm glad it's you, Jones. I'm... glad you ended it." Logan turned back to the yellow goalpost. His left knee was against it. Logan's voice was a whisper. Jones put his ear close to Logan's mouth.

"In American football this is *the end zone* but in Canada we call it *the dead line*. Ironic. There's hope when a guy like you finishes a guy like me."

"You are the 100th kill. Now, you will retire, for a season, from fear."

"You'll make a good president... Borg."

"Borg?"

"Adlai... Borg. You asked who sent me, back in Tripoli. The Consortium, they're behind... the attempts... then and now."

Jones felt Logan's warm hand turning cold.

Jones said, "That's not important now, what is important is your last thought and desire, before you depart this field."

Logan looks up.

"I can't see, Ahmad. Forgiveness! God, please forgive me."

Logan squeezed Jones' hand. There was a laugh, and then he murmured, "I can't move, Ahmad, can't move my head." Jones placed Logan's hand on his chest, then went through his pockets.

# 65

## Playing Wounded

THE SUV STOPS SHORT OF THE ASTROTURF alongside the BMW. Special Agent O'Donnell steps out onto the dirt and walks first to Marcus and then to Jones, who turns around and puts his hand inside his jacket. O'Donnell pushes his left palm out and puts his right hand on his pistol grip. Jones lowers his hand slowly.

O'Donnell looks back at Marcus, then at Logan, and then at Jones. "Ahmad, what happened here?" He takes his fingers off his pistol grip.

Jones struggles to stand up after having knelt near Logan's body. "Assassins, sent to kill me. I've got minutes left to make it to the studio by seven. How is Jack?"

"They took him to the trauma unit. He's going to be all right."

O'Donnell walks to Jones who is a few feet away from the goalpost. "That was quite an intense storm a few minutes ago. The lady cab driver briefed me about two men with guns and a hostage. She was crying. Thinks you're dead."

"Not yet. I have to do this broadcast." Jones lifts away the left side of his jacket. O'Donnell fixes his eyes on Jones' gunshot wound.

"Did it exit?"

"Still in there."

"You need emergency—"

"No time for that. If I don't do the interview, if I don't get to the studio..."

"Jack took a couple of bullets, so you could... but you could die."

"Only a half-hour segment."

"I don't know what to say."

"There's nothing to say, only to do."

"First aid kit is inside." Jones follows O'Donnell, past Marcus' body to the Tahoe. He opens the left passenger door and pulls out a blue plastic box.

Jones says, "Let me take a look."

"Make it quick." Jones opens the box, removes the lid and organizing tray. He takes out packages of gauze, a pair of trauma shears, tape, and antiseptic. He rummages around some more.

"What else, Ahmad?"

"A chest seal will do." O'Donnell points to it.

"Help me off with this, please." Jones slips his left arm out of his jacket and O'Donnell helps Jones pull his other arm out. Jones unbuttons his shirt, takes it off and lifts his undershirt above his chest. "Hold this, please," Jones says.

"The bullet is lodged in your side."

Jones slips on a pair of latex gloves and removes blood from the wound with an antiseptic wipe. O'Donnell lets go of Jones' shirt, sanitizes his hands, and puts on a pair of gloves. He takes out a three-inch gauze pack and opens it. Jones' breathing is labored but apparently under control. O'Donnell wonders why Jones isn't visibly in pain.

"No, I'll use the seal."

"You have to open it periodically to let it breathe. If you don't open and close it at times to release pressure, it—"

"I am aware of the risk to my life."

O'Donnell puts the transparent seal around the wound. Jones lowers his t-shirt and then grabs his dress shirt and jacket.

O'Donnell puts the first aid kit away. He says, "Ahmad, this is the golden time. You've got to wrap this up fast so you can get to a hospital. You know, necrosis and all."

Jones puts out his hand. O'Donnell shakes it. "Thanks, pal." Jones walks around the back and enters through the passenger door. O'Donnell gets in, puts the gear in drive and releases the brake.

"The lady in the cab says that one of these men took her keys."

"I have them." Jones pulls them out of his jacket pocket.

"I'll take you to her." The two men leave Marcus and Logan on the field. O'Donnell turns the car around and heads out to the main road, over the dirt and new paving stones. Olivia sees the brown Tahoe emerge and hesitates to get out until it gets to within ten feet of her. Jones gets out. Olivia is flabbergasted. O'Donnell gets out, too, and escorts Jones to the passenger seat.

"Can you get this man to the studio, now?"

Jones opens the door and slides in. Olivia, still in a state of disbelief, and with certain expectations says, "Not without my—"

Jones hands her the keys.

O'Donnell says, "I have to stay. Once you leave, I'll make the call for PPD and Bureau personnel. It's *The End Zone*, right?"

"Right."

O'Donnell notices Jones pull out a 1911 from his inside pocket. He didn't see it until now. "Where did that come from?"

"It's Olivia's, Agent O'Donnell. She has a permit for it. She slid it to me before I was taken. O'Donnell goes to the Tahoe to grab an evidence bag. Jones shuts the door and lowers the window. O'Donnell comes to the window and Jones drops the weapon into the bag.

O'Donnell seals the bag. "Both of you will have to be debriefed."

"Understood, as soon as I finish at the studio and get someone to attend to my situation." Jones doesn't let on to Olivia that he's been shot.

Olivia starts the cab and continues on past O'Donnell who waves goodbye. "Who are you, really, mister?"

"A former cop. I am also a guest on *The End Zone*. Do you have any water?"

"No, sorry." She turns to look at Jones and says, "Honey, you don't look so good."

"Had a *full* day."

"I smell blood. Are you bleeding?"

"Just a small wound. Those men were contracted to keep me from appearing on this show."


They covered another half mile and arrived at a checkpoint for the TV station. Olivia rolled down the left-side window.

The security guard, a balding man with a hearty smile under his handlebar mustache, said, "How're you doing, Olivia?"

"Okay. I'm fine, Neil. My passenger is gonna be with Max."

"May I have your name, please?" The security guard asked.

"Ahmad Jones, sir."

The guard guided his pen up and down the sheets on his clipboard.

"Okay, Mr. Jones. You're going to head for Building C. Good luck. See you 'round, Olivia."

They rode another two minutes, passing four direct-broadcast satellites about 200 feet away to their right. They turned left and drove up a circular incline for a few seconds. When they reached the top, Building C appeared straight ahead. "Well, Mr. Jones, here we are."

She continued to drive straight inside the large parking lot and stopped a few yards behind a burnt-orange Maserati that faced the front of Building C. The rectangular façade sported three sets of double doors, all plexiglass. Above them were two stories of desert-style architecture. The signage on the outer wall of the second story featured *The End Zone* in red-gold letters, which enlivened the exterior's beige coloring. Behind the plexiglass doors was a black wall with spectacular pictures of the most iconic football games ever played, like the Giants vs. Colts game of 1958, and the Packers vs. Cowboys championship of 1966, plus a smaller version of the same Vince Lombardi picture that dotted the landscape a few miles back. A young man came out through the plexiglass doors and walked past the Maserati to within a few feet of Olivia's door. He was tall and lanky, with a mercurial air about him.

Olivia said, "Well, that's nine-sixty."

Jones handed Olivia a twenty. "Keep the change. God bless you. You'd better go back to Agent O'Donnell." Jones opened the door and quickly exited the cab. Olivia got out, too, leaving the door wide open. The young man looked at his watch, considering the prep time for the next broadcast.

Olivia raced to the back of the cab and faced Jones. She was a couple of inches shorter than him. She took the pin out of her hair, which fell below her shoulder blades. She put the bill in her pocket and moved closer to Jones while looking intently into his eyes. Jones lifted the other piece of luggage out the trunk, as he watched Olivia getting closer. He was handling the ever-increasing pain in his side, but wouldn't be able to console Olivia, which he could do with a hug, or by entraining her rapid pulse with his. But his pulse wasn't steady but jumpy. Jones took a deep breath.

"I'm still processing what I saw," she said.

"The FBI will want you to describe it in detail."

Olivia rocked back and forth, first on her toes, and then on her heels, then she repeated the motion. "No problem."

Jones went around her, but she caught up with him and blocked him. The tall, lanky young man thought that the woman's actions were peculiar. "The man you saw with the FBI is Special Agent Mark O'Donnell," said Jones.

Olivia was within a foot of Jones. She smiled. "Got it. Are you married?" Up to this time she hadn't looked at his ring finger. She looked and her smile changed to a frown. "Oh, you're wearing a wedding ring. The good strong men are always married."

"But the other ring on your index finger looks like a Super Bowl ring."

"Yes, it does in some respects, but it's not. Olivia, I've got a show to do. Thanks for the lift. If you accept that as your reality, about all the best men being taken, then that's what you'll get. You can just as easily turn that statement into its opposite. Accept *that*, and you'll always have good strong men to choose from."

Olivia smiled and hugged Jones. "You think so?" Olivia's sudden gesture sent an unearthly pain through Jones side. He bent left but immediately straightened his body.

Jones dropped his bags and placed his hands on her shoulders and then stepped back. Jones winced a little, then lifted his bags and walked around Olivia. His steps were slower and more labored now.

# 66

## Third and Long

OLIVIA WALKED BACK TO THE OPEN DRIVER'S DOOR of her taxi and got in. She backed it away from the Maserati, winked at Jones, and then circled around and disappeared down the incline.

Jones walked up to the young man. "Mr. Jones, my name is Stew. The Program Director, Mr. Usman, told me to meet you and take you inside."

Jones put out his hand. "Glad to meet you, Stew."

"It's the other way around, sir. I read your book—twice! Here, let me help you with those."

"Twice?" Stew gathers the bags and hangs the straps on his shoulder.

"I read *Moby Dick* in less than a week. I read yours in one day—took me about two hours, no interruptions."

Still his gracious self despite his previous ordeals, wound, and Olivia's painful hug, Jones said, "Well, if you could read Melville's classic in one week, I imagine you *could* read my book twice in much less time. Where to from here?"

"This way through the center doors." Stew took Jones' bags to the doors, swiped his badge, held a door open for Jones and then followed him in. They proceeded left, traversing the marble floor past the sports pictures. Then entered a hallway that was carpeted in deep red. After fifty feet they passed between a slew of small production studios and rooms. They walked up to the fourth door on the right. The sign on the wall near the doorknob read

*Wardrobe & Makeup.* Inside there were seven large mirrors fixed on a black wall to the left, spaced two feet apart. There were also seven chairs before the mirrors and a long white counter that ran the length of the wall. Stew put Jones' bags on the floor near an adjustable cushion chair at the unmanned first station. There were several bottles of spring water in a milk basket below the counter. Jones took one and cracked the seal. He sat down and saw the restroom in the reflection. Perhaps he could check on his chest seal and put on another shirt.

"Mr. Jones?"

"Please call me Ahmad."

"Ahmad, Shirley will be in to get you ready. I'll be going back to the control room. Break a leg, Ahmad. Nice suit. Hey, is that—"

"Would you excuse me, Stew? I have to be alone for a minute."

"Oh, sure thing, Mr. Jones."

"Ahmad."

"Right, Ahmad."

"And thanks for reading my book, twice—a mighty compliment."

Stew breezed out. He wasn't certain if he saw a blood spot on Jones' shirt or not. Jones swiveled the chair around to face the bathroom; he got up, grabbed one of his bags and walked over to it. Inside he found an emergency kit replete with lots of gauze packages, tape and scissors. He shut the door behind him.

Twenty minutes later, three black Cadillac Escalades turned left off the road, up the incline, and into the parking lot. Six men in dark-blue suits got out and swept the area. Neil, from the checkpoint had notified Building C security in advance. There were three security guards at the plexiglass doors.

The head DSS Agent, named Reilly, towered over the Maserati, as he passed it and neared the three guards. "I am DSS Agent Reilly, a Mister Ahmad Jones is to be interviewed here at seven. And it so happens that is wife, the daughter of President Dewabuna of Afarland, is in Ohio on state business. She would like to watch her husband's interview inside."

The guards looked at the men, three of whom are huddled near the center SUV.

"Never heard of Afarland."

"Lots of people haven't. Have you heard of a country called Comoros?"

"Can't say that I have."

"These countries sit in the Indian Ocean and are a part of Africa's 6th region. Their names are not as well known as Nigeria, Libya, or South Africa. How do we secure permission to view the interview?"

"Okay, Agent Reilly. My name is Fletcher. I'm the head of security. I'll inform Mr. Usman and we'll try to get you into the viewing room to watch the show. Back in a minute." As soon as Fletcher opens the main door, several Peregrine police units file in the lot and surround the station. Fletcher sees four police units, and then hastens to Steve Usman's office. The two other guards just stand, waiting for their boss to return.

Steve Usman and the chief security guard arrived at the front door. Usman was five-nine with dark hair and a face full of the same. Before taking over as program director for *Sports Phase 4 TV,* he was a multi-sport athlete in college, and later a political-science professor. He checked out the law enforcement vehicles on studio property.

"I'm Usman." He was intimidated by four police cruisers, three federal vehicles and Reilly's height.

Reilly, who stands at six-three, says, "Good day, Mr. Usman. Ahmad Jones' wife is the daughter of the President of Afarland. She is wondering if it would be any trouble to watch the interview from inside?"

Marakie was sitting in the middle Escalade. A DSS agent opened the door and helped her out. She wore a black pantsuit with a crème blouse. Her handbag was gold. Three agents escorted her to the studio entrance.

"Good evening. My name is Marakie Jones, Ahmad's wife." She extends her hand.

Steve felt at ease, upon meeting Marakie. "Pleased to meet you, Mrs. Jones." Steve considers how the ratings will go if the TV audience becomes aware that the daughter of Za Dewabuna is in the studio to watch a show he's directing. He wonders how he can use this opportunity without coming off as political.

"Right this way into the VIP room. No, instead, I know just the place." Reilly and two other DSS agents follow Marakie, Usman and Fletcher inside. Local Peregrine police take up positions on the main road and inside the lot.

After twelve minutes, Usman spoke from inside the control room: "Standby, Camera One. Absolute silence in the studio."

Half a minute left. Dead silence on the set. The floor manager stood left of Camera One's mounted teleprompter. He watched the digital clock and motioned with his fingers: *Five, four, three...* and then pointed to the lead anchor.

The indicator lamp above the lens on Camera One glows red. Words scroll up the reflective glass. Steve Usman, the owner of the Maserati and the show's director, will call the shots for the fourth installment of the new sports program.

The clean-shaven, bald lead anchor talks to his television audience.

"Camera One's on air," Steve said.

"Welcome to *The End Zone!* Thanks for joining us. I'm your host, Max Brockwell. With me are Heather Brophy and Mike McGee. We bring you up to speed with the book, *Football's Astrological Measurements.* Yes, you heard right, and indeed we wonder... How do both football and astrology in the same sentence make any sense at all? We'll delve into this unusual matchup in the first half-hour. In the second half, we'll discuss the future of American football's popularity in the U.S. and abroad." Max turns to his fellow anchors.

Heather says, "As for me, I think this book is in the red zone toward best-seller status."

Mike adds, "And we're about to enter the preseason, folks. The author, Ahmad Jones, is with us in our Peregrine, Ohio studio today. Welcome, Ahmad!"

"Thank you. I am glad to be here."

Inside the production control room, Steve talks to the camera crew on the studio floor, calling for as many as five camera switches a minute.

Jones sat at the end of the table to the TV audience's right. Max opened the show with his comments before the montage of iconic images, the entrance music, and the title card. He jumped into the feature story with a cold open and snapped the new conversation into play—like the match that catches fire and lights the fuse on the opening to the original, *Mission Impossible* TV show. The co-anchors Heather and Mike each had a copy of Jones' book lying on the aqua-colored glass counter in front of them. Max turned to Jones with the book propped in the crease of his left elbow.

The director said, "Camera One, you're hot. We've got a clean product, so far... Focus, everyone! Let's keep it like that."

Max said, "I mean, man! Your book has football history and verifiable astronomic measurements that repeat themselves and show obvious correlations to football, even that one-in-a-billion astrological connection to the San Francisco 49ers in their first game against the Seattle Seahawks."

Max said, "What an unconventional mix! You have all the cylinders firing in your book, producing maximum power for a successful drive to bestseller."

Jones smiled as he talked, "Max, I appreciate those mixed metaphors."

Mike said, "Skeptic that I am—or was. I convinced myself before I ever turned a page that it was just about game predictions or the horoscopes of players—half-baked and for a certainty, inaccurate."

Heather asked, "Your wife bought it for you?"

"You guessed it! Just in case we happened to do a show about it, so I wouldn't be blindsided. After I skimmed the first few pages, I concluded that, man, my assumptions were all wrong."

Managing to keep most of his attire from being damaged from the blood inside his chest seal, Jones unlatched the two gold buttons to his Armani charcoal-colored two-piece, with his tie now front and center, as if he were on cue.

Steve was in heaven. He said, "There are no tonal mergers and Jones' wardrobe reflects light with elegance."

Heather said, "Tell us what inspired you to write this book and would you talk a little about its contents. By the way Ahmad, I've never seen a ring like that... it's striking."

There were enough seconds to see Heather's facial expressions. She laughed a lot as she spoke, which made everyone relaxed. She gave people the feeling of having a real interest in her guest. Her bright blue eyes sparkled with expectation—of a thrilling first half—along with the smiling expression on her cheekbones and tiny dimples.

Camera Two's light came on and captured all four in the central wide shot, the major shot for the show. Then the camera zoomed in on the ring. Jones' life—and moreover, his wife's life—were on the verge of changing in an extraordinary way.

"Thank you, this is a ring of state."

"A souvenir?" Mike asked.

"Not for long. You see, it was given to me three months ago. I'll explain how I received it—it's a fascinating story that ties in to my book—but first, I'll answer Heather as to what inspired me to write it. It all started with a simple addition problem and some Numerology theory. That was all. I used Astrology later to go another route." The three sportscasters were intrigued by that statement, as was the production staff, some thirty of them. Their ears perked up for what this peculiar guest was getting ready to say.

"He's got my attention," said Stew, sitting in the control room with Steve.

"The inspiration came when my wife Marakie and I were in Constantia, in Cape Town, South Africa. It was three years ago, on Monday morning, the 3rd of February 2014, on the night the Seattle Seahawks had beaten the Denver Broncos, winning the Lombardi trophy for the first time in 37 years. The digital satellite provider broadcasted the game throughout South Africa, and I also had my laptop set up so I could watch it online. There was talk that the American commercials weren't going to be shown on the cable network.

"I did a horoscope prep for Super Bowl 48 and went to bed at 8 pm. After five hours and twenty-eight minutes of dreamless sleep, I sprang up four minutes before kickoff, with an initial impulse to delve into the name, *Seattle Seahawks*. I felt there was a peculiar connection with the team's name and that game. I went with my vague intimation that something exciting was coming."

"How do you remember those times with such precision, while most people take those things for granted?" Mike asked.

"For me, the astronomic game clock is always ticking. If I notice something interesting, I'll look at my watch, record the time, and file it away. The local time tells me where the Earth is in its orbital rotation, and thus, what constellation is on the horizon at a given time, and the other planetary alignments and interrelationships. It's a habit that can yield useful information, such as when meeting someone for the first time, or the moment one begins a new job, or when a couple gets married, or the moment a football team arrives on the field for the very first time. By erecting a chart for those times and using it within the context of the event, one can get an understanding of the fields of energy at play in those moments and their potential unfolding over time."

Jones continued, "After I listened to Renée Fleming's rendition of *The Star-Spangled Banner*, I wrote down the 15 letters that made up the name *Seattle Seahawks* and placed underneath them their corresponding alphabetical number, like the number 19 for the letter S, and 5 for the letter E, and so on."

Mike leaned in to his left, with his elbow on the table and a clenched fist under his chin... evaluating. He squinted, as it helped him to concentrate.

"Then, with no further addition to reduce any of the double-digit numbers in the name, I added them and got the sum of 169. These are three of the numbers that make up the birth year of the Hawks' first season in the NFL—1976."

Heather nodded. She was drawn into Ahmad's conversational way of telling the story.

"At precisely 1:32 a.m. South African Standard Time, Steven Hauschka had just launched the kickoff drive for Seattle at Super Bowl 48."

Jones was feeling almost giddy as he felt excruciating pain. He wondered if any blood was pouring out of his shirt and onto the floor. His giddiness caused him, while giving this account, to journey back to that moment in Constantia. His eyes were far away now. A part of his being stepped beyond the studio and he was present at his home thousands of miles due southeast of this studio in Ohio. His words grabbed the attention of these articulate sportscasters. Anyone watching the show could feel that the three were engaged. The production staff was also interested, even the floor manager. He was aware of something that took hold of the studio.

The anchors crashed through space-time with Jones and boarded *his* time machine—but they had their job to do for the viewers. They were professionals and had to use a strong dose of self-restraint to continue to calibrate their surroundings and stay on their assigned task. Ahmad, still talking, felt some pain subside, but he knew he would have to endure more pain for the next 21 minutes. He had to give a good interview.

At 3 a.m. in Afarland, families in all eight provinces were huddled around flat screens, computer monitors and cell phones watching *The End Zone*. The majority was oblivious to the political re-engineering taking place. The murdered cabinet members had families and friends who had inquired about their whereabouts. Answers were vague: Alexander Whallun, the only living cabinet member besides the Prime Minister and Jones, said that, "They were in a closed session with the president," or "They left the capital and went to visit towns in their jurisdiction." Yet there were a couple of thousand who sensed that something wasn't right with their country. These people still retained the ability to intuit their surroundings by staying attuned to their Source.

Many Afarlanders had seen Jones with Marakie out in public and on local TV. The Joneses managed to secure the help of the African Union by having the technical support group send an alert to every Afarlander's cell, advising them to be up at 3 am to watch a program that would affect every citizen.

Back at the studio, Jones said, "I was too pinned to my laptop to watch Hauschka's kick. I only saw the blur of orange and blue and white jerseys at the upper edge of my eyes. I felt that the missing number seven was somewhere in the name, yet I was stuck without a play or an angle to extract it.

Then I looked upward through my window toward the cloud formation over Table Mountain and waited."

Max asked, "What came next?"

Jones drifted off again. He remembered pointing the remote, muting the transmission, and watching the game in silence. He peered through the ceiling-to-floor window to his left and into the darkness. He felt the life of the land. He looked at the dark outline of Table Mountain, standing at 3,358 feet. He had a memory flash of his attackers, from that day inside the tram. The mountain loomed over the vast expanse of land around his house. He saw *the tablecloth*, which is the cloud often covering the mountain's flat top. When Ahmad was sharing, he was engaged in second attention, an aside—he was remembering that just a minute before the last quarter of the Super Bowl began, his beautiful wife, appeared half asleep, in her long purple negligee. She meandered across their living room and sat on the couch. She snuggled up on his left side and settled her head under his left arm. He stopped work to sit back and share the field of love that preceded her into the living room.

She glided her left arm over his chest with her wrist perched above his right shoulder, her delicate fingers almost touching her husband's shoulder blade. He remembered how he had worked to a point of obsession and had felt in his body the strain from the intense pace of collecting, classifying, and processing so much new information.

He remembered the feeling of the heat and the rhythm of Marakie's breath and the intimate warmth of her body against his. Still, while sitting across from Mike, Heather, Max and the camera operators, and in front of millions of viewers, he was in two places at once and present in both.

He remembered when he and his beloved went to sleep on the couch after 62 minutes of the big game. He remembered how the rest of the time, the 22 men moved strenuously over the field, tackling, running, passing... crashing into one another like cars, only with no sound. And he remembered Terry McAulay's officiating announcements, appearing as digitized words, along with the commentators sharing their play-by-play accounts.

After he and Marakie drifted off, the Seattle Seahawks won the game: 43 to 8, mostly without a single sound from the TV set in the Jones' home. In one part of his mind, his remembering took all of three seconds, while through another part, he was engaged in explaining his initial calculations for his book...

Jones answers Max's question. "After a couple of seconds had passed, I did the number and letter match-up again, and this time I reduced any double-digit number to a single digit, like reducing 19 to 10 (1 + 9 = 10) and then to 1 (1 + 0 = 1), for the letter S and so forth. That finished, I got 34, which reduces to 7. And there was the missing number to the year 1976. Using numbers and letters was the angle to squeeze out the birth year of the Seattle

Seahawks encoded within that name. I also got that same number just by reducing 1+ 6 + 9 to 16 and adding 1 + 6 to get 7."

Heather smiled. She stretched out her arms, interlaced her fingers and settled them on her lap as if waking from a pleasant dream. She leaned back a few inches.

"Wow, I love that story, Ahmad!"

Heather had picked up on Jones' reminiscences; she perceived that he was somewhere else for that brief moment, even though she heard him breaking down those numbers. Heather had interviewed hundreds of male and female athletes in several sports before coming on *The End Zone* team. She enjoyed her associations with powerful people and how these athletes functioned at higher levels of action. They moved in the foreground from the masses. They *were* powerful. She interviewed athletes who were also authors and sports doctors, but this was her first author and astrologist combined. Heather could feel his physical presence. Perhaps Jones was a spiritual athlete. She knew that this type was out there somewhere. Now one of them was sitting across from her.

Heather sensed the emptiness behind the façades of many of these—the caricatures feasting on cheers, photo ops, interviews, and images on glossy covers. She could do this without criticism—it was just what she noticed at times. Yet, she acknowledged that these people were treading the path that Jones talked about on that Philadelphia astrology radio show she had listened to earlier that day. They were on a journey, like her and everybody else. Some knew who they were and played their game well and those who did not required reams of clues.

Jones had to keep talking. Had to wait for the right time to present Afarland's new president. The time had to appear organically from the show and not as an intrusion.

Heather said, "Our phone lines are open if you have a question for Ahmad Jones." Max said, "Yes, we invite callers who have read, are still reading, or haven't yet brought his book, *Football's Astrological Measurements*, to ask Ahmad anything. We hope that your questions are interesting."

The voice was sharp sounding and cold, "I have a question—it's more like a comment—for Mr. Jones."

Max, Heather, Mike and Jones all look out toward Camera Two.

"How y'all doing?" said the voice, "Name's Joe. I like the show."

"Joe, are you a poet?" Heather asked.

"No, not me. Couldn't rhyme even if I had the time... *oops!* No, definitely not me."

"Where are you calling from?" she asked.

"I make my home where *America's Team* makes theirs."

"Dallas! A great team," Ahmad said.

"That's right, born in Abilene, Mason Williams' home town. Your show is like *Classical Gas*."

"Oh, thanks, Joe."

"I still love my Giants, too. Anyways, Max always surprises me with something new during each program. I've watched from the git go... See? So, all right. Mr. Jones! I haven't checked out your book, and that parlor trick, you know, with the letters and numbers wasn't anything... spectacular. That's all there is to it."

"Get ready for a glitch in the matrix," Stew said. Steve said, "Stew, would you please brew another big pot of coffee for us? Thank you. Oh, can you also make me a latté, single shot, with foam, whip, and a pinch of nutmeg? Walk softly when you come back in here; there's millions worth of equipment."

"Sure thing, Mr. Usman."

"Please, Stew, call me Steve."

After Joe's remark, like people in the stands at a tennis match, the three anchors turned and faced Jones. They were preparing for a beatdown, either by Ahmad or Joe, but ready to defend Ahmad. The trustworthiness of their guest and the show's rep were on the line. They were at the beginning of a campaign for an ever-expanding viewership.

Did Jones have the tools? Was he shallow? Or could he catch a deep ball, and could he throw deep? Professional anchors are articulate and well pre-pared. They have information and verbal skills honed to a super-fine edge. They wait. A little tension makes for a good show. As of September, the DMA (Designated Marketing Area) for Peregrine was in the top 18 out of 210 tel-evision markets. *The End Zone* was considered solid and unique. To move up from the top 30 into the top 10 was plausible. Heather had not doubted that Jones would do just fine. She also desired to see of what mettle he was made. Could he outflank Joe, a heckler, a tackler? Could he be objective? Would he take it personally? Would he lose control? Would he find an A or B gap and outflank Joe without causing him to fall flat on his face—with just enough of a cut where he could move beyond his reach, so all Joe would contact was empty space while Jones went through the hole into daylight? Max and Mike were expecting to do damage control.

Jones' smile was polite. He said, "Thank you, Joe, for your comment."

Joe was silent, so Jones added, "Do you have a question for me?"

"Yes, what else do you got?"

Jones said, "Do you recall the final score of Super Bowl 48?"

"Ah... no, not off the top of my head," Joe said.

"The score was 43 to 8. The 43 is the reverse of 34. That was the Hawks' first Super Bowl win and they won it with a number whose digits are an integral part of their franchise name. To me that score had a deeper meaning."

Joe said, "It's possible that several teams could win a championship with numbers taken from their name... right?"

"Ouch! Ahmad, how do you address that?"

Max asked. He rattled his pen between his forefinger and middle finger.

Heather said, "Right, Joe, but he's using just the Seattle Seahawks for this example as it is germane to them."

"Fer cryin' out loud, *ger... what*?" Joe asked. The whole studio felt that and laughed hard. Joe continued, "Just playing with y'all. So, ah... Mr. Jones, hope you don't expect me or anyone else to quote *believe* unquote, in astrology, crazy numbers, or anything like that. Do you?"

Jones was feeing energized by the back and forth. He almost didn't remember the piece of lead in his side. "I was invited to the show to promote and discuss my book and answer questions. Now, it is possible to find tons of strange connections in just about anything. It's only information. Yet, I was intrigued by the amount of coincidences in this name. Here's another part of this number 43. Do you know what team was been lauded as having the best defense in the NFL?"

"The Seahawks," Joe said.

"Yes! And what's the common defensive scheme in American football?"

"*Hmm...* Great question!" Mike said. Heather uncrossed her legs and sat up straight when the conversation took this high turn.

Joe said, "Yes, I know what that is... I played defense in school and it's... *ouch!*"

There was a loud hissing sound, then *kachink.* Then no Joe.

Max said. "Joe, are you there? Did we lose him? Ahmad! I knew where you were going with that. If he redials the board operator can bring him to the front."

"Yes," Joe said, "I'm still here. *Cough! Cough!* Got smoke in my eyes...

*cough!* And I dropped my phone."

Heather asked, "Joe, are you having an emergency?"

"No, nothing like that." Joe said. I was fixin' to digest a genuine Fletcher Davis-style burger... Left it on the grill too long and it caught fire. Everything's back to normal now."

Steve relaxed in his chair, then sat back up. "This is priceless," he said.

Jones asked again, "So, Joe, do you remember the question: what is the basic defensive scheme? If you said it, I didn't' hear it."

Joe said, "Pretty good, Ahmad... to me, it's 4-3. Yeah, it's a common alignment in the NFL. I give you that. What about my home team, got anything cool about them?"

"Yes, I do. The Dallas Cowboys finished their first game ever against the Pittsburgh Steelers with a score of 28 in the year 1960. The number 28, which reduces to one, relates to 28 January 1960, when Clint Murchison, Jr. and Bedford Wynne were awarded an NFL franchise. The 28 was the Cowboy's score at the end of that first game, which was also the date that the franchise was awarded."

"Uncanny. What else?"

"Last one, please, Joe. We have other callers waiting," Max interrupted.

"If you use the number-for-letter system for the word Dallas, within that word there are two A's which represent one, and the letter S, the 19th letter, which breaks down to one. In total, there are three ones in the word Dallas.

"Now, Joe, if you zero in on my next comment, I believe you'll find it unusual. Dallas' record for their first season was zero, eleven and one. So, they won no games, lost eleven games, and tied one.

"There are 15 letters in the name Seattle Seahawks and when all their preseason games were over, they were one-five. For me, these curious correlations, combined with my love of football, were my first points of access that led to the ideas, which resulted in my book."

"Wow, man, that's outta sight! And I wish you could smell these burgers." The anchors took a breath of relief, as Joe added, "Did you play football?"

"Some."

"What position?"

"Halfback in sophomore year; tight end and second-string as a junior."

"Bye, Joe." Heather said.

"Bye, ya'll. I'll keep tuning in."

Mike asked, "Was that in the book? I don't remember seeing that."

"No, I made the Cowboy's observation after the book came out."

Max said, "Neither did you tell us you played football." Max rustled through some sheets of paper in front of him, squared off the corners and edges, then tapped the bottom edges twice against the table before laying them down. "It's not in your bio—"

Mike interjected, "So, give us the dope on your football career."

"You had a football career?" Heather asked.

"No, I didn't have a career. There's not much to tell. I played for Kaskaskia Township High School for two seasons. Got hurt a lot but no serious injuries. Well, except for one in my junior year, when I played tight end. I caught a bullet pass at mid-field. Just then the safety came up with momentum. As I turned, he rammed his right shoulder into my chest."

"That must've hurt," Mike said.

"A little, as I remember. Then the corner coming at me didn't stop in time; I was already off my feet going backwards."

"Some unnecessary roughness was about to happen," Mike said.

"You bet. The corner took out my legs a tenth of a second after the safety took out my upper body and I went horizontal for a moment, then made a strong impression on the turf with more of my back and less of my pads. Because I was quick off the blocks, I kept pads light. So, I absorbed much from those hits."

*Ohhh!* A chop block," Heather said.

Max asked, "Did you see stars?"

Ahmad laughed his answer, "No, it was still day."

After making a light thrusting motion with her pen, Heather said, "Touché!"

Jones said, "I finished out the season and then dropped out of football and got into gymnastics, in my senior year, a sport with a much lower violence quotient."

The studio was howling.

"Gymnastics?"

"Yes, does this surprise you? Gymnastics is no joke. I was flexible, had upper-arm strength, was a quick study, and made it to the state championship doing rings, parallel bars, horizontal bars, side horse, and floor exercise."

"That's impressive, Ahmad," Max said. "How did you do?"

"I received a medal for first place in all but the side horse and floor exercise."

"*Okay*... next caller," Max said. Heather and Mike were visibly impressed.

"Buster here, from Renton, Washington, home of my Seahawks. Hey, why are we losing Hawks? First it was Lynch, then, Lockette? I don't believe in that astrology stuff, but... what's your take brother?"

"Well, I looked at the basic planets' patterns in the horoscopes of these and other great players. You want to know how major shifts in their careers relates to their astrology?"

"Sure."

Max said, "Well, if Joe's comments seemed strident, Buster is presenting a little gauntlet! Does astrology have anything to say about these great players, Ahmad?"

Off camera, Matt, the Assistant Director, looks on in the colorful, semi-dark Production Control Room. His peripheral vision picks up a vague figure moving at him from his right. He moves the arms of his headset back, exposing his ears. "This ought to be pretty good," he said, still holding his set.

"This *better* be good!" Steve said from a couple of feet away.

"Ahmad executes. The whole group is electric and that *Joe* caller was gold. Come-on, Fletcher Davis?" Matt said, after taking off his earphones.

Steve said, "Well, give him credit for making the first fried beef patties with two slices, onions and pickles, and with mustard not ketchup. Maybe Joe is a purist. So far, the segment is informative. I've not read Jones' book, but the segment is grounded in a reality that I can appreciate and I think our viewers can, too. It's close to home and we're not out in some football field among the stars. They know where their heads are and where their feet are. Plus, Ahmad played the game, was an award-winning gymnast—"

"There's an athlete behind the astrologer—"

"And his wife is the freakin' daughter of the president of Afarland and watching the show from the inside of *my* studio."

Matt puts his earphones back on. Steve listens with only one earphone, while he stands watching the monitor.

Jones asks, "Buster, I guess you want to know what was going on when they got injured? I will tell you."

The sportscasters' faces dropped after that remark. Brows lifted. Heather's breathing was in peril and six pairs of pupils got smaller. The 18th spot in the television markets looked like it could go south. What if Ahmad Jones started spouting astrology jargon and this segment got a bad rating—or worse, became a laughing stock? They would never be taken seriously. Good for them that it would take more than this to shift the Nielsen ratings far off their present line.

Steve whispered into his mic, "Stew, make it a double espresso and make it quick, please. *Uh oh...*"

"Yes, Mr. Usman, sir."

"Call me... Oh, forget it."

Matt lifted one side of his headset. "Don't say it. Everything is gonna be all right. We're gonna have huge penetration by the time this is over. You watch."

"This will be good, or this will be bad," Steve said.

Jones said, "Those great players got injured because football is a rough sport, yes. I do have specific metrics on those and many other players. Read my book to get those answers."

The anchors breathed easier.

Steve said, "For the love of God!"

"I said it would be all right. He psyched us all. That was pretty damn good," Matt said.

Jones continued, "In the average 11 minutes of actual game play, 22 bodies are running into each other at full speed. They play while sustaining hits and hard falls to the turf."

"Ahmad, can you give us something really awesome, perhaps about our show, anything that will dazzle us even more?" Max asked.

Jones was now on the rim of a precipice. The pain in his side didn't go away quickly anymore but stayed longer. He grimaced. He took a breath and paused to weigh what he should say next. If he didn't get off the platform soon, they would have to take him off on a stretcher and the truth wouldn't have been told.

*Now is the time*, Jones thought. He turned and noticed Marakie, who was inside the studio sitting in a high-back chair and surrounded by agents. He thought of telling the anchors about the peculiar astronomic similarities between the Harvard and McGill game in 1874, the Harvard and Tufts game in 1875, the Rutgers and Princeton game of 1869, and the launch of ESPNs first show in 1979. But there was no time left.

"Well, I didn't mention the most important reason for writing *Football's Astrological Measurements.* If you will, I'd be happy to share it with your audience."

"Okay then," Steve said, "this is gonna be icing on the cake."

Jones' nuanced look was unfamiliar to the anchors. He was in pain. They knew that something different, extremely revealing, and probably controversial was about to happen. Jones was sweating through his makeup. He was in a desperate situation.

"I was shot less than an hour ago!"

# 67

## Touchdown

EACH ANCHOR LOOKS AT JONES. "You were what?" Heather asks.

"Shot?" Max asks.

Matt says, "Steve, we have to break for a commercial."

Steve pushes his hand up. "No... fucking... way. Camera One—"

Matt stands up. "Steve, what if he has a fatal wound—"

"I've got this and—"

"Usman, we don't know where he's been shot or the extent of his injury. We are in the dark, we have to cut to a commercial."

"Control, I've got this under control." Steve switches to Camera One. "I heard you, Mr. Johansson. I'm the director," he whispers into the mic. "Stew, call an ambulance right away, possible gunshot wound."

"Yes, sir."

The three anchors, who are standing after Jones' admission, sit down while Jones talks. Steve speaks to each anchor in their earpiece. "I know something that you don't about this, so keep talking."

Jones says, "I was writing my first book in Libya. In November of 2010, I was scheduled to speak at a gathering of European and African heads of state in Tripoli. That morning, two men arrived at my suite with weapons. I was unable to keep my first scheduled talk. Later, I was detained and was then let go after several hours."

Mike asks, "Excuse me, but why were you invited to speak in Libya, of all places?"

"I have a Master of Arts degree in government and political science."

"Now, there's a man after my own heart," Steve says.

"Astrology goes well with these, because I can talk politics in astrological terms and vice versa. That day, my talk would've been centered on trade. I had met with many heads of state from Europe and Africa before, talking about their national horoscopes with them."

Max looked through his paperwork. "Your bio keeps getting larger by the minute," he said. "I won't ask how you were shot, Ahmad, but shouldn't we end this segment and get you to a hospital?"

"After I answer your question and give the facts about the book."

Steve said, "Max! No one's going anywhere, not yet." Max was getting worried and so were Mike and Heather.

"The next day was 30 November 2010. That afternoon, I was sitting and writing under an umbrella near Green Square, when a tall man walked over, sat by me, and asked if he could talk with me. I said yes. After a few minutes, I was convinced that he knew more about me, and certain conditions that were unfolding n my world, than I even did. We talked for thirty minutes. Before he left, he told me to be ready for a test, a test that would strain all of my resources—mental, emotional, physical, and even my spirit. He reminded me of a teacher of mine, who I talk with regularly. So I left for my hotel, retired to my suite, and wrote until midnight. I then rested on my soft settee for a few hours. Then, I was awakened by three knocks on my door."

Ahmad took a drink of his water.

Steve said, "Stew, did you call the ambulance?"

"Yes, they said less than five minutes."

"Then," Jones said, "I answered the door and there were three men who said that they were from the Libyan Secret Service. They took me into custody. They wanted to know if I had executed five members of a certain paramilitary group."

"What?" The three anchors wondered where the show was going, and if Jones was delusional, after sustaining a gunshot wound.

"I told them *no*. They said that it must have been me because they found my keycard on one of the victims. They checked up on me, discovered that I was a former police officer, and concluded that I was the prime suspect."

"A police officer!" all three anchors said.

"They threw me into a private jail and said it would be for an indefinite period. I wasn't entirely surprised that this had occurred. After a month, my spirit was weakening—no one who knew me, not even my wife, was aware of my situation. Afarland's president asked about my whereabouts and was told that I had left Libya, for the states, on 2nd December. My name was entered on the manifest of a flight that left TIP, bound for JFK, I was told afterwards. By then, I had let go—relinquished, lost the vision—of ever seeing my wife, my family, or my country."

Jones looked down at the ring on his finger.

Back in Afarland, the ring of state was seen by all the citizens who were watching the program. There was an audible gasp. They were not sure why Ahmad Jones was wearing it.

"What I'm going to say next relates to the sport of football, my solitary confinement in Libya, and the love of my life."

Jones twirled the ring around, as the memory had awakened in him the deepest of feelings. He looked back up at Heather and Max, and said, "Marshawn Lynch, the Seattle Seahawk's running back, 2011."

"What does he have to do with this?" Max asked.

Jones was sweating more. His side, his entire body, was shaking almost imperceptibly. Jones talked faster.

"On 8 January, I was taken from solitary confinement by the guards and allowed to watch a Seattle Seahawks' game. It was against the New Orleans Saints. I could barely sit up on the small crate. There were three guards around me, laughing and drinking. I remember hearing the 12s during 2nd and 10. After the snap, the crowd was so loud I couldn't keep my head down. So, I watched... I watched... I—"

"Are you all right, Ahmad?" Mike asked.

"No. But I'll finish."

The crew beyond the cables and cameras had all stopped what they were doing. Jones took a deep breath. Marakie was standing now. She knew that

Ahmad could die up there without immediate medical help. She wanted to go up there and try to expose the coup in progress and get her husband off the stage. Was all this worth losing the man she loved? But she had a duty to her husband, and to take him from the scene would nullify everything he'd done, and his injury would have been in vain, including Hasta's death, and her father's suffering.

She covered her mouth as she cried. She wiped her tears. Reilly, standing next to her, looked at her and quickly turned away. He was ready to do whatever she deemed it necessary to do.

She had a duty to her country. In a few moments her husband would present the big revelation. The new President of Afarland had to be made of strong substance.

Jones said, "I watched a man shed at least a half-dozen attempts to knock him to the turf. It was Marshawn Lynch, number 24. It was Lynch's performance on the field that compelled me to endure this burden, until... until I could consciously move beyond the walls of my confinement and get that vision back. From that day on, I lived in my heart more and more. I knew that it was the awakened heart of that man, which broke those tackles.

Then one day, a month later, in late February, one of the guards came in. He said, 'Yatruk,' which means leave. He handed me a water bottle, some bread, and one hundred dinars. I went back to my hotel, where the manager was given orders to put me up in a suite. I ate my bread, finished my water, called my wife, slept, got up, showered, then went back to sleep on a soft bed. In the prison, I had to sleep on the bare floor."

The studio was silent as they watched Jones' emotions appear on his every facial expression. They didn't know what he had endured throughout the day, besides his gunshot wound. All he had survived was playing through his every gesture.

Jones tried to stand. Mike helped him up. Jones pointed to his wife. Marakie got herself together.

"I thank God for the celestial timing that allowed me to watch Marshawn Lynch rushing the ball down the field. Afterwards, I went home to my wife, and because of his example, I had something extra of myself to give to her." Jones' eyes met Marakie's. She nodded, favorably.

Heather wiped one of her eyes.

"Wow!" Max said, under his breath. He gathered his papers together, to straighten them out. He had to finish the segment.

At that moment, callers were waiting to give their reactions on the air. The switchboard was hot. The call screener answered a few:

*I thought this was a show about football, not politics!*

*Tell the director to make up his mind what this show is about.*

*Not into astrology, but your guest is handsome. I'm praying for him.*

*Is Ahmad Jones okay?*

*I ain't missin' your show after watching this!*

There was a call from a foreign correspondent in Doha, Qatar, who wanted to interview Jones. Several pay television concerns called for an exclusive. Steve Usman fielded the calls.

Heather said, "Ahmad, I hear an ambulance coming. If you're OK to continue, may I ask you about that ring?"

Jones turned to face Heather. "This is not my ring. It belongs to Afarland's new interim president. It's a long and convoluted story, but my wife is the new Provisional President of Afarland. I was merely carrying it, in a manner of speaking, like Marshawn Lynch carried the ball to the end zone."

Jones reached into his left jacket pocket and pulled out the mandate.

From the control room, Steve said, "Well I'll be... Zoom in on that document."

"This mandate, signed by Afarland's cabinet, is an official document that entitles the above-named Marakie Jones to govern the nation until the state elections begin next March. The people who shot me wanted me out of the picture, just in case I would show it on this program. They've been attended to by federal officers."

Jones continued, "Marakie Serapher Jones now has conferred upon her all the powers of the Presidency, including authority over the military. A coup d'état was going on today and President Za Dewabuna's cabinet voted her in as interim president just before most of them were assassinated." There was another audible gasp, this time, heard not only in the studio, but in Afarland.

Members of The Consortium shook their heads. All but one acted as if it were just another day at work.

Jones went on, "This document is one of two that were created. The other one isn't authentic. It's missing the seal of Afarland's government secretary. And neither is the other ring. The *fake* symbols of leadership were cleverly inserted into a private safe in the Presidential Palace, while I left with the real ones. This was the pre-arranged plan between myself and my wife's father, President Dewabuna because of the imminent danger I perceived was coming. If the coup planners and their inside man, General Garaka, had gotten to the real ring and mandate, they would be in control for a time. I've had them since March. Several people helped me to get here, in order to say, *this*. So, Heather, that's the story of the ring. It is Afarland's Presidential Implement of Office."

At that moment, Marakie walked up to the platform "Here comes my wife, the Interim President of Afarland," Jones announced.

Marakie walked on camera as all three anchors stood up.

Heather bobbed a curtsy, "Madame President, it is an honor to meet you."

"I am glad to be here, and I owe it all to my husband. Thank you."

Jones took the ring off his finger. Marakie walked to him with the dignity befitting a head of state, and with great admiration in her eyes. She made it to the end of the table and extended her index finger. Jones took it and guided the ring onto it. The entire studio began to clap. "Congratulations, Madame President Jones of Afarland." Max said.

"My husband, the ambulance is here," Marakie supported her husband's arm and they both walked off the set. "Honey," Jones said, "I'm going to be just fine."

Back in Afarland, the general assembly and a majority of the African Union member states supported Marakie Jones' presidential status. Alexander Whallun was in custody for treason. Marakie required 15 more trusted people to build a new cabinet.

The AU had sent coalition military forces to join with Afarland's forces, to seize all power from General Garaka and his muster, who were all under arrest. His troops stationed outside the Presidential Palace, the airport and major news outlets all put down their arms and surrendered to a peacekeeping force from Nigeria, an hour earlier. AU forces had continued to land and assist in the retaking of major communications buildings and their IT squad had restored the satellite feeds. They stood guard to ensure that the people of Afarland could see their new president on the air. Afarlanders felt happy that their country had a young woman president. *The End Zone* had been watched throughout most of the country.

"Jones' book sales are going to be ridiculous," Steve said. Matt nodded.

"All the best to you, and your country," Mike said as the Joneses exited.

"Standby Camera One for a close up on Max... Camera One on Max. Cue *Classical Gas.* Stand by to roll credits."

Max said, "Well, this wraps up the first half of *The End Zone*. Our phone lines are swamped with callers. Ahmad Jones and his wife, Afarland's interim president, have left the studio."

Outside the studio in the hallway, DSS agents on alert escorted the Joneses to the front entrance.

Jones had passed the pictures on the dark wall of the entrance. He felt no pain as he dropped to the floor like a puppet whose strings had been cut.

"Oh, my God, Ahmad!"

"Madame President, please stay back." Fletcher, the leader of the security team, knelt over Jones and placed his fingers on his carotid artery. "Mr. Jones, can you hear me?"

While lying face down, Jones said, "Had to... make it here."

The words could hardly come out of Marakie's mouth. "You're going to be fine, my husband... you're going to be well, okay?" She stepped back against the plexiglass door with her hand over her mouth. She took a deep breath. "Agent Reilly, you have to get my husband to the nearest hospital."

"Madame President, the ambulance is here." She turned and rushed out the door, running to the ambulance, which maneuvered around the Maserati, to within 40 feet of the entrance. The three DSS agents already outside, rushed to her to keep her safe.

Reilly approached the Peregrine Police, who were near the entrance ramp. "We have an injured man. We need you to clear a way to the hospital."

The officer at the wheel cut the engine on, "Dispatch, Unit 1, we have a 10-60 in progress."

Dewabuna was treated for his injuries. After enduring a beating, the fear of losing his only child, and watching members of his cabinet killed, the news that his daughter was at the helm of his country gave him such joy that his pains felt minimal.

Back in West London, Borg said, "We lost Afarland." His associates looked over at Hanson, the acting chairman, who left the room, suddenly. Borg lit a cigar. The other men got nervous. Borg looked over a list of other jobs being handled by skilled operatives. His main job was Afarland, which went bust.

Hanson ran into the room with his Beretta. He got to within three feet of Borg and pointed it between his eyes. Hanson's face was distorted with disgust.

Borg pleaded as Hanson pulled the trigger. Twice. Borg fell backwards with his chair; his cigar was still burning in his mouth.

"Did we, gentlemen, lose Afarland?"


Reilly followed Marakie into the EMS truck. The back doors were closed. Steve, Stew, and several members of the TV crew who had congregated in the front hallway, began to head back to their stations, for the start of the second TV segment.

"Copy that, Unit 1, 10-60."

Unit 1 drove off, followed by one patrol car, then followed by the DSS detail and two other patrol vehicles.

The sun was golden-pink.

# ABOUT THE AUTHOR

**Kevin D. Raphael Fitch** has used astrology as a consulting tool for his clients since 1981. He is the author of *Celestial Configurations of Africa and the Caribbean*, a 626-page volume that has been hailed by top astrologers and academics from America, London, and South Africa as a ready-made classic and valuable reference work—one that tells the story of Africa from the perspective of divine portents, revealing each nation's hidden connection to the higher world—greatly adding to the area of political astrology.

Most of the astrological charts depicted in this novel were calculated within the time frames depicted in the story. Each was discovered to relate precisely to the dramatic events experienced by the main characters in the book. Based on certain planetary cycles, the month that Robert Gabriel Mugabe of Zimbabwe stepped down was depicted in the story, while the author was writing it—several months before the event happened.

*Fitch is available as a speaker and dynamic presenter.*
*For more information, please visit his website,*
www.TheEndZoneNovel.com.